Frederick W Holden

with best wishes
Frederick W. Holden
2 October 2008

This Sorry Scheme of Things

Ah Love! Could thou and I with Fate conspire
To grasp this Sorry Scheme of Things entire,
Would not we shatter it to bits - and then
Re-mould it nearer the Heart's Desire!

Rubáiyát of Omar Khayyám
as translated by Edward Fitzgerald

Published by Fieldmouse Publishing
44 Tudor Hill, Sutton Coldfield, B73 6BH

First edition

A CIP catalogue record of this book is available
from the British Library

ISBN 978-0-9560174-0-6

Printed and distributed by York Publishing Services Ltd
64 Hallfield Road, Layerthorpe, York, YO31 7ZQ
www.YPD-books.com

Cover picture and design by F W Holden

This book is dedicated to my brother Brian, who encouraged me in many things including the writing of this trilogy, but whose sudden and untimely death meant he did not read a word of it.

Acknowledgements

With thanks to my wife Margaret, for her patience and forbearance during all the hours I have spent writing this trilogy.

My thanks also to Jean Agate, Sharon Goodridge, Kirsten Hill, Deanne Dowell and Barry Dowell, who together with my wife Margaret, proof read and commented on the original draft.

To Duncan Beal, Chris Mercer and the staff at York Publishing Services, for making the publishing of this book a pleasant and straightforward exercise.

CONTENTS

		Page
BOOK ONE		
The Moving Finger	1914 to 1936	7
BOOK TWO		
The Wine of Life	1930 to 1957	231
BOOK THREE		
The Fruitful Grape	1957 to 1982	473

Book One

(1914 to 1936)

The Moving Finger

The Moving Finger writes; and, having writ
Moves on; nor all thy Piety and Wit
Shall lure it back to cancel half a Line,
Nor all thy Tears wash out a word of it.

Rubáiyát of Omar Khayyám
as translated by Edward Fitzgerald

CHAPTER ONE

1914

YOUR KING AND COUNTRY NEED YOU - A CALL TO ARMS.

Frank and Tom stood side by side reading the cutting from the previous Saturday's Birmingham Daily Post, which Vernon Harper had pinned on the factory notice board.

An addition of 100,000 men to his Majesty's regular army is immediately necessary IN THE PRESENT GRAVE NATIONAL EMERGENCY. Lord Kitchener is confident that his appeal will be at once responded to by all those WHO HAVE THE SAFETY OF OUR EMPIRE AT HEART.

"Lord 'bloody' Kitchener can stay confident for all I care," said Tom, "'cause here's one who won't be volunteering. Three years being ordered about in the army? That ain't my idea of fun!"

"Oh I'm not so sure," replied Frank. "It can't be any worse than being ordered about in this place. We're not going to get anywhere here now that old Mr Harper's gone. He was the one who promised us proper training in the drawing office and he'd started to give us some interesting designs to work on. I don't know about you, but I'm getting totally fed up with the copying work that Mr Vernon is giving me. I reckon he's now giving me less important work than I was doing two years ago with old man Harper."

"Well the work he's giving me perhaps ain't as bad as that, Frank. But, yes, you're right! I suppose I'm going backwards instead of forwards as well. You don't reckon he's doing it to avoid giving us the pay rise the old man promised us when we reached nineteen, do you?"

"You can be damn sure he is. There's two things you've got to take into account when dealing with Vernon Harper. First, he's a mean and spiteful bugger. The old man never gave money away, but at least he was fair. Always was fair, according to my mother; even when she worked for him as cook. Strict but fair. And second; well that's family business. But God help me, if he was here right now, I swear I'd murder the bugger."

At that Frank gritted his teeth together, clenched his fists and turned to walk away.

Tom put his hand on Frank's shoulder and pulled him back, "Hang on a minute. What's got into you to say stupid things like that?"

Frank turned, as if spinning on his feet, anger showing in his face and his fists still clenched tight. For a brief second Tom thought he was going to hit him and stepped back in fear. On seeing his friend's reaction, Frank opened his fists, and held up his open palms towards Tom. A wry smile broke across his face as he reached out with his open right hand and gently patted Tom on the cheek.

"OK. You win old friend. You're right; doing him in wouldn't help anyone." Frank laughed as he said it, and Tom realised that much of the tension had gone out of Frank, for the moment at least, and decided to ask him about it.

"Look you've been in a foul mood all day. What the hell's got into you? I know you've never been keen on the guy, but that's a long way from wanting him dead. Come on, it can't be all that bad, can it? Maybe you'd feel better about it if you got whatever it is off your chest."

"You're right. I am going over the top a bit, but I'm not sure I want to talk about it. It's too personal. You understand, don't you?"

"No I don't, mate," replied Tom, "I thought we could talk about anything. Whatever it is, you know I'll keep it to myself if you want me to."

Frank pointed his finger at Tom and leaned towards him, using a half whisper, "OK, but just between the two of us, all right? Nobody else is ever to find out. I don't want my family business being gossiped about all over the place. So you say nothing to nobody, all right?"

"Sure my lips are sealed."

Frank put his arm round Tom's shoulder, "Come on, we should have got out of this place five minutes ago. Let's go and clock out, we can talk as we walk home."

At that, they each took their time cards out of the rack, clocked out and filed their cards in the 'out' rack. Frank put his arm back round Tom's shoulders as they started to walk out the factory, "You know how we both applied for a job on the factory floor when we left school and started at this place?" Tom nodded his head as Frank continued, "But after we started old Mr Harper sorted us out and offered us jobs in the drawing office. I never did quite understand why he'd done that. I thought he'd probably done it 'cause he knew my mother from the days she used to cook for his family before she got married. And, of course, she's helped out at the house plenty of times since, particularly when they'd got some special dinner on."

Frank stopped talking, taking side glances at Tom as they walked, trying to decide whether to continue or not.

"Come on, then," said Tom, his inquisitiveness getting the better of him. "Are you going to tell me or not?"

"OK. But just between you and me. Not a word to anyone else though?"

"No. Of course not! I've promised you I won't repeat it to anyone. We're mates aren't we? You know I won't let you down." Tom looking directly into Frank's eyes, a certain irritation in his voice, said, "Now, for God's sake, get on with it. You can't just stop now you've whetted my appetite. You really know how to get a chap going, don't you?"

Frank did not speak for a few seconds, merely smiling at his friend. Suddenly he laughed. "Well, it's obvious I'll never get any peace 'til I tell you something and you're right, it probably will help to talk to someone about it." He opened his mouth and took a long deep breath staring vacantly into the distance for a moment as he plucked up the courage to continue the story. Then almost matter of factually, as if he was relaying something he had read in a newspaper, he turned to Tom and said, "I heard my mother talking to Auntie Annie last night. They didn't know I was listening. They were talking about the time before Mom and Dad got married, when they both were in service. Mom working for the Harpers and Auntie Annie working for someone called Anderson; never heard of them before. Anyway, it doesn't matter 'cause the Andersons have got nothing to do with what they went on to talk about. They were both having a good laugh, just like a couple of girls telling stories out of school. Then Auntie Annie said something about it being a shame that old Mr Harper had died and would my mother ever go up to the Harper house again now that Vernon Harper would be in charge there."

"My mother almost cried out and quite clearly said, 'Not on your life. I haven't spoken to that man in over twenty years; since that night in fact, and I certainly don't intend to start talking to him now. I wouldn't work for him even if I was down to my last crust of bread.' And then good old inquisitive Auntie Annie said, 'You've made hints at what went on that night before, but you've never told me the whole story. What exactly went on?' Well as you might imagine, I crept closer to the door so that I could hear better after that."

"What are you pair of rogues whispering about? Going to let your old schoolmate into the secret?"

Frank and Tom turned round as Bill Turner came running up behind them. Frank looked at Tom and shrugged his shoulders. "No peace for the wicked is there?" And looking at Bill said, "Just working out tactics for the match on Sunday, Bill. Your side don't stand a chance against our superior eleven. We'll beat the socks off you. You don't stand a chance."

"No way," replied Bill and the three of them continued walking towards the factory gate chatting about the planned football match. Talk between Frank and Tom about other matters suspended for the moment.

A car horn sounded behind them as they were about to walk through the factory gate. They jumped to one side and the offending car stopped as it drew alongside them.

Everyone reckoned that Vernon Harper must have ordered the new Standard model S on the day the old man had died because he arrived at the factory in it only one month afterwards. Old Mr Harper had been openly opposed to, what he called those dirty, smoky, horseless carriages, and the story was that Vernon had been too frightened of his father to defy him and buy a car whilst he was still alive.

It was a warm August day and the hood of the bull nosed 'Rhyl' two-seater was down. Vernon Harper was at the steering wheel, his fat belly rounded towards it. He wore a bowler hat on the top of his head which neatly covered the bald part, leaving what hair he did have bordering the rim of the hat from ear to ear. Peering through the thick convex lenses in his gold rimmed glasses perched on his plump red nose, and the last three inches of his unlit Havana sticking out of his mouth, he did not look a bit like the dashing motoring ace he imagined himself to be.

He pointed towards Frank and Tom. "Matthews. Richards. Come here a minute."

Tom took hold of Frank's arm and squeezed it tight as if to say, "Take it easy mate. Let's have no trouble."

Vernon Harper reached into his pocket and took out a box of matches. He extracted a match, struck it against the side of the box and held it to the end of his cigar, sucking hard to get it lit. He turned towards Frank and Tom removing his cigar from his mouth and exhaling the smoke towards their faces.

"I've been meaning to have a word with you two about that wage review you say my father had promised you before he died. I can't find anything about it in his books, but I'll have a word with Miss Hill to see if she knows anything about it and then I'll come back to you. Look, why don't we say the end of the month? Yes that'll give me enough time to sort something out. That's right. Come and see me at the end of the month and I'll make a decision on it then."

Tom had still got hold of Frank's arm and held him back. Hopefully Vernon Harper took the move to be one of merely allowing him more room to manoeuvre his car out of the gate.

"Yes, thank you Mr Vernon, sir", said Tom, giving Frank a dig in the ribs and a look and a minute nod of the head which said, 'Go on say the same you idiot, before you cause trouble for us both'.

Frank got the message and said, "OK Mr Harper."

Vernon Harper flicked the ash off the end of his cigar and lifted his hand in a semblance of a farewell before adding, "See you at the end of the month then."

He put his cigar back in his mouth, inhaled the smoke deep into his lungs and blew it out of the side of his mouth in the direction of Frank and Tom, as if making some kind of gesture of superiority over them.

Tom was pleased Frank had already turned away and did not see the action, which in his present frame of mind, would surely have incited him into action.

Vernon Harper put the car noisily into gear and drove off. The three friends followed the car out of the gate.

"See you two in the morning," Bill said as he turned right at the main road, in the opposite direction to the way Frank and Tom went home.

"See you. We can get back to our tactical planning for Sunday's match now," replied Tom, laughing as he said it.

They had walked silently together for a good half-mile, before Tom could bear his curiosity no longer, "Well Frank, are you going to finish telling me what went on last night or not?"

"Ah! I suppose it's not the big deal I've been making it out to be. It happened years ago, and by all accounts nothing really happened anyway."

"Look, you've got to tell me now. You can't start telling me something like this and then just leave it."

"OK. But don't forget, not a word to anyone. Where had I got to? Ah yes! I'd just got to where Auntie Annie was asking mother to tell her exactly what had happened."

Frank became silent again, shaking his head from side to side and biting on his lip as if deep in thought. Suddenly, he turned to Tom, the anger rising in him once again, "You know what Tom? That fat, four eyed weasel, butter wouldn't melt in his mouth Mr Vernon Harper; (Frank was showing real contempt in his face as his spat out the words, particularly as he emphasised the 'Mister'); tried it on with my mother. That fat slob had the gall to think that my mother fancied him. Waited until he thought everyone had gone to bed and mother was alone in the kitchen tidying up, went up behind her, put his hands on her breasts and kissing her on her neck suggested that now they were alone, they could have fun together."

Frank spat out the word, "Fun?" again, followed by an even more aggressive, "With that bastard?"

He took a deep breath before continuing, "Well apparently Ma just laughed at him and told him not to be a silly boy and go to bed before he got into trouble. He just got more and more persistent, but she wouldn't have any of it and had to keep fighting him off."

Frank took a deep breath before exploding with, "Over sexed bastard! If Ma hadn't fought him off, he probably would have ended up raping her."

He took another deep breath, "He'd actually got her down on the floor and had hit her across the face to keep her quiet, when old man Harper came into the kitchen and pulled him off her. Apparently the old man was furious and sent him away somewhere. Ma said the old man kept apologising for his son's behaviour for ages after that, and kept asking her not to tell anyone about it."

He thought for a second before continuing, "You know, I reckon that's the reason old man Harper was always enquiring after my mother. He was always afraid she might tell someone, and I reckon that's why he was always so nice to me and why he offered us the drawing office jobs in the first place. Wanted to keep on the right side of my mother; the patronising bastard. And to think I always thought he was a good boss who recognised my talents."

Frank was obviously getting more and more angry as he spat out each word.

Tom butted in, "Come on, Frank, you'll blow a blood vessel the way you're going." He put his hand on Frank's shoulder but Frank immediately shrugged it off.

"OK. Have it your way but if you don't keep your voice down, you'll have everyone in the street hearing what you say, and you don't want that, do you?"

Frank turned towards Tom, gritting his jaw together under a semblance of a smile and, pointing a finger at Tom said, almost under his breath, "Look here, mate, I know you mean well but the way I feel about it, I couldn't bloody care if the whole world knows what the little fat git is really like."

"Calm down. Calm down," entreated Tom, "At least now I know what's been bugging you all day but as you said it happened years ago and bringing it all up now ain't going to help anyone; least of all your mother. Or you and me for that matter."

"I'm sorry, but I just haven't been able to get it out of my mind since I heard mother talking about it last night. And I certainly don't think I can carry on working at Harpers anymore. I just couldn't face having to take orders from that Vernon Harper. I'm sure I'd just end up hitting him next time he speaks to me, and as you say that won't do any of us any good. Look, why don't we go for a training run after we've had our tea? I might be a bit calmer after that, but I still think I'm going to give in my notice and leave Harpers."

"Now you are talking stupid! You shouldn't let private matters affect your work. Anyway what would you do if you left Harpers? And we might do all right if he does give us a rise when he sees us. I'll tell you what, leave it until the end of the month, then we'll go and see Mr Vernon together as he suggested. You'll probably feel differently about it then, and you never know he might make it worth your while to stay; even working for him!"

"I'm not so sure about that. You see my mother got up and came through into the kitchen to make a pot of tea, so I had to shoot up the yard and hide in the loo before she caught me listening at the door. The last thing I heard her saying before I shut the door was something about how, now that Mr Vernon was in charge at the factory, she was worried he might take it out on me for what had happened. Well as I said, I had to scarper before she caught me listening, so I didn't hear any more of what was said."

They were just about to enter the back yard of their adjacent houses but Frank pulled on Tom's shoulder and held him back. "Look, you're probably right. We should leave it until the end of the month and see what he's got to say to us and,"

Frank let out a little laugh, "I'll try and hold my temper, 'til then at least, but I'll tell you something, one way or another I'm going to get that bastard. I don't know how, but I'll get him even if takes me the rest of my life. I'll get him and his family and somehow I'm going to make sure my family don't have to keep kow-towing to the likes of him."

Frank seemed to be talking to himself now as if working things out in his head as he spoke, "Money! That's all it is, money! That's the only difference. That's why we bow and scrape to them; 'cause they've got money. Not 'cause they're better than us. I've never met one that was anyway. Money! I've got to get more money than them, and then they'll bow and scrape to me. That's it, that's how I'll get the bugger."

The two of them turned into the yard, "You know what," said Frank smiling as though he had worked out the mystery of the universe, "I think you're right about what you said earlier. It has helped to get it off my chest. I'm not quite so mad now. But, mind you, I will be if you talk about this to anyone else, so just keep quiet about it."

"Not a word to anyone. I promise."

Frank opened the back door to the house and turned to Tom who was entering his own back door opposite across the brick paved yard, "I'll give you a call in about forty-five minutes and we'll go for that run," said Frank.

"Sure. I'll be ready."

Tom's sister Grace was staring out of the window and waved to Frank. She was eighteen months younger than Frank and until quite recently had merely been Tom's little sister who always seemed to get in the way when the boys were together. But things had changed on a very hot evening a little over two weeks previously when after eating his supper Frank decided to get a breath of fresh air and walked across the field at the back of the row of small terraced houses in Brighton Terrace where he lived. He reached the canal about a hundred yards across the field and sat on one of the lock gates watching a couple of boys enjoying themselves by jumping into the water and splashing about.

He had only been sitting there a few minutes when Grace appeared at his side. "Hello Frank, it's very warm tonight isn't it?"

Frank had not seen Grace cross the field towards him, "Oh hello Grace, what brings you here?"

Grace felt her cheeks warm at this unexpected question and hoped they had not reddened for Frank to see, "Just out for a walk, it's too warm to stay inside, isn't it?"

Frank just nodded his head and for the first time ever, saw that Tom's little sister had somehow suddenly blossomed into a beautiful young woman and wondered how he could have missed such a fact before.

She sat on the lock gate next to Frank and they chattered away about anything and everything until they had to move to allow a horse drawn canal boat carrying goods on its way South to use the series of locks.

They watched the boat negotiate the first lock and then, although he had no idea why he did it, Frank suggested that perhaps they should go for a walk together along the canal tow path. Grace couldn't believe her luck and merely said, "OK," but inside she was shaking and hoped it was not noticeable. They continued chatting as they walked and Frank started to view Grace in a completely different light.

As they returned across the field back to their houses, Frank was surprised at how much he had enjoyed the walk with Grace and was even pleased that they had chanced across each other like that. He would never know that chance had nothing at all to do with it. Grace had seen him leave the house and cross the field on his own from the bedroom window and had rushed out so she could 'casually' bump into him.

Just before they turned into the back yard between their two houses Frank surprised himself for the second time that evening by suggesting that perhaps they go for a walk together again the following week. And so the wave from Grace this evening was to the man who had now gone for walks with her twice already. However the relationship had not progressed beyond that; no holding of hands and not even a peck on the cheek as they parted. Grace was sure it would progress further though, even if Frank didn't know it yet.

Frank smiled as he waved back to her and felt a flutter in his chest as he once more admired her curly ginger hair flowing over her shoulders framing her beautiful young face. The fiery red hair was the way that most of the Richard's clan was recognised. Grace's mother had the same flowing curly hair and so did Tom and three of the four other siblings.

Frank winked to Grace before turning to enter his own back door shouting, "Hi Ma," as he did so. His mother was working in the scullery getting his tea ready for him. He stood just inside the door, hung his jacket on the back of it and stripped off his shirt, "Will I be in your way Ma if I have a quick wash while you're finishing supper?" And without waiting for an answer, he eased past her in the narrow space to get to the sink.

"Are you going out tonight Frank, or are you going to stay and keep me company for a change?"

This was a regular question from his mother, but Frank knew that it was only part of the ritual; a ritual she had gone through almost every time she thought Frank was going out on his own since her husband's death some twelve years earlier.

Frank's father had also come in from work and pushed past his wife to have a quick wash before going out on the night he died. She had said almost the same thing to him, "Why don't you give your football a miss for a change Sam? It'd be nice to spend an evening together for a change."

But her husband had put his arms round her waist and lifting his hands to her breasts and kissing her on the cheek, had said, "I can't let the lads down but I promise I'll come straight back after the match. I won't go to the pub with the others. I'll come straight back home and we'll have an early night and a nice cuddle together."

She had forever wished he had gone to the pub with his mates, because as he came home on his own it had started raining heavily. A flash of lightning followed almost immediately by an enormous clash of thunder caused a horse pulling a carriage coming towards him to bolt. He stepped into the road to try to stop the runaway horse but slipped on the wet surface at the last moment and the horse and carriage had gone right over him.

Alice Matthews waited long into the night for her husband's return but it was not until two o'clock the next morning that the policeman came and told her of her husband's death. She was in total shock at the news and on the day before the funeral she lost the child she was carrying, her second miscarriage since Frank's birth.

Frank managed to avoid Vernon Harper quite easily over the next few days and then he was missing for the next three weeks. He had taken his family away on holiday to the South Coast. And so, by 31st August, when Frank and Tom were climbing the stairs to Mr Vernon Harper's office to discuss their expected pay rise with him, Frank had not seen him since they had met at the factory gates almost a month earlier.

The matter discussed between Frank and Tom on that same evening had not been mentioned by either of them again. Tom hoped Frank had come to terms with it and had put the whole thing under wraps. In fact, Frank had been able to convince himself that it wasn't in his mother's best interests to ever let her know he knew anything about the matter and he promised himself he would control his feelings about it for her sake. As far as his plans to get the better of Vernon Harper were concerned however, he knew they couldn't be achieved overnight and he would have to somehow make long term plans to achieve them.

Miss Hill, her black hair pulled tightly back into a bun, sat at her desk, guarding the entrance to Vernon Harper's office. She was, as usual, dressed all in black, except for her starched white blouse. Round her hair she had a neatly ironed black ribbon tied into a bow at the neck, the ends of which hung over the back of her blouse. The blouse was tucked into her long black skirt, fastened at the waist by a wide black belt with a large brass double clasp holding it together at the front. Even though she was dressed so severely, nevertheless with her classical 'hour glass' figure, or maybe because of it, she looked younger than her forty-five years, and she still turned the factory workers' heads whenever she walked down the stairs on to the factory floor. It had always seemed a pity to Frank that she had never married, but it was perhaps no surprise, as she always seemed to take a very superior attitude whenever she spoke to any of the men in the offices. And when she had to speak to any of the factory floor workers, it was as if she was almost choking with disdain.

"And what are you two doing up here?"

"Mr Vernon Harper told us to come and see him today," said Frank.

"He hasn't told me anything about that," she replied, "What's it about?"

"He promised to look into giving Tom and me more important work in the drawing office and a suitable pay rise to go with it. Mr Gilbert Harper had promised us a promotion after our nineteenth birthday and that was last month. Mr Vernon said he was going to ask you if Mr Gilbert had said anything to you about it, and he then told us to come and see him today for his answer."

Frank thought he saw a slight hint of a blush on Miss Hill's cheeks when she said, "I'm not sure whether he has time to see you about that today. I'll let you know when he can see you."

Frank was about to protest at this brush off but she saw the anger in his face and said, "Just stay here a minute and I'll go and see if he can see you."

She got up from her seat and went to knock on the door to the office, but she turned and in her usual officious manner, repeated the excuse for Vernon Gilbert not to see them, even before she had asked him, "He's very busy today, you know. He's got some very important visitors coming in a few minutes."

At that, she knocked on the door, and waited for the, "Come in", before entering the room and closing the door behind her.

Frank and Tom could hear them talking behind the closed door but could not make out the actual words. The conversation went on for some time, and then Vernon Harper's voice grew louder as if in a temper, such that Frank and Tom could clearly hear him say, "Well my father isn't here any more Miss Hill. I'm in charge now and what I say goes. You're not working for my father anymore, you're working for me. So you'll do as I say if you want to keep your job. Is that clear? Go on now and send those two in here. I'll soon sort it out with them."

Miss Hill came out of the office, and sniffing to hold back what Frank thought was a pending tear, she beckoned the two of them into the office, with, "Mr Harper will see you now."

Frank and Tom entered the office, which had been Gilbert Harper's, but which Vernon had taken over as his own even before his father had been buried.

Vernon Harper was seated in a large mahogany chair covered with green leather and with green leather padded arms, behind a large highly polished mahogany desk. The desktop was inlaid with matching green leather, which was edged with two gold embossed lines round its perimeter. A large sheet of unsoiled yellow blotting paper had been placed in the holder on the top of the desk. The only other items on the desk were an open box of Havana cigars; a large glass ashtray into which Vernon Harper tapped the ash from his cigar from time to time; an ornate ivory ink well holder with a carved elephant at either end; and two pens with ivory handles extending from the pen holders at the side of the ink wells.

The walls at the back and to the right were covered in mahogany bookcases, with cupboards at the bottom and leaded glass doors at the top. There were however, only six books on the shelves. The rest of the shelves were full of cardboard filing boxes, each with a 'date from' and a 'date to' clearly marked on the front. The wall to the left was composed almost entirely of three windows overlooking the front of the factory. The windows were covered up to half way with net curtains and to either side, heavy brocade curtains were held back with sashes made out of the same material. The floor in front of the desk was covered with a thick Indian carpet with a highly coloured, intricate flower pattern woven into it. Four mahogany visitors' chairs with matching green leather seat pads were placed around the carpet; two against the window wall and one either side of the door into the room.

The desk was totally devoid of any papers and Frank mused at how different it was to the way it had looked the few times he had been in the room when old Mr Harper had occupied it. On those occasions, there were always one or more filing boxes open and several working papers on the desk. Was Vernon Harper a much quicker and tidier worker than his father, or was it that he left all the work for subordinates to do? He guessed it was the latter. Frank also wondered whether he was sitting with extra cushions under him, because his torso seemed to extend above the top of the desk much more than his short body should have done.

Vernon Harper took his after lunch cigar from his mouth as Frank and Tom entered the room and indicated for the two young men to stand in front of the desk. As he did so he blew a large wave of smoke into the already tobacco filled atmosphere of the room.

He leaned back in his chair as Frank and Tom stood to attention in front of him. "Well now," he said, taking another puff on his cigar, "I've looked into this matter of the supposed promotion and rise you say my father promised you, and I have to say I can find no evidence of any such thing."

Frank bristled, and Tom looked across at him, trying by the sheer force of will through his eyes to prevent him from reacting to anything said. Frank got the message, and against all his instincts managed to settle into a more casual stance. He was determined not to lose his temper and thereby let Vernon Harper get the better of him.

But it seemed that Vernon Harper was enjoying putting the lads down when he carried on to repeat himself, "I've thoroughly investigated your claim and I've grilled Miss Hill about it for some time and she assures me that she has no recollection of my father ever promising such a thing to either of you."

Frank put his hand in front of his mouth, determined not to be roused into argument. After all, he had predicted to Tom exactly what Vernon Harper was now saying. He had also conjoined with Tom into a pact, whereby neither of them would say anything if the conversation went along these expected lines, deciding not to give Vernon Harper any excuse to accuse them of insubordination or rebelliousness.

Their pact was already having the desired effect. Vernon Harper looked several times from one to the other, clearly waiting for some response from one, or both of them.

He took another puff on his cigar. "I don't know why you made up such a silly story about my father. I'm not so stupid as to fall for every lie any Dick or Harry wants to say about what my father promised or did not promise. I think in the circumstances it would be better if you just went back to the drawing office and carried on with copying the work you've been given over the last couple of weeks. I never did think either of you were good enough for further training anyway and I'll tell Mr Lambert that that's the sort of work to give to you from now on."

There was a knock at the door and in walked a young man followed by a flustered Miss Hill, and an attractive young woman.

"I'm so sorry Mr Harper, I did tell your son you were engaged, but when I told him who was in your office, he just came straight in."

"That's all right, Miss Hill. Come in Mark. Come in Evelyn. I won't keep you a minute. I've finished with these two anyway."

Mark Harper and his twin sister Evelyn, were each the antithesis of their father. Just twenty years old, they had inherited their mother's stunning brown eyes and wavy blonde hair. Mark, almost six feet tall had the lithe figure of an athlete. He was dressed in light linen trousers tied at the waist with what looked like a school tie, a white open necked shirt and tennis shoes. But Frank was looking at his sister. Three or four inches shorter than her brother, she was also dressed for the warm summer weather, but not in the casual wear of her brother. She wore a cream silk dress flowing in folds from the waist and ending just above her neat ankles. The dress was embroidered with yellow and red flowers at the square shaped neck, round the edge of the short sleeves and at its hem. Her golden hair was hanging loose over her shoulders and she wore a large, but delicately woven straw hat with a large brim on her head. The hat was meant to be held in place by tying the multicoloured silk scarf, which was around the front of the hat and threaded through the brim either side, under the chin.

The scarf however was hanging loose, almost as an adornment to her flowing hair.

Frank was entranced by her beauty. How could the small bald man in front of him have sired such a goddess? The demeanour, elegance and sheer charm of the radiant young woman in front of him couldn't possibly be a result of Vernon Harper's genes! Such refinement and grace in a young woman was a new experience for Frank. He realised, at that moment in time, even more acutely than ever before, that his lowly social status in life would prevent him from ever being able to approach such a person on equal terms. His only means of achieving equality was the accumulation of wealth. That would be the answer to all his problems. He could then confront Vernon Harper, without having to bow and scrape, and he would be able to approach any lady, even one as charming and graceful as Evelyn Harper, without effacement or humility.

Frank was aroused from his dreams by Vernon Harper who motioned to him and Tom with a snap of the fingers and a flick of the wrist that they were excused and should now leave the room. They turned and walked towards the door, but Vernon Harper could not miss his chance of degrading them further, particularly in front of two witnesses.

"I don't know why you lied about such a thing. It must run in the family, Matthews. Your mother was always making up stupid stories. I don't know why my father ever kept her on."

Frank hadn't anticipated an insult against his mother. He turned to face Harper, fury and anger showing clearly on his face. Immediately, Mark Harper stepped in between Frank and the desk, preventing Frank from approaching his father.

He shook his head from side to side and spoke quietly to Frank, "Just leave it. He really isn't worth it. Believe me. I know."

Mark Harper's words although spoken in almost a whisper so as to be unheard by his father, were so positive and said with such conviction that Frank knew he was right. He turned again, glancing across at Vernon Harper in contempt as he did so. Evelyn Harper, standing behind her father, smiled at Frank, and puckered her face. A look that Frank felt was warm and compassionate. Frank was convinced by the look that she too, understood her father and was sympathetic to Mark Harper's comments, even though she almost certainly would not have heard them.

Frank knew he could not benefit in any way from further discussion, and with as polite a, "Good day to you all," as he could muster, he took Tom by the arm and pulled him out of the room with him.

As Frank and Tom were going down the stairs from the offices, and

Frank felt they were far enough away for no one to hear them, he turned to Tom, "I swear I'll do for that man if he continues to treat us in that way. I'm not going to stand it any more. I'm going to leave this place before he can have the pleasure of sacking us."

"That's easier said than done. If you leave here where do you think you'll get a job? I don't think Harper would help with any sort of reference."

"Well that's OK; 'cause I shan't need a reference where I'm going."

He reached into his pocket and took out two newspaper cuttings, "Read those."

Tom stopped on the stairs and unfolded the first cutting, which had been taken from the previous Friday's Daily Post. Frank had circled parts of an article headed, 'To Arms' and Tom began reading the highlighted bits.

Lord Kitchener has appealed for 100,000 recruits as an instalment of a contemplated new army of 500,000. Relative to other towns Birmingham has responded handsomely. But Birmingham can and ought to do much more. Lord Kitchener is asking for men aged between 19 and 30.

Tom noted that Frank had made a heavy pencil mark under the '19', and he jumped to the next bit of the article, which Frank had underlined a couple of paragraphs further on.

A time may come, when the country will demand instead of invite. We hope not, for it is infinitely preferable that we should fight for our national preservation under the simple stimulus of patriotism. For the present, at any rate, there is no compulsion, and every man can do his part with the abiding satisfaction of having acted voluntarily.

They heard voices coming from the offices above and realised that Vernon Harper was leaving his office with his two children.

"Come on, Tom. Let's get back to the drawing office and you can read the rest there."

He quickly took the cuttings from Tom and they both dashed back to the drawing office. Arthur Lambert, the drawing office supervisor, was nowhere to be seen and so, as soon as they had sat at their desks, Frank took out the cuttings again.

"Here, this is the one I want you to read." He handed Tom the cutting from Saturday's newspaper and pointed to the article headed, *'A CITY*

BRIGADE - WHO WILL JOIN - AN APPEAL FOR NAMES.'
Tom took the article and read it.

The suggestion that Birmingham should raise a battalion of non-manual workers to join Lord Kitchener's Army has met with the widest approval in the city, and efforts are now being made to secure the acceptance of the scheme by the War Office.

There is, we believe, every reason to expect that the battalion if formed, will be warmly welcomed by the authorities and that arrangements will be made to associate the force with the name of the City.

It is not possible to accept recruits but there is no reason why preparatory work should not be put in hand. Birmingham can, at any rate, effectively demonstrate its wish, to assist by raising the battalion.

To this end, the 'Daily Post' invites all who are willing to join the new battalion to send their names and addresses. These will be entered in the register and published in the columns of the paper.

Tom looked at Frank, "You mean to send off your name?"

"Well can you think of anything better than the old crow up there reading my name in the newspaper? His first inclination will be to send for me to tell me that if I want to join the army I might as well leave straight away. But, just think about it! Even he would realise what it would do to his reputation if I told the Daily Post."

Frank lifted his arm and indicated an imaginary line in the newspaper, "Can't you just see the headline, 'Factory Owner sacks employee for wanting to join the Birmingham Battalion'? Don't you see; the bugger can't win? He wouldn't dare sack me for doing my bit for King and Country and I just walk out of here when and if the Regiment's formed."

They both laughed. "But what about me? You don't intend to leave me out of it do you?"

"No of course not you idiot, but I can't volunteer for you can I? Anyway, you said the other week that you wouldn't join Kitchener's army!"

"I know I did, but this is different. You can't leave me in this place on my own."

"I'll tell you what. Why don't you think about it and instead of sending our names off to the paper, we'll go there on Saturday afternoon and hand our names in?"

At three o'clock on Saturday afternoon, two young men stepped off the train in Birmingham, having caught the train at Walsall station straight from work.

They marched side by side and could easily have been taken as brothers except for their hair. At five feet ten inches Tom Richards was a mere one-inch shorter than Frank Matthews, but they both had the same piecing deep blue eyes and the same tight set jaw. Neither of them carried an ounce of fat on their fit bodies and they both walked with the same sense of purpose and urgency. They were similarly dressed in black suits with waistcoats and highly polished shoes. Normally they put on clean stiff starched white collars twice a week for work, on Mondays and Thursdays. But today they had both put on clean collars which as usual, were rounded off instead of a point; almost two peas in a pod. However the one thing that set them apart was Tom Richards' mop of vivid red hair compared to Frank Matthews' light brown curly hair.

They did in fact, act and often think as brothers, for they had been born within three weeks of each other and had lived next door to each other all their lives. When Frank's father had been killed, Tom's mother had often looked after him so that his own mother could go out to work to keep paying the rent and look after Frank.

The two young men marched together to Victoria Square and stood outside the City Hall looking at the giant wooden barometer showing the recruitment in the City. The indicator was being reset several times each day and was already reaching the top.

As they stood looking at the barometer, a voice behind them said, "They'll have to build another section on the top soon."

Frank and Tom turned as the young fellow, who was grinning from ear to ear stepped beside them.

"They'll have to put it up another notch when I've signed on."

"Another three when we've signed on as well," Tom grinned in reply. He held out his hand and shook the lad's hand, "Tom Richards is the name and this here is my best mate Frank Matthews. We were just going to the Daily Post offices to put our names on the list for the Birmingham volunteers."

"Joe Hadley at your service," replied the young man, lifting an imaginary hat off his head and swinging his arm from left to right, whilst bowing low as if giving allegiance to royalty, "Pleased to make your acquaintance young Sirs and perhaps you'd be kind enough to let me join you?" He was laughing as he spoke and tottered slightly as he lifted up from the bow.

"You're very welcome to come and sign on with us but have you been drinking to get Dutch courage?"

Joe pulled himself straight, "Actually I haven't been drinking at all. I don't usually act as daft as this. I'm just a bit nervous see, and when I'm nervous, I always act a bit stupid. It's my way of trying to cover it up. God, I must be nervous. I've known you all of two seconds and I'm giving away my secrets straight away."

"What are you nervous about?" Frank asked. "If you're nervous about signing on, maybe you're frightened of becoming a soldier. In which case, it's my view that you really shouldn't be signing on."

"No it's nothing like that. I'm more sure about wanting to sign on and becoming a soldier than anything I've done before, but it's my Mom and Dad, you see. They don't know I'm here. They'll kill me when they find out. I'm frightened of telling them, particularly my Mom, she'll cry her eyes out. I know she will when she finds out her little boy is going to fight in the war. I just won't be able to take all her tears."

"Well, if it comes to that, I haven't told my mother yet," said Frank. "Have you, Tom?"

Tom shook his head from side to side.

"Well there's going to be showers tonight in three households at least," laughed Frank.

They all looked at each other and burst out laughing. Joe put two fingers under each eye and stroked them downward over his cheeks, pulling a face at the same time to represent the tears flowing, "Poor mothers! Who'd have them at a time like this?"

He put his hands together as if in prayer and bowed his head in supplication, a false quiver in his voice, "I'm sorry, dear mother. I love you dearly, really."

They all burst out laughing again.

Frank was the first to stop, "Come on you idiot, stop messing about. Do you want to come with us or not? You really should decide whether it's actually what you want you know. I doubt they'll let you change your mind once you've put your name to the bit of paper."

"No actually I feel much better about it now. I really don't have any doubts about wanting to sign on, and when I tell my Mom and Dad now, I'll just think about you two telling yours and I'll be OK."

He stepped between Frank and Tom and linked an arm with each of them, "Come on, let's go and join Lord Kitchener in his fight against the Hun."

The three of them marched, arm in arm across Victoria Square towards the special recruiting office which had been set up for the city battalion in

Great Charles Street. A recruiting sergeant stood guard at the door.

They unlinked their arms and the three of them marched up to him. "Is this where we sign on for the Daily Post's special Birmingham battalion?" enquired Frank.

"Sure is," replied the sergeant, "This way, gentlemen," as he indicated the door to them.

Frank was the first to reach the door, followed by Tom and with Joe at the rear. Frank opened the door and was about to go in when the sergeant put his hand on Joe's shoulder, "And how old would you be, young man?"

The three of them stopped and turned to the sergeant.

Joe stood as if to attention, "Seventeen, Sir."

"Sorry, not old enough. You'd better go away and come back when you're old enough."

The three looked at each other and Frank put an arm on each of the other's shoulders and led them away, "Come on, we'd better go and sort this out."

They walked back to the Square and went into a huddle. Ten minutes later, they marched in close order single file back up to the recruiting sergeant with Joe in the middle of the other two.

Tom, who was in the lead this time, headed straight towards the door, ignoring the recruiting sergeant.

"Oi! You three come here a minute," and pointing to Joe, the sergeant said, "And how old might you be?"

"Oh, he's just gone nineteen, sir," answered Frank.

"That's all right then. Off you go. Don't keep His Majesty waiting," and as they went past him, the sergeant stroked his waxed moustache and they heard him say under his breath, "God knows what they put in the water round here, but they sure as hell grow up fast."

"Make the most of this, Joe. This is the last meal you'll have in good old Blighty for a while."

The three of them were dressed in full kit as they waited their turn in the queue for breakfast. Corporal Matthews in front of his two pals. He looked across at the food being served out, "Good Lord, look at that lot; we've got the full works today, bacon, sausage, eggs, black pudding and fried bread. Come my hearties; eat your heart out. You'll need it for the journey. I bet they won't be feeding us up like this when we cross over into France."

"You two have never been on a boat trip or anywhere near the sea before, have you?" laughed Joe. "I just hope for your sake, that the weather's fine out there, otherwise you'll be bringing up everything you eat this morning."

He stuck out his tongue, put two fingers on it, bent his head towards the ground and let out a noise imitating a man being sick. He lifted his head, and moving his arm in a rolling action to represent a ship being tossed on the waves he laughed out loudly, "God help you if it's rough." He continued his arm rolling movement, "U....p and down. U....p and down. U....p and down." With each 'Up' he pulled in his stomach, leaned forward and opened his mouth to portray being sick. He burst out laughing again.

"Stop messing about, Joe," said Tom, pushing Joe forward in the queue. When Joe turned round and did his impression of a man being sick again, Tom looked at him quizzically, "It won't really be like that. Will it?"

Joe shrugged his shoulders, leaned towards Tom and shaking his head from side to side, said quietly, "To tell you the truth, mate, I haven't got a clue, I've never even seen the sea, let alone been on a boat either." He laughed again as he added, "But I've read about it and that's what the books say it's like!"

The queue had moved forward and Frank was holding out his plate to be served, "Well I'm going to have plenty of everything." He turned to Tom, who was obviously still thinking about what it might be like on the boat, "I suggest you just enjoy your breakfast Tom, and forget all about this being sick nonsense." He laughed, "Anyway, from what I've heard, it's better if you've got something to bring up!"

The three of them filled their plates and moved together to an empty trestle table to eat their meal. Frank looked round and suddenly realised how seriously everyone in the mess hut looked as they ate their meal. The usual rumble of conversation and the general laughter was missing. Few of the men were talking, but those that were, occasionally broke into nervous laughter. He noted how quickly the laughter stopped. It did not continue as was usually the case. *'Come to think of it,'* he thought to himself, *'even Joe is quiet today. Not acting the natural buffoon as much as he usually does. Even those antics about being sick on the boat: that was more out of nervousness than natural humour. He always goes like that when he's unsure of things.'* He looked across at him carefully and slowly eating his meal, obviously deep in thought about something. Tom was exactly the same.

Frank thought back to the first time he had met Joe, nearly fifteen months ago when they had signed up for this. *'God help us,'* he thought, *'What have we let ourselves in for? What is it going to be like in France?'*

He decided it would probably be better to think of the past rather than to worry about what was to come. He and Tom had become the best of pals with Joe since joining up. They had next met a year ago when they arrived at Sutton Park to start their training. The three of them were put in the same section, probably because they had signed on together, or at least that was what Frank thought. It seemed to Frank that they mostly spent the days digging trenches and then filling them in again, but that wasn't entirely true. They had been taught the elements of marching and then after they had been issued with uniforms, and later on still, with rifles, they had been taught to march and shoot with real earnest.

They still had to dig trenches on a regular basis but at least they hadn't had to fill them in quite as often, particularly when stores had been able to issue them with ammunition to practice firing from the trenches.

Frank had been surprised when he had been promoted to corporal in charge of his section. He was concerned at first how his pals might take it, but he need not have worried. The rest of the section and particularly Tom and Joe had readily accepted his being chosen as corporal.

They had been training in Sutton Park until July, and since this was so near to home, they'd managed to get home most weekends, and Frank and Tom often managed to get home for the odd evening in the week as well; sometimes missing the last bus to camp and having to walk the six and half miles back. Joe, who lived too far away to get home for an evening always joined them on these occasions and had rapidly become regarded as a member of their families.

Frank looked at Joe, "Do you realise I've only known you properly for just over twelve months? It seems much longer somehow."

"What on earth has made you say that, right now?" enquired Joe.

"Don't know really!" He shrugged his shoulders as he said it, "Just been thinking about how well we've got on together since we joined up. Do you ever wish the recruiting sergeant hadn't let you sign on?"

"A bit late to think about that now, ain't it?" Joe put his knife and fork down and thought for a moment, "No, not at all, I'd probably be daft enough to do it again." He laughed as he looked at Frank and Tom in turn. "But only if I met you buggers again and you conned me into lying about my age."

"Oh, come off it," said Frank, "you begged us to help you get past the recruiting sergeant. Anyway, it wasn't the only lie you told that day, was it?"

"You mean about my grandmother's address? That wasn't a real lie. I often stayed at her house."

"Well you should've made sure you were there more often then. Silly bugger! Just think about it, you might have been posted as 'absent without leave' on your very first day."

Frank laughed as he noticed others at the table listening to the conversation. He pointed a finger at Joe, "This is the guy who gave his grandmother's address in Yardley as his home address when he signed on 'cause he was worried that his real home in Bewdley wouldn't be accepted as a Birmingham address. Stupid bugger forgot to tell his grandmother though. When his call up papers arrived, she just put them behind the clock on the mantelpiece. Still been there now wouldn't they young Hadley if your mother hadn't badgered your old man to call to see how her mother was keeping on his way back from market on the day prior to the first parade." He laughed again, "All hell was let loose in the Hadley household that night, wasn't it, Joe? Mother crying! Sister crying! Father shouting poor old Joe's balls off! And there was Joe rushing round trying to sort out all the things he needed to bring with him and worrying how he was going to get to Birmingham in time for parade."

They all laughed and Frank slapped Joe on the back, "That's your story anyhow, ain't it mate?"

Joe looked at the others around the table listening to the story, "You lot can believe him if you want to but I tell you, every time he tells the story he adds a bit more to the tale. I'm not even sure what bits I believe myself any more."

Lieutenant Groves entered the mess and came up to Frank and tapped him on the shoulder, "Corporal Matthews would you mind sorting out all these chaps and get them lined up outside with all their kit? We have to be off in fifteen minutes to catch the train."

Frank stood up and giving a salute replied, "Yes Sir." and the Lieutenant immediately strode away and out of the mess.

"Always getting you to his dirty work ain't he Corporal?" said a voice from behind Frank.

Frank swung round but was unable to determine which of the men, all of whom were suddenly assiduously tucking into the remains of their breakfast, had spoken. He just stared at each of them as they lifted their heads to look at him, but without saying anything to them directly, shouted across the room, "Come on, all of you. If you haven't finished your breakfast in two minutes flat, you ain't going to. We're on our way. Pick up your kit pronto, and line up outside for the off. La France, next stop. Come on, you'll soon have your chance now to show the Kaiser and his merry men that they can't mess with us and get away with it."

Twenty four hours later, the men of 'C' company were 'enjoying' a very different breakfast of biscuits and what the cook tried to pass off as tea, but God knows what he had used for milk, or tea for that matter. As they huddled together trying to avoid the biting wind swirling around the hilltop and through the tents, they started to wonder whether they would ever get warm again.

Most of the men were still shivering from the most uncomfortable night they had ever spent under canvas and the wringing wet blankets they had been sleeping in. In fact they'd started to feel the cold as soon as they had embarked on the SS Invictor at Folkestone; the bitterly cold November wind cutting through the protection of the heavy greatcoats worn by any of the men who ventured on to the deck during the crossing; whilst those who chose to shelter below deck were nauseated by the stink of the disinfectant which had been swept on to the decks in bucketfuls to try to clear the stench of the vomit of the poor, injured wretches who had been brought back from France the previous night in what turned out to be a near disastrous crossing as the SS Invictor battled with the storm and the heaving waves.

The main eye of the storm had passed over by the time the battalion boarded ship but the effects of the disinfectant and the biting cold got the better of many of the men, on what was for nearly all of them, their first ever sea crossing or for that matter, their first ever sight of the sea.

Within ten minutes of leaving Folkestone, both Tom and Joe were heaving over the side of the boat discharging the remains of their last meal into the English Channel. Frank stood with his back to the rail, his greatcoat collar up around his neck, trying to hide from the wind, and with both eyes closed, trying to will himself not to be sick.

Afterwards he was not so sure he should have tried so hard. Tom and Joe seemed to be perfectly all right as soon as they disembarked at Boulogne and had planted their feet firmly on the soil of 'La France'. Frank's inside however was still heaving most of the way on the two mile march to Ostrohove camp and his stomach did not feel settled until he lay down to go to sleep. However, feeling warm and being dry were luxuries which they would all have to wait a long, long time for.

CHAPTER TWO

1916

Frank held his watch in his hand, squinting at the hands in the moonlight. As soon as the hands met at twelve o'clock he passed a greeting to each of the men in his section, speaking as quietly as he could, but loud enough to be heard by the men spread out along the sap, "Happy New Year chaps. Let's hope we can finish this bloody war soon and enjoy next New Year back home in Blighty. Never mind, only another eight hours before we get relieved out of this mud bath."

Tom and Joe were at the far end of the twenty five yard stretch of trench being held by Frank's section and he felt certain that they would not have heard his greeting. He did not want them to be oblivious to his New Year wishes, so he removed the bayonet from his gun and after placing it in his belt, he slung the rifle over his shoulder and, digging his elbows into each side of the trench, started the laborious journey to them.

It seemed that the rains of the last two months were going to remain permanently in the bottom of the ditches, turning them into seas of mud.

Frank tugged and heaved on his left leg until his foot finally emerged from the mire. Thank God his boot was still strapped to his foot; it would not have been the first time a boot had been lost in the oozing slime. Leaning forward to grab hold of the first man in the line with his right hand he pushed his left hand against the opposite side of the trench as he put his left foot back into the boggy mixture as far forward as he could stretch. He then slowly extricated his right leg and continued the process, leg after leg, praying that boot and sock would still be attached each time he disengaged a leg from the clammy, mucky treacle and hoping that his boot would not sink more than a foot into the quagmire, otherwise he might never get it out.

It took him a full ten minutes to reach Joe. He was just about to slap him on the back and wish him a 'Happy New Year', when he realised that Lieutenant Groves was heading towards him along the sap from the opposite direction. He too was progressing at the same slow and laborious rate as he painstakingly extracted one leg at a time through the mud; the men to the side of the trench having to hold him steady and prevent him from falling over into it.

Frank greeted him with a, "Happy New Year, Sir," when he had progressed to within two yards of him. “Quiet tonight! Perhaps they're seeing in the New Year by celebrating with the old Schnapps over there.”

“Exactly Corporal. Just the time to give them a surprise and spoil the buggers' festivities.”

The Lieutenant had reached Tom, who just managed to catch hold of him and prevent him falling as he tried to lift his rear leg from the oozing mixture.

After steadying themselves, Tom reached down to the officer's left leg, which he seemed incapable of lifting of his own accord. “Let me give you a hand, Sir,” he said as he tugged on the leg. His efforts finally succeeding in hauling out the leg and moving it forward a mere eighteen inches before dropping it back into the mud with a great 'plop'.

The Lieutenant just managed to keep his balance by grabbing the assault ladder leaning against the side of the trench, and by holding on to the rungs he was able to move his legs sufficient to twist and lean on it. He took out his hip flask, unscrewed the top, tipping his head back as he drained the last drops from it. After which, he held the bottle forward towards Frank in a form of salute, “And a happy New Year to you Corporal.”

He moved the flask close to his chest and after several attempts managed to screw the top back on without dropping it.

As he returned the flask to his pocket, he looked up and down the line of men, who by now were staring at him to a man. He looked back at Frank. “Corporal, we are going to give the buggers over there a very happy New Year. Go and fill your pockets with grenades, Corporal. You and me are going over there and help them see in the New Year with a few fireworks to liven up the party.”

“Have we been given orders to attack then, Sir?”

“We don't need bloody orders, Corporal. I'm giving the orders around here.”

He leaned forward and putting his hand on Frank's shoulder, moved his face inches from Frank’s and looking him directly into the eye said, “We're going to be bloody heroes, Corporal. If that's what she wants then that's what we'll give her. Come on Corporal, give me a lift up and let's go and sort the bastards out.”

Such fighting talk was quite out of character for the meek and mild Lieutenant Groves. In fact, he had something of a reputation in the battalion as weak and indecisive, and Frank was not alone in having a very low opinion of him as an officer. But as the Lieutenant leaned forward into his face, Frank could smell the reason for his bravado on this occasion. He had quite clearly been celebrating the New Year whilst tucked away in his own rabbit hutch and had obviously drunk far more than the mere contents of his small hip flask. Frank couldn't help thinking that the muddy floor of the trench and the narrowness of its sides to each other, was probably the only reason he had been able to keep upright for as long as he had. He was in no fit state to do anything, and certainly not to 'go over the top'.

"I don't think it would be a very good idea to attack without orders, Sir. Shall I just help you back and we can await orders?" And whilst he was saying this, Frank reached forward to steady the Lieutenant who was attempting to manoeuvre round to climb up the ladder. After a while he managed to release his left foot and get it on to the first rung of the ladder.

Frank was desperately trying to think of some way to stop him climbing the ladder and get him back to his foxhole to sleep off his inebriation. "Wouldn't it better if you tried to get some rest for now, Sir? We can always have a go at the Germans in a couple of hour's time if you want to. They'll all be well and truly plastered by then and that'll make the job easy."

"Not on your life, Matthews. We're going up over there to sort them out now and you are coming with me. I've told you we're going to be heroes; that's what she wants in a man." He pulled an envelope out of his top pocket and waved it at Frank, "A bloody hero is what she wants, so a hero is what I'm going to give her." On saying this he screwed up the paper and threw it in the mud. He pulled his pistol out of its holster and waving it at Frank said, "Come on, Corporal. Give me a hand up and let's go and show her who the real heroes are around here."

By now he had succeeded in lifting his right foot out of the mud and placed it on the second rung of the ladder. Frank reached forward, not to help him up but to try and prevent him going any further up the ladder. The Lieutenant, realising Frank's action, lifted his foot into Frank's stomach and pushed him reeling back into the mud.

Shouting at the top of his voice, he looked down at Frank, who, with the help of Joe was lifting himself from the muddy bath, "Now you give me a hand Richards and as for you Matthews, I've given you an order. Follow me over the top or I'll put you on a charge."

Tom helped the officer up the ladder as he had been ordered and Frank, shaking his head, tried to move towards the ladder as he had been ordered.

The lieutenant had, with Tom's help, reached the top of the ladder, his head and shoulders protruding over the ridge of the trench. He tried to lift himself on to the ground at the top of the sap but he was far too drunk to achieve it. He shouted down to Tom, "Give me a push, Richards."

Tom reached up to do his bidding as the sound of machine gun fire from the German trenches rang through the night air. Frank looked up and felt a splatter of warmth caress across his face.

He went to wipe the moisture from his eyes but instead reached his arms forward to try and catch the falling body of the lieutenant, which seemed to be flying through the air in slow motion towards him.

Seconds later, Frank was struggling under the weight of Tom across his legs and the weight of the lieutenant across his head forcing it into the treacly slush. He desperately tried to get his head above the mud before he suffocated in an inglorious death, but the harder he tried, the more he felt himself sinking deeper and deeper into the bog.

Just as his lungs were about to burst and Frank thought his end had come, the weight was dragged off his body, his flailing free arm was pulled taut and he was jerked upwards, releasing his head from the putrid and mephitic earth. His lungs were still straining for a fresh intake of air, his air passages still blocked by the pervading mud in his mouth and nostrils. He coughed hard and spat the rancid mixture from his mouth, and, taking a deep breath through his mouth, felt the cold oxygen flow through to his head like an opiate drug liberating him from a choking hell.

Frank was now sitting on his haunches in the mud bath, frantically wiping the sludge from his face, eyes and nostrils, whilst continuing to systematically take full gasps of air through his mouth to fill and refill his lungs.

Tom was sitting in a similar fashion facing Frank. "Are you all right, Frank?" but without waiting for an answer he opened his water flask and passed it to Frank, "Here mate, use this to wash your face and have a drink. It'll help clear your throat and nose of all that muck."

"Thanks. I thought I was a goner there. What the hell happened?"

Tom pointed to where Joe and Dick Glover were lifting the lieutenant into a sitting position. Frank noticed the hole, half an inch above the bridge of his nose, and as they twisted him round to lean him with his back against the trench wall, he saw the larger, messy exposure of brain tissue protruding out of the back of his head.

"Jesus Christ! You stupid sod! Why on earth did you have to go and do such a daft thing for?" He turned to Tom, "How on earth are we going to explain this away?" and turning back to the lieutenant he cried out as if in pain, "You stupid, stupid sod."

"We have to tell it as it was," said Tom. "He was drunk, we could all see that. And we all know you tried to talk him out of it, but he gave us orders and we had to follow them and let him go."

"Jesus, Tom, we didn't have to let the poor bastard go and get himself killed though. He didn't deserve that."

The men in the trench on either side of Tom and Frank were slowly moving towards them, inhibited from fast movement by the powerful suction of the persistent presence of the pervading boggy earth.

"Get back to your posts, all of you," shouted Frank, "There's nothing to see here so just get back to your posts."

The slow advance halted and the men turned wearisomely round to return to where they had come from, each man frustrated by the ever consuming mud; cussing and cursing as they tried to move, laboriously trying to lift one foot after the other without losing a boot in the process.

"A great welcome to 1916 this has turned out to be," said Tom, "Not only has he got himself killed but now we've got to try and carry him back through all this bloody muck."

Frank just laughed without comment and as he passed the water bottle back to Tom he noticed the envelope floating on top of the mud. He lifted it out of the earth and taking the bottle back from Tom washed the mud from the outside of the envelope. He held the envelope up, letting the water drip from it and as he returned the bottle to Tom said, "Look, I know we didn't think much of old Groves but we can't tell the powers that be what a stupid bloody idiot he was, and that it was all his own drunken fault."

He turned to look at the lieutenant again. The wide open eyes stared fixedly and coldly back directly at him and the mouth gaped open giving a look of utter astonishment on the face. "Oh, my God!" he yelled as he covered his own eyes with his free hand, "For God's sake close the bugger's eyes and tie up his mouth. It's enough to frighten anybody to death looking at something like that."

He continued the conversation as Tom took the lanyard from round the officer's neck and tied it round his head as a means of closing his mouth; the whistle still dangling from it under his chin, "Look, let's just say that he climbed up the ladder to see what was going on after we heard noises from the German trenches, and some German must have got in a lucky and accurate shot when Grovesy here popped his head up."

He looked at Tom and then across to Joe and shrugged his shoulders as he added, "Well, it's basically the truth anyway; isn't it? We don't have to make it worse for his family by saying he was drunk and stupid with it, do we?" At this, he shook the wet envelope once more and, folding it in half, placed it into the breast pocket of his tunic. He was about to button it up when he remembered the lieutenant's words as he had thrown the envelope to the ground.

He took the wet paper back out of his pocket saying, "She wants a hero, so that's what I'll give her. That's what he said, wasn't it? Do you think there's something in this letter that made him go over the top? If there is and we hand it in they may realise that our story isn't entirely true. Perhaps we'd better have a look, it's not as if that poor bastard will bother about his privacy any more, is it?"

Without waiting for an answer, Frank took the crumpled letter from the envelope and opened up the single page of pink notepaper, which had a printed address at the top of *'Rosemount, Bird Street, Lichfield'* and read the very short message.

Dear Cecil

I hope you are keeping well. All the family here are well and looking forward to Christmas.

I am sorry to tell you that I am calling off our engagement and I am keeping the ring safely in its box to give to you when you next return home. You see, I have met this wonderful Captain, who is home on sick leave. He was injured in the leg and arm, bravely fighting and killing several Germans before passing out from his wounds. Luckily he was able to get back safely when he came round.

I do love him so much and we plan to marry before he returns to the front. Mother says he will look so fine in his uniform at the wedding. A real hero.

I hope you understand. Take care.

With regards Henrietta

Frank handed the letter to Tom to read, "The vindictive upper-class cow. Couldn't give him the news gently, could she? Had to rub it in! No wonder he got himself drunk. You know what, Tom? I reckon the poor bastard was trying to prove himself a bigger hero than this Henriettta's Captain. Silly bugger, all he ends up doing is getting himself killed. Christ what a mess?"

He looked once again at the dead body, "You know what old fellow? I'm going to give your dear Henrietta her brave hero. When we get back to camp, I'm going to send her back this letter, with a covering letter from me saying how bravely you fought, and even though injured you carried on killing Germans to the last. And how, just before you died you handed me the letter and told me to write to her and wish her well with her Captain."

"Do you think I'll get it past the censors, Tom?" and without waiting for an answer added, "Probably not. I think I'd better hold on to it and go and see her when we get home. I can weave a jolly good story then. I'll make the bitch suffer."

He put the letter back in his pocket before continuing, "Do you think all women are like this, Tom? Or is it just upper-class women who are like it?" Your Grace wouldn't do the dirty on a chap like that, would she?"

Tom just shrugged his shoulders and said, "How would I know whether she would or not?"

"Well she's your sister, so you ought to know."

Frank had in fact been wondering whether Grace had done just that, because he had not received a letter from her since before Christmas. No special Christmas message or gift. Maybe she was not as keen on him as he had started to be of her, particularly since arriving in France. God, he had really begun to miss her, and how! Maybe she'd found someone else and didn't even have the guts to write to tell him?

He repeated the question, "She wouldn't, would she Tom?"

Perhaps Tom had not heard the question or perhaps he did not really appreciate the significance of it and the question remained unanswered, or at least until the post arrived two days later and Frank collected the parcel Grace had sent. It had obviously been opened by those blasted censors. What the hell did they think Grace was sending to him? Secrets for the Germans? No, just some gloves and a scarf she had knit and a small Christmas pudding complete with the essential silver three-penny bit in it.

When he read the letter she had sent with the parcel, the things she had written made Frank think that maybe she was missing him as well, and for the first time since reading Henrietta's letter to the Lieutenant he was able to convince himself that all women weren't the same.

Two months later, the brigade had moved to Arras to relieve the French at St. Nicholas, and was given rest and recuperation in billets at Agnez-les-Duisons. These provided absolutely luxurious accommodation compared to the front line mud bath trenches they had been guarding at the New Year.

At least here they were able to have hot showers and regularly change their socks, thanks to the industry of the ladies of Birmingham who must have been constantly knitting socks of all sizes to be sent in crates to the lads in their Birmingham Battalions.

Nevertheless for Frank, the different treatment of the men and the officers was a constant sore to him. If the officers were not dining on roast beef or roast duck or something equally delicious in their mess, they were away to the Hotel du Commerce in Arras where they could still get drunk on good French wine, whilst enjoying good French food served by pretty French maids. The men meanwhile dined under canvas or in the open air on some sort of vegetable stew, which from time to time may have included the added luxury of some form of meat. They could never quite make out what the meat was and Joe was always joking, “Well they have to get rid of all that dead horsemeat somehow, don't they?”

On Saturday night, when the lads were going to join the queue outside the mess for their evening meal, Frank stopped for a few seconds outside the window of the kitchen serving the officer's mess. He lifted his left leg on to the windowsill and retied his bootlace.

Afterwards he rushed up to Tom and Joe and grabbed each of them by the arm and in a low voice, so that none of the other soldiers could hear said, “Hang on, chaps, come with me. I reckon it's time we ate like Lords as well. Why should the officers always be the ones having the good food?”

He let go of their arms and spoke in his normal voice, “Looks like it's going to be a chilly night and I've left my scarf in the billet. Just hang on here for me, I won’t be a minute.”

He rushed back to the billet, where he collected his own and Tom's scarf and a box of matches that were lying on Tom's bed. He took his bayonet from its holster, covered it with his scarf, and carefully put it inside his jacket before rushing back to the officer's mess kitchen. But this time he crept closely along the wall to the door, opened it quietly and peeped in.

Charley Upton was the only person in there and he was whistling away as he prepared food with his back to the door. The two joints of beef Frank had seen earlier from the window were still sitting on the table not four feet away. He tiptoed over, watching Charlie Upton all the time, grabbed one of the joints and a loaf of bread, and managed to escape through the door without being seen.

He wrapped Tom's scarf round the joint and bread and went back to the lads. “Come on chaps, we're not eating in the mess tonight, we've got something rather special instead.”

An hour later all three were sitting around a fire in the wood a mile further away from the lines enjoying the barbecued steaks between slices of bread, both of which had been fairly crudely cut with the bayonet.

“Pity you didn't manage to get a couple of bottles of wine as well,” said Joe. “Go down a treat with a bottle of Beau Jolly would this.”

“A bottle of Beaujolais would be wasted on you, Joe. You wouldn't know a good bottle of wine even if we had it. Your 'common a garden’ Vin Rouge is good enough for you.”

"Well that's where you're wrong, Frank. I'm used to drinking the best wine in the whole world. My mother's home made elderberry wine would beat anything these Froggies make. Christ what I'd give to be out of this God forsaken hole, back home by the kitchen range eating Ma's steak and kidney pud with a bottle of her elderberry wine."

He went quiet for a minute and Frank thought he was going to cry, but he pulled himself together taking another good bite from his steak sandwich and with his mouth full, spluttered, "Best bloody wine in the world is my mother's elderberry. Tell you what, I'll get her to send us a bottle and you can taste it yourself." He let out a laugh, blowing part of the food out of his mouth as he did so, "Blow your bloody head off would Ma's elderberry wine."

They all laughed and continued the banter for some time, making enough noise to be heard from the road less than thirty yards away. Joe suddenly jumped up and stood to attention; trying to hide the remains of his sandwich by his left side, whilst saluting with his right hand, and whilst trying to hold the food in his mouth let out a, "Sir."

Tom and Frank turned round and jumped to attention themselves when they saw the officer; an officer whom they had never seen before.

"That's all right, chaps, you don't need to stand to attention here. Sorry to spoil your picnic, but my motorbike has broken down and now I've got stuck in the mud back there. Couldn't give me a push could you? I'd appreciate it if you could."

"Yes Sir. Straight away, Sir," said Frank, "Well that's as soon as we put this fire out," and at that he started to kick soil over the burning embers.

Tom bent over to pick up the last sandwich, trying to hide it from the officer.

"I say," said the officer, "that wouldn't be food you have there, would it? Couldn't spare some of it I suppose? I've been pushing that blessed bike for miles and I'm starving."

Tom looked across at Frank, who immediately took the food off him and handed it to the officer. "Sure, Sir, you are very welcome to it. We've had our fill anyway."

The officer took a bite and after chewing it for a while, waved the remains of the sandwich in his hand and said, "This is great! Do this sort of thing on your nights off instead of going into town do you?"

"Well no Sir, this is a bit of a special occasion," and without waiting for any further comment from the officer Frank said, "We really ought to get to your motorbike. The sooner we get it out of that mud, the better I reckon."

With that he kicked some more soil over the fire and marched off towards the road with the others following. "This way was it Sir?"

"Yes, down this way," said the officer frantically trying to keep up with Frank, who by now was almost running towards the road and trying desperately to think where he had seen the officer's face before and praying that he would never hear about stolen beef.

He remembered where he had seen the face before at Church parade the next morning, when the padre invited Lieutenant Harper to read the scripture, introducing him as the new officer who was officially joining the battalion for duty next day.

Frank put his hand up to his face and said under his breath, "Jesus Christ, I haven't got to take orders from a blasted Harper again have I? I joined this lot to get away from that. Not again please!"

No one could hear Frank, not even Tom who was next to him. On consideration, Frank hoped that the Lord hadn't heard him either, or at least if he had, he took it to be a prayer and not the profanity which it really was.

After parade Frank tried to get away as quickly as possible, pulling Tom along, "Do you realise that the new officer is Mark Harper, bloody Vernon Harper's son. Don't you remember him coming into Harper's office with his sister that day we went up to see Harper about our rise?" But without waiting for an answer added, "And now he's come here to haunt us and I bet he'll love dropping us in it over that beef we pinched."

No sooner had Frank said this than they heard running behind them and the Lieutenant shouting after them, "Corporal, can you spare me a minute please?" Their hearts started thumping rapidly and their mouths suddenly went dry.

Frank was about to pretend he had not heard but thought better of it and both he and Tom stopped and turned round. Lieutenant Harper stopped running and when he reached them asked them which part of Birmingham they came from.

"Well Sir, we don't actually come from Birmingham, we come from Walsall," said Frank.

"Thought so! You used to work for my father, didn't you? I've got a good memory for faces."

"Yes Sir. We used to work at Harpers."

"Yes, I thought I recognised you last night. Look I've a bit of a problem and I don't want to start off in the Battalion on the wrong foot, but there was talk in the officer's mess at breakfast this morning about half of our Sunday roast going missing. Someone suggested that a fox might have taken it but the cook said some bread was missing as well, so it's a bit unlikely to be a fox, don't you think? You wouldn't know anything about it would you?"

"No Sir," said Frank, shaking his head and pursing his lips, which he hoped Harper would take as disbelief that he had even thought he might know anything about it.

"Thought not, stupid question anyway," and with a broad grin across his face added, "I wouldn't expect anyone from Walsall to be involved in anything sordid like that. And, in any case I guess it's quite lucky for some that I don't actually start my duties here until tomorrow and I wouldn't want to create waves before I even start now would I?"

"No Sir, I .."

Lieutenant Harper interrupted before Frank could finish his sentence, "I suggest you don't say anything, Corporal. I might be new here but I'm not stupid and I wouldn't wish you to say anything that might turn out to be untrue. I think we've said enough. I'm not going to ask more questions about stolen beef, either here or anywhere else, but after today I shall look to any soldier from my hometown to be a model soldier. Understood?"

"Yes Sir," said Frank and Tom in unison.

"Right then and by the way I regard myself as a fair man, but I recommend that you don't take it to mean that I'm by any means a soft touch. I trust you understand what I'm saying because the way I see it, it would not be in your best interest to get on the wrong side of me, seeing as how, from tomorrow anyway, I shall be your commanding officer."

Frank nodded. "Understand perfectly, Sir."

"All right, see you on parade tomorrow morning then."

Frank stood there trying to work out whether the officer in front of him, was an ogre like his father and was playing cat and mouse with them, or whether, maybe, he was quite a nice guy trying to be friendly, whilst still keeping the distance between officer and men.

Frank was even more unsure when he looked at each of them in turn and said, "Thanks for your help last night with the bike, I appreciated it." He then gave a big grin and added, "I enjoyed the food as well!" and at that he walked away.

The battle of the Somme began on 1st July, and on 3rd July, the 'Birmingham Lads' started the long march from Agnez to Dernancourt, having lunch by the side of the road each day and finding the best billets they could each night.

In the country behind the lines, a myriad of army tents were pitched around every corner, and every spare farmhouse, barn, outhouse, village hall, school hall and church had been taken over to provide billets for the hoards of soldiers from the various divisions and battalions waiting in reserve and being prepared for battle.

The battering of the enemy lines with shells of all sizes had been going on for weeks. Although the lads had got used to the noise (or not as the case may be) of the guns pulsating away over the past six months, the fanfare greeting them as they neared Dernancourt was beyond belief. They had been used to the boom of German shells exploding in or near their trenches and the thunder of their own guns pounding shells into the German lines but at least you could count the shells being fired or hear the German shell on its way towards the allied lines. Here the distant sound was continuous, almost like a drum roll which never ended.

The Battalion was ordered to adopt 'battle order' on 19th July and after tying their greatcoats into bundles and handing them in together with any other unwanted gear, the men moved up to the battle zone. Each man was loaded down with all the accoutrements of battle; not only guns, ammunition and buckets full of Mills bombs, but food, cooking equipment, signalling equipment, rolls of telephone wire, rolls of barbed wire and a miscellany of other paraphernalia which, to those carrying it, did not seem in the least useful for killing Germans, and would certainly hinder their progress and manoeuvrability if and when they were sent over the top.

As they marched slowly up to the lines to the front, the noise of the guns became almost unbearable and when they were still a good mile from the enemy lines, all around were the vast lines of mighty siege guns. Each gun standing on ribbed wheels as tall as any of the men who were continuously feeding the heavy shells into their giant barrels and pounding the Germans faster than it was possible to count.

They continued their march through Caterpillar Valley towards the front, ready to support the trenches at the eastern end of the valley. The road they were on was packed from end to end with guns of all shapes and sizes and piled up all around and about were thousands of shells waiting to be fed into their barrels. Frank's first thought was what if the Germans fired a sixty pounder into this lot whilst they were moving past? All these shells would go off in one huge explosion and would finish the whole battalion off in one go. His second thought however was for the poor souls on the receiving end of the bombardment. He previously thought he'd seen the worst of war already but this was something beggaring belief.

He remembered when, only just over a month ago at Agnez, the Germans had started a bombardment against the front held by Frank's battalion and the 1st Norfolks on their right. The poor lads from Norfolk had been nearly obliterated by the mortar bombs and shells bursting all over the place. Their own supply lines and telephone communications had been cut off and the trench blown in half a dozen places. Several of Frank's pals had been killed and several other men had been severely wounded. Poor old Dick Glover had lost one eye and the last Frank had heard they weren't sure that he would be able to see through the other after they took the bandages off. And poor old Chalky White had lost both legs and was lucky to be alive, although Frank did not think that 'lucky' was the right word for it. He thought Chalky might have been better off dying out there than having to live without his legs. Wally Betts had been next to Chalky and he was in an even bigger mess when they found him; one leg and half his arm lying in a mangled heap some feet from his body. He had died before they had managed to get him out of the lines for medical attention. Maybe he was the lucky one?

It was after this that Lieutenant Harper had been made up to Captain and the new Captain Harper had had Frank made up to Sergeant to replace Sergeant Betts. Frank felt real bad about that; literally stepping into dead men's shoes didn't seem right somehow.

But the bombardment he was now witnessing was a hundred times worse. The earth shook incessantly as it was pounded by the crushing recoil of the heavy guns sending their shells screaming towards the German positions at Ginchy with an unbearable and painful ear shattering din and filling the air with swarm after swarm of flying torpedoes punctuating the relentless screen of smoke and dust thrown into the air as they exploded in fireballs on the horizon.

Frank felt sick in his stomach as he thought of what the poor young German cubs in the middle of that conflagration must be going through. He closed his eyes to shut out the carnage in front of him, but the noise was unremitting and he was unable to blot out any of it. God, what madness is this? How long will this slaughter of innocent young men, who were mere babes in their mother's arms so very little time ago, go on? Did none of the so called leaders of all the countries in Europe have any concern at all for the lives and well being of the poor souls under their care? Or were the men regarded as mere fodder to be fed into the mouths of their own insane scheme of things? Surely there's a better way of settling things than this?

The tired and frightened detachment of straggling soldiers under Frank's charge had finally reached the lines and Frank's main occupation now turned to positioning the men as best he could in the holes dug in the ground; holes covered here and there with the odd roof of corrugated iron and earth, none of which provided protection against any of the allied barrage falling short of its target, let alone any of the Germans' response to the onslaught. But Frank's mental discourse on the futility of war was soon taken over by thoughts of how to save his own skin and that of his comrades under his care.

At first he got the men to clear out the trenches and make them habitable for the night but soon they were uncovering dead bodies and parts of bodies. So after a while he stopped the nigh impossible and gruesome digging as being far more distressing than an uncomfortable night's sleep would be, so he concentrated on getting the telephone lines connected and working. After which they ate and tried to settle down for the night, but the noise of the continuous shelling from the sixty pounders firing from thirty or so yards behind them, meant that none had any real sleep.

For the time being Frank's Company were being held in reserve and were given orders to support the attacking troops of the West Kents and the 14th Warwicks, mainly by helping the injured back to the over worked medical staff and extricating as many of the men killed in the fruitless and senseless mêlée of the previous days' fighting as they could. The only ones they could reach safely were the ones killed before they had even got out of the trench or had been slaughtered a mere few feet from the trench.

A few days previously the 7th Dragoon Guards had led a cavalry charge across the fields of uncropped corn waving in the breeze and interspersed with splashes of crimson from the wild poppies whose petals glistened like rubies in the July sunlight. They rode up the slope to High Wood in classic formation at full gallop; heads down, lances pointing the way and ready for action, pennants flying and the plumage on their helmets blowing horizontal from the back of their heads; an extraordinarily brilliant and dazzling sight to all who saw it.

But the German's were waiting in the wood and as the cavalry galloped across the cornfields with each horse leaving a clear track of trampled corn as it sped forward, the German machine guns opened fire and the magnificent horses and men fell under the onslaught of bullets and shells.

A tragic, futile and ignominiously wasteful loss of life.

And now, only a few days later, the bodies of the men and horses had become bloated in the heat of the summer sun and turned a putrid black. Flies swarmed in their millions over the battlefield, feasting on each body, of no consequence whether it were man or beast. The incessant stench of the rancid corpses infesting and intruding into the very air the living soldiers in the trenches had to breathe; making the job of burying the rotting corpses an obnoxious, insistent and inescapable reminder of the absurdity and horrors of this inglorious war.

As the men dug a hole next to a horse and pushed it into it they found good use for their gas masks, but burying both German and English soldiers was even more horrendous. Dealing with the body of a man killed by gun fire was normally relatively straight forward, but bombardment of the area, by both the Germans and allied fire falling short of its target, had left very few bodies intact. A corpse with no head in a shell hole; bodiless limbs sticking out of the earth; innards welded together and lumps of flesh all rolled into one, making it impossible to decide whether it belonged to man or beast.

Burying bodies, keeping the area up to the front line trenches clear, delivering ammunition, food and medical supplies to the front line men, whilst trying to avoid both the enemy and allied fire was a sickening and thankless task, making many in the Company wish they could actually go over the top and have a go at the German bastards creating the carnage they were trying to clear up.

Perhaps their chance would come soon but not today. This morning had been the chance of the 14th division and Frank and his men in support had watched from six hundred yards behind the attacking line and witnessed the fruitless attack as the men going over the top were virtually annihilated; many falling before they had even cleared the ridge of the trench; whilst others had fallen merely yards into no man's land and now Frank was directing his men in sorting out the dead from the injured.

Tom collected the rifles with bayonets still attached from the dead and dying and placed them in a pyramid in a dug out at the side of the trench, whilst Joe was collecting name discs, pay books and other belongings from the dead and placing each man's in a separate bag to be sent back to their families. Others were attending the injured and dying as best they could or dragging the shattered dead bodies to the sap running at right angles to the main trench, where they were piling them in one heap.

All the men ducked in unison as the whiz of an enemy shell came closer and closer before landing just short of the trench where Tom was placing the last of the rifles. The blast sent an eruption of soil into the air destroying the side of the dugout and propelled Tom towards the stack of rifles with their bayonets pointing upwards. He twisted his arm to avoid the points, but the rifle he still had in his hand was rammed solidly into the side of the bulwark and as he fell the bayonet sliced off the index finger of his right hand and slashed a twelve inch channel along his arm. Luckily it was no more than half an inch deep at it deepest and as precise as any surgeons incision could have been. It finally penetrated right through his body three inches below his right shoulder breaking his shoulder bone in the process.

Frank heard his scream and ran to him, having to jump over several injured soldiers and the Samaritans attending them in the process.

"What the hell's happened, Tom?" but Tom had passed out and was unable to answer him.

Frank clawed at the soil around the rifle, freeing it completely and with the help of Joe and Bill Wainwright managed to turn Tom's still body and the rifle with bayonet attached in concert, thus avoiding any further damage. Frank disengaged the rifle from the bayonet leaving the lethal scalpel still lodged in Tom's shoulder.

He stared in horror at the blood pouring from the wounds and knew he had to act quickly if his pal's life was to be saved before he bled to death. He took another bayonet from the pile of rifles now lying in an untidy heap next to the body and used it to cut the tunic and shirt from Tom's inert body. He cut the shirt into strips and tied a piece of cloth as tightly as he could as a tourniquet around the small stub, all that was left of Tom's finger.

Next he had to stop the bleeding from the wound in the arm. His first reaction was to tie another tourniquet above the wound, but he knew that if he stopped the flow of blood completely and for too long, poor Tom might lose the arm altogether. If only he had the needle and thread he had left with his 'unneeded for battle' kit, back at Méaulte. He decided he would not leave it behind again!

For the moment though he had to do something about the wound. He decided the best he could do would be to cut the rest of the shirt into strips to use as bandage, and pulling the wound together as best he could, bind the arm tightly, but not too tightly, around the wound. He did this as rapidly and carefully as he could and then turned his attention to the bayonet still penetrating front to back of the shoulder.

He handed Joe two pieces torn off the remains of the shirt, "Soak these in water from your flask, Joe. Then squeeze as much of the water out as you can, fold them into pads and get ready to put them front and back right into this shoulder wound when I take the bayonet out."

He then turned to Bill Wainwright and another of the soldiers now looking on, "You two take the weight of his body and for God's sake hold him still while I take this out. Joe, are you ready? Now don't forget shove a piece of that cloth into the wound front and back as quick as you can."

He looked at the three men doing his bidding, "OK Joe. Get ready."

He wiped his hand across his mouth and looked at Tom, "I hope I'm doing the right thing here, Tom? Oh Christ, I hope that pulling this damn thing out won't make things worse? Right, here goes!"

He wiped the sweat from his brow and carefully took hold of the bayonet protruding from the shoulder in both hands. He hesitated for a moment and looked at Joe, who nodded as if giving his blessing and approval for what Frank was about to do. Frank slowly withdrew the steel blade trying to hold his hands steady so as not to cut any more flesh. It proved to be much easier than he had thought.

"Now, Joe. Now," he shouted and Joe responded be pushing the balls of damp cloth into the wound.

"Right, now let's bind up this wound."

There were only the sleeves of the shirt left, "We'll have to use these. Just keep holding him up whilst I tie them round to keep those pads in place."

He handed one of the sleeves to Joe, "Cut this into two strips and tie them together."

He took the other and passed it under Tom's armpit carefully tying it over his damaged shoulder. He took the other longer piece from Joe and tied it across Joe's upper body around both his arms, in an attempt to hold the swabs in place. Finally, he cut two strips from Tom's tunic, tied them together and used them as a sling for the wounded arm.

He looked at his handiwork, "Let's hope I've done it right? Christ I hope so!"

Walking back up the sap, he stopped at the point where two of his men had pulled a body off the ridge of the trench. The poor chap had half his head missing and was obviously dead. They were about to lift the body on to a stretcher to move it out of the way.

"Sorry, chaps," said Frank as he snatched the stretcher from under the collapsing weight. The dead body fell on to the ground unsupported. "My mate's need is greater than yours," and turning to the bewildered soldiers added, "Sorry, but you'll just have to carry him without this."

He returned to where Tom was lying and handed the stretcher to Joe and Bill Wainwright. "Right, you two, hold this while we lift Tom on to it."

He looked round and directed two other men to help him lift Tom's body carefully on to the stretcher. Frank took the head end and tried as best as he could to take the weight from underneath, without pushing on the damaged shoulder or arm.

When he was safely on the stretcher, Frank went to the pile of dead bodies, and removing the jacket from a dead officer's body, placed it over Tom's upper body.

"That should help keep you warm, old pal. That poor devil there won't need it any more anyhow." Tom opened his eyes as if to come round, but let out an "Oh God," with the pain and promptly passed out again.

"Right, Joe, I want you and Bill to take him as fast as you can back to the field dressing station, and get a doctor to look at him straight away. I know they'll say he's got to wait his turn, but just keep bothering them 'til they see to him and at least stitch up those wounds. When you know he's all right and only then, you can leave him and get back here and report back to me. If anyone asks any questions, just say Captain Harper sent you. I'll square it with him."

He turned to the other men around him, "Right, now you lot can get back to what you were doing. Come on let's get this mess cleared up before we get something to eat."

Tom and Bill got to the first aid station, which was no more than a shelter dug into the side of the hill, just as a doctor was coming out to take a break and have a cigarette. He watched as the two men carrying the stretcher came toward him and asked just as a round of heavy gunfire, blasted the air. "Who have we here?"

Joe had not properly heard what he said, but imagined he had asked, "Who has sent you here?"

Remembering Frank's instructions, he replied, "Captain Harper, Sir"

"Right let me have a look at him," and immediately Tom got the attention that Frank said they should demand. It was not until much later when they heard from Tom that he had got immediate attention because the doctor assumed the inert man on the stretcher was a Captain, thanks to the reply given by Joe and the dead officer's jacket which Frank had thrown over the body. Luckily for all concerned, Tom did not know what the hell they were talking about when he came round after the wounds had been stitched, calling him Captain. He quite genuinely did not know who had brought him in. The doctor had been too busy to take the matter any further.

Although weak from loss of blood, Tom was very quickly able to get to his feet and was moved to the base hospital at Rouen to have his broken shoulder set. The place was awash with beds and there was very little space between them for the nurses to move, but the casualties kept arriving and when they ran out of beds, they used stretchers in corridors or any other available space to place the injured. The doctors and medical staff were working non-stop and were at their wit's end as to how to deal with the continuing flow of men coming into the hospital whose wounds were far worse than Tom's.

This together with the total lack of adequate space proved to be to Tom's advantage as the doctors were anxious to reduce the number of wounded under their care as quickly as possible, whilst outside, the Transport Section had empty trains waiting to take the wounded back home. Nurses could not be spared to travel with the near fatally wounded, so in desperation they collected up as many of the walking wounded they could find, put them on the trains and sent them home. Thus Tom, who had been expecting to spend a couple of weeks in hospital or maybe at a convalescent camp somewhere in France before being sent back to the line for some duty or other, found himself in possession of a letter from one of the beleaguered doctors saying he was unfit for active service.

He had told Tom, that with his missing finger he wouldn't be able to fire a rifle and serve actively at the front line, but no doubt they would probably be able to find him a role in support, in transport, supplies, or even as a cook. Presumably he had meant to write all this down, but his letter merely said he was unfit for active front line duty and so Tom was on his way home out of this blessed war for good. His only regret was that he was leaving his pals at the front and felt particularly bad about this as he was left-handed and his missing finger was from his right hand. But for now he certainly was not going to point that out to anyone.

CHAPTER THREE

AUTUMN 1916

It was a bright clear night with hardly a cloud in the sky, and even though it was nine o'clock in the evening, the air was still warm from the day's hot September sun. Captain Harper was addressing his men, who had been making preparations for 'battle order' all afternoon, and were now standing at ease, listening to his instructions.

"Right chaps. This is our chance to show those Germans what the lads from Birmingham are really like. They've been playing silly buggers with us for weeks whilst we've been in support, but now the Generals are giving us the opportunity to get our own back. This time we're going to cross over no-man's land, right into their ruddy trenches and we're going to kill the bastards. Get rid of them once and for all."

Each man was loaded up with the paraphernalia of war; bombs; flares; Lewis guns; rifles; machine guns; extra ammunition et al., plus two day's rations and a full water bottle. Most of them had hung around their neck, or carried in their pocket, the lucky charm; ring; or other talisman given to them by a mother; wife; girlfriend; or sister prior to leaving England. Frank had punched a hole through the silver three penny piece Grace had put in the Christmas pudding, and now had it tied around his neck on a piece of string. He was no different to any of the others in the Battalion, who had been gripping their particular fetish all day and when they thought no-one was looking, had been kissing it whilst chanting unspoken prayers.

They had all had their share of danger in the front line before, but this was the big one; their first real time 'over the top' with the orders to take the enemy lines 'at all costs'. They had lived with the costs of this damned war for far too long and had all had their fill of the slaughter and of seeing the dead and maimed bodies; thousands upon thousands of them. And now, for some of them at least, it was their turn to experience the ultimate cost. How many of them would become just another single digit added to the number of dead? Each one feeling scared and guilty as they prayed for their own safety, hoping that it would be someone else's name added to the lists and not their own.

Frank was glad he had not asked Grace to marry him in his letters. It was true, that they had been getting more and more intimate since last Christmas, each expressing their feelings more openly without actually using the words 'love' or 'forever', but they had come mightily close to it.

Frank touched the silver piece around his neck. "Maybe if I come out of this I should write and ask her?" He spoke the words silently to himself, but then shook his head, his second thought being the same as always, "No. I can't ask her until all this is finished and I'm back home. It wouldn't be fair to do otherwise." He shook his head again, "No. It wouldn't be fair."

Frank had not noticed Captain Harper coming up towards him. "Are you all right, Sergeant?"

"Yes. I'm fine Sir, thank you."

"That's OK then. I just wondered what the nodding head was all about." He did not wait for an answer, "Look Sergeant, when the time comes, I'll be going over with your platoon and I want you personally to stay close to me. I want you right by my side when we go over. You can make sure Hadley and Naylor stay close to us with all that telephone gear. I have strict orders to keep HQ informed of our progress throughout this attack, so stay close."

He spoke once more to the assembled men, "Right men, all of you with watches, synchronise them with mine." He looked at his watch, waiting a few seconds before adding, "It's now 21.40 hours exactly."

He raised his hand high in the air, "OK, let's be on our way; as quietly as you can. Oh, and there's no need to march at attention, easily does it and you can smoke if you want to, at least until we get to the front line trenches anyhow."

The men appreciated the offer, even though they found it almost impossible to march, search for their cigarettes and light them, whilst carrying all that gear.

Captain Harper stopped his men at Angle Wood where the rest of the battalion was assembled, telling his sergeants and corporals that the men should rest as best they could for the next few hours.

The sun was rising when he called his officers and sergeants together to explain the operation orders he had been given. The German's were holding Falfemont Farm some hundred yards or so ahead of the front line trenches from where they would make their attack. Their objective was to take the farm and, as he put it, 'dismiss' all the Germans from it.

He continued with his orders, "The attack will commence at 0900 hours, at which time the French guns will bombard the farm to cause as much chaos, alarm and distraction to the Germans holding it as they can. This will give the 14th Warwicks over on our left and the King's Own Scottish Borderers on the right, who will be first to go over, the opportunity to take advantage of the confusion and advance on the farm. We'll be held in reserve and go over later in the morning to consolidate the position and advance further into the German lines. Right! Any questions?"

There was a general shaking of heads and no questions were asked.

As the sun rose slowly in the sky the intermittent gun fire of the night gradually increased in intensity from both sides, reminding Frank that no matter how grand and accurate the French cannonade of the farm, they would not silence the Germans entirely. If they were able to do that they would have done so already.

The Captain tried to encourage his men even further, "For miles on either side of us other divisions are all getting ready to advance at the same time to take all the German lines on a very wide front and shut them up once and for all. I'll give you all ten minutes to inform the men under your control what is expected of them and then we'll advance to the front line trenches and get ready for nine o'clock."

Frank, ready to do the Captain's bidding, organised his platoon in the middle of the battalion attack and the Captain was right by his side as they waited the appointed hour. The guns had been firing more and more frequently all morning but the French shells were certainly not falling on Falfemont Farm yet.

At 0900 hours exactly the advance commenced. Frank and the others watched helplessly at the death and destruction taking place on either side of them, as the enemy machine guns fired without hindrance into the advancing lines.

The Captain, in anguish, held his head in his hands, "Where the hell are those blasted French guns? They should be belting the hell out of the Germans by now. Christ, what the hell's going on Sergeant?" And, without waiting for an answer added, "Looks as though the bloody Froggies have let us down again. Does anything ever go right in this ruddy war, Sergeant?"

"Doesn't look like it, Sir."

Frank pointed to where he reckoned the French guns to be and then swung his arm round to point to the German positions to the East, "Looks as though the guns are firing over there instead, Sir. Looks like they're trying to silence the gun positions over there where those shells are exploding."

"That's no bloody good to the poor sods trying to take the farm. Look, there, and there, and over there, poor buggers don't stand a chance do they? And you know what Sergeant? There's damn all we can do about it, we've just got to sit here watching whilst waiting for orders to go over ourselves."

He turned to Wally Naylor who was holding the field telephone, "Naylor, that blasted telephone is hooked up isn't it? We aren't just sitting here waiting for their Lordship's orders and they can't get through, are we?"

Wally lifted the telephone to his ear and checked the equipment for the umpteenth time. "No, Sir, everything's working fine. I'll keep checking, but I'm sure no-one's trying to get through at the moment."

The Captain despaired at his own helplessness as he and his men watched the slaughter in no man's land all morning whilst at the same time trying to avoid the enemy shells falling all about them; some of which fell into the trench, killing and injuring several of his men before they had even had a chance of getting out of the line to attack the Germans.

At half past twelve the telephone rang and the instructions given for the battalion to support the 14th Warwicks and attack the Farm at one o'clock.

Putting the telephone down he took a swig from his water flask to moisten his parched mouth, which had dehydrated immediately on receiving the call.

He tried to wet his lips with his tongue as he spoke to the men either side of him, "Pass the word along, we're attacking and taking the Farm at 0100. We'll make the attack when I blow my whistle and I want everyone over together. Right, pass the word along."

Perhaps he had played the party game of 'whisper the message' too often and did not trust the correct instruction to get to the end of the line or maybe he just wanted something to do. Either way he turned and walked the length of the line, in both directions, giving the message personally and trying to give some encouragement to the men; an impossible task, considering what they had been witnessing for the past four hours.

Captain Harper, now back and standing next to Frank, stood whistle in his mouth, studying the watch on his left wrist as the second finger moved painfully slowly towards the appointed hour.

He counted off the last seconds, "Five, four, three, two, one.........," before blowing his whistle with all his might. He knew without looking that his men were scrambling up the sides of the embankment, using the banquette, ladders, stakes or whatever was available to get over and run forward as quickly as possible. How many deaths would be on his conscience within the next few minutes? Maybe he would never know, his own death might be first.

Frank's head was thumping as the adrenaline flushed through his body. He was running forward weaving from side to side to avoid the bullets and jumping over the shell holes wherever possible. He glanced over his shoulder to where Joe was running slightly behind him on his left, "Keep behind me Joe, hopefully that way, if one of us gets it, the other won't."

Until he spoke to Joe, the noise of the battle had somehow been obliterated from Frank's head. He had not been mindful of any sound since the blast of the Captain's whistle, but suddenly, like the vibration of thunder gradually increasing in intensity after the lightning flash, the initial battle roar of the men as they left the trenches reached his consciousness.

But the rhythm of this triumphant war cry rapidly changed, a wail here, a yell over there, the squeal of a man in violent pain behind, the shriek of men in terrible suffering over to the left, the howl of men being blown to pieces to the right and the screams of dying men all around. Other sounds and feelings reached his senses; the boom of the cannons in the distance, the smoke of battle and the smell of cordite pervading the air, but mostly the zzp, zzp, zzp, of the machine gun bullets flying all around like killer bees travelling at an unstoppable speed to be silenced only when they penetrated anything that got in their way.

Frank suddenly became scared, really scared. It had never felt like this before. He yelled out, pleading in prayer more than he'd ever thought possible, "Christ, help me, for God's sake help me. What am I supposed to do?"

He continued running, faster than his legs could really carry him, still dodging from left to right, disbelieving that he was still on his feet. The farm buildings and the enemy line came closer and closer. He could clearly see each individual German's position now and the separate flash from their guns as each shot was fired.

"I'm going to get the bastards. I'm going to get them." He was only fifty yards from them. Forty yards. Thirty-five yards.

He swung over to the right, his eyes fixed on where a shell had blown a gap in the rolls of barbed wire protecting the German line and shouted to Joe running immediately behind him, "There, over there, Joe. There's a break in the wire, we can get through over there."

Suddenly everything went into slow motion and the line of the Germans vanished from in front of him. "What the hell's happening? I can't feel anything so I haven't been hit. Or have I?"

He rolled down a slope and Joe tumbled down next to him. Seconds later, a screaming Captain Harper had clumsily followed them into the massive shell hole, falling on top of Frank.

Frank rolled the Captain off him and wiped his cheeks where Joe had thumped him with the field telephone as he had fallen. He looked at the blood on his hands. He felt his face again. There was only a small cut but he could already feel the throbbing around his eye and the swelling rising.

He turned to Joe who was lying at the side of him, inspecting his own thigh, “You’ve given me a right thump here, mate. I'm going to have a beautiful black eye soon.” He put his hand back over the bruised eye, “I can feel the bloody eye closing already.”

“Bugger your eye! I've been hit in the leg. The blighters have hit me in the leg.”

Frank rolled over to him, keeping his head well below the rim of the hole. Blood was running where Joe's trousers had been torn at the thigh. Frank made the tear bigger so that he could inspect the wound better. “You'll live, Joe, it's not that bad. You must have caught your leg as you were falling, probably on that bloody barbed wire, there look. You haven't been shot mate.” They all ducked down into the hole as the machine guns shells ricocheted off the ground all around them. Frank smiled at Joe as he added, “Not yet anyway.”

Joe looked scared at the remark and realising his stupid comment about 'not yet' he tried to brush over it as best he could, “Look mate, the three of us here are all alive and we’re going to get out of this mess.” He handed Joe a wound pad and a bandage from one of his pouches, “Here, put this over that cut and tie the bandage round your leg as quickly as you can so that you can come and help me to sort out the Captain here. He's in a bigger mess than you.”

Joe started to lift his head but Frank pushed it down as the bullets started to fly overhead again saying, “Keep your bloody head down, you silly bugger, that lot will soon knock it off for you if you give them half a chance.”

He inched his head to peer over the rear of the hole and looked at the carnage about him. The shells were still exploding all around causing limbs of dead and dying men to be scattered away from the rest of their bodies. Some of the men, who had dived for cover only yards from where they started from, were trying to scramble back to the trench as best they could, but the Germans were casually picking off each moving body. “You bastards,” he shouted, “For God's sake, give them a chance to get back.”

Once again the bullets zinged inches above his head as the Germans fired to where they had heard the shout. He quickly ducked down as low as he could get, “I suppose that means we’d better keep as quiet as we can. Best let them think we’ve had it, or they won’t give up ‘til they finish us off.”

He manoeuvred on his back the couple of feet to where the Captain lay.

“I don’t think I’m too bad, Sergeant,” the Captain said as he threw his head back towards the German lines, and with a pained look on his face said, “God, what a mess! We may have got a bit further than most of the other poor blighters but I doubt we’ll get any further.”

He shook his head, “Well I reckon we can count that as being one totally failed mission. We’d better let HQ know what’s going on.” He started to work his way towards Joe, “Have you got that telephone, Hadley?”

Frank leaned over him and held him down, “He's got the telephone all right, Captain. Banged me good and proper on the side of the head with it as he fell, he did. But it's no bloody good to us, is it? Poor Wally Naylor is out there somewhere with the roll of telephone wire he was supposed to unwind as he ran probably still in his hand, twenty yards from the rest of his body. Telephones! Waste of bloody time, if you ask me. No use to us here, is it? And as for Wally! Well it weren't any bloody good to him either, was it?”

He released his hold on the Captain slightly, “Forget the telephone, Sir and forget about HQ. I'm sure they’re better off than us right now, so let them look after themselves while we look after ourselves.” He moved on to his side facing the Captain, “Let me have a look at your wounds. They look as though they need more attention than HQ does right now.” He muttered under his breath, “Wouldn't be in this fucking mess if it weren't for fucking HQ.”

“Amen to that, Sergeant. Just as well with all this noise I didn’t quite hear what you said.” He smiled at Frank shaking his head from side to side, “But for the record I think you’d better remember that my hearing hasn’t been impaired yet.” He bit his lip to prevent letting out a scream as the pain hit him again, “Unlike the rest of me. Best have a look at the wounds, if you wouldn’t mind.”

The Captain had blood in several places on his body and face, but on careful inspection Frank realised that he had wiped most of it on to his cheeks and clothes when cleaning the blood from his left hand which had been running from the wound in his arm.

Frank undid the jacket and shirtsleeves but could not see the wound with the jacket and shirt on.

“Cut the sleeve, Matthews. No point messing about. Let's see what the damage is.”

Frank did as he was told and, taking his penknife from his pocket slit both jacket and shirt sleeves and rolled the material back to expose the wound. “Afraid its gone straight through, Sir. Clean entry and exit wound either side of the arm. I think the best we can do is just to bandage this one up and then have a look at your hip here.”

He attended to the wound on the arm as best he could to try and stop the flow of blood and then turned his attention to the hip. It was then that he noticed that the Captain's leg was bent out at a very awkward angle just below the knee. “Looks as though you’ve broken your leg, Sir, must have done it when you fell on top of me. Let's just see if we can straighten it a bit and then I'll find something to make a splint for it.”

The Captain made all the facial expressions of screaming with pain, but managed to hold back the actual outcry and no sound left his lips as Frank tried to straighten his leg. “Best leave it alone, Sergeant, for the time being anyway. It hurts too much to do anything to it at the moment. Let's look at this hip.”

At that he took Frank's penknife off him and cut his trousers away from the wound, “Well that's handy, it looks as though the bullet’s just bounced off my hip. Just a nasty surface wound but not enough to kill me off yet, I don't think. Let's just put a dressing on it. Here, use my shirt sleeve; it's no good for anything else now is it?” At that he tore at his shirtsleeve and ripped it clean off to the shoulder. He handed it to Frank with, “Here do the best you can with this.”

Frank reached for his water bottle and was about to clean the thigh wound when the Captain stopped him, “Don't waste your water on this, we don't know how long we’re going to be stuck here and we might be mightily glad of that soon.”

Frank put the top on the bottle and after putting the 'dressing' on the thigh as best he could, he took the penknife back off the Captain. It was only then as he turned over, trying to get more comfortable, that he felt a stabbing pain in his own leg. He twisted over on his side so that he could see the part of his leg where the pain was coming from. There was a neat hole in his trouser leg and a large crimson patch of blood around the hole. He took the penknife and slit the cloth either side of the hole to expose the wound. He winced as he touched the wound.

He looked at Joe and gave a short laugh, “Joe, I think I’ve got a bullet or something in there. It probably ricocheted into my leg ‘cause it’s not too deep. I guess you're just going to have to get it out for me.”

He handed Joe the penknife, “Your turn to do a bit of surgery now, pal.”

“Hang on a minute, Matthews, just have a swig of this first.” The Captain handed Frank his spare water bottle.

Frank removed the cap and took a mighty swig, thinking it was water. He gasped and spluttered as the neat Scotch whisky hit the back of his throat. He opened his mouth wide and his eyes nearly bulged out of his head as he gasped for breath. He handed the bottle back to the Captain, gulping once again, “Sorry Sir, I thought it was water. I'm not used to spirits, Sir. Well at least not in great mouthfuls like that.”

The whisky quickly had an affect and Frank felt himself going light headed. The Captain smiled, “Best get on with it quick, Hadley, before he gets used to it and wants the rest. Need some ourselves when the job's done.”

Joe wiped the blade of his penknife on his sleeve, his hands shaking quite noticeably as he leaned forward to attend to the wound. The Captain tapped him on the shoulder and handed him his cigarette lighter, indicating that he should use it to sterilise the blade. Joe lit the lighter and tried to sterilise the knife, but by now his hands were shaking too much.

The Captain took the knife and lighter from him and a few minutes later, as Joe held Frank’s leg steady, he had removed the bullet fragment and bound a dressing over the wound and round his leg.

Then he handed round the 'water' bottle, “Here have a swig out of this. Do you need anything for the pain? I've got some morphine here. They let us officers carry it when we come into battle like this.” He reached into his breast pocket and held out the phial towards him.

“No thanks, Sir, I'm OK. If we’re stuck here for very long, might all be in need of it later.”

“Maybe you're right, Frank, but I think I'm going to have some. Give you and Joe a chance to have another go at my leg then. I don't think we should leave it much longer. It’ll have to be strapped up if we’re going to crawl back anyway. I'll never manage with it twisted like that.”

Both Frank and Joe were taken aback by the officer's familiarity in referring to them by their Christian names. He must have realised their dismay, “And by the way, my name’s Mark. At least for as long as we’re in this mess anyway. The way I see it, if I'm going to die, I’d rather die with a couple of pals than with chaps that keep calling me Sir. So what do you say? We'll use Christian names all round, until we get out of this mess and then I expect 'fucking HQ' will expect us to go back to using formal titles won’t they Frank?”

The way he spoke the words 'fucking HQ' had clearly been an imitation of Frank's earlier words and was undoubtedly meant to put all three of them on an equal footing.

Frank grinned. Over the months he had begun to like this man more and more, even though he tried not to. And now he finally gave in, forgiving Mark Harper once and for all for being his father's son. “If that's how you want it Sir ..., I mean Mark, that's fine by me. If you’re ready we’d better get that leg straightened and then we can think about getting out of here.”

Frank did his best with the leg, using the remains of an old trenching tool, which was sticking out of the side of the shell hole, as a splint. Both he and the Captain knew that he hadn't made a very good job of it and further treatment would be needed, and soon, if the leg was to be saved.

Frank once more became aware of the noise of battle. The attack was clearly now over with the German's still holding the farm position. The chaos and the hullabaloo of battle had lessened, but both sides were still firing at the other's lines to let them know that whilst no side had gained anything, no side had lost anything either; except a few hundred more men to add to the lists of the dead! And what difference was that going to make? Nothing at all! Just a few more men who would not live a full life; a few more widows; wives who would never give birth to the children of their husbands; a few more girlfriends who would never enjoy their wedding day; a few more mothers and fathers who would never see their sons again and never know the joys of having grandchildren; mothers and fathers whose sons would not be there to mourn their own passing away and funerals with no children at the graveside. At least all of those back home would have a decent burial. Better than their poor sons and lovers here! Most of them will be lucky to be placed under the earth in one piece.

Frank shook himself out of his mournful silence, once more trying to clear his mind of all these morbid thoughts. “I don't think we'll be able to do anything until nightfall Si..... I mean Mark. Maybe the Germans will stop firing then and we'll be able to crawl back to our trench. I doubt they'll come and get us. Anyhow, with us crouched down this hole, I don't suppose they even know we’re here.”

“Right, Frank. Let's make ourselves as comfortable as we can, have a bite to eat in a while and then we'll decide how to get out of here. Either of you fancy a smoke?” He took the packet from his tunic pocket and offered Frank a cigarette.

No thanks, I don't smoke, but I'm sure Joe here would fancy one. Picked up all the bad habits since you joined up, haven't you Joe?”

Joe took a cigarette and Mark lit it for him and then lit one for himself. “You know Frank, you and I have never been able to have a good chat about things back home, have we? We might as well pass the time away chatting about the good old days, instead of depressing ourselves about all this lot. What do you say?”

“Not much,” said Frank, “I joined up ‘cause I didn’t think much of the 'good old days' and Joe here joined up 'cause he didn't fancy being a farmer. That's right ain't it Joe?”

Joe just nodded and took another drag on his cigarette.

“Come on Joe, tell us about life on the farm in Bewdley. I'm sure the Captain here, I mean Mark here would love to hear all about that.”

But Mark was determined not to let Frank take away his chance to find out more about his relationship with his father. Bearing in mind what he had heard from outside his father's office two years earlier he knew that it had quite clearly not been a particularly good one. He therefore just ignored Frank's encouragement to Joe and before Joe could answer asked of Frank, “Why did you want to leave Harpers and join up, Frank. You weren't doing too badly working for the old firm, were you?”

“Well no, I hadn't been, but it's a long and really rather personal matter. I'd rather not talk about it.”

“Oh come on Frank, it's been obvious to me for months that there's been something wrong between you and me. I thought it was me at first, but I couldn't see what I'd done to upset you so much. And then after a bit, when you let your guard down, I felt that we had a lot in common, particularly when it was just the two of us working out battalion matters.”

Mark tried to lift his broken leg and move it to a more comfortable position. He let out a gasp and screwed up his eyes with the pain as his manoeuvred the leg closer to the other. The bottom of the shell hole was not quite large enough for all three men to lie out fully so Frank edged as near to the side of the hole as he possibly could to give Mark more room to spread out. He rapidly ducked down again as the bullets once more careered inches above his head.

Joe started to get in a panic, “Frank we're never going to get out alive. The buggers know we're here and they don't intend to let us out and even if we leave it ‘til its dark to try and get out, they won't leave us alone even then. And what makes it worse is that our own side don't even know we're here, so if they see us coming towards them they'll probably think we're the Boche and start taking pot shots at us as well. Christ, what a mess!”

“Look Joe stop worrying,” said the Captain, “Once its dark I'm sure they'll stop firing and I'm sure we'll get out of here all right. Our own troops will be hoping that some of us are still alive and will be able to crawl back, so they won't be taking pot shots at us. Here have another cigarette and another swig of this whisky.”

He handed Joe the flask and took out his silver cigarette case and held it for Joe to take one, “I wish we had some means of telling HQ we are alive out here. They might then try to get us back somehow. God knows how, though.”

He turned to Frank and pointed to the field telephone on the ground. “You know Frank, those things are bloody useless in battle situations like this. I reckon it's about time they trained us all in using the new field wireless, I know there are a few of them about.”

Frank and Joe had heard of wireless, but had never come across any such equipment. “What exactly is this wireless, Sir?” asked Frank.

Well when I was at University, my main degree was in maths and physics, but I took wireless as a extra subject, so I do know a bit about it. Basically, as the name implies it’s a sort of telephone like that useless one down there, but it works without any wires. Wire less, you see. Enough of that anyway, I want to hear about you at Harpers.”

“Look I've said I don't wish to talk about it.”

“I'm sorry Frank but I can't accept that.” He smiled before continuing, “My father was the problem wasn't he? Perhaps it would help if I told you that I don't actually like my father either. You know, even though I missed my mother and sister terribly, I was mightily glad to go to boarding school, then University, then this lot; anything to get away from my father. He's just a born bully, so I do know how easy it is to dislike him. Incidentally, you are the only person, other than my sister, that I've ever told what I think about him.” He gave one of his little laughs as he added, “Must be the effects of impending doom, so come on, you can tell me your side of the story now, I heard his side after you’d left his office on that day.”

“What do you mean by his side of the story? What did he tell you?”

“Oh, just that you were a good for nothing waster, who’d fooled Grandfather into thinking you were worth promoting and paying more money to, merely because you were your mother's son.” Mark hesitated for a moment and then added, “He said Grandfather had a soft spot for your mother, even half suggested that the relationship was more than that of an employer and cook ought to have been.” He put his hand out and stopped Frank from saying anything, “And before you burst a blood vessel, let me say that I didn’t believe him. My Grandfather wasn’t like that. I know he wouldn’t have taken any liberties with your mother and that's why I’d like to hear your side of the story. You see I haven't found you to be a waster or shirker, so his story just doesn’t fit. So come on let me hear what you’ve got to say on the matter.”

This was the most unlikely of settings for any sort of discussion, let alone one as serious and painful to both Frank and Mark as this one. And so, during the course of the afternoon, Frank had, with Mark's insistence and encouragement from time to time, told the whole saga of what Mark’s father had done to his mother all those years previously.

“Yes that all adds up now,” said Mark, when Frank had finally finished. “I think my mother must have heard something of the episode after they were married, probably from one of the other servants, or maybe father just told her during one of their many arguments. I wouldn't put that past him. They always seemed to be arguing, and afterwards he always seemed to take it out on me. For all his faults I don't think he ever hit my mother, so when he got mad he always found some excuse to give me the belt. That's the main reason why I was so glad to get away."

The persistent roar and rattle of the fighting had subsided considerably during the afternoon's discussion and the battlefield was much quieter now. Both sides were still firing at each other whenever the opportunity arose, or when they wanted to let the other side know that they still existed. From time to time the air was chilled by the sound from a poor wounded soldier, somewhere out there in No Man's Land, a scream of pain, a cry of fear, someone hallucinating in a state of half consciousness, groaning in confusion and agonising distress.

"Look Frank, can you and I forget all about our parents, particularly my father's misdemeanours. I don't wish you to forgive him, not for a second, but for now we'd better have something to eat and a drink again. Perhaps we should keep to water this time though, and keep what's left of the whisky for our trip back. And then we ought to work out how we are going to get out of this hellhole. For my part, I assure you that I'm not like my father, more like my grandfather I think, so maybe when we get out of this blasted war, I'll be able to help you find some sort of employment, other than working for my father. Right what's for tea? Good old regulation issue biscuits?"

"No we can have something better than that," said Joe as he reached for his knapsack. He picked it up and inspected the hole in it, "Christ, the buggers have shot a hole in my birthday cake." He turned over the bag and inspected the other side. No hole.

He laughed out loud, "Must be my lucky day? Shot in the back, I've been. Must have been one of our own chaps?" He laughed again trying to be the comedian of the party, but this was not the usually amusing Joe, more a nervous laugh than real humour, "You don't think they were trying to hit me, do you?"

Frank took the knapsack from him, opened it, and took out the cake tin from inside. The bullet had gone into one side of the tin, almost through the cake and had just punctured the other side of the tin. "I reckon your mother's birthday cake saved your life Joe. You'd have been a dead 'un if you hadn't got this cake in here. Good job your birthday's tomorrow and not yesterday. What do you say?"

"What I say is, let's enjoy my birthday now whilst we can. Now, who wants a piece of mother's best birthday cake? Full of fruit." He prised out the bullet and held it up, "And who wants the one and only nut?"

Three hours later, they watched the sun set, a glorious opulent globe contrasting starkly with the desolation of the battlefield highlighted in its magnificent and brilliant glow.

"What do you say to us finishing the rest of this cake before we start back? I'm starving and I don't suppose there'll be any roast beef and Yorkshire pud left for us when we get back." Joe was the only one to laugh at his joke. "All right so it won't be roast beef. It probably won't be anything but dry biscuits and water, and that's if we're lucky. So come on let's eat this cake whilst we can. Don't want to share it with the rest of the lads anyway."

He took out the cake tin once again and begun to cut the remains of the cake into three pieces, whilst starting to quietly sing, "Happy Birthday to me, Happy Birthday to me." He stopped singing and beckoned to the others, "Come on you miserable so and so's, aren't you going to sing Happy Birthday to me."

He started to sing again, but this time at the top of his voice, "Happy Birthday to me," just as Frank became aware of a thud at the top of the mound protecting them from the German's. He turned just in time to see a Boche stick bomb rolling into the hole next to him. Without hesitation, in one movement, he twisted, picked it up and managed to get it back up the slope and over the rim of their protective chamber. The grenade exploded immediately it rolled over the rim sending soil and debris in all directions. They all covered themselves as best they could, but a stone, whizzing through the air, hit Mark on the side of his head, knocking him unconscious.

Frank let out a scream as bad as any Joe had heard from the dying on the battlefield, and Joe, suddenly feeling terribly alone and even more terrified than he had been all day, crouched into the foetus position and started to sob. He felt a tap on the shoulder and looked up. Frank was looking directly at him, a big grin on his face, waving his forefinger in front of his mouth, indicating to Joe that he should be quiet and said to Joe in a very low voice, "Sshh. I only did that to let the buggers think they'd killed whoever was here, otherwise they'll keep throwing those things at us. Now just keep quiet for a bit, while I try and work out how to get us all out of here."

"I don't think we're going to Frank. I've had this awful feeling in the pit of my stomach all day. I'm sure we won't make it."

"Don't be stupid Joe, of course we'll get out of here. Just have to wait 'til it's completely dark. The Germans won't bother us after that. We'll just have to keep our heads down."

"God I hope so, Frank."

Joe was quiet for a little, something obviously going through his mind. After a while he looked straight at Frank, "You know what's been going through my head all day today as well, Frank?"

Frank puckered his lips and shook his head from side to side. He gave a little chuckle and still shaking his head said, "No mate, I haven't a clue, why don't you tell me?"

"Well it's a bit embarrassing really. You won't laugh, will you?"

"Frank shook his head again, "No, of course not. I thought we were good mates, you don't have to be embarrassed at anything you tell me. And before you ask, I won't tell anyone else either." He hesitated a moment and then added, "That's unless you want me to, of course."

"God no!" blurted Joe, "You mustn't tell anyone else."

"OK. So what is it that's been bothering you?"

"Well I've been thinking." Joe hesitated again before adding, "For God's sake, don't laugh, but I don't want to die still a virgin."

Frank pulled his hand over his face, partially to hide his grin, but mainly to give him time to think about his reply.

"Look, Joe, I keep telling you we're going to get out of this OK and as soon as we get a pass, you'll be able to visit Madame's parlour and solve the problem for yourself."

"No I couldn't," replied Joe, "I wouldn't want it to happen that way. I know most of the blokes would think that I'm daft, but actually I want the first time to be with my wife whoever that might be. If ever that might be! God I haven't even got a girl friend, and never likely to have one unless this bloody war ends soon, and the way it's going right now, I can't see that happening, can you Frank?"

"Of course it'll end soon Joe, but first we have to get out of here, so let's get some rest so we've got the strength to pull the poor Captain back with us."

They were quiet for a few minutes, then Joe asked, "You won't tell the other lads about what I've just said, will you Frank? They'd only laugh and I couldn't take that."

"Don't be stupid, of course I won't, and anyway the way you're talking, anyone would think that you are the only virgin in this ruddy army."

"Well the way the lads speak about their exploits I'm sure I am."

"Don't you believe it, there are more of us about than you might think." Frank regretted the use of the word 'us' as soon as he had said it and tried to prevent giving Joe time to think about the remark by quickly adding, "I wouldn't believe half the stories the lads tell about their sexual exploits if I were you, mate. I'm sure most of them are lies."

But Joe had obviously interpreted the 'us' correctly, "So does that mean you've never done 'it' either Frank?"

Frank blushed, which he tried to hide by laughing, "Well if you must know, no I've never done 'it' either. Now can we drop the subject? I'm sure we're both going to die old men in our own beds surrounded by dozens of kids and grandchildren. So just let's drop the subject can we? Oh, and by the way, that's privileged information between you and me, so don't you go blabbing to the other lads." He pointed his finger directly at Joe saying accusingly, "You won't will you?"

Joe held up his hand as if taking an oath, "I promise." He too gave a little laugh, "You know I feel much better now, knowing we're both in the same boat. I don't think you're going to die in this war. I've always felt certain that you're a survivor so I guess if we're both in the same boat, then maybe I will die an old man in my own bed as well." He gave out a further laugh, "A bed that hopefully by then will have seen plenty of action. What do you say to that, Frank?"

"What I say to that Joe, is for God's sake let's drop the subject."

They both looked at each other, a new bond between them and Joe just added, "Amen to that," and that was the end of the matter.

They lay as motionless as they could, for what seemed hours to Joe, but in fact was only about an hour. Long enough Frank thought, for the Germans to lose interest in them long ago. Mark started to come round but was still in a complete daze and obviously in pain. Frank put his hand over Mark's mouth to try and get him to stay quiet, but the Captain was obviously still not fully conscious and soon drifted back to unconsciousness.

"Look I think it's time we got out of here, Joe. Do you think you'll be OK to drag yourself back, if I see what I can do with the Captain? Let's dump all our gear here. Bury it as best we can. No good trying to drag all that lot back as well."

"Yes sure," said Joe as he set about doing Frank's bidding as quietly as possible.

Frank meanwhile had cut the straps off the knapsacks to make a harness which he tied round the Captain so that he could drag him. With the job finished he turned the Captain on to his back and twisted him round as best he could, so that his head was facing the right way for the long haul back.

He watched and waited until a cloud blanked out the moonlight; took hold of the tackle around the Captain, and turning to Joe quietly asked him to give a help up the slope with the load.

"Right Joe, now as quietly as you can, you go on ahead and clear the way for me. Keep your head down and make sure we miss as many shell holes as we can.

And so the long laborious slog back continued. Frank needed to rest every few minutes to get his breath back and to check that the Captain, who was floating in and out of consciousness, was still alive. The wound in his own leg throbbing and paining him more and more with each advance forward. He dragged his own body ahead a few inches, to be followed by the enormous effort of pulling the inert load the same few inches; inch after inch over the undulating shell pitted land; inch after inch around the dead bodies and human detritus; inch after inch over the abandoned, broken, forsaken and rejected paraphernalia of war which littered the way. Slowly, inches turned into feet, the feet into yards and minutes turned into hours, as the home target became closer and closer.

At last they arrived at their own line and Joe stood and hobbled back to help Frank pull the Captain the last few yards to safety. Just at that moment the clouds drifted away from the moon and Joe's frame was silhouetted against the night sky.

The rat, tat, tat a tat, of the enemy machine guns broke the silence, and Frank screamed out an ear piercing "No.........." as the bullets zipped over his head and tore through Joe's body, splattering blood in all directions. Joe fell lifeless next to Frank whose scream turned to anguish as he wept uncontrollably clinging desperately to his friend, dead in his arms.

Frank was still sobbing at the loss of Joe when, five hours later as dawn broke, the Captain finally fully regained consciousness on the stretcher next to Frank. They were in the first aid station, having both been attended to and were awaiting transport to take them back to the field hospital behind the lines. Frank had insisted that the men, who had crawled over the parapet of the home trench to pull both Frank and the Captain to safety, should also pull Joe's body back into the sap. He was not going to let them chuck his friend's body into the general heap of bodies to be covered in earth and lost forever in this God forsaken hole. He insisted that Joe had saved both his and the Captain's lives and so had pleaded that they brought the body out of the line with the Captain and himself. Maybe it was in pity that they had agreed to his request or maybe it was in fear of some sort of retribution from the wild and distraught Frank if they did not. Either way, they had agreed, and there was Joe's body outside the tent, draped in a blanket, awaiting a decent burial.

Mark, next to him, becoming brighter by the minute, rolled over to face Frank, "Well Frank, you did it, you got us back safely. I must say I had my doubts that we'd make it. I'm going to recommend you for a medal for getting us out of there."

Frank decided he should, from now on, ignore the informality of the shell hole in No Man's Land and formally addressed the Captain, "No, Sir, we didn't all get back safely. Joe's lying here dead, full of bloody German bullets. If anyone gets a medal it should be him, not me. Joe's the one who should get it after all he's the one lying dead, not me or you. No Sir, I'm no hero, Joe is."

"God, I'm sorry Frank, I didn't realise he was dead. I knew they had brought him back here on a stretcher and I just thought he was injured. I'm so sorry. He was such a likeable chap."

"Yes, well likeable or not, it's not going to do him any good now, is it? It's his nineteenth birthday today and what does he get for it? He gets bloody shot, that's what he gets."

He turned to the Captain with real anger in his face, "You know if it hadn't been for me, he probably would never have been in this bloody army. He wasn't old enough, you see, and I encouraged him and helped him to lie about his age and join up. Lot of good I did him."

He was quiet for a while, torturing himself with grief and guilt at Joe's death, before he turned to the Captain, "Look, if you want to hand out a medal then give it to Joe. The poor bugger's got nothing else now, has he?"

"Come on Frank. I know I was pretty stupefied out there, but I wasn't so far gone all the time that I had no idea what was going on. I remember quite enough to know that it was you who treated our wounds, you who threw the bomb back and saved our lives, and you who dragged me all the way back to our lines. Believe it or not Frank, I'm as sorry as you are about Joe's death, but facts are facts and I have to put in as accurate a report as I can on this matter."

Frank became quite agitated at the Captain's words and now that he had the idea of Joe's death being marked by his being mentioned in reports and the possibility of a medal to mark his untimely death, he determined not to let the matter rest.

"Look, Mark, let us just get one thing straight, Joe died because he got up to pull you to safety. If you hadn't been injured out there, Joe would have got himself back to safety with no problem at all. Now I think I should help you to write your report correctly and make sure all those things you say happened because of me are properly stated as being up to Joe. You must remember how Joe pulled you all the way back and then stood up to lift you the last few yards back into our trenches. That's when he gave his life to save both of us. And I agree with you that Joe deserves a medal for that and I would be happy to countersign any report you care to write to that effect. Otherwise I think I'll have to say, how you were delirious out there and just don't remember things right. For God's sake let's give his mother and father something to be proud of him for."

"OK Frank, if that's how you want it, that's how it will be. Let's just hope the powers that be feel generous in giving out medals."

Joe was awarded the Military Medal. The medal, together with a copy of the citation, was sent to his parents along with his personal belongings. His body was given a decent burial in a marked grave at Montauban.

Frank and Captain Harper were moved back to the base hospital at Rouen, with the Captain always insisting, and managing to accomplish, that Frank should occupy the bed next to him. It was at Rouen where they met Captain Robert Fletcher, a friend of the Captain's who had been on the same course at University with him. After leaving University, 'Robby' Fletcher had helped set up the school for wireless operators at Farnborough. He soon found this a rather tedious life and so volunteered to come to France and use his expertise with this new wondrous means of communication at the front. Unfortunately within days, an enemy shell had hit the very first receiving station he had set up behind the lines. The equipment had been blown to smithereens and Robby had received shrapnel wounds, ending up in the hospital.

Robby soon became an ardent friend of Frank's and together with Mark, the three of them would talk into the night about the wonders of wireless and how it could change the nature of warfare if used properly and extensively.

Frank became obsessed with the subject and was quick to learn all he could about the topic from his new friend. His enthusiasm rubbed off on Mark and within a couple of weeks they had both learnt the Morse code and they spent hours tapping messages to each other on the side of their beds.

The wonders of wireless were not the only subject that Frank had become obsessed with whilst lying in hospital. The fact that Joe had died a virgin had played heavily on his mind ever since his death. He had never thought much about it before; at least not in the context of dying! It started to eat away at him, much in the way that it had obviously played on Joe's mind, particularly on that last day. Frank stupidly rationalised that if and when he went back to the front, he would not die if he was no longer a virgin.

Just before he was released from hospital Frank learnt that he was not going straight back to the front lines. Somehow Captain Harper had managed to pull strings somewhere, so that on their discharge from hospital, both he and Frank were going to be shipped back home for seven day's leave before reporting to the wireless operator's school at Farnborough to be officially trained in wireless operation.

On the Sunday at the end of this leave, an unusually warm autumn day, Frank and Grace were able to spend the day alone together walking in Sutton Park, having caught the train to Sutton station before making their way to Blackroot pool for a picnic lunch. They found a fairly isolated small stretch of grass surrounded by trees during their after lunch stroll and Frank had spread his greatcoat on the grass for them to sit on.

It was here that Frank finally professed to Grace his feelings for her, and asked her if she would marry him when the war was over.

She just looked straight into his eyes and said, "I love you too, and of course I'll marry you. Don't you know that I've always loved you, you idiot, and I always will? Come here."

At that she drew Frank's head towards her and kissed him full on the lips; a slow, gentle kiss at first, with both of them immersed in the sweet intimacy of it. Gradually, but surely, the veiled emotions of their love for each other became more and more ardent and more passionate as the long, long kiss progressed. Frank's hands held Grace on her shoulders. Slowly his right hand moved bit by bit forward, inside her open coat to her bare neck. The kissing stopped and with their faces only inches apart, they looked deep into each other's eyes. Frank's hand moved slowly downwards over Grace's dress to rest on her breast. He fully expected her to move his hand away but instead she held it firm against her breast with one hand whilst undoing the top buttons of her dress with the other. The task completed she took Frank's hand and placed it under her clothes and on to her bare breast. As she did so, she leaned forward and they kissed again, this time more passionately than ever before.

Frank was never able to be certain whether the impulsive and passionate love making that followed, would have happened but for the anxiety of the previous weeks over his virginity, or whether the time was right for both of them and was the right expression of the feelings they had for each other.

He just knew that at the time it felt the right thing for both of them. It was only afterwards, as they were rearranging their clothes back to a presentable state, that he started to panic about the possibility of Grace being pregnant through their love making and his own apprehensions about dying a virgin.

The one consolation was that he had asked Grace to marry him before their lovemaking. He would never have forgiven himself, if he had left it until afterwards. He would then always have had the misgiving that he had proposed marriage only because of their lovemaking, a fact that would have forever haunted him.

Grace, on the other hand, had none of these misgivings about the loss of her virginity. She had only just finished her period and had little worries about being pregnant. And if she were pregnant, so what, she wanted this man's children as much as she wanted to be his wife. For now, she could still feel his warmth inside her and she did not want to lose that feeling.

They were both quiet as they strolled back, arm in arm, to catch the train.

Eventually as they were about to leave the park, Frank said that he would like to keep their engagement a secret for the time being. He had to leave first thing the next morning to go back to his new camp and they would not have time to purchase a ring together. He wanted to do things properly and suggested that they should make it official on his next leave or maybe that it would better to leave it until the war was ended.

Grace protested against this and asked if he was having second thoughts about his proposal.

"No, of course not," was his passionate reply. "I want to marry you more than I can say, but what if I come out of this war as a cripple, or even worse, I don't survive it at all. I don't want you to be a grieving spinster for the rest of your life. If I'm crippled or don't survive, you mustn't spend the rest of your life fretting over me. Promise me that you'll find yourself another husband and have kids and forget all about me."

Once again Grace protested against his suggestions but eventually gave in when she realised that he was really fearful of ruining her life because of what might happen to him when he returned to France. And so she finally and begrudgingly promised that she would find herself another husband if anything happened to him. She had no intention of keeping her verbal agreement however. She was a young girl in love, and since she could not imagine ever feeling this way about any one else, the thought of being with any other man was a complete anathema to her. Some day she would tell Frank this, but not now. For now, she just wanted to enjoy the freedom of having and loving this man who, mentally, had been her secret lover for as long as she could remember and now had become her real lover, something that he could now never take away from her.

CHAPTER FOUR

SPRING 1917

Both Frank and Mark excelled during training at Farnborough, mainly because of their enthusiasm and previous knowledge of the subject matter. At the end of training, all of the thirty wireless operators on their course were formed into a new unit. Mark was to lead the unit as Captain and Frank was attached as his Sergeant.

On the very first day that the new unit paraded together, Mark told them that he had received orders for them to report back to France in eight days time.

On the Sunday afternoon everyone in the unit was busy checking their newly issued wireless equipment ready for the move to France. Mark had sent the men to have a break and get a cup of tea in the canteen. Billy Mallen came into the hut with a mug of tea for Frank and Mark, who were sitting together chatting about how they were going to organise things when they returned to France.

They each took a swig of the hot tea and after Billy Mallen had left the Captain asked, "What do you intend to do when this lot's over, Frank?"

"Do you mean when the war is over?"

"Sure, when you return to Civvy Street. Will you go back to working at Harpers?"

"No offence meant to you, or your family, Captain, but not if I can help it. I reckon I'll have had enough of taking orders by the time this war is over." He smiled and with a glint in his eye, which he was sure Mark would understand, added, "Especially from men I really don't have much respect for." Not wishing to offend Mark, he quickly added, "I don't mean you Sir, when I say that."

The Captain laughed, "No offence taken, Sergeant, I know exactly what you mean." His laughter increased, "Actually I could probably name one or two of them for you."

He took another drink from his tea. "So what will you do then?"

"Well I've been thinking about that all through this course. I really enjoy messing about with this wireless equipment, and even though I say it myself, I'm pretty good at mending them and making a few adjustments when necessary. And what I thought was, if and when the Post Office starts issuing licences again after the War, a lot of people will want to use wirelesses as a peacetime hobby. Well I reckon if I can buy some of the parts, I could make pretty good sets and sell them. In fact I've already made a few drawings of sets I think would work OK. All I need is some cash and some means of getting the necessary parts." He looked at the Captain and asked, "Do you think there would be money to be made from it, Sir?"

"Well Frank, I haven't really thought about it." He drank some more tea, obviously thinking over Frank's scheme. "You know Frank, I think there might be something in what you say. You're right it would be interesting work, even if not too profitable." He drained the rest of his tea before adding, "We'll have a chat about it again sometime Frank, but for now, let's get all this equipment tested and packed."

They had just started to check the equipment when a corporal from the Guardroom came into the hut and handed Mark a telegram. Mark read the telegram, and the colour immediately drained from his face. He stood in shock, his mouth open and shook his head from side to side as if denying the words in the telegram. He read them once more, rushed over to Frank and said, without giving any explanation, "I'm leaving you in charge Sergeant. I don't know when I'll be back, so make sure everything is ready for us to sail on Thursday."

Without waiting for any reply, he dashed out of the hut and went to the Officer's mess where he was able to phone Evie at home. After which he immediately saw the Commanding Officer who agreed, after much persuasion by Mark, that Sergeant Matthews was quite capable of ensuring the unit would be fully ready to go back to France on Thursday morning. On the strength of which, he agreed to grant Mark a seventy-two hour pass starting at midnight that night. Seventy-two hours would mean that he would arrive back at camp only hours before the unit was to leave for France.

That evening, after packing his overnight bag and sorting out his dress uniform, he went to see Frank in the Sergeant's quarters, but was told he had gone for a drink at the Tumbledown Dick with a couple of the other lads.

Mark immediately left on his motor bike for the Tumbledown Dick. The lounge bar was not as busy as usual and he saw Frank straight away leaning on the bar chatting away to the landlord's daughter Milly, who was the only barmaid on duty.

Mark took off his hat and walked up to the bar next to Frank, "A whisky, please Milly and give the Sergeant here another one of whatever he's drinking. Oh and have one of whatever you fancy yourself."

When Milly turned round to get the drinks he spoke to Frank, "I'm sorry to barge in like this Frank and spoil your fun but can you spare me a minute please?" Before waiting for an answer he continued, "Actually can we go and sit down at the corner table over there. I've had some news from home and I need to get back there as soon as I can."

Frank turned round and looked at the empty corner table, "Sure. Not bad news I hope?"

Mark flicked his eyes towards the other soldiers standing near to Frank at the bar, indicating that he did not wish to talk about it whilst other ears were listening. He nevertheless nodded his head with a very sad look on his face, "Mmmm. You go and sit down and I'll bring the drinks over."

Frank picked up his glass and drank the remains from it and, leaving it for Milly to re-fill, went and sat down. Mark downed his whisky which Milly had just placed on the counter and immediately gave it back to her for a refill. Mark joined Frank, with the refilled glasses.

Frank was questioning him about the 'news', before Mark had time to put the glasses on the table.

"What's the bad news, Sir?" Frank had never got used to the informality of using Christian names even though the Captain always seemed to want him to on occasions like this.

"Received a telegram from Evie this afternoon. Both my mother and father are dead."

"Oh my God." Frank was shocked and did not know what else to say. "Good God, I'm real sorry. How come? What's happened? Is Evie all right?"

"Yes, she's fine. Physically anyway. I managed to telephone her at home. They were both in a motorcar accident last night." He paused for a moment, a pensive frown on his brow, "Ironic really, my father only had the telephone installed last month. First time I've spoken to Evie on it. I've never phoned before. I always thought my father would answer it and I never wanted to speak to him. It would have been nice if I could have spoken to Ma before this happened though, wouldn't it?"

Mark picked up his glass and after lovingly stroking it for a moment, took a long slow mouthful from it. He held the warm, aromatic liquid in his mouth, and slowly released it down his throat before he spoke again, tears filling his eyes, "Why did my mother have to die?"

He looked questioningly directly into Frank's eyes as if the answer would spring from Frank's mind straight into his own. "Why, Frank? Why?"

Frank blinked, wishing to divert his eyes from the mesmerising gaze. He desperately wanted to distract Mark from looking at him so intently, knowing that he could not answer such an enquiry. He held out his hand and placed it on Mark's shoulder, "Do you know any of the details of the accident? How did it happen?"

Frank was relieved when Mark looked down at his glass and took another sip from it before answering the question, releasing Frank from the piercing stare. "Well apparently the old man took Ma and Evie to St Matthews late on Saturday afternoon so that they could help do the flowers for the Sunday services. Mother went to Church twice every Sunday, and did the flowers about once every month. Regular Church goer was mother, but the old man never went. Always take her to the door, but never went in. Never did know why that was. Anyway, he took them to the Church as usual and told them he was going to have a drink in the Wheatsheaf. Told Ma to come and fetch him from there when she'd finished and then they could go out for supper at the Bell on the Birmingham Road"

He drained the last dregs from his whisky glass.

"Would you like another one of those, Captain," asked Frank.

Mark handed him the empty glass, "Yes please, Frank. And for God's sake call me Mark while we're sitting here. I want to talk to a pal right now, not a subordinate."

Frank had never got used to Mark's trait of always wanting to wipe away the social differences between them. He had been acutely aware of his social status for as long as he could remember, and although he hated the bowing and scraping which this situation demanded from him, Mark's insistence on being called by his Christian name somehow emphasised the difference in status to him. Nevertheless, he intended that one day he would talk to Mark Harper, and everyone else for that matter, on Christian name terms as an equal, and not because they had condescendingly requested it. For now however he would do as Mark asked. This man, whom he had actually grown very fond of, was naturally very distressed at the news of his parents' death, and Frank had no wish to antagonise him in any way.

He picked up Mark's glass and held it out towards him, "Another one of these was it Mark?"

"Yes please," but then he called to Frank as he started to walk away, "No Frank, make it half a pint of their best bitter, will you? I'll get drunk far too quickly if I keep drinking whiskies one after the other."

Frank returned with the drinks, sat down, and they both took a sip from their full glasses before either of them spoke again.

"You were saying that your mother was going to meet your father at the Wheatsheaf after finishing the flowers," said Frank.

Mark looked up, awoken from his private thoughts, "Oh, yes. Well when Ma and Evie had finished helping with the flowers, they both went to meet the old man at the Wheatsheaf. Apparently, according to Evie, he'd already had plenty to drink; she could smell it on his breath. She told my father that Mary Rogers was waiting outside and they were going to walk home together. Mary only lives a hundred yards away from our house and she and Evie often go out together. Anyway Evie didn't go with Ma and the old man, thank God. She left and they went to the Bell for supper without her."

Mark looked at Frank, nodding his head, "God I don't know what I'd have done, if Evie had been with them and been killed as well." He wiped his open palm across his eyes wiping the moisture from them, "What on earth would I have done, Frank?"

Frank remembered the beautiful girl who had held him spellbound so long ago. He had often thought of her, or more accurately he had imagined his own Grace standing there in those same exquisite clothes, her hair hanging loose over her shoulders and the same smile on her lips. He blinked to try to clear his mind of the confused picture of the two women all rolled into one. Whenever this happened he could not clearly decide whether he wanted Grace looking like Evie, or whether he wanted Evie in the role of Grace. He loved Grace, he knew he did. She was what he wanted, but why did this confused picture keep coming to his mind? But for now, what did it matter anyway, Evie was still alive? Thank God she hadn't been with them. So don't feel sorry for yourself Matthews! This poor chap in front of you is the one who's in real pain, do something for him.

He reached out to Mark and touched him on the wrist, "Look Mark, she didn't go with them. She's all right. So stop torturing yourself with that one. You've got enough on your plate without worrying about things that might have happened."

Neither of them said anything for a good two or three minutes and Frank was beginning to wish he hadn't interrupted Mark's relating of the events. Mark was drinking heavily from his glass again and Frank felt he had to try to prevent him from drinking too much. He put his hand on Mark's drinking arm again, gently pushing it down, "So did the car accident happen on the way to the Bell?"

Mark was once more snapped out of his melancholy trance, "No, it happened afterwards when they were going home. Evie reckons that during the evening the old man must have had more to drink than to eat. God knows why mother let him drive home. She probably couldn't stop him though. The stupid bugger thought he could drive that bloody car no matter how pickled he was." He took another drink from his glass, but this time he only took one mouthful. "It was when they were going down the Arboretum hill leading to Lichfield Street. There was a chap on a horse, also going down the hill. The old man probably left it 'til the last minute to brake and pull out round him. Must have gone into a skid and went straight into the Arboretum wall on the opposite side of the road. Anyway that was that. He was catapulted right out of the car. Must have died instantly; broken neck Evie said. Poor Ma was still alive, but she died in hospital early this afternoon. Evie was with her all night. Poor girl didn't know whether to leave her to send me a telegram or stay with her. She knew I'd be more worried about Ma than the old man. Well, I suppose I am. Wouldn't have wished him dead though."

He looked at Frank, "Poor Evie, she's got it all to sort out. Says she'll try to arrange the funeral for Wednesday. I hope she can. I've got a leave pass until midnight on Wednesday. I'll be glad to see Evie. Maybe we'll be able to console each other a bit. What do you think Frank?"

Frank jumped with a start at the mention of his name. He had been reflecting with thoughts of Evie again and on how the sweet attractive young girl he had only ever seen the once would cope with the tragic loss of both her mother and father at the same time. "Yes I'm sure it'll help both of you to be together for a couple of days." He tried to think of something helpful to say, but could only say, "It would have been much, much worse for her, if it had happened whilst you were posted abroad though, wouldn't it? Perhaps you've got to be thankful that at least you can get home to comfort her."

"Yes you're right, I'm sure it'll help both of us to spend a little time together. Have to sort a few things out at the factory as well. Have to get Percy Lewis to run the place for a while. What do you think, Frank? He's a capable chap, isn't he?"

"One of the best. Worked there since he left school. Knows as much about the business as your Grandfather did and all the men respect him. Yes I'm sure he'll take care of everything and I'm sure Miss Hill will be able to see to all the bookwork. She always seemed competent to me even if she was a bit overbearing."

"Yes. I've got a lot to sort out in the next couple of days. Actually, I'd better go and get on my way. I know my pass doesn't officially start until midnight, but I don't suppose anyone will say anything if I get off now. But first I've got to sort out a few things with you about getting ready for the off on Thursday morning." And then, as if the mention of going to

France had changed what he was thinking about, he added, "Do you know? Another couple of months and Evie would have been in France herself, and then neither of us would have been able to get home for the funeral. She's joined the Red Cross as a nurse and has volunteered to work in France. Good old Evie. Always did have to get in the thick of it all. She never has been one for sitting at home, being a prim and proper lady."

The expression on Mark's face changed at this thought and he even managed a smile as he added, "My father never did understand her, he was always trying to get her to do the things he wanted, but she's always been determined to be a 'new age lady'. Fighting for women's rights, votes for women and all that. She used to drive the old man daft with all her talk." He shook his head slightly from side to side, "I was never sure whether she only said things to annoy him or whether she really believed in all that equality for women bit."

Frank liked the idea of Evie Harper standing up for her rights and was even more impressed with her now that he knew she had a very definite mind of her own. Yes, he could just see her standing up for her rights. The idea of her annoying Vernon Harper by standing up for herself and telling him what she thought of his privileged life amused Frank no end. So Vernon Harper didn't get everything his own way, not in his own home anyway. Yes, that amused and pleased Frank no end.

"You know Mark, I can just see her ministering to the lads in hospital in France. I reckon she'll make a great nurse."

Mark looked up from his drink and winked at Frank. A grin spread across his face, "You're absolutely right Frank she'll knock 'em dead, won't she?" His grin turned to an audible laugh as he added, "Figuratively speaking of course."

They both finished their drinks whilst Mark related a story of when he and Evie had been about eight years old, and three of his school friends had come to tea one summer's afternoon. "To start off, the lads had wanted nothing to do with Evie, but before the afternoon was over, Evie had been in charge, telling all of the lads exactly what to do. And we all followed her instructions absolutely, and all happy to do so. As pleased as punch to do everything she asked of us."

He smiled at Frank adding, "She'll have the whole hospital running round after her before she's finished, will good old Evie. She's a great organiser and a great one for getting things done. You know she's the only person who could get the better of my father; other than my Grandfather that is. The old man was always scared of Grandfather; but then you know something of that, don't you Frank?"

Frank had not thought about his real feelings towards Mark's father dying until this moment. He had been too concerned for Mark and his sister losing their mother. For the past three years Frank had had dreams of one day getting the better of Vernon Harper, and from time to time, the anger he felt towards him had been the main driving force within him. He had always been convinced he would survive this war to somehow vent retribution on him. Suddenly the object of his hostility was taken from him. How could you hate a dead man? At one time Frank had thought it would be easy to hate all his family, but he could never find it in him to hate his wife; a woman he had never met; and now dead. That certainly wasn't the way he wanted to gain retribution. And as for hating his children? And as for his son? Good God he actually liked and admired the man now sitting in front of him. There was a friendship between them that had somehow transcended the differences in rank, social status, education and wealth and there had been times when Frank had felt an equal partner to Mark in every way. He could not hate this man any more than he could hate the man's mother or sister.

Frank's reasons for this, however much he tried, were far more difficult to analyse. He knew he could never have anything but admiration for Evie. Once he had seen her that is! He had only seen the girl once and had never spoken to her, but he sometimes thought he had fallen for her the moment she had smiled at him, even though he knew that any sort of actual relationship between them was impossible. Anyway he knew his feelings for her were nothing like the feelings he had for Grace. Once more the conflict of the two women filled his mind. He couldn't 'love' Evie! He didn't even know her. It could only possibly be the vision of her that he admired.

He loved Grace, and given the clothes, the financial background and the leisure time granted to Evelyn Harper, Grace would be her equal. Money, or lack of it, was the only thing that differentiated the Harpers and himself (and Grace). They had money, he did not. It was as simple as that. He could mete out his vehemence towards Vernon Harper, dead or alive, by becoming the social equal of his family. That would make the man turn in his grave. He did not have to do physical harm to anyone, he just had to make enough money to become the equal of the Harpers. He didn't have to hate anyone. Once he and Grace were financially their equal, they could be real friends with this Mark Harper and his sister on equal terms, and that would be penalty enough for the dead Vernon Harper. He would have been the one to hate that situation.

"Are you all right, Frank? You've suddenly gone a million miles away."

Frank was instantly shaken from his musings by Mark's remark, but had not absorbed what he had said, "Sorry what was that?"

"I said, are you OK? You looked as though you had drifted into another world."

"Yes I'm fine. Just thinking that's all." He suddenly realised he ought to give some excuse for his dreaming before Mark delved too deeply into his real thoughts. "I was just thinking about your sister and how she must be feeling. Is she all on her own? I guess she'll be pleased to see you tomorrow. How are you getting home? On the train?"

"No, I'm going on my motorbike. I don't have to worry about train times or anything else then. Should get home in about four hours or so."

Frank pointed to Mark's empty glass and asked if he wanted the other half before going, to which Mark replied, "Actually I should get on my way. I probably ought not to drink anymore. I don't want to be another drunken driver like my father do I? Evie didn't say as much, but I'm sure she feels that Ma would still be alive if the old man hadn't drunk so much."

He stood up to go but immediately sat down again, "Actually, before I go I must sort out a few things with you. I've agreed with the C.O., or more precisely, the C.O. has agreed with me, that you'll be in charge of getting everything ready for the off on Thursday. Is that OK?"

They spent the next ten minutes discussing army matters but it was patently obvious to Mark that he had nothing to worry about on that score and that Frank was more than capable of looking after all the necessary detail.

At the end of their discussion Mark stood up again, "Can I get you another drink before I get on my way then, Frank." Frank declined the offer saying something about getting back to camp to get a good nights sleep so he could get up early to sort out all the things that needing doing for the return to France.

"Right I'll get on my way then. See you first thing Thursday morning." Mark thought for a moment, "Look, I really ought not to leave it until the last minute. If I can I'll try and get back before closing time on Wednesday. I guess you and the rest of the lads will be in here having a last drink of good old English beer before we sail for France, won't you?" He did not wait for answer but added, "I'll try and get back to see you and the lads on Wednesday then. I can then let you know how things work out at home and you can let me know if there have been any last minute problems."

"Sure. See you Wednesday then. Oh and give my regards to Evie. I'll be thinking about you both."

Mark merely replied with a quiet, "Thanks," and left the bar without looking back at Frank.

Frank was sitting in the same chair on Wednesday evening when Mark came into the bar almost at closing time.

"Sorry I'm so late Frank, but I've only just got back and I can't stop. The Colonel had left a note for me, saying he wants to see me tonight if I get back before midnight. Needs to go over orders with me, but I've managed to put it off for a bit, saying that I wanted to telephone Evie at home. Seemed to accept the excuse, but I must get straight back. Sorry I've kept you waiting all evening."

"No that's OK. Me and the lads were just about to go anyway. You need not have bothered to come, it wouldn't have mattered."

"No I must buy you all a drink." He called across the room to Milly. "Milly, give all these lads a drink of whatever they fancy, and let me know what the damage is before I go." He turned back to Frank, "Everything go all right this week? Any problems?"

"No, we've managed to get everything ready. Could have done with a few more spares, but there's never enough of those, is there? Everything go all right with you at home? How's Evie? Is she coping OK?"

"Yes she's fine but I'll tell you all about it some other time when I'm not expected elsewhere. Oh, by the way, Evie asked me to give this to you."

He took a small item from his tunic pocket and gave it to Frank, "It's a gold St Christopher medal. Evie gave it to me to give to you. Actually she gave me one as well. Said we are to take them to France with us to bring us luck and make sure we get home safely. Let's hope she's right?"

Frank took the medallion from Mark, "Why, on earth, has she sent this to me? She doesn't even know me."

"Well she knows that you saved my life last September and it's her way of saying thank you I guess. Anyway she said I was to give it to Sergeant Matthews with her best wishes. So there it is. Now I really must go. See you soon," and with that he got up, went and settled his bill with Milly and left the bar.

Frank studied the gold medallion, rotating it over and over in his hand until the landlord called, "Time Gentleman, please," and turned the straggling drinkers, including himself, out into the street.

All the way back to the barracks he pondered on why Evie Harper had sent the St. Christopher medallion. Was it merely a thank you gesture as Mark had suggested or was there more to it? Or was that merely wishful thinking on his part? He never did quite work it out but whatever the reason he was pleased to hang it next to the silver three-penny bit that Grace had sent him and he wore them together throughout the rest of his war.

"My God, all this waiting around is driving me mad!"

"Freddy, do you have to moan at everything? You can be a real pain in the arse at times, you know."

Freddy Anslow turned his back towards Billy Mallen, bent over, lifted his greatcoat, and wiggling his backside from side to side said, "That may be true old pal, but isn't that the most beautiful arse you've ever seen?"

Billy and Freddy were really the best of pals, but it seemed that the only way they could show their friendship was by continuously bickering at each other.

Frank shouted from the other side of the hold where he was checking that all the equipment was well battened down, "For God's sake, will you two just settle down. It's been a long day for all of us and I reckon that the only chance we've got of any sleep tonight is on this boat. So I suggest you pair of old wives just find some corner to settle down and get some rest. At least we can all get a break from your bickering then."

It had indeed been a long day and Frank had a lot of sympathy with Freddy Anslow's groaning. It seemed that every part of their journey had been delayed. First there had only been one truck available for the journey from the camp to the railway station. This was totally insufficient to take both men and equipment in one trip, so Frank and a few of the men, including Freddy Anslow and Billy Mallen had had to start off particularly early to go to the station, so that the truck could fetch the rest of the men from camp and return in time to meet the train.

When the train did arrive, almost two hours late, it was already packed with soldiers from Aldershot who had joined the train at Farnham. No matter how much Captain Harper cajoled and ordered the Aldershot men to make room, it made very little difference and most of his own men had to sit on their kit bags or on the floor. Several of them, including Frank, had decided to settle down in the guard's van. At least they were able to stretch their legs in there, albeit they were sitting on the wooden floor.

The train had made excruciatingly slow progress through south London, where they seemed to have to wait at every set of signals. But the train sailed through every station without stopping, which meant they didn't have a chance to stretch their legs or get a cup of tea. At every signal stop which had any sort of cover, most of the carriage doors were opened and soldiers were urinating onto the track, there being no corridors or toilets on the train.

Eventually in late afternoon the train had arrived at Dover and everyone was glad to stretch their legs and use to the station toilets.

The Captain managed to purloin a couple of greengrocer's barrows from the docks on which his men managed to transport the equipment to the awaiting ship. There was then further delay whilst the tons of ammunition, equipment and rations bound for the troops at the front were loaded.

All this activity and movement of war paraphernalia jolted Frank's senses, making him realise that he was going back to the awful carnage taking place across the Channel. He felt ill at ease for the first time in months and shuddered with fear at the thought of going into battle again. Would his luck still hold? Would he have a better chance of surviving if he were still a virgin? No, all these thoughts were stupid, but stupid or not, the panic grew uncontrollably within him. He touched the medallions around his neck and said a little prayer for a safe passage until he returned across this stretch of water.

The thoughts of his own mortality would not clear his mind and he began to experience the chronic debilitating panic he had seen in other men in the trenches. His legs were like lead, his mouth became dry, and he found himself staring into space for what must have been a very long time.

"OK chaps, time to go on board. Get your kit together and follow me." The Captain's words jerked Frank's attention, but his body did not want to respond. "Come on fellows. Let's show these other chaps that we still know how to march."

The men fell into marching order and Frank managed to drag himself to the rear of the ranks. The regimented discipline of marching helped him go with the others to the ship, but the pains in his body and the pounding in his head were screaming out to him to turn and run in the opposite direction. He understood at that moment why men just walked away from the front, with absolutely no concern that they may be shot for desertion. Frank's brain screeched silently inside his head, *"God help those poor bastards shot as deserters. They sure as hell didn't deserve to be."*

As soon as the boat transporting Captain Harper and his men back to the battlefields left the harbour at Dover, the Captain invited Frank to take a stroll on the deck with him. There was a wonderfully clear sky and even though it was a chilly March night the sea was particularly calm. The Captain took a cigarette from his silver cigarette case, lit it and inhaled the smoke deep into his lungs, as they each leaned on the handrail breathing in the cold but fresh sea air.

They did not speak for some time, just staring at the docks and coastline slipping further and further away from them as the ship chugged on its way back to France.

Eventually the Captain swung round, leaning with his back against the rail. He looked up into the night sky, took another draw on his cigarette, and after slowly blowing out the smoke into the night air, said, "I always think that on clear nights like this, the millions of stars up there are an awe inspiring sight."

Frank turned round and looked up at the sky, "Yes a truly beautiful sight." He pointed directly overhead in the direction of Ursa Major and added, "That's the Plough up there I think, but I'm afraid that's where my knowledge ends."

"Well you see those four stars almost forming a square, there look, a little higher in sky, with a tail of stars pointing to the North Star, looks a bit like the Plough on its side and a bit smaller, well that's the Little Bear." Mark then pointed further South in the sky, "And those there in that little group is Leo, and that group a bit to the left and down from Leo is Virgo."

"Know a bit about the stars as well as everything else then do we?"

Mark smarted at the rebuke, "Sorry, I didn't mean to be acting like a know it all." He turned and looked at Frank who could see the blushing in his cheeks, "I'm sorry I just get carried away sometimes. I didn't mean anything by it."

Frank was now the one to feel awkward about the situation, "Let's forget it shall we? I'm just feeling a little fractious at the moment. Not at my best. So I'm sorry about the remark. Probably some other time, I'd love to learn all about the stars."

Mark laughed, "Well actually I've told you most of what I know anyway."

He lit himself another cigarette and after exhaling his first puff of smoke, turned to Frank and asked him, "What is it that's bothering you then?" and without waiting for an answer he put up his hand and said, "Sorry, none of my business. I'm not being very tactful tonight am I?"

It was now Frank's turn to laugh and for the first time that evening he started to feel himself relax, "Look why don't we begin again and forget all this being embarrassed with each other?"

He turned round and leaned on the rail for a few seconds, then swung round again and pointing up into the sky, said, "Beautiful night tonight isn't it? Know anything about the star formations, Captain?"

They both laughed loudly after which Frank felt much, much better.

Mark nevertheless felt that a change of subject was called for, "Have you had any more thoughts about your idea of going into the wireless business?"

"No, not really, I've been too busy over the last week. What do you think of it anyhow? Do you think there's any mileage in the idea?"

"Sure," said Mark, "Been thinking about the idea myself. I needed something to take my mind of my mother's death."

Frank closed his eyes and shook his head, "Oh damn me, I'm so sorry, Sir. I was so wrapped up in myself, I'd completely forgotten about your grief. Please forgive me."

"Oh for God's sake, don't let's start that again. Look it's OK, it's not something I want to talk about at the moment. I'd much rather talk about your wireless business."

Frank smiled, "OK but I'd really like to know your thoughts on the subject, unless that's going to be maudlin for us as well?"

Mark took another puff on his cigarette, "No I don't think so. Actually, I thought it was a great idea. I'm sure you were right when you said that plenty of people will start getting interested in it as hobby after the war. That is, as soon as the Post Office allow private transmissions again. Have you thought about that, and how long it might be before folk will be able to use them legally?"

"Well, Yes and No. I've thought about it, but on the other hand I'll have to find some other work to give me a living anyway. So I guess I'll only be able to work on building new wirelesses to my design in my spare time anyway. And I won't have much spare cash to start much of a business, so I don't really suppose it'll get off the ground, but it's nice dreaming about making a fortune, even if I know in my heart it'll never happen."

"No you mustn't think like that. I think it's a great idea. There's no knowing what the future will bring and there's nothing better than being in on the ground floor of any new idea."

They were both silent for a while, but eventually Mark turned to Frank and said, "Now don't get mad at me again, but what I've been thinking over the last few days is that I really don't want to get involved in the family business and I'd much rather do something for myself." He was silent for a moment and looked directly into Frank's eyes, "Like going into business with you."

He held his hand up as to protect himself, "Before you say anything, I don't want to poke my nose in where it's not wanted, but we get on OK together don't we? And I reckon we could make it work between us. What do you say? Is it worth thinking about?"

After some thought Frank decided that there was no point agreeing to this thing without saying exactly what he felt, "Well I don't know really. I suppose it's an OK idea, but really we come from totally different worlds. I'm not educated like you and anyway I don't move in the same circles as you, and what's more I know in my heart I never will, no matter how much I resent it at times."

"Look," said Mark, "I'm not saying you should make a decision on this straight away, just think about it. And anyway you're wrong about the differences in our social status and education. Sure I've got more money than you, but I wouldn't want to make anything of that if we went into business together. And as for my contacts, well just think about it, they could be a real advantage. Any business needs the right contacts as well as capital. You've already said that money could well be a problem for you. Well, I've got money and before you say anything about that making me a boss and you an employee, then let me tell you that isn't how I see it. We would be partners, equal partners. We'd treat any initial capital I put into the business as a sort of bank loan, borrowed by the business at an agreed rate of interest; just the amount of interest I might get if I left the money in the bank. And as we make a bit of profit we, the business, will pay the loan back. Equal partners see."

He stopped speaking for a moment to let what he said sink into Frank's mind, but without letting Frank give any sort of answer continued with his thoughts, "And as far as my education is concerned. Well sure I've been at school a bit longer than you, but you know as well as I do, that you're a bright chap, Frank. One of the brightest I've ever met. You know perfectly well that on the course, you were picking up most of the ideas much quicker than I was. And look how quickly you learnt Morse code and you're certainly much quicker at sending it than I am."

He put his cigarette to his mouth and inhaled before continuing to speak, "No, Frank, it isn't you who would be using me if we went into business together, it's the other way round. You're the one with ideas and the one who knows he can design wirelesses better than the ones we've got at the moment."

Again he didn't let Frank say anything, "I don't want you to say anything about what I've said. Just spend some time thinking about it and maybe in a few weeks time we can chat about it again, and if you agree, maybe we can even start making some plans about how we might set things up."

He looked up into the night sky and as an indication that he regarded the subject as closed for now, pointed into the western sky and said, "And that over there is Cancer and if you look carefully below Cancer that blue star, well it's not a star, it's the planet Neptune and below that is Saturn."

Frank let out a roar of laughter, “You bugger! You know a damn sight more about it all than you said, don’t you?”

Captain Harper and his men had, for the time being, been posted to an airdrome situated at Bailleul where they were to train and liaise with Royal Flying Corps officers in trying to perfect effective wireless transmissions from aircraft to the operators on the ground.

Frank’s first impression of Bailleul was one of some surprise. He had been expecting the same paraphernalia of war that he left behind some months before; the columns of crawling khaki, camouflaged tents stretching in churned up muddy fields as far as the eye could see, on the otherwise barren and wretched landscape of war. The constant movement of traffic along dusty or impassable muddy roads, depending on the weather conditions, and ant like battalions of men moving to or from the front line, training and practising warfare, parading, exercising, playing games or just lazing about drinking mugs of tea and smoking a cigarette.

But all of this expected activity on and behind the battlefields of Flanders, was some fifteen miles to the east of them. Here at Bailleul there was a peace and tranquillity which Frank had not known at the front; a flawless line of large tents equidistant from the road and equidistant from each other, pitched by engineers with a wish for order and perfection. The side of each tent facing the field was strapped wide open, giving sufficient room for one of the two aircraft in front of each tent to be pulled back into it for maintenance and servicing out of the rain when necessary. To the west of the field was another row of six tents in which spares, tools and maintenance equipment was kept. Otherwise the field was only marred by the tyre marks which criss-crossed the flat grassy field. But on the other side of the road was another field filled with tents completely lacking the exactitude and precision of the layout he had just witnessed; a fact which expressed clearer than anything else that these pioneer military airmen regarded the needs of their aircraft much more important than their own needs. After all, sleeping, eating and other purely perfunctory human activities were mere interruptions to the real reason for living. Flying aircraft.

This was reinforced when Captain Harper reported for duty to the Commanding Officer, who having shook the Captain’s hand, walked over to the coat-hanger by the opening to the tent. He put on his leather jacket, snatched up his leather flying cap and goggles and strode purposefully out of the tent, indicating that the Captain should follow him.

As they walked he told the Captain to sort things out for himself, “Park yourself anywhere you like in this field. Just pitch your tents wherever you fancy. Have to look after yourself old chap, I'm needed across the road, right now. Have to love you and leave you, old boy. Come and see me when you've all settled in. Perhaps this evening, when it's too dark to fly? We'll sort something out then."

He shook the Captain's hand again, "Be seeing you then," and with that he crossed the road to the airdrome leaving the Captain a little bemused by the unusual informality of the arrangements.

For Frank who had managed to relax during the few months back in England, the lack of ceremony at the camp was ideal.

He enjoyed the company of the pilots and particularly their almost flippant attitude to everything other than aircraft and anything to do with them. For the pilots, life was to be enjoyed to the full, and it seemed that every evening was a party, at least that was how it seemed to Frank, who at first felt that here at Bailleul they were far enough away from the battlefields to be untouched by it all.

How wrong can a fellow be?

On the second of April, Frank heard the news that Ralph Rawlings and his gunner had failed to return from a mission; news that was just part of the nightmare for everyone at the camp but for Frank it was the beginning of the realisation that the joking and camaraderie of the pilots and their crewmen was a way of coping with their short life expectancy.

He had known the fear of death on the battlefield himself, but somehow in the trenches you always believed it would be the other chap who would 'catch it'. For these young pilots, many with less than twenty hours flying experience, there was no other chap to catch it instead of them. Often they were flying over the battleground on reconnoitre trips on their own against the far superior tactics of the German Jagdstaffeln. Soon plane after plane failed to return, and as 'Bloody April' progressed the number of casualties rose and the life expectancy of the new RFC pilots began to be counted in days not weeks.

Everything required of the airmen made their job an absolute nightmare of which keeping the plane steady and keeping an eye out for enemy planes was least important to the Generals.

The strategy Generals at HQ wanted them to change the photographic plates in the cameras in exactly the correct aerial position so that successive photographs could be pieced together to give a large area map of the battlefield. But the front line officers wanted them to provide immediate information on whether the long distance guns were hitting their targets or not. To do this they had to reel out of the aerial wire from the plane before trying to send messages on the new fangled wireless equipment that Captain Harper's team were training them to use.

Was it any wonder that so many of them failed to return home safely or were 'lost in action' before they had become fully conversant with the equipment?

As the number of losses increased the Generals became more and more annoyed at the lack of the vital up to date information they had requested and to Frank's utter dismay, a decision was taken towards the end of April that rather than train the pilots and their gunners in wireless operation, the operators from Captain Harper's unit should accompany the pilots and act as their gunners.

"Well they can all fire a gun can't they?" was the cryptic remark made by the Lieutenant who brought the orders from Headquarters.

Frank was not at all happy about going up in one of the airplanes particularly as so many failed to return from the reconnaissance trips.

Mark laughed at Frank's reluctance and said he could not wait to get up in a plane, as it was something he had wanted to do for such a long time, so he volunteered to be the first from the unit to try out the new arrangements.

This was to be the following Tuesday, but on the Monday evening he called for Frank and said, "Sorry Sergeant, but I've been called to a meeting at HQ tomorrow so you'll have to take my place as gunner instead."

Frank had a very restless night, but by the next morning had convinced himself he would enjoy it and was up bright and early for his first trip in an airplane. He was to accompany Buster Yates in his RE8.

Buster was one of the flying 'survivors' and was one of the first airmen that Frank had trained in the use and operation of the wireless. They become immediate friends and had spent many nights at the local hostelry, where Frank listened to his exciting airborne exploits; the engagements with enemy planes; the banking, loops and other evasion flying tricks used to avoid enemy fire and flack. It had all sounded terribly exciting at first, and Frank had almost taken up Buster's invitation to take a trip with him, but the news of Ralph Rawlings death was announced just a couple of hours before Frank was to go with Buster on a 'joy ride'.

Buster was pretty cut up about it as he and Ralph had been together at the same school and university and had joined the air corps together. He apologised to Frank and said he had to try and write a letter to Ralph's parents that afternoon and would not be flying. "We'll do it another day old chap." was his parting remark to Frank, but as the list of pilots and gunners killed in action rose, Frank had avoided the subject of flying with Buster and he felt certain that Buster knew why.

In fact Buster himself now seemed to avoid talking about flying (and so did many of other of the pilots) and gradually the evenings they all spent together became less and less boisterous and flamboyant.

And now on this clear, bright May morning just as the sun rose in the sky Frank was sat in the rear seat of Buster's plane on the orders from above. But this was not to be the joy ride originally promised; instead he was expected to act as wireless operator, photographer and gunner.

Frank's heart was in his mouth as they sped along the grass bumping over every indent in the meadowland previously made by the wheels of the planes taking off and landing. The engine noise increased unbearably as Buster increased the throttle before the final lift into the sky. They lifted high over the trees and Buster swung the plane round towards the rising sun, and the battlefields in the East. Suddenly the engine starting spluttering and after a few seconds cut out all together. Buster tried to start the engine again but nothing happened. They were falling rapidly, but fortunately back towards the field they had just left. Frank, thought his end had come, closed his eyes and involuntarily prayed to his Maker. He opened them only to see the ground rushing towards them. Buster was trying to keep the plane as level as possible but the inevitable was abruptly upon them. The plane hit the ground and the wheels broke off spinning in opposite directions rendering the brakes useless. The body of the airplane spun uncontrolled along the grass; various pieces of it breaking off and flying in all directions. Everything seemed to be happening in slow motion for Frank even though the far hedge around the field was becoming closer by the second. The trees grew larger and larger. The plane spun round and round. And then, Bang!

Frank woke up in a hospital bed twenty four hours later. He felt pretty groggy and when he opened his eyes he was totally disorientated. Who was this beautiful woman standing over him? He knew the face, the mere sight of which set his heart pounding faster, but where was he and what on earth was she doing holding his wrist and taking his pulse. Gradually he came to his senses and realised that he must be in a hospital bed.

"So glad to have you back with us at last. How do you feel now?" asked the nurse, giving Frank such a smile that he could feel the blood rushing to his cheeks. Surely she could see how much he was blushing?

She put his arm back on the bed and repeated her question, "How are you feeling?"

"Pretty woozy and I've got a hell of a headache. Where am I? And what am I doing here?"

"You've been in a plane crash and you're now in the Field Hospital."

Frank tried to lift his head but quickly dropped it back on to the pillow. "God that hurts," he said.

He put his hand to his head and felt the bandage and realised that his right forehead was obviously swollen, "That's really sore, what on earth have I done to it?"

"Don't you remember the accident?"

Frank closed his eyes trying hard to clear his mind. Slowly he remembered the plane trip.

"I remember going in Buster's plane and we had problems coming in to land. I don't remember anything after that." He suddenly panicked at the thought of Buster, the panic clearly audible in his voice as he almost shouted out, "How is Buster? Is he all right?"

"He's over there," replied the nurse nodding her head in the direction of the bed opposite.

"Hi, old chap," Buster shouted, "I reckon we were pretty lucky there. Nice to see you in the land of the living again. I'm OK. Be out of here in a couple of days. The plane's a bit of a mess though." He laughed out loud as he added, "They won't get many spares out of her."

Frank tried to move in the bed again. The nurse got a pillow from the next vacant bed and putting her arm under his shoulders, lifted his head and put the extra pillow under it before asking, "Is that better?"

Frank smiled and was about to nod his head, but thought better of it and just curled up his lips in agreement instead adding, "Yes that's fine thanks."

The nurse offered him a drink of water, and as Frank sipped from the glass he started to recall more of the details of the plane crash.

"Now I must be getting on with my work," she said, "Is there anything you need before I go and see to the others?"

"Well yes, there are a couple of things. First what have I done to my head and how long will I be in here?" Before she had a chance to reply Frank picked up the courage to ask the question which had been plaguing him since he had come round, "You're Evelyn Harper aren't you? We met once in your father's office in Walsall."

Frank was sure her cheeks were slightly flushed as she replied, "Yes I know," and as if to change the subject continued with, "Actually Mark was in here yesterday and reminded me that you are the Frank Matthews who saved his life and it was then that I recognised the St. Christopher round your neck." She smiled a gorgeous smile and held his arm with one hand as she touched the medallion with the other saying, "I hope this helped yesterday and thank you for saving Mark's life." Frank once again felt his face colouring.

"In fact Mark says that he should have been in the plane yesterday, not you. So I guess in a way you have saved him from injury yet again. I'm so sorry you've been hurt though. I'll just have to make sure you're given extra special treatment."

"Now as far as your injuries are concerned, you have a broken leg, which the doctor has put in splinters and that should mend fine in a few weeks. And, as you've already realised you've had a nasty bang to the head. Whilst you were out cold, the doctor couldn't tell what damage you'd done there. It's badly swollen but that may be a good sign. At least the swelling has come out which means any damage internally may be minimal. Let's hope so, anyway. And now I must go and let Doctor McPherson know you've come round. He wanted to have a look at you and talk to you as soon as you were conscious."

She smiled again at Frank, and now he was certain she must realise how much he was affected by this beautiful woman he had dreamt about so many times since the first, and only time, he had met her before. She squeezed his hand, raised her eyebrows and gave a big smile which sent his heart beat soaring as she said, "Must go and find Dr. McPherson now."

CHAPTER FIVE

1917

Luckily for Buster his injuries were quite minor cuts and bruises and he was declared fit for duty .

For Frank however things were not as straightforward. Dr. McPherson wanted to make sure the head injury and concussion were not serious and that he didn't have any internal brain damage. He therefore gave instructions that Frank should stay in hospital until the swelling had gone down when he would be able to check for any internal damage. In the meantime he insisted that Nurse Harper should keep a close eye on Frank and report to him immediately should Frank feel any grogginess or worse still, slip into unconsciousness again.

All this attention from Nurse Harper was manner from heaven for Frank. He had never met anyone quite like her. Her clothes were always so neat, so clean and such a perfect fit that Frank felt certain she must have brought a couple of her maids with her to sew, launder and iron her uniform. Her blond hair had been cut shorter than when he had first seen her. Then it had flowed freely over her shoulders but now it had been cut to fit into the nape of her neck. He remembered it as being wavy but now there was only a semblance of a wave as it curled under at the neck.

At first he felt he preferred it as he remembered it, but after a couple of days he had come to love the clean fresh lines of the hair under her nurse's cap. It always looked freshly washed and had a sheen about it that made him want to touch it. He never did of course. Her skin was so smooth and her hands and fingernails were beautifully manicured. She had the same brown eyes as her twin brother Mark, but somehow they appeared so translucent that they seemed to sparkle and smile even when there was no smile on her lips. She wore little or no makeup. She did not need to. She did however always wear perfume; and always the same perfume. It got so that Frank knew when she was heading his way, even when he had his eyes closed. He was sure he would be able to sense the fragrance from fifty yards away and when she spoke it was not with the coarse Black Country accent he had grown accustomed to from the women in his life, but neither was it hoity-toity but gentle and almost melodic.

Frank began to daydream about her and was constantly awaiting her visits. He hated it when she went off duty, but on a few occasions Mark came to visit him just as she was about to go off duty and the two of them sat on his bed chatting away for a hour or so. At first they reminisced and entered into their own world, laughing and joking with each other as if no one else existed. Frank silently watched as they avidly talked away to each other, his heart jumping a beat every time Evie looked at him or smiled in his direction, which she seemed to do quite often.

Gradually however, their conversation became more personal and revolved more and more on matters to which Frank was not party and he started to feel like the outsider. Here was a good comrade and a girl for whom he had intense feelings, chatting away to each other and, or so he felt, disregarding him completely. Was he imagining this or were they ignoring him? Perhaps he was not good enough for them! Perhaps he was not of their class! Recently he had not felt this with Mark, and even though there was the division of rank between them he had begun to look upon Mark as a friend, maybe a better educated and more eloquently spoken friend, but a friend and companion nevertheless. Now the bitterness of social standing rankled him once more and the anger and hatred he felt for their father started to well up inside him again. He had to admit to himself that the loathing had rescinded somewhat of late. What on earth was the point of hating a dead man? He started to have confused feelings towards the two people sitting on his bed, but suddenly the voices become more boisterous and Evie looked towards him, smiled and moved further up the bed to lean against the pillow next to him.

"You agree with me, don't you Frank? Tell this, this… obdurate and …. ob…. ob…. obscurant so and so that I am right."

Frank coloured, "I'm sorry I wasn't listening to what you were saying," and maybe because of his internal anger added, "And I don't know what 'obdurate' and "ob.." whatever it was you said, means."

Mark roared with laughter, "Neither does she! Go on Evie, tell him what they mean."

It was now Evie's turn to blush, eventually admitting, "Sorry Frank, I don't know what they mean either. Miss Malpass, my English teacher at school, once called my best friend Mary Hunt obdurate and obscurant during lessons. We looked them up in the dictionary but I can't remember what they mean. I just thought they sounded good and might impress Mark. I really can be a pig sometimes you know, but I didn't mean to embarrass you like that. I was only trying to get at Mark." She leaned towards Frank and kissed him on the cheek adding, "Please forgive me."

Frank was taken aback by her honesty and her obvious discomfort at being 'found out'. He leaned forward to return the kiss to her cheek, which she accepted quite gracefully, "I forgive you entirely and perhaps next time you can bring a dictionary with you."

They all laughed as the tension passed and the conversation from then on was three way, with Frank no longer the outsider.

Suddenly Evie turned to Frank and said, "Do you believe that there's a true love out there for each one of us, Frank? Mark thinks all relationships are pure chance and even if we met the 'true love of our life' we wouldn't know it. What do you think, Frank?"

"I've never thought about it, but it would be nice to think that there is a perfect partner for everybody and all we have to do is find them."

Mark said, "And have you found your 'true love' yet, Frank?"

Evie interrupted before Frank could answer, "Oh I do hope so. Frank is too nice a man to make do with second best."

Frank could feel his face turning red as she added, "He probably doesn't know he has though! Or do you know you've met her, Frank?"

"For God's sake, Evie, stop teasing the man. This may be the sort of stuff you girls talk about when you're together, but it isn't a man's subject."

"I'm not teasing him," Evie added indignantly, "I've always believed I would meet the 'love of my life' someday and I'd immediately know he was the one for me for ever."

She looked directly into Frank's eyes as she said this and he felt as if he was burning inside. Had she any idea at all what she was doing to him? He wanted to lean forward, take her in his arms and kiss her deeply; on the lips this time and not on the cheek.

The moment was broken by Mark thumping Evie on the arm and asking, "And have you met this love of your life yet Evie?"

Evie laughed, "Now that would be telling, wouldn't it? The real trouble though, is would I have the nerve to tell him and take the chance of him turning me down? It's just not the done thing for us women to take the lead in such matters." She again looked directly into Frank's eyes willing him to read the messages, "We have to wait for the man to say something to us, don't we Frank?"

Mark again broke the tension of the moment, "For goodness sake, Evie, let's change the subject, Frank doesn't want to talk about these things. Do you Frank?" He did not wait for Frank to answer before adding, "And anyway Frank has a girl back home waiting to marry him when he gets back from this nightmare of a war. That's right isn't it Frank?"

Frank did not know how to reply and merely nodded his head. He did not see the near tears in Evie's eyes as she suddenly got up and rushed away saying she must dash as she had work to do.

Mark also got up from the bed and said he also must go but would visit again if possible. Frank hoped he would as he wanted to discuss the question of going into business again. Doing so was one way in which he could stay friends with Mark and hopefully continue to see Evie.

Frank believed that the kiss that Evie had given him was only that of an acquaintance, and was of little significance to her. It probably meant less to her than the sisterly kiss he had seen her give to Mark each time they met and departed from each other. He could not believe there were sexual connotations to it. In fact he knew, or at least he thought he knew, that it meant absolutely nothing whatsoever to her. Nevertheless he could not get her out of his mind and began to fantasise over the return kiss he had given her. He closed his eyes and pictured her standing side by side with Grace.

Frank regarded Grace as a beautiful woman, and indeed she was, but she did not have the elegance of Evie. The two women were from different worlds and to Frank this difference was painfully obvious. He loved Grace and had every intention of marrying her when this awful war was over, but the more he compared the two women in his head, the more he realised that Grace always projected the image of what she was, a very attractive young woman, but a beautiful woman from a working class background.

Evie on the other hand, was from another world, and for now he could not help fantasising about what life would be like with Evie Harper instead of Grace. He knew (or thought he did) that she would never regard him as other than a friend of her brother's whom she may even quite like and that was as much as it would ever be.

A week later the swelling had gone down and Frank no longer had headaches. The doctor checked his vision, looked into his eyes, and asked him a load of questions to check that his memory and mental capacities had not been affected by the accident. Everything seemed OK and he declared Frank was fit enough to return to his unit provided they could guarantee he would only be given light duties and that he could avoid using his legs. It would take another few weeks for the broken leg to mend and in the meantime he was to use crutches and only carry out desk bound duties. He was to return to the Field Hospital in four weeks to have the splints taken off and the leg finally checked out.

Mark came to see Frank that last evening and seemed extremely pleased that Frank was able to return. "You see Frank, I haven't said anything until now because I wasn't sure whether you would ever be fit and able to rejoin the unit, but the day you went up with Buster instead of me, I had to go to HQ for an overview of the next big push being planned. I've been back today for the orders concerning our unit. They want us to liaise with the

19th, 23rd, 41st and 47th Divisions, and allot some of our men and equipment to each of the Divisions, so that when they drive forward, our wireless operators can signal back in coded Morse to HQ on the success of the advance."

After which Frank took the opportunity to bring up the subject of the wireless business again and was pleased that Mark still seemed keen and for the next hour they each became absorbed in talking about the matter.

Frank's only sadness was that Evie was not with them that evening and he felt quite jealous when Mark said she was spending the evening with some of the doctors and other nurses. He felt even worse the next morning when he realised she would not be on duty until later in the day, and that he would have to return to camp without seeing her. He left a note thanking her for looking after him, but felt unable to add anything of a more personal nature.

He reached camp at about midday and was told all the men in the unit were in the briefing tent. Frank shuffled across to the tent on his crutches and when he reached the entrance, he stood there for a while listening to Mark informing all of his men of the new instructions. A big cheer went up when Mark saw him and welcomed him back.

The next few weeks were hectic for the unit. Frank had never had so much paper work to deal with in his life. He longed for the day when his leg was mended and he could get rid of the crutches and get back to the hands on organising he was good at. The only respite he had from the paperwork was when experimental codes were received for the operators to practice the sending and receiving of messages in code. He enjoyed working with the lads on the exercises, but had to make sure they could interpret any of the code tables quickly and accurately, as the actual codes to be used would not be issued until the night before the advance. He just kept wishing that time would pass quickly so that he could go back to the hospital and get the splints off his leg and return to normal duty.

As soon as Frank had returned back at the camp, Buster came round to see him and invited him to join him later that day for a drink to celebrate their safe return and have a look over his new plane; a newly delivered Sopwith 1½-Strutter.

"I'll be able to show the Bosche what's what with this, old chap," boasted Buster as he pointed out all the features to Frank. Pointing to the forward facing Vicker's gun and then to the rear gunner's movable Lewis gun he added, "Be able to give them a bit of their own medicine with these. They won't know what's hit them."

"I'll have to fix it for you to come up with me again. You won't have to use your leg up there so there shouldn't be any problems. Give you a chance to have a go at the Germans yourself. Could be good fun for both of us. What do you say?"

"No thanks," was Frank's rapid reply, "I think I've had enough of flying, for a bit anyway."

Buster laughed, "Please yourself old sport, but don't forget the offer is there if you ever want to take me up on it."

Frank never did have the chance to take him up on it. Six days later Buster's plane failed to return from a reconnaissance flight and news reached them that he had been shot down over the battle ground, but only after his gunner had managed to take out two German planes. The gunner was Billy Mallen one of Frank's wireless operators, a great guy with a wonderful sense of humour, and a first rate Morse wireless operator. The loss of the plane was therefore a double blow to Frank. He had lost two more comrades in this unforgiving war.

Twenty-four hours after Frank had been given the all clear by Dr. McPherson, the unit moved with all of its equipment to the forward camps to the West and South West of Ypres. For Frank and Mark the war zone they returned to was equally as devastating and desolate as the one they had been invalided out of so many months earlier.

Ypres had been a thriving country town before the war but was now devoid of all local inhabitants and had long since become a ghost town. The piles of stone and rubble, unrecognisable as the remains of the ramparts and Gothic buildings and majestic high-gabled houses that once graced this noble medieval town with a proud history stretching back to the middle ages. The busy farms of the peacetime countryside round about, with their lush green pastures and fields flowing with wheat and hops, were now a wilderness of jarred earth reeking with the horror of three years of the devastating waste of human life. Every available square yard was heaving with putrefaction and splattered with all the garbage of the abandoned, broken and useless machinery of this lunatic war. Behind the lines, the grass meadow lands of peacetime had given way to mud fields covered with row upon row of bell-tents, broken only by the occasional field kitchen and ablution facilities for the dirty and hungry soldiers returning from their spells of duty at the front. In the whole of this war zone the only reminders that any vegetation had ever existed, were the remains of a few trees; stark sculptures of splintered wood, devoid of all greenery. The only suggestion that any of these wooden monuments had once had any life at all, being the occasional semblance of a branch jutting out from the desolate and impotent phalli.

But for the ravages of war, the otherwise flat reclaimed bog land of the Flanders plain was folded with the gentle slopes of the 'hills'; the name given by the military to the gradients delicately rising out of the shattered earth. Hills that were little more than bumps sweeping across the horizon and were surrounded on three sides by the small stretch of land which had been so stubbornly and catastrophically held by the British since 1914.

'Hill 35' - 35 metres high. 'Hill 40' - 40 metres high. 'Hill 60' - 60 metres high. Each a tiny salient not worth the loss of life of a single human being, but this few acres of land had already cost the lives of thousands of young men, with the list of dead and casualties still being added to each and every day. The Germans commanded the 'hills' and the undoubted advantage of control of all the land behind them, including supply railways, marshalling yards and an unhindered route right back to industrial Germany supplying all the equipment, ammunition, and supplies necessary for the continued madness of the conflict.

Over the previous three years these supplies had included thousands of tons of the necessary materials for the Germans to build concrete reinforcements around the hills facing the enemy. Lances of iron rods, over half an inch thick, had been embedded into this concrete, angled so as to impale any enemy forces stupid enough to try and get past them.

For their part the British forces had built an amphitheatre of concrete observation posts around the salient, with walls and roofs several feet thick. Sandbags and mud were placed around them for camouflage and more protection with the result that the German shells just bounced off them. And so, with both sides taking a strong defensive position, a total stalemate had been achieved and any skirmishes into enemy territory invariably resulted in loss of life to any forces stupid enough to attempt to advance.

Underneath all this devastation, reinforcements, camouflage and protection, the Royal Engineers' tunnelling companies, manned with ex-miners from the coal mines of Durham, Wales and the Midlands had, for the past twelve months been deep mining under the salient towards the 'hills' occupied by the Germans. Twenty-one tunnels, up to a hundred feet below the battleground were gradually being dug, inch by inch, and, by the time Captain Harper and his men arrived back at the front, the tunnels had already reached their destination, directly below the German front line fortresses. And each night, lines of soldiers were straining slowly forward to the tunnel entrances, through the firing zone of the Germans, each carrying a fifty pound bag of ammonal to be packed into the vast cavern which had been carved out at the end of each tunnel.

"Make sure you lads don't bunch up. Make sure you keep at least fifty yards between each of you," was invariably the last instruction given to the men as they started their journey to the pit shaft. Too many soldiers had already died for ignoring this instruction. Whenever a sniper's bullet had hit the bag of the man in front, it had not only blown him to smithereens, but the flying embers of the explosion had often exploded the ammonal being carried by the soldiers in front, or behind, or both, with equally disastrous results.

During the day, both sides continued their bombardment of each other, increasing daily the number of casualties of this pathetic war. The smug Germans glaring down from their superior position, totally unaware that they were now sitting on enormous time bombs lying silently in the graveyards reserved for them by the British waiting for the right moment to detonate the mighty volcanic eruptions directly below their enemy.

Moving slowly in the skies above were the British grey balloons and the German black ones, from which officers standing in the basket swinging gently in the breeze below were trying to strategically interpret the activities going on behind the enemy lines through their binoculars.

Frank was now able to observe at first hand the pilots of the Royal Flying Corps circling around the balloons and beyond in their planes. He was now quite an expert in recognising each type of plane; the Sopwith Pups, the larger Sopwith 1½-Strutters, and for the experienced pilots the highly manoeuvrable Sopwith Camels, all now armed with their Vickers machine guns, protecting them from the scourge of the German Fokkers.

He stood in horror as he watched the dog fights between enemy and allied planes wondering if the pilot and gunner were airmen he knew whenever a British plane was shot out of the sky plummeting in flames to the ground. He soon became sick of the sight and realised it was not the heroic frolics described by Buster, but just another catastrophic aspect of this awful and bloody war.

The powers that be decided that Mark and Frank should be the ones at HQ receiving messages and relaying them to the senior officers. However on June 5th, the Major co-ordinating all the signals arrangements, told Mark that he thought it would create better morale amongst Captain Harper's unit if they were part of the wireless operators supporting the attacking Divisions instead. Or at least that was how he explained the order to Mark, but that was not how Frank interpreted the change of instructions. He was certain the Major had decided on the switch to get back at Mark for arguing with him during the briefing session over the difficulties of setting up the wireless equipment and aerials on the ground in battle conditions, particularly if they were to be effective over greater distances.

The Major told Mark to stop making excuses, but by then it had became obvious to everyone, that the Major knew damn all about the requirements of wireless communications. But the damage had been done and it was only a couple of hours later that he issued the changed orders to Mark.

"What the hell is the point of messing up all our preparations like this?" Frank knew the answer for himself, but nevertheless felt obliged to ask the question. "Is there any advantage, other than getting you out of his way? You know I don't mind going with the attacking forces," Frank added with a wry smile, "Might even enjoy it! But why on earth do they have to tell us now and give us a mere four hours to have it all sorted and get our replacements here?"

"That's not all," said the Captain, "The orders are that we have to report to our new position by 0800 hours tomorrow morning."

"Good God, what does he think we are; miracle workers? What's the bloody rush anyway?"

The Captain just looked at Frank, smirked and shrugged his shoulders. He obviously was not in a position to answer the question.

"That's OK Captain, you don't have to answer, I'm pretty sure I've worked it out for myself."

It was obvious to Frank that the reason for the rush was not merely to get Mark out of the Major's hair. The hectic running about of the last two days by everyone for miles around had already made Frank think that a major attack was only days, or maybe hours away. The urgency of this new instruction just confirmed it.

Frank used his wireless equipment to contact Corporal Freddy Anslow to let him know that he and Charlie Bishop should return to HQ immediately, where the Captain and Frank would instruct them on their new duties. The Captain and Frank would then replace them by joining the Prince of Wales Yorkshire Regiment, as part of the Division preparing an attack on Hill 60.

Corporal Anslow and Charlie Bishop did not arrive until after 2100 hours that evening. They had managed, after much cursing and cussing, to get a lift part of the way back on an ammunitions supply truck returning on its way back to the dump to collect more heavy shells for the big guns. The truck had brought them within three miles of HQ and they had to walk the rest of the way. By the time the Captain and Mark had given them all the necessary information about the positions; call signs; frequencies and so on of all the men in each unit attached to the various divisions spread out on the eight mile front from Ploegsteert Wood to Ypres, and also told them of the officers at HQ who they should liaise with, it was two o'clock in the morning. If Mark and Frank were to replace them in the line in accordance with orders, they would have to leave for the front immediately.

Mark had managed to retain his motor cycle throughout all the comings and goings across France, and decided that this was the only form of transport that would get them to the front in time. Frank sat precariously in the sidecar holding on to all the signalling equipment that the Corporal and Charlie Bishop had just brought back with them.

"Why on earth didn't I just tell them to leave this somewhere handy for us to pick up instead of bringing it back to us?" Frank asked of the Captain as they drove off into the night.

The Captain did not answer. He was too concerned about finding his way to where they were supposed to be at the front.

After about fifteen minutes on a reasonable road surface, they turned off north towards Vierstraat. The amount of traffic was amazing. It seemed that trucks, ambulances, marching soldiers and horse drawn wagons were everywhere. The journey of less than ten miles took over three hours and they were both exhausted when they arrived at the 23rd Division rest camp a mile behind the front line. The sun had already risen and the activity seemed to be increasing by the minute.

"Frank I've had it," said Mark. "Let's stop here for a bit, we've got a couple of hours. Let's see if we can find somewhere to sleep for an hour or so and maybe get a bite to eat before we make our way to the front line."

Five hours later the Captain was shaking Frank quite violently, "Wake up Sergeant! For God's sake wake up, we've slept far too long. We should have been on our way hours ago. Just as well the push wasn't planned for this morning."

Frank had jumped up with a start, and was still shaking himself. "You didn't hear that last bit, Sergeant. No, better still, I never said it," implored the Captain.

"Don't know what you're talking about, Captain," Frank replied shaking his head. "Where the hell are we anyway and what time is it?"

"Time we reported to the Prince of Wales' Yorkshire Regiment, that's what time it is. We'll have to walk from here. God knows how long that will take. If the Major finds out that we haven't carried out his orders to the letter, he'll take great pleasure in putting me on a charge."

"Calm down. Calm down. He's not going to find out is he? And if he does so what?" Whilst he was speaking Frank was putting on his belt, jacket and boots, the only things he had taken off when he had flopped onto the bunk. "Look, we're already late now, might just as well have a quick wash, God knows when we'll get another proper one. And then maybe we should see if we can get a decent bite to eat before we start on our way. With a bit of luck, we can still be on our way in half an hour."

"OK. You're right yet again, Sergeant. But only half an hour and no more," Mark replied.

Thirty five minutes later they were on their way, this time on foot, with Frank carrying the A.T.M. Mark III short wave tuner and its two sets of Brown headphones, a battery for the wireless, a spare set of crystals, copper gauze earth mats and other miscellaneous bits and pieces. Mark was carrying another spare battery together with the thirty foot aerial mast in its eight cumbersome telescopic sections, the code book, note pads etc. and all the other sundry parts of unwieldy and bulky paraphernalia of the wireless operator's equipment. On their backs they each carried their knapsack containing front line food rations, emergency first aid kit, and other accoutrements issued to front line troops. Over their shoulder they each carried their rifle. Hand grenades, bullets and the other trappings of fire power hung in pouches from their belt.

It was an exhausted and weary pair who at three o'clock in the afternoon, were still trying to find the Prince of Wales' Own Yorkshire Regiment. They had been told they would find them at Battersea Farm. Eventually someone was able to point out the 'Farm'; a heap of ruins about two hundred yards from the point they had reached.

"Well I'm sure the farmer's wife will have a wonderful dinner waiting for us in the kitchen of that farm, Captain."

"I'm sure you're right, Sergeant," replied Mark, "But first I'll need to rest. I've nearly had it."

When they reached the 'Farm', it was nothing more than a few dug-outs around which was a pile of stones; the remains of what might well have been a farm, some three or four years earlier. Frank could not help thinking as he looked at the rubble and the waste land of war around it, that even if the war ended today, it would take years to create anything like a farm from this man made wilderness of ditches, concrete battlements, buried animal and human corpses, and all the discarded and wasted debris of war.

He was unaware of the further devastation planned for a few hours away, and no one was aware of the further destruction, loss of life and savageness to be played out on this landscape in the months to come. Perhaps if he had, he might have dropped everything he was still struggling to carry, and run and just keep running as far away from this madness as his weary legs would carry him.

In the cellars of the old farmhouse, the officers had tried to create some semblance of comfort for themselves. The Major in charge welcomed them both into the dungeon, where other men were resting, trying to ease the tension of the coming battle by writing letters, playing chess, reading a book or just smoking or snoozing, whilst others were listening to the music coming from the wind up gramophone in the corner. Every time the record finished a lieutenant would get up from his game of chess, wind up the gramophone and replay the one and only record they had.

"Help yourselves to a cup of tea and then you'd best get as much rest as you can," the Major said when they had divested themselves of their load. "I was given the final instructions just before you arrived. The balloon goes up at 0310 hours in the morning. We wait for the bang to clear and then we all go. So I should get as much rest as you can before then. Your Sergeant can stay here with you. He might as well for the few hours we've got left."

Frank was still not certain what 'the bang' was going to be, but for days snippets of whispered conversations he had overheard at Headquarters had been hinting at something pretty spectacular.

"Just check our equipment and call in to H.Q. first, Sir," Mark replied. "Better let them know we're here and receive any further instructions they have for us, Sir."

The Major responded with, "Just as you will, but I'd make it short if I were you, you look done in and you'll be no good to anyone at three in the morning if you don't get some rest before then. There should be some hot food coming up soon, so I'd try and get back in here by then if I were you. You can tuck in with us when it comes and then we'll all try to rest. Must go now and speak to the men. See you soon and good luck tomorrow. We'll all need it."

He started to climb what was left of the steps of the cellar, stopping on the second step, turned and spoke to all the men present, "Oh, and by the way gentlemen, we have to collect all the pay books and any Wills or last minute letters the men have completed and send them back with the lads who bring up the food. I'll give the men half an hour to write them, so I'd like you, Lieutenant Newman and you O'Dowd to come with me and organise it. And the rest of you can sort out your own amongst yourselves. You, Harper and your Sergeant, better put yours with ours, unless you've done it already, that is," and with that he continued up the steps followed by Newman and O'Dowd.

Mark turned to Frank after the Major had gone, "If he wants any letters for home in half an hour, we'd best just signal HQ as quick as we can and then get them sorted."

The food had just arrived when Mark who had been busy writing for some time, held out an envelope towards Frank, "Would you like to put this in with your letter home, Frank. I want you to have it and I don't want you to lose it whilst we are out there in action. You might need it when this lot is all over."

Frank looked puzzled, "Why what is it?"

"Well it's just a letter for you to give Evie to help you set up the business if you get out in one piece and I don't. I've left everything to her in my Will and that letter is just asking her to lend you any money you might need. I know you don't want any handouts so I'm asking her to lend you the money for as long as you like, without any interest charge."

Frank looked at the envelope, still being held by Mark, "There's no need for that we're both going home after this, so don't be so bloody morbid."

"Look Frank you know as well as I do what our chances are of being alive in even two days time let alone when this War is all over. So take it, I want you too. I'd have left some money to you in my Will if I thought you were not too bloody proud to take it. So this is the next best thing. I did think of putting it all in my letter to Evie, but I didn't want to say anything too morbid, and talking about what I wanted her to do if I'm killed."

He waved the envelope in Frank's direction, "Look, take it Sergeant, you don't want me to make it an order do you?"

Frank took the envelope and sealed it before waving it back at Mark. "I'll tear this up unopened and unread when we're having a drink celebrating the end of this War together back in Blighty, but for now I'll just humour you and take it." He then folded it and put it in the pocket of his tunic.

By two-thirty the next morning, all the officers had left the cellar to be with their men for the attack. As Mark and Frank climbed the steps of the cellar, the big guns, which had been pounding away for what seemed forever, fell silent. The effect was unrealistic and eerie as they crept the hundred yards to the front line trenches carrying all their gear with them.

The Major who was standing looking over the top of the parapet in this total silence, his binoculars lifted to his eyes, turned to the Captain, "You might like to come up here to get a better view, Captain. It should be quite a sight when the mines go up."

One of the men standing in the trench next to Frank whispered to him, "Mines! What the hell does he mean, Sergeant? Mines! What mines?"

Frank just replied, "I guess we'll find out in a few minutes, mate. Just keep your head down."

The Captain moved up the trench ladder next to the Major and peered over the top. The Major looked at his watch, "I make it almost 0310 hours. What time do you make it, Captain?"

Mark took out his watch and checked the time in the moonlight, "Ten seconds to go, Sir."

The Major started to count out the seconds, "Ten, nine, eight, …." It seemed as though every man around had stopped breathing as they listened to the Major count down the seconds.

When he reached 'zero', there was still silence. The men looked at each other and for the man standing next to Frank, the anticlimax after all the tension was too much for him. He looked at Frank and let out a great roar of laughter but as he laughed the ground began to move and his laughter suddenly turned into a cry of shock horror. The movement seemed to last forever, although it was only a few seconds before the most almighty thunderous roar came rumbling from Hill 60. The earth continued to shake beneath their feet and the men wondered if this was an earthquake. The roar increased to a violent ear-shattering boom, so deafening that it caused panic fifteen miles away in Lille, and was heard in London over one hundred miles away. Men covered their ears to relieve the pain. The boom was followed by another from a different direction, then another, and another, and another, as nineteen of the twenty-one man made volcanoes erupted, lighting the night sky and sending earth and debris into the air, to fall on anything, everything and everyone in its path.

For most of the Germans on the front who were not amongst the 20,000 instantly killed or maimed by the explosions, the shock left them completely sterile and unable to react in any way to the events.

The Major and most of his men stood glued to the spot, unable to truly believe the spectacle unfolding in front of them. The noise! The colours bouncing into the sky! Here was a 'Guy Fawkes Night' unlike any other.

It was not fireworks however that caused the vision in front of them, but a series of enormous mushrooms of earth being blown into the sky as over a million tons of ammonal exploded below ground. The landscape changed shape all around them as the lethal blasts sent everything above them, whether animate or inanimate, living or now dead, into the air and back to the ground with awesome force.

Suddenly a whistle blew about a hundred yards along the line. Then another. Then another.

Frank came round in hospital several days later, not knowing who he was, unsure of where he was, and totally unable to work out how he had got there.

He was lying on his stomach and seemed to be totally bathed in bandages. He tried to look around, but was unable to do so. He tried to speak but was powerless to do more than utter a grunt. He tried to move on to his side but the throbbing in his head and particularly the stinging in his back was excruciating. He passed out again from the pain and had no idea how long it was before he came round again.

He spent the next three weeks lying in this position, unable to turn on to his back. Each day a nurse would come to change his dressings, and each day whilst the bandages were off, the nurse would try to remove any pieces of the shrapnel lodged in his back which were exposed through the surface of his skin. Or at least the skin that was left on his back!

The day after Frank had come round, the nurse quietly hummed 'the Londonderry Air' as she gently bathed the raw and exposed skin. Frank felt some comfort in her careful and tenderly soothing touch and for the first time, he was able to relax sufficiently to take some notice of his surroundings.

The nurse was just over five feet tall and was rather dumpy, but Frank only noticed the beautiful smile she had on her pretty, smoothed skinned face. She had sparkling dark brown eyes and short black hair which gleaned as if freshly washed, under her newly starched white cap. The sun shone through the doorway directly behind her, creating a halo effect around her head. Frank thought that whilst he would not describe her as an altogether beautiful woman, he nevertheless felt that she had one of the prettiest faces he had ever seen. Her smile was so infectious that Frank was soon smiling back at her, causing her to smile an even broader smile, which seemed to spread into her eyes making them shine as if full of love and compassion.

She continued humming the Air as she put down the small bowl from which she had bathed his back, and picked up a pair of tweezers off the trolley.

Frank had not yet spoken a word but decided that this administering angel would be sympathetic to his inner turmoil, "Where am I, nurse? How have I got here? And who the hell am I? What's my name?"

"Oh dear," said the nurse in a broad Irish accent. "My poor pet, don't you remember anything? The bang on your head must have been worse than we thought."

Frank just looked at her, a bemused look on his face as he stumbled over his words in an effort to explain what was going on in his befuddled head. "No, I don't think so. I've got this rumbling noise in my head most of the time and whenever I close my eyes, it's just as if everything in front of me is lifting into the sky."

"Well," said the nurse, "Let's see. Where shall I start? First things first." She put the tweezers back on the trolley, went to the foot of his bed and removed the clipboard containing his medical notes.

She read from the clipboard, "William Northwood, that's your name. Is William the name you prefer to be called? Or do you prefer Bill or Will?"

Frank looked at her and gently shook his head, "Ouch! That hurts to move my head like that. William Northwood, you say. No I'm sorry that means nothing to me. Neither does Will or Bill."

"Oh dear," said the nurse, the smile no longer on her face, "At least I can tell you where you are. You are at the No 11 Casualty Clearing Station at Godwaersveldt."

"Sorry, but that all means nothing to me."

"Well, I suppose all you need to know is that you're in hospital."

"Frank smiled, "Yes I realise that, but what's happened to me and how did I get here?"

The beautiful smile returned to her face as she re-hung the clipboard on the bottom of his bed, "We don't know exactly. We can only guess what happened from the extent of your wounds."

She went and fetched a folding chair from beside the bed opposite Frank's, placed it at the side of the bed close to Frank's head, and sat down. She took his hand in hers and held it in her lap, "As far as we can tell you must have been quite close to a shrapnel bomb when it exploded."

She continued to hold Frank's hand in her left hand, but she took a handkerchief from her apron pocket, moistened it in the dish on the trolley, and began to stroke Frank's forehead and cheeks with it.

"You have been very badly wounded, but luckily for you," she stopped and thought for a moment, "No of course I don't mean you've been lucky, I just mean that it could have been much worse. You must have been sitting on the ground at the time with your head bent forward, and, fortunately for you," she stopped again mid sentence, "Sorry I don't mean you've been fortunate either, but you must have been wearing your helmet and there's no doubt that if you hadn't been, whatever hit the back of your head would undoubtedly have killed you. As it is, it put a big dent in your tin hat, and has obviously still done enough damage to cause you to lose your memory."

She squeezed his hand and held it firmly against her. Frank could feel the warmth of her stomach against the back of his hand and he wondered if she realised that her compassionate actions were beginning to have a more stirring effect on him than was intended.

The same thought must have crossed her mind at the same time, because she suddenly placed Frank's hand back on the bed by his side, stood up and picked the tweezers again from the trolley, and spoke quite abruptly, "Better finish off tending to your poor back."

The action of standing up had quickly recomposed her and the smile returned once more, "This may hurt a bit but I must try and get these bits of metal out of your back."

Frank held on to the sides of the bed with his hands as a defence mechanism against the expected pain as she leaned over him and started to extricate the first small piece of shrapnel from his back.

She continued to talk about his wounds as she worked, "You must have been sitting down when the shrapnel hit you. It's only hit you in the back."

She pulled on the metal and Frank gave out a yelp as it left his skin. The antagonising piece was dropped in to the metal dish on the trolley with a mild clank. The nurse reached over to deal with another piece of metal on the far side of his back and in doing so her leg touched against Frank's hand. She moved it away as soon as she realised that it was Frank's hand and not the bed she was leaning against, and once more an abruptness entered her otherwise gentle and lyrical voice, "We've had many a man in here who was standing up when one of these things hit him in the legs. Sometimes they damn well near chopped them off. You'd be surprised how many times we've had to finish the job and remove their legs after gangrene set in. Lying out there in the muck and mud too long before they brought them in here, I reckon. Pity, nice lads most of them are."

Frank let out a yelp as she pulled on the second piece of metal from his skin, which by now, had started to heal around the offending foreign body. The gentleness in her voice returned, "I'm sorry but I'm going to have to loosen this. I'll try not to hurt you too much."

She picked up a small scalpel and leaned over, her leg once more pressing against Frank's hand. Frank was uncertain whether she was unaware of it this time or not, but she did not remove it as she gently cut the skin around the metal. There was another clang as she dropped the removed item into the metal dish close to Frank's head, and continued inspecting his back for further pieces of metal, her leg innocently gently caressing Frank's hand as she did so.

She started to bathe Frank's back again, "This is a bit of a mess though. It's such a shame."

For the first time since she had started to attend to his back again, Frank spoke to her, "What's a shame? What's the matter with it?"

Her leg moved against Frank's hand again and this time Frank was convinced that the movement was not accidental. He was certain of this when he stretched his fingers and she responded by moving her leg from side to side against the back of his open hand.

She eventually answered his question, "Goodness, I'm sorry I should have said. I should have told you. Oh, dear me! You see, you weren't only hit by metal pieces in your back, but the heat of the exploding metal must have set your tunic on fire and your back was badly burned."

She continued bathing and checking his back and eventually declared, "I can't see any more metal at the moment so I'd better leave it for now and put a new dressing on."

She turned away to pick up the dressing, but when she turned back again her leg was neatly placed against Frank's hand once more, but Frank had turned his hand round and this time it was the palm of his hand against her leg. As she put the dressing on his back, Frank closed his eyes and at the same time gently moved his fingers; the muscles in her leg gently tightening and relaxing in unison to Frank's movement. Frank smiled to himself as he considered the advantage of his lying on his stomach. At least she would not witness what was happening between his own legs!

She finished the dressing and as she reached to pull the sheet over Frank's back she stroked Frank's hand with her leg a couple more times before removing it with a, "That's you done for the day. I'll have another look at your back tomorrow."

She gave Frank a broad smile as she tidied up the trolley and the effects of her actions began to subside in Frank.

"See you later William. Or should that be, see you later Bill. I think I prefer Bill, it's more friendly, so I think I'll call you Bill from now on. Is that OK?"

Frank could not quite make out her responses and by now was uncertain whether her previous intimacy had been mischievous; whether she had acted that way with him specifically or whether she acted that way with all the patients. He decided to avoid any reference to what had occurred and just answered her question, "Yes that's fine. Bill will do fine." Then he added, almost as an afterthought, "And what do I call you?

"I'm Nurse Kelly," and continued to walk away to attend to the other wounded.

When she came back his way Frank called to her, "Nurse Kelly, can you come back here please? I think my bandage has moved."

She returned to the bed, removed the sheet and looked at the dressing, this time making certain of a distance between the side of the bed and her legs. The gentleness of the administering angel was back in her voice, "No, the dressing is fine. Your back has bled slightly where I took out that last piece of shrapnel, but it's stopped bleeding now so it should be fine."

She covered him with the sheet again, "See you Bill"

"No don't go yet, Nurse. I don't know why but Bill doesn't sound right. What's your name anyway?"

She grinned and raised her eyebrows, "I've told you, it's Nurse Kelly."

"Yes I know, but what's your first name, Nurse Kelly?"

"The Sister doesn't allow Christian names, so you must never use it, but my name's Alice. Alice Kelly."

"Alice. That's a nice name. Alice, I like that name. Actually, my mother's name is Alice."

They looked at each other and smiled.

"Are you sure?"

"Yes," Frank replied. "Yes. Alice. That's my mother's name."

He began to look puzzled, "Well, yes, or at least, I think that's her name."

"I'm sure it is," the nurse said, "You said it straight out without thinking, Bill, so I'm sure it must be Alice."

"Alice. That's right. Alice is my mother's name." He was silent for a moment, and then added, "But why does Bill sound so odd?"

"Well maybe they call you something other than Bill at home. Maybe it's Will. Or perhaps they do call you William."

Frank shook his head, and once again smarted at the pain at the back of his head as he did so, "No, none of it sounds right. William, Will, Bill. None of them mean anything to me."

"Well I'd stop worrying about it if I were you. I'm sure that now you have remembered one thing, you will start to remember other things." She touched his cheek gently as she turned to go, "And don't forget, it's Nurse Kelly if anyone is around."

Frank winked at her, "Sure Alice," and gave her a big grin.

Alice Kelly tended Frank every day for the next week, and as she did so, she talked incessantly about herself, her childhood and strict Catholic upbringing in Southern Ireland. And then, when she was ten years old, about her move to Liverpool, along with her three younger brothers, when her mother had died in childbirth, her little baby sister only living for two days. Her father had put them on the ferry to live with their mother's sister.

As she related her own story, she constantly asked Frank questions about himself, but he was unable to answer any of them. He was certain that she was using this technique to try and help back his memory.

Each time she tended to his back, she made sure her leg did not touch his hand but then on one occasion it did, purely accidentally. However she did not immediately snatch it away as Frank had expected, but let it remain there just long enough to cause no embarrassment to either of them.

Then on about the eighth day, Alice started talking about her boyfriend, Archie. How they had met in Liverpool just before the war and how, against her wishes, he had joined up as soon as he could in 1914. He had been posted as 'Missing presumed dead' at the battle of the Somme in 1916, and she had heard nothing since.

It was whilst she was saying all this to Frank that, with tears in her eyes, she had once more pressed her leg tightly against his hand, almost inviting Frank to caress it.

"I wanted us to get married before he went to war, but his Mam and my Auntie Annie both said we were too young and should wait 'til it was all over. You know the first time I saw you lying face down in the bed, I thought you were him. He's got the same wavy hair as you. Same colour, same waves and everything. I thought they'd found my poor Archie and he weren't dead at all."

Her leg caressed Frank's hand as she said this and for the first time Frank realised that she wasn't flirting with him, but was caressing her dear Archie. Frank felt sad for her as he realised that for this very upright Catholic girl, letting Archie caress her leg through her skirt was probably as far as she had ever allowed his advances to progress. He released the pressure from his hand and, with an understanding and tenderness that was no longer sexual in any way, he gently touched her dress with his fingertips, so sensitively and lovingly that Alice understood his compassion immediately. She looked deeply into Frank's eyes, tears running down her beautiful face, "You've got the same blue eyes as my Archie, and the same smile."

She bit her lips and with her fingers wiped some of the tears, which were now streaming down her face, "I do love you so much Archie and I miss you every minute of every day. Please, please come home safely to me."

She pulled her handkerchief from her apron and roughly wiped her tears, "I'm sorry I didn't mean to be silly like that."

Frank gently touched her leg before slowly taking it away, "You aren't silly at all. I just wish I were your Archie. It would be nice to know who I am and be loved by a pretty girl like you."

She smiled at Frank and tilted her head to one side as she admitted, "You know don't you that the first time I bathed you and took the bits of shrapnel from your back, I felt as though I was healing my Archie."

"I do now. I'm sorry if I did anything to hurt you. I didn't mean to hurt or embarrass you."

She gave one of wonderful smiles, "No I didn't really think about you at all. I'm the one who should say sorry."

She was silent for a moment as if pondering over what to say next. She finally said, "Can we be friends?" She then gave a delightfully lyrical laugh as she added, "I would like you as a friend."

This was the first time that Frank had heard her laugh and he knew instantly that any awkwardness between them over the touching was now history and that her question was not lightly asked, but was a request to fill a void in her life, without any sexual connotations whatsoever. She would never again regard Frank as her missing Archie, but wanted to feel close to someone who would always remind her of him and her love for him. Someone who she could openly talk to about her Archie and who would always understand the way she felt about him.

"Yes I would like us to be friends," Frank replied. And as if to reinforce his understanding of the situation he then added, "Yes I would like us to be special friends and if I get out of this lot safely, I promise you can always count on me."

Having said all that he decided that it was time to change the subject and without thinking about what he was saying, declared, "You know you said that your Auntie Annie didn't want you to get married, well I've got an Aunt Annie."

They both laughed out loud putting the seal on their new, understanding relationship.

"It's working isn't it? All your talking about yourself is helping my memory to come back."

She squeezed Frank's hand and gave him the biggest smile yet, "See you tomorrow, pal, we'll talk some more then. I think I've said enough for one day, don't you?" And with that she was off.

That night when Frank closed his eyes, the noise and vision of everything lifting into the sky, became more detailed in his head. The images became more specific and gradually the spectacle of the exploding mines under the 'Hills' took on a real vision for him. He saw the erupting volcanoes, the light display in the sky, and then he felt a revulsion and nausea as he realised that in the millions of tons of rising earth were thousands of men being slaughtered without any hope of escape. Although he still did not know what it all meant, the visions gradually became clearer and clearer giving him an uneasy, restless and painful night as he tried to make some sense of it all. The visions may have became clearer but he still could not believe what he was seeing in his head were real images. How could they possibly be? Surely this vision of Armageddon was some dreadful hallucination?

"I just can't get the picture of it all out of my head," he said to Alice as she tried to extract another bit of shrapnel from his back. "Why on earth should I keep having these appalling dreams?"

She listened quietly as he described his tormenting apparitions in detail. She had redressed his back and was sitting beside him by the time Frank had finished the account of all the pictures in his head.

Alice held his hand and told him about the mines dug by the clay kicking miners under the Messines Ridge. How the mines had been packed with explosives; how the mines underneath the German lines had been blown up on June 7th and how he had been with the first line of soldiers to attack on that day.

"What you've been seeing in your head isn't your imagination playing tricks, Bill. It really happened and you are remembering the sight you actually saw."

Frank drew in a deep breath as he tried to come to terms with the horror and reality of it all, "But what happened after that? If I knew that perhaps I would remember more."

"I'm sorry, but I really don't know. All I do know is that you must have made it to what was left of the German front line, because that's where they found you injured, and brought you here later . The only other thing I know about you is that when they brought you in here, someone had covered you with your greatcoat and we found your dog tags in the pockets."

She got up from the chair, saying, "Hang on a minute, I won't be long. I'll just get something to show you."

When she came back a couple of minutes later, she was holding a wallet in her hand. She sat down and held the well-worn, dirty, black leather wallet in her open palm for Frank to see. "This is your wallet, it was in your greatcoat. I don't know whether there's anything in it to help your memory. I don't think there is though. I'm sure they'd have said so if there was."

She looked at Frank with sadness in her eyes, "Do you want me to show you what's in it? Maybe there'll be something to trigger your memory?"

Frank lifted his eyebrows as a means of saying, "I suppose so," without actually saying anything.

She opened the grubby wallet and took out its contents one by one, naming them as she did so.

"One ten shilling note." She placed the note on her lap, took out more notes and counted them, "Three French francs notes." She placed these on top of the ten-shilling note, "One, two, three playing cards." She turned them over and as she placed them into her lap with the other items, showed each to Frank in turn, "Ten of Clubs, Queen of Hearts, Jack of Spades. Good at 'Find the Lady' are you Bill?"

Frank shrugged his shoulders and shook his head, which he could now do gently without any pain, "They mean nothing to me. It's almost as if the thing doesn't belong to me"

Next she took two postcards from the wallet. They were placed face to face and neither had anything written on the back. She parted the cards and looked at the fronts. She immediately pushed them back together and colour rose in her cheeks.

Frank laughed and spoke in a questioning tone, "You're blushing? What is it? What have you found now?"

She shook her head, "I think you must be right. I don't think this can be yours," and with that started to put the postcards back in the wallet.

"Oh come on now. You can't do that. Let me have a look at them."

She took the cards back out of the wallet and with a rapid movement held one in each hand facing Frank, inches from his face.

"Oops," was all that Frank could say as he looked at the picture of a naked woman on each of them. And, as soon as he said it, Alice snatched them back and placed them face down on her lap with the other items.

"I'm not going to find anything else like that, am I?"

Frank looked deep into her eyes and struggled to find the right words. There was an element of pleading in his voice when he eventually said, "Alice, you don't know how much I wished I could remember everything right at this moment. I know I keep saying the same thing but none of it means anything to me. I don't think I've ever seen those before. And like you say, it doesn't feel like me. None of it does. Oh God, please help me remember."

Alice took his hand in both of hers and gently stroked it with the one on top, "I pray that you'll get your memory back as well. Every night I do."

Frank wrapped his fingers round her bottom hand and squeezed it. "You're a good girl, Alice and I'm glad you're on my side. It's nice to have one good friend around."

There were almost tears in both of their eyes as she moved her hands away and returned to inspecting the wallet

"Here what about this?" She took out a bent up card from the wallet and unfolded it. "It's a Christmas card, shall I read it? She then thought about the previous items and quickly added, "Or is it private?"

"No, I want you to read it. I've told you none of it means anything yet."

She looked at the writing inside the card. It had the printed inscription 'Merry Christmas' and underneath in very large and quite wobbly childish writing were the words, 'All My love Hilda', followed by two very large X's. Alice looked at the words and they reminded her of the first attempts at writing by her youngest brother Timmy when he was six or seven years old. She felt certain that the writing had been copied, probably by someone unable to read or write. She was about to say something to Frank when she suddenly realised that it could have been written by someone with an illness or affliction who was trying to hold their hand still. She started to wonder who Hilda was. Was she a girlfriend? Or maybe it was a little sister and her first attempts at writing.

Frank interrupted her thoughts, "Well what does it say? Is it in a foreign language? Is it rude or what?"

Alice smiled one of her wonderful smiles, shook her head, and said, "No, it just says, Happy Christmas, all my love Hilda. Here do you want to have a look at it?" She held out the card to Frank so that he could read it.

He once more puckered his lips and carefully shook his head from side to side, "Nope, it's a total blank to me. Who's Hilda anyway?"

"Maybe it's your little sister?"

Frank laughed out loud and gave her a wink, "Or maybe the girlfriend? No, maybe it's my wife?"

Alice hadn't thought of that. She swallowed hard and shook her head, "No, I don't think so. You don't look the married kind to me."

"And what would one of them look like then?"

"One of what?"

"A married man, of course."

"Dunno really, but I've never thought of you as being married. Anyway I don't think a married man would have items like these in his wallet." She lifted the offending postcards off her lap and slapped them back down again.

"Please don't be like that, Alice. Is there anything else in there?"

"No, nothing else." She started to put everything back into the wallet, "I don't see much point in doing this anymore Bill, and to be frank with you, I've had enough….."

Frank interrupted her before she had time to finish the sentence and shouted out in excitement, "That's it, that's my name. Frank. That's my name. Frank. It's not Bill at all. It's Frank."

They stared at each other and Frank nodded his head up and down and added in a much more relaxed tone this time, "Yes Alice, I'm sure of it. My name isn't Bill, or Will, or William for that matter, it's Frank. Frank…….." He looked puzzled and stumbled over what come after 'Frank'.

"Frank what though? Oh, damn this memory of mine!"

Alice gave one of her smiles and immediately felt relieved that maybe the wallet was someone else's. She started to push everything back into it, not concerned about how roughly she did so. She then realised that she was only thinking of herself and how the thought that the wallet belonged to someone else had given her immediate contentment and satisfaction.

"I'm sorry Bill." She stopped herself mid sentence and corrected herself. "I'm sorry Frank," she said placing considerable emphasis on the 'Frank' as she waved the wallet in the air, "I'm so pleased your memory's coming back and that we can put this away and hope it finds its true owner soon."

The relaxed friendship between them returned and Alice never doubted that Frank was the very special friend she had come to value ever again.

CHAPTER SIX

AUTUMN - WINTER 1917

Everyone continued to call him Northwood, except Alice that is, who always made a point of using the name Frank as many times as she could in conversation. Every time she spoke to him, each sentence either started with a 'Frank', or ended with a 'Frank'; sometimes both. And sometimes there was a 'Frank', or even two or three, in the middle of the sentence as well.

After about two days Frank asked her to stop saying 'Frank' so often. She agreed, but it nevertheless continued to be a word used in almost every sentence. Frank let it go at that. He knew she was well intentioned and was only trying to get him to suddenly come out with his surname, as he had done with his Christian name when she had used the word 'frank'.

One day she suggested that she should say all the surnames she could think of to him, to see if he responded to any, but after ten minutes of listing all the ones she could think of, Frank stopped her, "Look, I'm pretty sure none of those are my name."

He smiled a sympathetic smile and said, "Please don't be offended, I know you're only trying to help, but most of those names sound Irish and I don't think I'm Irish."

She just laughed out loud at him, "What you Irish? With an accent like the one you've got. I hate to disappoint you but I'm damn sure you've never been anywhere near Ireland."

Frank was relieved she had taken his comment in good spirit and they both laughed together as she asked, "Or an Irish woman either, or have you?"

"Not one like you, anyway," was the best reply he could think of.

"Actually I'm surprised you were in the Prince of Wales' Yorkshire Regiment. You don't sound much like a Yorkshire man to me either."

"Why, where do you think I come from?"

"Well I'm no expert, but we've had a few lads in here from Dudley and West Bromwich and you sound more like them. So perhaps you were born in the Black Country and moved up to Yorkshire for some reason."

Frank thought hard about what Alice had said on the subject of his accent, but it meant nothing to him and the more he pondered on it, the more agitated he became. He eventually fell asleep but was soon awakened by his usual nightmare of the explosions in front of him.

When the doctor did his rounds, he told Frank he had healed enough to be shipped back to England to complete his hospitalisation and treatment in the Home Counties.

"I must tell you though, that you still have some healing to do, but I'm afraid we need your bed here for more urgent cases. I'm sure you'll be glad to be back in Blighty and away from this lot for good. I don't think they'll be sending you back here. Your back should heal even though it will be badly scarred where you were burned the worst. I also think that you still have some of the shrapnel lodged in your back. I know the nurses have tried to get out as much as they can, but I bet there are still some bits in there. Probably give you some pain from time to time, but it should be OK if they don't move. Sometimes the bits work their way to the surface; it's easy to get them out then. Trouble is, if they move inwards and damage you inside; your lungs or something, then it could be dangerous. Anyway all the best old chap. Look after yourself and give my regards to the White Cliffs of Dover when you see them." He gave Frank a half hearted salute as he added, "I wish I could come with you, you lucky blighter."

With that he turned and walked to the next bed.

Alice came to Frank about an hour later. "I'll miss you, Frank. I'm glad you're going back to England but I shall miss you. I've got quite fond of you over the last couple of weeks." She laughed and added, "In a sisterly sort of way I mean."

"Well, you're pretty special to me." He thought for a moment before he continued, "Please don't take this the wrong way, but I'd be proud to have you as a sister. Whatever happens I'll never forget what you've done for me. You've helped to keep me sane and I don't want to lose your friendship, so can we keep in touch?"

"There'll be trouble if you don't and anyway I'd like to know who you are when you remember." With that she got a piece of paper and wrote both her full military address in France and her aunt's address in Liverpool on it.

As she passed the paper to Frank she made him promise on oath that he'd write to her regularly and let her know everything he remembered.

"I'm sorry but I'll have to write to you under the name of Northwood until you let me know differently," she apologised and as he took the piece of paper pleaded with him, "You will write to me, won't you?"

Frank held out his hand to her and she gave him hers, "You're the best friend I've got. Of course I'll write to you."

Alice looked quizzically at him, "I'm the only friend you've got at the moment." She laughed as she added, "Or at least the only one you can remember."

They both laughed but nevertheless wondered if they would ever see each other again. Frank knew he must have gone through this sort of parting before but he could not remember it.

The visions of the explosions were still a regular nightmare to Frank and sometimes he dreaded closing his eyes for fear of the emotions the pictures in his head evoked in him. However, by the middle of October, his back had healed sufficiently well for him to be moved into the garden and enjoy the views over the beautiful Suffolk countryside and the warm autumn afternoon sunshine.

Slowly, the peace, the quiet and the solitude, subdued the anxiety he felt over his identity and his past, with the effect that his nightmares became less and less disturbing.

He remembered the noise more clearly now. He remembered the colours bouncing into the sky more vividly and he even remembered thinking of it as a Guy Fawkes' night unlike any other. He remembered the landscape changing shape all around him, but most clearly of all, he remembered his revulsion as the lethal blasts sent everything above them. Whether they were manmade, living or now dead, it mattered little, as everything was forced into the air with awesome power and intensity.

These thoughts were no longer nightmares but clear memories of real events, and gradually the visions of the explosions moved on from the event itself and he saw the eruption fall back to earth and the dust begin to settle.

And then one night he awoke from his nightmare with a start and soaking with sweat. He closed his eyes again hoping for sleep, but this time the vision of explosions and pyrotechnics moved on, and he shook again in startled surprise as he remembered a whistle blow about a hundred yards along the line. Then another whistle further away; then another, this time closer by.

He slept very fitfully that night as he tried to remember what happened next but could not. However, little by little over the following weeks, he remembered more and more of the events following the explosions. He remembered standing in the advance trench with other soldiers, all glued to the spot, unable to truly believe the spectacle unfolding in front of them.

As he recalled these events he tried hard to focus on the faces of the men around him, but they were always a blur, and totally unrecognisable to him.

But he did remember how, after the whistles signalling the advance blew, the war cries of 100,000 men followed as they scrambled out of the trenches and ran towards the German front line, or at least what was left of the German front line after the explosions.

Some men ran straight forward as fast as they could, whilst others zigzagged from side to side as they ran to avoid the expected enemy fire. But no such fire or counter attack came. Most, if not all of the front line Germans were either dead, wounded or totally dazed and befuddled.

Frank then remembered that after the majority of the troops around him had left, an officer next to him indicated it was their turn to follow, but no matter how hard he tried he could not put a face to the officer. However he did remember the two of them running and progressing as fast as they could, even though the heavy equipment they carried made their progress slow and laboured. He remembered also that the slowness of their advance was not only caused by the weight of all their equipment but by the high explosive and gas shells which had started to explode around them. The Germans in the rear positions, unaffected by the explosions, had recovered from their initial astonishment and surprise at the devastation to their front lines and had quickly begun to retaliate with long-range gunfire.

Next came the obstacle of an enormous crater created by one of the explosions. Both he and the officer slid down the side of it and by the time they had managed to scramble up the other side, the first troops had reached their objective and had started to take prisoners and dig in on the top of the newly captured ridge.

He could not believe the advance was going so well, but suddenly Germans in the second defence line, who had been ready to retreat from their positions, were mustered by an officer, and began using their machine guns to fire on the advancing troops.

Frank's abomination of war returned and he felt physically sick as he heard the men scream and once again watched dying men fall ahead of him, mowed down by the gunfire. More fodder to the slaughter.

The officer fell to the ground and shouted to Frank to do likewise, "Keep your head down, Sergeant, we'll crawl from here. Those bloody bullets are getting far too close for comfort. You'd better put your mask on as well; some of those shells might have gas in them."

Progress after that was painfully slow and although neither would ever have admitted it, the initial rush of adrenaline had now vanished and they had both became more and more scared of the situation as they inched forward.

But now, with the advance halted at the target line, the Germans were able to really reorganise themselves at the rear of their lines and their bombardment of the new allied front line grew in intensity by the hour.

He remembered digging in for the night, having something to eat, and he remembered someone calling from what remained of a German concrete bunker to his right. He remembered moving some sort of equipment to the bunker, but somehow his mind would not allow progress beyond that.

He wrote a letter to Alice twice a week telling her in detail about the small but detailed extensions of his memory, including the memory of the officer calling him 'Sergeant'. *'Surely if he called me sergeant,'* he wrote, *'then I can't be Private William Northwood, can I?'*

Alice normally sent him two letters each week but he received them rather spasmodically because of the efforts of the censor and other exigencies of war, and he hadn't yet had her response to this letter.

On the second Sunday in November Frank received two unexpected visitors.

He wore a cap and had wrapped a blanket round him as protection from the wind as he sat outside enjoying the wonderful view over the valley in front of him. This was the first dry day for a week and he was pleased to enjoy some fresh air.

He could just make out two rowing boats through the trees lining the bank of the river winding its way along the valley half a mile away. Racing coxless pairs he thought, but they were moving quite quickly and he only caught the occasional glance of them as they passed the breaks in the trees.

The midday sun cleared the clouds and there was a gentle breeze blowing. He was amazed at the myriad of autumn colours in the trees as the wind propelled their dead leaves all around him. He wanted to imprint on his otherwise troubled mind the peace and beauty he felt at that moment, so he closed his eyes, tilted his head back and relaxed into a dream world, enjoying the short spell of unexpected heat before the sun was once again covered by the clouds drifting rapidly across the sky.

The Ward Sister's voice boomed out from about thirty yards behind him, "Private Northwood, your wife and mother have come all the way from Barnsley to see you. Poor souls have been travelling all night to get here."

Frank was suddenly rigid with horror. Would he recognise them? What would his wife look like? He hoped she was pretty. He did not know if he could bear an ugly wife whom he did not recognise.

The thought going through his head as he stood up and turned round to face them was, *'God, please make her pretty. Please make her pretty.'*

The two women were rushing towards him as he turned, but both stopped abruptly when they saw his face. The elder of the two screamed out. Frank did not recognise this little thin woman dressed all in black, who looked about sixty, but was probably only in her forties. She wore circular wire rimmed glasses on her large sharp nose below which was a line of facial hair which gave the appearance of a moustache.

As she came closer to Frank, she realised that he was not her son and let out a piercing shriek as if in great pain, "This isn't my Willie! Where's my Willie?" and without waiting for any reply immediately ran towards two other recuperating soldiers who were sitting on a bench to Frank's right, sobbing into her hands as she ran.

The other, much younger woman, just stopped frozen to the spot, staring wide eyed at Frank and opened her mouth in a totally horrendous scream. Tears ran down her face and she took deep breaths as she tried to overcome her shock. Eventually she let out one long continuous howl, which Frank thought would go on forever. He walked towards her to try to give her some comfort; his only thought as he walked towards her with a look of complete anguish and bewilderment on her face, was how pretty she was.

She was obviously dressed in her Sunday best, and Frank thought that maybe she had purchased the clothes especially for this visit. She was a young lass of no more than eighteen or nineteen with long flowing blonde hair which glistened in the sunlight. Perched on her head she wore a pert wide brimmed straw hat with a coloured band around the brim. She was about five feet eight inches tall and Frank was drawn towards the wide open deep brown eyes glistening from the tears, which were now streaming down her otherwise radiantly beautiful face.

When Frank had almost reached her, she stopped screaming and put her hand to her mouth for a moment before pointing directly at Frank screeching, "Keep away, keep away, you're not my husband. Where's my husband? What have you done with him? Where's my Will?"

Frank stared back at the girl. Some things about her seemed so familiar. Why should she look familiar? He tried so hard to work out what it was that had triggered this thought. He closed his eyes and had a flash of memory of another girl; another pretty girl about the same height; same hair; same eyes and similar hat? The image vanished as quickly as it had appeared and his head started to hurt as he willed back the memory, but it would not come back. He opened his eyes and looked at the girl again. He was sure he did not know this girl in front of him, but why did she look so familiar then?

She waved her hands in front of her, "Go away. Go away, you're not my Will. Go away."

The hands she held out were those of a working girl; broken nails; rough skin and grime in the pores which no amount of scrubbing would have removed. He suddenly had another flash in his head of the beautiful manicured hands of a lady. He looked again at the girl's hands shaking in front of him and he knew for certain that this was not the girl he knew. Although he again could not bring the full image in his head he was nevertheless convinced that the woman he knew was a much more delicate and refined lady and she certainly did not have the washer woman hands of the girl in front of him.

For her part, the girl just continued saying, over and over again, "You're not my husband. You're not my husband. Where's my husband?"

After a short while, Frank let go of his own thoughts and the girl's words began to sink in. "I'm not her husband," he shouted to all around. "I'm not her husband." As he repeated the words he felt this enormous swelling of relief inside him as he realised that this girl was confirming that he was not William Northwood. His immediate reaction then was to tell her to stop bleating on about her husband. Couldn't she be as happy as he was that he was not the said person?

The Sister put her arm around the sobbing girl and tried to comfort her as best she could. The other woman was now on her way back to join them after her inspection of all the men sitting outside enjoying the sunshine. She was coming up the slight slope towards them, stopping every few yards to get her breath. Her breathlessness made much worse by her constant sobbing. Frank went towards her to help her up the slope.

As he reached her and tried to take her arm she swung her handbag at him, "Get off me, young man. What have you brought me all this way for, when you're not my William?"

"I'm sorry, ma'am, but I've never said that I was your William. I didn't know you were coming and I certainly never asked for you to come."

Her suffering now turned to anger, "If you didn't say you were my son, who the hell did say you were, then?"

Frank was relieved when she turned her anger towards the Sister, "If he didn't say he was my son, who did? And who said we should come here?"

She grabbed hold of both the Sister and her young charge, "Come on just show me where William is." She dragged the two women towards the open French windows of the hospital ward, "Come on Hilda, let's go and find Willie."

The young girl, who Frank realised must be the Hilda on the Christmas card, now spoke for the first time, "We'd better go home mother. We're not going to find Willie here. He isn't here. They thought that man back there was Willie." She took her mother-in-law's arm and started sobbing again, "Oh, I do hope this doesn't mean that Willie is dead."

After walking a few yards, she turned her head towards Frank, "Best of luck, I hope you find your wife and family soon."

Frank watched them walk all the way back to the hospital building before he suddenly remembered the wallet. He was just about to call after them, when he recalled the pictures of the nudes and decided it would best if he removed them before giving the wallet back to the Ward Sister to send back to the poor wife. He sat down again but was unable to recapture the peace and quiet he had been enjoying half an hour earlier. He kept thinking of the tragic young girl whose heart must have just been torn out as she realised that her husband was probably dead. God knows how both of William Northwood's dog tags had ended up in Frank's pocket. And then an even worse thought hit him, if William Northwood's dog tags were not on his body, the authorities would never be able to tell whose body it was if it was found and the girl may never know whether her husband was dead or not.

Frank spent a very perturbed few days thinking about the girl and struggled harder and harder to work out who he was, who William Northwood was, and how the mix up had come about.

He was so troubled and agitated about the mix up that he began to question his own sanity and couldn't find the energy and will to write to Alice about the visit. He had not heard from her either for the past two weeks and had started worrying whether she was all right and was even contemplating that perhaps something dreadful had happened to her. He stopped worrying however as soon as the nurse came and gave him five letters that had arrived that same morning.

Alice always addressed her letters to Frank? C/o Private William Northwood, and this had sometimes caused problems to the censors trying to decide why they were so addressed, and they had invariably opened every one of the letters. The salutation inside was always 'My dearest Frank,' and there was always a 'with all my love' annotation at the bottom.

The letters themselves however never included any of the usual 'lovey-dovey' sentiments contained in most soldiers' letters to loved ones and this must have been frustrating to those censors who enjoyed the power they had to read the most personal of letters. The result of their disappointment with the contents of Alice's letters must have made them check them more closely, because the censor's pencil was invariably evident whenever any mention was made of names, places or enquiries that Alice had been making to find out Frank's real identity.

Nevertheless, Frank was able to guess the gist of the deletions and on occasions treated this as a game or crossword.

He opened all the letters he had just received and placed them in date order. He was almost surprised how reading them and reinserting the censor's deletions quickly lifted him from the depression of the past days. His spirits were boosted even more at Alice's obvious excitement when she was commenting on Frank's memory gains, particularly the one about the possibility of his being a sergeant.

Here the censor had deleted several lines, but even though Frank could not decipher the exact words, he knew Alice well enough by now, to be certain that the obliterated portion would contain the names of all the men and officers, together with their battalions etc., whom she had spoken to, to see if they had a Sergeant Frank ??, who was missing. He quickly checked the next letter, but since the envelope was still addressed to 'C/o Private William Northwood', and the letter itself contained no further reference to the Sergeant enquiry he realised that she must have met with a total blank.

As he reread the letters for the third time, and came to the one about his recollection of the officer referring to him as Sergeant, he tried unsuccessfully to relive more of the memory, but this time his inability to do so did not seem to disturb him so much. He had felt so relaxed since his women visitors had proved that he was not William Northwood, but now that he knew for certain who he was not, he needed to know who he was more than ever. He decided to write a letter to Alice straight away, hoping that the writing of it would help bring back more memories.

He was quite excited as he wrote about the visit of the two Mrs Northwoods. *'I am definitely not William Northwood'* he wrote and then added, *'Mind you the younger Mrs Northwood was quite a good looking lass, perhaps I should have pretended to be her husband!!!'* He hoped that Alice would find that comment amusing but to make sure, he added, *'Not really, only joking!'*

As he wrote he became even more relaxed and started to rethink about the flashes of memory he had had to date. He began to write again. *'You know Alice I am always relaxed when the bits of memory come back. It's as if, the harder I try to remember, the more difficult it is. So I must learn to relax as much as I can and not try so hard to remember things'.* He spoke out aloud as he wrote this, "Yes I must learn to relax more."

Reggie Davies who was sitting opposite him in the day room, took his pipe from his mouth, blew out a great billowing of smoke and said, "What did you say, mate? Didn't catch what you said, I was miles away."

"It doesn't matter, Reggie. I was talking to myself. You know me, off my rocker I am. Haven't got a clue who I am, nor where I come from."

"I wish I could lose my wife and mother as easily as you, mate. Especially my mother, silly old cow. Driving me mad she is. Every time she comes, its nag, nag, nag, all the time. She was getting on to me again last Sunday, asking what I'm going to do without any legs. What job will they give me back at the factory? How will I be able to support the wife and kids? Anybody would think I'd chopped me bloody legs off myself. No mate, you're better off, off your rocker. At least you ain't got my bloody mother on to you all the while. What, I'd be in heaven if I'd got no-one to nag me every time I said I was going to the pub for a drink. My bleeding wife's started on to me now as well. Thinks she can get away with it whenever me mother's by her side. Wait till I get her home. I'll knock her bleeding head off if she starts it then."

He replaced his pipe in his mouth and took several puffs until his cheeks were full of smoke. He rolled the smoke around in his mouth and slowly blew it out in one continuous stream. "I'd stop worrying about who I was, if I was you, mate. I'd be taking a different tart home with me every night, I would. I might have lost my legs but I ain't lost the important bits. Give me the right woman and I'll still do the business." He let out a great guffaw and shook his head at Frank when he realised that Frank, who did not find this crude talk in the least amusing, was not laughing. "You just don't know what a lucky bugger you are. You wouldn't want some old bat as a missus would you?"

He laughed even louder and waved his pipe at Frank as he added, "Mind you, your wife might turn out to be some gorgeous big busted blonde who's got the hots for you. I'd be dead jealous of you then, mate."

"Big busted blondes aren't my cup of tea," Frank replied.

"Oh my God, you aren't a fucking nancy boy are you?"

"Hell no," Frank quickly responded, "It's just that I prefer a different sort of woman. I'm not a 'bust' man, more a 'leg' man."

"Well I suppose it takes all sorts, but I'd be careful if I were you mate. Sounds to me as if your memory's coming back."

They both laughed out loud and each returned to their individual thoughts.

Frank smiled inwardly to himself with the certainty that whatever he could remember, or more to the point could not remember, he was sure that any attraction he had to women had never been directed towards the big busted, crude women that Reggie seemed to be attracted to. In fact Frank felt revulsion for Reggie's attitude to women generally. The more he thought about it, the more he realised how uneasy he felt about allowing himself to be dragged into such a 'macho' style discussion on women generally, even to the limited extent he had done so.

Frank sat back in his chair, closed his eyes and started to drift into his own thoughts, but began to get irritated by Reggie's constant wafts of smoke being blown into his face.

He got up, gave Reggie a, "Just going for a lie down," and returned to his bed. He was disappointed in himself for feeling that he needed to give Reggie a reason for leaving. Why had he felt it necessary to do that?

He lay on his bed and was soon fast asleep. The nurse awoke him with, "Nice cup of tea here for you." Frank felt it was a shame that she never called him by name even though he had asked her to call him Frank on a couple of occasions. The one time she had called him Frank the Sister had been nearby and he was certain she had said something to the nurse about not calling patients by their Christian name. He could just imagine her saying, "After all this is a military hospital, and we must keep military protocol here."

The nurse had avoided calling him anything after that except Private, and then when he told her about the Sergeant memory, she had stopped calling him anything at all. He got used to this but somehow he found the Sister still calling him Private Northwood, even after the visit of the two Mrs Northwoods, as most distasteful.

And then two days after Boxing Day Frank got a letter from Alice saying that she was accompanying a train load of badly injured soldiers back to England in time for Christmas, and was hoping to arrange a few days leave whilst back in the old country. If she could, she promised to try and come to see him.

Frank was elated as he read the letter, particularly as the Doctor had told him on the day before Christmas Eve that his burns and other injuries had now healed as well as they would and as they could do no more for him medically, he would have to give up his bed in the New Year for more deserving patients.

"You'll be all right though," the doctor had added, "I'm pretty sure the medical board will agree with me that you are permanently unfit for active duty, so you'll be able to go home and return to a near normal life again."

"How the bloody hell can I return to a normal life?" Frank had shouted at the doctor, "I haven't got any frigging idea who I am. Where the bloody hell am I going to return to?"

The doctor had been taken aback by this outburst and tried to dismiss the problem as quickly as possible, "Well soldier, I've done my bit, and got you well again; as well as anyone can get you anyway. The problem of your lost memory, if that's what it is, is not my problem. Just consider yourself lucky that you're not as bad as some of the other poor buggers in here, they'll never be able to look after themselves."

The doctor turned to walk away and Frank realised that there was no point in continuing the discussion. The doctor turned back again before he reached the door, "Guess you'll be out of here, the first week in January, so I'd start making plans if I were you," and then, almost as an afterthought added, "Merry Christmas."

The thought of 'going home' had ruined Frank's Christmas. He just could not get his head round what to do with the rest of his life.

In the evening Frank was sitting in the ward re-reading Alice's letter. He started scratching his head with one hand and tapped the arm of his chair with the other, as the same problem which had bugged him constantly since the doctor's visit pounded through his head, "What am I going to do? What am I going to do?"

He moved his hand to the table and continued his tapping. Di da da, di di di di, di da, ……….. "WHAT THE HELL AM I GOING TO DO? WHAT THE HELL CAN I DO?"

"Oh, for God's sake, Frank, stop that bloody tapping," Reggie took another puff on his pipe and added, "You're always bloody tapping away like that. Give us all a break and stop it before you drive us all daft."

"What are you going to do about it anyway?"

Frank turned to look at the soldier who had just been wheeled into the room. He had never seen him before.

Frank shook his head, "Sorry, what did you say?"

"I said what are you going to do about it? That's what you were tapping out in Morse code, wasn't it?"

Frank looked totally bemused by what the soldier had said. He started tapping again but this time more slowly as he listened intently to the beats he was making.

Di da da, di di di di, di da, da, "Bloody hell IT IS Morse code" he shouted out as his fingers moved faster tapping out the letters. Da, di di di di, di.

He shouted out, "What the hell am I going to do?" Suddenly, his head was filled with blurred images and memories. He closed his eyes to try and make sense of them.

He was jolted out of the nightmare images in his head by a familiar woman's voice. He looked towards the door and saw Alice rushing towards him with her arms outstretched. Frank started to get up but she reached him first and took his head firmly to her bosom. She held him for some time and when she let go, Frank realised that there were tears in her eyes.

She looked straight into his eyes, "Frank I think I've found out who you are. It was one of the chaps I was escorting on the boat coming over who told me. It all fitted with what you'd told me. I'm sure it was you he was talking about."

She spoke so rapidly that when she stopped to catch her breath, Frank took her hands in his, and pleaded with her to, "Slow down, slow down. Come and sit down. I'll get you a cup of tea and you can tell me if what you've found out agrees with what is going on in my head right now.

"What do you mean, have you remembered any more? Have your remembered who you are?"

Frank was quite calm, even though his head was buzzing with rapidly returning memories. He knew he needed to take things gently, afraid that if he got too excited it would all suddenly vanish.

"Well I think so, but I think we need to take things slowly. I want to get it right this time so let's have that cup of tea, and you can tell me slowly what you've found out."

He got up and left Alice sitting there. She had been so on edge since she had spoken to the injured soldier on the boat, wanting to rush to Frank straight away, but had been obliged to accompany the injured men to a hospital in Devon and had not been allowed to leave until this morning. She had got up at four o'clock to catch the mail train and had spent all day getting here. She had wondered whether to try to speak to Frank on the phone to tell him what she had found out, but knew it wouldn't be easy to actually speak to Frank himself, even if she could have got access to a phone. And anyway she wanted to see Frank's reaction to what she had to say, so she had controlled her excitement all over Christmas, and now all Frank could do was leave her to fetch a cup of tea!

Frank returned with the tea before Alice's frustration was able to turn to anger. He passed her the tea, placed his own on the table, sat down and took Alice's hand once again, "Now begin at the beginning and tell me slowly what you've found out."

"Well I wrote and told you that I had to accompany a train load of injured soldiers from the front line to recuperate in Devon. On the boat over, I was tending to a poor chap from the Prince of Wales Yorkshire regiment, who'd lost his right arm and his right leg below the knee. I asked him how he'd received his injuries and he told me that it was his own 'bloody fault'. He'd been at rest in a camp behind the lines and had been about to steal some apples from a food supply wagon passing the camp. The driver had stopped the wagon for a call of nature and he thought he could pinch a few apples for himself and his mates. He'd climbed on to the wagon and filled his pockets with apples out of a sack when the driver came from the bushes and saw him. The driver shouted at the top of his voice, the horse bucked, he fell off the wagon and the horse settled himself pushing the wagon backwards a few feet straight over the poor chap's arm and leg. They were crushed too badly for the doctor's to save them."

"You know nurse, he said to me, first over the top we were when those bloody mines went up and I got through all that murderous fighting and slaughter and got through all the carnage that followed without a scratch and then end up doing a stupid thing like this for a few bloody apples."

"Well, when I heard he was there with the Yorkshire Regiment, I asked him if he knew a sergeant with the Christian name Frank. Well I knew he was going to say no. So I then asked him if he knew anyone by the name of Bill Northwood and you know what he said?"

Frank laughed not only at the excitement in her voice but also with immense joy at the old memories flooding through his own head. Looking straight into her eyes, he replied, "No, No. What did he say?"

"Oh stop laughing at me, Frank. This is serious."

Frank drew his hand over his mouth to turn the smile into a solemn look, "I'm sorry, I'll try to be serious, but it's really good to see you, and anyway I'm bubbling over to tell you my news, but you finish your story first."

"What's your news then?"

"No it'll keep for a bit, please tell me what happened."

"He said that Bill Northwood had been his best mate and that they'd been together when the mines went up. He told me that Bill had nearly been killed on the day after the mines had gone off. Apparently a crazy German had nearly cut his throat, but a sergeant from signals had saved him."

Frank erupted at the mention of a sergeant and signals, "A sergeant from signals! What else did he have to say about him?"

"Well as you can imagine I was beside myself when he mentioned a sergeant in the same place as William Northwood on the day you'd been injured. So I asked him if he knew the name of the sergeant."

"And what did he say to that?"

"He said he had no idea. Both the sergeant and his mate Bill had been injured when the German had thrown a stick bomb. He said he hadn't heard anything about Bill after that. Most of his platoon had been killed in the later attack and so had the Captain who'd been with the sergeant."

"Did you ask him, how come the German had got that close to them all?"

"Well yes. I thought the sergeant might have been you and somehow your identities had got switched, so of course I asked him to tell me what had happened exactly. And in detail."

"And did he tell you?"

"Yes, but his story doesn't help identify you any more than I've already told you. So tell me your news first."

He smiled and stroked her cheek, "It's just that I think my memory is coming back. I've got some idea in the last few minutes of who I am and if you tell me exactly what he said, maybe it'll help clear things in my head."

Alice could not contain herself with excitement, "You know who you are? Who? Tell me what your real name is. What memories have come back?"

"Nothing really, I'm still not sure who I am, but things seem to be coming clearer. I realised just as you came in that I know Morse code and since then various memories keep forming in my head and I know they're real memories. So if you tell me what he said about the signals sergeant maybe I'll remember it too."

"All right, I'll tell you everything he told me. He said that the advance after the mines had gone off had been easy. They'd all reached the Germans' line safely, and those Germans that hadn't been killed in the blast, had raced back to German lines further back or were so dazed that they just gave themselves up as prisoners. He was expecting the officers to give orders to continue pushing forward to the next line, but no such order was given. They were told to clear what was left of the trenches and dig in, whilst they awaited further orders from HQ. Well he and his mates found what was left of a concrete bunker system so they cleared it of bodies or at least the bits that were left and then settled down for a smoke. They received no further orders that day so they just relaxed. There was a captain and sergeant from signals who'd followed them forward and they'd set up their equipment near the bunker because it was the highest bit of ground around. They just spent the rest of the day sending messages and passing on any messages they received for the Major. Later their own Sergeant came along and told them to get something to eat, clean their weapons, and get some rest for a possible advance the next morning. So that's exactly what they did. The pair from signals joined them to eat and they all settled down for the night. By now the Germans further back had sorted themselves out and were firing at them again, so they didn't get much rest."

Frank put his hands over his eyes for a moment before looking at Alice, "That all seems familiar. I'm sure I was there. I must have been the signals sergeant." He took Alice's hands in his, "So what happened next?"

"Nothing 'til the next morning. Apparently the Germans had obviously been well provided with rations in their concrete bunker. The lads found a barrel of water but they didn't know if it was safe to drink, so they decided to have a good wash in it. At daybreak the lads started washing and several had stripped off to the waist, including Bill Northwood and the signals sergeant, after they had put a billycan on a paraffin stove to make a mug of tea. Well apparently Bill Northwood decided he wanted to pee before he washed, so he walked five or six yards up the concrete trench to where it had been breached by the previous day's explosions and the fractured concrete was blocking the trench. He started to pee up against the broken concrete when suddenly the biggest block of smashed concrete fell towards him, pushing him over. Before anyone realised what was happening a German soldier emerged from behind the concrete. He must have been hiding there since the previous morning. Anyway he emerged with his bayonet in one hand and a stick bomb in the other. He pulled Bill from off the ground and held him in front of him with his bayonet across his throat, obviously ready to slit his throat if anyone moved. Everyone was scared, including the German apparently. He shouted something in German but no one understood what he was saying. The signals sergeant, who was nearest to him held his hands up in the air and very slowly inched towards them, talking all the time, telling the German to take it easy, not to worry, no-one was going to hurt him and so on. Anyway the German just kept waving the stick bomb and babbling away in German. The sergeant suddenly darted the last couple of yards, and grasped the German's arm. Bill Northwood managed to duck out of the way, but the German in a panic threw the stick bomb and it landed where they'd put the paraffin stove. Well the bomb went off whilst the signals sergeant was still struggling to get the bayonet off the German. He got the full force of the splintered paraffin stove and billycan and God knows what else in his back. The paraffin and metal fragments hit him full force in the back, setting fire to it. He was screaming in pain but he nevertheless managed to twist the German's arm and carved it across his neck. The bayonet the German was holding sliced through his own throat and he dropped down dead with blood gushing from the gaping gash across his neck."

Alice continued the story without giving Frank any opportunity to butt in, "Apparently, the German fell across Bill Northwood and the signals sergeant fell across both of them. The other lads picked up a jacket lying nearby and used it to put out the flames on the sergeant's back. They pulled the men apart and then realised that the bayonet had not only become embedded in Bill Northwood's arm but the fall of the two men on top of him had resulted in him getting a broken leg. They moved the dead German to one side, covered the two injured men as best they could, and waited for the medics to take them back from the front line to the field hospital."

She looked at Frank with a big grin on her face, "So what do you think? I reckon you were the signal's sergeant and that somehow they'd used Bill Northwood's tunic with all his papers in it, to put out the flames and cover you with. As to what happened to the real Bill Northwood, well, we'll probably never know. Maybe he got killed on his way back to the hospital. There were plenty poor sods who did."

Frank reached forward, took Alice's face in his hands and pulled her towards him. He kissed her full on the lips. A short, hard smack of a kiss and looking straight into her eyes, said, "You're wonderful. You are the only person who's ever really believed that I'm not Bill Northwood." He laughed and added, "Until his wife and mother turned up, that is."

He took his hands from her face and held her hands tightly, "You might say this is an odd coincidence but just before you came I realised I knew Morse code. That new fellow over there told me that that was what I was tapping out. And you know what? Once I realised that he was right; that I did know the Morse code; then things started to slip back into place. Yes, I was a signals sergeant and do you want to know what my real name is?"

Alice's eyes had not left Frank's since he had kissed her, "Of course I want to know your real name. What is it? What is it?"

"Frank Samuel Matthews. That's what it is. Frank Samuel Matthews." He laughed out loud and shouted out, "My bloody name is Frank Matthews,"

He pulled a face, tensing the muscles in his neck, as he realised that everyone in the ward was looking at him. He raised his hand and waved it around the ward, "Sorry folks, I'll keep quiet from now on."

He turned and looked at Alice again, "And you know what, my mother's name is Alice and she's a wonderful woman just like you."

At this Alice realised that this comment confirmed what she really already knew, that the kiss had merely been a joyous reaction to his recognition as to who he really was and was not in any way a sign of sexual passion. She really liked Frank, and yes, she did love him, but she knew the love between them would only ever be as close as that between brother and sister, or maybe between son and mother? Ah well, even that was better than no feelings at all, but she preferred to be his sister rather than his mother.

They spent the rest of the evening talking and Frank gradually remembered more and more of his past. And finally he remembered both Grace and Evie. He spoke at length about Grace but only mentioned Evie in passing when he was talking about Mark.

When Alice came back the next day Frank was already making plans to go home to Walsall. He was so excited at the thought of meeting them back home and at last get clear images of them all, rather than the fuzzy pictures he still had in his head. He didn't admit it to anyone, and certainly not Alice, but he had a very clear view in his head of Evie, particularly the first time he had met her when she was wearing the straw hat with the silk scarf round it. He then realised that this had been his first clear memory following his memory loss, but he just did not know whose image it was. And it was Evie who he was thinking about when he had seen Bill Northwood's wife; the way she had been dressed had reawaken that first memory of Evie. Would he ever meet Evie again? He hoped so.

Other memories returned quite quickly and he was soon able to convince the doctors of his real identity. They wanted to send a telegram to his family but Frank asked them not to, as he didn't know what story they had been given. Presumably they'd been told he'd been 'lost in action presumed dead'. If he was allowed to go home in the next few days he preferred to be there so that they could see him in the flesh when they got the shock news.

Alice did not entirely agree with him. She thought Frank's family should be given the news as soon as possible, but Frank was adamant. "They've probably already received one telegram too many," he said and would not discuss the matter any more.

Unusually for the Army, or so Frank thought, things moved quickly. Later that same day, just as Alice was about to go back to her lodgings in the town, he was told he could go home on the following day for a week's leave. The only proviso was that he should come back at the end of the week to be assessed by the board for a medical discharge.

"You know Alice, I'm a bit scared of meeting everyone," he said after the doctor had left. "Do you think I'll remember them all, and their names? Oh God, they'll be so upset if I can't remember them."

Alice put her arms round him, "Don't be silly, they'll be so glad to see you alive it won't matter that you've got a bit of a memory loss." And then, without really thinking, she added, "Shall I come with you? I don't have to report back for another four days."

Frank leaned back without completely taking his arms from around her, "Would you? It would be good to have someone with me who could take over if I become confused."

And so it was agreed that Alice would accompany Frank on his trip back home and to his loved ones, who hopefully, he would remember.

CHAPTER SEVEN

1919

Alice and Grace were eating breakfast at the parlour table when there was a knock at the front door. Neither of them had yet dressed and they were still sitting in their dressing gowns covering their nightdresses. There was a second more urgent knock at the door. Grace started to get out of her seat to answer it.

"No, I'll go," Alice said, "You just sit there and enjoy your last meal as a single woman. Anyway, who on earth would be knocking on the front door? Everybody knows the back door's always open."

"Well it's probably Mary and Tom with the flowers. I asked Mary to make sure Frank doesn't see them before he sees me at Church. That's the trouble with living next door to the chap you're marrying!" But Alice did not hear the last bit as she was already on her way through the front room and answering the door.

The postman greeted her with a, "Parcel for you missus. Can you just sign here for it?"

He handed a sheet of paper to Alice and fumbled in his top pocket to find a pencil, which he also handed to her. He pointed at the paper, "Just sign there if you don't mind, only it's a special delivery see and I have to get a signature for them."

"Well I don't actually live here so can I see who it's addressed to please, then I can get you the proper signature?"

Alice stretched her hand out to take the parcel but the postman held it from her. He took a step back and read the label, "Addressed to a Miss Grace Richards. Does she live here?"

"Yes sure, I'll just get her. It's probably a wedding present from someone. She's getting married today."

"Oh that's nice," replied the postman, "She's got a lovely day for it. Going to be a scorcher today, it is."

Alice went back into the parlour and spoke to Grace, "It's the postman, Grace. He's got a parcel for you and he needs your signature. Sorry but you'll have to go yourself after all."

Grace went to collect the parcel and sign for it. As she went to close the door the postman held his foot against it, "Sorry love, I just wanted to wish you all the best today. I hope you have a great wedding and that you and your hubby will have a long and happy life together." With that he removed his foot from the door and turned to go.

Grace closed the door with a, "Thanks, I'm sure we shall."

She returned to the table, sat down, placed the parcel in the centre of the table, picked up her knife and fork and started to tuck into the rest of her bacon and eggs. She put a forkful of egg into her mouth without taking her eyes off the parcel. The box was about the size and shape of a shoebox, was neatly wrapped in brown paper and tied with string, with all the knots and places where the string crossed being sealed with red sealing wax. The name and address were written in bright blue ink in a neat, precisely executed, flowing script.

She finished the mouthful of food, put down the knife and put her hand to her chin, "What do you think is in it? Why would anyone send us a wedding present just addressed to me? I think I should leave it and open it with Frank when we come back from the church, don't you?"

"Not at all," replied Alice, "It's addressed to you, so it may be nothing to do with Frank. It might even be from Frank. It would just be like him to send you a surprise this morning. Anyway, if it was sent to me I'd have ripped the paper off straight away. Forget Frank and have a look at what it is. Put us out of our misery." She shouted into the scullery, "What do you think Ma?"

Hannah Richards was in the scullery making more tea and cooking more eggs, bacon and sausages to take up to Grace's father Tom, who was still in bed. He normally had to get up at five-thirty each morning to walk the three miles to work before clocking in at seven-fifteen. So, as usual on a day off work, he was having a lie in. His wife always got up first to cook him some breakfast before he set off to work, and on his days off, she always got up earlier than him to cook breakfast and take it to him in bed. Today was no different even though it was his daughter's wedding day.

"What was that, Alice? What do I think about what?" she shouted back from the scullery.

"Oh Ma, just come here a minute will you?" demanded Grace. "Dad can wait for his breakfast a bit longer, can't he?"

Hannah turned down the flame on the gas cooker and moved the frying pan to an unlit hob.

"I haven't got time to mess about, not today of all days," she muttered as she walked from the scullery wiping her hands on her freshly starched white apron. "What on earth do you want?"

Grace grinned and pulled a face to Alice at her mother's fussiness, but quickly composed her face again when her mother entered the room.

"Well," said her mother, "What is it you want? We haven't got all day you know. You'll have to think about getting a wash and putting your dress on soon."

Grace picked up the parcel and held it out toward her mother, "This parcel has just been delivered addressed to me. I think it's probably a wedding present for Frank and me. So do you think I should leave it 'til Frank can open it with me when we come back from the church?"

Hannah Richards had never opened a letter or parcel in all her married life. They rarely received any mail and she would not have dared to open any of it. Such things were a husband's duty, not a wife's. And anyway her husband was the much better reader and she didn't really enjoy the difficulty of making sense of hand-written script.

"Of course you should leave it for Frank to open. Now finish your breakfast and let's get on with things," and with that dismissal, she turned and went back into the scullery to finish her husband's breakfast.

"Well that's told you," Alice whispered across the table so that Grace's mother could not hear, "It's your own fault for asking her."

"Well I think I'd prefer to leave it anyway," retorted Grace and pointing a finger at Alice so as to emphasise the point added, "And that's not 'cause I'm scared of Frank like Ma is of Dad."

Alice decided to let the whole thing drop and they both finished their meal without any further comment.

Just as they were about to clear their plates and cups off the table, they heard Tom's voice at the back door, "It's only me, Ma." He went into the scullery and gave his mother a kiss on the cheek, "That for me, Ma? I could just eat one of your Sunday breakfasts."

"Haven't you had anything to eat yet? Sit yourself down and eat this. I can soon do your father some more."

"No don't be daft, Ma. I'm only joking. I've already eaten, and anyway I must go next door and do my best man duties. Mary's waiting at the end of the street with the flowers and I've had strict orders to make sure Frank ain't looking out of the front window when you let her in."

With that he walked into the parlour just as Grace was coming out with the dirty dishes. He put his arms round her lifting her off the floor, "And how's my favourite sister then? All ready for the big day?"

He put her down and spun her round plucking at the material of her dressing gown, "Don't think much of your wedding dress, Miss. Is this the best you could do? Don't think you'll send Frank into a tizz wearing this young lady." He turned her round once more, "Don't know though, if that's all you're wearing it might be just the thing to get him going tonight."

"Shut up you idiot, Ma might hear you."

He laughed out loud and then whispered in her ear, "You never know she'd probably be turned on by a good looking chap like Frank herself."

Grace nudged him out the way with her elbow, desperately gripping the plates so as not to drop them, "Just get out of the way, you idiot. We've got more important things to do than play with little boys like you, you know."

Suitably admonished, for the moment at least, he walked across to Alice. "I suppose I hadn't better comment on the wedding outfit you're wearing, had I, Alice? You could get a chap all hot and bothered wearing an outfit like this, you know."

Alice had had to deal with Tom's flirtatious comments ever since the first occasion she had met him, when she had accompanied Frank from hospital almost eighteen months previously. She had immediately fallen in love with Frank's family and friends, although she sometimes found Tom and his father a little difficult to deal with. It wasn't that she didn't like the older Tom; it was just that he never said much and she just did not understand what made him tick. And as for Tom himself, well he wasn't the same as Frank, but he was Frank's friend so she would never do anything to spoil that relationship for Frank. She had instantly taken to Grace and Tom's wife Mary though, and the three of them had quickly become inseparable friends. A friendship destined to last the rest of their lives.

Tom had been immediately attracted to Mary the very first time he had seen her, when he and Frank had visited Joe and his family during their last leave before going to France. Fearing he may never see her again, he had managed to speak to her alone and asked if she would write to him if he wrote to her from France. After he had been invalided out of the army following his war wound, he started to court Mary and they had married less than twelve month's later.

Alice did not respond immediately to Tom's comment but stepped towards him and grabbed hold of his left ear pulling him painfully towards her. She leaned towards his ear and whispered directly into it, "Don't bugger around with me today, you pathetic moron. This is Grace and Frank's day and you'd better behave and make it special for them. Don't you dare do anything to spoil it for them or you'll have me to answer to. And I'm a nurse so I know exactly where to lift my knee to inflict the most pain."

With that she let him go. He pulled back raising his hands up in front of him, "Steady, old girl, you've got me all wrong. I'm only joking." He shook his head and repeated, "You've got me all wrong, old girl."

Alice stepped towards him once again and he recoiled anxious at what might be coming. However, Alice did not touch him this time. "I'm not your 'old girl'. In fact I'm nobody's old girl and I've been around soldiers long enough to know how to read the male mind, so I don't think I've got it wrong at all." She was about to add more, but Grace returned from the scullery, so she changed what she was about to say, "Well, OK Tom, you go and look after Frank. I'll give you a couple of minutes and then I'll let Mary in through the front door with the flowers."

Tom turned and went out of the door, "See you Sis, see you at the Church, and you Ma."

Two hours later, Grace watched Frank, Tom and Frank's Auntie Annie setting off to walk the mile or so to St. Paul's church. She felt it was so sad that neither Frank's mother nor father would be at their wedding. His father had died years ago and his mother had never got over receiving the telegram saying that Frank was 'missing in action'. She waited day after day for news with Grace sitting with her each evening. As the days stretched to weeks and then to months, they had both believed Frank to be dead and Grace had reconciled herself to being a spinster for good. It seemed to Grace that Mrs Matthews was getting older and more frail each day and unfortunately, Grace herself was not able to give her any comfort as she was totally distraught herself. Neither of them were eating well and much of the time they only ate to please each other and at the other's insistence. They had both lost weight and Grace who had lost half a stone worrying about Frank when he had last gone back to France, lost another stone and was only a little over seven stone. Frank's mother who had always been a well-built woman who enjoyed her food; plenty of suet puddings and the like, had lost almost three stones in as many months.

By Christmas, Grace was beginning to feel that Mrs Matthews would not last out the winter, but then after Christmas, Frank and Alice had arrived and everything was wonderful again. Frank's mother had improved overnight and by the time Frank had been discharged from the army on medical grounds, she seemed to be back to her old self, although she never put back all the weight she had lost. Grace herself had started to eat well as soon as she knew Frank was safe and would not have to go back to the front in France. Everything had been fine with Mrs Matthews until the beginning of November when she had been taken ill with the flu pandemic. Half the people in the street had been taken ill; a situation repeated throughout many streets in the country. Mrs Matthews had been unable to cope with the illness and got worse not better. She died on the evening of 11 November with all the church bells ringing in the town to herald the armistice and the cessation of fighting on the western front. Unfortunately, Grace's younger sister Harriet had caught it a few days later and died a week later. Tom and Mary's baby daughter, Mary had died from the epidemic later that same week. Luckily, Grace and Frank had gone for long walks together over the summer and had become really fit. They both caught the flu bug, but managed to fight it off with a few feverish days in bed.

Alice, who was also standing at the window watching Frank go, turned to Grace and watched her wipe a tear from her eye. "What on earth are you crying for Grace? Today should be the happiest day of your life."

"I know, I was just thinking how much I miss Harriet and Frank's mum. Harriet was so thrilled when I asked her to be my bridesmaid. I do miss her, especially right now. And Frank's mum held me together all through the time Frank was away in France. I loved her almost as much as I love my own Ma. She always said I made up for the two daughters she always wanted but had been unable to carry to full term. All through the war she talked about me and Frank getting married. She would have loved it today."

"I know," said Alice, "I only met her a few times, but she always made me feel so welcome and even special. And Harriet was the prettiest and liveliest girl I've ever known. Still, I'm sure they'll be there in spirit looking down on both of you today. So just wipe your eyes, we'd better get you dressed before Mary, your Ma and me, get ourselves off to the church. So come on, put on this dress, and let's get going."

Grace's father was grumbling and his wife Hannah was struggling with his front stud and trying to put on the new stiff white collar and tie bought specially for the occasion when Grace and Alice finally came down the stairs. He was wearing his one and only suit, which had been taken out of mothballs and specially sponged and pressed for the occasion. Luckily Grace had coerced her father to try it on after she had pressed it two nights earlier only to find that he had put on weight since he'd last worn it and he couldn't fasten all the buttons on his trouser fly. A couple of hours of unexpected sewing had followed as Grace let out as much of the waistband and backside of the trousers as the material would allow. Just enough for him to fasten all the fly buttons.

Her mother was wearing her best black dress, which had been lovingly washed and ironed before she had sewn on a grand cream lace collar she had bought at the church jumble sale. She wore the cream bonnet she had purchased at the same jumble sale. Mary, bless her, had come this morning and pinned two red roses and some green foliage on her hat and had pinned a corsage of flowers and foliage on to her dress.

Neither her mother nor father had heard Grace coming down the stairs. They were too engrossed with the collar and stud. "Damn you woman, you're pinching my neck. Do I have to put on this damn thing? Bloody weddings and funerals! Why do I have to wear a collar and tie at weddings and funerals?"

"Now Dad," interrupted Grace as she gently eased her mother out of the way and took hold of the collar, "Today isn't any old wedding, it's my wedding, and I want you to look special for me. So come on, just relax a bit and we'll soon have this fixed and you can take it off as soon as the wedding is over and we're on our way home. I promise. Just do it for me, will you Dad?"

He took hold of Grace's hands and looked her straight in the eye, "Aye lass, aye, I'll do it for you, but only you mind and only this once. I ain't ever going to wear it again, not for you, not for nobody."

He delicately pushed her away from him, "But first, let's look at you." Grace thought she detected the semblance of a tear in his eye as he added very slowly, wetting his lips and squeezing her hands as he did so, "Aye, lass you'll do, you'll do. That Frank Matthews ought to consider himself a very lucky fella having someone as pretty as thee to marry." Grace knew that her father was a man of few words and that a comment like 'you'll do' was praise indeed coming from him.

He let go of her hands brushing his left eye as he did so. Grace smiled. Now she knew it was real pride and approval from her father. No matter how casual he tried to make the movement she knew it was indeed a tear he was wiping from his eye. He immediately composed himself and beckoned her towards him as he added, "Now come on lass, let's get this blessed collar on and get ready for your wedding." He pointed towards his wife, "And you woman, you'd better get off to the church, or we'll be there before you if you're not careful."

"Not so fast. Not so fast," interrupted Hannah Richards in such a sharp voice that Grace hoped her father did not interpret it as a defiance of his bidding, "I want to have a good look at my daughter before I go. It's a mother's privilege to see that the bride's perfect before leaving for the church."

Grace turned towards her mother, smiled and then slowly twirled all round so that her mother could view from all sides the dress she and Mary had made from white dress material bought from the Co-op in town. And particularly the delicate flowers that Alice had lovingly embroidered on the bodice, around the waist and at the hem. "Do you think I'll do, Ma?"

"Do! I'll say you'll do, take no notice of your father, love, you look beautiful, really beautiful." This time it was obviously tears that her mother was wiping away from her eyes as she stepped towards Grace and took her in her arms. "Your Dad's right about one thing though, that Frank Matthews is a very lucky fella."

With that she gave Grace another hug, kissed her on the cheek and turned to Mary who had been sitting quietly on a chair at the table whilst all this had been going on, "Come on Mary, let's get going." She turned to Alice, "And you, Alice. Come on. I want to be waiting at the church when Grace arrives and you know I can't walk that fast." She turned to Grace, kissed her on the cheek once more, and spoke quietly to her, "You look lovely love. See you at the church." She leaned forward and spoke in her ear, "He'll be all right at the church love. You won't hear a peep out of him with all those people about." She turned to Mary once more, "Now Mary, where's my handbag?"

Mary handed her the handbag and with that she added, "Right girls, let's get going," and without a break in her movements was on her way out of the back door with Mary following her. Alice just managing to give Grace a kiss on the cheek and pick up her hat and handbag as Mary pulled her after her. She pulled free of Mary at the backdoor and turned back to Grace, "You do look beautiful, you know Grace," and then turned back to catch up with Mary and Ma.

"Right Dad, now let's fix your collar."

Ten minutes later there was a knock at the front door. Grace shouted through the back door to her father who, for the third time since getting up, had had to dash up the yard to use the toilet, "Come on Dad. Hurry up. They're here to take us to church."

He shouted back, "Won't be long love. Go and let Mr Hancox in will you and give him a drink?"

John Hancox, a local haulage contractor, was a drinking pal of her father's, who had agreed to provide a horse and cart to take Grace and her father to the church. Grace went to the front door to let Mr Hancox know that they wouldn't be long, and was pleasantly surprised to find that his wife was at the reins not Mr Hancox.

"Oh, Hello Mrs Hancox, thanks for coming. We won't be long. Do you want to come in a bit?"

"That's all right, Grace love. We'll be fine here, won't we Elsie?"

It was only then that Grace noticed the six year-old girl sitting next to Mrs Hancox as she nodded her head to her mother's remark. "I hope you don't mind little Elsie coming along with us, but she wanted so much to see the bride when I told her what we were doing. You don't mind, do you?"

"No, of course not, Mrs Hancox. It'll be lovely to have her along with us." Grace was looking at the horse and cart. It wasn't quite as her father had described it when he had boasted at how he had fixed transport up to take her to the church. The horse was a shire horse and the cart was obviously one used for moving goods. *"Oh God,"* she thought. *"I do hope it's not the one Mr Hancox uses to deliver coal."*

As if she read Grace's mind Mrs Hancox said, "You'll be all right in here Grace love. We've cleaned it out pretty well this morning, haven't we Elsie? Come and have a look Grace. We've put a rug on the floor of the cart, and we've put some nice cushions on the bench we've put for you to sit on, so you'll be fine in here won't she Elsie? Come on Grace, have a look."

Grace did not want to upset Mrs Hancox, who had obviously made a considerable effort to make the cart fit for the occasion, so she went and had a look at the cart. It did look clean and the sides still showed signs of slight dampness where they had obviously been scrubbed that morning. Bunting had been pinned to the sides and wild flowers clipped to that. The horse had a few wild flowers in his mane. It was obvious that considerable effort had been made to make it a little special.

"Is it all right Grace? We've tried to make it all right, haven't we Elsie?" The little girl, who had been staring at the bride in awe all the time since she had arrived at the door, nodded her head once again.

"It's lovely, Mrs Hancox. It's grand." Grace wanted to say something to show she appreciated the effort that Mrs Hancox had obviously made, so she added, "I'll feel like a real princess travelling in that."

As she went past the horse he turned his head and Grace, who was unused to horses, pulled away quickly.

"Don't worry love," said Mrs Hancox, "Old Herbert might be pretty big, but he's as gentle as a kitten. He wouldn't hurt a fly. That's right ain't it Elsie?"

Elsie, still without taking her eyes off the bride, spoke for the first time, "Yes Ma. Herbert's lovely."

"I'm sorry Mrs Hancox, it's just that I'm not used to horses," and with that she turned into the house, "Won't be long. Just get my veil on and get my Dad."

"Right, Grace my love. I'll turn old Herbert round whilst we're waiting so we're facing the right way and then we'll be ready for you."

The horse and cart next appeared in Brighton Terrace just over two hours later, with the bride sitting as close as she possibly could to the groom, without actually sitting on his lap, proudly smiling to all the neighbours who had turned out to welcome them back home. She was still gripping tightly the large bouquet of red and white gladioli set off with some fern leaves which Mary had picked from her garden that morning, and with her usual flair for these things, had created a spray of flowers which Grace was delighted with. The children of Grace's two elder brothers and elder sister, were running aside the slowly plodding horse, as they had done all the way back home from St, Paul's Church.

The rest of the family, or at least those that could keep up, were walking behind the cart arm in arm, most of them had big grins on their faces. Alice and Mrs Richards were trailing way behind with Grace's father Tom, collar and tie already removed, between them. They were walking much slower than the rest and both Alice and Mrs Richards were holding on tightly to one of his arms. It looked like a picture of two women who were fond of the man between them, helping each other with the long walk. This was partially true but it was also Mrs Richards' way of making absolutely sure that her husband did not stop off at the pub on the way back. If that had happened they probably would not have seen him again until closing time and she wanted to make sure that he was around for the celebration meal that had been prepared back home.

As soon as the neighbours had waved Grace and her father on their way to the church, they had gone into both Grace's and Frank's houses, removed the tables into the yard, and set about creating a surprise wedding supper for the bride, groom and all the guests. A surprise arranged by Grace's mother.

Freshly starched white tablecloths were laid on the tables, on which were placed plates of sliced meat. Beef, ox tongue and boiled ham, all cooked by Hannah Richards whilst everyone was at work the previous day. Dishes of lettuce, tomatoes, cucumber, pickled onions and pickled red cabbage, and plates of thickly buttered slices of home made bread, which had been baked in the oven next to the fire in the black leaded grate in the parlour on the previous afternoon, were carefully placed on the tables. Scones, little decorated fairy cakes, a caraway seed cake and two sponge cakes followed. On a small table at the top of the yard, were placed two barrels of ale, a very generous wedding gift from Grace's brother Tom and his wife Mary.

And finally the two-tier wedding cake, lovingly cooked and covered with marzipan and decorated with delicately patterned white icing by Agnes Williams, was placed at the head of the table. Agnes Williams was a kindly old neighbour, whose husband had died before Grace was born and who, having no children of her own, had made a fuss of Grace and her sister Harriet from the moment they were born. She had looked after them as babies and later when they came home from school until their mother returned from work. There had always been a piece of one of her wonderful cakes waiting for them together with a glass of milk. She had taken the place of the grandmother they had never known and they always referred to her as Nanna Agnes.

Grace had wanted her to come to the wedding but she had said that the arthritis in her hips and legs made it too painful to get about and would not be able to make it to the Church. She nevertheless wanted to do something for Grace on her wedding day and had been absolutely thrilled when Hannah suggested that she make the cakes for the wedding meal, and was even more delighted when Hannah insisted that she join them for the meal.

Agnes was sitting on a chair outside the front door of the Richards' house when the bridal pair returned. Grace spotted her as soon as the horse had turned into the Terrace. She gave a big grin and waved her bouquet in the air as a greeting to her. Mrs Hancox pulled on the reins and gave a "Whoa Herbert" and the horse pulled up just beyond the house, so that Grace was exactly next to the seated Nanna Agnes.

Agnes painfully got up from her seat and stretched out a hand to Grace, "Welcome home Mrs Matthews."

Grace leaned forward and just managed to reach low enough to give her a kiss on the forehead. Frank held on to her arm so that she did not topple over. "Thanks for being here for me, Nanna Agnes. It was a lovely wedding." She sat up and gave Frank a kiss on the cheek, "At least I thought it was." She kissed Frank full on the lips this time, "It was, wasn't it, Frank?"

He kissed her back and winked at Mrs Williams, "Yes of course, the best wedding ever."

Frank got down from the wagon, picked up the chair Agnes Williams had been sitting on and, placing it at the back of the wagon helped Grace down. He led her round to the front to where Mrs Hancox and her daughter were sitting and thanked them for a comfortable and steady ride.

"Yes it was lovely of you to make the wagon look so special," added Grace, "Thank you very much." She stepped round the horse and gave little Elsie a kiss on her cheek, "And thank you Elsie for being such a special driver's companion. Won't you both come in and have a drink with us before you go back, Mrs Hancox?"

"No thank you love. Must get back and get Mr Hancox's tea and feed old Herbert here." She leaned forward and gave Herbert a gentle slap on his backside, "You deserve something to eat by now don't you old boy?"

Frank and Grace helped old Agnes back into the house, and when they went through into the parlour they were puzzled as to where the table and chairs had gone. And then they looked through the window and saw the table outside laden with all the food. Grace dashed outside into the yard and became excited when she saw all the bunting hung all round the yard. Bunting which had been made by everyone in the Terrace for use at the street Armistice celebrations following the war and which Nanna Agnes had kept especially for this occasion.

"Come and have a look at this, Frank. Oh it's so lovely Nanna."

She then noticed the wedding cake finely decorated with piped scroll icing and beautiful little white roses. On the top was an iced heart with an arrow through it and the names of '*Grace*' and '*Frank*' so carefully written on either side of the arrow.

"Oh Frank, just look at this beautiful cake. Where did it all come from?" She then noticed the grin on Agnes' face. "You did it, didn't you Nanna?"

Agnes nodded her head, and Grace came and gave her another big hug. "Thank you Nanna Agnes. It's lovely, and such a surprise. Thank you."

By now, the rest of the family and friends were coming through the house and Grace made a point of kissing each of them as they walked through the back door. It was indeed the most exciting and happiest day of her life.

It was way after midnight by the time the last guests had left, with most of the men well imbibed with the drink, leaving their women folk to carry the little children back to their homes. Nevertheless everyone agreed it had been a great day and a great wedding party.

Grace's brothers had earlier taunted Frank about the night that lay ahead of him, and had mischievously tried to encourage him to leave the party and take Grace to her wedding bed. He resisted all the taunts, and in an effort to ensure that Grace did not hear their vulgar comments, tried to keep them away from Grace as they become more and more drunk. They stopped their taunts when Grace's mother overheard their comments and had promptly cuffed both Tom and his eldest brother Bill around the ears and told them to behave themselves or she would tell their father about them. As youngsters, they had received the sharp end of their father's thick leather belt and got to know the extent of his anger well. Whilst they were now much bigger than their father and would have stood up to his wrath on other occasions, they decided for Grace's sake, and their mother's, that they would not want him to get angry tonight and spoil Grace's wedding day. The taunting and whispering to Frank only occurred after that when the men managed to get Frank on his own. After the third time however, Frank did manage to avoid them and their taunts for the rest of the evening.

Alice, Grace and her mother cleared away the remnants of food that had been left on the table after all the goodbyes had been said to the rest of the family leaving. Frank removed the tablecloths and started to bring in the first of the chairs from outside but Mrs Richards stopped him, "There'll be plenty of time for that tomorrow Frank. Just leave them all outside. It's a nice night so they won't hurt outside for now. Anyway it's about time we all went to bed," and with that, she turned to her husband who was at the top of the yard trying unsuccessfully to get the last few drops of beer out of the second barrel, "Come on Tom, it's time we left these youngsters and let them have a chance to be by themselves for once." She turned to Alice, "Come on Alice, time we all went up to bed." She kissed Grace on the cheek as she gently pushed her outside, "Goodnight love, it's time you were with your husband."

As the door was closing, Grace remembered the parcel that had been delivered that morning, "Just a minute Ma, there's something I want."

She pushed open the door, went into the parlour, and found the parcel on the floor in the corner where the neighbours preparing the food earlier in the day had placed it. She picked it up and with a grin so wide that it could not hide the pleasurable anticipation she was feeling towards the first night she would spend with Frank, kissed her mother, father and Alice on the cheek and dashed outside to where her husband was waiting for her.

Frank watched the gas lights being turned down by Mrs Richards and then taking his wife tightly in his arms and for the first time that day, felt the full softness and warmth of her body against his own. She responded by pressing her hips forward to feel the warmth rising in her husband, and gave him the long lingering luxurious kiss full on the lips, which they had both been waiting for all day. As Frank eased his lips away from hers, Grace noticed the tears in his eyes, "There's no need to cry my love, we're together now and no-one can keep us apart any more."

"I know sweetheart. I'm just so happy. I can't believe we're finally married and can go through the same door together." He pointed to the door of the Richards' house, "I've died every night I've had to let you go through that door," and then pointing to his own back door behind him, added, "Then having to go through this door on my own." He gave her another squeeze before adding, "And you know what was worse than that?" He did not wait for an answer but just continued, "Knowing that when you were in bed there was only a single wall separating us. You just don't know how difficult that's been for me."

"Oh yes I do. Don't you think it's been the same for me?"

Frank grinned and bending forward picked her up in his arms, "Not any more, Mrs Matthews." He pushed open his own back door with his foot and carried her into the house, "And what's more we've got the whole house to ourselves." He kicked the door shut with his foot and carried her through the parlour and awkwardly carried her all the way up the narrow stairs.

At the top of the stairs he managed to take the key out of his jacket pocket and open the front bedroom door with it, without dropping Grace. He again kicked the door open and carefully placed Grace on the edge of the bed, which smelled of freshly laundered sheets. There was a vase of flowers on the bedside table and several flowers strewn on the pillows. It was obvious that Frank had taken particular care to make the bedroom special for her. He had also taken the precaution of locking the door and keeping the key with him so that no one, particularly Grace's brothers could get in during the day and spoil it for them.

"What about the back door, Frank? Don't you think you should lock it?"

"Well I'm not leaving this room now that I've finally got you to myself." He held up the key he had just used to unlock the bedroom door and re-locked it, "That'll do the trick." He leaned forward and kissed her, slowly lifting her from the bed at the same time. The parcel dropped out of her hand on to the floor. Frank picked it up, "What's this?"

"It's a parcel that came this morning. It's addressed to me but I thought it could only be a wedding present, so I thought we ought to open it together."

Frank put it on the bedside table next to the vase of flowers. "Not tonight we're not. We've got far more important things to do."

Grace smiled and looked directly into his eyes and he put his arms round her back and started to unfasten the buttons at the back of her dress. She put her arms to her back to help in the task, "Let me do it, Sweetheart, I've had more practice than you."

They undressed slowly, watching each other until they were looking at each other's naked bodies. Frank pulled back the sheet, picked Grace up and placed her on the bed. He walked round the bed to lie beside her. They tentatively touched each other's bodies and gradually became more and more passionate in their embraces until Frank finally entered her and made their marriage complete.

They woke early the next morning and made love again. Afterwards they were basking in the pleasure of being warm and close together, when Grace remembered the parcel.

She reached across and took it off the table, "Let's see what we've had sent to us."

She held it out for Frank to open. He looked at it and passed it back, "It's addressed to you. You should open your own mail."

He put his hand under the sheet and started to caress her belly again.

Grace took his hand and moved it away from her, "Just be a good boy for a bit then."

She fiddled with the string on the parcel trying to undo it as Frank moved his hand back. "Well all right if you must," she said, "but don't you dare move your hand down any further or we'll never get this parcel open."

Frank started to do exactly what she had bid him not to do, but moved his hand up again when she gave him a very disapproving look, "You'll have to go and get some scissors to cut this string. I can't get it off otherwise."

Frank reluctantly reached across to his trousers hanging over the back of the chair, took out his penknife, opened it and cut the string. He flicked back the blade of the knife, put it on the floor and returned his hand to its warm, soft resting-place. Grace took the paper off the box and removed the envelope pinned to the outside of the box.

She put the box back on the bedside table, opened the envelope again addressed to her, and started to read the first of several pages quietly to herself and then let out a gasp, and sat up in bed.

"What's the matter Grace? What on earth does it say?"

"Just be quiet a bit," she replied. "Just listen to this." She began to read the letter out aloud.

"Dear Miss Richards

I hope you will forgive me for writing this letter to you, but I did not know what else to do with the contents of the box. They are the personal belongings of Sergeant Frank Matthews, who was killed in action in June 1917 at Messines Ridge. He was my brother Mark's sergeant and I believe they became quite close.

I met Frank on a few occasions. He was a fine man. I liked him a lot and I know my brother had a lot of respect for him and his undoubted abilities. We met in 1916 when I was a nurse in a field hospital and

Frank had been injured in a plane crash. Frank spoke of you very affectionately then and my brother told me that you had become engaged.

I don't know what the army told you and Frank's family about his death. Just the usual 'Died in action' I guess, but I thought I should write and tell you the little I know of the events surrounding his death.

Mark would have written to you himself but he didn't want to believe that Frank was dead and didn't want to write to you before he knew what had happened. Frank had been injured saving a fellow soldier from being killed by a German. The other soldier had also been injured and both of them were shipped out to the field hospital.

Mark ordered that the dead German should be moved out of the bunker and it was then that they found Frank's identity tags in the German's hand. He must have pulled them off Frank's neck when Frank killed him. Mark collected Frank's knapsack and his personal belongings out of his jacket which was lying beside it, intending to try and get them back to him in hospital. However shortly after that the Germans started to shell their positions and all their wireless equipment was lost. Mark also heard that the original barrage of shells that had overshot their target had killed some of the injured men being moved out and feared that Frank was one of them.

Mark returned to his base to collect more equipment and took the opportunity to see me at a field hospital and asked me to make enquiries about Frank in the various hospitals. He also left Frank's papers etc. with me to give to Frank, when I found him.

Mark returned to the fighting zone as soon as he had his replacement equipment, but was killed in action on his first day back at the front. As you can imagine I was extremely upset when I heard the news, as he was the only close family I had left after my mother had died. Although I did make further enquiries about Sergeant Matthews at the various medical units and at H.Q. there was no information about him and by then anyway I learned of the official news that he was 'missing presumed killed in action'.

I am sure you must have been devastated by the news and I know there is nothing I can say that will help. I hope that time is a healer for you and that you will meet someone eventually to make you happy again.

The items in the box are Frank's personal things that Mark asked me to pass on to Frank when I found which hospital he was in. I'm sorry I have not been able to let you have them sooner but I have only recently returned from France myself and it took me a little time to find out your address.

I hope you will find some comfort in receiving them.

With my kindest regards

Evelyn Harper

Grace finished reading the letter and looked at Frank. He had a blank look on his face as if he was thinking of things miles away. She leaned over and kissed him on the cheek, "Are you all right sweetheart?"

"Sorry. I was just thinking about Captain Harper. He was a good friend to me as well as one of the very few officers I had any respect for. I suppose I've just tried to blank all thoughts of the war out of my mind since I came back home. I guess in a way I knew the Captain was dead. I'm sure he would have got in touch with me otherwise. I just didn't want to think about it all."

His shoulders started to move and soon he was sobbing uncontrollably on Grace's bare shoulder. His tears running on to her shoulder and gradually down on to her breast.

"I'm sorry sweetheart I just didn't want to think about it. How many more do you..........?" He was unable to continue speaking as he held her so tightly that it hurt her; his whole body shaking, as the emotions he had held to himself since his first encounter with death and the horrors of war in 1916, came pouring out.

He released his hold slightly, but Grace did not want him to pull away completely. She knew that this was something they had to share together if Frank was to get the demons out, so she held him to her. "It's all right, sweetheart. It's all right," but she left it at that, not wishing to stop the flow of emotions that her husband needed to get out of his system.

She had worried for some time that he hadn't been able to talk about his war experiences. In the early days she just thought it was a case of missing memories, but gradually she realised he was deliberately avoiding the subject and he always either, just drew into himself and stopped talking, or changed the subject whenever she tried to ask him about it.

Gradually the shaking and sobbing abated but by this time his body was saturated with sweat and tears. Grace's own body was soaked from the tears and the moisture from his body. At that moment she ached so much with love for him that she felt she would burst. She lay down in the bed and wrapped the whole length of her body against his. They lay like that for some time and slowly Frank began to breathe more slowly and easily and she knew that his torment was gone, for the time being at least, and he was again able to just enjoy the warmth of her body against his. She wanted so much to show him how special he was to her, and even though she was not sure it was the right thing to do at that moment, she lay on her back, rolled him on top of her and eased him into her, "Just lie still for a while sweetheart."

They lay inextricably linked together until she knew that the demons had finally left. He lifted himself up without leaving her, and looking straight into her eyes said, "I'm so lucky to have you. I love you so much."

The magic was broken by Grace's mother shouting up the stairs, "I've got breakfast here for you pair. Are you going to get up at all today? You'll have to soon if you're going to go to church."

Frank did not move as he replied, "We're just getting dressed Mrs Richards. Just leave it on the table we'll be down in a minute."

"The table's still outside love. I'll put it on the hearth for you."

They waited silently, trying to hold back their laughter, until they heard the back door shut, and then, the moment of intimacy totally gone, both burst into guffaws of laughter.

"I told you, you should have locked the back door," said Grace easing herself away from her husband, giving him another hug and then taking his face in her hands, kissed the last remnants of moisture from his eyes.

"Well I'll lock it from now on, I assure you. We can't have your mother, or anyone else for that matter, spoiling our married life; can we?" and with that he pushed his hips against hers before rising out of the bed.

"I suppose we'd better eat that breakfast your mother has cooked for us, before it gets cold."

He reached for his trousers and pulled them on. Grace started to get out bed. "No, you stop there, Mrs Matthews. I'll bring the breakfast up and we can eat it in bed." He reached in his pocket and found his house keys. "And if your Ma's not about I'll lock the door, before they get any ideas about bringing all the furniture back into the house."

"You can't lock the door now. Ma knows it's open. What'll she think if she suddenly finds it locked?"

"Probably that this is our house, and she'll be welcome when she's invited but not otherwise. Now stay there and I'll get the food and then we can have a look in the box."

Grace reached across and picked up the under-slip she had taken off the night before and started to put it over her head. As he went past her Frank gently took it from her, "I like you as you are. Plenty of time to put that on after we've eaten."

Mrs Richards had cooked them a full breakfast; eggs, bacon, sausages, mushrooms, black pudding, tomatoes, fried bread and toast, together with a large pot of steaming hot tea.

"I hope you won't expect this every Sunday morning Mr Matthews? Because if you do you're going to be disappointed. Maybe egg and bacon or egg and sausage, but not this lot."

Frank ignored her comment and he eagerly ate all the food on his plate whilst rereading the letter from Evie. He put his empty plate on the floor, poured himself another cup of tea, and placing the letter on the bedspread, turned to Grace and said, "I'm sorry about earlier sweetheart. Just the reminder of all that death and all of my friends dying was just too much for me. It won't happen again I promise."

Grace put down her knife and fork and took hold of his hand, "Oh yes it will. I don't want you to hold it back any more now that we can be on our own," she laughed as she added, "And after we've locked the door to keep everyone else out you can talk to me about all the horrible things you had to endure. You don't have to keep it all to yourself anymore." She looked beseechingly into his eyes, "We can share it, can't we?"

He nodded his head and without saying a word reached over, picked up the box and took the lid off it.

Grace went back to eating her meal slowly. She realised that talking about Frank's war experiences was a matter about which she would have to deal with very carefully if she was to help him without antagonising him and she remained silent as she watched him inspect the items in the box.

The first thing he took out of it was a pile of letters tied together with a piece of string. They were the letters which Grace and his mother had sent to him during the war. He contemplated re-reading some of them but thought that this was probably not the time or place to do so. Maybe they would read them together one winter's evening when it was cold and damp outside and they were sitting enjoying the warmth from the parlour fire?

He placed them on the bed on top of Evie's letter.

Next he took out his identity tags, the St. Christopher and three-penny piece still lying next to them. He held the three-penny piece for Grace to see, "Do you remember giving this to me? I wore it all the time to keep me safe." He laughed as he added, "Even if I did forget who I was without it."

She put her plate down on the floor and put her arms in his, "There was a time when I dreaded that these would be the only part of you I might get back. I'm pleased that they've been returned safely but I'm so glad I got you back first."

She held on to his arm as he delved back into the box. He took out his leather wallet, extracted the money from inside it and laid it out on the bed in front of Grace, note by note. He placed two pound notes, three ten shilling notes, and then placed several different denomination French franc notes beside them. He then put his hand back inside the wallet and took out four pieces of white paper, which had been folded into small packets. After unfolding the first piece of paper he took hold of Grace's hand and placed the five-pound note into it. He unfolded the other three pieces of paper and gave her the three further five-pound notes adding, "I was keeping these for our wedding, my sweet. So I guess they're really yours to spend now."

Grace, who had never held even one five-pound note in her hand before, let alone four, held each one in front of her in turn. She studied every facet of them, turning each one over carefully and holding each up to the sunlight streaming through the window.

"Where on earth did you get this much money from, Frank; you didn't steal it did you?"

Frank went into himself as he thought about how he had come by most of the money. He couldn't admit to Grace that he'd won much of it (including the five-pound notes) when the Captain had taken him with him to a card game with a group of officers. Officers who had more money than sense and who, by the end of the evening had been too drunk to care about how much they were losing. Frank had felt a little guilty the next morning about walking away with so much money and wanted to give it back, but Mark had just laughed and told him that that was the last thing he should do. "They actually expect to lose and you'd just embarrass them if you tried to return it to them. Gambling losses are a matter of honour to them, so don't even think about giving it back." He had given a chuckle and smiled at Frank as he continued, "Anyway you won it fairly and squarely. You didn't cheat, did you?"

Frank had shook his head and added indignantly, "Surely you know I wouldn't cheat, don't you?"

"Of course I do, Frank. I wasn't trying to suggest you were a cheat. I know you're not. I wouldn't have taken you to the game if I'd thought that. No I just meant that you'd won by playing a better game than they did. Look just put the money in your pocket and forget all about it. Just keep it and send it to that lovely girl you're going to marry."

Grace shook Frank to bring him out of his thoughtfulness, "Frank, are you all right? Did you hear me? I just asked where did you get all this money, but it doesn't matter if you can't remember."

Frank shook his head, "No it's OK sweetheart. I suppose I just managed to save it. Nothing to spend your money on out there, you see." He deliberately did not tell her how he had obtained it in the first place.

Grace knew that Frank could not possibly have saved all this money from his pay in addition to the money he had sent home. Just before Frank's mother had died she had given Frank his Post Office savings book that she had been keeping for him. Both Grace and Frank had been staggered to find that she had saved most of the money he had sent to her from his pay; especially the balance of £44.12s.6d shown in the book; money that was still sitting in the account.

In order to change the subject Frank picked up the French francs, "Don't know what we can do with these. Might be worth a few bob, but we can't spend them as they are can we?"

Grace took them from him, knowing that the question of where the other money had come from was now closed and she decided it was best not to raise the subject again. "Perhaps I can take them to one of the banks in town and see if they'll give us anything for them?"

Frank shrugged his shoulders, "I suppose you could, but I don't know if they'll serve the likes of us." He wanted to add some comment about how the 'bloody upper class' were given preferential treatment everywhere they went but thought better of it, and just stared into the wallet at the other items without taking any of them out, before placing it on the bed.

He went back to the box and took out a brown envelope. Reaching inside the envelope he took out two further envelopes from it. He held out the first towards Grace; a dirty pink envelope that had obviously been screwed up and straightened out. "I've had this for far too long. I ought to have done something about it on the last leave I had. Trouble was the leave was so short and I wanted to spend as much time as I could with you."

"Why what is it?"

"It's a letter that was sent to Lieutenant Groves by the girl he was engaged to. The thought that he was going to marry her was probably the only thing that kept the stupid bastard going. But you know what?" He waved the envelope furiously in the air, "This letter told him she was going to marry someone else. The silly bugger got drunk when he read it, went over the top and got himself killed. The daft half-witted bugger just got himself killed." He shook his head as he continued, "Absolutely pointless it was. Couldn't have done a better job if he'd shot himself in the head."

He put the envelope back in the brown envelope he had taken it from. "The girl only lives in Lichfield and at the time I promised myself that I'd visit her to give the letter back and make up some story about how he'd died a real hero's death. I just wanted to make her feel bad about what her letter had done to him. Seems a bit foolish now though don't it?"

"I don't know, perhaps you should let her have her letter back." She realised that Frank was still very angry about what had happened to the lieutenant and that this was one of the many demons still haunting him; demons that she wanted to help him overcome if she could.

"Whatever it was that happened and whatever caused it, maybe you should go to Lichfield sometime and just let her know he died bravely and give her back the letter. But don't pass the blame for his death on to her, even if it's true. I'm sure that if the lieutenant really loved her he wouldn't want her to feel guilty about his death. If she'd realised that he'd received her letter just before he died, she probably feels guilty enough anyway."

"Yes I suppose you're right. I'll just tell her what a great guy he was even though he was a pain in the neck most of the time."

He held up the other envelope. This time it was a plain white one. He looked at it puzzlingly, as if bewildered as to what might be in it.

He turned the envelope around in his hand, looking at it from all angles, but there was no writing or marks on it to give him any clues. Eventually, he took it in his left hand, lifted the flap with his right and took out the piece of paper that was in it.

He read the contents of the paper silently to himself.

"What is it Frank? What does it say?"

"Well you can read it if you like," and with that he handed her the letter. She read it slowly as Frank watched her without saying another word.

My dear Evie,

I am giving this letter to Sergeant Frank Matthews in case I don't get out of this hellhole alive and he does. You know he saved my life once and it may be stupid but whilst he is with me I actually feel quite safe so hopefully he won't need to use the letter.

You see, he and I have often talked recently about setting up some sort of business together when this lot is over. He's proving to be a great engineer with the wireless equipment. Can mend any of it can Frank. Knows how the things work and even has plans on how to improve them and make better ones. He even talks about using them in peacetime in people's homes to receive national news etc. I'm sure that he could build one that would do the job brilliantly and he's so enthusiastic that he has got me enthusiastic as well.

I've offered to lend him the money to get him started and I thought that maybe I could perhaps market the things for him.

Anyway, if I shouldn't survive this lot, everything I've got should come to you, and if he's not too proud to come and see you, then I'd like you to lend him the money I had promised him. Don't ask for any interest on it and if the business doesn't work for him don't ask him for any of it back either. He's a proud and honest chap who's also got his head screwed on straight and if my judgement of people stands for anything at all, then I'm sure he'll be successful and you'll be OK as a sleeping partner for him.

I hope for all our sakes that there'll be no need to use this letter, but you know as well as anyone the chances of two comrades both surviving this mess.

Please help him as much as he needs and bear in mind he'll probably need a lot more than he asks for

.

With all my love Mark

She folded up the letter and passed it back to Frank, "Why haven't you ever told me any of this, Frank? You've never said a word about setting up business for yourself. Do you think you could do it?"

"To be honest I haven't thought too much about it since I came back home. It's been more than I could do to get my life together without thinking about risky things like going into business for myself. Anyway this wireless business is all new, and nobody really knows where it will lead." He had a big smile on his face, "I did enjoy messing about with it all though."

"What would it all entail, if you did try to make and sell these wirelesses?"

Frank started to talk enthusiastically about the matter, eventually confessing, "Actually, it isn't true that I haven't thought anymore about it." He looked rather sheepish as he continued, "I've already written to the General Electric Company, Marconi's Wireless Telegraph and others and I've got loads of technical details from them. I've also just heard from a Dutchman I met in France. His brother works at Phillips and he tells me that Phillips started manufacturing valves last year and he sent me details of them. They'll make all the difference to wireless manufacture. If I could be in at the start then maybe I could make a success."

She noted that as he said all of this, he had a glint in his eye, such as she had not seen since his last leave. He had been so quiet and introvert when he first came back home with Alice. He had refused to go back to work at Harpers, giving no reason for this but just said that he didn't want to.

When Grace had started to question why, Frank's mother quietly suggested she let it drop, and so Grace had never really questioned his actions after that.

Frank had taken work in the foundry where Grace's father worked, but she knew he hated it. She had never understood the diagrams he drew from time to time. He just told her that they were electrical things he'd learnt about during the war. She now realised they were plans for wireless equipment, thus confirming how untrue it was when he said he hadn't thought much about it.

She decided that she had worried far too long about Frank's bouts of depression and at last saw a possible way to bring back the old positive and strong-minded Frank who had left to go to war. She was determined to help him and decided to encourage him over the next few days to talk about this interest and revitalise him back to his old self.

"Could you get some of these valves?"

"Possibly, but the best way would be to go to Holland, see Hans Van Beek, that's the Dutchman I mentioned, and get all the information on the valves and then try to design a really up to date wireless."

She waved the five-pound notes in the air, "Well that's how we'll spend this. On a trip to Holland. You can take me on a belated honeymoon when we get our annual holiday week in August."

She started to collect together all the items from the bed and put them back in the box. Before Frank could object or interrupt she said, "We'll talk about it again later, but for now we'd better get up before mother comes back from church and starts banging on the closed door."

CHAPTER EIGHT

AUTUMN 1919

Frank, wearing his best wedding suit, mounted the two steps up to the front door of 'Rosemount' in Bird Street, Lichfield and pulled on the bell chain. He felt in his pocket to make sure he still had the pink envelope containing Henrietta's letter and waited to find out whether she had married her Captain or whether she still lived at this address.

Over the months since their wedding he had gradually told Grace some of his war experiences and she had realised that the only way he would rid himself of the nightmares was to take positive action; whatever that may be.

In the case of the anger he felt about the death of Lieutenant Groves she had come to realise that talking to the girl herself was probably the only way for Frank to clear his head about it all. Frank had agreed that showing his anger to Henrietta would serve no purpose at all and they had rehearsed together what he was going to say.

The door was opened by a young maid wearing a white pinafore over a black dress, and hands covered in flour. "Yes what can I do for you, Sir?" she asked as she wiped her hands on the tea towel she was holding.

Frank started to speak the lines he had so carefully rehearsed with Grace, "Does Henrietta still live here? I'm sorry I don't know her surname."

The girl looked flustered. She had never seen this man before and she was unsure how she should answer his question. The Major was quite strict about checking out visitors before letting them into the house, but she was saved from making a decision as the Major and the Colonel came walking down the stairs and into the hallway. They were both in uniform and they both stopped as they reached the maid.

The Major took his gloves from his belt and starting to pull them on. "Betty, when Mrs Radburn returns will you please tell her that the Colonel and I will be back for lunch at around one o-clock." He looked at Frank on the doorstep and then back at Betty, "Is everything all right, Betty?"

"Yes Sir, thank you," but Betty realised that was the wrong answer. "Well no Sir, not really, this gentleman was asking after Mrs Radburn, Sir."

The Major looked directly at Frank and eyed him up and down, "Can I help you? What did you want my wife for?"

None of Frank's preparations with Grace had covered this particular situation. He had expected to meet Henrietta's mother at this address and, expecting that the father would be at work at this time of day, just have a gentle chat with her. He and Grace had decided that Frank would not mention the letter and allow them all to think that he had died without receiving it. He would say that he'd been with Lieutenant Groves when he died ensuring that he embellished the circumstances of the death to make the lieutenant look the hero, and not the fool who had virtually invited his own suicidal death.

They also decided that Frank would say the lieutenant had spoken of how he was to marry Henrietta and had died with Henrietta's name on his lips; a slight distortion of the truth! Frank was certain that Henrietta's mother would pass on all he said to her and he would have discharged his obligation to tell how Lieutenant Groves had died a 'hero'.

Meeting the husband had never come into their role play and Frank did not know how to deal with his present predicament, but then remembered they had decided to pretend the letter had not been received and so he said, "I'm sorry Sir, I was looking for a Henrietta who was engaged to Lieutenant Groves and who I understood lived at this address."

The Major looked a little uneasy and shifted on his feet, "Right Betty, you can run along now. I'll deal with this."

Betty gave a courtesy and a "Thank you Sir," as she hurried back to the kitchen.

Frank could now see the Colonel, who had been standing a few feet behind the Major quite clearly, and felt that there was something familiar about his face, but his thoughts were interrupted by the Major's, "Yes, yes, my man. My wife was once engaged to Groves but what is that to you?"

Frank now wondered if he should go into the routine practised for the mother. Taking a deep breath he decided to do just that.

"Well Major, I was in the same regiment as Lieutenant Groves and I was there when he died."

The Colonel, who had not said a word up to this moment suddenly stepped forward and studied every inch of Frank's face, "It's Frank, isn't it? Frank mmm," he snapped his fingers and frowned as he struggled to remember the surname. "No don't tell me it'll come in a minute." He continued snapping his fingers, but suddenly the frown went and the clicking of the fingers stopped, "Frank Matthews, that's it. Frank Matthews. You were with Mark Harper weren't you?"

He reached forward and grabbed Frank's hand shaking it vigorously. "How are you Frank? How have you been keeping?"

Frank remembered the bubbly voice and mannerisms of Robby Fletcher as soon as he had started talking. "I'm fine thank you, Sir. Nice to see you again. Oh and congratulations on the promotion to Colonel, Sir."

The Colonel shrugged off the compliment, "Stay in this man's army long enough and we all get promoted. That's right isn't it Major?"

The Major looked a little uneasy with the comment and merely nodded his head.

"Are you still in the army, Frank?"

"No Sir. I was invalided out last year."

"Sorry to hear that. Nothing too serious I hope?"

"Badly burned back and a bang on the head. But no Sir. it isn't that bad and at least I'm still here. Not like a lot of the other lads. So I consider myself pretty lucky really."

The Colonel looked thoughtful at that remark, "Yes the ones who came out of it are pretty lucky. Have always considered myself damned lucky to have survived it all. How about you Roger?"

Robert Fletcher did not wait for an answer but turned to Frank and added, "We're just off to The Swan up the road for a drop of liquid refreshment before lunch. Would you care to join us Frank?"

Frank pursed his lips together and shook his head, "I don't think so, Colonel. You don't want me with you. I'm sure you have plenty to talk about without me."

"Yes we ought to go now Colonel if we are to get back for lunch. I'm sure Frank has plenty of other things to do," interjected the Major.

"Absolute nonsense, Roger. You haven't got anything to do right now, have you Frank?"

He did not wait for an answer but took hold of Frank's arm and led him down the steps and towards the Swan Hotel, quietly saying, "And no more of this Sir business, you're not in the army any more, so stop calling me Sir. The name's Robbie remember." The Major followed like a lost child.

"What's your poison, Frank?" the Colonel asked when they had arrived in the lounge bar of the Swan.

"A pint of bitter please, if that's OK."

"Sure that's OK, Frank. I think I'll join you." He turned to the Major who was still waiting behind them unsure what to do, "Two pints of bitter for us, Roger. We'll just go and sit at that corner table over there. Come on Frank, I want to hear what you've been doing with yourself."

The Major walked up to the bar to carry out the orders given him. He was not a beer drinker, thinking it an 'other rank's' drink and not a drink for officers; at least not senior officers. But maybe today he ought to drink it. He had so wanted to impress the Colonel and thought he had a wonderful chance to do so by having him stay at his home and not putting him up in barracks as the Colonel had suggested. He ordered three pints of bitter. "Who the hell is this Frank Matthews?" he muttered, "And why on earth is the Colonel being so friendly to him." He never did realise that the Colonel had been bored out of his mind by his small talk and all his sycophantic actions since he had arrived the previous evening, and the arrival of Frank, whose company he had thoroughly enjoyed during his stay in hospital at Rouen with Frank and Mark Harper was a gift from heaven for him.

Frank however knew none of this and was as puzzled as the Major why the Colonel was giving him all this attention. They'd got on well together for the short time they had been in hospital and had had some laughs and Frank had been fascinated by his chatting about wireless for hours on end. But he was an officer and a friend of Mark Harper's and Frank had regarded himself as a mere bystander when the three had been together, and he would never have anticipated this sort of welcome from him.

They sat down at the corner table. "Let me see now," said the Colonel, "When we met you were with Mark Harper. How is Mark? Do you know?"

"Well yes Sir. I only learned quite recently that he'd been killed a week or so after I was injured. I liked Captain Harper a lot so I was really sad to hear he'd died."

The Colonel looked down pensively, "Yes so am I, this war has taken far too many. I only hope we can all learn from it." He looked up at Frank, "Mark was a good chap. We got on really well together at Oxford. As you said a lot of good chaps never came back. Such a waste. Such a waste."

They heard the Major order the drinks and say to the barman, "Just bring the drinks over to the table and I'll settle up with you before I leave."

The Colonel leaned over to Frank, speaking quietly so as not to be overheard, "What rank were you, Frank?"

"A sergeant, Sir."

The Colonel continued to speak in a whisper, "Yes I thought so. Listen Frank, I want you to stop calling me Sir all the time and certainly not whilst the Major is with us. And don't let him know your rank. It won't do any harm if he thinks you were an officer, not for now anyway. Oh and don't give him any reason to feel superior to you. He's the sort of chap who would enjoy putting you down if he could."

Frank was puzzled by the request but decided that he had best do as Robbie suggested.

As the Major returned to the table and sat on the chair opposite the Colonel, the Colonel sat back and caught hold of Frank's arm, "You're not in the Army any more now Frank and I know I've been promoted since we last met but you can still refer to me by my Christian name and stop calling me Sir." He let go of Frank's arm and turned to the Major, "And this Frank, is Roger Radburn." He smiled to himself as he added, "Frank can call you Roger can't he Major?" knowing that this would rankle the Major. The Major just nodded his head as he busied himself passing round the beers, which the barman was placing on the table.

Robby Fletcher took a long drink from his glass winking at Frank as he put it down on the table, "Now Frank, tell us what you've been doing with yourself since you left the Army." He winked again as he picked up his glass to take another swig.

Frank remembered what the Colonel had whispered to him and took the winks to mean 'just embellish what you say as much as you like'. He decided to go along with the charade without actually lying.

"Well I've recently come back from Holland; went to see the people at the Phillips factory to talk to them about the new wireless valves they're now producing. I managed to get all the technical details from them and brought a box full back home. Have been playing about with them ever since. Unfortunately, like all amateurs I haven't yet managed to get a licence, and officially I shouldn't even be experimenting with these new parts, so you won't drop me in it will you? I've managed to send signals between the different sets I've made and I'm sure that when the Post Office starts issuing licences and I can erect my aerial, the equipment I've produced will work fine over much longer distances. What I plan to do eventually is go into business to produce equipment for other enthusiasts."

The Colonel nearly choked on his drink, but just managed to contain himself. He put down his glass and roared with laughter. Frank just looked at him in astonishment. What had he said that was so funny?

The Colonel continued laughing as he slapped Frank on the back, "What a coincidence. Isn't that a coincidence Major?"

"Yes Sir. Quite a coincidence Sir," replied the Major.

The Colonel just continued laughing and Frank had to start to laugh with him, without understanding the joke or why it was a coincidence.

The Colonel picked up his drink and this time drained the glass before passing it over to the Major, "We'll have another one of these all round, Major. Just do the honours again will you old chap?"

The Major had only taken a sip from his own glass and Frank's glass was still half full. "Another one for you Frank?" he asked, but the Colonel did not give him time to reply. "Of course he wants another one." He caught the arm of the barman who was now serving the people at the next table. "When you've got a moment can we have the same again please, Barman?"

He shook his head from side to side, "You cannot imagine what a coincidence meeting you here and now is Frank. Do you know why I'm here today seeing the Major? No of course you don't!"

He turned to the Major and looked at his watch, "Twenty past twelve. Forty minutes before lunch. Just not enough time." He continued to study his watch as he realised that with Frank here it was an ideal opportunity to get out of having lunch with Henrietta and Roger Radburn, but knew that if it was a choice between having an extra guest rather than having no guest at all, the Major would probably invite Frank to lunch as well. He would have to choose his words carefully, as the last thing he wanted was to expose Frank to lunch with the boring Radburns.

He turned to Major Radburn, "Roger, I think it would be very useful if we included Frank here in our discussions don't you?" He continued without waiting for an answer, "And we don't want to bore your good lady with all our army talk, so why don't you just run along and let, what was her name, Betty wasn't it? That's right Betty. You just run along and tell Betty to let your good wife know that we've been joined by other parties to our discussions and we'll be staying here for lunch." He waved his hand at the Major whilst he said this, "Give dear Henrietta my sincerest apologies for messing her about like this, but I'm sure she appreciates by now that these things happen in army life." He put his hand to his mouth and thought a little, "Yes give her my apologies and tell her to let my man have my things at three o'clock when he calls to collect me. My bag is already packed."

The Major got up and Frank had to smile to himself at the way the Colonel was so dismissive of him. The Colonel called him back as he reached the door, "Major, would you be good enough to ask your good wife to tell my driver to come and pick me up from here after she's given him my bag? I'm sure the kitchen here will be able to rustle up a plate of cold meats for us and we'll be able to keep chatting about business whilst we eat it. Be able to sort everything out before my three o'clock deadline that way."

He dismissed the Major once again and turned to Frank, "That'll suit you, won't it Frank?"

Frank, who did not know what the hell was going on, just nodded his head.

After the Major had gone, Colonel Fletcher took a long drink from his freshly delivered beer, “He’s such a prat, Frank; one of the many officers who got their commissions through the 'old boy's' network and family connections. I suppose he’s not as bad as some I’ve met, but I wish he’d just have a realistic conversation with me instead of trying to please me all the time. And his wife! God bless her but she’s even worse.”

He took several more swigs from his glass, “Not a bad drop of beer this Frank.” He put his glass down and continued with his discourse on the Radburns. “Old family. Landed gentry. His grandfather was an Earl. The title has gone to his uncle now. Unfortunately for him, he’s the son of the old Earl’s youngest daughter. So he’s got all the breeding but none of the land, title or, and this is even worse, none of the money. Hence an army life was the only thing left.”

“Me now Frank, I’m second generation new money. That’s why I got on so well with Mark Harper at Oxford. He and I were both 'new money' you see, unlike most of the others who were of the Roger Radburn school. Except that Mark wasn’t second generation money, he was third generation money, his grandfather started the business. Nice chap, his grandfather, I met him once when he came to visit Mark at University. Mark thought a lot of his grandfather. Had a lot of respect for him and wanted to emulate him as much as he could. Didn’t have the same regard for his father though and couldn’t wait to get away from him.”

He finished his drink and signalled to the barman for a refill. “How about you Frank, do you want a refill?”

“No thanks, I’m fine with this one for the moment.” He looked into his glass for a moment and then looked at the Colonel, “I’m puzzled why you are telling me all this and why is my being here a coincidence?”

He stared at Frank quite hard and quite pointedly said, “I’ve told you that Mark had a high regard for his grandfather, well when we were in hospital he compared you to his grandfather. Said you had the same ability to grasp things and learn new things very quickly and easily and like his grandfather, you had a high level of integrity, honesty, tenacity and what was the other thing? Oh yes reliability. Praise indeed from someone like Mark, who like me, was one of life’s cynics when it comes to trusting other people. That’s why I remembered you, and why I’m telling you all this and why I’m going to include you in the discussions later.”

He leaned further forward, “Look Frank, I don’t want any of what I’m saying about Radburn, about Mark, or about you and especially about me ever repeated. I have to trust you on that and on the basis of Mark’s assessment of you, I’m pretty sure I can do just that. So I’m going to tell you a bit more about me, stuff that I'm by no means ashamed of, but I don't want it talked about in front of Radburn." He looked Frank directly in the eyes, and added, "Or anyone else for that matter. OK?"

"Sure. Whatever you say is safe with me, but I'm still bewildered about it all."

He nodded his head and smiled, "I know Frank, but all will be revealed in due course, I promise you."

The barman brought over the fresh drink, but this time the Colonel just let it sit on the table in front of him, "My father was a soldier. He was a sergeant who fought in the first Boer war and stayed out in the Transvaal when his tour of duty came to an end. He liked it out there and got involved in security for the mines and he soon realised that there was money to be made by arranging the import of equipment and other goods the miners and settlers needed. He set up a trading company and was quite successful in the import export business and then he met my mother, married her and came back home to run the business from here. I was born and we went back to South Africa several times in my childhood. My father always insisted on us travelling with him, until I was ten anyway. Up until that time I always had a personal tutor who travelled everywhere with us."

"He was, is, a great father. Always had time for me. He is also a great judge of character and has always reckoned that that, more than anything else, is the secret to his success. Every time we went out to South Africa he would take out the new managers he had personally picked and trained in the business back here, to open new depots and trading stores. He always paid them a good wage and a commission based on their business turnover on top of that. Made most of them quite rich men and in the process made himself a very, very rich man. He always said I could do and be anything I wanted to be with the right education and always made sure I got the very best available. He had very little formal schooling himself before he joined the army, but once in the army he read everything he could get his hands on and because of that can hold his own in any company."

He called the barman again, who came over quickly, tray in his hand and towel over his arm. He was a young lad of sixteen or seventeen, who was obviously new to the job and trying hard to do the right thing and please customers.

"Another drink, Sir?"

"Not at the moment thank you," replied the Colonel, "but we would like some food please."

"Lunch is being served in the restaurant, Sir. Shall I show you the way?"

"No thanks. I think we'd prefer to eat something here."

The lad looked a little flustered and not sure how to deal with the request. "Well I'm not sure that's possible, Sir. I'm sure you'd enjoy the meal in the restaurant, Sir."

"Tell me young man what's your name?"

Now the lad looked really concerned. Had he gone too far? Was this Army officer going to report him for bad service? "My name's Pardoe, Sir. Robert Pardoe, Sir."

"Robert, that's a very good name Robert. Well Robert, what does your mother call you, Bob, Rob, Robbie?"

"I'm called Bobby at home, Sir."

The Colonel reached into his pocket and took out a handful of coin. "Well Bobby, I want you to go into the kitchen and use all your persuasive skills to get the chef to let you have three plates of cold meat, together with a dish of salad, a dish of pickles, some nice fresh bread and a dish of dairy butter." He selected two half-crowns from the coins in his hand and put them into Robert's hand, "Now you just put that in your pocket and you can tell the chef that if we enjoy the meal there'll be five bob for him when we've finished."

Frank could not believe his generosity, and neither could Bobby whose eyes lit up as he put the money in his pocket. He put his finger to his brow with a, "Thank you Sir," and rushed away to the kitchen.

The Colonel ignored the gesture and continued the conversation, "Other than making sure I had a good education my father never tried to influence what I did. I always wanted to be a soldier though, so here I am."

"And now Frank, I suppose you're wondering what all this chatter is about. Well there are two reasons, and I have to admit that both of them are quite selfish. But they should be to your benefit as well; or at least I hope they will."

"The first and main reason for telling you my personal life story is that I would like very much to emulate my father, particularly his ability to chose the right man for the job and reward him handsomely to everyone's advantage. Meeting you has given me, or at least I hope it has given me, a real opportunity to do just that. How, will be the subject of our discussion when Major Radburn returns? The second reason is that I'd like you to understand what makes me tick. I hope you'll then be entirely honest with me and only make me promises later if you're convinced you can carry them out. I'm trusting you for no other reason than I have a gut feeling that you can deliver what I'm going to suggest."

Major Radburn came rushing back into the room. He nearly tripped over himself in his attempt to get back to his chair as quickly as possible to hear what was being said. But the Colonel merely cut off his conversation with Frank and turning to the Major continued without a distinguishable break in his flow of words with, "Everything all right with Mrs Radburn? I hope she wasn't too upset with my cancelling lunch at such short notice?"

He then turned to Frank and continued his discussion with him, ignoring the Major's breathless attempt to give an answer to the polite question asked of him about his wife and lunch. "By the end of the War many of the Generals had become impressed with the advantages of wireless communication. So much so, that I've been given the task of implementing a programme to not only unify the introduction of a workable and realistic wireless communication system across all regiments, but also to ensure the most up to date, flexible and reliable system. A pretty tall order as you can imagine."

The barman returned from the kitchen carrying a tray. He put the plate of bread and dish of butter from it on to the table, "The kitchen staff are just preparing the meat and other things for you, Sir. They'll be out with them in a few minutes. In the meantime would you like me to get you any drinks to have with your meal?"

"I'm fine for now, Bobby. How about you Frank? Anything for you Roger?"

Both Frank and the Major declined the offer and the Colonel thanked Bobby for sorting out the lunch before continuing the conversation. "And now that Roger has come back, Frank, I'll explain the real coincidence. I've been speaking to Roger this morning about the progress I'm making and the things I want him to do within the South Staffs Regiment to implement our strategy. But the interesting thing was that as we were coming out for this drink I was telling him how last week I was talking to these Electrical Engineering post-graduates at Birmingham University who are doing research into wireless communications. They've come up with some brilliant designs that I'd love to use, but they don't want to lose the uniqueness of their plans by getting one of the bigger established companies to build them. So they've been looking for someone to manufacture their equipment as an equal partner. That way they can share in the profits made from their work rather than just receive a one off payment."

Two waitresses came from the kitchen and placed three plates of cold meat, the pickles and knifes and forks on the table in front of the men, and with a petite courtesy left them to eat their meal.

The Colonel cut a piece of beef and started to eat, indicating that the others should also start eating by waving his fork at their plates. He swallowed the beef, "How about it then Frank? How do you fancy producing the equipment to their designs for the army's use?"

Frank could not believe the conversation, and wondered if he was dreaming. He knew that if it was for real, then this was an opportunity of a lifetime and a miracle he couldn't afford to let slip. So whilst his head was wrestling with all the problems he was letting himself in for and urging him to be cautious, he nevertheless jumped in feet first. "Yes, I'd love to be involved with them but what about licences?"

"Don't worry about that," the Colonel added as he took another mouthful of meat, "I'm sure we'll be able to get you the Post Master General's approval for work you'd be doing for the army." He chewed and swallowed the meat before continuing, "You'll need to arrange the necessary capital, premises and equipment pretty quickly though. Can you do that?"

This was 'make or break time' for Frank and he knew it. He either had to take the plunge now and hope he could sort out all the other problems later, or tell the truth that after the trip to Holland he had less than thirty pounds to his name and make a very embarrassed exit. But didn't he still have Mark Harper's letter? Didn't he merely have to see Mark's sister Evie and all would be arranged? His head was throbbing with the words, *'God I hope so,'* as he replied, "No problem at all, the money's sitting there just waiting for such an opening."

"Good, that's fine then. Now let's get down to talking about the production time-scales and delivery dates."

The Colonel reached into his briefcase and gave Frank a pencil and a pad of writing paper to make notes and for the next two hours Frank's head was in a total spin as both the Colonel and the Major gave Frank names, dates, quantities and other details of their requirements. As the conversation progressed Frank became convinced that he was agreeing to things that he could not possibly deliver, but he was in far too deeply by now and he just had to hope that the miracles would continue to happen. God knows how he could deliver on the entire shopping list in front of him otherwise!

As he sat on the bus home, Frank's head was throbbing with a headache the likes of which he had not had since he had woken up in hospital with no memories. He took out the notes he had made from his jacket pocket. The pink envelope containing Henrietta's letter fell on to the floor. He picked it up and held it in his left hand and his notes in the other. He looked at the two items for several minutes before deciding that it was too late now to do anything about the letter, so he returned it to his pocket; an episode to be forgotten. He started looking at the notes of the meeting that he had just left. The more he sat contemplating the scribbled notes, the more his heart and head pounded with anxiety. His concentration was broken when the conductor came to collect his fare; the action of paying it being sufficient to interrupt the daze he had been in, and he determined that worrying about the items would not solve anything. So he took a series of deep breaths, turned to a fresh sheet of paper and wrote *'ACTION LIST'* at the top and then started to list all the things he had to do over the next two days beneath it.

The first item on the list was *'Ask Grace's dad to let the factory know I'm not going back – make sure he gets me the money I'm owed.'*

He would have to withdraw the remaining money in the Post Office bit by bit to keep going until the money started to come in from the Army. After all he couldn't expect Evie to lend him money just to pay his own household bills, could he?

He thought about this carefully and wrote above his first item, *'Talk to Grace about post office money,'* and by the time he got off the bus to walk home his *'ACTION LIST'* covered four very full sheets of paper.

Frank was out of bed at six o'clock the next morning as usual. So many things had been going through his head all night that he had slept very little.

He had a lot to sort out before going to see Evelyn Harper. He first wanted to see if there were any vacant premises for rent that might be suitable to set up his workshop. The main problem was making sure that they had an electricity supply. Without it they would be no good. The other problem was that he had no real idea how large the premises should be, but if he could sort out two or three of different sizes, then at least he'd be able to put a minimum and maximum rental figure in the cost calculations he proposed to show to Evie. He and Grace had talked until after midnight the previous evening, discussing all the unbelievable happenings of the day, and working on his 'action list' and the financial calculations.

It was still not light outside and he shivered with the cold as he got out of bed. He pulled on his trousers and put on his thick sweater as quickly as he could before going downstairs, trying not to disturb Grace. He shivered again when he went outside and up the yard to the toilet. A blanket of autumn fog limited visibility to a few yards and Frank hoped it would soon clear. Once back inside he cleaned out the grate and lit a fresh fire, which was well ablaze when Grace, with a thick blanket swathed around her, came down the stairs half an hour later. Frank had made a pot of tea and they both sat drinking it with their hands wrapped around the mug to get them warm.

Once warm Frank took the fresh kettle of boiling water off the hob above the fire and went into the scullery to shave and wash. Grace followed him and put her arms around him as he shaved.

"Do you think it will work out all right sweetheart?"

Frank twisted round in her arms and, ignoring the shaving soap, which he had just lathered on to his face, kissed her before replying, "Everything will be fine. I think I've sorted out most of the problems." He laughed as he wiped the shaving soap from her chin adding, "At least I have in my head. All we need now is for everything to fall into place in the way we planned last night."

He wiped the last bit of shaving soap from her face, "Getting the money from Evie Harper is the essential bit. Once that's in place I'm sure I can sort out the rest." He gave her a quick kiss on the cheek and as he wiped the soap away, said, "I think I'd better finish this shave don't you? I need to look smart when I meet her."

"Oh, it's like that is it? I'd better keep my eye on you."

He smiled and kissed her again, "You have nothing to worry about, it's just that I need to impress her if I'm to get this money."

This time Grace wiped the shaving soap away herself. "Me thinks the man protests too much," she said as she picked up the kettle and pushing Frank away from the sink, filled it with water, before going back to the warmth of the parlour fire.

She placed the kettle on the hook hanging over the fire before sitting in the armchair. She drew her legs up beneath her and pulled the blanket tightly around her shoulders. She bit her lip as she pondered on all the thoughts going around in her head. For the very first time since Frank had become her 'boyfriend', she did not know how to discuss her worries with him. She had just missed her period for the second month and was now pretty certain she was pregnant. But how could she put the worry of an expected child in the way of Frank's dreams of starting this business? She now wished she had mentioned the first missed period to Frank, but she had decided to wait until she was a week late before telling him. The day before she was going to mention it her sister-in-law Mary had announced she was expecting and everyone had been so excited about it, that Grace had not wanted to spoil Mary's announcement and had decided to be more certain before she said anything to Frank. Now Frank had said he was giving up work and they would be short of money for a while. Would the news of a child change his mind about going into business? He had been so excited over everything that had happened the previous day. She could not spoil his dreams could she? Leaving it another few days wouldn't hurt and anyway her period could just be late and maybe in a few days she would not have anything to worry him about.

And then quite suddenly she started worrying about what might happen when Frank met Evelyn Harper again. Grace knew from the few times he'd mentioned her that he found her a very attractive woman. He had never said so specifically, but the warmth in his voice whenever he talked about her, made Grace realise that she was something special to him. She always felt some envy towards Evie Harper at such times, but had not been too bothered in the past as she knew it was unlikely that Frank would ever meet her again. But now he was not only about to meet her again but they could become business partners. Would this mean that they would be meeting on a regular basis? Good Lord, she hoped not! And then she shuddered as she suddenly had another, even worse, thought come into her head. What if Evie Harper fancied Frank? Maybe she was the sort of woman with money who would enjoy playing around with a working class man. She tried to push the thought out of her mind, but the more she tried the more the worry increased.

Frank came in from the scullery, freshly scrubbed and cleanly shaven. He positioned himself next to where Grace was sitting so that he could look into the mirror over the fireplace. Grace thought that he was inspecting his appearance too carefully as he stood combing his hair. The kettle started boiling and Grace took her legs from off the seat, leaned forward, took the kettle off its hook and placed it on the top of the fire's oven. "Shall I make you some breakfast? Do you fancy a couple of boiled eggs and some toast or something else?

"Just toast would be fine, I'm too nervous about this meeting to eat anything more than that." With that Frank turned from the mirror and went back upstairs to dress, leaving Grace to worry again about his meeting with Evie Harper.

She shook her head and told herself not to be so stupid. It was probably all this pregnancy business that was giving her these stupid thoughts. Frank would never try to enter into such a relationship, if for no other reason than he would not wish to be rejected. He was too proud a man to deliberately put himself in a position where someone could treat him as being of a lower social status. She knew how difficult meeting Evie Harper today and asking her to lend him money was for Frank. He was a very proud man with an aversion to owing money, and to become financially indebted to someone like Evie Harper was a very hard thing for Frank to do.

No she must stop these silly thoughts and look on the bright side. With a bit of luck and some hard work on the part of Frank, in twelve months time they could have started to be better off and there would be a bit of money to provide for the baby. After all she was only just pregnant, if at all, and it would be months before they needed money for the child. And as for Evie Harper, well worrying about her was just stuff and nonsense.

By the time Frank came down the stairs again dressed in his wedding suit, and wearing a new stiff white collar with the tie she had bought him last Christmas, she had toasted three slices of bread for him on the fork in front of the fire and had made a fresh pot of hot tea.

She walked up to him as he entered the room, "My you do look smart. You give me goose pimples all over when you dress up like this," and with that she hugged him tightly and gave him a long hard kiss fully on the lips.

"I'll have to dress in my best clothes more often if that's the effect it has on you," Frank said before he gave a long return kiss, after which he added, "I don't know how late it'll be when I get home tonight, sweetheart. I'm going to see Leonard Oakes and Russell Rhodes at Birmingham University this afternoon to talk about their wireless designs and what we'll need to manufacture it. That's assuming I get the money off Evie Harper. God I hope I do! I don't know what I'll do if I don't."

Frank had not contemplated that scenario before and shuddered at the thought, "What on earth will I do if I can't get the money to start the business?"

Grace hugged him tightly; suddenly feeling stronger knowing that Frank had worries too. "You will go and see your boffins in Birmingham and sort everything out, and then you'll come home and we'll have to have another think about where the money's going to come from. Banks lend money, don't they? Maybe we can borrow it from them."

"Good Lord, I've never been in a bank in my life. They wouldn't lend money to the likes of me."

"You've always said you're as good as anyone else, so stop worrying about it."

"You're right, I shouldn't worry unnecessarily and anyway when we've got the business going we'll have to have an account in one of the big banks, won't we?"

Without waiting for an answer he added, "I don't know how long I'll be with Oakes and Rhodes. I could be quite late. Will you be OK?"

She hugged him tight again, "You are a fusspot. I'll be fine. Anyway, Mary is meeting me out of work today and she's coming back here to spend an hour with me whilst Tom is at his football match, so I'll be able to have a good natter to her."

Grace let go her grip on Frank and suddenly felt much brighter. She knew she would be able to talk confidentially to Mary about her worries and hoped that by the time Frank returned she would have gotten her concerns about this Evie Harper out of her head.

Three hours later Frank stopped at the end of Mellish Road to catch his breath before going the next few yards to where Evie lived. He concluded that he should not have walked the mile or so from town at quite such a pace. He didn't want Evie to see him sweating like this. He took out his handkerchief and wiped the inside of his collar to remove the moisture from his neck, but as soon as he put the handkerchief back in his pocket, he felt the sweat returning. He leaned on the wall and decided to wait a little and as he did so, a removal van drove out from the Harper's house. Or at least he thought it had come from the Harper house.

He took out his handkerchief and once again wiped away the sweat from his neck. He brushed his hair into its parting with his hands and walked up to the Harper house.

Frank walked past the van parked in the drive and up to the open front door, just as two men were coming through the doorway carrying a large mahogany dining room table.

"Out of the way, mate. Can't stop with this now, we're half way through the door."

Frank retreated back down the steps as the burly men manoeuvred the solid table through the doorway and down the steps. A much smaller man dressed in a black suit with waistcoat and wearing a bowler hat followed them to the van, giving instructions all the way. Such a slight small man looked quite comical against the mass of the two heavy weights carrying the table. He reminded Frank of Charlie Chaplin in the film he had seen some months earlier and almost burst out with laughter at the memories of the antics of Charlie Chaplin, but just managed to hold back as Charlie shuffled round his men giving instructions on how to lift the table on to the van.

Frank re-ascended the steps and pulled the bell handgrip.

The men returned from the van and Frank stepped to one side to allow them to enter the house once more. The largest of the men stopped to speak to Frank, "Lucy's upstairs mate, she's packing the last of the mistress's things. I'll give 'er a shout for you." And with that he entered the house, stood at the bottom of the stairs and in a voice that seemed to make the whole house shake, shouted, "Lucy luv you're wanted. There's a gent 'ere wants to see somebody."

He turned back towards Frank, "That'll shift 'er mate. If she ain't here in a couple of minutes, I'd give 'er another shout if I were you." After which he followed his two comrades into one of the downstairs rooms.

Frank waited for several minutes without any sight of Lucy. He was just about to follow the bruiser's instructions and shout at the bottom of the stairs, when the maid appeared at the top of the stairs puffing and panting as she struggled with a leather trunk. Frank stepped into the house and shouted to her up the stairs, "Can I give you a hand with that?"

The maid looked startled and almost slipped. She managed to regain her composure as she looked at Frank in surprise, "Well I'll be blowed. It's Frank Matthews ain't it?"

"Yes, but how do you know my name? I hadn't told Miss Harper I was coming."

The maid brushed the front of her apron as she descended the stairs to get a closer look at Frank, "Don't you remember me Frank? I'm Lucy Evans. We were at school together."

Frank remembered the name, but somehow wasn't able to recognise this curvaceous and buxom young woman, as the awkward thirteen year old girl he had last seen at school. "Well you've grown somewhat since I last saw you Lucy."

Lucy smiled a grand beam of a smile and wiggled her shoulders and hips as she descended the last few steps. She moved to within a few inches of Frank, placed her hands on her hips and expanded her chest, "Grown for the better I hope Frank?"

It was just as well she didn't wait for an answer as Frank was becoming a little flustered by her closeness and familiarity. Instead she just let out a laugh, took hold of Frank's hand and led him up the stairs. Frank began to pull back but she turned round with the same beam of laughter in her eyes. "Don't worry Frank, I'm not going to eat you, but you did offer to give me a hand with this trunk and it's a bit too heavy for me on my own."

She let go of Frank's hand at the top of the stairs and stepping around the trunk, bent forward to grasp the handle, giving Frank a close view of her heaving breasts as she did so, "Right Frank, grab the other handle and let's get this trunk on the van."

As they carried the trunk down the stairs Frank began to wonder what had caused the change in this girl. This was certainly not the Lucy Evans he remembered. The Lucy he knew was a reserved girl who always went red in the face and struggled over her words whenever he spoke to her.

It was almost as if she read his mind, "Have I changed that much Frank? You're almost acting as if you don't know me."

"Well you must know how much you've changed since I last saw you. I remember you as a thin girl and I'm sorry to say this but I also remember you as quite a reserved and clumsy girl. And now! Well you don't strike me as being reserved."

"And I'm not thin and flat chested now either am I?"

By now Frank realised she was playing with him and decided to join in the fun, "Not in the least ma'am."

They almost dropped the trunk as they both burst out laughing, in the middle of which, Lucy managed to signal she wanted to put it down.

With the trunk safely deposited on the drive by the van, they both continued laughing, the intensity of which increased each time they looked at each other.

Tears were streaming down both of their faces when the removal men came out carrying a large mahogany dresser. They stopped laughing when they saw the men and Frank took out his handkerchief to wipe his eyes whilst Lucy lifted up her pinafore to wipe hers.

"Come on Frank, it's time I made these workers a cup of tea." She took hold of Frank's hand again and led him into the house. "You can come into the kitchen and give me a hand while you tell me what you're doing here."

As they went through the door one of the removal men shouted after them, "You dain't tell us your boyfriend was coming Lucy. A bit of all right he is. We don't mind waiting a bit for our tea, but don't be too long, you can do whatever it is with your boyfriend later."

The two heavyweights laughed at the joke but 'Charlie' shuffled up to them and said in a high squeaky voice, "Come on lads, we haven't got all day you know, and we certainly haven't got time to fool around."

"We're only having a joke Mr Jones. No harm in a little joke is there?"

"There is when it stops you working. Lift this dresser on to the van and let's get this job done."

Inside the kitchen Lucy looked at Frank, "Sorry about that Frank. You weren't too embarrassed by what they were saying were you? They've been like that with me all morning since the mistress went."

Frank was suddenly jolted back to the purpose of his visit by the mention of the mistress, "I take it that Miss Harper isn't here then?"

Lucy had filled the kettle and was lighting the gas stove with a match.

"No Frank, she left about an hour ago. Was it her you wanted to see then?"
"Yes it's pretty important that I see her today. What time will she be back? Perhaps I can call later."
Lucy sat on a chair at the kitchen table and signalled to Frank to sit at the chair opposite, "She's not coming back today, Frank. In fact she's not coming back at all."
Frank felt the panic rising in his chest, "What do you mean by she's not coming back at all? Where's she gone? Has she gone to the factory? Perhaps I can see her there?"
"The only place you're going to see her Frank, is up in Scotland. She's on her way to Edinburgh to get married. This house has been sold and she don't have anything to do with the business anymore. We're just packing everything up for her. She's paid me up to the end of the month and she's given me a bit extra to see me through till I've found another job, but we ain't going to see Miss Harper in Walsall again. She says there's no one left here for her to bother coming back to."
Frank put his head in his hands and muttered, "Oh my God, what am I going to do?"
Lucy reached across and took hold of his hand, "What's the matter Frank? What did you want to see her about?"
"Oh it's nothing and everything. Never mind I'll just have to sort it out some other way. If she's not here I better get on my way. No point staying if she's not coming back, is there?" With that Frank started to get up from his seat.
"You just stay where you are Frank Matthews. You're not getting away that easily. I want to know what it's all about."
She went to the boiling kettle, "I'll just make the tea and take it to the men out there and then we can sit here over a nice cup ourselves and you can tell me all about this 'nothing and everything'."
Lucy turned out to be a good listener and a very good counsellor. She told Frank enough about her own life since leaving school to put Frank at ease before enquiring further about his visit.
By the time they had finished their second cup of tea Frank had learned that she had married at eighteen and had spent three days with her soldier husband before he had been posted to France. He had only been in France ten days before being sent to the front line and he had been killed on his first day in the trenches. She even told Frank that she had been a virgin when she got married, but that in the three days she had spent in a hotel with her husband, she had learned to love the passionate side of marriage so much that she still ached for her husband every day. She added rather

quickly, as if to make sure that Frank did not get the wrong idea, "And I haven't been with another man since and I've got no plans in that direction either. I know I flirt a bit Frank and I'm sorry if I flirted a bit too much with you, but it's my way of coping with the hurt. You do see that, don't you?"

This time it was Frank's turn to take her hand, "Yes I think I do understand Lucy. He must have been a very special man?"

She looked up at Frank, tears again in her eyes, but this time they were tears of sorrow not tears of laughter, "Yes he was and I know he loved me as much as I loved him."

She took her hand from Frank's and wiped the tears away, "And now Mr Frank Matthews that's enough about me, let's hear about you."

By now Frank had warmed to her. She was so different to the girl he had known. But too many young women had had to grow up and had aged too quickly through the pain and madness of the war. He decided to tell her about his problems and in no time at all she knew all about his memory loss, his marriage to Grace, his business plans, his friendship with Mark Harper and the promise of financial help in setting up a business. He also told her about the letter from Evie and why he had come to the house to ask her for the loan that Mark had asked her to give him.

In between telling her all this he learned from Lucy that Evie was going to Edinburgh to marry a doctor she had met in the field hospital in France. He also learned that the doctor was the person who had managed to hold Evie together when she heard of the death of Mark. She had only recently brightened up as plans for the marriage were being made.

"Why don't you write to her in Scotland? I can let you have the doctor's address. She let me have it in case any letters came for her before I finish here at the end of the month."

"I'm not sure. Perhaps it's not such a good idea bringing up memories of Mark again with her. Maybe I can get some money from elsewhere."

"Well, the mistress was quite generous, she gave me twenty pounds. I could let you have that. Would it be enough?"

Frank got up from his seat and moved round the table to where Lucy was sitting. He leaned down and kissed her on the forehead. "Bless you Lucy. Thanks for the offer, but I wouldn't take your money. You'll need it. I'll just have to find some other way to raise the money."

She looked up at him, "It's all right Frank you can have the money if it'll help. Anyway I shouldn't have too much trouble getting another job. Miss Harper's given me a good reference and mentioned me to a couple of people from the church. She even said I could go to Scotland and be her maid up there, but I don't think I want to be a live in servant any more. There's more to life than that, ain't there?"

Frank put his hand on her shoulder and gave it a squeeze, "There certainly is Lucy, and you deserve a bit better luck than you've had over the last few years. Anyway I must be off now. Thanks for the tea."

He turned to go out of the house, but Lucy stood up and grabbed hold of his arm, "You know Frank I always fancied you at school and I never knew what to say when you spoke to me. I knew you didn't feel the same way about me though. I'm glad you're married and happy with your Grace. It's nice to know things can work out for some people." She shook her shoulders and her blond hair, which was pulled into a bun on top of her head bounced about. She noticed the look of apprehension again in Frank's face. She gave a little laugh again, "Don't worry Frank. I got over you years ago and what I said about being glad for you, well that's exactly what I mean. It's not jealousy or anything as stupid as that."

She smiled and touched his cheek, "It's been grand seeing you again Frank and I hope everything sorts itself out for you. Maybe we'll meet again somewhere. It'd be nice to meet your Grace again. It must be three or four years since I last saw her in town. Yes it must be four years. It was just before I married my Kenny. Actually you might remember him, Ken Evans, he was two years above us at school. No relative at all, but being an Evans my name's still the same. I'm still Lucy Evans. Married or not."

She suddenly stopped talking before the emotion took over again, rushed towards the door and did not speak again until they reached the front steps. "If you're after any good workers when you set up your factory Frank, you won't forget about me will you? You can always contact me through my mother. She still lives in the same house on Green Lane."

"I'll bear that in mind, Lucy. I'll mention to Grace that we met. See you sometime and thanks for the tea and chat." He gave her a little wave and walked up the drive without glancing in the direction of the workmen who he sensed were staring at him.

It was almost midnight when Frank arrived home. Grace had been getting increasingly concerned about his whereabouts for the last two hours. He had said he might be late but she did not think he meant quite this late. She had been looking out of the window more and more often since about eight o'clock, but she could not settle and had been standing permanently staring out of the window for the last hour.

As soon as she saw Frank turn into the back yard she raced to the back door, flung it open, and threw her arms around him. She wanted to shout

out, 'where on earth have you been?' but thought better of it and just gave him a kiss. She could smell the beer on his breath.

Frank kissed her back and slowly led her to the fire in the parlour. The fire had almost gone out, so he bent over and put another couple of pieces of coal on to it.

Grace could not contain herself any longer, "Well. How did you get on?"

"Just make a cup of tea and then we can sit down and I'll tell you everything that's happened today."

"Yes all right, but you did manage to sort everything out didn't you?"

"Well, yes and no. We'll talk about it when you've made the tea."

Grace did not recognise the melancholic man in front of her as the same bouncy, confident man who had left that morning. She looked deeply into his eyes as if trying to read his mind, "You didn't get any money from Miss Harper did you?"

Frank's head jolted back in surprise, "How did you know that?"

Grace saw the total chagrin in his eyes and wanted to comfort him as one would a child. "I didn't, but I was hoping in a way that you hadn't."

"Why on earth were you hoping that? All this afternoon's plans are for nothing if we can't get the money to start the business."

She kissed him, her anxiety of the last few hours starting to ease, "I've been busy myself today and I think we can sort it all out. So just sit down and I'll make that tea."

She went into the scullery to refill the kettle, and as she did so she shouted to Frank, "You didn't tell Rhodes and Oakes that you hadn't got the money did you?"

"No. Funnily enough, the subject never came up, so I just didn't mention it. I guess they just assumed that everything was in place, or maybe they just assumed I had money of my own. Why do you ask that anyway?"

She walked back in with the kettle and placed it over the fire. She poked the new coals with the poker to create more flames and heat, "Oh, no real reason. Now tell me about your day."

Frank started at the end and told Grace how he had spent the afternoon with Lenny and Russell, "That's Leonard Oakes and Russell Rhodes. They're nice chaps, I think you'll like them. Bit older than us. I'd say they're thirty'ish. Went back to University to do what they call their doctorate after doing their stint over in France, and that's how they came to work together on these wireless experiments."

"Do you think they liked you?"

"I think so. It was a bit awkward at first. I think they were testing me out, but when they realised that I understood most of what they were talking about, it got much easier. After a while they seemed almost pleased to be able to explain and teach me some of the bits I didn't understand straight away. They insisted that I go to the pub with them to continue the conversation whilst we grabbed a bite to eat. That's why I am late. Sorry about that."

Grace deliberately did not reply to the comment about being late but asked what had happened about Evelyn Harper and the money.

Frank then went into a great rigmarole about the removal men and Lucy Evans; even remembering to mention that Lucy had asked to be remembered to Grace, without once mentioning Evie or anything about her.

By now Grace was becoming quite annoyed with what seemed to be his avoidance of the issue of money and Evie Harper, "Are you going to get to the subject of the money or not? Wouldn't she lend you the money?"

Frank looked at her sheepishly and by the look on his face Grace knew he was finding it difficult to answer the question without considerable emotion. He bit his lip and shook his head slightly from side to side, "No, it's not that, she wasn't there. I'd just missed her. She's sold the Mellish Road house and had already left to go to Edinburgh to get married and she isn't coming back apparently. So I've no idea where we go from here."

His eyes brightened a little as he added, "Lucy gave me the Edinburgh address of the doctor Evie's marrying. I'll write to her, but it's not as easy as seeing her face to face."

Grace knelt on the floor in front of Frank and putting a hand each side of his face pulled his head toward her. She smiled when their faces where almost touching, "It's all right. Mary and me sorted it all out this evening. There's no need to go to Evie Harper. We can keep it in the family."

Frank snatched his head back, looking quizzical, "What on earth do you mean? How could you and Mary sort it out? You know how much money we need. Where are we going to get that sort of money and keep it in the family?"

Grace grinned as she took hold of Frank's face again. "Well it's my turn to tell you a story now." She gave him a quick kiss on the cheek. "Did you know that Mary had an uncle in Australia? Her dad's younger brother apparently. Well when Mary's grandfather died and the farm went to Mary's dad, Joseph, that's her uncle's name, went to farm in Australia. As toddlers Joe and Mary had played a lot with Uncle Joseph's two boys, who were a little older than Joe and Mary. Little Joe, Mary's brother, was named after his Uncle Joseph, and Uncle Joseph had always been very fond of both Mary and Joe. He always remembered their birthdays and

Christmas and Mary had written to her two cousins regularly."

"Both of Uncle Joseph's boys joined the Australian Army at the beginning of the war; much to the dismay of their mother and father. But they wanted to see a bit of the world and thought they might even get to see a bit of England again. It wasn't to be though; they were with the forces at Gallipoli, where they were both killed. Mary's Uncle received a telegram telling of the death of the younger brother on one day and then a telegram about the older brother's death three day's later. Their mother never got over the shock and died about twelve months later. Mary reckoned her Uncle never really got over the boy's deaths either, and then losing his wife had been too much to bear. He died about eighteen months ago leaving everything he had to Mary."

"Mary received about a hundred and twenty pounds a few months ago and thought that was everything her uncle had left her. They bought us the beer for the wedding out of that apparently. But then she had a letter the other day saying that the farm in Australia has now been sold and a banker's draft for the remainder from her uncle's estate was enclosed. She didn't tell me exactly how much it was for, but from the way the conversation went I guess it could be as much as a thousand pounds."

Frank let out a, "Good God, as much as that?" He took Grace's hands from his face and held them tightly in his lap, "But it doesn't really matter how much it is, we still can't ask Mary to lend us the money. I can't be grabbing like that, just because we know they've been left some money."

Grace lifted off her knees and sat on Frank's lap, snuggling up closely to him, "You don't have to ask her for the money. Seemingly, ever since they received it Tom has been saying how it's a golden opportunity for him to set up a business for himself. He made that bicycle trailer for that chap that went into the chimney sweeping business and he thought he might start making those and selling them, but Mary doesn't feel there'd be a big enough market for them, and says she'd really be much happier if Tom could go into a business with you, particularly one where you seem to already have some orders. She also said she trusted you. She thought you were much steadier than Tom and would control things much better than Tom might. Tom's a bit too over optimistic in his expectations and too easily led is how she put it. But you won't tell Tom she said that will you?"

Frank shook his head signifying that he wouldn't and Grace just continued talking, "Anyway the result of all our chat was that she asked me to see if you'd let her invest in your business and take Tom on as a partner. She said I could let her know after work tomorrow if you were interested.

So what do you think?"

"I think it's too much to take in for one day. I know it seems the perfect answer to everything, but we need to think about it before we commit ourselves. If Tom becomes a partner, he'll presumably want a share of the profits and since I've already agreed with Russell and Lenny that they'll be paid a commission on every wireless sold, anything Tom and Mary get paid will have to come out of our share."

He looked at the clock and lifted Grace from his lap, "Look it's nearly two o'clock and I'm whacked. I can't take any more of this in. Part of me thinks it's a wonderful idea and part of me is saying 'be careful'. Let's sleep on it. I'll give it all some thought tomorrow and then I'll meet you out of work and we'll go and see Tom and Mary together."

He started to lead Grace towards the stairs, "How was Mary anyway? Is she keeping all right with the baby?" He grinned and added, "Maybe we should follow suit."

"Funny you should say that," replied Grace.

Frank gave her a quizzical look, but Grace decided that she would break the news about her pregnancy when they were tucked up in bed.

CHAPTER NINE

1926

Lucy Evans ran up the stairs to the office at Richards and Matthews; her handbag and coat, which she dragged behind her, bumping on each step as she did so. She stopped in the small waiting room at the top, taking deep gasps of air to try and get her breath back after running all the way from home; her weariness made all the worse by the heat of the morning sun. She took the scarf from her coat pocket and wiped the sweat from her face, neck and shoulders before opening her handbag. She took out her powder compact and dabbed powder on to her face, making sure that she put plenty on her cheek just below her left eye. She returned the compact to her bag, took another deep breath, pushed open the door and entered.

Frank was sitting at his desk at the far end of the office, studying the papers spread out in front of him and did not look up as she entered the room. The large office was in the top floor attic space of the factory premises in Hospital Street. The only daylight in the room was from two small garret windows in one side of the roof. Electric light bulbs hanging from the ceiling in several places enhanced the otherwise poor light. Although the sloping roof on two sides and the separately constructed waiting room at the top of the stairs made the office look much smaller than the factory workshops on the three floors below, it was nevertheless large enough to contain five desks, and a number of filing cabinets. Two of the desks were pushed against the sloping wall giving the minimum of daylight to people working at them, but electric wires led from the dual bulb sockets in the ceiling and a separate light bulb hung over each desk from the wires. The walls had been painted white a long time ago and now were mostly a dirty grey. A small well-worn green rug covered the centre of the floor and a calendar was pinned on the end wall. These, plus a couple of electric fires which were used in the colder weather, were the only signs of any comfort in the room. The one luxury, as Tom called it, was the telephone sitting on Lucy's desk with an extension on the side table between Frank's and Tom's desks. Frank had insisted on the need for a telephone when they first started the business and Tom had only recently agreed that it had proved useful.

Richards and Matthews initial workshop had quickly become too small and they had moved into these larger premises the previous year, allowing space to separate the office functions from the factory floor. However, Frank had deliberately decided that he would not fall into the trap of having any signs of luxury in the office which might create a barrier between him and the other workers. He remembered only too well the opulence of Vernon Harper's office, and how he felt that such extravagance had immediately created a barrier between him and his workers. He did not want to make the same mistake, but had perhaps taken the 'I'm only one of the workers' approach a little too far. Tom had said that at least they ought to put a fresh coat of paint on the walls. Frank agreed but they hadn't yet got round to doing it.

Lucy relaxed a little when she noticed that Tom's chair was empty. He was probably in the workshop where he spent most of his time. She pondered whether she should just sit at her desk and get on with her work but decided against it and walked across the room to where Frank was sitting, throwing her coat and handbag on to her desk as she did so.

Frank did not look up until she started speaking, "I'm sorry I'm late Frank. I had to sort out a bit of a problem at home. I'll work through my lunch break to make up the time, if that's OK?"

Frank looked up for the first time, "What on earth have you done to your face?" He got up from his chair and walked around his desk to where Lucy was standing and gently touched the swelling on the left side of her face.

"How on earth did you do that?"

"Oh I banged it against a door just before I came out. It's nothing really, it'll be OK by tomorrow."

Frank placed his hands on Lucy's upper arm to look at the swelling more closely. She flinched and let out a small cry of pain as he did so. He immediately moved his hands away, "He's been hitting you again, hasn't he? What reason did he give for hitting you this time then?"

Frank did not wait for an answer; he knew only too well that none would be given. "What other damage has he done to you besides your face and your arms? Where else has he hit you?"

"Nowhere Frank, you've got it all wrong. I've told you, it's all my fault. I just banged myself against the door."

Frank shook his head from side to side and struggled hard to contain the anger within him, "For God's sake Lucy. How long are you going to let him keep doing this to you? You've got to get rid of him or he'll kill you one of these days. Is he still at home because if he is I'm going to sort him out and I'll break his bloody neck for him?"

Tears were already running down Lucy's cheeks, "Please don't do that Frank. Please don't." The uncontrollable tears were now flooding down her cheeks and her shoulders were shaking as she sobbed, "It's OK really Frank. It's not his fault. It's all my fault. I shouldn't do things to make him so mad. I don't want you interfering. I deserve it, really I do."

"Lucy, Lucy, Lucy. What are we going to do with you? It's me Frank you're talking to and you know I'm not that daft. It's perfectly obvious what's going on. Doors don't swing out with a right hook and for God's sake stop saying it's your own fault. Nobody deserves what he does to you."

Not wanting to touch her bruised arm again he took her hand and led her to her chair and told her to sit down, before taking the chair from the nearby desk and sitting next to her, "When I met you at the Harper's house and when you came to work for me, you were such a positive person even after the pain of losing Kenny. I know you missed him, but this bloke's not really a substitute for Ken, is he?"

She wiped the tears from her cheeks, but they kept coming, and although she was calmer now, there was still a quiver in her voice as she spoke, "I thought he was when I first met him. He reminded me so much of Ken, so loving and caring."

Frank got up from his chair, "Now just stay there and take it easy. Tom's gone out, so I'm just going downstairs to make us a cup of tea and when I come back we'll have a good chat about this and see if we can't sort you out."

Frank went down to the ground floor to the small kitchen and made some tea. He did not know what to do about Lucy. After leaving the Harper household, she had used the money Evie had given her to pay for lessons in both typewriting and bookkeeping and when she joined Richards and Matthews five years ago, this had enabled her to quickly become an indispensable assistant in the office. Her bright and breezy temperament had been a joy to have around, and when she first met Walter Nelson about eighteen months ago, she also began to have a glint in her eye that Frank hadn't noticed there previously. Within a couple of months this Nelson guy had moved in with Lucy.

Lucy had wanted to get married rather than 'live in sin' as her mother put it, but this, or even the pretence of it, was impossible, as everyone knew that Walter had a wife and two small children, who had been abandoned and left with his wife's mother in Cannock.

Frank had noticed a change in Lucy almost as soon as they had started to live together. She was not her usual light-hearted and cheeky self and over a very short period of time she became more and more withdrawn and her work began to suffer. And then about six months ago Frank accidentally brushed against her on the stairs and she let out a cry of pain. That was the first time she gave the excuse of some minor mishap at home. He started to become suspicious about ten days later when she arrived late for work limping on one leg and hardly able to write. Another unfortunate slip down the steps at home!

But this time, Frank could not let the matter go and tried to talk to her about it. She had, of course, flatly denied that it was any of Walter's doing, just as she had flatly denied it on every occasion since. Her work was suffering to the point where Tom, who for some reason seemed oblivious to the real cause, had proposed that they should seriously consider sacking her. Frank had merely indicated that she was going through a bad patch, and they should leave it a bit longer. Tom made some muttered comment about Frank having a 'soft spot' for her, but nevertheless would leave it for Frank to sort out. For his part, Frank felt he should keep to himself the real reason for Lucy's poor quality of work, but was finding this increasingly difficult as the mishaps were becoming more and more frequent.

He poured the tea into two cups, adding milk and sugar to both, and carried them back upstairs to where Lucy was still sitting, her head resting in her hands on the desktop.

As he entered he shouted across the office to her, "Here we are Lucy. Tea's up."

He sat on the chair next to her again and took her hand. He kissed the back of it lightly in a gesture that was more out of pity than for any other reason, but immediately wished he hadn't done it, when Lucy pulled his hand back to her and placed a warm, firm kiss on the back of his hand before holding it firmly against her undamaged cheek.

Frank wanted to pull his hand back and Lucy must have sensed this as she looked up at Frank and for the first time in weeks, she smiled.

"Don't worry Frank I know you care for me but I also know it's nothing more than friendship. I knew that when we were thirteen at school and it's never changed for you, has it? Your Grace is a very lucky girl and if I've hit on unhappy times, then it's my own fault and not your concern, is it? Don't worry I'll sort it out. He's not as bad as you think, he really isn't and he's always sorry and loving afterwards."

Frank was relieved that Lucy had finally admitted the truth that Walter had hit her, but even so he felt the anger welling up inside him, "For God's sake Lucy, you can't carry on like this. I know it's the least of your worries at the moment, but it's affecting your work and you've got to do something about it before we have to do something about your job."

Frank thought that mentioning the possible loss of her job might upset her, but clearly she was still living in her dream world believing that everything would be fine from now on, "It's all right Frank, Walter said he was sorry, and that it wouldn't happen again. I asked after his wife and kids and it just made him mad. Say's they're nothing to do with me and I shouldn't talk about them, so I'll just avoid that subject in the future and everything will be OK."

Frank was about to tell her yet again that it wasn't her fault and that she should get out of the relationship but he heard footsteps on the stairs and decided to leave it until the next time!

When Tom entered the office they were both drinking from their teacups.

"I could just do with one of those. Be a good girl, Lucy, and go make me a cup." With that he turned to Frank and handed one of the envelopes to him, "The postman handed these to me as I was coming in the factory. This one looks as if it's the new drawings and ideas from Lenny and Russell. You'd better have a look at the amendments they're suggesting. You'll understand it all better than me."

Lucy left the room to make the tea as Frank started to pore over the papers Tom had given him.

It was almost ten o'clock when Frank arrived home that evening, and when he entered the parlour Grace shouted to him from upstairs.

"Is that you Frank? Can you come up here; I'm worried about Kathy. She doesn't seem at all well."

Frank threw his jacket on to the fireside chair and ran up the stairs into the children's bedroom. Grace was sitting on the side of Kathy's bed wiping her brow with a wet cloth. Three year old Kathy was crying and shaking her head from side to side. Frank had always loved to see his wife shake her head like this, making her gorgeous long red hair sway and float in the air, particularly on a summers day when the sun shone through it, making it quiver and tremble like the autumn sun shining through the bronzed autumn foliage of the trees on a windy day. But now, Kathy's usually bright and shiny hair, so much like her mother's, was soaked with her sweat and stuck closely to her head and shoulders without the usual vibrant movement.

As Frank crossed to the bedside he saw that her radiant clear and bright brown eyes also inherited from her mother, were now bloodshot and swollen. Her usually divine face was puffed out with the pain and constant crying. When he reached his wife he could smell the stench of vomit on the bedclothes. "What's the matter with her? How long has she been like this?"

Grace got up from the bed and passed the damp cloth to Frank. "Where've you been 'til this time? I've been waiting for you to come home for hours?"

Frank started to answer but Grace cut him short, "It doesn't matter, you're here now. Just sit and try and comfort her a bit. She's been so hot for ages and she's been sick a couple of times. I think we'd better move her into our bedroom, we don't want Philip and John catching this, whatever it is."

She walked over to the bed which eighteen month old John shared with the eldest of their children, Philip, who was now almost six year's old. Neither John nor Philip had their mother's red hair. Both had their father's mousy coloured hair and blue eyes. John was fast asleep but Philip was sitting up in bed crying. Grace put her arm around him and told him to lie down and go to sleep. "But what's the matter with Kathy, Mummy? Why is she crying and being sick?"

Grace wiped the tears from Philip's cheeks, kissed him on the forehead and helped him to lie down, "She's poorly, sweetheart. Now you just be a good boy and go to sleep for Mummy and Daddy, then we'll be able to look after Kathy and make her better."

Philip sniffled and turned to hug his mother around her neck, "I'm frightened Mummy."

"Don't be silly, sweetheart. There's nothing to be frightened of."

He sniffled again, "I don't like it when Kathy's poorly."

"Just go to sleep sweetheart. She'll be all right."

Grace started to leave the room, "I'm going to see if I can find some clean sheets. We should then try and move her into our room for the night. In the meantime Frank, see if you can cool her down a bit and get her to sleep."

Suddenly Kathy bounced up off the pillow, taking deep breaths and heaving, and almost immediately vomited over Frank's shirt. She continued retching but did not seem to have anything else to discard.

Frank started to wipe the vomit off his shirt with the cloth, "Bloody hell what a mess!"

Frank's outburst frightened poor Kathy even more. She screamed and began crying. Philip sat up in bed and started snivelling again. Grace dashed back into the room, by which time little Johnny had been awoken by all the commotion and had also started yelling.

"What's the matter now? What's going on?" Grace cried as she rushed to where Kathy was sitting up in bed gasping for breath in between coughing. She snatched her from the bed and held her over her shoulder, gently rubbing her back in an attempt to ease the child's discomfort.

"My throat and head hurt Mummy. Make it go away Mummy."

By now Frank was at their side and gently rubbing the child's back in unison with Grace, "What should I do, love. Do you want me to fetch the doctor?"

"I think you'll have to soon if it doesn't get any easier. Look; go down stairs and get her a cool drink. I boiled a kettle ages ago. The water should be pretty cool by now. Just bring a glass of that. I shouldn't think it'll do any harm. You'd better bring a glass for the boys as well."

Frank started to go out of the room. "Oh and bring the aspirins, maybe one of those will help her."

It was almost two hours later by the time Grace and Frank had settled the children enough to start undressing ready for bed. The boys had got back to sleep quite quickly after Frank had moved Kathy's mattress out of the back bedroom and on to the floor of their own room. Kathy had taken much longer to settle but was now asleep on Frank and Grace's bed, although she was still breathing heavily and noisily.

Frank felt that after all the problems of getting her to sleep they should not disturb her any more, "Let Kathy stay where she is, she can sleep with you tonight. I'll sleep on this mattress here and I think we'd better get the doctor to call in the morning if she's still breathing like that."

Grace put on her nightdress, kissed Frank on the cheek and carefully climbed into bed next to Kathy, "I think you'd better call in at the doctor's in the morning Frank, and get him to come and look at her anyway."

Frank nodded his head in agreement as he slipped under the sheet covering the mattress on the floor.

At four o'clock, Frank was on his way to fetch the doctor. Kathy had slept for less than two hours and had awoken with a rasping dry cough, which produced no phlegm and just made her cry and distressed. Her temperature had risen again and she was complaining once more that her throat and head hurt. They gave her another half of an aspirin and a drink of cool water but this did nothing to settle her.

Frank knew that the doctor lived above his surgery in Littleton Street some half a mile or so away. He rode his bike to the surgery, a thing he had not done for almost two years. The tyres were much flatter than they should have been but he decided not to waste any time trying to pump them up at this time of night and anyway he was, by now, extremely worried about Kathy's illness.

When he arrived at the surgery he banged on the door but did not seem able to arouse the doctor. He banged even harder and after what seemed an inordinate and for Frank a totally unacceptable length of time, (but was only about two or three minutes), a light appeared in the surgery and someone shouted from the other side of the door, "What the hell do you want at this time of the night? Go away and let me get some sleep. Call again in the morning. Whatever it is you want, I'll sort it out then."

Frank's heart sank as he heard the footsteps moving away from the door and immediately started banging even harder than before, "For God's sake open the door, my little girl's really ill and we don't know what to do."

The doctor came back to the door, and Frank heard the bolts being pulled back. After a short while, the door opened and the doctor just looked at Frank. He was sipping something from a glass and was dressed in his nightgown with a large multicoloured crocheted woollen blanket pulled around his shoulders.

"What on earth's the matter?" but before waiting for an answer he added, "I had a rough evening last night and could do with going back to bed. I'm really not up to a house visit at the moment, so tell me what the problem is and we'll see if we can solve it without my coming out."

As he stepped forward Frank could smell the alcohol on the doctor's breath and realised that the 'rough evening last night' had nothing to do with attending patients. He was, by now, beginning to get very angry with the doctor's response, or lack of it, but knew that losing his temper would not get the doctor to visit, so he took the gentle and pleading approach. He explained the symptoms and the distress that Kathy was in. He considered exaggerating the symptoms but as he went through them, the headache; the throat pain; the vomiting; the fever and high temperature; the coughing and the difficulty in breathing, he realised there wasn't much he could add even if he were lying, so he just told it as it was.

"You say she managed to get a little sleep after you gave her the aspirin?"

Frank nodded his head.

"And your wife was giving her another aspirin when you left?"

Frank nodded his head again.

"Well I've no doubt your little girl will be asleep again when you get back. So tell me where you live and I'll pop out to see her in the morning."

He said "Goodnight" and started to shut the door but Frank stepped forward into the doorway to prevent it being closed. He was by now extremely angry with the doctor's casual attitude, but once again just about managed to keep composed.

"Look I know you were probably attending to deserving patients late into the night but I really would appreciate it if you could visit my little girl right away. I really do think that there's something seriously wrong with her."

Frank repeated all the symptoms again and refused to allow the doctor to go. The doctor continued to sip from his glass and whether it was the effect of the liquid in the glass or whether it was Frank's persuasiveness and persistency, eventually the doctor seemed to become more alert and started listening to the symptoms described by Frank.

"Well yes, that doesn't sound too good. Just go back home now and I'll get dressed and be with you as soon as I can."

Frank doubted the sincerity of the doctor's remark, thinking it might merely be a ruse to get rid of him. "I'll wait here for you if you don't mind and then I can show you the way."

For the first time since the doctor had opened the door Frank thought he recognised a slight look of compassion on the doctor's face, "Don't worry; I know where you live so I won't need your help to get there."

The doctor smiled and added, "I really will come as soon as I can. You go home and help your wife. I'm sure she needs you more than I do. I can find my own way to your house."

The doctor diagnosed diphtheria as soon as he had examined Kathy. He gave her some medicine from his case. This seemed to give Kathy a little comfort and for a while eased the coughing.

He scribbled out a prescription and handed it to Grace, "Get your husband to take this to the Chemists as soon as they open in the morning and give her two teaspoons every four hours. If she needs it you can give her just one extra single teaspoon full about two hours after the first dose, but don't keep that up, else it'll do her more harm than good."

He locked his case and turned to leave the bedroom, "Let me see now. You have other children don't you?"

"Yes we've got two boys. Philip, he's six and John, he was born in October the year before last."

"Well I'll call to see Kathy again after surgery tomorrow morning." He took out his fob watch, opened it and looked at the time, "I'm not going to get much sleep before then am I?"

Frank, who could not believe that this gentle bedside manner was from the same man who had been so difficult a little earlier, shook his head and added, "I'm sorry I was such a pain earlier doctor, but I was so worried about her."

"And rightly so. She's not a well little girl and unfortunately may get worse before she gets better, but if you give her the medicine and follow my instructions, hopefully we've caught it in time."

He put his hand once again on Kathy's forehead and tutted. He pulled himself straight, "Right, I'll see you after surgery. I'll check out your boys at the same time, but in the meantime keep them as far away from Kathy as you can."

Frank went to the factory as soon as the doctor had finished checking out the children on his visit after surgery.

"I know these changes are what the military want," he said to Tom as soon as he entered the office, "but they're going to cost quite a bit more to produce than the existing model. I just hope we can get them to pay for them." He took off his coat and sat down at his desk, "We'd better get on to pricing the changes straight away and then I'll arrange to see Robby Fletcher as soon as I can and try and get him to accept an increase in price. How do you think we should play it with them Tom?"

Frank had given no explanation as to why he had turned up at midday instead of his usual seven-thirty, and Tom did not therefore answer the question but asked his own, "Any problem this morning, Frank? Everything OK at home?"

"Kathy isn't well. Doctor say's she's got diphtheria and he thinks Johnny might have it as well, so it'd probably be as well if you keep Edward away from our house for a while. Don't want him catching it as well, do we?"

"OK, I'll tell Mary, but is there anything we can do for you? Do you want to go home? We can sort all this lot out another day."

The anxiety of the past twelve hours and his anger with the doctor in the night suddenly overwhelmed him, "No we can't bloody well leave this 'til another time. It's got to be done now, so let's get on with it."

Such a tirade was not in character for Frank, and Tom, taken aback with it, decided to ignore the comments and just do Frank's bidding.

"If we're going to make any bloody profit at all this year then we've got to get the military to cough up more money. I was hoping we could increase production on our home wireless sets soon. I'm sure that's where the money's going to be in the future, particularly now that the BBC's regularly broadcasting across the country. Believe me it won't be long before everyone's got a wireless set in their home and we really ought to be making and selling hundreds of them soon or we'll lose out to the other manufacturers."

The doctor came to check on Kathy again the following day but by then she was much worse and baby John was beginning to show early signs of the same illness. Within a week Kathy had died and although baby John survived the diphtheria, over time Grace noticed that he had difficulty in breathing and sleeping. When he was three years old the doctor admitted that the diphtheria had damaged his heart and he would probably never be a very fit boy.

Both Grace and Frank were distraught over the death of Kathy and neither of them ever fully recovered from the shock. Unfortunately however more distress was to follow before the year was out.

Frank had found it particularly difficult to cope with the death of Kathy. He did not like to admit that she was not only his favourite child, but she was the daughter he'd always wanted since marrying Grace and the fact that she was the image of her mother had enhanced his love for her.

When she started to walk and talk, he played with her for hours and was never happier than when she demanded a hug and kiss from him before going to sleep at night. He had always given the boys a hug and kissed them goodnight as well and whilst he loved them both dearly, it was not quite the same as the spontaneous affection his daughter gave him.

He immersed himself in work as the only analgesic which gave any sort of relief from the pain he felt. The doctor gave both him and Grace some pills to help them sleep, but they both quickly dispensed with them. They just seemed to increase the intensity of their nightmares whilst at the same time making their memories fuzzy.

Grace soon noticed that Frank was getting some relief from his pain by increasing his workload, and decided that perhaps she should find something to similarly occupy her time. Philip was now at school and Grace's mother offered to look after John until he started school. Grace had often helped Frank at the factory, particularly in the early days when he could not afford the wages for someone else and since then she had helped out at busy times, assisting Lucy with the month end and annual accounts.

After Kathy's death, occasionally helping Lucy like this did ease the constant hurt, but she needed something that demanded her full concentration if she was to find the same remission that Frank appeared to get by engrossing himself in work.

The idea came to her one evening when she and Frank were having supper after putting the children to bed. Frank continued to avoid the subject of Kathy's death and often talked about his work in the evening.

He had always told Grace how things were going at the factory, and she was always willing to listen, but these days, it wasn't to keep Grace involved in his life and work that he spoke about things that had gone on during the day, it was his means of keeping his mind concentrating on office problems, thus leaving less room for the loss of Kathy.

All throughout supper, Frank talked about the potential market in wireless sets for home use and how he'd designed and had made several attractive sets, housed in a polished oak, mahogany or beech veneered cabinets. He had brought one for Grace to see and she was amazed at how more impressive it was than the exposed valve and separate loud speaker model he'd built for their own use.

"I'm impressed Frank, that's a really nice piece of furniture."

Encouraged by her comment he took some papers from his briefcase and showed her drawings of several of the other cabinet designs.

"I've talked to Tom about going into production but he feels it's too risky, particularly now we've started to get a few orders for the Air Force and Navy as well. He thinks we shouldn't make stuff that may not sell, particularly as we don't have any means of sales and distribution for them."

Frank continued talking and changed the topic to some other work related matter, but Grace was only half listening to him, her mind was in overdrive thinking about what he had said.

She was distracted from her concentration when she heard Frank mention some problem involving her brother Tom and suddenly started listening to him again, "He's fine when things are going OK, but I still get nervous when we introduce design changes or different parts or anything that requires watching carefully over the workers whilst they're learning the new procedures. I went down there today, and God knows what mess we'd have been in if I hadn't stopped and checked on one of the first models made to the new design. They'd got the valves the wrong way round. It would have just blown up when it was switched on. Then when I checked further all the others were the same. Luckily they'd only made eight so far, so I was able to save a major catastrophe. It's a good job we test every one before we send them to the army, we could have lost our contract if these had gone out without being tested."

She had always known that Frank had been reluctant to go into partnership with Tom and would have preferred a sleeping partner to provide the capital to start up the business. Or better still someone, such as Evie Harper, to lend the money at interest, but have no other connection with the company. Things had been difficult for Frank at first, he'd wanted to make all the decisions himself without Tom's involvement, but eventually as the business grew, he and Tom had each been able to forge their own none conflicting roles. Tom almost naturally moved to the role of works manager looking after the production side, whilst Frank concentrated on design, distribution, component purchases and general administration.

Grace had always felt some responsibility for bringing Tom, with Mary's money, into the business, as it was her insistence that had prevented Frank from contacting Evelyn Harper in Edinburgh to borrow the money. She continued to mull over the things Frank had said, whilst still trying to keep some semblance of interest in his conversation which had now changed to some other topic.

She could not sleep that night, but the reason was not her normal preoccupation with Kathy, but were the thoughts going round in her head to do with the extension of the business Frank had talked about. She had an idea which could perhaps solve Frank's current problem, whilst at the same time giving her a real personal involvement and go a little way to salving her conscience over the money business.

After taking Philip to school the next morning, she asked her mother to look after Johnny and spent the rest of the day, putting her thoughts and plans on to paper and walking round town to find suitable premises. She surprised herself at the amount of preparation she was able to cram into the day before having to collect Philip from school.

She noticed another mother collecting a child from school holding on to the hand of a little girl about Kathy's age. Tears came to her eyes as she realised that she had not thought once about Kathy all day. Was this how it was for Frank? Maybe if her plans meant she would forget about Kathy then she'd rather forget them!

By the time she arrived home with Philip and had collected Johnny from her mother, she had thought long and hard about her plans. She realised that if she was to go ahead with them, she probably would be thinking about other things most of each day; things that were merely what people called 'getting on with your life', but she didn't want these things to mean that she forgot Kathy. Nevertheless, she decided that she would definitely put her ideas to Frank that evening, and start getting on with her life.

Within two months Frank and Grace had used the money they had saved from the profits to set up G & F Matthews. They purchased the lease on a shop in town and agreed a contract with Richards and Matthews to purchase home wireless sets to Frank's designs. After some initial doubts Tom had agreed that they would manufacture the wirelesses and sell them to Grace with the same profit margin as they had from the Army sales.

Grace had spent two weeks tidying up the shop, painting the walls, fitting curtains and generally getting it ready for business and in the evenings Frank taught her enough about wireless and wireless installation for her to knowledgeably sell the wireless sets to customers and at weekends he taught Harry Skidmore how to install frame aerials and the wireless sets into people's homes.

Harry, an ex soldier, had been almost buried alive when a shell exploded in the trenches where he was standing, and had often told Frank that he found the atmosphere at the foundry where he worked too claustrophobic. When Frank suggested the job to him he jumped at the chance to work outside at his own pace even though it would be for less money.

The shop proved a complete success. Initially Grace only opened from nine-thirty until three to fit in with taking Philip to school, but interest and sales were much higher than expected and she had to take on an assistant to help in the shop and another fitter to install the aerials. All of the sets sold ran off car batteries as most people still didn't have electricity in their homes, and soon Grace had a thriving trade providing a weekly battery recharging service, employing two schoolboys to collect and deliver the batteries in the evenings and weekends.

Both she and Frank still mourned the loss of Kathy as soon as they relaxed, but mostly they were so absorbed in their work that the pain was unbearable less often.

By November of that year, the hectic pace of sorting things out at the factory and the shop had settled into a more regular routine and Grace had even started to plan the family Christmas celebrations.

Frank had also started to find some time to work on a design for wireless sets powered from electric lighting circuits which he wanted to introduce the following year. He had found it difficult to sleep the previous night thinking about an improvement to them and so he got up early, trying not to disturb Grace as he did so, and arrived at the factory before seven o'clock.

He was surprised to find the light shining through the window over the office door and was even more surprised to find Lucy curled up asleep on the floor.

He bent over her still body, and noticed once again the telltale signs on her head of Walter's mistreatment of her. Lucy's work had certainly improved since his chat to her some months ago and although she never mentioned it, Frank had assumed that things with Walter had improved. He stepped around her deciding to let her sleep, at least until the other workers started to arrive.

He worked at his desk for the next half an hour, looking up to check on

Lucy from time to time. He heard women's voices chattering away on the floor below and knew that the first workers had clocked on for work. Time to wake Lucy before Tom came in.

He bent down and gently shook her shoulder, "Time to get up, Lucy love. Time to get ready for work."

She let out a scream as she bolted upright, a look of sheer horror on her face. The look vanished when she saw Frank's face and realised where she was.

"You'll have to get up off the floor now Lucy, Tom will soon be coming in and we don't want him jumping to any stupid conclusions if he comes and sees us both on the floor like this, do we?"

Lucy gave a weak smile and painfully lifted herself up. She stumbled and obviously found it difficult to stand. Frank held her arm and helped her to her seat.

He could now see more of the injuries she had sustained; both her lips were cut and bruised; her left eye was swollen and closed; a red gash on her forehead above it, and her hair was matted with blood from the wound. Frank guessed that both her arms had been damaged and from the way she held them across her chest, he realised she'd been punched in the ribs as well. And by the way she limped to her desk he also thought her left leg was injured. He could not hide his anger at Walter's treatment of her, "What on earth has Walter been doing to you this time?"

Lucy sensed the anger in Frank's voice and pulled back in her chair with fear on her face. Frank realised that her recent beating had made her tremulous of further hurt, "It's all right Lucy, I'm not going to hurt you. You're safe here. We'll look after you."

She seemed to relax at this but was still shaking and silent.

"How long have you been here Lucy, and how on earth did you get here in that state?"

At first, she spoke so quietly that Frank could hardly hear what she said. "Do you think you could get me a glass of water Frank, while I tidy up my face ready for work?" She reached for her handbag hanging on the back of the chair, but she obviously found the effort very painful.

Frank reached around her, took the handbag off the back of the chair and placed it on the table in front of her. He put his hand over the top of it to prevent her from opening it, "No Lucy, I don't think putting make-up on top of those wounds will do anything to hide them and anyway you need them seeing to. You're not going to do any work today, so just sit there a bit and I'll fetch you some water and find some excuse when I see Tom to stop him coming up to the office for an hour or so."

He put his hand gently on her shoulder, "You'll be all right for a bit won't you?"

She nodded her head but winced with the pain.

By the time Frank returned with the water she seemed to be much less agitated, and Frank decided to try and find out what had happened this time. He placed the glass on the table and gave her a wet towel to wipe her wounds, "How long have you been here Lucy?"

She took a sip from the glass of water, "I crept out of bed at about two o'clock this morning when Walter was snoring soundly. I'm sorry Frank, but I couldn't go to my mother's house. I didn't want to worry her with all this, so I came here. And anyway my mother's will be the first place Walter will go to try and find me. He wouldn't look for me here, not in the middle of the night anyway."

The look of fear suddenly returned, "Oh God, what if he comes here now?" She looked at Frank as if waiting for an answer, but when one didn't come immediately said, "If he's slept all night he might just think I've come to work and not bother about me for the rest of the day, and I won't see him 'til I go home."

Frank cautiously touched her hand, "Don't worry Lucy, we'll have you out of here well before that. I'm going to send for an ambulance to take you to hospital. You need all those cuts and bruises seen to."

Lucy became agitated by this suggestion, "No Frank, I'll be fine. I don't want to go to hospital they'll only want to know how I ended up like this, won't they?"

He patted her hand, "OK, OK, just relax for now, we'll sort all that out in a minute. How did all this happen anyway? You seemed so much better lately and I haven't seen any marks on you for ages."

She put the damp towel to her face and started sobbing.

"It's all right Lucy. You don't have to say anything if you don't want to."

She wiped her right eye with the towel and delicately dabbed her swollen left eye with it, "No Frank, you've been so good over all this that I think I at least owe you some sort of explanation." She held the towel to the left side of her face, "Just after you spoke to me that time, Walter got a job in the pits in Cannock and went back to live with his wife and kids. Then a couple of weeks ago he came back and everything was fine. He was his sweet, gentle caring self like he was when I first met him. I don't know what happened yesterday, but last night when he came back home late and drunk, he just started shouting at me. I told him when he came back that I wouldn't stand him hitting me again, so when he started shouting I told him to get out and go back to his wife."

She smiled at Frank realising now her own stupidity at standing up to him like that, "Pretty daft of me to do that weren't it Frank? I should have known he wouldn't take any lip from me." She shrugged her shoulders, "Well that's it Frank. He laid into me, but this time he just kept hitting me, over and over again and when I fell to the floor he started kicking me. He's never done that before."

She was now weeping unconstrainedly and once again squirmed as she held her arms round her chest. She spoke through her tears, "I'm sorry Frank. This is such a mess."

"I've told you not to worry about it, we'll sort something out, but for now I really do think we need to get you to hospital. Your chest is hurting you as well, isn't it?"

She nodded her head, "It feels as though I might have a broken rib where he kicked me."

"And I wouldn't be surprised if you don't have a broken leg as well. How on earth did you get here like that in the night?"

She smiled at him and merely added, "Painfully."

She seemed more relaxed now but was also finding it very difficult to keep her right eye open. Frank was worried that she might soon faint from the pain and decided to send for an ambulance. He reached for the phone and when the operator answered he asked for an ambulance. Lucy immediately took the phone from him and told the operator it wasn't needed. "I've told you Frank I can't go to …. hos…pi…. tal."

She started to fall off her chair and Frank just managed to catch her and gently lower her to the floor, before rushing out of the office and shouting down the stairs for some help.

It was Tom who shouted back, "I've just got something to sort out down here Frank. I'll be with you in a couple of minutes."

Frank yelled at the top of his voice, "No Tom, now, I want you here now."

Tom noted the panic and urgency in Frank's voice and ran as fast as he could up the stairs, "What's up Frank? What's the panic? I was just starting to sort out the stuff to go on the van for Grace's shop."

He nearly ran into Lucy as he rushed into the room, "Oh my God what's the matter with Lucy?"

Frank did not answer the question but asked if the van they hired for deliveries to the shop was outside at the moment.

"Sure, it's just arrived, but we haven't put anything on it yet." He pointed to Lucy on the floor, "But what's the matter with Lucy?"

"She needs to get to hospital. Just go and get the driver to give us a hand to get her in the van. We'll go down the back stairs so nobody needs to see her in this state." Tom just stood there looking at Lucy. "Come on Tom. She needs help quick so go and get the driver." Tom started for the door, "And come back up the back stairs, Tom. Don't forget use the back stairs."

When Frank returned from the hospital Tom was sitting at his desk eating his lunchtime sandwiches, "How is she Frank? Is she all right?"

He did not want to go into too much detail with Tom but realistically knew he would find it hard to avoid giving more details of her injuries. "She'll live. She came round before we got to the hospital, so they don't think it was concussion. They think she just fainted from the pain."

He walked over to Tom and picked up the teapot, which was on a tray on his desk, "Any tea in this? I could murder a cup of tea."

"Yes, help yourself."

Frank took a cup from the top of the cabinet and poured the tea.

"How did she get her face messed up like that? Walter Nelson's doing again, was it? That animal wants locking up."

Frank had not realised that Tom knew of the beatings Lucy received from Walter, but obviously it was more common knowledge than he thought.

"I guess so, but she's got to do something about it this time. We can't let it happen to her any more."

"Well I've tried to tell her in the past but she won't listen to me." Once again Frank was surprised that Tom had also spoken to her about it, "I've told her at least three times to chuck the bugger out. In fact I thought she had, she seemed so much better lately."

"He had left, Tom, but he came back a few days ago. Poor cow; took everyone's advice and told him to clear off last night. Telling him to go is the reason she's in hospital now with two cracked ribs, a possible broken leg and God knows how many other cuts and bruises. That's on top of all that damage to her face."

Frank took his cup of tea to his desk and sat down, "I'll maybe pop and see her tonight, but for now let's see if we can catch up on the work. Did you manage to get all that stuff off to Grace? I sent the van back as soon as we got Lucy to the hospital."

"All done, he got back in no time at all. Said he wouldn't charge us any more for the extra time he wasted."

Frank was a little surprised at the comment but decided to let it drop.

There was a sudden commotion and raised voices at the bottom of the stairs. Both Frank and Tom went into the waiting area to listen to what was going on.

The shouting got more urgent and louder, "Get out of my way, I'll knock your bloody block off if you don't clear out of my way."

Frank started to go down the stairs but Tom held him back, "Let Big Billy sort it out Frank. That's Walter Nelson down there, sounds as if he's drunk again. He's no match for Billy. Billy'll soon send him on his way."

Frank decided to do as suggested, particularly when he heard Billy's gruff voice declare, "Right, you little twerp, bugger off. I've told you Lucy isn't here, so just bugger off."

"No, you bugger off. Get out of my way." There was a sudden thwack and Frank thought that Billy had hit Walter, but realised it was the other way round when he heard running footsteps up the stairs and Walter shouting, "Lucy, where are you Lucy? Come down here, I want you here now. Do you hear me?"

Walter Nelson appeared on the landing below them. He continued up the stairs waving in front of him the broom with which he had hit Big Billy on the head. He was trying to run up the stairs, but was obviously drunk and almost fell as he staggered up the steps.

Frank and Tom stood together at the top of the stairs blocking his way. He continued shouting, "Get out of my way, I want to see Lucy."

Frank spoke whilst he was still coming up the stairs, "She isn't here, so you might as well just turn round and go back the way you came."

Walter stopped three steps below Frank and Tom. He poked the broom at them like a lance, "Just get out of my way. I know she's here, so just shift before I make you."

Tom was holding the head of the broom that was pushed into his stomach. It was now his turn to answer Walter, "Look Walter, you've been told she isn't here so there's no point coming any further, so just go before you get yourself into big trouble."

Walter reacted by pushing as hard as he could on the broom whilst ascending the last few steps and pushing past Frank, "Out of my way. You and your sidekick here ain't going to stop me. So just shift yourself before I knock your bloody block off."

Tom was sent reeling backwards and doubled up with pain and he fell to the floor banging his head on the wall behind him as the broom head was bulldozed into his stomach. Walter snatched the broom out of Tom's hands as he held his stomach and tried to catch his breath.

The assailant turned to Frank, "Now you! Out of my way." He swung the broom back towards Frank, who ducked and caught it in his hands, wincing as it stung into his palms. He held on to the brush and tried to jerk it out of Walter's grasp, but Walter held on tight and propelled forward with all his strength. Frank was sent backwards down the stairs as the brush handle slipped from Walter's grip. Frank rolled over and over with increasing speed down the steps, his body seeming to bounce on each tread as he did so, finally coming to rest in a misshapen heap against the wall. Blood ran from his leg where the broom handle, broken on the way down, had scored his leg. Walter, who realised the damage he had done, ran down the stairs, kicking Frank in the leg as he lunged past him. Big Billy who had been sitting on the bottom step holding his head and just about managing to stay conscious was booted in the back as Walter went swaying and lurching on his way out of the building.

Billy's first reaction was to run after him but he heard Tom from above shouting for help. He stumbled up the stairs to where Frank was lying in agony unable to move. Tom was trying to help him into a more comfortable position but Frank screamed in pain each time he tried.

Billy saw the blood running from Frank's leg and went to get a cloth to wrap round it, "Just leave him there for a minute, I'll give you a hand to move him as soon as we've seen to that leg."

Tom asked Frank if he could move into a more comfortable position. Frank moved his head from side to side, "I can't Tom, I can't move my legs at all and my back's killing me."

"OK, we'll sort you out as soon as Billy comes back. Shall I call for an ambulance?"

"No, my leg isn't that bad, it's just a flesh wound. It doesn't hurt and it'll be OK with something on it to stop the blood running."

Billy came back with a first aid box, tore a bigger hole in Frank's trouser leg and quickly bandaged the wound. He and Tom then each took hold of an arm and lifted Frank up off the floor.

"It's no good chaps, I can't feel my legs. I can't stand up on my own. You'll have to let me sit down again."

"No Tom, don't let him go, just hold on to him a second longer," and with that Billy put one arm under Frank's legs and the other around his back and lifted him up and carried him down the stairs.

Tom was guiding Billy down the stairs and giving some support for Frank's sheer weight, but when Frank passed out, Billy said, "I think you'd better get an ambulance Tom. I don't know what he's done but things don't look too good to me."

Lucy was let out of hospital two days later; her leg in plaster and her cracked ribs bound with bandages for support. She had received six stitches on the cut over her eye and the swelling was starting to abate. But the doctor was not certain whether her eyesight would be affected and had suggested that her left eye should be left bound up for a while to give the healing process a chance to restore as much sight as possible. When she heard what had happened to Frank she vowed never to see Walter again. A promise that was easier to keep than she expected. Tom had called in the police and made a complaint about the injuries inflicted on himself, Billy and Lucy, but particularly the injuries that Frank had received. When Walter heard that the police were looking for him, he decided to get as far away as possible and no one ever found out where he went.

Lucy not only returned to work straight away, but insisted on working the long hours needed for her and Tom to sort everything out whilst Frank was missing. Grace was mostly able to leave the shop in the hands of her assistant but the shock of Frank's injuries, so soon after the loss of Kathy, took a terrible short-term toll of her health. She seemed to age fifteen years overnight and within two months her once beautiful red hair had turned completely white.

Frank was finally released from hospital on Christmas Eve. There was nothing more they could do for him. The external injuries had quickly been dealt with but the fall had twisted his lower back, dislodging a piece of shrapnel that had remained in his buttocks since his war injury. Whether it was the movement of the shrapnel or the force of the fall itself the doctors never decided, but Frank's spinal cord was damaged leaving him paralysed from the waist down, never to walk again.

CHAPTER TEN

1936

Tom handed Leonard Oakes the bundle of paper as soon as he walked into the office saying, "Frank has asked me to give you these Leonard. It's the stuff you gave us to look at last Friday. He apologises that he's not here to see you, but he's got a hospital appointment this afternoon, so he hoped you'd stay and have dinner at his house this evening when we can agree on the final changes." Leonard sat down and looked at the top sheet as Tom continued talking, "I checked them on Friday and Frank looked at them over the weekend and we've made a few suggestions which should make manufacture a bit cheaper."

Tom went to leave the office saying, "I know you'd prefer not to have any distractions, so I'll leave you to it," but turned as he reached the door, "Oh by the way I've got a Council committee meeting later this morning, so if you need to discuss anything with me, I'll be back about three. I'll get Lucy to bring you a drink, and if there's anything else you want just give her a shout." He smiled as he added, "She'll be able to discuss costs with you a lot better than me anyway."

Tom becoming a labour councillor was only one of the changes that had taken place since Frank's accident. In the first twelve months the firm had struggled to keep on its feet, particularly as Tom had panicked at every decision he was required to make in Frank's absence. It was Lucy who eventually told Grace that things were failing to get done properly and they were in danger of losing the military contract if matters didn't improve.

Once Grace realised what was happening, it not only gave her the fillip she needed to pull herself together, but gave her the incentive to organise all that was necessary at home and both businesses to keep things going.

Lucy and Alice proved to be her greatest allies in this. One Sunday after visiting Frank in hospital, the three women had walked back to Grace's house and had a grand powwow about all the problems, each pitching in with their suggested solutions. Alice, who now lived next door as a lodger with Grace's mother, said she would give up her nursing job at the General Hospital and be a carer for both Frank and the children, allowing Grace the opportunity to involve herself full time in both businesses.

Alice convinced the others of the need for this when she said, "Frank is too positive a person to let this get the better of him, and I'm sure he'll soon be able to get involved in work properly again, maybe as soon as the New Year. But I know Frank, once he realises he can do things again he'll get so involved he won't bother to look after himself, and that's where I'll come in. He'll need daily exercising on his legs if they're not going to whither away, and he'll need help to get washed, dressed and all the other things. I can make sure he's properly looked after and between doing that, I can look after the children, taking them to school et cetera."

Grace reluctantly agreed to this as a short term solution until other arrangements could be made, but nevertheless immediately felt a great weight lift from her at this realistic solution to Frank's care. She insisted however that they pay Alice the same money she was receiving as a nurse. This caused some disagreement initially as Alice felt it was more than they could afford, but eventually agreed when Grace pointed out that the arrangement would enable both her and Frank to work virtually full time.

"Right, now that's sorted out, let's get something to eat and then we can concentrate on the factory and the shop."

The discussion went on until after midnight and was only interrupted by the making of more pots of tea.

Grace was staggered at the unequivocal and positive contributions made by Lucy. She had always considered Lucy to be a bit of a flighty character but by the end of the evening had changed her mind completely. Lucy obviously knew the business inside out and Grace became convinced that she was more than capable of running the office side of things.

"Tom is great with the workers and he really is good with the practical side of manufacture," she said after their third pot of tea, "But he just doesn't seem to cope with the paper side of things. He worries too much about it and I'm sure he'd be better off sometimes if he just left it to me."

"I know exactly what you mean, Lucy," Alice interjected, "we've got a doctor at the hospital who's just like that. He's brilliant with diagnosis and the patients, but when it comes to the mundane things, paper work and the like, he's hopeless. Mind you," she added, "I do sometimes think it's a deliberate ploy just so we do it all for him."

"I don't think Tom's like that. He really does get confused about it all."

"He's always been a bit like that, Lucy. Very practical and great with his hands but he never was the best at writing and arithmetic." Grace got up to refill the kettle ready for their next pot of tea, "I'll have a word with him and get him to leave all the office work to you."

Lucy was bothered by this and was unsure of such an approach, "No don't do that, he'll think I've been complaining to you."

Grace stopped on her way to the scullery, and turned to Lucy, "Relax

Lucy, he's my brother after all. I think I know him well enough to say the right things and besides if we're to get through this crisis it's got to be done, hasn't it?"

They all agreed and also agreed that this impromptu meeting had been successful in solving the immediate problems, probably in a much more practical way than the men would have done. Particularly two men, one of whom was lying in a hospital bed and the other who was lost without him.

Over the following years the three women had many such meetings, always without the men's knowledge, but with united and carefully planned subterfuge, they always managed to improve things and make both businesses more profitable.

Frank had left Grace to run the shop very much on her own and with the help and practical solutions from the other two women, by 1936 the one shop business had expanded into a thriving empire of thirty seven shops around the country. Grace had expanded the range of equipment being sold and no longer exclusively kept to the Richards and Matthews' radios, but included other manufacturers and other equipment, such as radio kits for the DIY enthusiast, record players, the latest records from home and America, and all ancillary bits and pieces.

Early in 1936 Grace and Frank finally moved from Brighton Terrace. The house was really too small when Frank came out of hospital and they had to use the front room as a bedroom for Frank as there was no way he could have got up the stairs, but all the money they'd saved had been used to set up Grace's business so they couldn't contemplate a move of house before.

After that, any profits made went to buy the freehold of shop premises in high streets of various towns. The properties being bought in Grace's personal name, with her leasing them back to the business. A practice repeated each time she expanded the business.

The new house in Little Aston was big enough for Frank to have his own office and workshop and a separate bedroom on the ground floor, and for Alice to live in a small adjoining flat so she could give Frank his daily physiotherapy. She had however returned to work three years earlier when the boys no longer needed her full attention.

The house was several miles away from the factory, which meant that Frank could not get there under his own steam in his wheelchair. He had been able to do this whilst they lived in Brighton Terrace and that was another of the reasons they had stayed there for so long.

In anticipation of the house move, they had purchased a Lanchester car the previous year and both Alice and Grace had learned to drive the preselector gearbox car very quickly. Both the front and back doors of the car were of sufficient size for Frank, with a little help, to pull himself out of his wheelchair and into the passenger seat or back seat of the car.

By 1936 Frank and Grace had been married for seventeen years, most of which had been very troublesome and hard work for both of them; but now they were able to relax a little and enjoy the rewards of their hard work.

Two years earlier, the year in which both businesses had been made private limited companies; Russell Rhodes was offered the Chair of Electrical Engineering at the University and as such, no longer had time to be directly involved in the design work for the company. Russell had always been more interested in his academic career than research and development and it had become obvious to Frank quite early on that Leonard Oakes was the one with all the ideas and the design flair and after some persuading by Frank, Leonard Oakes had agreed to spend more time on design work for Richards and Matthews.

Frank had invited him to join the company as a full time director and design engineer but Lenny had said he was not interested in management and preferred to stay as a lecturer at the University and keep to the existing arrangement whereby he received a commission on each set sold; an arrangement that worked well as Lenny was still able to call on the talents of his students from time to time to help with experimental research.

Frank had also wanted Lucy to be made a director of Richards and Matthews Ltd., but Tom wouldn't agree to it, but after some persuading by Frank, he had reluctantly accepted that Lucy should be given more responsibility, and pay, and she had been placed in overall charge of the office and administration and been given the title of 'Office Manager'.

Grace however had insisted that Lucy should be made a non executive director of the separate retail business and knowing how well the two women got on together, Frank had agreed to her request when Grace convinced him that it would not affect her work at the factory. The same offer had not been made to Tom and Frank felt that this, more than anything else, had been why he had objected to Lucy being made a director of the manufacturing company.

For Frank the new arrangements meant that he no longer had to spend every spare moment at the factory and he decided to take the whole day off and spend the morning relaxing with his eldest son prior to his hospital visit in the afternoon.

Philip was very much like his father. Not only did he have his father's good looks and features, but he had also developed a passion for radio and everything to do with them. He spent many hours in his father's workshop watching him work, asking him questions, pouring over the drawings and in the last year or so, occasionally making suggestions for improvement.

When Philip realised that his father was not going to the factory he asked if he might spend time with him in his workshop.

"No, Philip, I feel like a bit of fresh air so I'm taking the day off. How would you like to take me to the Arboretum for a walk round the lake? And then we can have some lunch together in town before I go for my check up at the hospital."

Philip did not much like the idea but decided not to upset his father, "Yes, sounds a great idea, but how are we going to get there?"

"That's easy. I've already asked your mother to drop us off on her way in to work."

Philip was a little niggled that such arrangements had been made before he had been asked, but his mother interrupted before he had a chance to make any untoward comment, "It'll be nice for both of you to spend a little relaxing time together. Make a change from the hours you spend together in the workshop." She got up from the breakfast table, "I'll be ready to go in about ten minutes, so you'd better hurry with the rest of your breakfast Philip. I said I'd pop and see Lucy at ten this morning and I don't want to be late."

Grace pulled up outside the Town Hall and helped Philip with the folding wheelchair, before they assisted Frank from the car into it.

Grace gave both Philip and his father a kiss on the cheek before wishing them a pleasant day and telling Frank she hoped his check-up went OK. Philip hated being kissed by his mother like that, particularly in public. Thank goodness none of his school-friends were around to see it, he would never live it down if they had been. He really must pluck up the courage to ask her not to do it.

When Grace had got back into the car and about to drive off, his father let out a laugh and shook his head at his son, "Not overly fond of your mother doing that, are you son?"

Philip could feel the colour rising in his cheeks. "Is it that obvious? I just wish she wouldn't do it in places like this where someone might see me."

Philip took hold of the wheelchair handles and started to push his father from the town centre along Lichfield Street towards the Arboretum, "I don't suppose you could tell her not to do it, could you Dad?"

His father let out another laugh, "Not up to me to tell her, she's your mother and it's you she's kissing. So why don't you just ask her not to do it? She'll be upset but I'm sure she'll understand." He continued laughing.

"It's not that funny, you don't know my school-friends, they'd have a field day if they knew my mother kissed me like that every time we parted."

Frank found it difficult to stop giggling. "Sorry son, it's just that I was thinking that it won't be long before you start kissing girls of your own age. You'll find that quite a different experience. That's assuming you haven't already started kissing them. Have you?"

Philip replied a very indignant, "No I have not," for which Frank was somewhat relieved. Not that he was bothered whether he had or had not. In fact he thought it was high time that his son had found a girlfriend, but he had realised as soon as he had asked the question that he no right asking such a blunt question of a sixteen year-old.

They were both silent for the next few minutes, but after a while Frank decided he should perhaps take this opportunity to tell his son a few of the facts that no-one had ever bothered to talk to him about.

"Tell me to mind my own business if you want to, but I've never heard you talk about any girlfriend. Is there a girl you fancy?"

Philip frowned and pulled a face behind his father's back. Several months earlier, he had been awe-struck with Sadie Taylor, the seventeen year-old girl, who worked in his mother's shop and he had found an excuse to go into the shop on his way home from school, whenever he knew his mother wasn't there.

Sadie was always friendly with him and seemed to enjoy playing the latest records for him. He just couldn't stop thinking about her. At night when he was in bed he would dream about her, envisaging her lying beside him, her big blue eyes staring at him and her ample breasts warm against his chest. He had never actually seen a woman's breasts let alone touched them, and could only therefore imagine what they would be like. He eventually plucked up enough courage to ask her if she would go to the cinema with him but she just laughed and said he was far too young for her. The rejection was more than he could bear, particularly the thought that Sadie might have told his mother about it.

Was his father asking about Sadie? He decided to bluff it out and tried to speak as nonchalantly as he could, "Well there are a couple of girls I'm friendly with, but nothing serious, I haven't met a girl I really fancy yet."

"Well hang on to that. Just enjoy the company of girls for now and don't get too involved. You do know what I'm talking about don't you?"

Was he talking about Sadie? His head pounding he decided to continue to bluff, "No not exactly but if you're talking about the birds and bees then yes I know all about that. I've done biology at school, you know Dad, so I don't have any problems in that area." He was however lying. Biology lessons at school had never even discussed the sex life or sexual organs of animals, and as for human sexuality, well that was almost a complete mystery to him.

For Frank, who had learned from Grace of Philip's attraction to Sadie Taylor, Philip's answer was something of a relief. Grace had said that Sadie was a good worker and an excellent salesgirl, but that she was too precocious and too aware of her own femininity and the effect she had on young men to be the right girl for Philip. She had asked Frank to talk to Philip and make sure that she was not taking advantage of him! Frank had not wished to interfere in such matters with his son and felt that he was old enough to make his own choices and decisions. He had certainly not wanted to get on to the subject of the 'birds and bees' as Philip had put it, and was happy he could now tell Grace that the matter had been dealt with and not get any deeper into this subject with his son.

"Good I'm pleased about that son, but don't forget if you're ever worried about anything you can come and chat to me about it."

Philip went along with the charade, "I know I can Dad, but there really isn't any girl, not one I'm bothered about at least, and anyway there's plenty of time for all that after I leave school."

"Yes you're right son, there's plenty of time yet. I just hope you wait 'til you meet the right girl and don't make the mistake of settling for second best."

Philip sensed his father's unease at the way the conversation had gone and resolved not to let his father off the hook just yet. He had for some time wondered about his father's relationship with his mother particularly that although they had separate bedrooms, he knew that his mother frequently spent the night in his father's bedroom.

He was more concerned however that his father seemed to spend far more time with his Aunt Alice and with Lucy Evans than his mother. He knew his father depended totally on Alice for physiotherapy and generally looking after his physical welfare, but had been puzzled that both Alice and Lucy seemed to be with him so much of the time. Perhaps now was the time finally to bring his concerns into the open, and so trying not to be too obvious asked his father if his mother was the only girlfriend he'd ever had.

"I guess I was lucky, I always knew your mother was the girl for me, right from the first time we went out together."

"Did you never have any doubts about her or meet any other girl you fancied? I heard Mom talking to Auntie Mary once and she said that

Auntie Alice and Mrs Evans were both in love with you."

Philip had achieved his objective and it was now Frank's turn to feel uneasy at the question and put on the spot by his son. He decided to keep quite calm. He ignored the first question and just dealt with the second.

"First let's put the record straight about your Aunt Alice. She was the only person who had any faith in me when I lost my memory, and yes we did become quite close, but never in the way you're suggesting. She's more like the sister I've never had."

Frank seemed quite sad that Philip had even suggested a romance between him and Alice, "And any love she has for me, or you and the rest of the family for that matter, is purely that of a sister, do you understand what I'm saying?"

"Yes Dad, I know all that really. I was only pulling your leg."

Frank ignored the remark and continued, "And as for Lucy Evans. Well you're not the only one pulling my leg; she's been doing it for years. It's all a big joke for her about how she fancies me, but it's all just talk and your mother and everyone else knows that. Do you know how I came to end up in this wheelchair?"

"Of course I do. Mrs Evans' boyfriend at the time had beaten her up and then he came and pushed you down the stairs."

"That's right and Lucy still bears the mental, as well as the physical scars from that day. She blames herself for what happened to me and no matter how many times I tell her it wasn't her fault, she still can't forgive herself. On the one hand she feels she owes me, and on the other the experience has left her afraid of ever getting close to a man again. The only man she trusts implicitly is me; and all this talk about fancying me, is just her defence mechanism to save from getting entangled with any other man. But let me assure you that that's all it is; nothing more and nothing less."

Frank turned his head so as to look Philip in the eyes, "So for your information there's nothing going on between Alice and me, or Lucy and me. There never has been and there never will be, OK?"

Philip now looked sheepish and wished he had never raised the subject, "I'm sorry if I got the wrong idea."

"That's OK, son. Now let's just enjoy the peace and quiet of the park."

They entered the main entrance of the Arboretum just as the clouds started to break up and the sun shone, immediately warming up the air. Philip started to push his father in an anticlockwise direction around the lake.

"No Philip, let's go round the other way for a change. We can take in the air for half an hour or so and then get a cup of tea and a bun at the café."

Philip did as his father asked and they spent the next hour walking around the park, watching the adventurous swimming in the lake, and the less adventurous in rowing boats. They chatted at great length about the business and Frank mentioned that the BBC planned to start broadcasting television programmes from Alexandra Palace later in the year.

"I hear that they plan to experimentally transmit television programmes to Radiolympia in August so how would you like to come to the exhibition with me. We can stay overnight and do something else as well. Do you fancy that?"

Philip was thrilled at the idea of going to Radiolympia again. His father had taken him twice before, and he had even spent some time with his father on the Richards and Matthews stand. "I'd love to. That would be great, thanks." Philip was tremendously excited about seeing television for the first time and asked his father if he had any plans to make television sets at the factory.

"Well I've discussed it with Leonard and we've drawn up some designs, but I'm not sure we should start manufacturing. We could only sell in the London area around Alexandra Palace and a lot of people don't think it will spread to other areas, not for a long time anyway. What do you think? Do you think we should?"

They had reached the café and Philip had some difficulty manoeuvring the wheelchair up the steps. "I don't really know whether it will take off or not, but a lot of people thought that radio was just for the enthusiast when you started the business but look at that now. Maybe in another ten or fifteen years it'll be as popular as radio is now."

They found an empty table and Frank gave his son the money to get a pot of tea and a plate of cakes. The conversation about television continued as they drank their tea, "Does it really matter that much whether you make televisions or not, Dad. After all we now have plenty of shops so why don't you and Mom start to get contracts with other manufacturers to sell their television sets? If you get in early enough you can make all the profit on sales without all the headache of manufacture."

Frank was surprised at his son's perception. The shops had proved more profitable in the previous year than the factory, and Grace was intent on opening more shops. "I reckon you might have something there son, I'll talk to your mother about it. Maybe she should come to Radiolympia with us?"

Philip was always afraid of letting go of the wheelchair when he was steering his father down steps and leaving the café was no exception. By the time the wheelchair had reached level ground outside his arms were really hurting from the strain of trying to control it.

"Do you think I could sit on that bench over there a minute Dad? My arms are killing me."

His father laughed, "Sure, but maybe you should come with me when Alice is making me do my exercises. I'm sure she could suggest some to give you more strength in your arms."

They both laughed and Philip agreed with a, "Maybe," and hoped his father had forgotten the suggestion by the time they returned home.

He wheeled his father to the side of the bench, put on the wheel brake and sat on the bench. They both watched the boys diving into the water on the other side of the lake.

After a while Philip became aware that his father was staring at a woman and a boy of about fifteen or sixteen who were walking across the grass from the greenhouses towards the lake walk. The woman was talking to the boy and was oblivious to Frank's stare.

She looked much younger than her forty-one years and was immaculately dressed in a very pale green wool suit. The long belted jacket and the straight skirt which almost reached her ankles made this slim woman look quite tall, but as they came nearer Philip realised that she was probably no taller than his mother. She wore a large brimmed cream coloured felt hat with feathers on one side, which cast a shadow across her face obscuring most of her features. Her leather gloves and shoes matched the colour of her hat and she carried a leather handbag in the same colour over her arm.

This attractive woman, who seemed to glide across the grass, soon transfixed Philip, and when she looked up in their direction, unlike his father he was unable to divert his stare away from her.

She smiled directly at him and for a moment he saw the beautiful features of her face. She continued smiling for a few seconds almost demanding Philip's attention and giving him permission to continue looking at her. He was fascinated by the deep brown eyes staring at him, the loveliness of her face enhanced by the soft make-up she had used, and the lips, painted with a soft almost transparent red lipstick, smiling at him.

He felt the colour rising in his cheeks and was relieved when she turned back to the boy and continued talking to him. The boy pointed to the café and said something to the lady. They both stopped; she took off her gloves, opened her handbag and gave the boy some money from out of it. She stood where she was as the boy ran into the café and returned a few minutes later carrying an ice-cream.

Whilst the boy was in the shop, both Frank and Philip started talking to each other again, both consciously trying to avoid looking at the woman.

Frank glanced at his own clothes and took some satisfaction that he was wearing his best suit, a clean shirt and a new tie for his hospital visit. His own clothes were now tailor made to measure and of the best cloth. He had always believed that the saying 'manners maketh man' was only partly true as in his opinion 'clothes and money maketh man' was a much more apt description when it came to differentiating between the classes. As he looked at this woman in all her finery he was at ease with himself and felt he could raise his trilby hat to her as an equal and not out of deference.

As the lady and the boy walked towards where Frank and Philip were sitting, they both tried to act natural and unconcerned about her approach. The woman however seemed to be taking more interest in Frank the closer she came. She stared hard as she neared them and stopped a mere three feet from where he was sitting.

"Hold on a minute, Alaistair," she said to the boy as she turned and stepped back to Frank, "Excuse me for interrupting your leisure, Sir, but you remind me of someone I once knew, and I wondered if you were perhaps a relative of his."

Frank looked clearly at the woman's face for the first time, and let out a gasp, "Evie Harper, it's Evie Harper isn't it?"

"That's right, well yes but it's Evie McPherson now." It was now her turn to show shock on her face, "It is you Frank, isn't it? But I thought you had been killed in the war." She shook her head at the stupidity of her remark. "No of course you weren't killed, you wouldn't be here if you had been."

Frank motioned towards the bench, "Move along a bit Philip and let Mrs McPherson sit down." After she had sat beside him Frank inquired, "What on earth are you doing here, Evie? I was told you'd moved to Scotland when you got married."

She laughed at this remark as if mocking Frank a little, "So you checked up on me did you?" Her laughter turned to a gentle smile and she touched his arm, and gently kissed him on the cheek as she added, "It's really nice if you did."

Philip noticed the kiss but was unable to catch what the lady had said to his father. The questions of earlier in the day about Alice and Lucy were nothing to the thoughts that were flashing through his head at the moment, *'Who is this lady?' 'How on earth does she know Dad?' 'Why is she so familiar with him?'*

It was if Frank heard the questions. "You must have heard me speak of Captain Harper, Philip. Well this is his sister, Evelyn."

Philip still looked puzzled as if demanding further explanation. "You've seen the Military Medal at your Aunt Mary's parents' house; the one her brother won for saving the Captain's life? Well that was Captain Harper and this is his sister. We last met in a field hospital in France where she was a nurse looking after me."

Frank decided that was enough justification for his talking to Evie for the time being and suggested that Philip should go and talk to the boy. Philip did as he was told, got up from the seat and went to chat to the lad. Frank now turned his attention once more to Evie.

They looked at each other for several minutes, neither knowing how to continue the conversation, but eventually Evie asked, "Have I changed so much that you didn't recognise me, Frank?"

"No not at all." He checked that Philip was out of listening distance before, to his own surprise, he added, "You are just as beautiful as you've always been. It's just that I couldn't see your face clearly under that hat and anyway I didn't want to make it so obvious that I found you an attractive woman to stare at."

They both laughed and she touched his arm again. He placed his hand on hers. "How come you didn't recognise me then?"

"Because I wasn't looking at you I suppose. I take it that is your son?" Frank nodded as she continued, "Well I was just so taken with him. He looks exactly like you did when I first met you. I was just so taken aback by him. I couldn't believe my eyes and I suppose that's why I had to stop and ask."

The boys were starting to make their way back to where Frank and Evie were sitting. "Are you in any hurry to get away?" Frank asked.

"No not at all."

Frank reached into his inside jacket pocket and took out his wallet. "What would you say then if the boys took themselves off for half an hour in one of the rowing boats on the lake and we sit here and I can perhaps catch up with what's been happening in your life for the last twenty years? Would that be OK?"

Evie agreed to the suggestion and Frank took a ten-shilling note from his wallet and gave it to Philip with the instruction, "Bring back the change but you can each have an ice-cream on your way back as well," and soon the boys were running around the lake towards the boathouse.

As soon as they were out of earshot Evie motioned towards the wheelchair, "I take it you ended up in this as a result of war injuries?"

For both Evie and Frank the following half an hour was a mixture of emotions as they recounted their own life stories since they had last met. Evie told how she had almost gone to pieces when Mark had been killed.

She had been working with Dr. McPherson at the time and he had been instrumental in keeping her sane. Over the twelve months following Mark's death they had grown very close, "And I suppose," she said, "we fell in love."

"The day before Mark was killed Mark had given me all of your papers and asked me to find which hospital you were in and return them to you. I know he should really have handed them in to the authorities but quite honestly he said things were in such a mess that he didn't trust any of the administration people to make sure you got them."

Evie held Frank's hand again and Frank was once more taken aback by this intimacy, "I did search for you but all of the field hospitals I got in touch with said you weren't in there and well, to be honest, after I heard of Mark's death, I just didn't make any more enquiries for several weeks. When I did enquire again at HQ, I was told that you were missing presumed dead."

She wiped a tear from her eye and returned her hand to Frank's and squeezed it tightly, "I wish I'd known you were still alive Frank. I'm sure it would have helped a great deal to know that. I was very fond of you and I know that Mark was too. You've no idea of the mess I was in. I felt so utterly alone. I had no family left."

Frank was unsure where the conversation was leading. Evie had always evoked uneasy emotions in him, and right now he was beginning to feel drawn to her again. He had often wondered whether their relationship would have been much closer if he had been of the same social class. Was this attention she was giving him now anything to do with the fact that he would no longer be considered working class? Should he now take advantage of the situation and see how 'fond' Evie was of him, and whether she had any similar feelings for him?

"Do you really think my being around would have made any difference?"

She did not answer immediately, but took a cigarette case from her handbag and offered a cigarette to Frank.

"No thanks, I don't."

"You don't mind if I do, do you?" and without waiting for a reply, she took out a cigarette and, after lighting it, inhaled the smoke deeply into her lungs. "Now what were we talking about?"

"I was just asking if you thought it would have made any difference if I'd been around when Mark died."

Evie pursed her lips together and shrugged her shoulders, "Maybe." She looked directly into his eyes as she said this but after a moment's hesitation she averted her eyes and said, "Maybe not." She touched his hand and squeezed it again, "But I know that the thought that you were dead added greatly to my depression. I think it would have been nice to know that you, at least, had survived all that waste of lives."

Frank was pondering what he should say or do next when they heard a scream from the lake. Evie jumped up from the bench and ran towards the railings around the lake and Frank released the brake on his wheelchair and pushed himself after her.

The commotion revolved round two rowing boats about fifteen yards from the opposite bank of the lake; one was empty and the occupants of the other were bending over the side of their boat with their backs to Frank and Evie.

"Oh my God! It's Alaistair and your Philip," shouted Evie.

"Calm down a bit Evie, they seem to be all right. It looks as if the people in the other boat are the ones in trouble. Let's get round to that side of the lake and then we'll be able to see what's happening much better."

Evie started to run but almost immediately turned round and came back to where Frank was manoeuvring his wheelchair, "I'm sorry Frank, I forgot about you in my rush. I'll give you a push."

Frank gave a laugh, "No I'm fine thanks. You get going. Once I've got this thing moving I'll probably overtake you."

It almost became a race between the two of them and they were both puffing and panting when they reached the boathouse. Evie helped Frank move his wheelchair to the edge of the landing platform, where several people were shouting advice to the protagonists of the spectacle. A group of teenagers standing near the edge of the lake about twenty yards away were laughing and pointing and generally enjoying the free show. All the spectators far more interested in watching the life or death pageant unfolding in front of them than in helping the unfortunate actors taking part.

Philip and Alaistair had managed to pull a young boy out of the water and all three were gripping the coat of an older man who was holding on to the side of the boat. Each time he tried to pull himself into their boat, it started to sway and the three boys in it were almost toppled overboard.

Someone on the bank shouted to the man and told him to swim to the shore. The man was violently shaking his head and Philip shouted back, "He says he can't swim."

Frank shouted at the audience, "For God's sake can't someone do something?" He pointed to the lifebelt hanging on the stand at the water's edge, "Evie, get that and throw it to them," but before she was able to, a young boy in swimming costume grabbed it, jumped into the water and swam the fifteen yards or so to the wobbling boat.

He had to fight to get the flailing man to loose the side of the boat and hold on to the lifebelt. Eventually the man grabbed the safety ring with both hands and the swimmer gradually swam to the shore pulling the life belt and the man behind him. As they reached the shore it was as if all the spectators suddenly wanted to take part in the show. Many of them rushed to the water's edge to help drag the poor swimmer and sodden man on to the bank. The remainder of the onlookers were applauding the participants.

Philip had already told the younger boys in the boat with him to sit down and was rowing towards the landing platform. The rescued man dismissed all aid from the many people around and was now standing, with the water dripping from him, waiting for the return of his son.

The boatman, who had merely been an onlooker at the back of the crowd, suddenly stepped forward to the water's edge and shouted at Philip, "Oi! What about the other boat, can't you pull that in with you?" He pointed towards the oars from the vacant boat now floating away on the water, "Grab those oars and bring them with you as well."

Evie ran up to the boatman, a look of sheer anger on her face. Frank looked on flabbergasted as he fully expected her to hit him with her handbag. However she merely pushed him out of the way, telling him, "Leave those children alone. Go and get your own oars and your own boat." She then shouted to a confused Philip, who was trying to manoeuvre to pick up the oars, "Just get yourselves back here safely, leave those oars and the other boat where they are and let this idiot here get them."

The boatman now turned to the rescued man who had taken off his jacket and was trying to squeeze some of the water out it, as he waited for his son's return. "You man! You hired the rowing boat. It's up to you to go and get it and bring it back safely."

Once more it was Evie who took control, "You stupid man. can't you see the trouble the poor man is in? Get the boat yourself."

Frank smiled to himself as the crowd cheered with cries of, "Yes get the boat yourself," and "Leave the poor lads alone."

Realising that the audience were obviously against him, he decided to take the matter no further, and Evie ignoring the boatman's mutterings turned her attention to the boys' boat which had now pulled up against the landing platform. She took each boy's hand in turn and helped him to safety. An onlooker stepped forward and held the boat steady as she did so. When the three boys were all back on firm ground, the man, who had been steadying the boat, stepped into it and took up the oars, saying to Evie that he would go and get the lost boat and oars to save any more trouble.

On seeing the man settling into the boat and taking up the oars, the boatman once more leapt into action, "What do you think you're doing? You can't take that boat until you've paid for it," and without waiting for the man's reply tried to grab hold of the oar as the man pushed it against the landing stage. As he leaned over the water, the temptation of his backside so close to her was too much for Evie and as she led her son away she deliberately nudged into it sending the man off balance and head first into the water. The crowd roared with laughter at the continuing pantomime, but Evie, who suddenly realised the seriousness of what she had done, grabbed hold of Frank's wheelchair with the pronouncement, "I think we'd best leave here as fast as we can."

"I think we had," was all that Frank could say in between his own laughter as they left the landing stage as quickly as they could. They did not stop again until they had reached the park entrance; all four of them doubled up with laughter.

"Did you push that man in deliberately, Mom?" Alaistair asked his mother, when they had all calmed down a little.

Evie looked at Frank, hoping for some support from him.

"No she slipped a bit on the wet planks," Frank lied. "But it was his own fault for getting so close to the water, wasn't it?"

Both of the boys laughed again, "Come on lads, enough is enough," Frank suggested, "We shouldn't really be laughing at the poor man's misfortune." He then added as an afterthought, "I do hope he can swim." A remark that set all four of them laughing again.

This time it was Evie who stopped the laughter. She straightened herself up, ran her fingers across her eyebrows and suddenly became the very beautiful, prim and proper woman that Philip had admired earlier in the morning. "I think we've had enough fun at other people's misfortune for one day." she said, with what Frank detected as a slight Edinburgh accent. "I think it's time we thought about going back, don't you Alaistair?"

"Which way are you going?" Frank enquired.

"Into town, back to the hotel."

"That's the way we're going. We'll just come with you if that's all right?"

"Fine," Evie said and turned to Philip, "Why don't you walk on ahead with Alaistair, Philip, and I'll push your father."

As the boys moved forward, Evie took a cigarette out of her handbag and lit it before taking the handles to the wheelchair to follow the boys.

"Where are you staying, Evie?"

"We are at the George for tonight and then we're catching the overnight sleeper back home later tomorrow."

"Look," said Frank, "We were going to have lunch in town, probably at the George. Perhaps you and Alaistair would like to join us. It really would be nice to chat a bit more."

Evie looked at her watch, it was twelve-thirty, "That would be very nice, Frank, but we don't have much time. I have a meeting arranged with the Solicitors this afternoon."

Frank did not want her to go without spending at least a little more time with her, so he interrupted before she had time to completely decline the invitation, "That's all right, I have to be at the hospital for a check up at two-thirty. So we'll be having a fairly quick lunch ourselves. What say we work our way back to the George? We'll have a quick lunch, and afterwards Philip can push me up to the hospital for my appointment and you can go to see your Solicitor."

She still looked a little unsure, until Frank added quietly, "I really would like to spend a little more time with you. It could be another twenty years before I see you again."

Evie smiled and nodded her head, "Very well. It would be nice to have lunch together and chat for a bit more."

The boys were waiting at the entrance to the George Hotel as Evie pushed Frank across the Bridge past the statue of Sister Dora and as she reached the boys she asked the doorman to give a hand to lift the wheelchair into the hotel but he appeared reluctant to move from his post. Philip went to his father's side and beckoned to Alaistair to assist him, but Evie stopped them. She stepped up to the doorman, took his arm and led him towards Frank, "Come on young man; help this gentleman up these steps."

Embarrassed at such rough handling, the doorman reluctantly took hold of the one side of the wheelchair whilst Philip took the other. Once inside the doorman wheeled the chair into the dining room and Frank gave him a shilling for his trouble.

Unlike the doorman, the Headwaiter had seen Frank several times before in the restaurant and was used to finding him a suitable table. "Good morning, Mr Matthews, table for four?" Frank nodded.

"Would you like the table by the window over there," and without waiting for an answer took hold of the wheelchair and pushed Frank to the table. He first pulled a chair out for Evie to sit down, who immediately lit up another cigarette. He then moved the chair opposite to the side to make room for Frank. He beckoned to the boys to sit on the other two chairs but Evie interrupted, "I think you boys should go and wash your hands before you sit down to eat."

Philip and Alaistair went to find the washrooms and the Headwaiter left the menus with Frank and Evie. The wine waiter was at their side almost immediately. Evie declined the offer of wine with the meal and said that she would just have water and Alaistair would have a lemonade. Frank ordered lemonade for Philip and a scotch and water for himself.

"Is Alaistair your only child?" Frank asked when the waiter had left.

Evie seemed a little embarrassed at the question and dragged deeply on her cigarette before answering, "Yes, I didn't find it easy carrying Alaistair and Bertrand said it was probably best if we didn't have any more. and so we never have." She was silent for a moment as if contemplating whether she should add to the comment, but suddenly sat upright and asked, "Do you have any other children?"

"Yes. We have another boy, John. He's eleven now." Frank was in two minds about mentioning Kathy but on balance saw no reason not to, even though he still found it difficult to talk about her. "And there's Kathy of course. She was the apple of her father's eye, but she caught diphtheria and died in the same year that I had my accident."

Evie leaned forward and touched Frank's hand once again, "I'm so sorry Frank, that must have been dreadful for you and your wife."

Frank felt a tear coming to his eye, "Yes it's still very painful for both of us, but we were lucky in that we had the boys and of course we had each other," and without really knowing why, he added, "It helped that Grace and me have always been very close. Still are. And that helps."

Evie squeezed his hand, "I'm glad you've got each other. I'm sure it must help. You're very lucky to have that. I envy you."

Frank was puzzled at the implication of the, I envy you, comment. He had also found the earlier comment that Bertrand had said they shouldn't have any more children rather odd. Did it mean that Evie had no part in the decision? He decided to change the subject, "Tell me a bit about your life in Edinburgh then."

She smiled and shrugged her shoulders, stubbed out her cigarette and lit another one, "Nothing much to tell really. We live in a large house and I spend most of my time running the household and generally looking after that and my son." And then she quickly added, "And my husband of course. When he's around that is."

"Why does he have to go away much?"

Evie laughed at the question, "No, in fact the consulting rooms are part of the house but they're out of bounds for me except when I know they're empty and I'm checking on the cleaners. Bertrand also lectures in medicine at the University and then of course, he has his club and meetings on many evenings. That's when he's not visiting patients in their own homes on top of everything else. I sometimes don't see him for days." She gave another laugh, "You know Frank, some mornings when I get up and he's not around, I check his bedroom to see if his bed's been slept in."

Frank was shocked at the realisation that Evie did not sleep with her husband and thought it best not to pursue that subject any further either.

"I remember a Dr. McPherson treating me when I was in hospital in France. The same time that Mark was in hospital. But he was much older than us." He did not allow Evie to comment but continued talking and asked, "Is your husband in practice on his own?"

"Yes, well he has a secretary and a couple of nurses but there are no other doctors working at his consulting rooms." She went quiet for a moment, as if contemplating what to say next. Frank was just about to change the subject again when she added, "And yes my husband is the same Dr. McPherson who treated you in France. And yes he is twenty years older than me." She smiled and looking down at the tablecloth added so quietly that it was almost as if she was speaking to herself and not Frank, "Maybe I should have married someone younger."

She lifted her head, gave a little laugh, and looked directly at Frank again. "His father and grandfather were medical men and I guess that Alaistair will follow in the family business. I quite enjoyed nursing during the war, and so when Alaistair started school, I suggested that I might help in the surgery as a nurse or even with some of the paperwork, but Bertrand said it would not be right for his wife to work, and so it never happened."

Frank was relieved that the boys returned from the washroom at that point as he felt that Evie was perhaps being too critical of her husband and was glad to be able to change the subject yet again.

When everyone had been served with their choice of lunch, the boys started talking again about their excursion on the rowing boat and having a good laugh at the (mis)adventure. Whilst this was going on, Frank considered all Evie had said about her life in Scotland, and particularly the comments she had made regarding her husband. It was obvious to Frank that she and Bertrand did not have the same relationship he had with Grace.

It was true that he and Grace had had separate beds since his accident, but even now after so many years, Grace would still come into his bedroom saying that she needed him. She would pull back the sheets and take off his pyjamas before stripping herself naked and getting into bed beside him.

They would both enjoy the warmth of being so close and talk sweet nothings to each other, just as they had done when they had first married. After a while they would inevitably start to touch each other, exploring each other's body and eventually bringing satisfaction to the other in the ways they'd patiently learnt together since Frank's accident.

Frank looked closely at Evie as he watched her speaking to Philip and then to Alaistair. This was the woman he had so admired for such a long time and he had never really exorcised her from his memory. Today he had been given the opportunity to do just that.

The woman in front of him was a very beautiful woman, but so was Grace. She was undoubtedly a very likeable person and really good company, but so was Grace. Frank looked intently at her almost trying to see behind the beauty at the real person inside. Was she as close to her husband as he was to Grace? Probably not! Was her husband distant to her or was it in fact Evie who kept her husband at a distance? Perhaps not! Would she have been the same with a younger husband? Maybe she would, but did all this matter? Definitely not! Would Frank's life have been any better with someone like Evie rather than Grace? Absolutely not!

"Are you all right Frank? You seem to be in some sort of trance."

Frank shook his head, "I'm sorry, I was just thinking of all the things that have happened since we last met and wondering how much we've changed."

"Well we've both grown a little older Frank. I know I have. But other than that you seem much the same Frank Matthews I met all those years ago." She put down her knife and fork before continuing, "God Frank, where have all the years gone? I wonder sometimes what I've got to show for all of my life. My father ruined my childhood for me and since I got married! Well I don't know what I've got to show for that." She turned and touched Alaistair on the side of his head, "Other than Alaistair of course. You're the best thing that ever happened to me, aren't you sweetheart?"

Once more Evie had referred to some measure of unhappiness in her life and although Frank wished afterwards that he hadn't been so direct in his comments and hoped that Evie had not read it as a level of boasting on his part. "Well I'm certainly glad that we had children, but when I look back, both Grace and I have had a very eventful life. We've worked very hard and had a fair bit of success and I'm pretty sure I'm speaking for Grace as well, when I say that we've thoroughly enjoyed doing it all."

"You're a very lucky man then Frank and Grace is a very lucky woman to have you."

For quite a time no one spoke as they all busied themselves eating their lunch. The lull in the conversation was however becoming a bit of an embarrassment and Frank, trying to choose a subject less intrusive into Evie's private life, asked, "Have you been here in Walsall very long?"

"No, I came down the day before yesterday. I brought Alaistair with me because I thought it'd be nice to show him where I used to live and a little of the town. That's how we came to be in the Arboretum this morning; just showing Alaistair one of the town's better aspects." She put down her knife and fork. "But the main reason I'm here is to see my Solicitor."

Before he thought about what he was saying Frank was once more asking personal questions, "I trust seeing your Solicitor isn't because of a loss in the family or anything like that?"

Evie smiled, "No nothing like that, I don't have any family left in this area at all."

"I'm sorry, I really shouldn't be asking you about your private affairs, it's none of my business. Let's talk about something else."

"No that's fine. Actually I come down here to finally sell the business. Percy Lewis's wife died a couple of years ago and he's seventy now and really doesn't want to work any longer, so I've had to do something about it." She took a sip of her water before continuing, "Do you remember good old Miss Hill? Well she and Percy Lewis are going to get married, so we're losing her as well." Evie laughed at herself as she added, "You know I don't think I've ever heard anyone call her by any name other than Miss Hill. I haven't a clue what her Christian name is." She took another sip of water, "That's a terrible admission isn't it? She must have worked at the factory all of her life and I haven't a clue what her name is. Anyway, I've never had any interest in the business. I hate going there and I don't know why I didn't sell it years ago. I always feel I'll find my father sitting in his chair and he'll start ordering me about and telling me what to do."

She shuddered as if she had encountered a ghost as she spoke of her father, "I shouldn't talk about my father like that should I? I miss my mother but I'm glad I don't have to deal with my father any more."

She continued talking about the interest from both Austin and Morris cars to which they had been supplying components for years, but Frank was listening less and less intently. He was surprised at Evie's comments about her father, or was he? He remembered how she had recoiled when her father had approached her and kissed her in the office all those years ago and how Mark had never had a good thing to say about him. His mind began to wander with thoughts about the anger and hostility he felt towards their father. How his loathing for the man and what he stood for, had driven him in the years of the war and for a long time afterwards. Perhaps he should make an offer for the business; that really would be the final nail in Vernon Harper's coffin. The old man would turn in his grave at such a thought! Frank Matthews buying his business! Frank audibly laughed at the thought.

"What did I say, Frank? What's so funny?"

"Oh nothing, I'm sorry, it's nothing you've said, well not directly anyway. Just carry on with what you were saying."

"You can't just leave it at that Frank. What did I say?"

Frank knew he had to say something but was aware of the two boys sitting listening intently to everything being said, "It'd be best if I left answering that for a minute." He called the waiter over to clear away the empty lunch plates and asked Evie if she wanted anything from the sweet trolley.

"No, I'm fine. I'll just have a coffee, but you have something and I'm sure you'd like something wouldn't you Philip?"

Before they could answer Frank said, "Of course he would, and I bet you would too, wouldn't you Alaistair?"

He turned to the waiter., "Could you please bring the sweet trolley over and let these boys have what they like from it." He winked at Alaistair as he added, "Make sure you give them a goodly portion, they're both growing lads." The waiter gave a "Yes Sir," and turned to go away, but Frank called him back, "Mrs McPherson and I will take coffee in the lounge."

He turned back to the boys, "Enjoy your sweet lads, we'll come and fetch you in a while." The waiter again turned but Frank held his sleeve and said, "Sorry to bother you, but would you mind wheeling me into the lounge?"

Evie jumped up from her seat, "Don't worry Frank, I'll do that. Let the waiter feed these boys."

When they were seated in the lounge Evie lit another cigarette before asking Frank to explain what he had been laughing at earlier.

Whilst sorting out the arrangements for sweet and coffee, Frank had had time to think through his feelings about Vernon Harper. Perhaps this was the opportunity to release forever the demon that had been in him. Nevertheless he would have to choose his words carefully if he was to avoid offending Evie.

"I was just thinking of something that happened years ago, before I joined the army. In fact it happened at Harpers, when your father was running the business and I worked there. You grandfather had made a promise to me and after he died your father wouldn't honour that promise. I'm sorry to say that I really despised him for that."

Now that the boys were no longer around, Evie also felt she could be even more open about herself than she had been up to now. She too had been holding resentment towards her father all her life, or at least that was how it seemed to her. Since the loss of Mark she had had no one to talk to about it. She missed that, and Frank was certainly someone she found it easy to talk to. He had been close to Mark as well, so that made it even easier. And the real bonus was that she probably would never see him again, so would not be embarrassed in the future by anything she said now.

"You don't have to feel bad about feeling like that towards my father. He really wasn't a nice man. He never treated me properly as a daughter. I don't want to go into detail but if it hadn't been for Mark I'm sure things would have been much worse. Anyway his own children didn't like him, so you certainly shouldn't feel bad about not liking him."

Frank was unsure what she meant by her father not treating her properly as a daughter. He hoped she didn't mean that she'd been abused but feared that was indeed what she had meant. They both sat in silence as the waiter brought the coffee and served it to them. After he had gone, Evie continued, "You've probably realised from what I've said that my marriage isn't the biggest success in the world either. Oh, we get on well enough I suppose by many people's standards, and Bertrand has been good to me in many ways, but maybe I expected that marriage to him would solve all my problems in a flash, but of course it didn't."

She took a sip from her coffee, "Bertrand was always so kind to me in France, and looking back I think that maybe I saw him more as the loving father I'd never had, when I should have been looking for a loving husband." She stubbed her cigarette out in the ashtray and looked directly at Frank, "But no sooner had I met the man I thought might fill that bill, I was told he was dead."

Evie could not believe what she had just said and felt the colour rising in her cheeks, hoping that Frank did not understand its significance.

Frank was about to comment but she spoke before he had chance to. This time it was Evie who changed the subject before she said much more than she ought, "That's enough about me. My father doesn't still bother you does he?"

"You know what," said Frank, "I've just realised that no, he doesn't. He was a big problem to me twenty years or so ago, and I spent years of my life trying to prove something. Trying to prove it to everyone, but I suppose mostly to myself and to your family, the Harpers; to your father; to

Mark and probably even to you. I laughed in the restaurant there because I suddenly realised that it's all totally unimportant now. Maybe I've proved everything I needed to. Maybe I have and maybe not, but what I do know is that it matters not a jot anymore. Seeing you today and chatting to you has really exorcised the demons once and for all."

She smiled, "Do you think you could exorcise my demons as well Frank?"

He smiled back at her, "Don't let the past ruin the rest of your life Evie. I'm sure if you really thought about it you would realise that the past is really past and you could get rid of the demons yourself."

He reached into his waistcoat pocket, took out a card and handed it to Evie, "And if they ever come back and you want to talk about it, then my works number is on that card. Just give me a call anytime you need to."

She put down her cup, got up from the chair and stood behind Frank, putting her arm around him and kissing him on the cheek, "I'm so glad I met you today Frank. I'm now going to sell the business, go back to Edinburgh and I don't think I'll ever come back to Walsall again, so maybe I won't have to face the demons again either."

She left her hand on his shoulder and looked at the card in her other hand, "I hope I don't need to telephone you with my troubles after today, but I will keep this safe. Perhaps we might meet again, I hope so. I've enjoyed being with you today and now we have met again I wouldn't like to lose touch with you all together, so if I ever feel lonely and in need of a good friend, perhaps I might phone just for a chat? Would that be a problem to you if I did?"

Frank turned his head and kissed her on the cheek, "I wouldn't like to lose touch with you either, so no, it wouldn't be a problem if you phoned. I do hope we can meet up again some day though, but in the meantime, let's both say goodbye to the demons forever."

She squeezed his hand, "That's a promise."

Book Two

(1930 to 1957)

The Wine of Life

Whether at Naishápúr or Babylon,
Whether the Cup with sweet or bitter run,
The Wine of Life keeps oozing drop by drop,
The Leaves of Life keep falling one by one.

Rubáiyát of Omar Khayyám
as translated by Edward Fitzgerald

CHAPTER ELEVEN

SUNDAY 3 AUGUST 1930

Grace Matthews had been awoken by the first crash of thunder at around two in the morning and for the past hour she had been standing at her bedroom window watching the persistent rain bounce relentlessly on the road below. Every few seconds, a streak of lightning bounded across the night sky exposing the roofline of the terraced houses opposite and the iron works' chimney stack less than half a mile away in Green Lane.

At the next lightning flash, she counted the seconds until the roar of thunder jolted her eardrums. Only seven seconds had elapsed. *'Thank goodness, at least that one was nowhere near the boys'.*

The constant rain beat unremittingly against the windows and the guttering was so full that most of the water ran straight off the roofs cascading like a waterfall to the ground below. Any rain reaching the drainpipes ran so rapidly down them that the soakaways were unable to take it away. The water was gushing straight out of the pipes into the narrow street below making it look more like the canal that ran through the field at the back of the house than a road.

Grace's mind was in a total whirl worrying about her son on his first camping trip. How on earth will he manage? Oh God, please, please look after him, she prayed. Fearing the worst, she imagined that if it were raining in Bewdley like this, the boys would be washed out of their tent and might even have been swept into the river.

She tried to convince herself that she was worrying unnecessarily, but could not. She'd had so much to worry about over the years that worrying was now almost part of her nature.

Frank, her husband, slept downstairs in the front room, as he had done for the last four years since becoming paralysed from the waist down. The shrapnel lodged in his back had moved and severed the nerve when he had been pushed down the stairs at the factory.

She knew Frank would be awake but did not wish to concern him with her worries. God only knows, his nights were restless enough without her adding to his problems unnecessarily. Even so she guessed that tonight this thunder and lightning would almost certainly be adding to his sleeplessness. Each burst of lightning and every crash of thunder bringing back painful memories of the persistent artillery bombardments from both sides on the Somme. Unlike some of his comrades, Frank had managed to retain his sanity during those dreadful days, but memories of the horror of it all still brought him out in a cold sweat. He still dealt with these terrible memories on his own; preferring that his wife should not be upset by his anguish.

After the accident the doctors had advised Grace to let her husband sleep in a separate bed. Frank had agreed with the suggestion, insisting that Grace would get a better night's sleep that way, particularly as he often stayed up late at his drawing board working on new design ideas.

At first she had resented not being able to sleep with her husband every night, but had not pushed the idea with Frank. She knew how guilty he already felt about his disability and she had reluctantly agreed that the front parlour was not big enough to take a double bed, Frank's wheelchair, his drawing board, his desk and all the bits of electrical and wireless equipment he was always working on.

She had however only waited a week after he had come home from hospital before going to Frank's bed and now she used every excuse possible to spend a night snuggled up against him in the single bed with his arms around her.

She longed for him now. Tonight her anxiety over Philip meant she missed his comfort unbearably. She felt certain he couldn't possibly be asleep with all the noise of thunder going on. Perhaps she should go down to check if he was all right, and squeeze up in bed beside him. He had never refused to comfort her and she knew that if she went downstairs to him, he would welcome her into his bed and satisfy her need. And afterwards he would hold her and after listening to her worries would undoubtedly manage to convince her to stop being silly as the boys would be fine. She could almost hear him telling her.

The next fork of lightning flashed directly into the bedroom lighting up the room and giving her silver hair an unnatural glow. It was the shock of losing her three year old daughter with diphtheria and then having to deal with her husband's accident and paralysis all within a twelve month period that had turned her hair to grey.

Last night was the first night ever that Philip had not been around to give his mother a goodnight kiss. He was growing up and perhaps he would not be giving her a goodnight kiss for much longer.

By the next flash of lightning she had made up her mind that her brother Tom would look after Philip and make sure he came to no harm. She would go to the public phone box in the morning and phone Nathan Hadley at the farm in Bewdley to make sure everyone was all right, and for tonight, she was going downstairs to lie with her husband, even if neither of them got any sleep in this awful weather.

Philip Matthews had woken early the previous morning, excited about the adventure that lay ahead of him. This ten year old boy had been romancing about the trip for some weeks. It was the first time he had ever been away from home and the idea of camping out with his cousin, hopefully with no adults around was thrilling beyond belief. He visualised it as a real expedition; an endeavour the likes of which can only be imagined by a boy not yet out of short pants, who believed himself to be a man.

He washed in a bowl of cold water in the scullery, not bothering to waste time boiling water on the range, and raced through his breakfast before fetching his bicycle out of the coal shed at the end of the backyard. When he returned into the house, his mother was just putting a pair of socks she had been darning into one of the canvas pannier bags, which had once belonged to his father. Philip took the bag from her, closed it, and picking up the other one, fastened them both to the back wheel frame of his bike. He was now ready for his holiday, so he went into the front parlour to say farewell to his father.

Frank was sitting at his drawing board when Philip walked in, but immediately swung his wheelchair around to give his son a hug.

Philip returned the hug and saying, "Bye, Dad, see you next week," was quickly on his way out of the room.

"Oi, hang on, young man. Come back here a minute."

Philip turned round towards his father, who had wheeled his chair over to his desk and was opening the top drawer. He took three shilling pieces out of the drawer and gave them to Philip.

"Here, enjoy yourself. Don't do anything silly and remember to send your mother a postcard, you know she'll be worrying about you."

"Thanks Dad, I've already put a pencil in my bag so that I can send you all a card," and waving the money in his clenched hand repeated the, "Thanks for this Dad, see you next Saturday," and was once more on his way out of the room.

His mother and little brother John were waiting for him by the scullery door to say their farewells. Grace reached into her apron pocket and gave him another two shilling pieces. He had never had so much money in his life. He put the money safely in his trouser pocket, and with a "Thanks Mom," reached forward and gave her a kiss and an extra special hug.

The three of them walked along the path at the back of the terraced houses until they reached the road. He gave his mother another kiss before jumping on his bicycle and riding off. He looked back and gave his mother and John a final wave before he turned the corner into Green Lane.

He hated riding his bike down the cobbled road of Green Lane and was pleased when he reached the smoother surface of Littleton Street. Half a mile further on at the end of Littleton Street, he passed the Queen Mary's Grammar School, where his father hoped he would be going in twelve month's time. He looked up at the clock over the entrance to the Arboretum, its fingers stretching straight across the clock face and looking like a highly waxed sergeant major's moustache. A quarter past nine. *'Good.'* he thought to himself, *'I should make it easily by half past.'*

He continued on his way, pedalling as hard as he could up the Arboretum Hill, refusing to get off his bicycle and walk up the steep incline. Ten minutes later he arrived at his Uncle Tom's new house.

None of the Richards family was as prepared for the holiday as Philip had been. His Aunt Mary was busy packing spare clothes into Edward's pannier bags, neatly folding the new socks and pants she had purchased for him a couple of days previously. His Uncle Tom busied himself putting a strap around his leather case and tying a rope around the canvas bag containing the ex army surplus bell tent he had purchased at the Army and Navy store.

Philip, who was standing at the open front door, could see them both as they fussed about in the hall.

"Come in old boy," shouted Tom, with his usual big friendly grin all over his face. "You ought to know by now that you don't have to wait to be invited in."

His cousin Edward, wearing only his pyjama trousers came out of the bathroom still drying his hair, which was exactly the same fiery red as his father's, on the towel. He peered over the banister, and shouted down to Philip, who was now standing in the hallway watching his uncle's efforts at sorting out the equipment, "Looks as though we're going to have another scorching hot day, Philip. Let's hope it stays like this all week." He turned and threw the towel into the bathroom, "I say, why don't you come up here and help me sort out some of the things I want to take with us?"

Philip squeezed past his Uncle and the pile of camping equipment. He raced up the stairs and nearly fell over Edward who had suddenly decided to pick up the towel in the bathroom before his mother complained about his untidiness yet again!

Edward was obviously as excited about the holiday as Philip was. He talked about all the things they were going to do, almost without stopping for breath between sentences.

"You know, my Dad says we'll be able to go fishing in the river near to where we're going to camp," he said. "He's going to ask Granddad if it's OK, but he's pretty sure it will be. It should be more fun than fishing in the canal, shouldn't it?"

"Well, I guess so," replied Philip, "But why didn't you say about it before. I haven't brought my fishing rods with me." The disappointment sounded in his voice, "Do you think I've got time to go home and fetch them," his voice lifting, as he suddenly realised that maybe he wouldn't be left out of it after all.

Tom, who had heard the bantering from below, shouted up the stairs, "I wouldn't worry about that Philip, I've got some spare rods you can borrow." Remembering how independent Philip liked to be, he quickly added, "I suppose if you really want to use your own though, we can ask your Aunt Mary to call in at your mother's and collect them for you before she comes down to Bewdley in the car."

"Oh no, I don't want to put Aunt Mary to all that trouble, I guess your fishing rods will be fine. So if you don't mind, I'll use those."

"Sure, old boy. I'll make sure they're packed for you. I'll tell you what," he added, "Why don't you come down and sort them out. They're hanging up in the garage, and I'm sure old Ted there will get dressed much quicker if he's left on his own."

"Yes," added Mary, "You've been messing about getting washed far too long, Edward. Hurry up, it's about time you were down here giving us a hand to sort out all these things we need to take with us."

Edward pulled a face, and shaking his head mouthed imaginary words, imitating his mother's telling him off. Philip put his hand to his mouth to stifle the laugh he was about to make, but in reality, he never did quite understand why Edward made fun of his parents behind their backs.

"I'm coming, Ma, I won't be a minute," and in an attempt to make Philip laugh again, pulled his mouth down with his fingers and nodded his head.

"Oh, before you go down," Edward said to Philip, "have you got your swimming trunks with you. It'll be fun to go swimming in the river."

Philip smiled, relieved that he had remembered to pack them. "Sure," he said, "My Mum's also let me have the big towel so that I can lie on it after we've had a swim. We'll be able to sunbathe and get a super suntan in this hot weather," and at that he dashed down the stairs. "Must go and sort out those fishing rods. I'll sort out your rods as well shall I?" he shouted back to Edward, but he did not wait for a reply.

For the next hour everyone helped to get things ready. Tom reversed the black Austin 7, which had been purchased for £125 12s 6d, part of last year's profits, out of the garage so that Philip could search more easily for the fishing rods. Meanwhile Tom fixed the luggage rack, which he'd designed and built at the factory the previous week, to the roof of the car.

Unfortunately the little car with its 747cc engine could not take too much weight, but as Mary would be the only person travelling in the car, it would be possible to put some of the camping gear in it. Tom and Mary's cases where accordingly put on the back seat, Edward's bicycle was tied on to the roof rack and after a little pushing and shoving the bag containing the tent was also manoeuvred on to the back seat.

Tom was glad to be getting away from the factory for a week. Unlike Frank who always seemed to enjoy nothing more than working on a new design and thinking up ways to extend the business, Tom always regarded it as just a job and preferred to go fishing, or enjoy an evening with his new found friends at the Labour Club. He kept telling Frank to relax a little but since Grace had opened the shops neither of them seemed to relax much.

Frank had even had another go at him only yesterday saying that there was an enormous market for well designed radios and he was convinced they could expand the home radio business dramatically if they tried hard enough. He also thought they should try and sell some of their military radios to foreign countries as well.

Tom thought that perhaps Frank was right, he usually was, but there was no point letting it get in the way of the holiday. Next week would be time enough to worry about the business again. He knew what Frank's reaction would be though if he didn't do something about it then. He would get angry at his disability and say, "Damn it man, if I wasn't stuck in this bloody wheelchair, I'd get out there and sell the damn things myself."

He was jerked out of his pondering by Philip who had found the fishing rods and asked where he should put them.

"Oh, just drop them here, Old Boy, and then perhaps you and Ted can bring the rest of the stuff out of the hall and we'll pack it away."

"OK," he replied, and soon he and Edward had brought all the camping gear out of the house, and spread it out on the driveway; pots, pans, buckets, Primus stove, blankets and everything else you could think of were soon littered all around the car.

Mary came out of the house and saw all the paraphernalia lying on the driveway, "I think you've forgotten the kitchen sink." she mused.

Tom laughed, "Oh dear, that won't do," he chuckled, and turning to Philip he said, "Philip just go and fetch it for me."

Philip, without thinking turned to go into the house and both Tom and

Edward immediately fell about with laughter. Philip stopped and turned scarlet as he suddenly realised how stupid he had been.

On seeing Philip's blushing face, Mary realised his action was instinctive and wished she could lessen the poor boy's embarrassment, but could not think of anything to help. She nevertheless pulled faces at her husband and son, without Philip seeing, in an attempt to get them to stop laughing.

Realising Philip's discomfort, Tom stopped laughing and told Edward to fetch the tandem out of the garage. "And can you go and fetch the trailer from round the back of the house, Philip?"

The tandem, which Edward and his father were going to ride to Bewdley, but would be used by Tom and his wife whilst on holiday, was wheeled out of the garage. Philip went through the gate to the back garden and returned with what looked like a box on two bicycle wheels, with a tubular arm projecting from the front like a swan's neck. The box on wheels was, in fact, a bicycle trailer built by Tom.

He had originally made it for a Chimney Sweep friend, but after it had been built, he decided on some changes to make it lighter and more quickly fixed to and dismantled from the back of the bicycle, so he built a 'mark two' version for the Chimney Sweep and kept the original for himself.

Tom had thought about going into business building and selling them to tradesmen whose only form of transport was a bicycle, for carrying their tools and other bits and pieces in, but he never did and went into business with Frank making wirelesses for the military instead.

As he was bolting the trailer to the tandem, Tom cursed under his breath about the awkward fixing clip, made worse by the difficulty he had in using the second spanner in his right hand which had the index finger missing.

At that moment, the spanner slipped out of his hand and he let out a, "Bugger, bugger, bugger," loud enough for everyone to hear.

When Mary told her husband to "Go and wash your mouth out with soap and water," Philip forgot his previous embarrassment and laughingly asked his uncle, "Do you want any help with that, Uncle Tom?"

The grin spread across Philip's face, and Tom remembered how Frank had laughed at him in the same way when he had first tried to fix the trailer to a bicycle. He looks just like his father did at the same age, he thought; the same unruly mousy hair, the same deep blue eyes, and the same infectious grin which stretches from ear to ear when he laughs.

Tom grinned back at Philip and with a lump coming to his throat as he remembered how energetic Frank had been before his accident said, "No thanks I'll manage." He so wished Frank was still as fit as he used to be.

He certainly missed him at the factory on the days when he worked at home.

Philip and Edward went back into the house to fetch the last of the camping gear and at last Tom managed the task in hand. With the trailer secured, he set about packing all the gear into the trailer box.

Tom was just packing the last few pieces when his wife shouted from inside the house, "Don't forget all of this,"

They all turned to find out what had been forgotten. "Go and see what your mother's got for us," Tom said to Edward, just as Mary came out of the house carrying a cardboard box filled with food under each of her arms.

"And before you say anything, don't blame the boys for not bringing it out before," she implored Tom, "They didn't know it was tucked away in the larder cupboard"

Tom let out a few unspoken expletives under his breath, but actually said out loud, "Heavens above! Now I'll have to repack this darn thing."

Both of the lads let out a roar of laughter and stated to unpack, spreading things all over the drive again.

"Hang on a minute, lads," said Tom, "there's no need to empty everything out. I'll tell you what, just go inside and make a cup of tea for us all. I'll have this all repacked by the time tea's ready and then we can all get on our way as soon as we've drunk it."

Once all the others had gone inside he started to repack, swearing as he did so. This time not under his breath, but still not loud enough to be heard inside. He did not want to get another public reprimand from his wife.

Ten minutes later as he and the lads sat on the front doorstep drinking their tea, Tom decided that everything was finally ready.

Mary came out of the house again, this time carrying a smaller parcel in each hand. Holding out her right hand, she said, "This is your picnic lunch," and holding out the bag in her left hand added, "and in here is a bottle of lemonade for the boys, and a bottle of beer, for you, Tom."

Tom took the packets from her and put them on top of everything else in the trailer. "Thanks," he said as he gave her a kiss on the cheek. "Right lads, let's be on our way, or we'll never get on our holiday. I reckon that by the time we've ridden to Dudley and over Dudley hill, we'll just about be ready for these sandwiches, and I'm sure we'll be ready for something to drink. It's going to be thirsty work riding our bikes in this heat."

Philip climbed on his bike, whilst Edward and his Uncle Tom said their farewells to his Aunt Mary.

Mary shouted to Philip, "Don't I get a kiss from you as well, Philip?"

"Sorry," he replied, as he got off the bicycle, leaned it against the wall and walked across to his aunt, to bid her farewell.

With all the expected hugs and kisses completed, Philip remounted his bicycle whilst Tom and Edward mounted the tandem; Tom at the front and Edward at the back. They all pedalled out of the drive waving farewell to Mary, who would follow on behind in the car after she had tidied up, fed the cat and taken her to the next door neighbour who had promised to look after her for the next week.

Mary was not going to rush herself however as she had no intention of leaving for at least another hour. She did not wish to arrive at the farm in Bewdley before the rest of them.

It was however nearly three hours before she finally got on her way. First she had stopped to chat to Hattie Brookes, her next door neighbour when she took the cat round and they had sat on the deck chairs under the shade of the big oak tree in the back garden. It must have been nearly 90 degrees in the direct sun. She hoped the boys were not finding the ride too strenuous in this heat.

Then, after tidying up at home and safely locking all the doors, she drove to her sister-in-law's house to let her know that Philip, Edward and Tom had all set off safely, and ended up spending time chatting to her friend without the usual interruptions from Tom and the children.

Mary had met Grace during the war, when Tom and Frank had come to see her brother at her father's farm in Bewdley and had brought Grace along with them. It had been the boy's last leave before sailing for France, and Mary recalled how pleased her mother and father had been to meet Tom and Frank. They had worried about Joe being in the army and were relieved to know that he had made such good pals with Tom and Frank and were even more pleased to know they were looking after their young son.

At first, the three soldiers went off along the river to enjoy the freedom of not being ordered about by an officer for the first time in weeks, leaving the girls, who were following behind, to chat away to each other. The girls quickly realised how similar they were, particularly in their likes and dislikes, and by the end of the afternoon were giggling and laughing together like two thirteen year old schoolgirls who had known each other all of their lives.

Frank, who was 'walking out' with Grace, had on this occasion chosen to stay with his pals, but Tom found the opportunity before the end of the day to talk to Mary and ask if she would mind if he wrote to her occasionally. She had readily agreed.

The girls become firm friends over the following twelve months and regularly wrote to each of the boys as being their way of doing their bit to cheer up the lads fighting the Huns, and would often meet in Birmingham on Saturday afternoons to read the boys replies to each other.

For some time the letters were jolly and humorous but gradually the ones between Grace and Frank, and between Mary and Tom, started to become more personal to the point where Grace and Mary would deliberately miss out bits when reading the letters to the other. When the boys reached the front, the letters became more serious and although there was still humour in them, the girls realised the boys were no longer on the jolly ruse they had previously talked about and started to worry more and more about them.

It was then that Mary realised her concern about Tom's safety was equal to that she had for her brother's safety. She still wrote letters to both of them and to Frank, but gradually the letters to Tom became longer and it was always his reply letters she anxiously awaited.

One Saturday afternoon, Grace confided to Mary about her true feelings for Frank and she wasn't surprised when Mary told her that she had similar feelings towards Tom. Thereafter they discussed their feelings to each other in much greater depth than they would ever dare put in their letters. During the next few dreadful months, as news of the tragedies on the Somme became known, they were able to find some comfort talking to each other about it and built up a closeness and intimacy that was to last the rest of their lives.

Mary parked the car in Birch Street and walked along the alleyway at the back of the row of terraced houses in Brighton Terrace. She knocked on the back door of Grace's house but did not wait to be let in before walking through the scullery into the back room. Grace, who was bending over the black leaded grate shooed 'The Colonel', the cat, out of the chair for Mary to sit in it. The coal fire was burning brightly even on such an intensely hot summer's day.

"I'll sit over here if you don't mind, Grace. It's a bit too hot to sit that close to the fire," Mary said as she moved over to the table and sat in one of the upright wooden chairs against the wall, as far away from the fire as she could get.

"Yes, I don't blame you," said Grace, "It's really too hot for a fire today but I've promised to take young Johnny and some of the Sunday school children on a picnic to Barr Beacon on Monday. I'm baking a few scones and some bread to take with us. I wouldn't have lit the fire otherwise." She turned back to the fire saying, "Let me just take these scones out of the oven and then we can have a cup of tea and a good old natter."

At that, Grace picked up the oven cloth and knocked the latch to the black leaded oven door next to the roaring fire open, and proceeded to take the scones and bread from the cast iron oven.

The smell of freshly baked bread filled the room and Mary was reminded of the times she and her brother Joe had stood as children at the door in the farm kitchen at home when their mother was baking bread, waiting for her to take it out of the oven so that they could share the hot steaming crust off the end after their mother had spread it thickly with freshly churned butter.

Grace put the bread and scones on the table to cool and fetched the second batch from the scullery where she had left them to rise in the cool and placed them in the oven to cook.

"These smell wonderful." said Mary pointing to the scones.

"Yes let's spoil ourselves and have a couple with a cup of tea," replied Grace.

"That'd be lovely, It'll keep me going 'til I get to Bewdley and have something to eat with the others."

"Oh, I'm sorry, I didn't think," said Grace, "If you've got to wait that long for something, I'll do you something more substantial. There's a little salad left over from the yesterday's lunch. Would you like that?"

"No, a couple of your scones would be fine, I don't really feel hungry but they smell so gorgeous I just can't resist them. Is there anything I can do to help?"

"No, I'll just make the tea," replied Grace as she picked up the teapot, and put in two heaped teaspoons of tea out of the tea caddy that stood on the mantelpiece above the fire. She filled the teapot with water from the steaming copper kettle on the hob above the fire's oven and placed the teapot on the table to brew. She went to the scullery to refill the kettle and fetch her last jar of home made blackberry jam from the larder cupboard. Returning, she placed the kettle on to the hob and handing the jam to Mary, proceeded to pour the tea.

"Would you just put some jam on a couple of scones for Frank and I'll take them to him with a cup of tea."

"Yes sure. How is Frank these days?"

"He manages most of the time especially when he has some new design idea, but he misses the hustle and bustle of the factory so much. The trouble is that when he does go there, he gets so irritated and angry at all the things he can't do, that he comes home in a foul mood. I sometimes think it's much better for everyone when he stays here to do his work. Lucy pops in with the mail and keeps him up to date with things at work, but enough about Frank and the business, let's talk about something else for a change."

The two women chatted away for the next hour, occasionally checking through the window to make sure that John was still safely playing in the back yard outside.

Grace suddenly jumped out of her chair, "Oh I almost forgot the bread." She reached for the oven cloth, and using it carefully to avoid burning her hand, opened the oven door and took out the bread.

"Another few minutes and the children would have been having toast on Monday," Grace commented, and both women laughed.

"I'd better be going soon," Mary dropped into the conversation a little later, and she started to get out of her seat. "By the way I've just remembered, can you sort out Philip's fishing rods? Tom's promised to take the lads fishing and although Tom's put in a spare set of his for Philip to use, I'm sure he'd rather use his own."

Grace went outside to the coal shed and came back carrying the fishing rods. Mary was washing up the tea cups at the scullery sink.

"There's no need to do that, Mary, I'll clear up when you've gone."

"No, I'll just finish this bit of washing up, and then I really must be going." replied Mary, who by this time had started to wash up all of the bowls and other cooking utensils Grace had used for her cooking.

John followed his mother into the scullery. "You look all hot and bothered, Johnny, I hope you haven't been out in this sun too long." Grace filled a glass from the tap, "Here, sit down a minute and drink this water while I help Aunt Mary finish the washing up."

Grace took up a tea towel, wiped dry all the crockery and placed it in the appropriate place on the shelves.

Whilst saying their farewells, Mary promised to take good care of Philip and make sure he returned safely the next Saturday, probably late in the afternoon.

Mary eventually arrived at the farm just after three o'clock by which time Tom was beginning to worry about her safety.

The boys were stretched out on the small lawn at the front of the farmhouse, filling themselves with the cake and lemonade provided by Grandma Hadley.

Mary apologised for her late arrival, but this was soon forgotten as they all helped carry the heavy tent across the fields. They were all glad to drop their load about thirty yards from the river on to the grassy patch chosen as the campsite.

Erecting the canvas bell tent was no easy task for one man, assisted by two small boys and one woman. Nevertheless, the boy's enthusiasm made up for their lack of a man's strength. Once they had all heaved the weight of the canvas on to the centre pole, Philip and his Aunt held on to the pole, whilst Edward helped his father bang in the pegs and tie the guy ropes securely to hold up the whole configuration.

The task completed, the boys went back with Tom to fetch the bicycle trailer. Once they had safely dragged it across the bumpy field, they took the tarpaulin groundsheet from it and carefully laid it on the grass inside the tent, clipping it to the fixings around the base of the tent. The remaining camping gear was then taken from the trailer and put inside the tent.

"You'll be as snug as bugs in a rug in here boys," said Tom, half-wishing he hadn't made the arrangements for his wife and himself to stay in the farmhouse. He would have loved to camp out with the boys.

"Right lads, now let's sort out some supper for us all. Edward you take the bucket and go and ask Grandma if she'll let you have some drinking water and Philip you take this billycan and ask her if she'll fill it up with milk for you."

"Oh, and while I think about it, when you come back you can go and collect some firewood from the wood over there," he said, pointing to the small copse which lay about fifty yards away to the left along the river. "And don't forget, when you do collect the wood, don't go anywhere near the river, and only collect wood that's already lying on the ground. You mustn't break any branches off the trees."

"Be careful you don't spill any of it on your way back," Mary shouted out after the boys as they went racing off across the field towards the farmhouse.

Tom had soon cleared a small area of grass on the bank above the river and gathered a few stones in a small circle to form a suitable safe place to light a fire. He collected the Primus stove, a small bottle of methylated spirits and the matches and set about lighting the Primus to boil the water.

Meanwhile, Mary spread a blanket on the ground a few yards from where Tom was busy pumping the stove to get it going, and fetched bread, butter, a knife and a plate from the tent and started cutting the bread and spreading the butter on to it for their meal.

The butter had melted in the heat of the day, making the task rather messy. She would have to try to keep the remaining butter in the water bucket to keep cool if it was to last for another day.

When she had finished, she covered the plate of bread and butter with a tea towel to keep it free from flies and other nasties and went back to the tent to collect the chicken she had cooked the previous evening. She also collected lettuce; tomatoes; a jar of her home made tomato chutney; a jar of her pickled onions; and the caraway seed cake Grace had given to her.

By the time the boys returned, she had four plates of roast chicken and salad laid out on the blanket in front of her, and Tom soon had a steaming pot of tea ready to accompany the meal.

The boys were ravenous after the hard day's cycling, followed by the work of preparing the campsite and Mary had to spread more bread and butter for them and Tom, who was having no trouble at all eating as fast as the boys.

After the meal, Tom went off with the boys to collect firewood and Mary tidied up the supper things. Tom lit a wood fire, and managed, by manoeuvring the larger stones with a stick, to provide a firm base for the kettle to sit over the fire.

As they waited for the kettle to boil again, the sun became lost in the sky behind the clouds gradually drifting in from the west and the cool air rising from the river gave a very welcome change from the heat of the day.

But soon the clouds became darker and heavier obliterating all the remaining light from the sky and Mary became very worried that the boys would be washed out in the storm that was obviously on its way. "Perhaps they should come and sleep in the house tonight? I'm sure Mom and Dad would be really pleased to put them up."

The boys who heard the comment, both gave a resounding "No" to the suggestion and Edward pleaded that they should be allowed to stay in the tent, "We'll be fine Mom, really we will."

"Well you stay with them tonight Tom," Mary said, "I really won't sleep if they're out here getting soaked while we're tucked up in bed."

Tom laughed at the suggestion, "But it'll be all right if I get soaked will it?"

Edward who had been planning a midnight feast with Philip protested at the suggestion and after much discussion, and very much to Mary's disapproval, it was decided the boys could sleep on their own, provided that Tom came to look after them if the rain became too heavy.

Mary and Tom made sure the boys were snugly tucked in before they extinguished the camp fire, said goodnight to the boys, and walked across the field back to the farmhouse to enjoy an hour's peace and quiet with Mary's parents before going to bed themselves.

Tom was woken by Mary sometime after two-thirty. She usually gave him a punch in the arm to stop his snoring, but tonight she was shaking him violently.

"For goodness sake, wake up," she was crying, "How on earth can you sleep with all that noise outside? Can't you hear the thunder? It's enough to wake the Gods!"

Tom merely rolled over; his usual response to the 'snoring' prod, but the shaking and the crying out continued until he was sufficiently awake to sit up in bed.

"What on earth's the matter?" he mumbled whilst rubbing his eyes, "Just calm down and tell me what the problem is."

"Are you deaf or something?" she berated him, "Can't you hear that thunder?"

She suddenly drew in a sharp breath, "Oh my God, look at that lightning! Can't you hear the rain? It's been like this for the last quarter of an hour and all you can do is snore peacefully away, as sweet as a baby."

"But what's the matter?" was his sleepy reply, "What's the problem?"

"Oh, for goodness sake! The 'problem' as you put it, is the boys, you idiot! They'll be getting drowned in that tent out there. It's been thundering and lightning like this for ages and you promised you'd go and fetch them if it rained, but all you can do is lie there snoring away."

Tom decided he had best get out of bed before he got into more trouble. He went to the window and pulled the curtains open wide. A flash of lightning lit up the room, followed very quickly by the roar of thunder.

Mary was soon standing by his side and they both stared out of the window, looking towards the river where they had pitched the tent.

Another flash of lightning streaked across the sky somewhere the other side of the river and for a brief second, Tom thought he could make out the shape of the tent, but he wasn't absolutely certain.

"I'm sure I saw the tent just then," he said to Mary, "Did you manage to make it out?"

"I think so, but I'm not at all sure, it went dark again so quickly," she replied, "But you'd better get dressed and go to them."

Tom ignored the comment, "If we both concentrate on that spot, we should see it when the next flash of lightning comes."

"What good's that? With all this rain they could be swimming in that tent. Poor lads are probably frightened out of their wits. You'll just have to put some clothes on and go over to see if they're all right."

"I'm sure they'll be fine and in any case I'll get soaked to the skin before I get to the gate to the field," was his immediate response. "Why don't I leave it a bit to see if this rain abates?"

"No, you have to go now, there's no knowing what trouble the lads are in out there, and anyway you promised you would. You have to go; we promised Grace and Frank we'd look after Philip and I'd never forgive myself if anything happened to him or Ted while we're just standing here watching."

Another flame forked across the sky but this one was too far to the left and did not give any light to the area where they were looking. The next flash of lightning seemed to bounce straight into the field at a point not more than two hundred yards away.

"Look you have to go," said Mary, "The next one like that could hit the tent and then what would happen?"

"Oh all right," said a very reluctant Tom, "But I don't know what I can do about that, assuming I get there that is."

At this he started pulling on his trousers without bothering to remove his pyjamas. "Did you pack that thick woollen high necked sweater you knitted for me last winter?"

Mary went to the wardrobe and returned with the navy blue woollen bundle, "Yes, here it is. It's a good job I remember some of these things, or you'd be in a fine pickle, wouldn't you?"

Tom did not bother to answer but quickly pulled it on over his pyjama jacket.

Mary went back to the wardrobe and returned with an oilskin cycling cape and his boots. She handed him the oilskin, "It's a good job I thought to put this in the car after you'd left this morning."

"You're an angel," he said to his wife and pulled on the oilskin before giving her a kiss on the cheek.

Several rounds of thunder shook the room which was lit at irregular intervals by the lightning.

"I think I'll get dressed and come with you?" said Mary.

"No, you stay here, there's no point both of us getting soaked. Look, I'll take some matches with me and when I get there, I'll light the candle lamp, and if this damned rain doesn't put it out, I'll wave it in this direction to let you know everything's OK. When you see it, you can light that candle over there, and wave it across the window to let me know you've seen my signal. Provided everything's OK I might as well stay with the boys until morning. I think that'll be the best thing to do, don't you? No point getting the boys soaked as well if we don't have to."

"I suppose so," his wife replied, "But you'll make sure you see my signal first though, won't you?"

"Of course I will and then you get back into bed and stop worrying."

He picked up his matches, making sure there were a few left for his wife to light the candle which was standing next to the alarm clock on the table at the side of the bed. He gave his wife another kiss, "Now stop worrying, I'm sure this rain can't keep on like this for much longer."

Just as he opened the bedroom door, the door opposite opened and Grandpa Hadley stepped out wearing his old green chequered woollen dressing gown, tied at the waist by an old leather belt. He had obviously lost the original cord. Grandma Hadley followed him from the room.

"Do you think the boys are all right, Tom?" she asked.

"I'm just off to check," Tom replied.

Grandpa Hadley walked over to Mary who was still standing looking out of the window, "I had a feeling we'd get rain tonight but not this bad. I do hope my cows are all right in the barn."

His wife let out a scream at him, "You and your blessed precious cows! It's the boys we're all concerned about."

"So am I, you silly woman, I only made a comment about the cows. Nothing wrong in that is there?" and turning to Tom said, "Let me know if you need anything for the lads. By the way, it'll be pretty muddy out there by now. You'll find some Wellingtons by the back door. If you can find a pair the right size, you'd better put them on. Shall I come with you?"

"No thanks, no point us all getting soaked," he replied, "And thanks for the offer of the wellies, I'll have a look at them as I go out. And thanks for your offer of help as well, but I'm sure the lads will be OK. You get back to bed and get your sleep. You'll need it if you've got to get up at six to milk the cows."

Tom did not bother with the Wellington boots, but went straight out of back door and across the farmyard towards the gate leading to the field were the tent was pitched. "Damn," he said to himself as his boots squelched into the ground, "Nathan was right about this mud, I should have borrowed those Wellingtons."

The rain was still falling as vigorously as ever and was soon running down his neck. He continued in the general direction of the tent, just about managing to get some sort of bearing when the lightning lit up the sky.

At the next step, his foot went into a deep puddle and the water ran over the top of his boot soaking his sock and collecting under his foot. "Oh God." he cried, "Who's bloody stupid idea was it for the lads to camp out? By the time I get over there I'll be soaked to the skin."

He was indeed 'soaked to the skin' when he eventually reached the tent, but very relieved to have got there in one piece and to find the tent still standing. He unfastened the opening and when he was inside, he managed to find the candle lamp and light it. Both boys were fast asleep, totally oblivious to the weather outside.

"Jesus, what a waste of my bloody time," he said to himself, not knowing whether to be pleased that they were safe or angry that he had defied this weather; got soaking wet for his trouble; and lost his night's sleep; only to find that there was nothing to worry about after all.

He signalled that the boys were safe to his wife, but she was obviously having some difficulty seeing the signal as it was some time before he got the agreed reply signal from her. After which, he got back into the tent, took off the wettest of his clothes, found a towel and dried his head and feet, then lay down between the boys to try to finish his night's sleep.

A little after six o'clock they were all woken by Mary's voice shouting from outside the tent, "Are you all right in there? It stopped raining ages ago." She opened the tent flap a little and crawled inside, "Thank goodness you're all safe," she said.

Edward sat up and rubbed his eyes, "What time is it?" He looked at his mother, "What are you doing here?" He then saw his father lying on the floor beside him, "What's Dad doing here? Didn't you trust us to look after ourselves?"

All was quickly explained but neither of the boys could understand what all the fuss was about. Philip was particularly bothered, as he was not sure whether he had done wrong by staying asleep. He thought it must be all right though when his aunt gave both Edward and him a hug.

"Actually it looks as if it might be a nice day again," said his Aunt Mary. Philip peeped out of the tent and looked up at the sky, feeling the warmth of the early morning sun as it broke clear of the remaining clouds.

Mary laughed with relief that the boys were fit and well, and gave her husband a friendly kick with the suggestion that he'd had enough sleep.

"Why don't you all get up and come across to the farmhouse for some breakfast? Grandma's been as worried as I have, and she insists on you all coming over for breakfast. Mind you, she thinks you must have been awake all night like the rest of us. Perhaps you'd better not tell her you slept through it all. Anyway, it'll do you good to get a cooked breakfast inside you so hurry up."

During breakfast, Philip asked about the medal attached to the picture frame which took pride of place on the mantelpiece. Inside the frame was a typewritten document, and in an identical picture frame next to it was a picture of a young soldier. Edward's grandfather immediately got up from the table, took down the two frames and handed the one of the soldier to Philip.

"That's our son, Joe." He then handed him the other frame, "And that's the Military Medal he won for his gallant action in saving the life of his Captain in the War. You read the citation and it tells you what a brave man he was."

He then spent the whole of breakfast telling the story of how his son Joe had saved his Captain's life in 1916. The story he told of his son's valour was the story that Philip's father had told him. Frank Matthews had completely reversed the roles played by himself and Joe in the way that Captain Harper had been dragged across no-man's land back to their own trenches; the only true part of the story being the final bit where Joe had been fatally shot. It would be another fifty years before Philip learned the true story and the fact that the medal really belonged to his own father.

After finishing their breakfast, Edward and Philip asked to be excused from the table so that they could return to their camp whilst Tom and Mary went to church in the town.

"Yes, that's fine lads," said Grandpa Hadley, "But if you don't mind, can you just help me get the cows into the field before you go off to enjoy yourselves?" All three went out of the house into the farmyard and Nathan Hadley walked over to lead his cows out of the milking shed. "Be good sports, lads, and go open that gate over there for me?"

"Sure, Mr Hadley," Philip replied, "Race you to the gate," he shouted to Edward, but he'd already started to run and was several steps ahead before Edward joined in the race. Philip easily reached the gate first and rushed to open it but in his haste he stepped back right in front of Edward who crashed into him and fell on his backside into the mud.

"Yeahhhh," Edward screamed as he scrambled up, water dripping from his trousers, mud all down the back of his legs and his hands covered in something even worse. He had managed to find a cowpat where he had put his hands to the ground behind him to halt his fall.

"Yeehhh," Philip echoed, "What a mess! You'd better clean all that muck off you."

Edward turned and looked to see if his grandfather had seen his mishap, but he was still in the milking shed prodding the last of the cows out of the stalls and had not seen the fall.

"Look don't let my Grandpa see this mess," Edward pleaded, "Let me stand on the other side of the gate and you can stay between me and him so that he can't see the mess I'm in." Holding his hands up in front of him, he walked towards Philip and said, "Let me wipe this off on your shirt."

Philip stepped away and was saved from the threat by the appearance of Grandpa Hadley coming out of the shed prodding the cows along with his stick, "Right boys, just hold that gate open and make sure all the cows come through it."

Edward stood behind the gate furthest away from his grandfather to make sure he couldn't see all the muck on his back. Nevertheless his grandfather saw his dirty hands.

"What on earth have you been playing at?"

"Oh nothing, I just slipped in the mud."

"Look, let me get these cows into the field and then you can get cleaned up. You'll find a tap just inside the milking parlour, go and wash your hands there. You'd better help him Philip and get some of that dirt off your shoes as well. Just leave the gate, I'll shut it when I've finished, but don't forget when you've washed that muck off your hands, shut this gate and the one at the other end of the field when you go back to your campsite. I wouldn't be at all pleased if my cows managed to get near the river."

Both boys moved towards the milking parlour with Edward moving in a crab-like sideways move so that his Grandfather could not see his backside.

"I'll go back to the tent and change into my spare pair of trousers when we've washed our hands," Edward whispered to Philip, "Do you think we can wash these dirty ones before my Mom and Dad see them?"

"We can try," Philip replied not at all certain how they would do so.

"What do you think is the best way to wash them before mother sees them," said Edward as he was changing into a clean pair back in the tent.

Philip thought about it for a minute, "I'll tell you what," he said, "Let's take them down to the river and wash them like the Red Indian squaws do. The sun's shining quite brightly now. I'm sure they'll be dry in no time at all."

"That's a great idea," replied Edward as he fastened his belt round his clean trousers, picked up his dirty trousers, donned his fishing cap and set off for the river.

The rainfall in the night had already worked its way into the river flow, which was now running rapidly as it washed against the riverbank. Edward stood at the top of the embankment looking down at the river some six feet below him. The bank, which had been quite dry and firm when they visited the spot the previous evening, was now quite wet and muddy.

As the boys looked down at the swelling river, the noise of their laughter disturbed a water vole in the reeds near the water's edge and it went scampering up the slope to the right, quickly getting lost in the ferns growing near the top of the bank.

"Did you see that," said Edward, "I'm not going down there to get bitten by one of those. I know what we'll do Philip; I've just had a great idea. You go and fetch that piece of rope Dad used to tie the tent up with yesterday. I'm pretty sure it's lying just inside the tent. We can tie that round the trousers and dip them into the river from the top of the bank here, without going down there near any of those horrible rats."

Philip quickly returned with the rope and passed it to Edward, who rolled the trousers into a bundle and tied the rope round them. He swung the rope outward, so that the trousers did not drag against the muddy bank. Unfortunately when the rope reached its full length and pulled taught, the trousers continued on their way, slipping out of the rope and falling some ten yards up stream.

"Strewth!" Edward cried out, "What are we going to do now? My mother will kill me when she gets back! For goodness sake, Philip, what on earth are we going to do?"

Philip was just looking at the spot where the trousers had fallen, his mouth wide open in astonishment. He brought his left hand up to his mouth, his eyes stretched open in horror as he turned to look at Edward lost for words.

As if on a given signal, both boys ran up stream to where the trousers had fallen into river.

"Look there they are," shouted Philip,. "Down there look, they're caught against that branch hanging in the river."

"I know what we can do," he suggested, "We can go and put our swimming costumes on and go down into the river and get them back. Come on, let's go and get them on quickly."

"No, that's no good," replied Edward, "Look at the way the water's pulling at them in the current. If we don't get them out quickly they'll be washed down river and we'll never get them back."

"OK," said the ever-resourceful Philip, "You go and fetch my swimming costume, I'll get undressed here behind this bush and go and retrieve your trousers and when you bring me the swimming costume I can put it on and come out of the water."

At this, Edward made his way back to the tent, whilst Philip quickly stripped off all his clothes and started to make his way carefully down the slippery bank. He reached for the branch to steady his descent, but snagged his hand on the stub where a small branch had been broken off.

"Damn," he muttered to himself as he sucked the palm of his hand to try and stop the bleeding. Luckily, it was only a scratch and would soon mend.

He continued to edge into the river, taking in a big gasp of air as he lowered his body into the cold water. The water was only about three foot deep at this point and so, with his feet on the bed of the river, he was able to keep his head above the water as he safely retrieved the miscreant trousers.

He heard Edward running back to him with the swimming costume. He appeared at the top of the bank, waving the costume triumphantly in the air.

"Here we are, Philip. Here's your cost...u....m......e...." The word dragging out into a long cry as Edward slid unceremoniously down the slippery bank.

Philip watched the unfolding event in amazement. It seemed as if he was watching one of those silent film comedies. Edward came down the slope, waving his arms about in almost slow motion. The spectacle came to a sudden end as he reached the bottom of the bank and went 'plop' into the water; the noise of the splash breaking the spell on Philip.

Edward let out a scream as his body entered the freezing water. Splashing about, he quickly managed to stand upright a few feet from Philip.

"Are you all right?" Philip enquired as he made his way to Edward and put his hand on his friend's shoulder.

"I think so," replied Edward, "I can't feel any pain anywhere, except in my bum where I bounced down that slope. But even that's not too bad." he laughed as he added, "I think this water's giving it the 'freeze' treatment and it's feeling better already."

Philip joined the laughter at the joke before asking Edward for his swimming costume.

"Here you are," he said as he handed it to him, "I don't know why we bothered though, you should have just jumped in fully clothed like me!"

Both boys let out another loud laugh, and once they had started the laughter continued for some time as each boy thought how stupid the other looked. The laughter would cease for a brief moment but then Philip would look across at Edward, fully clothed, cap still on his head, water dripping from the rim, and fall about laughing again in that over demonstrative way that ten year olds seem to indulge in from time to time. Philip's laughter would bring about a repeat performance from Edward and vice versa.

Eventually Edward put his hands to his face to wipe the tears of laughter from his eyes and in doing so wiped a streak of blood across his chin from a cut he had acquired on his slide down the bank.

Philip's laughter stopped abruptly, "You've got blood on your face," he said, pointing to Edward's right cheek.

"Where?" said Edward as he stroked the middle three fingers of his right hand down his cheek and then checking them for the signs of blood. When he looked at his hand he could see the cut across the palm which, aided by having been constantly held in the water, was now bleeding quite freely.

"Oh, damn," he said, "I've cut my hand. I must have done it on the way down."

"Snap," shouted Philip, as he held up his right hand and displayed the cut on the palm of his own hand, which was still bleeding slightly.

The boys looked directly into each other's eyes and, as if orchestrated, they lifted their right hands in unison and clasped them tightly together at eye level. "We are now blood brothers," quipped Philip.

"Yes," replied Edward, "We should make a solemn vow of everlasting comradeship and promise to always look after each other, like the Indians do in the films."

"I so promise," said Philip.

"And so do I," replied Edward.

The chugging of a boat's motor coming from up river broke the trance. The noise increased as a pleasure boat carrying a group of schoolgirls rounded the bend. One of the girls saw the boys and quickly pointed them out to the others and soon they were all waving profusely and some of the girls started to throw them kisses.

The boys gulped, as they felt the blood rush to their cheeks. Goodness knows what the girls thought of the sight they saw. But then both realised that the water covered them almost up to their necks and the girls had no way of knowing that one of the boys they were waving to was fully clothed whilst the other was totally naked.

The thought that the girls could not be aware of their predicament brought a wry smile to each boy's face, and once again they each lifted their right hand and clasped them together. "One for all and all for one!" they shouted in unison as they waved back to the girls.

It was not until the boat had vanished round the next bend in the river that Philip realised the banners he had been waving at the girls were his swimming costume in one hand and Edward's trousers recovered from the river, in the other.

CHAPTER TWELVE

SUNDAY 3 AUGUST 1930

Megan Prior had been unable to get to sleep. She was now almost two weeks overdue and the bulk of her unborn child made it impossible for her to lie comfortably in any position.

Lawrence, her husband, lay peacefully asleep at her side. She had become somewhat irritated over the last few weeks that he'd been able to fall into a deep sleep almost immediately on getting into bed. Thank goodness he wasn't a snorer; that would have really niggled her. She on the other hand, had been having some fitful nights with little sleep. The recent hot weather had been almost unbearable and she had lain in bed for several nights bathed in sweat. Tonight was no exception; but her discomfort and unease were made worse by her worry over the unborn child.

Both the doctor and the midwife had told her everything was fine with the baby and they were sure she was going to have a very healthy child. Nevertheless, she still had very vivid nightmarish memories of her first child being stillborn, and the subsequent miscarriage. She so desperately wanted this child and hoped it would not be much longer before it was born, but would happily wait a few days more if the midwife was right and it would be a healthy baby. She had however been having twinges for the last hour or so but was unable to decide whether these were real contractions.

She felt another 'pain' in her stomach. Was this it? It didn't seem as bad as the pains she had when she lost her first baby. Still that last pang seemed longer than the previous ones and was certainly more of a real pain.

The silence of the room was broken by the sound of rain starting to beat against the windowpane; a patter of rain, which very rapidly increased in both its velocity and it's intensity.

She lay quietly in bed going through all the names they had contemplated for their child, when suddenly she felt an urgent need to go to the toilet. She certainly did not wish to go to the toilet at the bottom of the yard in this weather. Damn! She'd have to use the commode; a thing she preferred not to do if she could avoid it. It always felt so undignified. Still she could not hold herself much longer and this rain certainly didn't seem if it was going to abate at all. So commode it would have to be.

She eased herself out of bed and walked over to the commode. As she was doing so she felt another twinge in her stomach. This one took her breath away. She sat back on the bed and waited for the pain to ease. She was sure they were lasting longer now.

'How long ago did I have the last twinge?' she thought to herself. *'I'd better start keeping a note of the time.'*

She picked up the alarm clock sitting on her bedside table. Two minutes past two o'clock. *'I'll have to try and remember that. Let's say two o'clock. I'll remember that easier.'*

She put the clock down and went to the commode, lifted its hinged seat and sat herself on it. She no sooner sat down than the room was lit up by a distant flash of lightning. As she sat, she tried to decide whether the pains were the real thing or not, she didn't want to wake Lawrence unnecessarily.

Another flash of lightning lit up the room.

'I wish I'd pulled the curtains together. I don't want anyone seeing me sitting here!'

She was just about to get up and close the curtains when a boom of thunder reverberated around the room.

"My God, what was that?" yelled Lawrence as he was awoken from his slumber and sat bolt upright in bed. "What's happening? Are you all right?" he said, looking across at his wife.

Megan was grinning back at him, highly amused by this sudden activity on the part of her husband. And, as she was still not absolutely certain the pains were often enough yet to chase after the midwife, she was pleased she hadn't been the one to unnecessarily wake him.

"Well that was thunder," she said, "but I'm fine except that I think the thunder is heralding the arrival of the baby."

"Oh heavens! Are you sure? How long? Oh heavens, I'd better get up and go and fetch the midwife. Will you be all right whilst I'm gone?"

Megan grabbed his arm and prevented him getting out of bed, "Calm down, calm down. There's no need to rush out of bed like that, I don't think I'm far enough to get the midwife out in this weather yet."

She eased herself back into bed next to him.

"Let's just lie here a bit. You can give me a cuddle and we'll see if the pain comes back."

She was more certain however, when the next pain came. It was much stronger and lasted longer than the others but the crashes of thunder and flashes of lightning were much more frequent than her pains and she was sure that they must have awoken everyone for miles around.

She looked at the clock, "Just after quarter past two. Fifteen minutes since the last one. Yes, I think it's the baby coming. We'll just wait for two or three more to make sure and then perhaps you had better get up and get ready to fetch the midwife."

Half an hour later they decided that Lawrence should fetch the midwife even though the storm was still as bad as ever.

Lawrence got out of bed and quickly dressed. He folded his pyjamas and lifting his pillow went to place them there as usual.

"I don't think you'd better put them there," said his wife. "We don't want the midwife getting all excited when she sees those, do we?"

"No we shouldn't give her too many distractions." He leaned over and gave Megan a kiss on the cheek, "I'll put them here in the drawer with my other clothes."

"Look, shall I dash next door and ask Mrs Pratt to come round to look after you whilst I fetch the midwife. She did say she'd be happy to wait with you if we wanted her to. I know she's a bit of a chatterbox but I really don't want to leave you on your own and goodness knows how long I might be in this rain."

"No, there's no need just yet and anyway we'd better get the bed and everything ready for the baby's arrival. Where's the list Mrs Gibson gave us. I'm sure I've put everything ready but we perhaps ought to check it off again."

Lawrence handed her the list that Mrs Gibson, the midwife, had provided and they checked the items piled in various places around the room against the list.

They checked the things for the baby first. Nappies, nappy pins, rubber pants, vest, blankets, woollen socks and gloves, nightgown, shawl, ...

Next came Megan's clean clothes etc. for changing into after the baby's birth. Then things that Mrs Gibson would need, a pile of freshly laundered but old towels, strips of linen, cotton wool, a bowl, a bucket, a water jug and washing bowl. And so the list went on, everything requested present and correct, as Lawrence knew it would be. It had, in fact, been ready for the last month and had been checked off by Megan every morning on getting up and every night before getting into bed, and for all Lawrence knew, probably several times each day as well.

Megan felt another twinge, this time more painful than previously. "Yes, I'm sure the baby's coming now. Let's put these clean sheets on the bed."

Lawrence reached over and started to pass her the almost new sheets that Megan's mother had lent them for the occasion.

"No, not those," said Megan, "The old ones underneath. It doesn't matter if those old ones get marked and soiled. Here let's get these dirty sheets off the bed first and pass me that rubber sheet to put on first. We don't want to soil the mattress if we can help it do we?"

After making the bed, Megan climbed on to it and lay down, whilst Lawrence folded up the sheets which they had removed and took them downstairs into the scullery. When he returned he enquired whether he should now fetch Mrs Pratt from next door and then go to fetch Mrs Gibson.

"Not right now, the pain is coming again. Wait 'til it's over and then you can fetch her," said Megan. "Perhaps this rain might have slowed down by then. You'll get soaked to the skin if you go out right now."

"If you're sure," said Lawrence as he lay down next to his wife, putting his right arm around Megan's head and laying his left hand lightly on her bulging stomach. Megan grabbed the hand on her stomach and squeezed it tightly as the pain came. She gulped a deep breath and said, "There's another one. Yes, I'm sure it's the baby coming. You can call Mrs Pratt after it's eased off and then fetch the midwife, but when you go for Mrs Gibson please rush back as quickly as you can, I don't want to be left here too long with Mrs Pratt and I certainly don't want her here for the actual birth. You will get rid of her when the time comes won't you? Oh I do so hope everything will be all right this time!"

"Don't worry, everything will be fine. I'll get rid of Mrs Pratt as soon as I get back with the midwife and I'll stay with you this time. Just calm down and everything will be OK. Look, I'll just be gone a few minutes now whilst I fetch Mrs Pratt and then I'd better dash off for Mrs Gibson. I'm sure she wouldn't stand any nonsense from Mrs Pratt anyhow."

Lawrence looked down at his wife as he fastened his bootlaces. She was pulling her face and biting her bottom lip, "I'll have to use the commode again as soon as you've gone, so make sure I'm back in bed before you bring Mrs Pratt in."

Lawrence smiled at her. He never ceased to be amazed that someone as beautiful as Megan had consented to marry him. At thirty-two she still looked as lovely as when he had first met her at twenty. He secretly hoped that the baby would be a girl and grew up as beautiful as her mother. He so hoped that the baby would have its mother's good looks, but for now he just wanted everything to be OK.

"I love you sweetheart," he said as he bent over to kiss her, "You're the best thing that ever happened to me."

She looked up at him and smiled, "You don't have time for all that nonsense now, just get going and hurry back." The emphasis placed on the 'hurry back'.

Lawrence gave her another kiss and rushed downstairs. He put on his mackintosh in the scullery and opening the back door was taken aback by the ferocity of the rain. With all his concern for his wife he had been almost oblivious to the storm outside. He went back to the scullery and took his old trilby off the coat hook, put in on and went out of the door, making sure it was firmly closed behind him.

The house was one of a line of terraced houses and the Pratt's back door was directly opposite theirs about six feet away but there was a low wall separating the two sculleries which were single storey buildings attached to the back of each house. Because of the wall he had to run to the gate at the end of their house, through the gate, through the gate at the end of the Pratt's house and up to their back door. A short enough journey, but by the time he was knocking on the Pratt's back door he was soaked.

He was sure they must be awake in this weather. Surely this thunder must have awoken them already. Perhaps they thought the banging was merely more thunder. He waited for a break in the thunder and lightning and gave the back door a series of bangs as loud as he could. A candle light materialized in the back bedroom and he could see John Pratt's puzzled face staring down.

At that moment, a flash of lightning lit up the yard and Lawrence waved up with one hand whilst banging the door again with the other. John Pratt responded by waving his arms about in a manner that Lawrence took to mean he was on his way down.

What seemed like an eternity to Lawrence, but was probably only about a minute or so, the back door was unlocked and John Pratt stood there in his pyjamas with an old cardigan pulled over the top. Lawrence thought that the cardigan must have belonged to Sybil Pratt, his wife. It was much too big for John and hung off his narrow shoulders and dreadfully thin frame like an oversize, but extremely short cloak. Many a time he and Megan had laughed when they saw the Pratts together; her short and tubby body contrasting against his tall spindly frame.

Their name didn't help either. Megan always referred to them as the Sprats and sometimes quietly repeated the 'Jack Sprat' nursery rhyme in her head. Lawrence had to admit that it was an apt comparison but the Pratts were extremely good neighbours and he prayed that Megan would not accidentally call them Sprat to their face one of these days.

"What's up mate? What's the problem? Come in you're getting soaked out there."

Lawrence stepped into the scullery and closed the door behind him. The water dripping off him making a pool on the tiled flagstone floor. John passed him an old towel, "Here dry your face a bit. What's up anyhow."

"It's Megan, she's started, can Mrs Pratt come and stay with her while I go for the midwife?"

Lawrence removed his hat, shook the water off it into the sink and started to wipe his face on the towel that John Pratt had given him.

"I don't think I can ask her to come out in this," said John. "She's scared to death of this thunder and lightning. She's huddled under the bedclothes and I'm sure she won't move. I daren't ask her, and to make matters worse, Betsy is all huddled up beside her. The blessed dog is no damn good as a guard dog in this weather. As scared as her mistress she is."

A despondent Lawrence was trying to work out what to do next and was just about to say, "No matter I'll go and ask someone else," when John added, "Look give me a minute. I'll get dressed and I'll come and stay with Megan. She'll be all right with me, she will."

Lawrence was none too sure about this proposition but felt he didn't have much alternative but to accept the offer in the circumstances.

His concern and hesitation must have shown in his face for, before he was able to answer, John said, "Don't worry old boy! I know I ain't going to be your wife's favourite minder in the circumstances, but it'll be all right, I promise you. One good thing, she won't have to listen to Sybil's chatter all the while. She's got a good heart, but she does go on a bit, don't she?"

He laughed at his own remark but Lawrence decided it would be best if he did not join in the laughter or worse still, agree with the comment. "Oh, and listen," John continued, "don't you worry if the baby starts to come while you're gone. Had plenty of experience, I have. Been there to help old Betsy with all her litters and she never come to no harm."

Lawrence was beginning to think that this time it was John who was 'going on a bit'. Maybe it was because his wife wasn't there to dominate the conversation for a change. He was also horrified at the thought of him helping with the delivery, but was desperately anxious to fetch the midwife so he had to accept the proposal.

"Well thanks for the offer then. Yes I'm sure Megan would be pleased to have you sit with her," he lied. "Look, I'd better rush and fetch the midwife else you might have to deliver the baby."

He looked at John Pratt trying to anticipate Megan's response to having him as a minder, but realising that there was no alternative just repeated, "Yes, thanks for the offer, I'd better be off then," before retrieving his hat, dashing past Mr Pratt and out of the door.

A rather startled Mr Pratt shouted after him as he ran the maze back to his own back door, "Right, you go and let Megan know I'm coming and go and fetch the midwife. Don't worry, I'll let myself in. Front bedroom she's in, is she? I'll just go and get dressed then. Won't be a minute. See you later."

When Lawrence reached his back door he shouted back, "That's great thank you. See you in a bit." And with that he rapidly removed his hat and mackintosh, and dashed up the stairs to inform Megan of the arrangements.

She was not at all pleased at the thought of John Pratt looking after her whilst Lawrence was away, but realised that there was no alternative. She had thought that John Pratt could fetch the midwife whilst Lawrence stayed with her, but then she remembered about Mr Pratt's bad leg, injured in a factory accident, and she realised that Lawrence would be much quicker on his bicycle, particularly in this weather. In any event, her pains were not that close yet and Lawrence ought to back with Mrs Gibson before the baby was born, so she decided not to interfere with the plans made.

As soon as he heard John Pratt shout up the stairs, "All right for me to come up?" Lawrence shouted back, "Yes," before once again kissing his wife good-bye, and turning to go knocked into John Pratt as he entered the room. He apologised adding, "Really must go. See you in a bit."

Luckily, Mrs Gibson, the midwife, lived only a little over half a mile away, but nevertheless Lawrence was completely soaked through by the time he arrived at her house a little under ten minutes later.

Lawrence admitted to himself, as he cycled to her house, that he found all this thunder and lightning a little scary. The street gas lamps along the way, created pools of light in which the heavy rain leaped inches above the road like fountains bouncing off a pool. In any other circumstances, he felt certain he would have found an excuse not to go out on a night like this. Perhaps Mrs Pratt had the right idea after all; being wrapped up in a warm bed was much better than this.

As he knocked on Mrs Gibson's front door he hoped he didn't have the same problem making her hear as he had making John Pratt hear and was relieved when the light went on in the bedroom almost immediately. A little later Mrs Gibson appeared at the door, wrapped in a long woollen dressing gown, an extremely frilly pair of bright red slippers on her feet and with hair curlers in her hair which was covered with a thick brown hair net.

Lawrence viewed her in some amazement. This was quite a different picture to the one he had previously seen of a very prim and proper nurse, dressed in her blue and white starched uniform and with her frizzy hair covered with her starched white nurse's cap.

"Hello there, Mr Prior. Megan's started then, has she?" and without waiting for his reply, she continued with, "Do come in out of the rain a minute. How often is she getting the pains then?"

"About every ten minutes when I left," he replied.

"And she's all right, is she?"

"Well, yes. A little anxious, I think, but, yes, she's fine. I think she's glad it's finally started."

"Ah good, well you'd better get back to your wife and I'll be along as quickly as I can. Oh, and make sure you've got plenty of hot water on the boil by the time I arrive. It won't take me long to get dressed and get my things together. You be off then. See you shortly."

"Thank you, I'll get back then if you don't mind. I've left Megan with the next door neighbour looking after her, but I'm sure she'll be glad to have me with her. Look I'm sorry I've had to fetch you out in the middle of a night like this."

"Now don't be silly, young man," she replied, "I'm used to getting up in the night this. Babies always seem to pick the middle of the night to be born, but I must admit your baby has picked a corker. By the looks of you, I think I'd better bring some spare dry clothes with me. You're soaked to the skin, so off you go and get out of those wet clothes. I won't be far behind."

The ride back home was all downhill, and the round trip to alert Mrs Gibson was therefore completed in a little less than half an hour. Lawrence was pleased he hadn't been away too long and was certainly pleased that he could get out of this incessant rain.

He parked his bicycle against the wall outside the back door; not wasting the time to put it back in the garden shed. He entered the house, pulling off his hat and mackintosh as soon as he had closed the door. His boots came next and his soaking wet jacket quickly followed. His mackintosh had given him little protection against the rain tonight.

He filled the kettle with water from the scullery tap, lit the burner on the gas stove and put the kettle on it, before dashing up the stairs. Jack Pratt was holding Megan's hand, who was lying on the bed puffing and blowing in obvious discomfort and pain from the contraction she was experiencing at that moment.

Lawrence rushed round the bed and taking hold of her other hand, asked if she was all right.

She continued huffing and puffing for some time before answering him. "Does it look as if I'm all right, you idiot," and quickly realising her husband's question had been asked out of concern, added, "I'm sorry dear, I shouldn't have shouted, but when the pain comes, it bloody hurts."

Lawrence was somewhat taken aback by his wife's use of 'bloody'. She rarely, if ever, swore and he realised her pains must now be much worse than they had been before he had left.

He squeezed his wife's hand tightly, "Try not to worry now, dear. Mrs Gibson is on her way and I'm sure she'll be able to help with the pain when she comes."

"Look," he said, "I put the kettle on when I came in, do you think you could manage a cup of tea? Do you think that might help?"

"No," she replied, a wry smile on her face as if by way of mild reprimand, "I don't think I could manage it at the moment. Let's get this all over with first then perhaps I might enjoy one." Her face again being pulled into distortion as the next labour pain arrived.

Lawrence gave her hand a gentle squeeze, "Mrs Gibson's sure to be here soon."

Before Megan's pain had subsided, there was banging on the front door. John Pratt got up from his seat and headed towards the bedroom door. "That's probably the midwife now. I'll go and let her in, shall I? And then I'll make myself scarce. I'm sure you don't want me around anymore, do you Megan? Best to leave you in the hands of the professionals."

He was through the door before he'd finished speaking and did not wait for a reply to any of his queries. Half way down the stairs, he stopped and shouted up to them, "Look if there's anything you want me to do just give me a shout. Anything at all, I shan't bother going back to bed now, so just give me a shout and I'll be only too happy to help."

They heard him open the front door and usher Mrs Gibson into the house and out of the rain. He made some comment about it not being a fit night to send the cat out. They did not quite catch Mrs Gibson's reply, but it was obvious from the tone of her reply that his joke had not been well received.

Mrs Gibson shouted up the stairs, "Won't be long now, folks, I just want to get out of these wet clothes. Are you all right up there? Soon be with you and have everything under control."

In no time at all she was on her way up the stairs and when she entered the room Lawrence was quite surprised at how prim and proper she now looked in her uniform. Quite a change from the woman who had opened her door to him half an hour earlier. He would have to remember to tell Megan about her night attire later.

She marched across the room and took Megan's hand from Lawrence and felt her pulse, checking it with the nurse's watch hanging on her left breast.

Everyone in the room was perfectly silent as she carried out the procedure.

"That's fine, my dear. Now how are you feeling? How often are the pains coming now?"

"Oh, about every five minutes," Megan replied, and then remembering the first question added, "I don't feel too bad at all, just starting to get a bit weary."

"Nonsense," said Mrs Gibson, "You've got a long way to go yet. We've got a lot of work to do yet, this is no time for getting weary."

She crossed over to the bedroom table where she had placed her bag. "Now young man, I want you to go downstairs and boil me up some water, plenty of it now. Best boil a couple of saucepans full as well as the kettle. When it's boiled, you can bring the kettle and one of the saucepans. Now just go and do it while I give your wife a check up down below to make sure everything is going as it should."

As soon as Lawrence had left the room to follow out her orders, Mrs Gibson took the blankets and top sheet off the bed and folded them up. "Won't be needing these tonight. I'm sure you're plenty warm enough in this heat anyway, aren't you? It really is still quite muggy even though this blessed rain has cooled it down a bit. Never mind I'm sure we need the rain after all the sun we've had over the last couple of weeks."

"Now let's just see how you're getting on." At this she sat on the bottom of the bed, lifted Megan's nightdress and started to examine her.

Megan flinched very slightly as Mrs Gibson touched her.

"Now, now, dear, no point being embarrassed about this, it's just got to be done I'm afraid. By the way, you said something last week about having your husband here during the birth. I don't usually have husbands around you know. If you're embarrassed about me checking just to see how you're progressing, are you sure you want your husband around?"

Megan could well see how Mrs Gibson usually got her own way about keeping husbands out of the room during births. Mrs Gibson's 'military' manner could certainly be off putting, and Megan could understand how some women would be dominated by her, but she had got to know her quite well over the last few months and knew her to be a very caring midwife whose main concern was the well being of mother and baby. Megan felt her posturing and ordering about was all part of an act to make sure that whatever needed to be done in the best interests of mother and baby got done with emotion and feelings kept under control.

"Yes, I am sure about having Lawrence around. He wants to be with me and I want him here, and I'm sure I'm no worse than any other woman when it comes to internal examinations, now am I?"

Megan stressed the 'Now am I', not so much as a question but more as a positive statement which she was defying Mrs Gibson to contradict.

Mrs Gibson smiled, realising that there was no need to bully this mother into following her instructions, "No, you're quite right my dear, none of us really like being poked about, do we? Never mind, I've finished for the time being and everything is coming along fine. We've got a wee bit to go yet. Your waters haven't broken, but we can easily do something about that later if necessary. For now, everything's fine."

Megan went into another contraction. Mrs Gibson held her hand and Megan knew from the way she held it that she really was as gentle and caring as anyone could be.

"Now I know it's not easy dear, but it really will help if you try not to tense up so much when the pain comes. I want you to relax even though I know that's probably quite impossible. Anyway you know what I mean, so just breathe slowly and deeply."

Megan followed the instructions, deliberately taking a deep breath, followed by a slow breathing out.

"That's it," the midwife said with a smile on her face, "Now just do that every time the pain comes, and it should really help."

Mrs Gibson knew about Megan's previous medical history and wanted to make sure that this birth went well, probably more than usual. She also knew that Dr. Wilson had wanted Megan to go into the Maternity Hospital for this birth and had been quite put out at Megan's insistence about having the baby at home. Dr. Wilson had told Mrs Gibson how Megan had firmly stated, "I know I'll feel much more comfortable at home in my own surroundings with my husband around. And, in any case, I'm sure that Mrs Gibson can look after me as well as anyone else can in the Hospital."

Mrs Gibson felt quite proud that one of her 'mothers' felt this confident in her ability. She would do everything she possibly could to make sure her patient's confidence was well founded.

Lawrence came into the room carrying the kettle in one hand and a saucepan full of steaming water in the other.

"Careful with those, young man, we don't want any accidents do we? Put them on the mat on the table over there next to my bag."

She followed him to the table and taking a metal tray from her bag, laid it on the table and took numerous medical instruments out of her bag and put them into it. She took the saucepan and poured the steaming water over them. "I did sterilise these instruments properly yesterday, but I always feel it's best to do this, just in case."

She passed the almost empty saucepan to Lawrence, "Now take that back downstairs, fill it with water again, and put it on a very low gas. We shouldn't need any more hot water just yet. Did you put any more hot water on the stove?"

"Yes, there's one more saucepan. Do you want me to bring it up?"

"No, just turn the gas off from under that one. You can soon boil it up again if needed."

She got more bits and pieces from her bag as Lawrence left the room. "And now, young lady, let's get you ready for this birth."

Two hours later, Megan was in an almost sitting up position with all the pillows in the house behind her back. Lawrence was sitting on the bed next to her with his right arm supporting her head and was grasping both her hands with his left hand. Mrs Gibson was kneeling at the foot of the bed; her sleeves rolled up above her elbows and was gently massaging Megan's tummy between Megan's open legs. The pains were now coming quickly one after the other and were lasting almost a minute.

Poor Megan had started to get a gnawing backache between the contractions and Mrs Gibson had suggested a hot water bottle. This had helped a little but had made Megan sweat even more profusely.

At the next contraction, Mrs Gibson suggested that they all breathe together, "Breathe slowly with me, that's it! Deep breath. WONDERFUL! That's it, just let it happen. Feel yourself opening up. Look at me, that's it, you're doing fine." The contraction started to ease. "The pain going away now?" Megan nodded. "Good. Take it easy for a bit and get ready for the next one. How's the back now?"

"It's really hurting," said Megan, "I think it's worse than the contractions themselves, at least I feel something's happening when they come."

Mrs Gibson put both her hands on Megan's stomach and felt the position of the baby, "I think it might help if you lay on your left side for a bit. Lawrence, just get rid of those pillows and help Megan on to her side."

Lawrence did as he was told and disposed of the pillows under the bed.

"Right," said Mrs Gibson, "Now I want you to lift your right knee up so that you're almost lying on your tummy. That's it. That's fine!" She got up from her position at the bottom of the bed. "Now Lawrence come round this side of the bed and sit close to Megan's back. You can gently rub it where it's hurting her most."

Once more Lawrence did as he was told, asking his wife to tell him when he had found the right spot to massage.

Each time a contraction came, all three in the room had got into the routine of breathing together. Megan cried out with pain, and started to become very irritable particularly towards her husband, who, picking up on

Mrs Gibson's words of encouragement, had begun to join in with the, "That's it, deep breath and let it happen."

Megan rebuked her husband when he added on one occasion, "You're doing fine," followed with, "It won't be much longer now."

"How do you know that everything's fine and it won't be much longer? You haven't got a clue what it's like, have you?"

Poor Lawrence was at a loss for words and tears began to form in his eyes, "I'm sorry," was all he could find to say as he looked at his wife like a lost schoolboy.

Megan realised how hurtful her remark had been and added, "So am I. Give me a hug and then let's get on with it, I don't think I can stand much more."

The massaging by Lawrence, and the encouragement from Mrs Gibson did little to ease Megan's discomfort, the pain from the storm of contractions, and particularly the constant backache, wore away at Megan's previous positive approach to the birth. Contraction followed contraction and Megan began to feel that the process of birth would never end. She began to feel more and more weary. It seemed the pains had now taken over the whole of her body, overwhelming her very being.

She shouted out as the pain welled up once more, "Oh no, no more, I can't take any more. Please, please take away the pain."

Mrs Gibson said, "Actually you're doing really well. I know it's not easy, but please try and relax. If you can I'm sure baby won't take much longer in coming. I'll tell you what. Just get up for a minute. Lawrence walk her round the room again and see if we can't get rid of the backache once and for all."

Lawrence set about lifting his wife from the bed, and as she moved on to her feet, it felt that the baby moved round with her swinging movement and suddenly the pain in her back was gone and she felt a gush of warm wetness between her legs.

She put her hand between her legs to catch the flow, "My waters have broken and I think my back pain's gone! What's happened?"

"Back on the bed, young lady," Mrs Gibson replied. "I'm sure that what that means is that your pelvis has finally finished opening wide enough for baby to get through and baby really is on its way. Back on the bed, and let's get ready for the next contraction."

As soon as Megan was back on the bed in the birthing position, the next contraction came, but this time Megan felt much more at ease. Her eyes moved from Mrs Gibson to her husband, the glimmer of a smile on her face as all three took a deep breath in unison.

When the contraction was over Mrs Gibson put her stethoscope to Megan's tummy and listened for baby's heartbeat. Megan and Lawrence both held their breath and were perfectly silent as if they were expecting to hear the boom of a heartbeat themselves.

"Yes baby's doing fine" said Mrs Gibson as she placed the stethoscope back round her neck, "Now when the next one comes, let both Lawrence and me help you more. Look at me and we'll take a deep breath together, and when you feel the urge to push, give a nice strong and steady push."

The three of them soon got into a routine and with each contraction they all took a deep breath and as they each held their breath, Megan gave a firm but strong push, going slightly red in the face each time. Lawrence held her left hand tightly in his and gently stroked her forehead with his right hand. From time to time he would take the towel and wipe away the sweat from her face and body.

Megan's previous anxiousness and agitated state had now subsided and she began to 'enjoy' the pleasure of pushing through the pain. She was much more relaxed now that she could push, and with each contraction tried to record the feelings she was experiencing; storing them in her head, so that she could recall them at some later time.

Mrs Gibson once more took a ball of cotton wool and wet it in the basin of warm water lying beside her. She wiped the birth canal and beamed as she looked directly into Megan's eyes. "I can see the top of baby's head now covered with hair. Right, now next time you get a contraction, I want you to look directly at me, try to relax and breathe with me and PUSHHHHH!"

Now with each contraction, she was using such words as "BEAUTIFUL" and "WONDERFUL" and "Yes baby's really on its way now."

She invited Lawrence to look at his child entering the world and at one stage took the mirror from the dressing table so that Megan could see her child's head appearing. But, just as the baby's head had fully emerged, she spoke firmly and authoritatively to Megan, "Stop pushing! Hold it there! I don't want you to push no matter how much you feel you need to."

Megan puzzled at this change to the routine, tensed up and implored, "Why? What's the matter?"

Mrs Gibson again spoke quietly and almost matter of factly, "Nothing to get upset about, my dear, I just need to deal with the cord. It seems to have got wrapped round baby's neck. Now just do as I've said and everything will be fine."

Both Megan and Lawrence had come to have complete confidence in Mrs Gibson over the last few hours, and Megan did exactly as she was told, leaving Mrs Gibson to deal with the matter.

Mrs Gibson was relieved as Megan merely panted at the next contraction and did not push. It was just as well that neither she nor Lawrence had realised the sudden panic she had felt when she saw the head emerge and the obvious distress shown on the poor mite's face. Luckily she had seen straight away the cause for the distress; the child was being strangled by its own umbilical cord wrapped several times around its neck.

She quickly took hold of the cord and after clamping it, cut it and unravelled it from around the child's neck. She took a fresh wad of cotton wool and, after wetting it in the basin, wiped the mucus and blood from the mouth and nose. She reached over to her instruments lying in the tray on the dressing table and taking the mucus extractor put the syringe in baby's mouth and gently suctioned, clearing an air passage for baby to breath.

"Ah, that's better," said Mrs Gibson, "Poor little mite had the cord round its neck three times. I've never had one that wrapped up in the cord that many times before. But baby will be OK now. No need to worry."

Baby's face gradually grew less agitated and became pink as air started to reach the lungs.

"Right!" shouted Mrs Gibson, "Baby is fine now, so at the next contraction you can push as hard as you like. One last long and very strong push. Right. Deep breath. PUSHHHHHHH!!"

Megan did as she was told and, with great relief, felt the baby finally slide from out of her, ably aided by Mrs Gibson, who gently pulled the baby as Megan pushed.

The baby cried as soon as Mrs Gibson held her out for Megan to hold.

"Congratulations," said Mrs Gibson, "You have a fine healthy girl."

Lawrence beamed at Megan as she took the newborn child to her breast. He had never seen a newly born child before and was somewhat shocked at the wrinkled, blood smeared, tiny thing held by his wife.

Megan, on the other hand, was immediately filled with awe at the wonderful and beautiful child she held closely to her. It was the most exquisite baby she had ever seen and she immediately felt at one with this little baby girl, who was already rolling her open lips over Megan's breast, searching for the nipple to suck.

She smiled at Lawrence and leaned her head forward to give him a kiss. They held each other for some time unable to speak with their joy.

Lawrence whispered in Megan's ear, "Thank you," and "I love you." She looked at him and mouthed the words, "I love you." She turned to the baby, giving her a hug as she almost shouted out, "And we love you to death; you gorgeous little girl."

Mrs Gibson, who had been busy all this time, cleaning and tidying up, passed a clean towel to Megan and suggested that she wrap it around the baby to keep her warm. She then passed her a damp flannel and suggested that she use it to wipe away some of the mucus from the child.

A few minutes later, Mrs Gibson asked Megan to push again, as the placenta was ready to come away. Once this was delivered, Mrs Gibson took it and wrapped it in the thick brown wrapping paper, which was one of the items on her list of items given to Megan in preparation for the birth.

This task completed, she went into a frenzy of cleaning up. The baby was taken from Megan to be washed and given the once over to check that all the vital parts were present. When the baby had been dried, she was powdered, wrapped in a cotton shawl and then handed to Lawrence to hold, whilst Mrs Gibson took out a metal curved tray hanging from a spring attached to weighing scales. She held the spring firmly in both hands and asked Lawrence to place the child very carefully in the tray. He did this, and then Mrs Gibson proudly announced the weight, "Six pounds twelve ounces. A good healthy weight for a little girl."

She asked Lawrence to remove the child from the scales and then she dressed the child.

Lawrence was amazed at the difference now compared to the newborn child of half an hour ago. The little girl now placed in the cot, had pink cheeks, wisps of fine blond hair and gorgeous blue eyes like her mother. She really was beautiful.

"You'll have plenty of time to stand gawping at her later," Mrs Gibson chided, "Right now why don't you go and make a nice cup of tea for us all." She looked across at Megan and added, "And I'm sure a nice bacon sandwich wouldn't go amiss after all that hard work, would it dear?"

"Actually I do feel a bit peckish now," replied Megan.

"That's right, off you go then young man, whilst Megan has a wash, and she'll look all beautiful for you when you come back."

Lawrence once more did as he was instructed, and when he returned fifteen minutes later with a pile of bacon sandwiches and hot cups of tea, the bedroom had been transformed. Megan was sitting up in bed once more holding the baby, hair combed, clean nightdress and bedclothes, and the curtains had been opened letting in the bright sunshine.

"Good heavens," said Lawrence, "It's stopped raining! When did that happen?"

"I guess it stopped ages ago," replied Mrs Gibson, "Anyway, it looks as if I'll be able to keep dry on my way back home, thank goodness. Let me just have a cup of tea and one of those sandwiches and I'll be on my way."

Lawrence handed her the tea and a bacon buttie. She took a swig of the tea before adding, "I'll let Doctor Wilson know you've had a lovely baby daughter, and I imagine he'll pop in to see you later this afternoon. What are you going to call her anyway?"

Megan looked across towards Lawrence and raising her eyebrows and shrugging her shoulders replied, "Well we're not quite sure yet. Lawrence likes Samantha; but I'm not certain about it."

Mrs Gibson took another sip of her tea and, after thinking for a moment, said, "Yes I think she'd make a fine Samantha, but you'll have to make up your mind soon. Can't leave the poor little girl without a name for too long, can you?"

She finished her tea and bacon sandwich and picking up her bag, leaned over Megan to look at the baby once more, "See you later, sweetheart," and glancing across at Lawrence added, "Or is it Samantha? Anyway must be on my way now. I'll pop in to see you again later today and if there are any problems you know where I live. Don't worry about seeing me out. Just put Samantha in the cot and let your wife have another cup of tea. I'll see myself out."

She swept out of the room leaving the new family alone together for the first time. When they had both finished their tea and sandwiches, Lawrence moved the cups and plates onto the dressing table and lay on the bed beside his wife.

"Do you think it will be all right if we just have Samantha between us for a little while. It won't hurt her will it?"

"Of course not, silly," replied his wife, "So it is going to be Samantha is it?" and without waiting for his reply added, "OK, Samantha it is. Just pass her here."

They lay quietly together for some time with baby Samantha lying peacefully on the bed between them, savouring the happiness of the moment. It seemed that they had both waited so very long for this moment and everything about it seemed perfect.

Megan gave her husband another hug and kissing young Samantha on her cheek said, "I wonder what sort of life she has in store for her. I do hope that when she grows up, she meets someone as nice as you to love and marry."

Little did she know that the boys, who were to be the men in Samantha's adult life, were at that very moment standing in the River Severn, one fully clothed and the other completely naked, swearing an undying brotherly bond to each other.

CHAPTER THIRTEEN

1936

Philip was pondering the morning's events as he pushed his father up the hill towards the General Hospital for his six monthly check-up. How did his father know the Mrs McPherson they had met in the park that morning? His father seemed to know her so well. In fact at one point over lunch, he had sensed a level of intimacy between them that had made him feel quite uncomfortable. And yet he had never heard his father, or his mother for that matter, ever mention her name. His father had spoken about Captain Mark Harper once or twice, but he had never mentioned that Captain Harper had a sister or that he knew her.

Frank was also quietly and privately reflecting on the feelings and emotions he had experienced that morning on meeting Evie again. The first time he had seen her, over twenty years previously, she had epitomised the perfect woman to him, and for most of that twenty years he had regarded her as beyond his reach both socially and emotionally. But this morning; although the woman he had seen in the park, was at first glance a beautiful and perfectly groomed cultured lady, she was on closer observation, no grander than his own wife Grace.

He started to compare the two women in his mind. Grace was now a naturally handsome, socially confident and successful businesswoman, who dressed elegantly and needed little make-up to be the strikingly fine-looking woman of whom he was immensely proud. Evie on the other hand, now wore considerable make-up; too much in Frank's opinion and she smoked far too much, but then he had never liked to see women smoking. He had never seen her smoking before and she had never used much, if any, make-up when he knew her during the War.

He started to re-live their conversation and consider whether his assumptions about her life and particularly her relationship with her husband had been correct, but Philip asking if he had met Mrs McPherson much over the years interrupted his thoughts.

"No, I first met her in her father's office at Harpers where I worked before the War. I then met her again during the War. She was Miss Harper when I knew her, Miss Evie Harper. She was a nurse at the field hospital where I was a patient. Mark, her brother was my Captain, and the three of us spent a few evenings chatting together. Anyway that was a long, long time ago, and I haven't seen her from then until today. But it was nice to meet her again. It would have been nice if your mother could have met her."

"Why? Does Mom know her then?"

Frank was somewhat thrown by the question and seemed to become quite distant and lost in thought. Philip, who could not see the pensive look on his face, thought his father had not heard the question and repeated it, wrenching Frank out of his musings.

"I'm sorry son, I was miles away. No, I don't think your mother has ever met her. In fact, other than the few times we met in France, I only ever met her that once in her father's office. Well met isn't entirely true; I just saw her when she came into the office, we didn't speak or anything".

"Does she still own Harper's factory then Dad?"

"Well she does for the moment but she said she was going to sell it. So I guess she won't be coming back to Walsall any more."

They crossed the road towards the hospital entrance, and Philip had to push hard to negotiate the slope up to the main doors. Once inside Philip went to the reception and gave his father's name and the name of the consultant he had come to see to the nurse. She made a phone call and after she had put down the phone, said someone would collect his father in a few minutes.

Philip returned to his father who immediately started talking, "I'll tell you something that Mrs McPherson told me years ago when she was nursing me in the field hospital. It's to do with what we were talking about earlier; relationships and girlfriends?"

Philip wondered what was coming next and hoped his father was not going to embarrass him.

"She told me there are hundreds of girls out there, and no one should settle for the first one that comes their way. It's not an easy lesson for a young lad to learn but you should wait and make sure that the girl you marry is the right one."

"And did she tell you how you know she is the 'right one' as you put it?"

"Well that's the dilemma isn't it? Until you meet her you'll never know she even exists. I laughed when she told me but I do now happen to believe that there is a 'love of one's life' out there somewhere for everyone, and I also believe that we all meet them at some time in our life. So the trick is to make sure that you haven't 'buggered' it all up by having settled for someone second class before you meet them."

Philip wanted to ask him what the hell he was talking about; why he had chosen to offer these words of wisdom now and whether his mother was the 'love of his life'. But just then a porter came up to them and took Frank to see Mr. Edmunds, so he didn't have the chance to ask.

"You just wait here, Philip. I shouldn't be too long."

"OK Dad, see you soon," and with that he sat down and watched the porter wheel his father out of the waiting area and towards the lifts. He couldn't understand why his father had mentioned the things about 'love of one's life' and hoped he never brought the subject up again. He never did!

Ten minutes later Philip was beginning to get fidgety and wished he had brought a book to read. Even reading the new Physics book his mother had bought him for his next year at school would have been better than nothing. It would at least have kept his mind busy and stopped him from the nausea he felt as he watched the workman who had just been brought in with a blood soaked towel wrapped around his arm. The poor chap, who couldn't have been much older than Philip, was dressed in the filthiest overalls he'd ever seen, and was covered in what looked like coal dust from head to foot.

Philip came to the conclusion that he possibly worked in one of the local steel foundries shovelling coal into the furnace, or maybe he was a coal-delivery man? Whatever his job, he was ashen faced and obviously in great pain. Blood was dripping through the cloth and Philip's mind went into overdrive thinking about the injury to his arm. He was mesmerised by the sight of the dripping blood, and the thoughts of the damaged arm under the now deep red cloth was making him feel quite faint. He turned his eyes away from the suffering man in an attempt to take his mind off the blood, when he heard a female voice calling out behind him.

"Matthew Phillips."

No one answered and the nurse repeated, "Is there a Matthew Phillips in here?"

Philip turned round and looked at the nurse, "Sorry, but did you say Matthew Philips?"

"Yes, that's right, are you Matthew Phillips?"

"No, my name's Philip Matthews. Are you sure you've got the name right?"

The nurse laughed as she walked up to Philip, "Well I'm sure that's what the Sister said but she always calls everyone by their surname, so perhaps she gave me the surname first and the Christian name last. So whether it's Philip Matthews or Matthew Phillips you'd better come with me. We don't want to keep the Sister waiting, do we?" She then added, just loud enough for Philip to hear, "Everyone has to jump to it when Sister gives out her instructions."

She beckoned to Philip to follow her. He stood up, but felt quite wobbly as he went past the pool of blood that had dripped from the injured man's arm. The nurse reached out and held his arm, "Are you all right? You look a bit pale."

Philip stood up straight, and not wishing to admit to his uneasiness at the sight of the blood, snatched his arm from her grasp. The nurse was taken aback by the way Philip pulled away from her. She felt she had offended him by holding his arm and she blushed as she apologised for her action.

Philip saw the colouring of her cheeks, as he looked directly at the nurse for the first time. He smiled and was pleased that she returned the smile.

He had expected a much older woman and was surprised that she looked about his own age, but more importantly he was taken aback by how pretty she was. She was slim and about six inches shorter than his own six foot, with shoulder length black hair beneath her nurse's cap. She had a beautiful wide smile and her deep brown eyes seemed to be trying to read his thoughts. She was not glamorous like Sadie Taylor who worked in his mother's shop, but had a natural and almost plain beauty that affected him as much as Sadie had. He was surprised at how he felt as they both stared at each other.

The careful examination only lasted a few seconds but it seemed much longer to Philip, who was relieved when she nodded her head towards the door and said, "Come with me and we'll soon have you sorted out."

Philip followed her as she moved away and they were half way up the first flight of stairs before he even started to wonder why he was following her anyway, "Where are we going?" and suddenly thinking about his father asked, "Is my Dad OK? Nothing's happened to him has it?"

"Sister didn't tell me the name of the other patient so I didn't know it was your father but I'm sure everything will be fine. I don't know all the ins and outs of what they're planning to do, but I'm sure it's all very straightforward, and he'll be sorted in no time at all."

"Well what's the matter with him then? What are they doing to him?"

Deciding that the least said about the state of the patient waiting to go into the operating theatre the better, she smiled at him and shook her head slightly, "They don't tell me what they're planning, but Mr Allen is the best there is. So don't worry, everything will be fine."

"Mr Allen? Who's Mr Allen?" Philip queried as they turned the bend at the top of the stairs and headed along the corridor towards the operating theatres.

"Mr Allen is the surgeon who's going to sort out your Dad's problem."

"But I thought my Dad was seeing Mr Edmunds?"

The nurse looked a little bemused and stopped outside the door to the operating theatres, her hand on the door handle, "Look I've told you they don't tell me anything. I don't even work in theatre usually. In fact I've never been inside one before today. I usually work on the old men's ward but they're a bit short round here today, so they sent me here to do the theatre Sister's bidding. So I'm sorry I can't answer your questions, but, as I've said, I'm sure everything will be all right. Just stop worrying."

She started to open the door, but Philip took her arm and stopped her, "But what do they want me here for then? I've never been with my father before when he's had any treatment."

"Oh I didn't realise it was your first time, I thought you'd given blood before."

"Given blood! What on earth are you talking about? What do they want my blood for?"

"Well I think it's because your blood will be OK to give your father. Perhaps they always have a member of the family, I just don't know. Like I said before, I'm new round here." She went to take Philip's hand from her right arm with her left, "Come on they'll be waiting for you and I'm supposed to get you settled before they need you."

Philip did not move his hand preventing her from opening the door, "Will the Sister explain it all to me when we get inside?"

"Well she probably will, but if I were you I wouldn't bother her. She can be a real battleaxe if people don't do just exactly what she says. I'd just do what she says and keep her sweet if I were you. Now come on before you get me into trouble," and with that she pulled Philip's hand away and opened the door and led him into the room.

Philip had always been aware of the disinfectant smell as soon as he entered the hospital, but here in this room the smell was overwhelming. There was a trolley to the side of the room on which was a rubber-covered mattress and the nurse led Philip towards it. The mattress had obviously been scrubbed with disinfectant; the smell became stronger as they walked towards it.

"Now just strip to the waist and lie on the mattress. You can leave your vest on but I need both your arms free. I'll be back in a minute," and with that the nurse turned and walked out of the door they had just come through.

It was at least five minutes before she returned, by which time Philip had stripped to the waist as instructed and was lying on the mattress. The rubber was cold against his bare back. Perhaps he should have put his vest on, but he rarely did so in the summer, even though his Aunt Alice was always on to him to wear it every day of the year. "You can still catch colds and the flu in the summer you know," was her reason every time she found he was not wearing it. Thank goodness she had started to give him some privacy whilst dressing in the last two or three years. Even so his back was getting more and more chilled on this sanitised bed.

"Ah good, you're ready," she said as she entered the room and shrugging her shoulders added, "I'm sorry but they're not ready for you yet though, so you'll have to wait for a bit."

Philip was becoming embarrassed at the nurse standing so close to his half naked body. She seemed to be studying his prone figure on the trolley and he started to fantasise that any minute she would start to stroke his bare chest. He tried to get rid of these thoughts and hoped she was not aware of how much he was being affected by the nearness of this girl he found particularly attractive. He deliberately shivered and said, "If I have to wait can I put my shirt back on? This mattress is pretty cold."

The nurse giggled and stared directly into his eyes as if she was deliberately trying to unnerve him, "I'll get you a blanket. I won't be a minute." She once more headed towards the door and Philip was certain that she mumbled, "But it'll be a shame to cover up that gorgeous torso."

When she came back with the blanket, Philip almost snatched it from her to cover himself. "Will I be here long? And what are they doing to my father that's taking all this time?"

The nurse touched him on the shoulder, "Just relax, I've told you they won't be long." She looked at the watch pinned to her apron, "It's almost three o'clock. No I'm sure they won't be too long now. Did you say this was the first time you've given blood? When Sister sent me to fetch you I'm sure she said that you'd know what to do."

"No, I've never given blood before. Does it hurt much?"

"No, of course not," was her immediate reply, but then she seemed to have second thoughts and added, "Well I shouldn't think so."

Philip winced a little at this reply and decided to change the subject. "How long have you been a nurse then?"

She didn't answer immediately and seemed to be adding up the dates in her head, "Just over two years, I started here when I left school."

"And do you like being a nurse?"

"Yes it's fine. I feel I'm just beginning to do some proper nursing. Up to now it's been mostly feeding the patients, cleaning, emptying bed pans, and generally running round for Sister and the other nurses. But we've just had another girl start on the ward, so I'm no longer the youngest and they've started letting me change bandages and the like."

Philip was only half listening to her as she continued talking about what she did and what was wrong with some of the patients. He was more interested in the girl herself than what she did in the hospital. '*Should I ask her what her name is, or would that be too forward? What do you say to a girl when you want to ask her out?'*

She suddenly stopped talking, "Are you OK? You seem miles away."

Shaken out of his musings, Philip decided to ask the girl if he could see her again outside the hospital, "And what do you in your spare time?"

"And why would you be interested in that?"

Philip coloured a little but determined to stay with it and ask the girl out. "Well I wondered if you'd like to go to the cinema with me some time."

"Very forward aren't we?"

"I'm sorry I didn't mean to offend you. I understand perfectly if you don't want to. I really….."

Taking his hand in hers she interrupted before he could say any more. "Yes I would like that, but I think we'd better talk about it later. I think I can hear someone coming and, if it's Sister, I don't think she'd like us talking about making a date in her operating theatre. She doesn't think nurses should fraternise with patients at the best of times."

Philip was just about to say that he wasn't a real patient when the door opened and in walked the Sister. She was nothing like the frumpish and elderly Sister that Philip had been expecting. Instead, a very attractive woman of about thirty came walking towards him. She had the most wonderful smile, and lying down as he was, he was able to see her perfectly formed ankles peeking from her skirt.

"Right Phillips, We'll be ready for you in a couple of minutes so we'd better make sure you're ready."

"It's Philip, Sister, not Phillips," Philip said quietly, not wishing to offend or incite the 'Sister's wrath' that the nurse had spoken of.

"I beg your pardon, what did you say? You'll have to speak a little louder than that if you need anything." And then as an afterthought she added, "Yes whilst I think about it, I should ask you not to speak at all in the theatre. Mr Allen doesn't like any talking in his theatre whilst he's operating, so please only speak when you're spoken to."

Philip nodded his head. However, since she did not ask him again what he had said; he resolved only to acknowledge her requests when he was spoken to from now on and not bother her with all the questions about what was going to happen that had been going through his head ever since he had entered this room.

The Sister looked at the clipboard she had brought into the room with her. "Right Mr Phillips can you confirm your name please?"

"Philip Matthews."
The Sister nodded and ticked off 'Phillips – Matthew' on the form.
"And we have your blood group here as Moss group 3. Can you confirm that's correct?"
"I'm sorry I don't know what my blood group is."
Again the Sister just ticked off the form, adding in a very forceful voice that reminded him of the nurse's description of the Sister as a battleaxe, "You should really try to remember your blood group you know. It's very important."
Philip decided to do as the nurse had suggested earlier and just keep quiet and not annoy the Sister.
The double doors opposite the door Philip had been brought through suddenly crashed open. Philip lifted his head to see what had caused the noise, but the Sister immediately pushed his head down again.
"Can you bring the donor in now Sister, Mr Allen will be here soon and we'd better get him into theatre before they bring the patient in."
The Sister objected with, "But I haven't finished checking off the list yet."
"No time for that now, Sister. The patient is already on his way down so just wheel the donor in."
The speaker had by now reached where the Sister and the nurse were standing and Philip could see the man for the first time. He was dressed in a white gown and had a white cap on his head under which wisps of black hair were protruding. He took the clipboard from the Sister, adding once more, "Just wheel the donor in."
Philip's mood immediately changed from one of bemusement, to sheer panic as he was pushed into the operating theatre. He could feel his heart beating rapidly and started to find it difficult to breathe. The nurse seemed to notice the change in him and once they had stopped in the operating theatre, she took his hand and winked as she smiled to him, "You'll be fine. Just take it easy and breathe slowly. It will help."
The Sister snatched the nurse's hand away from Philip's, "Of course he'll be all right you silly girl. Why wouldn't he be? He's done it all before."
Philip wanted to protest at the Sister's comment and let her know that he'd never done this before, but he was too scared to say anything to the 'battleaxe'. Instead he panicked even more and found it increasingly difficult to breathe. He followed the nurse's advice and deliberately took slow deep breaths. It seemed to help.
By now, the other occupants of the room had left him alone and were busy preparing the operating table which was in the middle of the room.

The man who had fetched Philip was now checking what Philip took to be bottles of anaesthetic. He looked at the dials attached to the bottles and then laid the tubes leading from them on to the small table at the side of the main operating table.

"Switch all the lights on, please Sister," he shouted across the operating table and the Sister went to a small panel on the wall and suddenly the room was ablaze with light.

Philip turned his head and looked round the room. In the far corner he could see another nurse standing next to a large oblong metal container with steam pouring out the top of it. The nurse reached into the steaming cauldron with a pair of metal prongs, and took out all sorts of surgical instruments. Philip was fascinated with all the various implements she took out and carefully laid on the tray next to the sterilising unit. At first they were small instruments, scalpels, tweezers, clamps and such. But then she reached into the bottom and started to bring out much larger instruments, which Philip felt would be more at home in a butcher's shop. Saws, great carving knives and what Philip thought looked too much like a machete for comfort. He turned his head away before she took out anything that was even more horrendous.

Meanwhile, the nurse had crept back to be by Philip's side and was about to take his hand, when the Sister came bounding across the room to them. "I think we can manage without you now, nurse. You can go and wait next door until we've finished with this young man and then you can look after him until he's ready to go home again." The nurse smiled at Philip and touched his arm as she said, "See you soon, and don't worry you'll be fine."

"I said you can go now, nurse," boomed the Sister, and the nurse hurried out of the room.

"Now young man," the Sister looked directly at Philip as she said this, "We like to let donors know a little bit about the person they're giving blood to, so that they know what to expect."

She picked up the clipboard the anaesthetist had previously taken off her and folded over the top two pages. "Yes, here we are, today Mr Phillips, you'll be giving blood to a man who was brought in an hour or so ago. He's been in a nasty accident at work and has lost a lot blood. His leg is very badly damaged and Mr Allen thinks we have no option but to amputate it, but Mr Allen wants to give him some blood before he does so. He fears he might lose him altogether if he doesn't. So that's why we sent for you."

Philip wanted to say that nobody had sent for him, but the Sister did not give him a chance to say anything. She just continued talking.

"Now if you're squeamish, just keep facing the wall over there away from what Mr Allen is doing. And don't worry, Mr Allen will give the man your blood, and you can be out of here before he starts work on the man's leg."

She looked down at the sheet again, and Philip was about to protest about everything that was going on, when she looked up from the papers and said, "Now you know the procedure don't you?"

Philip meekly shook his head from side to side.

"Well it will be exactly the same as before," the Sister said without giving him any opportunity to say anything. "As soon as the patient is brought in and the anaesthetist has got him asleep, Mr Allen will be here and will put the needle into your artery and connect the tube up to the other man's vein. And then we'll wait whilst the blood is transferred. Once that's done, we'll take you out of here and nurse will look after you, give you a cup of tea and a biscuit, and make sure you're safe to go home."

Philip decided that enough was enough and that he really ought to pull himself together and be more forceful. It was now or never. If he didn't object to what was going on, it would soon be too late.

He took a deep breath and started to speak to the Sister, "I really don't know what all this is about. I'm only here with my father."

But the sister had gone before he had finished the first sentence. The double doors had been flung open and the poor victim who was going to lose his leg was wheeled in at great speed. As soon as the trolley appeared all the hospital staff seemed to jump to attention and the atmosphere suddenly became electric with activity.

Philip felt he had to do something, NOW. "Sister" he shouted, "I need to speak to you right away."

"Yes dear, I'll be with you in a minute. Just don't worry everything will be fine," and with that she just carried on putting on her mask before tending to the patient.

Once more Philip was in sheer panic. He took deep breaths as the nurse had suggested, but this time it was no good, he just could not get his breath at all and he felt he was going to pass out. No one was paying him the least bit of attention.

"I really must get up and get out of here", he thought to himself. But he just couldn't move. He was hyperventilating and felt certain he was dying.

The door swung open again and in walked a tall, thin gentleman, who shouted to all inside as soon as he hit the door, "What is going on here? I thought you were ready for me and yet I've just bumped into this man outside the theatre. He says he's come to give blood. I thought you would have him prepared by now."

The Sister rushed over to where Philip lay, "But we have got him ready, Sir. Here he is all ready."

"Well who is the man outside who says he's been sent for to give blood as an emergency. He says his blood group is Moss 3, which I understood was our patient's blood group. Have you sent for two donors Sister?"

"No Sir, just the one."

The Sister searched around for the clipboard and found it lying across Philip's legs. She picked it up, and read the name, "Mr Phillips is the man we sent for and that is the young man here."

"Well you'd better see the man outside, because he said his name is Phillips and he insists he had a call at work to come here. He wants to get back to work as quickly as he can, so if we have sent for two Mr Phillips, you better decide which one we are going to use pretty quickly and let the other go. I'm going to scrub up now so have it sorted by the time I'm ready." With that the surgeon stormed out of the room and the poor Sister was left shaking. Everyone else in the room had dropped their heads to avoid being implicated in the faux pas.

Philip decided it was time he spoke up. He took deep breath, gulped and through his dry lips shouted as loudly as he could, but it still only came out as a rasp that sounded nothing like his usual voice, "I am Philip Matthews. Matthews is my surname, not Phillips. So get me out of here."

All the heads suddenly lifted and five sets of glaring eyes burned into Philip.

The Sister's mouth opened but no words came out for what seemed like an age to Philip. Without closing her mouth, she looked at the clipboard again, as if not believing what she had previously read on it. She took a great gulp and suddenly the words came tumbling out, "But we checked your name and you agreed it with me,"

Philip had now lost his earlier apprehension and fear of this woman and unexpectedly felt in charge of the situation. Why hadn't he felt like this before he had got into this mess! "No ma'am, I did not agree my surname was Phillips. I quite clearly told you my name was Philip Matthews. Philip, as in 'Christian name', Philip; and Matthews as in 'Surname', Matthews." The moisture had started to come back to his mouth and lips and the final 'Matthews' came out much louder than the rest.

"What the devil are you doing here then? This is not a game you know. You said you were here to give blood."

"No, you said I was here to give blood. You just didn't give me a chance to say otherwise. I thought I was here to help my father."

"The patient is your father?" squealed the Sister.

"No, I haven't a clue who that man is, but I thought my father was going to be the patient and you needed me."

Philip decided he had probably said enough and should get out before any more mishaps. He lifted himself up and sat upright on the trolley, "I'll go now then shall I?" He didn't wait for an answer but jumped off the trolley and went to dash through the doors he had come in through to collect his clothes.

The Sister caught him by the arm, "Not so fast young man. You just stay here whilst I check the man outside properly," and with that she went out through the other doors and into the corridor.

All of the others in the room started to snigger, but several put their hands to their mouths so that their laughter was kept in check sufficiently for it to be unheard by the Sister, who was now outside in the corridor talking to the other Phillips.

The anaesthetist said to Philip, "Somebody will be for it when she gets back, she's the last person to accept that anything could possibly be her fault, so she'll have to blame someone."

Philip's previous nervousness and trepidation was now turning to anger and he replied quite indignantly, "Well she hadn't better blame me. I'm the victim here. It's me who should be complaining about her."

The Sister flung open the doors just as he was saying this. A man in working clothes being pushed into the room ahead of her.

Once in the room she held on to his arm and said, "Before we go any further can I just check your name again?"

"Matthew Phillips. You've already asked me that outside."

"Yes I know but I want to make sure before we have any more mix-ups. Now, 'Matthew' is your 'Christian name' and 'Phillips' is your 'Surname'? That's right isn't it?"

"Yes, of course, 'Phillips' is my surname, and 'Matthew' is my first name.

"So your name is Mr Matthew Phillips?" she asked once again, emphasising the 'Phillips' part.

The man was starting to get rather irritated by the continuous checking of his name and the annoyance sounded in his voice, "Yes, that's what I said. Matthew Phillips is my name. So do you want me or don't you want me?"

The Sister blushed scarlet at this and finally deciding that everything was now correct she nodded her head as she ticked off 'Phillips – Matthew' on the chart in front of her again.

She now looked across at Philip, "And who are you going to complain to, young man?" But once again she did not wait for an answer. She pushed the man towards the trolley that Philip had vacated, "Strip to the waist and lie on that trolley. You do know the procedure don't you Mr Phillips." The 'Mr Phillips' was emphasised as she turned her head to Philip, as if trying to make a point.

"Yes Sister," replied the man, who was already stripping off as he said it.

"Good, you obviously know the procedure, Mr Phillips." The Sister once again stressed the 'Mr Phillips' as she stared directly at Philip with a searing look that would have disintegrated him in a puff of smoke had that been possible. "Just get up on to the trolley. Mr Allen will be here in a moment to sort you out."

She now turned her attention to Philip, "And you young man had better get out of here as quickly as you can."

He started to leave the operating theatre, but the Sister shouted to him, "Just wait there a moment. I want the nurse to make sure you find your way back, without causing us any more trouble."

Philip was about to protest that it was not him who had caused all the trouble, but decided it would be best if he went quietly without making any more fuss.

The Sister took Philip out into the corridor and told him to wait whilst she fetched the nurse. She was back in no time with the poor nurse hurrying along behind her, "Now nurse, I want you to take this young man back down stairs; back to where you found him and when I've finished here I want to see you in my office."

She turned to Philip who was leaning against the wall wondering when the Sister was going to vent her wrath on him, "Right Mr Matthews." She emphasised the 'Mr Matthews' and Philip shuddered in trepidation but in fact she continued to speak in a quiet gentle voice, which immediately calmed him. "I must apologise for all this confusion, I do hope we haven't upset you too much. I will be having a further word with Nurse Hunter about this mix up and when I've finished with her she won't make the same mistake again."

"But it wasn't her fault," Philip blurted out in an attempt to stop the girl getting into trouble. The Sister started to speak but Philip was intent on taking the blame and with his heart pounding so much that he wondered if the Sister could hear it, continued speaking, "She called the name of Matthew Phillips and I was the one who answered her. I don't think you should blame her, it really was my fault."

The Sister looked intently at Philip trying to work out what had caused this outburst. He was obviously perturbed that the nurse was likely to be reprimanded and he was certainly trying hard to save the girl's skin. "Well she should have checked much more carefully, but I suppose if I had given her Mr Phillips record sheet she may not have made the mistake. Maybe I will be a little gentler with her." She put on a stern face and looked straight into the nurse's eyes, "But she must learn that such mistakes could have disastrous results in a hospital. She mustn't make such a mistake again."

Philip pursed his lips together and tilted his head to one side, as he tried to impress the Sister with the pleading in his eyes to go easy on Nurse Hunter. A thought suddenly struck him and he said, "I don't mind giving blood anyway. You can wheel me back in if you like and take whatever blood you want, then all this mix up won't matter will it?"

The Sister laughed out loud before replying, "It's not that simple Mr Matthews. We have to make sure you are fit to give blood and that your blood is the right type needed; maybe some other time."

Philip was still anxious to make amends for the nurse. "Well what do I have to do then? I really would like to help if I can."

The Sister smiled again, "That's not possible today, Mr Matthews, but Nurse Hunter can take your details if you're sure you want to be on our donor register."

Philip smiled inwardly. So he would be seeing the nurse for a bit longer, and be able to continue their previous conversation. He wanted to find out her Christian name and complete the arrangements to see her. Even if meeting her socially was a complete flop, he would at least find out what punishment, if any, the Sister dealt out to her.

Now that all the panic was over the Sister felt quite relieved and smiled at Philip again, "Right Mr Matthews, I must go. I'm needed in theatre."

She turned to look at the nurse as she opened the door to the theatre, "And you nurse can take Mr Matthews back to where you found him as soon as you have his details. I'll tell you what to do with them when you see me in my office at the end of your shift."

The poor nurse coloured at what she took to be another reprimand and feared what was to come later.

"And make sure you get all the details down correctly. We don't want any more slip ups, do we?"

Nurse Hunter thought she detected a faint smile from the Sister as she said this, but dared not smile back in case she was mistaken. "No Sister. I'll make sure of everything this time," and with that she took Philip by the arm and led him along the corridor.

Once they had reached the stairs she let out a big sigh and started talking rapidly with the relief of having escaped the Sister, for the time being at least. "Oh my goodness, what a mess; I'm sure to be in for it later. You don't think she'll sack me, do you? I really enjoy this job and my mother would kill me if I got the sack. She was so proud when I got the job. I daren't tell my mother about this, whatever happens."

Philip rushed to get in front of her and held out his arm for her to stop, "Whoa a bit; try to stop worrying. I've told Sister that it was my fault, and not yours. I'm sure she won't be too hard on you."

"And a lot you know about it, Mr Know It All. At the very least she'll give me a good telling off and probably have me doing nothing else but emptying bedpans and cleaning for the next couple of months; just when I'd started to be given some of the really interesting nursing stuff to do."

She was obviously very concerned about the punishment that awaited her and Philip was at a loss to know how to take her mind off it. He wished he could say something that would diminish her worry and anxiety. "I'm sure it won't be that bad," he said as he was deciding whether he dared ask her out again. He resolved to leave it for a bit longer. She looked too agitated at the moment and he felt sure that she would turn him down if he asked her right now. "What do we have to do about my giving blood, then?"

They had reached the bottom of the stairs and were almost back in the reception area. The nurse pointed to a few empty seats, "We'll sit down over there and you can give me your details."

They were walking over to the chairs when Philip heard his father shouting from the other side of the room. He started to wheel his wheelchair towards them. "There you are, Philip, where on earth have you been? I've been waiting here for you for the last twenty minutes."

Philip thought that if his father came any nearer, he would lose the opportunity to ask this girl out for ever and wished he had sorted it out whilst they had been coming down the stairs. "No Dad, you just stay there. I need to sort something out with this nurse. I'll tell you about it later. It's a bit of a laugh really."

His father continued to come towards them. Philip was encouraged when the nurse interrupted, "Yes Mr Matthews. You just stay there. I need to sort out a few details with your son. We'll just sit over here and your son will be with you in a moment."

She went over to the reception desk and collected a piece of paper from the receptionist. "Right Mr Matthews," she said as she sat down next to Philip, "Now give me your name and address and we'll contact you shortly to come and give us a sample of your blood so we can sort out your blood group and put you on our register to donate if and when we need you."

Philip gave her the information she requested and ended with, "Now Nurse Hunter perhaps you would like to tell me your name," and before she could answer he raised his eyebrows and added, "And your address?"

She said that her name was Teresa, but declined to give him her address, smiling as she suggested she might let him know where she lived once she got to know him better.

"So, you will meet me sometime for a date then?"

This time she laughed out loud, "Well I wouldn't go as far as saying I'll go on a date with you, but yes I'll meet you in town for a coffee." She looked hard at Philip for a moment trying to make up her mind about him, but quickly came to a decision by adding, "And yes, we can then go to the cinema together if you like."

And so arrangements were quickly made to meet each other on the following Saturday evening outside the Gaumont cinema.

CHAPTER FOURTEEN

1938

Philip switched off his alarm clock just before it was set to go off at six o'clock. He had been lying awake for the last twenty minutes excited by the prospect of the trip he was about to embark on with his cousin Edward. They had been planning the trip for months and now that their examinations were over, they would be off today for a six week journey through France.

Originally they told their parents that they wanted to travel to Spain to see a bullfight; a thing Philip had wanted to do since reading Ernest Hemingway's 'Death in the Afternoon' the previous year but the suggestion was quickly squashed by both sets of parents because of the civil war there.

Their second suggestion had been a trip to Germany. Here their argument had been that it would be a tremendous fillip for both of them to polish up their German before going to University, but again their parents had been totally against it. They were not surprised at this response as they were themselves concerned about all the news about Germany and Hitler in the newspapers, and really would have been upset if their parents had said yes, because in truth they had only proposed trips to Spain and Germany to soften up their parents for the planned trip to France. And so after several evenings arguing with their parents about trips to Spain or Germany, their plan worked and the parents gave in easily when the trip to France was suggested as an alternative.

Philip got out of bed and opened the curtains. There was not a cloud in the sky and he felt the warmth from the sun through the open window. It was going to be the glorious summer's day he had hoped for. At least the first day of the trip to Southampton should be pleasant and dry.

Edward was going to call for him at seven o'clock and they planned to leave immediately at that time as everything had been packed in the pannier bags and sidecar of Edward's Triumph 650cc motorcycle on the previous day.

The motorbike had been a seventeenth birthday present from his parents but both boys had learned to ride so that they could share the driving. They had packed a small two-man tent to use if they ran out of money or could not find anywhere cheap to stay. To this end they had joined the YHA and were hoping to get a warm bed and a good wash cheaply in a youth hostel.

Philip rushed to the bathroom and quickly washed and dressed. He was down stairs in the kitchen in less than ten minutes where he found his mother and Auntie Alice fussing over a cooked breakfast for him. As soon as he said "Good morning", his aunt picked up the freshly brewed pot of tea from the table and started to pour him a cup.

"Sit down, lad, and get this down you. Probably the best cup of tea you'll get in the next six weeks."

Philip was about to protest that he was perfectly capable of making a good cup of tea but thought better of it. He knew that both his aunt and his mother were quite concerned about this lengthy trip to a foreign country; particularly one that his aunt had such dreadful wartime memories of.

He had tried, over the weeks following his parents' agreement to the trip, to talk to both his father and Aunt Alice about their experiences in France, but neither had wanted to say much about their war service.

"Things were a lot different then," had been his father's comment and his aunt had added, "You just can't compare wartime with anything else. Your father's right, I'm sure things are a lot different now."

"Yes, I know that but I was just wondering about the people. What are the French people like?"

"The few I met seemed fine, but we didn't meet that many did we Alice?" was his father's response.

"I don't remember meeting any," said Alice, "And anyway, I didn't understand a word of the language. At least you and Edward won't have that trouble," and with that she once again changed the subject to something else.

When Philip mentioned it to Edward later, he said, "My Dad's just the same. How is it that parents seem to manage to change the subject so easily when they don't want to talk about something?" Philip just shrugged his shoulders and they too started to talk about something else, without realising they had just done exactly the same thing.

Philip took a sip of the hot tea his aunt had just poured him as Alice turned and switched on the radio. Almost immediately his mother, who was breaking another egg into the frying pan, shouted to be heard over the music that blared from the speaker, "Turn that down a bit, Alice. I can't hear myself think," and without a break in the sentence added, "And how many slices of toast do you want with your breakfast, Philip?"

"Two or three rounds please, depends how much bacon and stuff you're cooking."

Alice rushed forward and picked up the bread knife and switched on the new toaster that had only been purchased the previous week, and was still a novelty for all to use. “Don’t worry Grace, I’ll do the toast. I’ve been waiting for a chance to try it out. You just look after the rest of the lad’s breakfast.”

A couple of minutes later, Philip’s mother put an enormous plate full of bacon; three eggs, sausages, black pudding, tomatoes, and baked beans in front of him. “Get that down you, son. That should keep you going until lunchtime.”

Philip laughed, “I should think this’ll keep me going ‘til the middle of next week.”

“You just get it all down you, you need to keep your strength up, and I doubt if you’ll get anything as good as this in France, young man,” his aunt said as she put four slices of toast in front of him. She picked up a knife and started to ladle a thick layer of butter on one of them and almost pushed it into Philip’s mouth when the toast was covered to her satisfaction.

“Ladies, ladies, there’s no way I can eat all this,” and then, not wishing to offend them, added, “I’m really too excited to eat much, and Edward will be here soon. I wasn’t expecting you to get up and do all this for me.”

“You just eat as much as you can. We’ll make a sandwich with what you don’t eat and you can perhaps eat it in a couple of hour’s time. I’m sure you’ll be hungry again by then.”

“Yes and last night we put up some nice beef sandwiches for your lunch, I’ll fetch them for you from the larder,” his aunt added.

Philip decided not to protest any more, and to do just as he was told. Long experience had taught him not to argue when his mother and aunt were fussing over him like this; he knew he would hate it even more if they never fussed over him.

Philip was awoken the next morning by Edward, who was excitedly pointing out the French coastline gradually coming into view. Poor Philip felt he’d only just managed to doze off after spending most of the night trying to get comfortable on the bench against a wall of the passenger deck.

The previous day’s journey from home along the A34 had been horrendous. It seemed that they were held up behind every lorry and tractor in England. No sooner had they managed to find a straight run to overtake one tractor than, half a mile further on, they were being held up by another; or at least that was what it seemed like. As a result the journey had taken much longer than planned and they had caught the overnight ferry at Portsmouth with only minutes to spare and by the time they had secured the motorcycle on the car deck and found a couple of benches on which to sleep, the ship was already leaving port.

Settling down for sleep on the uncomfortable slatted seats proved almost impossible even though they were both worn out by the journey. As the night progressed it began to get quite cold and they wished they had brought a blanket on deck with them.

Philip rubbed his eyes and went to the side of the boat where Edward was, "Couldn't you have left me a bit longer? I've hardly had any sleep."

Edward responded by merely pointing out the coast of France where they could already clearly make out the shape of the port buildings at Le Havre.

"I've still got the bacon and sausage sandwiches mother made me yesterday morning. Do you fancy one before we dock?"

Philip reached into his rucksack and took out the remains of the squashed pack of sandwiches. He opened the greaseproof wrapping and viewed the contents, "Perhaps not! They look a bit worse for wear to me."

"Never mind that," said Edward, "I'm starving. Here let me have one," and in no time at all the two boys had devoured the sandwiches and were back by the motorbike well before the ship had docked.

Many long evenings had been spent preparing for this trip. They wanted to see as much of rural France as possible so maps had been purchased and marked with a route south mainly along secondary roads. Once they reached the Mediterranean, they planned to take seven or eight days travelling along the coast from west to east, eventually visiting Nice and Monaco. Then they would travel north along the Rhône - Saône valley to finally spend a few days experiencing the delights of Paris before returning home via Calais and Dover.

After leaving Le Havre they travelled the short distance to Honfleur, hoping to meet some pretty girls sunning themselves, whilst drinking coffee outside the cafes along the inner waterfront.

They found a spot by the river to leave the motorbike and walked the short distance to the marina and before crossing over the cantilever bridge they stood for a while admiring the colourful six, seven and eight storey buildings facing the sheltered inner harbour. Each building seemingly so narrow that it would surely have fallen down had it not been held up by an equably tall and narrow building on either side.

Philip was mystified as to why each building had clearly been designed quite separately from its neighbours. Each roof was a different height; some with skylights; some with small garret windows, whilst others had quite handsome gabled windows. Each building apparently built of different bricks and materials, and there appeared to be no consistency in the room height of adjacent buildings as there was no uniformity in the level of the windows; some windows with flower boxes dripping in green and crimson glory; others with painted shutters; others with coloured awnings.

He was amazed that in all this confusion of styles and lack of conformity there was a profound architectural beauty; a beauty that was enhanced even further by the array of tables and chairs on the quayside outside each restaurant and bar; brilliant red, green, yellow and blue tablecloths blazing on the tables beneath equally colourful parasols. The gloriously coloured panorama enhanced by the multitude of people sitting at the tables drinking, or eating from plates piled high with gourmet creations of sea food, or just walking along the quayside admiring the yachts of the rich playboys.

Philip took out his Kodak camera to take a photograph of the scene. What a pity the black and white print would not show the real multi-coloured effect of the scene! Looking through the viewfinder he realised he would not be able to capture the whole view in one shot, but he did not want to use up too much of his limited film supply so early in the holiday, so he made do with just one shot of the middle section of the full view he really wanted.

The boys crossed over to the other side of the harbour and started to walk along the quayside weaving around the tables, whilst having a good look at the delicacies being eaten by the different diners.

They spent the next two hours walking round the harbour but were disappointed at not finding any unattached young girls to talk to. Finally they decided to sit outside one of the bars and each ordered a glass of the cheapest vin rouge on the drinks list. When it came they were surprised to receive it in a glass tumbler filled to the brim. They smiled at each other and simultaneously said “Cheers” as they each carefully raised their glass to their lips, making sure that none was spilt.

Philip merely wet his lips and the tip of his tongue with the deep red liquid, but Edward took one huge gulp, filling his mouth. His cheeks swelled out; his lips tight together and his eyes almost popping out of their sockets as he tried to decide whether to swallow the dry, sour wine or whether to spit it out all over the table. In the end he took an enormous breath and swallowed. This was immediately followed by a series of deep breaths and wagging of his tongue outside his mouth as he tried to get rid of the dry acrid taste.

Philip burst out laughing at Edward’s antics. It was obvious he hadn’t tasted such a dry wine before. Edward joined in the laughter but they stopped abruptly when they realised the other diners were staring at them.

"Jesus," said Edward, "What sort of wine is that?"

"Have you never had a dry red before?" queried Philip.

Edward looked almost guilty as he replied, "Not like that I haven't."

Philip chuckled, "You mean you haven't drunk any kind of red wine before."

Edward decided to come clean, "Never drunk any wine before, except a few sips of my mother's sweet sherry or her Madeira. I thought they were quite nice." He picked up his glass again and putting it to his lips declared, "Tasted nothing like this stuff before."

The glass remained at his lips as he tried to decide whether to drink more of it, but finally plucked up the courage and after declaring, "Waste of money if I don't drink it," he raised the glass towards Philip and added, "To experience," before taking another much smaller mouthful.

Although Philip had previously tasted a dryish red wine at home, he had never tasted anything quite as rough and dry as this, but nevertheless both boys persevered until the last drops of liquid had been drained from their glasses; a task that took well over half an hour.

"I suppose one could get used to the taste. Maybe we should try some more. We might actually get to like it?" Edward suggested.

"I don't think so," replied Philip, "Not right now anyway. We'd better get going and find somewhere to camp for the night."

"And get something to eat," countered Edward.

The boys stood up, but unused to the effects of wine, especially a tumbler full of wine taken on empty stomachs, they each felt rather light headed.

Philip sat down again, stating that the wine must have been stronger than he thought and had gone to his head, and pronounced that they'd better eat something sooner rather than later.

Edward declined to sit down again stating that he liked the feeling and added, "We'll have to get some of that to drink later."

Philip shook his head before standing up again, "Come on let's get something to eat."

The next morning Philip did not wake until after ten o'clock; his mouth thick with foul tasting mucus, and his head throbbing with the first hangover of his life. He looked across to Edward stretched out asleep beside him in the small tent.

He pulled on his clothes before shaking Edward out of his slumber, "Hey! Wake up, you lazy so and so."

Edward rolled over, his eyes tight shut. Philip shook him again, but it wasn't until Philip threatened to throw a mug of cold water over him, that he made any real outward sign of waking up.

He rubbed his eyes with the ball of his hand for some time before finally blinking and asking, "What time is it?" Shaking his head and rubbing his eyes again, he added, "What did we get up to last night?"

"Twenty minutes past ten and I don't think we should have had two bottles of that wine," and in the firmest voice he could muster, Philip pronounced, "And we're not doing it again!"

Edward pulled the blanket tightly around him as Philip implored him to, "Come on, let's get moving, we'll never get anywhere on this trip if we keep acting like this." He placed his palm against Edward's, laughing as he said, "A quick dip in the river will do us both good so come on blood brother. We'd better be more careful this time than we were the last time we went swimming in a river together."

Edward slapped his hand against Philip's, "All for one and one for all. Last one in's a sissy," and with that he pushed Philip over and tried to hold him down while he struggled out of his pyjamas, opened the tent flap and went running naked to the river.

The water was pretty cold and the boys were soon out, dressed and had eaten the remains of last night's bread, whilst the water came to the boil on the Primus stove. After two cups of coffee to wash down the nuggets of dry bread they dismantled the tent.

As they were doing this, clouds started to drift across the sky obliterating the sun and the temperature dropped quite quickly. Both lads unpacked their sweaters and pulled them on.

But by the time the tent was packed away and all their goods loaded on to the motorbike, a cold north wind was blowing in from the sea making it even colder. Despite this change in the weather the boys nevertheless decided to keep to their plans and drive the few miles down the coast to Trouville. However, on reaching the sea the wind was blowing even more strongly and the beach was virtually deserted. The few people walking along the board walk were hugging themselves to keep warm and a small group of elderly ladies walking towards Edward and Philip were hanging on to their elaborate hats, clearly afraid that if they let go their precious bonnet would be blown away.

The young girls that Philip and Edward were hoping to meet were totally absent. Surely this part of the coast was the playground of the Paris set, both young and old? Obviously not today!

After walking the length of the promenade the boys turned round and made their way back. As they did so, they ceased to scour the practically empty beach for the non existent girls and instead began to take an interest in the row of fine large houses adjacent to the wooden walkway.

The sand beach stretched right up to the elaborately designed walls surrounding the houses and one could almost imagine the houses had been built on the sand itself, but for the fact that between the wall and the house, were finely laid out gardens, with lawns and an array of flower beds.

Each house was of an individual design seemingly trying to be more ornate and elaborate than its neighbour and each had tall chimneys of highly crafted decorative brickwork. Most of the first floor rooms had balconies facing the sea; some with intricate structured roofs, whilst others had colourful awnings protecting them. Many had fine cane or other outside furniture ready for the occupants to relax and sunbathe when the sun was out, but today none were prepared to endure the cold and wind unnecessarily and the sunbathers were all missing.

Edward looked at his watch before they reached the end of the 'promenade de planches'. "Hey, look at the time. It's way past lunch time and I'm starving." He laughed as he added, "And maybe by the time we've eaten there'll be some girls around."

"Some chance in this cold," Philip replied as they took refuge from the wind by huddling together against the side wall of one the houses.

Edward removed the large baguette, and the half kilo of the cheapest pâté they had been able to find, from his rucksack and they each took half of the baguette and spread a thick layer of the pâté on to it.

In no time at all they had devoured it all and they snuggled up against each other to keep warm. They were soon asleep and it was almost two hours later when they were woken by a small terrier dog barking at them.

The sky had cleared, the sun was shining and the wind had eased. Philip tried unsuccessfully to shoo the persistently yapping dog away and finally in desperation he barked back at it. The startled animal froze for a moment before yapping once more and immediately running off over the beach.

A young mother, with her back to Philip and Edward was playing nearby in the sand with two small children. She shouted towards the dog, "Reviens petit diable." The dog stopped, looked at the woman, and started to run round and round in a circle as if he did not want to return to her but did not want to go too far away either.

The eldest child, a boy around four years old, was concentrating on making sure that no sand fell out of the bucket as he overturned it to add another turret to his sand castle. The mother, who had her arms round the little girl of no more than eighteen months of age, let her go and stood up intent on running after the dog, but as soon as she was free from her grasp, the little girl scrambled forward and waving her arms from side to side totally demolished all of the sand castle's turrets. The boy screamed and the woman just managed to grab hold of his spade as he swung it towards his young sister.

"Tu es mèchant. Il ne faut pas attaquer ta soeur avec la pelle."

The boy went into an even greater rage, banging his fists in the sand. "Mais c'est sa faute. Elle a démoli le chateau," and with that he picked up the bucket and emptied all the sand in it over his sister before tossing it as far away as he could.

Now it was the little girl that was screaming. The mother picked her up in an attempt to calm her, whilst frantically trying to brush the sand from her head and face. The boy still sobbing, looked on for a short while, but all of a sudden he jumped up and started to run towards the sea, shouting back as he ran, "Ce n'était pas de ma faute. Je vais dire à maman que tu as crié et que tu m'avais dit de le faire."

Edward, who was the better linguist, had been trying to give Philip a translation, but Philip could work out most of it without his help. He was nevertheless surprised when Edward told him that the little boy had said he was going to tell his mother that the woman had 'made him do it'. It was only then that they both realised that the woman was at least not the boy's mother but just someone looking after him. Could it be that she wasn't the little girl's mother either?

It was now the poor woman's turn to start crying. She got up, and still trying to knock the sand off the girl in her arms, chased after the boy. The dog decided to join in the fun and started running in circles around the woman instead. The dog nudged her leg and she fell to her knees just managing to save herself from falling completely and dropping the girl. As if he knew he would be in trouble if he stayed around any longer, the dog turned and chased towards the sea after the boy.

Edward determined to be the Good Samaritan, stood up and raced to her rescue and as he helped her back to her feet, he said in his best French, "Reste ici une minute. Je vais chercher le garçon."

This was the first time he had seen her face; she was not only a very pretty girl but was probably no older than himself. They smiled at each other before he ran as fast as he could to the boy's aid, who had now stopped at the water's edge trying to decide what to do next. He saw Edward rapidly gaining on him and suddenly made his decision and plucking up his courage ran forward to face the waves just as Edward was about to snatch him up.

The dog, who had been running alongside Edward, turned to protect his young charge and Edward in his desire to reach the boy and also avoid the dog's teeth, slipped on the wet sand and fell headlong into the next wave.

The boy stopped, and pointing a finger started to laugh at Edward as he flapped about trying to get up before the next wave hit him.

Edward was still struggling to his feet as the girl reached the boy and, still holding the small child in her left arm, grabbed him with her right and pulled him, now screaming again, out of the water.

Edward got to his feet dripping wet and the girl let go of the boy as she tried to stifle a laugh. Edward looked straight into her eyes as he waved his arms and legs about to shake off the water. He started to pull a face at his predicament and soon everyone was laughing at the situation.

Philip had now arrived on the scene and hoping his French was accurate said, "Donne-moi le bébé pendant que tu t'occupes du garçon." She handed over the child and immediately picked up the boy, shouting at him so fast that even Edward could not follow everything she was saying. The boy's laughter quickly turned to more tears as the girl continued to reprimand him at the same rapid pace, from which Edward was only able to pick up the occasional word and phrase. He did however manage to understand the bit when she told the boy to stop snivelling and be good or she would be the one telling tales to his mother about how naughty he had been.

The boy puckered up his lips and continued sniffing as he tried to control his tears. Suddenly he pointed to a girl coming across the sand towards them and shouted, "La glace. La glace."

"Si tu ne t'arrêtes pas de crier tu n'auras pas de glace."

For the moment this final threat from his carer of no ice cream seemed to have the desired effect and he stopped crying.

They all reached the spot of the destroyed sandcastle at the same time, where the girl spoke to the new arrival, "Heureusement que tu arrives Madeleine. Je m'en suis vu quand tu n'étais pas là. Si ce n'était pas pour ces gallants hommes je ne sais pas ce qu'il se serait passé."

Philip put the little girl down on the sand next to where the older girls were now sitting, "Come on, Edward, we should let these girls sort themselves out now."

The first girl looked up and said, "You are English? How lovely. Sit down and talk to us. We at least owe you a lick of our ice cream."

The look of astonishment on Edward's face at her perfect English was a joy to see. "Now I'm confused, I thought you were French."

"I am French, well half French. My father is French, but my mother is English. They met during the war, got married and have lived in France ever since, but mother visits her family in England several times a year and Grandma and Grandpa are always visiting us over here. So I almost speak English as much as French."

And with that she laughed; an infectious laugh that Edward thought made her even more beautiful. Her shining black shoulder length hair framing her enchanting face; her deep brown eyes revealing the same infectious laughter and her petite nose were all a delight to behold, and her smiling mouth with such sweet soft lips would surely be a joy to kiss! He could easily fall for this girl.

Philip looked at his watch and then across at Edward who was staring intently at the girl and rapidly showing facial signs of a smitten lovesick imbecile. "We should be going soon and find somewhere to stay. We haven't really got the time to sit and talk."

Edward awoke from his trance and realised that this was Philip's excuse to get away from these young women with children in tow, and possibly find some unattached girls. But he had noticed that neither girl was wearing a wedding ring or any other kind of ring for that matter. And now that they were up close, neither girl looked really old enough to have children. In any case he had already fallen for the first girl, so he quickly replied, "No, we've plenty of time, and I need to dry off a bit first," and with that he sat down and whilst taking off his shoes and socks asked the girls what their children's names were.

The girls looked at each other and laughed.

"They're not our children, they're our cousins. We're looking after them for the afternoon."

Edward was inwardly ecstatic at this reply and as he removed his last sock he made sure he moved slightly closer to the girl.

She, for her part, pointed to the little boy and said, "This is Emile," and putting her arms around the little girl said, "And this little beauty is Thérèse." She pointed to where the dog was sitting, his eyes darting from each of the ice-creams being eaten, as if waiting for his share of the spoils, "And that little troublemaker is Georges."

She looked across at the other girl, "And this is my sister Madeleine, and I'm Juliette. Now are you going to introduce yourselves?"

"Well, hello, Juliette," said Edward as he held out his hand to shake hers even though he had an overwhelming desire to pull her much closer.

He let go of her hand reluctantly and far sooner than he wanted to, before holding out his hand to shake each of the other's in turn as he added, "Hello, Madeleine, hello Emile and a special hello to you my little Thérèse."

He continued as if speaking to the baby girl, "My name is Edward and this is my cousin and best friend Philip. Can you say 'hello' yet Thérèse?"

The little girl shook off Edward's hand and squirmed from Juliette's grasp so that she could continue to attack her ice cream, not caring how much of it was becoming plastered all over her face.

Philip looked at the second girl, "So Madeleine, if you are Juliette's sister, do you speak English as well?"

"Sure, of course I do," she said in an accent that had hardly any trace at all of her French origins.

She then leaned over towards Juliette and put her face against Juliette's, "We are not only sisters but are twin sisters." She laughed out loud as she added, "But you wouldn't guess would you? We don't actually look like twin sisters, do we?"

Juliette moved her head away and looked at Madeleine, "Actually, I was born a year before you, so I'm not sure that you could call us twins."

Madeleine dug her in the ribs, "Here we go again, she's always telling this story. The truth is that she is only ten or fifteen minutes older than me, but she was born just before midnight on New Year's Eve and I was born just after midnight on New Year's Day. So officially we were not only born on different days but were also born in different years."

"That's exactly what I said; I was born a year before you."

They all laughed at the story and Philip thought that even though Juliette and Madeleine were twins, they were so obviously not identical twins.

Juliette had the hour glass figure, eighteen inch waist and perfectly symmetrical face of a budding film star; the sort of beauty that Edward had always been attracted to and so different from Madeleine who had what Philip regarded as the sweet natural beauty he felt more at ease with.

She was an inch taller than Juliette and had a slightly fuller figure. She had auburn hair which curled at the ends, a cute nose with the slightest hint of a kink in the middle, sparkling blue eyes, full pink cheeks and a delightful smile even when she stopped laughing.

As they continued talking and laughing, the clouds gradually cleared away and it become warmer and warmer until it was now quite hot and Philip needed to take off his jacket. He rolled up the sleeves of his jumper and checked his watch. It was just after four o'clock. Could they perhaps leave it for another half an hour before they needed to head towards Caen looking for somewhere to stay the night?

He considered the situation and decided that they ought to be able to find somewhere to pitch their tent later, even if it were dark. After all, they had finally found the ideal two girls they had been looking for. Surely they could stay and enjoy their company for a little longer, couldn't they?

What was the worst that could happen? Pitching the tent at the side of the road somewhere wouldn't present any difficulties, would it? And as for food, well they had a few biscuits in their rucksack and if necessary they could wait until morning for something more substantial.

In any case when he looked across at Edward who was almost whispering to Juliette and moving closer to her with every passing minute, he knew instantly by the way he was looking at her that he had no intention of moving before he was forced to. Food and where to camp for the night were the last things on Edward's mind!

Philip told himself to relax and enjoy the moment like his father was always telling him. He could hear his father now, saying, "I've had enough experiences in my life, some quite beautiful, and many quite horrific, to know that you should always enjoy the beautiful ones and make them last as long as you can. You never know what tomorrow will bring. So always enjoy the moment, son."

He turned to speak to Madeleine only to find her waving to a man and woman walking towards them along the promenade de planches.

"Regarde Emile, voilà papa et maman."

The reaction from both Thérèse and Emile was instantaneous. Emile pushed the last remnants of his ice-cream into his mouth, stood up and immediately started to run towards his mother and father. Thérèse, who was sitting on Juliette's lap, also stood up and started waddling forwards in the same direction; the remains of her ice-cream falling on to Juliette's dress as she did so, and before Juliette could do anything about it, the dog had pounced on to her lap and was licking up the remains of the ice-cream.

Poor Juliette didn't know whether to push the dog off her or allow him to clean the worst of the mess from her dress. She decided on the latter and sat there, somewhat embarrassed, as the dog licked away.

In the meantime, Madeleine got up and followed the children to meet their parents. Emile ran straight to his mother, who immediately picked him up and started to hug him close to her, kissing him on the top of his head.

Thérèse did not progress towards them at the same pace as her brother, but her father ran towards her, sweeping her into his arms as he reached her. He lifted her high above his head and she screamed with delight.

Madeleine gave both her aunt and uncle a kiss on the cheeks and in no time at all they all reached the spot where Juliette was still wrestling with the dog as he pushed his head deeper and deeper into her lap to get to the last remnants of the ice-cream. They all watched in amazement without saying anything until Juliette pushed the dog away after he had finished the final vestiges of his feast. She stood up and brushed the front of her dress in an unfruitful attempt to clean the wet mark from it.

Philip noticed that her cheeks were flushed with the embarrassment of Georges' antics. It was as much as he could do to stifle his amusement, but not wishing to add to Juliette's discomfiture, he managed not to laugh out aloud as all the others were doing.

The man was the first to speak, "Arrête d'en faire tout un plat Juliette. Ta tante Marthe te lavera la robe avant de rentrer chez toi demain. Tu peux le faire ce soir et ce sera sec avant demain, n'est ce pas Marthe?"

The woman replied, "Bien sur, tout ira bien, et je la repasserai demain matin. Tu peux même la mettre pour rentrer si tu veux." She moved a little closer to Juliette, turning her back to Philip and Edward, who had already picked up their rucksacks ready to leave, and asked Juliette as quietly as possible, "Qui sont ces jeunes hommes? Ils te dérangent?"

"Oh non Tante. En fait ils se sont occupés d'Emile et Thérèse avec moi, quand Georges est devenu fou furieux et s'est enfui." She turned towards the boys and in her perfect English, she declared so that all could hear, "They have been a great help to us. Haven't you?" And without waiting for an answer, pointed to Edward, and said, "Aunt Marthe, Uncle Victor, I would like you to meet Edward," and then pointing to Philip, added, "And this is Philip. They are from England."

Both Philip and Edward, shook hands with her Uncle Victor, who managed to do so, by holding Thérèse in his left arm, but when they came to shake hands with Aunt Marthe, she had to put Emile down on the sand, before holding out her hand to each of them in turn.

"And what part of England do you come from, Philip?" Victor asked in slow and carefully formed English. He obviously knew the language well, but was not as fluent as the girls.

"We come from a place called Walsall, which is near Birmingham, Monsieur ..... I'm sorry I do not know what your name is."

"My name is Guilbert, the same as everyone else here. I am the younger brother of Juliette and Madeleine's father, but you can call me Victor, if you wish." He continued speaking without waiting for any sort of acknowledgement from Philip, "I have heard of Birmingham but I have never been there although I did spend a few months in London just after I qualified, polishing up on my English. Did you know that Madeleine and Juliette's mother is English? In fact she was the one who helped me to learn your language. I try to keep up the English by speaking it every time I am with my sister-in-law and her family. Parlez-vous le français?"

“Je ne parle pas bien le français, Monsieur, mais vous parlez très bien l’anglais,” replied Philip, who could not translate the rest, so he reverted to English, hoping that Victor would understand , “But actually Edward is the linguist. His French is much better than mine.”

Victor turned to Edward, “Génial. On parle français?”

An embarrassed Edward replied, “Je préfère l’anglais monsieur, si cela ne vous dérange pas.”

“OK,” said Victor but gave a hearty laugh as he nevertheless continued speaking in French, “Et vous comptez rester combien de temps en France les garçons?”

Edward realising that he was playing games with him, decided to have none of it and answered in English, “Providing the money lasts out, we are hoping to be here for the next six weeks. If it doesn’t, we shall have to try and find a few days work or head back home as quickly as we can.”

The game continued for a while; the conversation moving back and forth between French and English, with Juliette and Madeleine jumping in with either an English translation for Philip and Edward, or a French translation for their uncle or aunt; particularly their aunt who had only a smattering of English, and was continually asking Juliette what was being said.

Victor told them that they lived on a smallholding with a large apple orchard near a place called Hèrouvillette, a few kilometres to the east of Caen, and looking at his watch, said, “Good Heavens, we must be going and get the children home. They will be falling asleep in the car if we do not go now, and then they will wake up when we arrive home and we will not be able to get them to sleep later.”

They all got up as if on a signal, and started to collect their things together. Victor still holding Emile in one arm lifted Thérèse in the other, but Marthe, with a scowl of disapproval, instantly took her off him. Victor was equally disapproving that his wife did not trust him to carry both children at the same time, but nevertheless took the heat out of the occasion by turning to Edward and asking, “Where are you boys staying?”

“Oh, we’ll no doubt find somewhere to pitch our tent on our way to Caen,” he replied, knowing full well that Victor and his wife lived on the way towards Caen.

He got the exact response he was hoping for when Juliette piped up with, “They could pitch their tent in your orchard, couldn’t they, Uncle Victor? It would save them wasting time trying to find somewhere else, wouldn’t it?”

“Quite so Juliette, and I suppose the suggestion would have nothing to do with your wishing to spend a little more time with them, would it?”

Juliette coloured at the remark, but he took no notice and turning to the boys asked how they were getting about. He seemed impressed when they said they had a motorcycle with sidecar, and on being told that it was on the quayside behind the casino, he said, "Well my car is by the casino as well, so why don't I show you exactly where it is, and then you can follow us home. I'm sorry but we don't have a spare bedroom whilst the girls are staying with us, but you can either camp in the orchard as Juliette suggested, or you can sleep in the hay loft above the horses stable. It should be quite warm in there, and it will save you the bother of putting up your tent and taking it down again."

"That would be great, Sir," interjected Edward, with a great grin on his face, before Victor had any chance of changing his mind.

"Right then, is everyone ready? Then let us go." He turned to his wife, who obviously was not quite sure what was going on and said, "J'ai dit à ces garçons qu'ils peuvent rester avec nous ce soir." Marthe shook her head in dismay, but relaxed when Victor told her that he had only offered for them to sleep in the hayloft.

At that they all walked off towards the casino, where Victor pointed out where his car was parked. Philip and Edward ran around the other side of the casino to their motorcycle and chucked their rucksacks into the sidecar. Edward jumped on to the saddle and Philip jumped up behind him, and they drove to where Victor's car was as fast as they could, not wanting him to change his mind and leave them behind.

Later that evening, the boys were sitting with the rest of the Guilbert family around the table on the porch at the back of the house. The garden was little more than a mowed grass field, although near the house was a small flower bed; a flower bed mainly composed of unattended rose bushes interspersed with an abundance of what looked like weeds to Philip. Clearly no-one cared for the roses, as the number of dead and dying blooms hanging from the stems seemed to greatly outnumber the few fresh flowers on the plants, making the roses only slightly more attractive than the weeds.

An old swing and an even older slide resided on the grassy area, and a few yards further away was a circular track worn into the grass. Philip guessed this had probably been caused by the children's pony when Victor, standing in the middle and holding the halter tied round the pony's neck as a check on both the pony's and the child's movements, was teaching them to ride.

Over to the west was a large orchard; the fruit trees already loaded with apples, pears and plums. Although the fruit was still too small to pick it was in sufficient abundance to signify a healthy and bountiful harvest in a few months.

But Philip was fascinated by the view to the South beyond the garden area where the field had been left fallow and was now a mass of colour. Brilliant red poppies interspersed with ox-eye daisies stretched all the way to the rolling hills in the distance. Philip wondered if this was anything like the fields of poppies on the Somme his father had mentioned to him. Perhaps not! This view was far too beautiful and peaceful.

The children had insisted that Juliette and Madeleine should put them to bed and read them a story and their mother had readily agreed, as this gave her time to prepare the evening meal for everyone. Meantime, Victor took Edward and Philip to the stable block to show them his pride and joy; a four year old, smoke grey Holstein stallion, called L'etoile d'argent, which Edward roughly translated as meaning Silver Star.

Philip was spellbound by the size of the horse. He had never been this close to a stallion before. He was amazed at the innate strength and breathtaking physique of the horse. Its muscles shimmered in the light gleaming through the open stable door and every move the horse made, no matter how small, echoed the power and strength of the superb animal.

What would it be like to ride on the back of this wonderful beast, with the wind blowing through one's hair; taking one's breath away as one sped through the countryside, jumping over hedges and flying through the air as the horse cleared ditches in a leap that would seemingly last for a lifetime?

Philip was shaken out of his dream and brought back to the here and now when Victor tapped him on the shoulder, saying, "Do you ride Philip?" and without waiting for an answer asked, "Have you ever ridden such a magnificent creature?"

It took Philip a moment to regain his senses and take in where he was and what was being said to him. He nevertheless could not take his eyes of the stallion, whilst answering, "Sorry, what did you say?"

Victor smiled a knowing smile, delighted in the realization that Philip was fascinated and in awe of his beloved mount, "I said, do you ride?"

"No?" was all Philip could say.

"That's a pity. I would have loved you to have a ride in the morning, but I'm sorry, he's much too precious to let you out on him if you have no experience." He turned to Edward, who had taken very little interest in the horse, and who kept looking towards the house, so obviously waiting for the girls to come out and join them. Victor realised that unlike Philip, Edward was not impressed in any way by his prized possession. "I take it that you don't ride either Edward?"

Edward wondered whether he should say "Yes", thinking that it may in some way impress Juliette, but he was thrown by the negative way the question had been asked, and decided to be truthful, "No I've never ridden."

"In that case, perhaps I should show you Emile's pony," grinning as he added, "It may be more suitable for you." He closed the door to Silver Star's stable saying, "Come with me, we keep the pony in the next stable."

They walked round the back of the stable block where Victor opened the top part of the door to another stable. Philip had to go right up to the door and look over the lower half to see the sweetest Exmoor pony.

Victor laughed out loud, "Sorry, Edward, I don't think Petit Joseph is quite big enough for you."

Philip joined in Victor's laughter, but Edward did not think the remark in the least bit funny. Nevertheless, he did give a little smirk, hoping that Victor would not make any further comments about his lack of riding ability, but Victor had already picked up a bucket and was filling it from the outside tap. He returned with the bucket, entered Petit Joseph's stable and poured the water into his small trough before making a fuss of the pony, and without saying another word to the boys, went to refill the bucket and make his way back to Silver Star's stable, where he went through the same ritual.

But this time he seemed far more affectionate to the horse as he patted him on the head and stroked his neck whilst talking into the horse's ear. Silver Star responded by rotating his head closer and closer, obviously enjoying the attention and affection being shown to him by his owner. Although neither Philip nor Edward could hear what was being said, they nevertheless felt almost like voyeurs watching such a level of fondness between man and beast. Victor eventually stepped back and said quite softly and affectionately, "Dormez bien mon cher ami. A demain matin."

He quickly picked up the now empty bucket and patted Silver Star one last time before closing the door.

"Come on boys, I'll show you the hayloft and you can put your things in there before joining us for supper. I'm sure the girls will have it waiting for us if we stay out here much longer.

The wine had flowed freely before the meal, and Philip was surprised at how much richer, smoother and altogether more enjoyable it was compared to the wine they had drunk since landing in France.

Everyone seemed to have all the time in the world to enjoy the good food, the good wine, and the good company; nothing was rushed, and everyone acted as though it mattered little whether the meal took all night or not.

First, an enormous plate of mussels was placed in the middle of the table next to an equally large dish full of pieces of what Edward referred to as 'French bread'.

Everyone helped themselves to the bread and mussels, with both Philip and Edward putting far less of the mussels on their plate than anyone else. However, after tasting the first few, they had both accepted the invitation to refill their plate with many more.

Whilst eating the mussels Philip was talking to Victor and found out that he was a civil engineer with an office in Caen, and that his work took him all over the continent often for weeks at a time. But Edward was more interested in Juliette and as soon as there was a break in the conversation he asked her, "And what do you do, Juliette?"

Soon the two of them were chatting to each other as if there was no-one else around the table. He quickly found out that she was seventeen and lived in a place called Goupillières, a small village just north of Thury-Harcourt, and some twenty-five kilometres south of Caen and would be returning there the following morning. Her father Raoul, was a vet and Madeleine wanted to follow in his footsteps and join the family business.

"And are you also going into the family business?" he asked.

"No way!" was her strident and forceful response. "I don't intend getting up in the middle of the night to get all dirty and wet attending to cows in labour." She shuddered and pulled a face to show her revulsion at the thought, "There has to be better things to do in life than that, so no, I'm not going to be a vet. In fact, I've had enough of school, so I'm going to tell my father that I'm going to leave and become a hairdresser."

Victor laughed out loud, "Take no notice of what she says. She's what you English call, 'pulling the leg'."

"No I am not," was Juliette's vociferous and positive response. "I am going to leave school to be a hairdresser." She turned to Madeleine adding, "I'd make a good hairdresser, wouldn't I, Madeleine?"

"Yes, but with your brains you'd make an even better veterinary surgeon," was her Uncle's immediate retort, at which they all laughed, but neither Edward nor Philip was really certain whether Juliette was joking or not.

After clearing away the remains of the mussel shells, Marthe and the girls all vanished into the house to return some time later with dishes piled high with potatoes, salad and more bread, which they placed in the centre of the table. They went back into the house and almost immediately returned with a separate plate for each on which was a grilled sea bass.

Wine glasses were refilled as everyone helped themselves to the potatoes and salad before Victor restarted the conversation by asking Edward, "And what about your family, Edward?"

Edward took the opportunity to boast somewhat about their fathers' family business and how it had been built up from nothing after the war into a very successful and thriving enterprise.

Victor seemed fascinated when Edward spoke of the work they did for the armed forces and started to ask more about it. Philip did not think there was anything sinister in his interest, but nevertheless felt uneasy about the ever detailed questions being asked, as his father had always told him that information about the military contracts was to be kept confidential.

So he quickly changed the subject by saying, "Unfortunately, neither of us know much about the technical aspects of any of the military equipment produced at the factory," and moved on to talk about his mother's business.

"She originally opened a shop locally to sell wirelesses produced in the factory, but now she's got shops all over the country and sells a far greater variety including from other suppliers." Once he'd started Philip couldn't help but do some bragging himself as he continued, "She sells musical instruments, gramophones and records, and after seeing the television sets at last year's Radiolympia exhibition, she opened a shop in London where she has television sets for sale."

Juliette had never heard about televisions and Philip was soon in his element explaining all about them. At first she thought that Philip was 'pulling her leg' as she did not believe that pictures could be sent through the atmosphere and was somewhat embarrassed when her Uncle Victor laughed at her ignorance. Philip wished he hadn't been so enthusiastic on the subject and quickly tried to change the topic of conversation again, but this time Victor was having none of it. He obviously knew something about the subject and he and Philip soon became embroiled in discussing the differences between the Baird and Marconi-E.M.I. systems; why the BBC had chosen the 405-line system; and even who were making the best sets.

Marthe realised that everyone else was getting bored by all this technical talk and interrupted Victor mid-sentence to tell him to clear away the plates and bring them into the kitchen. She stood up and passed her own plate to Victor who immediately stopped talking, collected the plates together and followed his wife into the house.

As soon as he had gone, Madeleine asked Philip, "Where do you plan to visit over the next few weeks?"

"We have no definite plans, other than seeing something of France and getting to know the people a little."

"And what sort of people do you want to get to know?" asked Juliette.

Edward answered with, "Well, I'd like to get to know you a lot better, if that's O.K," and Philip was staggered when he added, "We were planning to go to Bayeux tomorrow to see the tapestry and then we were travelling south, passing through Thury-Harcourt, but we could miss out Bayeux and come straight to Thury-Harcourt, so that we could meet up again later tomorrow, if you have nothing better to do."

Philip had seen Edward using his charms to try to date girls before but this was different. Usually, he was not as direct as this, preferring only to hint at things and waiting for the girl to suggest meeting again. That way he made sure he was never the one to be turned down. Perhaps on this occasion he knew she wanted it as much as he did, but even so, Philip could not believe it when he said they planned to pass through Thury-Harcourt. They had no such plans. In fact Philip had never even heard of the place before this evening, and he was certain that Edward had not heard of it either.

Madeleine quickly interrupted before Juliette had time to answer, "Maybe you should talk to Philip before you start making plans to change your arrangements like that. Perhaps Philip still wants to go to Bayeux and may have different ideas on how he wants to spend his holiday rather than wasting time in Thury-Harcourt. After all there's nothing special about Thury-Harcourt is there Juliette?" but without waiting for an answer she turned to Philip and asked, "What do you think, Philip?"

Philip gave a non reply, "I haven't really thought about it but we did have our route and timescales pretty well sorted out before we came."

Edward jumped in, sounding quite angry, "Yes, but nothing was written in stone. We always said we'd be flexible and change parts if necessary."

This was true, but whilst Edward had often spoken about meeting and chatting up any French girls they met, Philip had never taken it particularly serious and only ever imagined it as being half an hour of fun on a beach and was pretty sure Edward hadn't intended anything different either.

Edward had always played the fool around girls thinking that was the way to impress them, but he had not been acting in the same way today. During the bike ride from Trouville, he had been talking constantly about Juliette and asking Philip what he thought about her. "Have you ever seen a girl like her before? Do you think she likes me? Do you think I have a chance with her? Shall we rearrange things to spend more time with the girls? We won't miss that much if we do, will we?"

Philip had immediately made it quite clear he did not wish to spend all the time in France chasing after girls, but Edward said he wasn't interested in chasing after girls and just wanted to make sure he didn't lose this particular girl. He even suggested that this was the girl he was going to marry. Philip had taken it as a joke when he first mentioned it, but by the time they pulled into the Guilbert's smallholding he was seriously beginning to wonder whether Edward really meant it.

To make things even worse, Philip had sensed a growing intimacy from Juliette towards Edward all evening. He was no expert in such things but he was pretty certain he wasn't imagining it.

He did not want to prevent Edward from meeting Juliette again but neither did he want it to change all their plans to see the rest of France. For himself, he did find Madeleine both amusing and pleasant to be with, and maybe it would be fun to spend another day, or perhaps two at the most, with the girls, but there was no way he wanted it to last any longer than that.

He had only recently ended, once again, the on and off two year friendship with Teresa Hunter. Teresa was good fun to be with and Philip enjoyed the time he spent with her, but all too often for his liking, she had made overtures about a more intense and permanent relationship.

Whenever she did this, he made the excuse that he needed to spend more time studying, or to spend more time helping his father and would not be able to see her as often. But he always found it difficult to actually tell her he did not wish to see her at all as he did not want to again suffer the emotional reaction from Teresa that had happened on the one occasion he had done so. He had no plans to commit to any girl; at least until he finished university, and was always hoping that Teresa would find another male friend so that he didn't have to go through upsetting her again.

He did like her but he had always felt he would know straight away when the right girl came along, and he had never felt that Teresa was that girl.

As soon as he had thought this, it struck him that maybe Edward had found the right girl in Juliette. Had Edward felt straight away that Juliette was the one and only girl for him?

Philip shuddered as he realised that that was exactly what had happened, and that unless he chose his words carefully, Edward would opt for Juliette over the rest of the holiday with him without a second's thought.

He looked up and immediately felt Madeleine's eyes staring straight into his own. She was waiting for his response about meeting up again in Thury-Harcourt, or not as the case may be. How could he say he didn't want to without upsetting Edward and Juliette? But he didn't want to offend Madeleine either, and right now he couldn't decide whether her remark had meant that she did not want them to meet up again.

The decision was taken away by Juliette who had no intention of letting Philip or Madeleine say anything that would prevent her and Edward meeting again when she said, "Well, if you're going to be in Thury-Harcourt anyway, yes it would great to see you again." She shrugged her shoulders and added, "But it wouldn't be easy to see you tomorrow as Dad is picking us up from the station. So you could still go to Bayeux tomorrow and we could all meet up the day after."

Madeleine would have none of it however, "Oh, I think this is far too pleasant an evening to talk about making plans right now, why don't we all sleep on it, and sort it out in the morning before we set off on our way?"

Juliette was about to disagree when Victor came out carrying a tray with another carafe of wine and six clean glasses. He was followed by Marthe carrying another tray containing cheese and clean plates. She placed the cheese on the table before giving each a fresh plate. Victor followed her, placing a glass at the side of each plate. He then went round again filling each glass from the carafe.

When he got to Philip, he showed him the carafe asking, "Have you ever had this before, Philip?"

Philip looked at the thick liquid and shook his head, "I don't think so. What is it?"

"This young man, is calvados made many years ago by my good father. God rest his soul. This area is called Calvados and this is a local drink made by distilling cider, the other drink made in the region. Father left a barrel of this to each of his sons and daughters when he died. You won't buy calvados as good as this in any shop."

He reached across and took his own glass, filling it to the brim from the bottle. He lifted the glass and beckoned to everyone, "A toast."

He turned to Edward, raising his glass as he did so, and then raised his glass to Philip, "May your trip be as successful as you want it to be; and may good luck follow you throughout your travels," and with that he lifted his glass to his lips and drank from it.

Before speaking, Philip pretended to take a sip as he did not want to appear an ungrateful guest. He then raised his glass back to his host and then to Marthe, "Thank you for your wonderful hospitality," adding, "I think we should propose a toast now, don't you Edward?"

Edward nodded and prodded Philip, "Stand up then and do it properly."

When he was standing Philip raised his glass to each of the others around the table in turn, and finally said, “A toast to the wonderful Guilbert family.” This time he not only raised the glass to his lips but emptied the glass in one gulp. Next moment tears were streaming from his eyes as he coughed and spluttered from the fire in his throat.

Both Marthe and Madeleine jumped to his aid, patting him on the back and passing him a drink of water. The other three, however, were just sitting back in their chairs engulfed in laughter. Victor laughed so long and hard that he eventually started to cough and splutter. This time however no one went to his aid. Madeleine merely adding, “It’s your own fault, Uncle Victor. You shouldn’t have been laughing at Philip’s misfortune so much.” And at that, she too started laughing, to be joined very quickly by everyone else, including both Philip and Victor; both of whom had to drink water every now and again to prevent further spells of coughing.

From then on, it seemed that no-one could say anything without everyone falling about in bouts of laughter. There was no more sensible conversation that evening and it was well after midnight and several more glasses of calvados before the party broke up with everyone wishing one and all a “Good night.” “Sleep well,” and “See you in the morning.”

Philip was asleep immediately he lay down in the hay barn and so there was no mention that evening about plans for the next few days and whether they were to see the girls again or not.

He woke the next morning at almost seven o’clock with an urgent need for a toilet. He pulled on his trousers and rushed out of the barn looking for somewhere suitable. He did not want to go into the house disturbing everyone else at this hour, so he went to go round the back of the barn, expecting to be able to relieve himself there. But as he was about to turn the corner he heard voices and realised that Edward was already there talking to Juliette. Had they arranged to meet like this the previous evening? If so Philip did not know when or how.

He peered round the corner to check exactly where they were. Juliette had her head on Edward’s shoulder and he was stroking her hair with one hand. His other arm was around her waist gently stoking her back. They were so clearly wrapped up in themselves that they probably would not have noticed Philip unless he deliberately bumped into them.

But Philip’s need to spend a penny was now pretty desperate so he crept away and found a suitable place round the side of the barn facing away from the house. He then crept back to the barn, lay down and went back to sleep.

He was woken at eight-thirty by Edward, shaking him, “Are you going to sleep all day? Victor is about to go to work and he's taking the girls with him to catch the train in Caen. So if you want to say goodbye to them you'll have to hurry. I'm off, see you outside in a bit," and with that he was back down the ladder and out of the barn.

Philip rubbed his eyes before putting on the clothes he had taken off the previous evening. He took his towel and tooth brush; went out of the barn; and round the side to the tap which Victor had used the previous evening to fill the water buckets for the horses. He hurriedly washed his hands under the icy cold water then splashed it on his face. The cold water had the desired effect and quickly revived him from his sleepy demeanour and after cleaning his teeth under the running water he felt quite perky.

He walked up to the house and found Victor already putting the girls' cases into the boot of his car. Marthe was trying to control Emile who was tugging at her skirt, without dropping Thérèse out of her arms, whilst at the same time trying to give Juliette a hug.

Seeing her dilemma Philip stepped in and took Thérèse from her. Poor Emile obviously felt left out of the hugging and kissing, and was trying to squeeze between Marthe and Juliette to get in on the act. Edward decided to help by picking Emile up, but he would have none of it and was soon screaming and struggling in his arms.

Marthe quickly broke away from Juliette, took Emile from Edward and spoke quietly and lovingly to her son, but Emile was inconsolable and it took several minutes for him to stop shaking and crying, by which time Thérèse had started howling. She started struggling to get out of Philip's arms with arms stretched towards her mother. This time, it was Victor who stepped in and peace was quickly restored.

Once he had Thérèse safely in his left arm, Victor held out his right hand to Philip and as they shook hands with a firm grip, Philip smiled and again thanked him and his wife for their hospitality.

Victor released his grip of Philip's hand but instead of stepping back as Philip expected, he stepped towards him, put his free arm round him and gave him a warm hug. "I have enjoyed your company. Make the most of your trip and I hope you will come back to our country again, and if you do don't forget to drop in on us." He gave a laugh as he added, "We'll be pleased to let you sleep on the hay in the barn anytime you want to."

He went through the same routine with Edward before kissing his daughter and son on the forehead. He handed Thérèse to her mother. "Come on girls. We must be going if you are to catch that train. Say your farewells to these boys and let's go."

The boys shook hands with each of the girls and as Philip shook hands with Juliette she said, "I hope we shall see you again soon?" But when shaking hands with Edward, she held on to his hand, pulled him towards her and kissed him on the cheek, whispering in his ear, "See you soon, my sweet."

Philip did not realise that Juliette had whispered anything to Edward, and he certainly had not heard the arrangement she had made. No-one had said anything about meeting again so he assumed that after sleep, both girls had decided against the idea. Perhaps that was what Juliette had been saying to Edward at the back of the barn earlier that morning?

After the car had pulled away out of the drive and onto to the road, Marthe turned to the boys and speaking in broken English said, "I make petit déjeuner for you, if you come with me."

Once inside the kitchen she placed the children on the floor. "Look after les enfants and I make food. You like café?"

Philip was quick to reply and help her out of her dilemma of trying to speak English, "Oui, café au lait, s'il vous plaît, Marthe," and for the rest of the time they spent with Marthe and the children both Edward and Philip, spoke in French. It wasn't long before Edward brought the conversation round to Juliette and by the time they left an hour later even Marthe was aware of how infatuated he was of Juliette.

The first chance Philip had of talking to Edward about the day's plans was when they were packing their things back in the barn, "I'm pleased we haven't made plans to see the girls again. I certainly don't want us to go out of our way and waste precious days of our holiday in a place I've never heard of before."

"Well I'm sorry to disappoint you, Philip, but that's exactly where you're wrong. I've told Juliette I'll meet her outside the church next to the town hall in the centre of Thury-Harcourt at ten o'clock tomorrow morning. I wanted to see her later today but she said her Dad wouldn't be pleased if they wanted to come back into town as soon as he'd picked them up and taken them back home. You should be all right though. She said she's pretty sure she can convince Madeleine to come with her or at least she hopes so! Hopefully, if Madeleine comes her father will be OK about them coming into town."

Philip was aghast that his friend had made all these arrangements without even discussing things with him, "And what will you do if I say I don't want us to change our plans?"

It was now Edward's turn to be put out, "You don't really mean that do you? No you can't mean it! I've told Juliette we'll be there and anyway, she feels certain that Madeleine would like to see you again."

"And what if I don't want to see her again?"

"Of course you want to see her again," Edward said, but he really wasn't sure whether Philip was being serious and actually had no wish to see her again. "But you do want to see her again, don't you?"

Philip was now really irritated with Edward, "The point is not whether I want to see her or not. If we were at home maybe it would be OK, but we're not at home and we've spent weeks planning what we're going to do, and here we are, two days into a six week holiday and you're changing things already."

"Oh, come on, I haven't changed all our plans. All I've done is changed one day and we both said before we came that we could spend an extra day in a place if we liked it."

"And that's all you've done, is it? Decided, without asking me, that we'll spend a day in a place that neither of us had ever heard of before yesterday?"

"Well yes I suppose so. Look, I'm sorry you're so upset, but the truth is I really like Juliette and I want to get to know her better. You wouldn't begrudge me that would you?"

"Edward, it was obvious to me yesterday, that you're smitten with this girl, and OK, I don't mind us going to somewhere we hadn't actually planned on. It's just that I wished you'd checked it out with me first."

Edward leaned forward and put his arm round his friend, "Thanks. It means a lot to me."

"So we're agreed then, are we? We go to Bayeux today as planned, then we travel to this Thury-Harcourt just for one day, and we'll be back to our original plans on the day after."

It was obvious from the look on Edward's face that he wasn't happy at this, but he nevertheless decided not to tell Philip right now about the full plans he'd made with Juliette that morning. He had actually told her they would stay in Thury-Harcourt for several days and when she had said that the family was going on holiday the following week to the south coast near Nîmes, he had suggested that they could meet up again there. He thought he would tell Philip about all that tomorrow perhaps.

Edward looked at his watch, "Come on let's get going to Bayeux then. We've got a big day ahead of us and it's after ten o'clock already."

The arrangements became a more and more aggravating issue for Philip as the holiday progressed and the boys argued about it on and off for the rest of trip. At one point Edward even threatened to do his own thing and let Philip go and do whatever he wanted, but since they only had one motorcycle, and that actually belonged to Edward, Philip thought better of it, and gave in to Edward far more than he wanted to.

The result was that they spent four nights camped out in the Grimbosq forest, which was even closer to where Juliette lived than Thury-Harcourt. They spent the best part of a week near Nîmes, concertinaed four weeks plans into two weeks, spent only one day in Paris before crossing country back to Thury-Harcourt for three days and then back to Paris for another night before making their way back home via Calais as planned.

Increasingly Philip realised that for Edward this was not a holiday fling but something far more serious, and he agreed to all these changes of plans less and less reluctantly. By the end of the holiday he was convinced that this was a relationship that was destined to last for a long time to come, however much Edward and Juliette would be apart.

CHAPTER FIFTEEN

JUNE 1941

Both Frank and Tom had been spending more and more time at the factory trying to meet the orders being placed by the military for communications equipment needed for the ever increasing numbers in the armed forces. The job was not made any easier by the loss of their trained male employees who had joined one or other of the armed services.

The task was made even more difficult since even the few trained male production line staff they had left were unable or unwilling to put in the hours of overtime needed to meet the production schedules. All the men still working, including those too old for military service, had, since Herbert Morrison's regulation at the end of 1940, been compulsory required to perform fire watching duties in addition to their work. Frank had been excused from this because of his disability, but Tom had immediately joined and had in fact quite enjoyed the camaraderie of his fellow fire watchers.

Frank had always been happy to employ women on production and after initial reservations Tom had readily agreed that for the most part they were as adept and as good as the men, so they replaced the lost men with more women, but now, even the women were required to do their stint on fire watch if they worked less than 55 hours a week. In the need to meet production quotas, this had to some extent worked to Frank's advantage however, as most of the women were willing to do extra paid work on what was regarded as essential war work in order to avoid the fire duties.

Lucy Evans was also spending more and more time at the factory and Frank had become more and more dependant on her. These days, she not only kept the office in order, acting as chief bookkeeper, taking orders and sending out all the invoices, but had become an expert in reading the design blueprints, which she then used to create all the production schedules. Using these she made sure that all the components were purchased in good time and available to the production workers when needed.

Frank now regarded Lucy as the most important and totally irreplaceable individual in the factory. He had known for some years that whilst she would almost certainly be able to keep things turning over perfectly well without him, he would not be able to manage without her invaluable knowledge and expertise. He argued this point with Tom over and over again and when they had become a private limited company, Frank had suggested that they take Lucy on as a director and properly reward her for her work. Tom almost certainly knew that Lucy was indispensable but would never actually admit to this and to date had not agreed to the suggestion, always arguing that she was amply rewarded because of the annual bonus system.

The business profits had increased substantially over the last five or six years and the bonus scheme had been Frank's suggestion for sharing out some of the rewards of this success to employees, as recognition for their loyalty and hard work in achieving the increased profits.

At first, Frank had great difficulty in convincing Tom of the benefits to be gained from this and it was only when he said he was going to do it anyway, even if it meant paying it out of his own share of the profits that he managed to embarrass Tom into agreeing. Even so, in the first year, Tom only agreed to a bonus of two day's extra pay, but each year Frank argued the case for more and last year a bonus of two week's pay was made. Tom had not only finally got used to the idea, but had even recognised that the bonus scheme was one of the reasons why workers were intent on making sure that the planned monthly production figures were always achieved or exceeded.

The annual bonus was, once again, top of Frank's agenda. He and Lucy had spent the whole of the previous weekend and each of the previous two evenings until after midnight completing the last financial year's accounts up to the end of May. The final figures showed the biggest ever profit and Frank was trying to decide what size of bonus he should suggest to Tom but was finding it somewhat difficult to concentrate.

The reason for this would have been obvious to anyone else, but somehow never seemed to register with Frank. He had not been home since the previous Wednesday, a full week earlier. He had spent each night asleep on the bed that had been set up in his office some two years earlier. A bed that had never been intended for sleeping on, but merely a bed on which he could receive the physiotherapy treatment he needed each day to keep his muscles and the blood flow in his lower body in some sort of order.

Alice Kelly, who still lived with Frank and Grace, had religiously given Frank the necessary treatment every morning and every evening since he had first come out of hospital after the accident in 1926.

However, at the beginning of 1938, she had complained that, as the two boys were now grown up and no longer needed her to look after them she had too much spare time on her hands. And so, encouraged by Frank, she had applied to the General Hospital for a full time nursing post. The hospital offered her a position but she refused the post when told she would have to work shifts. Grace was puzzled at this until she realised that the only reason for Alice not wanting to take the job was because it would mean she wouldn't always be around to give Frank his physiotherapy.

It was then that Grace came up with the idea of the bed in Frank's office, saying that Alice could give Frank his treatment both before and after her shift, either at home or at the office, depending on where Frank was at that time. Alice was delighted at the suggestion, and had readily agreed to it.

Frank however, would have none of it, "I'm not going to let you undress me in my office. Everyone can see right into it from the factory floor and the door is always open. Anyone could come in just when you're helping me out of my pants. No, definitely not. I'm not having it."

Grace, ever the peacemaker, rarely interfered in Frank's affairs, but she was as protective of his physical welfare as Alice, and had become more furious than Alice had ever seen her. "You, stupid, stupid man, how dare you be so insensitive? Alice has been here looking after you, day in and day out, for years. She has never complained at your grumbles. She has always fitted her life around you, getting up at some unearthly time to give you your physio before you go to work, no matter how early that's been, and then waited up 'til God knows what time, to do the same thing before you get into bed. Now she's offering to still fit it all in round her hospital work and you're just dismissing it out of hand."

She waved her fist at Frank and her voice became even louder and angrier, "Now selfish Frank doesn't want her to help any more does he? How dare you treat Alice so dismissively, you selfish bugger?"

Frank had never heard Grace use words like this before and when she stepped towards him he thought she was about to hit him. But, without taking a break for breath, she put her face inches from his and continued her attack, "You will have your physio and you will apologise to Alice for treating her this way. All your stupid excuses are irrelevant. I'm going to sort it all out, even if it means coming to the factory and dragging you out of there in front of all your precious workers to bring you back home when Alice is here. And you don't want that, do you?"

She turned to look at Alice, "Alice, I'm going to get some blackout material today and I shall get Lucy to help me put it up over Frank's office door so that no one can see in. And I'm going to have a word with Tom about putting a lock on the door and building some sort of bed on which you can give this ungrateful so and so his treatment."

She turned back to Frank, "Now apologise to Alice, and let's get on with it."

And so the arrangements had been made, but Frank insisted that the blackout should be fixed on a rail so that he could still see the production area when Alice was not there. He also insisted that Alice's visits should only occur when most of the staff had gone home, and even though Alice ignored this whenever her shift patterns meant she had no other alternative, on such occasions Frank always seemed to be having a meeting in his office and over time the sessions became less and less regular.

When Frank first used the bed to sleep on all night, Grace had had second thoughts about how good her idea had been in the first place. There had been another telling off for Frank when he arrived home the following evening, but this time it had no effect at all, and within a short space of time Frank was often sleeping overnight on the bed.

These sleepovers were mostly for the odd night every couple of weeks, but Frank had spent so much time trying to sort out the accounts that he had slept on the bed every night for the past week. To make matters worse Alice had worked extra shifts over the previous weekend, so she had only managed four treatment sessions with Frank since the previous Friday.

It was now Wednesday and a furious Grace was on the phone, once more giving vent to her anger that he had somehow managed to get out of his session with Alice on the previous day.

"I promise I'll be home this evening and Alice can give me all the treatment she wants to then." Frank gave a final "I promise," before putting the telephone down just as Tom walked into the office, and without looking at the clock on the wall, Frank knew it was now seven-thirty, the exact time Tom turned up for work every morning without fail.

"Morning, Frank. How goes it?"

Tom, as ever, was immaculately dressed in a freshly laundered white shirt and his neatly ironed suit with a precise crease down each trouser leg.

Frank could smell Tom's freshness and suddenly became aware of his own dishevelled self. He badly needed a wash and change of clothes.

He felt his beard, now almost pure white and matching his hair which had turned grey and then white over the past few years. He told Grace he had grown the beard because he though it statesmanlike and gave an air of authority, but Grace was not fooled and knew the truth was that it saved him the time and effort of shaving each morning. As he stroked the beard, he smiled. He knew full well that Grace had not only grown used to the idea of the beard but had actually grown to like the look of it.

"Fine, except I've just had Grace on the phone again, bending my ear about making sure I go home tonight."

Tom looked across at the unmade bed behind Frank, "By the look at that, I take it you've been here all night again then? I agree with Grace, you really should get a good night's sleep at home every night, and not make do with this excuse for a bed. I bet you haven't had anything to eat yet either?"

"Lucy said she'd bring me something when she comes in. She'll be here soon."

"And I suppose you kept her here half the night again. Anyone would think there was something going on between you pair. Just as well we all know that you're too much of a slave driver to waste precious work time on things like that."

Frank was suddenly concerned about Tom's observation, "Nobody actually thinks that, do they? I wouldn't want to put Lucy through anything like that." He thought about it for a moment before adding, "Perhaps Grace was right just now on the phone, when she said I had become a selfish so and so who never thought about other people properly. Does it really look like that? I'm only trying to keep up with all this work you know, but I would hate to get Lucy talked about like that just because of my stupidity. They don't really think that something's going on, do they?"

"Calm down, old boy, I was only joking. And no, I don't think anyone thinks that you'd have a fling with Lucy; or anyone else for that matter. Who'd have you right now anyway? You look as though you haven't washed in a week and that's the same shirt you had on yesterday, and Monday, isn't it?" He took a deep whiff, put the fingers of one hand to close his nostrils and put his other hand across his mouth. "No self respecting girl would look twice at a smelly object like you, and as we all know, Lucy is far too nice a girl to get involved with a married man, even if he were all spruced up."

Frank decided it was time to change the subject but after Tom's last remark he was nevertheless pleased that he had said he would go home that evening. Perhaps he ought to ask John to take him home as soon as he arrived so that he could have a bath and change his clothes, but looking again at the mound of papers on his desk he decided that going home would have to wait until later.

He picked up the sheets he and Lucy had been working on, "Here, have a look at these. If the figures are right, and I'm sure they are, we've made an even bigger profit than ever before."

He handed the papers to Tom, adding, "It just seems a little immoral to me that we're making all this profit out of the military orders, when the country is at war and things are getting tighter and tighter for everyone else."

Tom took the papers, sat down on the chair opposite to Frank, and started to inspect the figures. "You know your trouble Frank, you're too soft. You'd give all the profit away if it was left to you. Thank God, Lucy's got a business head on her shoulders, and gives realistic prices for all our products. I sometimes don't know what we'd do without her. Best thing you ever did when you gave that girl a job. She's the best thing that ever happened to this business."

Frank could not believe the words coming out of Tom's mouth and decided the time was right to bring up Lucy's position in the firm with him again. He was sure he would not get another chance as good as this.

"For once Tom, I agree one hundred percent with all you say. It is about time we all recognised her worth as much as you obviously do. Why don't we make her a director? I'm sure that one of these days we'll both want to take it easy and who better to look after things than Lucy?"

Tom let out a guffaw of laughter, leaning back on his chair so far that he quickly had to pull himself back again to prevent himself falling right over. He did not stop laughing however and his amusement continued for so long that he eventually starting coughing. When he managed to stop he looked accusingly straight at Frank, "You old bugger, you've been waiting for me to drop myself in it like that for years, haven't you?"

Frank merely smiled and waited for Tom to continue.

"Actually, Frank, I have been thinking about it lately and I think you're absolutely right, we should consider Lucy's position. We should talk about her becoming a director and how we best achieve that whilst still keeping overall control ourselves."

He looked down at the papers in his hand again, "Wow, am I reading this profit figure right? That's nearly half as much again as last year, isn't it?"

"You're reading it absolutely right, and that's after we've already accounted for a bonus the same as last year. We could of course be more generous than last year, but Lucy thinks it would be wrong to increase it this year in case we can't do the same thing next year. She did make what I think was a very good suggestion though. She suggested that we might give something to the wives of the chaps who've joined up and won't be benefiting this year. What do you think?"

"Come on old chap, let's not run away with ourselves. You'll be suggesting we give some of it back to the military soon."

Frank smiled and shook his head, "Well would that be such a bad idea?"

Tom jumped up. "You are joking, aren't you? But in case you're not and want my answer, then yes it would be a bad idea. I give in on one thing and you're immediately trying to get me to go that bit further."

Frank waved his hand up and down at Tom, "Oh for goodness sake Tom, sit down. Lucy's already convinced me that it wouldn't be the right thing to do. She also said that it wouldn't be right to cut our prices either, as that would give the impression that we've been overcharging up to now."

Frank thought for a moment before continuing, "She did wonder though if there was any way we could make the military equipment more robust without adding to the weight or maybe even reducing it. If you could come up with a solution even it cost more per unit to make, we could perhaps charge the same price and thus continue to be in the military's good books. What do you think?"

"I don't suppose she told you how I should do it, did she? I sometimes wonder if I'm the director in this business or if it isn't Lucy who's already the director instead of me. You always seem to have these little tête à tête's together about how to run the business, and what's more they always seem to be when I'm not around."

"Don't be like that Tom. You know that's not true. We're all on the same side, and you ought to know by now that Lucy only ever makes suggestions for the good of the business and everyone who works here. And as for us talking when you're not around, well we were only chatting about things in general whilst finishing off these figures last night."

Frank knew that Tom had always felt somewhat embarrassed that Lucy was terrific at doing all the office work that he himself had failed to keep on top of following Frank's accident, but had never directly dealt with the matter with Tom. Perhaps now was the time to put the record straight.

"You know Tom, you and I have always been the best of pals, but we are different in so many ways. Your strengths are not my strengths."

He looked down and slapped both his legs, "And I'm not talking about these bloody useless legs, either. You are brilliant at sorting out all the silly little niggling production problems they seem to have out there. The men respect you and the women all love working for you."

He smiled as he added, "You know that don't you? I'm sure little Dorothy out there would jump straight into your pants anytime you'd let her. But, somehow you can deal with all that, all the problems, all the mess ups they sometimes make, without upsetting any of them and they'd all jump through hoops for you if you asked them. I'm not daft, you know, I know they wouldn't do it for me, and what's more I don't think they'd do it for Lucy either. Yes, she's good at her job, no, that's not true, she's actually brilliant at her job and we both know it, but so are you brilliant at your job."

Frank looked directly at Tom, "I've suggested we make Lucy a director, not because I think she's better than you, and certainly not as a replacement for you, but because I think this business is successful because all three of us each do the things we do best, and together we cover all aspects of the business brilliantly. Actually, if I'm honest, I think that out of the three of us, I'm the one that could most easily be lost."

"Now, who's the one being a silly bugger?" said Tom.

Much to Frank's relief there was a knock at the door before Tom was able to go on with what Frank feared would prove to be an untrue embellishment of his own attributes.

Tom got up and opened the door, "Oh, hello John, come in."

John entered the room carrying a tray of drinks and a plate of bacon sandwiches. He nodded to Frank and then to Tom, "Morning, Dad. Morning Uncle Tom. Mrs Evans said I was to bring you these bacon butties to eat with your tea."

John put the tray on the desk and Frank took one of the bacon sandwiches, "Where on earth does Lucy get this gorgeous bacon from?" He was about to take a mouthful, but instead winked at John, saying, "Perhaps we shouldn't ask. I'm sure it's not with her food coupons so we might not approve of the answer. What do you think John?"

John shook his head from side to side, "No, don't ask her."

Frank detected a slight reddening in his son's cheeks and wondered if he knew the answer to the question, but soon realised the blush was caused by John picking up the courage to pass on his mother's message when he added, "Oh, and Mom told me to tell you that she was expecting you at home for your supper tonight and that she wouldn't accept any excuses."

"I know son, she's been on the phone already telling me off. So, if you don't mind, perhaps you could stay behind tonight when Uncle Tom's finished with you and then you can take me home."

Getting John to learn to drive had been another of Lucy's brilliant ideas, just as it had also been her suggestion that they should give him a job at the factory as soon as he was old enough to leave school.

John had always struggled at school and even though Frank and Grace had paid for the best education they could get for him, he had nevertheless only managed to leave school with the barest of educational ability. He struggled with both reading and writing but managed OK with numbers.

It was Lucy who noticed one day how rapidly he could add up a column of figures, when years ago whilst he waited for his father, she had given him a piece of paper to scribble on and he had immediately copied down a set of her figures lying on the desk, drew two lines under them, and proceeded to add them up. After he'd gone she picked up the paper to throw it into the wastepaper basket, but decided to check his total first. She was surprised to find the correct result at the bottom of the page. Lucy, being Lucy, had thereafter given him more paper each time he came, and was soon so impressed with his ability, that she started giving him columns of her own figures to add up. He was not always one hundred per cent accurate but she nevertheless found it a good way of double checking her own additions.

When he was about to leave school and Frank was anxiously telling her that they did not know what to do with him, Lucy suggested he should give John a job in the factory. At first, Frank dismissed the idea, saying he wasn't going to have his son doing all the menial tasks in the factory, such as sweeping up. It was only then that Lucy admitted what she had been using John for from time to time. She had assumed wrongly, that Frank knew of his son's ability at maths, and it therefore took her sometime to convince Frank to give him a chance. On that occasion however, Tom had been the first to back her up.

He had always had a soft spot for his nephew, and enjoyed the occasions when John visited him in his workshop at home and had shown enthusiastic interest in all the wood and metalwork Tom dabbled with in his spare time; things that his own son Edward, had never shown any interest in.

In the event, working at the factory had been far more successful than anyone had expected. John always had a smile on his face and seemed somehow to make people pleased, or even feel better, for having seen him. He was not an expert at anything, but was always willing to step in anywhere to help anyone asking for his help. He would fetch boxes of parts, happily assist when someone wanted something holding whilst some intricate bit was soldered into place, and still added up columns of figures for Mrs Evans on a regular basis.

Lucy had often told him to call her Lucy the same as everyone else did, but he had called her Mrs Evans since the first time he met her as a four year old and found it impossible to change it now.

John was about to leave the office when Frank suddenly realised that other than when he had brought his tea each morning, he had not spoken to his son in a week. Perhaps it was about time he started thinking of others! He called to his son just as he opened the door to go out, "As usual son, Lucy's done far more sandwiches than we can eat, do you want one?"

John turned and nodded his head.

"Fetch yourself a cup of tea then and when you come back you can tell me how everyone is at home, and what you've all been doing with yourselves for the past week."

Tom and Frank usually had lunch together in Frank's office talking about all the current plans and problems and today was no exception. Mostly they chatted about the accounts and the bonus, but they had also spoken at length about Lucy and the directorship arrangements they would offer her.

Frank was surprised how much Tom's suggestions were very much in line with his own and it became obvious that, for some reason he was unaware of, Tom had obviously changed his mind totally since they had last spoken on the subject several months previously.

"So when do you want to tell Lucy about this then," Tom asked. "I think she should be told sooner rather than later. Why don't you tell her this afternoon?"

It was only when Frank did not answer that Tom become conscious of the fact that he had been doing all the talking, and that Frank had just been sitting there saying nothing.

"Are you having second thoughts about it, Frank?"

Frank merely shook his head from side to side.

This sort of non verbal response was most unusual and suddenly realising that Frank looked quite pale, Tom got up from his seat and went round to Frank's side of the desk. "Are you OK, Frank?"

"Yes, I'm fine, I just feel so tired. I haven't felt this tired in ages. Perhaps Grace is right when she says I ought not to push myself so much."

"It's not just Grace that says that. That's what we all feel. Look why don't I go and ask John to take you home right now. I can spare him for the rest of the afternoon and he could help you get into the bath and have a long soak. I'll tell him to make sure you get a proper lie down in your own bed for a few hours afterwards. What do you think? Shall I go and fetch him?

"No, I'll just sit here for a bit and have another cup of tea. I'll be fine after that. Anyway, Lucy wants us to sign some papers the bank needs first thing in the morning and I don't think she's even prepared them yet."

"Forget it, you're not staying here any longer, not even for another cup of tea, and certainly not for papers from Lucy. That can all wait 'cause you're going home right now. I'll check the papers this afternoon and you can sign them in the morning before she goes to the bank."

At supper that evening Frank did in fact feel much better. He had managed to relax completely in the bath, and if John had not gone into the bathroom to check on him after fifteen minutes, he would undoubtedly have fallen fast asleep in the water. John had helped him out of the bath; dried him; put on his dressing gown and wheeled him into the bedroom, where Frank lifted himself on to the bed, falling asleep almost instantly.

At five o'clock Alice arrived home and reluctantly woke Frank for his physiotherapy. There was a small bedroom that had been especially set up for Frank's treatment, but on this occasion Alice decided to treat Frank in his bedroom. She had taken the decision to wake Frank on the basis that he ought not miss out on any more physio and, if she treated him where he was, he could go back to sleep again straight afterwards.

Frank had not slept again, saying he felt quite awake and would not be able to sleep later if he slept any more now.

"Have it your own way for now then. I suppose a full night's sleep will make a change for you anyway. But don't forget I insist that we have a full two sessions again tomorrow, and you can either have the first at the factory as soon as I've finished my shift. Say about nine o'clock. Or, you can wait here 'til I get back and we can sort you out here before you go to work. Please yourself which, but I insist that we get in two sessions tomorrow."

It was not unusual for Alice to speak to him like this, but she knew perfectly well that if he chose to do so, Frank would take absolutely no notice of her instructions. He always managed to get his own way, even things he was physically powerless of doing without assistance. Alice hoped this was not because they felt sorry for him. Frank would hate that as much as she hated the fact that he was so dependant on them. What she would give for him to have the use of his legs back again!

Whilst clearing away the supper things, Grace asked if Frank would like to have an early night, adding, "It won't hurt for you to get to bed early for once."

"Well actually, Alice said she thought I should lie-in in the morning until she got back from her night shift and then she could treat me before I go to work, but Lucy needs some papers signing for the bank first thing."

"Tom said he'd sign them and leave them on my desk and I could sign them before Lucy has to go to the bank. So I thought that if John runs Alice to work, I could go with them, and after we've dropped her off, he could drive to the factory, leaving me in the car whilst he nipped into the office and fetched the papers for me to sign. I wouldn't need to even get out of the car and John could put them back on my desk, all signed and waiting for Lucy to pick them up. If Alice doesn't mind turning up for work a bit early we could go straight away and be back here in an hour, so I can still have an early night. We could all have a nice late breakfast together in the morning and I could leave going into work until after lunch if you like."

Grace put down the plates she had collected, "And now what are you up to?"

"I'm not up to anything, love. Lucy really must have those papers signed for first thing in the morning."

"And what else do you intend to do whilst you're there?"

"Absolutely nothing, I promise." He looked at his watch, "It's only just gone half past seven. If we go straight away, we could drop Alice off, I could check and sign the papers and we'd be back here by nine at the latest. I'll be in bed by nine-thirty, no problem."

Grace smiled and shook her head, "Nine-thirty? That'll be a first."

Frank held up his hand in the scout's salute, "Back by nine, scout's honour."

Grace this time, laughed out aloud, "Scout's honour? My ****." She mouthed the '****' but no word came out of her mouth. "Anyway, Alice's shift doesn't start 'til ten, she'll be much too early if she goes now."

Alice immediately cut in, "Oh, I don't mind being early if it means that Frank gets a full night's sleep for once. Anyway, I'm sure there'll be plenty I can do on the ward."

Alice suddenly realised that in saying this she had taken away from Grace the means of possibly preventing Frank going out. She looked directly at Grace and mouthed an apologetic "Sorry."

Grace knew she would lose any argument she put forward so picked up the plates again saying, "I suppose if you have to go, then you have to, but if you're not back here by nine, then ......" She shook her head as she tried to think what would be the appropriate threat to make.

"Then what, my love?"

"You'll find out if you're not back at nine."

The tension and anger had gone from her voice and Frank started laughing at her and held out his hand towards her, "Nine o'clock I promise. Now come here and give me a kiss."

Grace joined in his laughter and as she put down the plates for the second time, she took his hand and planted a kiss on the top of his head.

"Not like that. I want a proper kiss."

Grace yanked her hand from his grasp, "You can have your proper kiss at nine o'clock." She wagged her finger at him, "And you'd better be here to claim it, or else." Once again she failed to say what the 'or else' was.

When the telephone rang at almost half past ten, Grace had been sitting in the dark for almost two hours. She had all the lights off in the house so that she could keep the lounge blackout curtains open in order to see the car as soon as it arrived on the driveway outside.

At half past nine and still no sign of Frank, she phoned the work's number but there was no reply. She phoned Tom at home and asked him if he knew whether Frank had been to the factory, adding that he should have been there over an hour ago."

"No. I haven't seen him since he left just after lunch. Is everything OK?"

Grace explained the situation and he replied by saying, "Well everyone, including me, left at nine when the late shift finished but Frank certainly hadn't arrived by then. I'll go back to the factory and look for him if you want me to."

"No, don't do that. I'm sure he's fine."

"Yes, I'm sure he is. You know what he's like, probably seen someone on his way and is chatting away oblivious to the time passing. Are you sure you don't want me to go and find him? Mary can easily keep my supper warm for a bit longer."

"No, don't do that I'm sure he won't be long."

"Well if you're sure. Look, I'll tell you what, I'll give you a call when I've finished eating and if he's not back I'll go and find him for you."

"No don't do that. I'll ring you if there's any problem. You just enjoy your supper and forget all about Frank."

"OK but you just stop worrying, I'm sure everything's fine."

She relaxed a little after speaking to Tom, but nevertheless moved her chair nearer to the phone so that she could reach it without losing her view of the drive outside. Every five or ten minutes after that she rang the factory number again, letting it ring for longer and longer each time she tried.

She looked at her watch for the hundredth time, "Twenty-eight minutes past ten, where on earth can they be?" Grace had been staring at the phone willing it to ring for what seemed like hours, but when it did ring, it was nevertheless something of a shock and she jumped up out of her seat and just looked at the phone, unsure what to do. In seconds all sorts of things flashed through her mind. Had they had an accident? Were they in hospital or even worse? Was it the hospital ringing? Or maybe even the police?

She snatched the phone off its base, her anxiety level evident as she shouted "Yes," into the mouthpiece.

"Hello, Mom, I'm real sorry we're late, but we've had a bit of a problem with the car."

Grace was unaware that she was still shouting into the phone, "What sort of problem? Where on earth have you been? Are you all right? Is your Dad all right?"

"I'm real sorry about it all, Mom, but Dad says I'm not to worry about it and to tell you not to worry either. He says to tell you that everything's fine and to tell you that I'm OK and that he is OK Oh, and I'm to tell you that the car is OK as well, just a couple of burst tyres to sort out."

"Two burst tyres? What on earth have you done?"

"Me? Nothing! Well actually, I suppose it was me who drove over the milk bottles, but they shouldn't have been there in the road should they?"

Grace was immensely relieved to hear John's matter of fact voice saying that both of them were unharmed, but as the tension that had built up over the past few hours was released she started to shake and felt uneasy on her feet. She pulled the chair towards her and sat down.

"Right, now tell me the whole story, slowly from the beginning."

"There isn't a story to tell. We dropped Auntie Alice off at the hospital, and as we were driving up Green Lane, and you know how bumpy that is over all the cobbles, well someone's milk bottles must have got knocked off their front step and rolled into the road. Dad said it was probably a cat. Anyway, I didn't see any milk bottles, and 'cause of the bumpy cobblestones, I didn't even feel them when we ran over them. It was Dad who said it had suddenly got bumpier in the back and that I should stop and have a look. And there it was; a flat back tyre."

"You said you had two burst tyres?"

"Yes, well I didn't know that at first, did I? It took me ages to get the tyre off. I just couldn't turn the nuts. Goodness knows what sort of strongman they'd used to tighten them up! Anyway, I eventually got the spare on and was just about to get back into the car when I noticed that the front tyre was as flat as a pancake and without another tyre we were stuck weren't we?"

"And all of that's taken you over two hours has it?"

"Well no, I had to ask someone to help me get Dad out of the car and into his wheelchair, didn't I? And then we had to walk here."

"And where is here? Where are you now?"

"We're in Dad's office and I'm just about to make us a cup of tea."

"If your Dad is there with you, why isn't he the one to phone me? Are you sure he's all right?"

"I told you he is fine, absolutely fine."

"So, why are you the one who phoned?"

Grace sensed the sheepishness in John's voice as he said, "Well Dad thought it would be better coming from me."

By now Grace had stopped shaking and had calmed down completely. "And your Dad is all right, isn't he?" and without waiting for his answer, added, "Let me speak to him."

She could hear the mumbling at the other end of the phone, but eventually Frank spoke, "Sorry about all this Grace. I know you must have been worrying but it couldn't be helped."

He then delivered what he knew would take all the sting out of anything Grace was about to throw at him. "None of this was anyone's fault and it certainly wasn't poor Johnny's. He feels really bad about it all, but I keep telling him that neither of us has been hurt so there's absolutely nothing for him to worry about. He's said he's sorry at least a dozen times already and we don't want him to think you are mad at him, do we? We'll get the tyres mended in the morning and everything will be fine. So don't worry any more, just get to bed and we'll see you in the morning."

Up to now, Grace had only been concerned to know what had taken place and that nothing untoward had happened to her son and husband and had not given any thought to anything else. She had just assumed that both of them would soon be home albeit later than expected. "What do you mean by see you in the morning?"

Frank had been dreading this question. "I know it's not what you want to hear, but the truth of the matter is that we'll get to bed much sooner if we just bed down where we are. John has gone off to make a cup of tea and when we've had that we'll just curl up here and be asleep in no time. John has already said that he's looking forward to sleeping in my office with me. It'll be something for him to talk to the girls about in the morning. And it's not as though I haven't slept on this bed before is it?"

Grace did not know whether to laugh or scream at Frank, as she replied, "You can say that again." She decided that anger would have no effect so let out a loud laugh before continuing, "You know exactly how to press the right buttons to get me to agree with you, don't you? But don't for one minute think I'm fooled by any it."

It was now Frank's turn to laugh, "I wouldn't dare, my love, I wouldn't dare."

He did not wait for any further response from Grace, but just continued, "So, you just do the same. Have a bedtime drink and we'll be back home in the morning as soon as the tyres are fixed. Night, night. Sleep tight," and with that he put the phone down before Grace was able to argue with him.

It was pitch black in the room when Frank was awoken by John shaking him. "Wake up Dad; can't you hear all that noise outside?"

Frank was usually a light sleeper, but tonight he was out cold, the shortage of proper sleep over previous nights having caught up with him. The sirens were going off all around warning of the incoming bomber planes.

"Make sure the blackouts are pulled to John, and then switch on the lights."

"But Dad, shouldn't we be going to the nearest shelter?"

"I'm sorry John, but I haven't a clue where it is. I suppose one of the houses opposite might have an Anderson in the back garden but by the time we get there and find out where it is this will all be over." He took John's shoulders, "And in any case, they're probably just panicking. I doubt if there are any planes on their way. And certainly not here, they're more likely to be over Birmingham. I'll tell you what, now that we're awake, why don't you go and make us a nice cup of tea and we can enjoy that while we wait for this to pass over."

The sirens stopped as John turned to check the blackout curtains. He was just about to turn on the light when they heard the drone of the planes approaching.

"No don't switch on the light Johnny, they sound a damn sight closer than Birmingham. Come here and get under this bed of mine. Tom made it high so that I could slide off my wheelchair and back on to it easily, so there should be enough room under there. And knowing Uncle Tom he'll have made the whole thing stronger than any Anderson shelter."

John went to join his father, "If it's all right by you Dad, I don't think I want to get under there. I'd rather just sit on the bed by you."

Frank was just about to speak in reply, when he heard a noise that he hadn't encountered in over twenty years. The sound of an explosion as a shell hit the ground some distant away.

The memories of such an event came flooding back, but unlike events on the battlefield in France when he had accepted the possibility of his own death as each missile headed his way, this time it was totally different. He had not been scared at the thought of death then and he was not scared of his own death now either, but this time there was an enormous difference; a difference that petrified Frank. His son was with him now. He still felt the loss of little Kathy every day, and the thought of losing another child sent shivers through his whole body. He knew Grace would never survive such a loss again.

Another bomb exploded, this time nearer. And then Frank heard the drone of a plane coming closer and closer.

He grasped hold of John and pulled him to his chest. He crushed John against him and shook with the fearful thoughts in his head. Why had he been the selfish idiot that Grace had accused him of? Why had he insisted on coming here tonight? Why had he been so egotistical and obstinate? They could both now be reasonably safe in the cellar at home, which Grace had furnished just for such an eventuality, instead of this lean to wooden structure that Tom had created as an office for him, against the back wall of the factory on the ground floor.

Frank had been delighted with Tom's efforts to give him somewhere to work after his accident. There was no way he could have got to the existing offices in the attic space of the building, or at least, not unless someone, or several somebody's, carried him up the stairs each morning and back down again each evening. Tom had even built a separate private washroom and toilet facility with extra wide access and special bars so that Frank could manage things himself without the embarrassment of having to get someone to help him every time he needed the toilet.

But now was this personal sanctuary that Frank had been so pleased with, going to become his tomb? If that was to be so, why had his self-centred actions on this occasion meant that his son was here as well? If only he could turn the clock back a few hours!

This time, instead of merely hearing the explosion as the bomb hit the ground somewhere, Frank listened to the unmistakable hiss of a bomb falling directly towards them. He had been able to distinguish the noise of shells heading his way as opposed to those heading in other people's direction, on the Somme. But somehow the Gods had always spared him, even though he had often been covered with the flying earth as the missile hit the ground too close for comfort, and often killing others only feet away.

But this wasn't a shell, this was a bomb and bombs fell straight down didn't they?

As he held his son waiting for the end to come, time stood still and every second seemed like an hour. He clung to John more tightly and managed to say, "Sorry son, I love you," as he listened at the sound of the bomb coming towards them.

He could not prevent the uncontrollable fear rising within him and his whole body started to shake as he waited in expectancy for the bomb to come crashing though the roof. He heard the whistle as it sped towards the ground and felt a brief moment of enormous relief as he realised that it was not going to fall directly on top of them.

Only fractions of seconds separated the unfolding events, but to Frank everything was now moving in slow motion. He was acutely aware of each and every distinct instalment of the disastrous events happening around him and as he identified the source of every new sound, his heartbeat pounded faster and louder and the level of terror within him increased.

How he managed to differentiate between each event and why it was all happening so slowly was a mystery to him. He recalled that Captain Harper had once told him that that was what happened to anyone killed in action. Their last moments of life seeming like an eternity.

But how would anyone know that that was the case? No-one in that situation had ever lived to tell the tale, had they?

His relief at realising that the bomb had not hit the factory was overtaken by the immediate return of alarm as the room was scorched in a searing flash of light that, but for the blackouts, would surely have blinded him. This was immediately followed by the most enormous bang. A blast to end all blasts; an explosion more deafening than any exploding shell he had ever experienced in France. It reminded him of when Hill 60 had exploded, but then the eruption had been some way away on the German side of the battle field. Now the eruption was so near that Frank thought his ears were going to explode with the violent vibrations.

John let out a scream and this time it was he who was clinging to Frank rather that the other way round. Frank wanted to comfort his son, but he was powerless to utter any words. Why was the inevitable taking so long? In the fields of Flanders, Frank had always assumed that death had been instantaneous for most of his fellow combatants being slaughtered daily on the battlefield. One second they were alive and in less than the blink of an eye, they were gone and knew nothing of what had happened to them. He had always felt sorry for the poor buggers who had merely been injured and lay in excruciating pain and suffering as they waited to die.

"God, please don't let it be like that for John. If we have to go, please make it quick."

As the roar of the explosion died away, it was replaced by the rumble of falling timber and masonry. Next came the sound of flying debris hitting the east wall of the factory. Shattering glass exploded in rapid succession as window pane after window pane burst out of its frame smashing into whatever was in its way. Frank could differentiate each separate eruption as sheet of glass, followed by an ever nearer sheet of glass, was smashed to smithereens in the blast.

The window of Frank's office disintegrated, the flying glass tearing the blackout curtain to shreds as the roar of speeding debris, smoke and foul air spread across the room towards them, showering them with dust and wreckage. A piece of flying glass shattered into smaller pieces as it hit John on the leg.

The chimneys were next. A slow rumble as the mortar cracked and fractured; followed by the cacophonous clatter of brickwork rolling down the roof bringing with it the splintered parts of the skylight windows to the loft offices. This wreckage had not hit the ground before the rattle of loosening tiles, sounding like shingle being moved by rolling waves started, quickly building up to a crescendo of falling pieces of rubble, smashing on to the ground in rapid succession.

They jerked against each other in unison at the sound of each shattering missile. But now the very room they were sheltering in was trembling from the onslaught. And then it came! The rest of the loosened chimney came roaring down the roof, bouncing against the exposed drainpipe before shooting at an angle to crash through thc fragile roof of their refuge. It landed on the desk destroying it beyond recognition, to be followed by several roof timbers crushed by the impact of the falling masonry, destroying the wall opposite them in the process.

For a moment they could see flashes of moonlight through gaps in the collapsing building but within seconds the air was filled with choking dust as their crumbling sanctuary buckled around them.

They both lay in utter dread, clinging to each other as they waited for the next devastating episode which would end their lives. But none came. Gradually the noise abated as the flying debris settled. The fog of dust steadily fell and came to rest in a layer of grime on everything around, including themselves.

Eventually there was silence broken only by the heavy breathing of both of them gasping for air. They were still alive! The beams of the shattered roof had come to rest at a crazy 45 degree angle against the wall at the side of the bed creating a sloping canopy trapping them where they lay, with no room for movement. Was this to be a tomb from which there was no escape? Frank closed his eyes and silently prayed for the nightmare to end. He sensed that time was now moving at its proper and normal pace and for the first time he was actually able to speak to John.

First however, he kissed him on the cheek and held him tightly once more. "Are you all right John? You're not hurt are you?"

John released his grasp on his father and lifted his face to look into his eyes. "I'm fine, or at least I think I am. How about you?"

"I think so. You've saved me from most of the falling debris."

John managed to roll over until he was lying at the side of his father and in doing so rolled onto the shattered glass lying on the bed. He felt the splinter tear his trousers and scrape his leg as he moved. He now moved very cautiously as he shifted his position to try to inspect the damage.

He ripped the torn trouser leg and saw the blood running slowly from the cut across his calf. "Well I was all right 'til now, but I don't think this scratch will take much healing."

He tore the bottom of his trouser leg completely off and used it as a temporary dressing to stem the flow of blood. He looked around him and realised that trying to move off the bed was probably not a good idea as there was too much damaged roof precariously balanced around them.

Frank who had similarly assessed the situation clung on to his son, making sure that he did not try to climb off the bed.

"I think we'd better stay here son. I know it'd be nice to get out and breathe some fresh air, but I haven't heard any more planes in a while and I'm sure someone will be here soon to dig us out. Best just stay where we are and try and get some rest whilst we can."

It was almost midday before the debris had been carefully removed from around them and they were finally freed from the ruins of their mutilated shelter. Unbelievably, Frank's wheelchair, which John had folded and placed at the bottom of the bed, was removed from the wreckage undamaged. It was merely covered with the same coating of muck that covered John and Frank, making them look like black minstrels.

As Frank was lifted up and carried to Tom's waiting car, he said he wanted to inspect the damage to the factory. Grace, who had been tendering John's cuts and bruises as the rescuers were lifting Frank free, immediately barred him from such a thing, insisting that she would have her way for once and that he was to be taken straight to the hospital to be checked over.

"I don't need to go to the hospital. I'm fine. Just let the chaps get me into the car and then Tom can take us home. I need a bath and by the look of Johnny, he could do with one as well." He turned to his son, "You OK, John? Do you need to go to the hospital?"

"No, Mom's fixed the cut on my leg and like you say, I think I need a bath and then get to bed for some rest."

The two men carrying Frank turned him to make placing him in the back seat of the car easier and for the first time Frank was able to see the damage to the factory. Every window in the place had been blown out and one of the chimneys was missing. But other than the total destruction of his office on the west side of the building and an area of missing tiles, the building was still standing and looked structurally sound. However as they twisted him around the open door of the car, he saw the devastation further down Hospital Street. The brick and wood structure of William Bate Ltd. was completely gone and in its stead stood an enormous crater.

"My God, I hope there weren't any poor buggers in there."

His two bearers looked at each other, reluctant to answer the question.

Frank realised what their silence meant, "There was, wasn't there?"

This time they could not avoid the question, "Well we managed to get two chaps out of there this morning. In a right mess they were, but we've just been told that they have since died in hospital. I reckon the other three of their mates must have died instantly. Christ I hope so, for their sakes anyway. I tell you we put bits of 'em in more than three bags. You don't know how lucky you are mate. When we heard you shouting we thought we were going to find you in the same state that we pulled out the other two. Thank God for some small mercies."

Frank tried to relax as he sat in the back of the car but the trauma of the last few hours hit him again and he was forced to relive the calamitous events of the previous night. He felt his heart rate increase and had to take slow, deep breaths, to stop himself from fainting. The voice in his head reminding him of how scared he was of losing his son and how, if the bomb had been dropped only a fraction of a second earlier, it would have been him and John that would have required several bags for their dismembered body parts.

The next morning, after a fretful night's sleep, Frank insisted on being taken to the factory to see the extent of the damage for himself. The broken glass and other mess had been cleared away and men on ladders were already measuring up the windows for new glass.

As soon as Tom saw Frank he shouted to him from the top of a ladder where he, with the help of several men whose heads were poking out of the hole in the roof, was spreading a large piece of tarpaulin over the missing section of roof. "You shouldn't be here Frank. Get him back in the car, John, and take him back home. There's nothing he can do here 'til we've sorted this lot out."

Frank and Johnny watched as they completed the task and secured the tarpaulin in place. When Tom joined them, he told them that with a bit of luck, they would have it all sorted by evening time and be able to start production again .

"I've told you Frank, that there's little you can do until then, so go home and come back again tomorrow. I'll try to get you a table and some corner to put it in, so you can work at it tomorrow. So, go home and get some rest for once."

Frank knew that Tom was doing what he was best at; organising the workforce and handing the tasks that he wanted each of them to carry out. But as for going home and out of the way, he would have none of it and insisted that John should wheel him round the factory to see everything for himself. When he had done that he sent John to try and get some bread and bits and pieces so that they could make sandwiches for the sweating workers so busy around them.

On Friday night Frank spent another fearful and fretful night during which he experienced over and over again the traumatic events as the bomb dropped. He had never known such paralysing fear until that dramatic night with John, not even on the battlefield.

During the war he had accepted danger and the possibility, or even probability, of death as part of the risk of being a soldier. He'd seen others shaking with fear and had seen men distraught with the effects of shell shock. He'd also heard of men who had walked away from the battlefield completely broken, only to be accused of desertion and executed by firing squad. He had been shocked when he had first heard of such an execution and had believed the officers, when they said the men had been shot for cowardice and desertion, and was only thankful that he had never been required to be part of such a firing squad.

Alice had told him many times since the war, that those executions were a disgrace. It was the British Army hierarchy that had brought dishonour to the country by the treatment of these men and it was most certainly not the other way round. The men were not cowards, but gravely sick men, made so by the trauma of war. They were damaged men; mentally damaged men who needed help, and should not have been treated so scandalously.

Frank had always nodded his head in agreement but whilst he understood how men could be scared on the battlefield, he had never quite understood why men were still so greatly affected after leaving the battle.

He had sympathised with them, always talked to them and tried to calm them, but nevertheless had never quite understood why they still could not control their shaking, even when they had left the trenches and were now safe and sound in the camp several miles back from the front. But in the middle of that sleepless night he had understood.

He too had been shaking uncontrollably; he too had been staring, eyes wide open, but seeing nothing; he too had been silently crying into his pillow without really knowing why. It was all over, they were both safe, so why, oh why did he still feel like this?

The next morning when Grace noticed his shivering, he merely replied that he must have caught a chill during the dreadful bombing ordeal.

"Shall I call the doctor? You don't want it to get worse."

"No, I'll take a couple of aspirin, I'll be fine after that. Anyway, Tom has arranged for everyone to come in this weekend to try and catch up on the missed production, so I really must support them and show my face."

"But you're not going in tomorrow, are you?"

"Well yes I was planning to. That's not a problem is it?"

Grace glared back at him, "You've forgotten haven't you?" Frank was so grateful that she did not wait for him to answer the question, but just continued, "I'm fetching Philip back from university today and we're all supposed to be spending the day together tomorrow to celebrate the end of his course."

Another example of the tricks his mind was playing. He had found it difficult to concentrate on anything during the last couple of days.

It had been Frank himself who had suggested the celebration a couple of weeks ago and it had been he who had arranged for the tickets to see George Formby, Evelyn Laye and Fred Emney at a special 'one off' performance at the Savoy cinema on the Sunday afternoon. How could he have forgotten such a thing?

"Sorry love, I've just got too many things on my mind. I'll tell you what, why don't I just pop in today until lunchtime and I won't go in at all tomorrow. Instead we'll all have a great time together for once."

But the next morning after another fretful night, Frank did not feel at all well, and Grace did send for the doctor. He had had a mild stroke during the night, and the doctor instructed him to stay in bed and rest.

Frank insisted that the family should go to the concert at the Savoy, saying that it would be a shame to waste the tickets.

Grace agreed saying she would stay and look after Frank. However a short while later at the time that the others were enjoying George Formby on his ukulele and the humour of Fred Emney, Frank started complaining of severe headaches and Grace sent for the doctor again. But before the doctor arrived, Frank was dead from a second massive brain haemorrhage.

Philip insisted that the coffin should be carried both into and out of St. Paul's church by members of the family at the funeral on the following Friday. He did not want his father carried by unknown pall bearers hired for the occasion.

After the service, the coffin was lifted onto the shoulders of Philip and John at the front and Tom and Edward at the rear. Philip was surprised at the weight and felt that the funeral director should have advised them that they ought really to have had six bearers. The walk back down the aisle was deliberately being taken at a slow pace. Nothing about the final farewell to his father was going to be rushed.

As soon as they turned round to face the back of the church for the walk down the aisle, he became aware of a woman sitting on her own on the back row pew. Why he was drawn to this particular women he did not know, but her eyes were firmly fixed on the coffin as it moved slowly and majestically down the aisle, and once he had seen her he could not take his eyes off her. She seemed totally oblivious to everything but the coffin. She was obviously moved and distressed, tears were streaming down her cheeks and she was making no attempt to wipe them away.

This was not someone he knew, but there was something vaguely familiar about the slim woman. She was immaculately and expensively dressed in a black cashmere coat, which, instead of a normal collar, had a sort of scarf, made of the same material, one end of which was thrown over the shoulder, whilst the other end hung down across her breast. On her feet was a pair of fine black leather strapped shoes, that had just the right height of heels to fully enhance the briefest amount of her attractive calves and her neat ankles showing beneath the coat. Her hat was quite large, the brim of which put her face in shadow. It was not however, the ostentatious sort of hat that many mature women seemed to wear, but was the perfect canopy to capture the smooth beauty of her face.

When the coffin drew level with her she moved her eyes from the coffin to Philip. She nodded her head to him, and as if she suddenly became aware that other people were around, she quickly raised her black gloved hand and wiped the tears from her face with a white lace handkerchief. Philip noticed that she was holding a single red rose in the other hand.

Her eyes returned to the coffin and fresh tears ran down her cheeks as the pall bearers moved passed her and out of the church.

The family waited outside as the coffin was being put into the hearse ready for the journey to Ryecroft cemetery for Frank's burial in the grave next to that of his daughter, Katherine Grace, who had died of diphtheria aged three years. The grave having been purchased in 1926 at the time of Kathy's death, so that Frank and Grace could join her when their time came.

The rest of the congregation filed out of the church, all standing around in a large group as the coffin was lowered and carefully placed into the back of the waiting hearse.

Philip and John joined their mother and as the funeral director's staff carefully positioned the wreaths around the coffin, Philip was helping his mother into the car when he saw the mystery woman move from the back of the rest of the waiting mourners and swiftly walk to the hearse. As she reached it she placed the red rose into the back of the car. She kissed her fingers and then touched the coffin with those same fingers and quickly continued on her way, away from the car, and out of sight. Her actions had been so swift that no one, other than Philip, had witnessed them.

Drinks and refreshments for the mourners had been arranged in a private room at the George Hotel and after making sure that his mother was being looked after by Alice and Mary, Philip felt it was his duty to act as principle host and greet and talk to everyone as they arrived. The task was not easy as he had seen little of his father over the last three years whilst he had been at university; a fact that weighed heavily on him.

He was thankful that the last Saturday with the family had been a joyous one, but it had all been centred on him, his father sitting in his chair, unusually quiet as he himself answered everyone's questions.

"How were your finals? Did you think you've done all right?"

Before he could answer his mother's questions, Alice had interrupted. "Of course he's done all right. What I want to know is has he found himself a girlfriend yet?"

Philip had replied in the negative, "I've been doing too much studying to have any time for girls. There'll be plenty of time for that in the future. I need to get myself sorted out with a job first. What do you think, Dad?"

His father seemed oblivious he had been asked a question and only answered when Grace poked him and repeated the question.

"Sure son, actually I wanted to talk to you about joining the firm and giving me a bit of time for myself. I'm sure your Mom would be glad of you helping her side of the business as well. Plenty of time to talk about all that though, and as for girlfriends, maybe you could pick up where you left off with that nice girl, Teresa. I always liked her. What's she doing these days?"

Philip said he had no idea, but Alice interrupted again, "She's still at the hospital and has recently been promoted to Ward Sister."

Philip decided to change the subject, but nevertheless thought maybe he should get in touch with her again. After all they had got on well.

He did not think the opportunity would be presented to him so quickly and certainly not in these circumstances, but when Teresa had told Alice she would like to attend the funeral service, Alice, being Alice, had not only told her that that would be fine, but had invited her to both the cemetery and here to this gathering following the funeral.

And here she was, standing against the opposite wall talking to Lucy.

Philip hadn't spoken to her yet, but knew he would have to soon, or it would not only appear rude but would indeed be just that. There had never been any animosity between them, and whilst Teresa had considered that they had broken up when he went to university, Philip had never really considered that there was anything to break up. He should really go over and speak to her, but decided to find the toilet that he had so badly needed since arriving at the hotel.

He was returning across the foyer when he noticed the mystery woman talking to the clerk at the desk. He waited until she had finished and then deliberately walked in her direction so that she would have to acknowledge him in some way.

She no longer had on her outdoor clothes. The coat and hat were gone and she wore a plain fine wool black dress expertly cut to fit her slim, but perfectly rounded figure, set off by a double row of pearls round her neck.

When they were a few feet apart, Philip took a step to the side so that he was directly facing her, and both had to stop. She stared at Philip. He was the last person she had expected to see here at the hotel. She pulled herself together quickly. "Hello," she said, and then added, "It's so sad about your father, he was a good man. I'm sure you will all miss him."

Now that he was up close to the woman, he realised that she was probably older than the late thirties that he had thought in the church. Maybe she was in her forties. The figure was as perfect as he had first thought, and was still capable of sending many a man into blissful delight at meeting her. Her blonde hair was immaculately sculptured as were her delicately manicured nails on her slender hands. But under the finely applied makeup, the face was perhaps not as perfect as he had thought. Were they the first signs of age lines under her eyes? Although there were no tears now her deep brown eyes still reflected the sadness she had so obviously felt in the church.

She desperately wanted to ask him what he was doing here at the hotel; surely he had not come to find her? She willed herself to act as naturally as she could and to control her emotions in front of Frank's son, "You are so like your father. You look just like he did when I first met him. He must have been about twenty then and you look exactly like I remember him at that age."

She held out her hand, waiting for Philip to shake it. Her grip was much firmer than he expected, not in any way the limp effort that so many women employed on these occasions, "If I remember correctly, its Philip isn't it?"

Philip suddenly remembered where he had met this woman before, but could not remember her name, "Yes, I'm Philip and if I remember correctly your son is Alaistair, isn't he?" He did not wait to be answered before adding, "But I am so sorry I cannot remember your name."

"My name is Evelyn McPherson, but everyone calls me Evie. So please call me Evie."

"Yes it's coming back to me now. The last time we met was actually right here wasn't it? We all had lunch together in the restaurant. And Alaistair and I spent the morning on the boats in the Arboretum. But I thought you lived in Edinburgh. What are you doing here?"

She did not answer immediately. She had thought she would attend the funeral service and leave without needing to speak to any of Frank's family or friends. She had not wished to interfere with their grief, and had certainly not expected to meet Frank's son here at the hotel.

She now regretted even staying overnight in Walsall, she could so easily have stayed in Birmingham and gone straight back there after the funeral. But now she had to talk to Philip and answer his questions.

"That's right. I live in Edinburgh. Still live in Edinburgh and I'm going straight back there tonight. I've just been getting the staff here to confirm my berth on the night train from Birmingham."

Philip was now a little puzzled, "You say you're going straight back there, does that mean you haven't been here long?"

Evie decided that total honesty was the best policy; after all she had nothing to be ashamed of. She had merely attended the funeral of an old and good friend; nothing more than that.

"I came down yesterday and stayed here overnight, but I have nothing to keep me in Walsall these days so that's why I'm going straight back." She did not know why she then said, "I'm not sure I have anything for me in Edinburgh either, but that's where I live, so it's back to Edinburgh."

"What about Alaistair; and your husband?"

"My husband is away in London most of the time. He's been commissioned back into the army. He doesn't talk about his work much, but it must be something to do with organising medical facilities for the army. And, as for Alaistair, well I don't hear much from him. He left university as soon as war broke out, just walked out and enlisted in the Army. I don't even know where he is right now. What about you, what are you doing?"

"Just finished my degree," and then he surprised himself when he continued with, "I intend to enlist myself as soon as I can." He had no idea why he said this as until that very moment he had never considered enlisting before he was conscripted to do so.

But Philip didn't want to talk about himself any more. He wanted to know why this woman had come all the way from Scotland just for his father's funeral but didn't want to ask quite such a blunt and direct question as, "Why have you come to my father's funeral?"

After a little thought the question he asked was, "How did you hear about my father's death?"

Evie had hoped she would be able to end their conversation without such questions being asked, but thought that the best way of dealing with this question and the ones that might follow, would be to deal with everything at once and quickly change the subject back to something else.

"Lucy Evans phoned me to tell me and before you ask the question, I've known Lucy for over twenty years. She was my maid, when I lived in Walsall. I had lost touch with her, but when I met you and your father in the Arboretum and we had lunch here, your father gave me his business card, saying that if ever I wanted to chat to him, I should ring."

She pointed to a group of empty chairs, "Why don't we sit over there for a bit, I was just going to order myself a pot of tea? Why don't you join me?"

"Well, that would be nice, but all the family and friends from the funeral are in the function room over there. Mother has organised plenty of drinks and refreshments, so why don't you join us?"

Philip immediately recognised the look of terror on Evie's face, "I'm sorry, I didn't realise your whole family was here. It was years ago when I knew your father. In the last war, he was a very good friend to my brother, even saved his life. So when I heard of your father's death, I merely wanted to pay my respects. I've never met your mother or any of your father's family or friends and would feel a bit of an intruder. But, you must go and look after your mother, so if you don't mind I'll stay and have a drink out here and then I'll be on my way."

She had hoped that this would be a sufficient hint for Philip to leave her, but to her surprise, he said, "Yes I understand that, but it won't hurt if I stay with you a little while," and without waiting for her to object, he walked across to the desk and ordered tea and cakes before rejoining her and pointing the way to the empty chairs.

When they were seated, he picked up the conversation where Evie had left off, "So you say Lucy told you about Dad's death, and you were telling me how that came about?"

Evie was now obliged to tell Philip how she had indeed telephoned his father but omitted to say how often this had happened. She did not wish to tell him how, without the fairly frequent calls to Frank asking for his opinion and advice she would not have had the strength to turn her life around so dramatically.

After going back to Scotland following her chance meeting with Frank all those years ago, she had come to realise how much her husband controlled her and her life. Frank had shown her that she was responsible for her own life and she had decided to take charge of it herself again.

Knowing that it was merely a crutch, she had stopped smoking. Next she looked for something meaningful to do that took her outside of her home and she ignored all of her husband's protestations that he did not want his wife to go out to work.

Initially this had caused some awful arguments, but the new Evie was determined to do what was best for her no matter what this meant to the relationship with her husband. She knew him well enough to realise that he'd always keep up the pretence in public that theirs was a loving marriage whatever happened. He would never go so far as to damage that image.

She had no wish to publicly upset him either, and knowing he would consider paid work as beneath his wife, she had taken on volunteer work at the hospital.

Initially he did not like this but had quickly dropped his objections, at least publicly, and had even started to announce that the idea of such volunteer work had been his, by boasting to all his friends, "It seemed to me that it's a waste of Evelyn's skills not to utilise them properly, particularly for the poor who cannot pay for normal nursing services."

Evie continued explaining things to Philip, "I just needed your father's advice occasionally and he was very kind to give it. The very first time I telephoned, Lucy answered, and we talked about old times. Women's stuff really, but I enjoyed having someone to chat to from the old days."

"I often called for a chat after that and it was Lucy who phoned to tell me about your father's death. I was so shocked and felt I had to pay my respects. I hope you don't mind?"

"So you just came down for the funeral?"

"In normal circumstances I may have stayed a bit longer to catch up with things with Lucy, but when I spoke to her on Wednesday, it seemed that she had so much to sort out at the factory, that she wouldn't have any time to spare. So I didn't want to waste her time whilst she is so busy, so, yes, I came down yesterday and back tonight."

Philip wanted to stay and ask her more questions, but she did not give him the time to do so, "I'm sure you have a lot to do as well, so I'll let you get back to your family."

She stood up and held her hand out for Philip to shake, "I am so pleased that I've had a chance to speak to you. And once again, I'm so sorry about your father."

Philip thought he detected a faltering in her voice as she continued, "I'm sure he'll be missed by so many people, he was a good friend to me."

Philip was now standing and took her hand, "Yes, I'm glad we met as well. I do hope that we'll meet again."

"You are so like your father, and I don't just mean in looks. Give my regards to Lucy and tell her I'll phone her sometime," and with that she turned and made her way to the lift, leaving Philip standing where he was.

CHAPTER SIXTEEN

1944

Both Philip and Edward had enlisted soon after Frank's funeral, and on completion of officer training, were appointed to serve with the 6th North Staffs, part of 176 Infantry Brigade attached to the 59th Infantry Division.

To date the 59th had spent all of its war service on home soil and Philip was beginning to wonder if he would ever see service abroad, but in March 1943 the 59th was moved to another home posting in Kent where the 59th became part of the newly formed 21st Army group and when training for a possible landing began at the end of July, rumours quickly spread amongst the men that at last they were going to cross the channel to retake the Calais Dunkirk coast from the Germans, and then progress on to retake Paris.

Before long it seemed that the whole of Kent was covered with the tented camps of the thousands of troops taking part in Exercise Harlequin. Time after time the men had to practice moving through embarkation assembly areas as far as the actual landing craft. But by October, when the division was moved to winter quarters near Canterbury, the talk had changed and the men began to doubt that a landing would ever happen. There was even a suggestion that the whole thing was just a bluff to get the Germans to move men to the Channel coast instead of the Mediterranean where the real attack would take place. The conspiracy theorists talked for hours about bluff and double bluff, but in truth none of the men had the slightest idea what was going on.

1944 came and each month brought more exercises and troop movements. So much so that Philip became concerned that if this carried on much longer his men would be battle weary without even going into battle.

At the beginning of June the theorists were totally confused when news broke that the invasion had taken place on the Normandy coast. Perhaps the talk about bluff and double bluff was justified after all!

Philip felt quite let down that after all their training they had not been part of the landing and he started to think that the war would soon be over and he would never see any real fighting. He had almost convinced himself of this, when a few days later, orders were received to prepare for embarkation. On 17th June the units were moved to camps on the north bank of the Thames near to London docks. Perhaps he would see action after all.

On arrival at the embarkation camp there was a restlessness amongst the men that Philip had not seen before. All the rumours and all the gossip were no longer there. In their place was a mixture of excitement, apprehension and trepidation, but in a few Philip detected the sheer terror of frightened men who were doing their best to cover their feelings.

Things were not helped when junior officers were instructed to ensure that each of their men completed a will. As the regiment had now been placed under orders for action, the simplified will form without witnesses could be used. All wills had to be completed and returned no later than first thing the next morning. Philip took this opportunity to talk to his men and after supper he was still helping some of them to complete their wills.

He deliberately left Jimmy Turnbull until last as he knew that he was one of those scared at the thought of battle. Jimmy, and his twin brother Len, had been called up together and were now both under Philip's command. Their mother, Agnes, had worked at his father's factory for over ten years and when she learned that Philip was her sons' officer, she had pleaded with Grace to write to him and ask him to take special care of her sons.

James and Leonard Turnbull may have been twins but they were chalk and cheese. They had some physical similarities, such as their black hair and size, but emotionally they were quite different. Leonard was a strong, enthusiastic and very competent soldier, who was not only well liked and respected, but was also trusted by all his fellow soldiers as a reliable and dependable comrade. It was obvious that Len was not only capable of looking after himself in any circumstances, but that he would also be there for others when needed. As a result, he had quickly been promoted to corporal; a promotion that was well received by all the men in his section.

Jimmy, on the other hand, was a very sensitive individual. In training and exercises he had the physical strength and stamina to keep up with the best of them, but Philip realised early on that Jimmy did not have the heart for fighting and had done his best to watch out for Jimmy without getting too close or showing any particular favouritism. Today he once again sensed the tension in Jimmy and wanted to lift his spirits as much as possible.

He found Jimmy sitting on a bench writing a letter to his mother, "Hi there! How are you finding things here Turnbull? Have you sorted out this will business yet?"

Jimmy jumped up and saluted; his papers falling on the floor as he did so. "Yes Sir, I have it here." He picked up the papers and rummaged through them until he found the will. He handed it to Philip, putting the rest of the papers on the bench.

Philip took the form and spoke in a voice that could not be heard by any of the others milling around, "Sit down and carry on with what you were doing, soldier." He then said in a softer voice, "Do you mind if I sit down with you for a while?"

Jimmy jumped up again, collected his papers together and offered a space on the bench for Philip to sit, "Sorry Sir, but we don't have much space round here Sir."

Philip took his arm and eased him back down as he sat next to him, "We'll be all right you know. The worst part of the attack was the initial landing itself and now that's over I'm sure we'll have no problems at all. I'm sure we've already got the Germans on the run and whatever's left for us to do will be a piece of cake."

He put his hand on Jimmy's shoulder, "We've all been training for this for an eternity, and if we're not ready now, then we'll never be. We're all anxious about what's ahead and some of us might even be a bit scared, but we've got a great squad of men and I know we'll get through the next few weeks just fine. So just take things easy, get a good night's sleep and let's go and get this war over and done with, and get back home."

"I'm sure you're right, Sir, but I'm not scared for myself. I'm not even afraid of dying. If that's my fate, then so be it."

"You're not going to die. It won't come that. In a few months time you and I will be having a drink together in a pub in Walsall and we'll wonder what all this apprehension was about."

Philip went to stand up but decided against it and sat down again, "If you aren't scared for yourself, then who are you scared for?"

Jimmy looked at Philip; was about to say something, but immediately screwed up his lips and slowly shook his head, without saying anything.

"OK, we'll leave it at that, unless there's anything else you want to say?"

"No, Sir. Well nothing I could say to a fellow soldier, Sir; and certainly not to an officer." His face immediately reddened as he realised that he had said far more than he should.

"Well what if I said that for the next few minutes anything you say is just between a couple of Walsall lads chatting and not between a soldier and an officer."

"No, I think its better not said, Sir."

Philip did not wish to add to his embarrassment, so decided to leave things well alone, "If you're sure, then I'll leave you to finish your letter, but don't take too long. Get plenty of sleep, we've got a big day tomorrow." And with that he stood up, and, wishing all the men around a "Good night" left to prepare his own will and write a letter to his mother.

During the night it started to rain and the weather in the Channel deteriorated so badly that they all had to kick their heels in the marshalling yards for the whole of the following week. The Division finally set sail on 25th June, arriving at the Normandy coast the next day.

They couldn't have asked for a better start to what was for most of them, their first posting on foreign soil. The shipment of men and equipment was completed without incident and they were all settled in unexpected comfort in Normandy without a single casualty. For the next few days, it was a case of resting up and checking equipment as it was unloaded from the ships.

The relaxed atmosphere soon changed however when the divisional battle orders for Operation Charnwood, the military plan for finally taking Caen, were received. British troops had been trying to capture Caen, some twenty miles south-east of where the 6 N. Staffs were now getting ready for battle in reasonable comfort and safety, since the first D-day landings, but the Germans were hanging on as steadfastly as ever, and the allied troops were getting battle weary in their failed attempts to win control of it.

Whilst Philip and Edward were having a drink together on the last evening before the move south and their first taste of a real battle, Edward once again brought up his concerns about the fate of the Guilbert family; a subject he had regularly spoken about ever since the Germans had occupied France and driven the British expeditionary force out at Dunkirk.

Following their visit to France in 1938, Edward had lost none of his feelings for Juliette. They had written to each other every week and in 1939 Edward had spent all his holidays visiting her in France. But the letter writing had ceased in the summer of 1941 after the evacuation of Dunkirk, and following the spread of German troops across the whole of northern France, he had received no further news of her or her family.

Since then it seemed to Philip that it was impossible to have a conversation with Edward without the subject of Juliette being raised by him at least once or twice. It had been even worse following their arrival on French soil. Now it was impossible to have a conversation with Edward that was not about Juliette; so much so that it seemed that Edward's mind was more engaged in thoughts of Juliette than his responsibilities as an army officer. Philip tried to put his mind at rest as best he could, but tonight he found Edward almost uncontrollable with worry.

"What if Victor is still working in Caen? Worse still, what if Juliette is in Caen? We could be the ones to send in the shells that kill her."

Philip did not quite know how to respond to this question and merely said, "Look Edward, they wouldn't be so stupid as to put themselves in that position. They all live miles from Caen and I'm sure that they're all tucked up in their own comfortable beds."

"Yes but what if…?"

Philip interrupted to stop the rest of the sentence, "What if, nothing! Any Frenchmen that can do so will be as far away from Caen as they possibly can be at the moment. None of the Guilberts I met would be so stupid as to put themselves in any unnecessary danger."

"Yes but..?"

Up to this point Philip had responded sympathetically to Edward's concerns, but now he reacted almost angrily.

"Look Edward, the Guilberts are wherever they are, and there's nothing we can do about it. If you want to see Juliette again the best thing we can do is drive these bloody Germans back to Germany, and maybe, just maybe, when you find Juliette you'll be able to do what you've threatened to do for so long and ask the poor girl to marry you. She might even say yes, and we'll have an end to this continual bleating I get from you about her. Stop thinking about her and think about what we have to do tomorrow. Start acting like a soldier and not some love sick teenager."

Edward had tears in his eyes at this outburst and Philip felt terrible that he'd been so belligerent towards his friend.

He took Edward's hand and turning it over pointed to the very faint small scar. The similar mark on his own hand had long gone. Nevertheless he pressed it into Edward's hand, "Remember that day in the river at Bewdley?"

"Two stupid kids playing stupid kid's games," was Edward's response.

"Maybe it was a stupid kid's game but we promised to look out for each other then and that hasn't changed, has it?"

Edward let go of Philip's hand: wiped the tear from his eye; threw his arms round Philip and hugging him tightly said "All for one and one for all," before whispering in his ear, "Thanks mate. I love you too."

He let go quickly and stepped back and saluted Philip, "You're quite right, Lieutenant. There's too much to do right now, without wasting time worrying about things we can't do anything about," and with that he gulped down the rest of his drink and left, waving to Philip as he went, "See you in the morning, soldier."

Twenty four hours later, as they made their way south to the battle, Philip wondered if Edward's fears were well founded. Could any of the family possibly be in Caen? He tried to push such thoughts out of his mind, but once he'd had the thought, try as he may, he could not do so.

It was just after midnight when Philip turned to the men in his platoon, and putting his hand to his mouth gave clear instructions for no more talking as they moved the last mile forward to their allotted position north of La Bijude. The night was clear, the moon and the myriad of stars providing ample light to see their way forward without any additional lighting.

A couple of hours earlier, the silence and eeriness of the place had been broken when the night sky was filled with the noise and spectacle of heavy bombers as they streamed on their way to attack enemy positions in Caen.

Drove after drove of planes just kept coming; so many it was impossible to count their number. The sight of so many British planes attacking the German positions brought an immediate sense of relief to the men as they realised the enormity of the back-up systems supporting them.

Philip was reminded of the night three years earlier when it was German bombers over the Midlands that had caused so much damage to the factory and had been, in his opinion, the cause of his father's death. He not only felt a huge release of tension as soon as he realised that these were British bombers and not German ones but had felt an immediate sense of joy at the thought that it would be Germans suffering this time, and only just managed to stop himself shouting out, *"Serves you buggers right. What does it feel like to get a taste of your own medicine, you blighters?"*

His elation quickly subsided however, as his mind reverted back to the previous evening's conversation with Edward and he realised that probably a lot of French people would also be casualties of the bombs being dropped; and in reality he had no genuine wish to see anyone killed, French, German or any other nationality.

At half past twelve, Philip directed his men to their positions ready for the hour set for their first battle. Edward's platoon was spread out to the left of them and Tommy [Dusty] Miller's men were to his right.

Philip went along the line, shaking the hand of each of his men as he did so. He tried to say something encouraging to each man, but soon became overwhelmed with the thought that this could easily be the last time he spoke to some of them, or even all of them if he became a casualty, and so, after shaking hands he merely gave each of them a thumbs up sign; a sign that soon became reciprocated by each of them.

When he reached the end of the line, he walked up to Dusty Miller and shook his hand adding, "Well this is it, Tommy, here's hoping we all come out of it safely."

He thought he detected a tremble in Tommy's voice as he replied, "I'm sure we will, after all the bombs dropped by those planes I bet there's nothing left of the enemy."

Philip merely smiled and nodded his head, before turning round and walking the full length of his men again, patting each one on the shoulder or head as he did so until he reached Edward who was chatting to his sergeant a few yards from the end of Philip's line of men. He held out his hand towards Edward, but instead of taking it, Edward stepped forward and gave Philip a quick hug. No words were said as the hug said everything.

As they waited for 'H hour', the air got cooler and cooler, and Philip felt that he had never been in such an evil place. It seemed that the only life around was the men who were all waiting to kill or be killed. How on earth did man get himself into this position?

The silence was again broken at 0420 'H hour', and the men heard the opening roar of battle as the British artillery and Royal Navy guns sent missiles zooming over their heads towards the enemy positions.

This was the signal to move forward and Philip carefully led his men towards La Bijude. Dusty Miller on his right immediately rushed ahead of his men urging them to follow and in no time at all they were thirty or more yards ahead of Philip's platoon. But Philip was much more cautious as he made his way through the corn; encouraging his men to keep their heads down below the level of the standing crops and avoid wherever possible the lanes where it had been flattened by the enemy.

Philip halted his men at the end of the first field where most of Dusty Miller's platoon were crouching in the corn. Ahead of them was a strip of open ground, and there sprawled out at the far side of the tract were the broken and shattered bodies of at least twelve of the platoon, including Dusty. All had been shot before reaching the safety of the rising corn beyond.

Philip inched forward to the edge of the open ground to take a count of the injured men. It seemed to him that only two were moving, one being Dusty who was lying in a pool of his own blood gushing from the large exposed wound on his left side. He could hear Dusty's moans, but as Philip tried to work out what to do, these got quieter and softer, and it was obvious that Dusty was either passing out or was, as was more likely, dying. In a very short time the moans ceased altogether and Philip decided that even if he could get across the open space safely, he would only have a dead body to drag back.

The other injured man, who was a mere six or seven feet from Philip, was trying to move himself back towards the relative safety of the cornfield. Philip signalled for him to keep still but he ignored his signs and continued to move forward. As soon as he lifted his head there was a burst of machine gun fire throwing the poor wretch into convulsions as the bullets ripped through his body and whipped his skull into sudden jerks, wrenching his brains from his head and splattering them on the ground around him.

Philip could not believe that he had witnessed such a catastrophe in less than ten minutes after starting the advance, and even though he had great difficulty preventing himself from throwing up, he could not avert his eyes from the awful sight in front of him. He began to shake uncontrollably and felt that his legs and body would not move.

He did not know how long this had gone on; it was probably only a few seconds but it seemed an age. A tap on the shoulder and the sound of Edward's voice shook him out of his trace, "What's going on mate? We can't all stay here, we must move on."

Philip pointed to the dead men, "We can't go this way." Edward almost threw up when he saw the bloodbath in front of him but Philip ignored his friend's distress and pointed to the right adding, "There are Germans up there with at least one machine gun focussed directly up this line of open ground and they're shooting at anyone who moves across it."

Edward shook his head and merely remarked, "Christ, what a mess?"

Both men moved back into the field as Philip continued, "I reckon we have two options. One, we can skirt round to the left for as far as we have cover and try to find a less exposed crossing place. Or secondly, we can try and take out the Germans holding that position. What do you think?"

"What do I think? I think we should do both."

"Right then! I suggest one of us stays here with the men, whilst the other takes out those German gunners."

Philip crouched on his stomach and inched forward inviting Edward to do the same. He stopped just before the open ground and with his right hand pointed up the cleared tract, "I think they're about sixty yards or so up there, but they must be dug in 'cause I can't see them." He handed Edward his binoculars, "If you look carefully you can see a slight rise in the ground. I think that's where they are. We'd probably be able to see them when light comes but we can't afford to wait that long."

Philip pulled back to let Edward get a better view. "I can see something glinting, probably from their machine gun. I'm sure that's where they are." He also moved back adding, "You stay here and I'll go and sort them out."

"No way! We'll toss for it," and without waiting for a response from Edward, he took a coin from his pocket, tossed it up, caught it in one hand and covered it with the other, "Heads or tails?"

"Heads"

Philip uncovered the coin, "Sorry, tails," and with that he immediately put the coin back in his pocket. "Right, you stay here and I'll take Dusty's sergeant with me. I'm sure he'd love to get his own back on the buggers for taking out his men. I suggest you send Corporal Turnbull to reconnoitre over to the east and see if there is a way forward well out of the sights of those gunners. Turnbull's a good man and if he comes back and says he's found a safe way to cross, then you can bet your life and the lives of all these others, that he's found a safe route."

Edward knew it would be a waste of time to disagree with Philip; time they did not have, so he just took Philip's hand and shook it, "Best of luck." He looked at his watch, "I make it 0440 now, if Turnbull's found a way through and you're not back by 0500 hours, then we're off to do what we're supposed to be doing. OK?"

"Fine, we'll catch up with you later."

Philip immediately told Sergeant Jackson what he wanted them to do and, without any further delay, they were crawling through the corn towards the German position as fast as they could.

When Philip thought they had gone far enough he moved slowly towards the edge of the field and peered out to see if he could make out the German position any better, and there, some twenty yards further up the slight incline, he could see the machine gun pointing down the open strip.

Hoping that all the Germans' attention was on the position they had just left, he decided the best thing to do would be to stand up and lob a couple of hand grenades into the dugout before they realised that he and Jackson were there. If the grenades failed to hit the target he knew they would take no time at all to swing the gun round and he would stand no chance of getting out of the way of their bullets.

As a very small child his father had loved to play football with Philip, but after his father ended up in a wheelchair the only ball game he could play with his father had been throwing a tennis ball to each other. His father had insisted that Philip go further and further away each time he threw, and with the resultant accuracy of his throw Philip had many a batsman run out by demolishing his wicket from twenty or more yards away. He prayed for the same accuracy now.

He crawled back to Jackson and quietly told him what he planned, "I want you to stay well back. If I miss or they see me before I get them, there are going to be bullets flying all over the place around me. I've no doubt you'll want to have another crack at them if they get me, but just in case, my official order is that you don't even try but that you get back to the others and try to get through with them further down in the other direction."

He sat on his haunches, the top of his head less than half an inch below the top of the corn. He took a deep breath and removed two grenades from his belt, holding one in each hand.

He practiced the move in his head. Straighten up above the crop and in the same move pull out the pin, swing arm over head, and release grenade in hopefully the right direction with the right angle and speed to reach the right spot. Then swap the second grenade into right hand and repeat the throw before the Germans know what's happening.

The adrenalin was flowing again and his heart was throbbing as he took another deep breath, *"God, I hope I can do this right,"* and with that thought he was up and releasing the first missile. The second followed before the first had landed. *"No bullets coming back? Thank God!"* and he fell back into the protection of the cover.

He had hit the ground when the first explosion came, and then another, followed by a third.

"We got the buggers, Sir," came the response from Jackson who was standing tall above the crop a mere four feet behind him, as he threw another grenade in the direction of the trench.

But the sound of Philip telling him to get down was totally obliterated as Jackson's second grenade fell far further than the dugout, and whether by design or a miss throw, a fourth enormous explosion erupted as it hit the rest of the Germans' ammunition supply.

The blast sent Sergeant Jackson flying and made Philip's ears ring.

"I don't think there'll be much left of them now, Sir. Sorry about ignoring your order Sir, but I wanted a go at them as well. They won't be killing any more of our chaps now."

Philip was a little surprised and somewhat disturbed by the sheer delight and exaltation he felt in Jackson's words. He knew that what they had just done was absolutely necessary in the circumstances, but he nevertheless felt remorse for those poor ordinary Germans blown to pieces for no reason of their own making. They were just doing what they had been told to do; the same as he and Jackson and everyone else was doing. The vision of his own soldier having his brains blown out flooded his mind again and he just managed to tell Jackson to get back to the others before he quietly threw up out of his sight.

When they arrived back with the others, Edward was already sending the men safely across the open space and on to La Bijude.

The adrenalin increased rapidly as they reached their objective and the battle started. But their enthusiasm quickly changed to fear when they were met with a barrage of bullets and shells coming from the enemy, and soon everything was overtaken by the dreadful screams of comrades falling all around. Nevertheless, La Bijude was finally captured at 0730 hours, but at a high price in casualties, which included both company commanders leaving it to the subaltern to take over and fire the success signal.

The success was short lived however and the enemy were by no means a beaten force. Germans to the south of La Bijude, who were well ensconced in trenches missed by reconnaissance and both the aerial and artillery bombardment, immediately carried out a fanatical counter attack driving the brigade back out of the village.

The 6 N Staffs withdrew to a position some two hundred yards north of the village, but as the counter attack continued more and more casualties fell amongst Philip's comrades as they tried to hold their new position, of which Corporal Turnbull, who received a serious leg injury was just one.

They successfully retook La Bijude with the help of further troop and tank support by early afternoon, but the Germans, who had also suffered tremendous losses, nevertheless still had a very able and ferocious fighting force ensconced in the strong trench system south of the village.

Philip received a field promotion to Captain overnight and his men, along with the rest of the 6 N Staffs, were ordered to make a full scale attack on this German's trench system at 0930, resulting in this remaining German resistance being finally overcome by early afternoon.

Over the next few days other brigades had many successes and failures, but by 11th July the 59th Division had completed its overall objective and won the battle for Caen, at a huge cost in lives and casualties.

Philip, Edward and all their men now enjoyed a welcome rest; a chance to a get a cooked meal; a bath; and laundered uniforms. However the break was short lived when the division put Operation Pomegranate into effect starting with an attack on Noyers, a village to the south west of Caen, and then to continue further South before turning towards Paris.

They gradually moved south over the next three weeks. Some days were reasonably militarily successful and others were less so. Nevertheless, successful or not, every day brought its share of deaths and casualties.

By the time they entered each conquered village and hamlet most of the buildings were just heaps of rubble and mere carcases terribly scarred and shattered by the shells from both sides in the battle.

"God help us, but we must be killing as many poor Frenchmen as Germans the way we're battering their houses," Edward professed to Philip and with each passing day as they moved further south and closer and closer to where the Guilbert family lived, he became more and more depressed and more concerned about Juliette and her family.

By the beginning of August the advance was progressing southwards more rapidly and by the 4th had reached a position only a few miles north of Goupillières, the nearest village to where the Guilberts lived.

Edward was panicking when Philip saw him that evening. "I'll have to do something to make sure they're all right or I'll go out of my mind."

"Look there's nothing we can do about it so try and stop worrying. Anyway, as I remember it their house was some way east of the village, so they should be OK. And with a bit of luck we'll be able to find out what the situation is in the next few days."

"I can't stop worrying and nothing you or anyone else says can stop me worrying."

Philip had no answer to that. He sympathised with his friend, and had always tried to console him, but the more Edward brought up the subject, the more concerned Philip became about the Guilberts as well.

The division advanced rapidly the remaining seven miles towards the river Orne, but on nearing the river near Goupillières the leading troops once more came under heavy mortar fire from the enemy ensconced along the bank. The Germans had large guns positioned on the opposite bank and these caused considerable damage to the leading tanks. Nevertheless by the time darkness came the enemy had been mostly driven from the near bank and across the river.

In conference that evening, the officers were considering the problems they would encounter in battle the following day; the main ones being how to cross the river and how to identify the strength of the enemy on the other side.

As soon as the discussion started, Edward told the commanding officer that he, and to a lesser extent Philip, had spent time in this area before the war and knew its layout and contour reasonably well.

"Right, perhaps the two of you would like to describe the area and particularly what cover might be available for our troops."

Edward stood up and pointing to the map, he started with their present position and illustrated the difficulties ahead.

"From Goupillières there is this one road to the only bridge around, here at Le Bas." He pointed to the road and the bridge on the map and then to the river north of it. "The ground this side of the river is very steep and the ground falls rapidly all along the west bank. The road itself winds through a cutting with high banks on both sides. Added to this is the fact that there is plenty of tree cover on either side making excellent cover for any Germans waiting to attack troops using the road."

He pointed to the bridge again, "This bridge is the only real crossing point along this stretch of river. There is a further bridge at Thury-Harcourt but that's a good three miles further south." He moved his pointer to show the position of the bridge at Thury-Harcourt, merely adding, "Here."

"If, as we believe, the Le Bas bridge has been damaged by the retreating Germans, we need to consider other possible crossing points. Fortunately, although the river all along the whole stretch north and south of the bridge is about fifteen or sixteen yards wide, it shouldn't be too deep at this time of year and should be fordable in several places."

He again pointed at the map, "I've fished here; about a mile north of the bridge; just about opposite this village of Grimbosq. The infantry could probably cross here and in several other places along the bank; but definitely not the tanks and heavy weaponry as the bank is too steep."

"The one advantage of this side of the river is that there is ample cover from the trees and undergrowth, giving good observation across the river. The downside is that we are much higher than the river here and for the last hundred yards or so the ground is extremely steep along the whole stretch of the river north of the bridge. Added to that is the problem that the bank itself is very high; too high and steep to even scramble down in many places. The east bank of the river is reasonably gentle, and on that side of the river there are plenty of orchards, little hamlets and isolated farmhouses until you reach the Grimbosq Forest."

"This reasonably flat area on the east side is quite narrow and soon starts to rise. Although the rise is less steep than on this side, unfortunately the forest runs right up to the river only slightly further north and is never more than about half a mile from the east bank for a good two mile stretch southwards. The Germans can hide unobserved in there and, if we are not very careful, could just wait for us to cross the river and cut us up as we try to cross the more open ground leading up to it."

He again pointed to the bridge at Le Bas, "My own view is that this is the only place where the tanks could safely get down to the river to cross and, if the bridge has been damaged, they still could not do so without some form of temporary bridge or causeway."

At this point the commanding officer stood up and thanked Edward for his contribution.

"It's obvious that we have to check things out at the river before we do anything. I suggest we send out some patrols to identify possible crossing points." He faced Edward saying, "Perhaps you would like to head up one right away Richards? I want you and Matthews to choose a couple of men to go with you and check along the bank where you suggested. Where you had fished, wasn't it?"

Edward and Philip stood up, saluted and left as the choosing of other patrols and their objectives continued.

When they had reached outside, Philip turned to Edward and asked, "When have you ever gone fishing?"

Edward laughed, "Well I couldn't say what I was actually doing in the long grass along the bank, could I?"

After they had walked only a few yards, Edward moved closer to Philip, "We almost have to pass the Guilbert's house on our way down to the river, so this is my chance to check that things are OK there. It won't take more than ten minutes or so."

"Not on your life, we have to get this job done first, Maybe we could go the slight detour on our way back if we find a good crossing point fairly quickly, but if not, you'll just to have to wait for another day."

"Well all right, we'll get the job done first, but on the way back I'll be taking that detour, whether you come with me or not."

They agreed to take two men with them, and chose one each. Philip chose Jimmy Turnbull and Edward selected Ralph Freeman. Philip considered Ralph Freeman to be a bit of a maverick and guessed that Edward had deliberately chosen him as the one most likely to cover for him if he went to check on the Guilberts.

Ten minutes later, after they had briefly outlined the task to Freeman and Turnbull, and after all four of them had blackened their faces, they were leaving the compound. The sun had already set as they headed east towards the river, avoiding Goupillières and crossing the road north of the village. They now moved much more slowly and carefully as they made their way across the fields, keeping to the cover of the hedgerows wherever possible.

By the time they reached the wooded area a couple of hundred yards from the river, darkness had fallen completely and the only natural light was from the moon and stars that shone through the breaks in the clouds.

Philip stopped the party as soon as they had the cover of the trees, "I suggest we spread out here; probably about eighty to a hundred feet apart."

He took Edward by the arm, and pointing to the north, "I suggest you go about fifty or sixty yards that way." He then turned to Freeman, "You go with the Lieutenant but move down to the river from about thirty yards in that direction. Turnbull, we'll go in this direction with you heading to the river after about thirty yards and I'll go a further thirty yards or so before I turn down to the river. We can compare notes later and decide whether any routes down are easier than the others."

He then deliberately directed his advice to the two privates as he did not wish to offend Edward, who almost certainly knew the facts anyway, "Be very careful when you reach the bank for two reasons. Firstly, we know that the river bank itself is a virtually vertical drop of several feet in most places along the bank, so approach it very cautiously, we don't want you slipping over the edge and breaking your neck by falling into the river." He smiled as he added, "But what would be far worse than a broken neck would be your making such a noise that any Germans on the other bank know of our whereabouts."

Jimmy Turnbull returned the smile, "Assuming we don't break our necks Sir, what's the second reason?"

"Well we don't think there are any Germans left on this side of the river, but they are almost certainly spread out somewhere along the opposite bank. So get as close to the bank as you possibly can and I then want you to make a note of three things. One, how high the bank is? You'll have to take an educated guess at its height but mainly I want to know whether you think it is far too high to jump down if it's decided to cross the river along this stretch. Two, try and make some assessment of how deep the river is. Not easy I know, but it will probably appear to be running faster in shallower areas. And lastly, use the binoculars to check out the opposite bank and note any movement that could be the enemy."

He turned to Edward who was standing at his side, "Have I said everything necessary?"

"I guess so. I'm sure we all know what to look for, but don't you think we should spread out more? We'll get a better idea of a wider stretch of ground that way."

"Maybe we could spread out a few yards more, but we don't know what other patrols the Colonel has sent out and we don't want to run into any of those and get treated as enemy. I was also hoping that we don't get so far apart that we lose total contact with each other."

Philip did not want Edward to feel left out of the decisions however, so he added, "What do you suggest? Shall we spread out at say fifty yards rather than thirty?"

"I guess so, and I suggest that as we check the bank, we all move back into the middle and meet at the bank down there." He pointed directly ahead, eastwards to the river.

Philip looked at his watch, "I make it 2334 hours. Why don't we arrange to meet together at say 0030 hours? Do you think that's long enough?"

"I would think so. We need to have time to recheck particular places if necessary."

This agreed, they all synchronised their watches and moved to their allotted start positions before turning to the river.

Within a few yards the ground became much steeper and Philip had to steady himself from slipping by hanging on to branches on the way down but even so he nearly fell over as he stepped into what he thought was a rabbit hole. He winced at the sudden jerk of pain and held his breath to avoid letting out any sound as he tentatively put his weight on the foot to test the extent of any injury. There was an immediate increase in the pain but it was bearable and probably nothing more than a twisted ankle. He continued slowly down the slope, avoiding putting his full weight on the injured foot as much as possible, but by the time he reached the bank the pain was becoming unbearable.

Thereafter his progress was painfully slow and it was almost a quarter to one when Edward, who had come to look for him as he had not arrived at the meeting point by the allotted time, found him.

Philip put his finger to his mouth to prevent Edward speaking as soon as he saw him and when they were close up very quietly said, "I'm sure I spotted movement over on the other side a little while ago, so I stayed checking it out for a bit."

"And is there anyone over there?"

"Well I'm not sure. I thought it was maybe a couple of men on observation duty but I haven't seen any more movement so perhaps I was wrong." He pointed to his leg, "But the biggest problem is my leg. I twisted it back there and it's hurting like billy-oh now." He looked at his watch, "Sorry I've kept you waiting but I can't walk very quickly. How have you all got on?"

"Turnbull thinks he saw movement on the other side as well. So you are probably right about the lookout. Other than that I guess there are a few places we could cross, but we can talk about that later. For now we better get you back to base and have that ankle looked at."

Climbing up the slope was even more painful for Philip, and by the time they had cleared the trees and were back on the farmed land, he was finding it more difficult to put any weight on it.

Just before they reached the end of the field Edward looked across at Philip, "You'll be OK from here won't you? I just have a little detour to do. I'll catch up with you before you get back to base," and without waiting for a response turned to go, but he suddenly stopped and held back the others.

"Shush. Did you hear that?"

They all froze at the sound of people talking in the field on the other side of the road. "Wir solten von hier aus sicher runter zum Fluss kommen"

"Hoffentlich" came the response.

Edward mouthed his words to the others, "Bloody Germans and they're coming this way."

Philip mouthed back, "How many do you think there are?"

Edward held up two fingers, then three, then four. Then he shrugged his shoulders to imply that he had no idea at all.

Philip signified that they should get back to the cover of the bushes. He then put the bayonet on his rifle, indicating to the others to do the same.

They heard a rustle in the hedge on the opposite side of the road, and Edward held up his fingers again counting the sounds of boots crossing the road. He held up one finger after the other and was eventually holding up five fingers.

The footsteps became quieter when they reached the grassy verge on the other side of the hedge bordering the field where they were all waiting anxiously.

"Herr Hauptmann, hier können wir durch"

One by one the Germans squeezed through the gap in the hedge and started moving towards the point where Philip and the others were waiting. They were bound to be seen soon.

Edward quietly ordered them all to lie on the ground with their guns at the ready. Pointing to Turnbull's rifle, he put up one finger and pointing to the Germans signified that Turnbull was to take out the first German. Pointing to Freeman's gun he held up two fingers. He held up three fingers for Philip, and pointing to himself he held up four fingers. He then held up five fingers and swung his hand showing that they should all have a go at number five as soon as they could after hitting their first target.

Holding his rifle at the ready he counted down with his fingers; five; four; three; two; one. Immediately the shots rang out and two of the Germans fell. The others dived into the hedge firing back blindly as they did so. The fifth man darted back to the gap in the hedge just as Philip got in his second shot. He let out a squeal as he scrambled through the hedge dragging his machine gun with him, so Philip did not know if he was wounded or not.

Freeman, who had missed his man, aimed a second shot at number two but the man was now lying on the ground and he only managed to hit him in the shoulder.

Number one was running towards them firing his pistol and succeeded in hitting Freeman in the thigh. Turnbull was struggling to get in his second shot but Edward's second shot was aimed directly at Turnbull's target and the officer immediately let out a yell as he doubled up holding his stomach. Edward's third shot hit him a second time and he fell to the ground without any further sound, his pistol flying out of his hand as he did so.

Number two, although injured, was still shooting at them but the moon had once more gone behind a cloud putting him in the dark shadow of the hedge but even so, Philip managed to finish the job and the firing stopped.

Edward, quietly gave out a "whoopee" and added, "four down and one to go. Shall we let him go or shall we chase after him? I'll go and have a look to see if he's still around," and started crawling on his stomach towards the road.

Philip was just about to suggest that they had more important things to do than to chase after him in the dark, when a new batch of shots came flooding through the hedge. Freeman, who was now kneeling trying to stem the blood from his wounded side, let out a short yell before flying back into the hedge as the barrage of bullets hit him.

Edward also let out a yell. The other two ducked down as bullets flew inches over their heads.

Philip decided that he had to deal with this maverick soldier before they were all killed and as soon as the shooting stopped he signalled to the others to stay down and keep still. Hoping that the machine gunner would continue aiming any more shots to the edge of the field where they were, he chose to go out into the middle of the field, trusting that when he reached a point at right angles to the gap in the hedge he would be able to get a good shot at the troublemaker before he realised he was there. He put a bullet into the chamber of his rifle and silently crawled across the field, staying as close to the ground as he could.

Another burst of gunfire came from the machine gun and from the flashes as the bullets left the gun Philip was able to see exactly where he was but before Philip could take aim someone shouted at the top of their very shaky voice, "Hör auf zu schiessen, du Idiot! Die sind schon alle tot."

Philip thought he recognised Edward's voice and held his breath as he waited to see if the German was taken in by Edward's German. Perhaps the noise of the German's own gun had masked Edward's voice but it was obvious that he had thought the instruction to stop shooting as all the enemy were dead was from one of his comrades as he immediately stopped shooting and replied, "Sind Sie sicher das alle tot sind?"

Edward replied with a simple, "Ja."

The gunner got up from his prone shooting position, moved into the field and walked towards where he imagined his comrades to be.

Philip now had to act quickly before the German reached his dead comrades who were less than ten yards away. Should he shoot him in cold blood? The German was dragging his machine gun behind him and Philip guessed it would take him several seconds to be in a position to use it. It was now or never, so he jumped up, pointed his rifle directly at the German, and in his own best German shouted, "Halt! Oder ich schiesse."

The poor man did not know what was happening. He stopped, dropped his gun and promptly put his hands above his head.

"Shoot the bastard," came the immediate but weak response from Edward. "He's just blown poor Freeman to bits."

Philip ignored the plea and went to frisk his conquest and make sure he had no other weapons before shouting across to Edward, "What's the German for kneel, Edward?

It was noticeable from the weakness in Edward's voice that he was now finding it difficult to speak, "Auf die Knie!"

But before Philip could tell the man to "Auf die Knie!" Turnbull shouted across to him, "Sir, you need to come here quickly, the Lieutenant's got blood spurting out of his leg and I can't stop it."

Philip pushed his rifle into the man's back forcing him to walk to where Turnbull and Edward were and once there he told the man to, "Knien," and handing the rifle to Turnbull told him to, "Make sure he doesn't move and if he does just shoot him." Philip did not know which one, Turnbull or the German was most shocked by this instruction, but it was obvious by the sudden look of fear on each man's face that both had fully understood the gravity of what he had said.

He now turned his attention to Edward. He ripped his bloody trousers away from the injury. The wound in his leg was not large but the bullet had obviously gone right through his leg severing the femoral artery. The blood was still spitting out from the wound into a pool of blood beneath in unison with Edward's weakening heart beat.

Edward was still conscious but his eyes were gradually closing and his breathing was now very slow and heavy. Philip took off Edward's tie and tied it around his leg just above the injury as tight as he could but blood was still coming from the wound. Philip looked around and found a short thick stick, which he twisted into the tie pulling it tighter until the bleeding stopped. He then took off his own tie and tied it around the leg to keep the stick in place.

"We've got to get the Lieutenant some help before he loses any more blood. He's lost too much already and I don't think he'll last if he loses any more. We're going to have to carry him; he's in no fit state to walk."

He turned to Turnbull, inspecting the blood on the arm of his torn jacket, "And what have you done to that?"

"They got me in the arm, Sir, with that last round of bullets."

Philip quickly inspected the arm, deciding that it was merely a flesh wound. He took out a pad and bandage from his first aid kit and wrapped the wound as best he could. Although the wound was in no way life threatening, it was obvious that he was in no fit state to carry Edward and neither was he with his sprained ankle.

He looked at the German, realising for the first time why he'd been the one chosen to carry the heavy machine gun. He was forty or so years old, was at least 6ft 3ins tall and looked as strong as an ox, so Philip summed up the best schoolboy German he could and said, "Hey, Du!" and pointing to Edward added, "Heb ihn auf."

The man immediately moved to Edward, put one arm between his legs, and bending low down took Edward's arm and stood up with Edward over his shoulder in a fireman's lift. The German turned and looked at Philip as if to say, "And now what?"

Jimmy Turnbull had the same look in his eye as he turned to Philip, "What now, Sir? It's quite a way back to camp. Do you think the Lieutenant will make it that far?"

"No, I don't, but I know someone who lives not far from here; or at least he used to. He's a vet so if he's still there, he might be able to help," and prodding the German in the arm he signalled the way he wanted him to go.

Philip quickly checked on Freeman but he was beyond any help. He turned to Turnbull, "You follow the German and make sure he doesn't do anything stupid. Keep your gun on him and shoot if you have to."

Given this instruction, Turnbull started to visibly shake and tears came to his eyes.

"What's the problem, soldier?"

"Can I just shoot him in the leg, Sir? I don't think I can kill him in cold blood this close up, Sir."

In the five or six minutes it took to reach Guilbert's house, Philip had his first real chat with Jimmy Turnbull since they had spoken together before leaving England. This time he was able to get him to talk about his fears and learned that although he was quite prepared to die himself, the thing he was really frightened of was taking another man's life.

"But we've been in several battles together including tonight and as far as I'm aware, you've always done what was required of you."

"You may think so Sir, but I just point my rifle, close my eyes, and shoot; praying at the same time that I don't hit anyone."

Poor Philip didn't know how to deal with this admission and felt that it would have been better if he hadn't heard any of it. "I'm going to forget you ever said that to me and for what it is worth I'm sure you won't need to shoot this German but don't let him know that."

They turned a corner in the road and immediately Philip was able to change the subject, "See that house standing back from the road over there, that's where we're going."

He again prodded the German in the arm and pointed to the house. It looked to be undamaged but was in total darkness. *"Please be there,"* the only thought repeating over and over again in his head.

They reached the front door and Philip was just about to bang on it when Jimmy Turnbull said, "What if there are Germans in there, Sir?"

"Too late for worrying about that now," and he banged on the door. There was no response from inside so he continued banging and yelling "Monsieur Guilbert, it's me, Philip Matthews. We met a few years ago. I have Edward Richards here. Do you remember him? He's badly injured and we need your help."

He was about to start banging again when he heard movement inside, "Qu'est ce que tu veux?"

Philip understood the question but his schoolboy French had deserted him, so he just answered in English, hoping that whoever was inside would understand, "We have an injured soldier here and we need your help, Sir. It's Edward Richards and he needs medical help quickly."

The use of Edward's name seemed to do the trick, because he heard a female voice urging someone to open the door and let them in. The bolts were drawn back and the door opened a few inches. A torch shone through the crack in the door and Philip put his face directly into the beam.

Juliette flung open the door, "It's Philip, Pa."

There was some consternation when she saw the German uniform on the man standing in the shadow, but she was more concerned by the sight of the now unconscious Edward flung over his shoulder.

Her father now took control, "Bring him to my surgery and we'll see if we can patch him up." He bolted the door behind them before turning to his wife and daughters and told them to return to bed. His wife did as she was instructed. Madeleine said a quick, "Hello," to Philip adding, "See you in the morning if you're still here," before following her mother back to bed.

Juliette however refused to leave them, insisting that she wanted to stay and help. Once in the surgery the blinds were checked before the lights were switched on. Raoul Guilbert now looked at each of his visitors' faces and smiled as he looked at the German. He pointed to the scrubbed table in the centre of the room and surprised Philip when he spoke German to Edward's bearer, "Stefan, leg ihn hier hin. Vorsichtig."

The German did as he was asked and with Raoul and Philip's help, put Edward on the table carefully so as not harm him any more. Juliette had tears in her eyes as she kissed Edward on the forehead, "My poor Eddy. What have they done to you?"

"Move away sweetheart," said her father, "He's in a bad way and will be even worse if we don't sort him out quickly."

He started to loosen the tourniquet but immediately tightened it again as a spurt of blood shot up into his face. Wiping the blood from his eyes he declared, "I'm going to have to try and mend this artery or he'll bleed to death." He looked at Edward's ashen face, and touching his forehead shook his head at the feel of Edward's cold skin.

"I've only ever operated on animals before so I don't know if I can help him."

"But you must," said Philip, "It's his only chance, and it's a sure fact that he'll die before we could get him to the medical unit back at camp. You must help him, Sir."

Juliette hugged her father and with tears streaming down her face, begged him to try to save Edward.

He kissed his daughter's forehead, "Well I suppose there is a first time for everything, sweetheart. I'll have a go, but don't hold out too much hope, will you?"

Juliette's sobs were now filling the room and the German took her by the arm and, leading her away from the table, put his finger to his mouth as a signal for her to be quiet.

Philip moved forward to protect her as soon as the German took Juliette's arm and Jimmy pointed his gun at him but before either of them did anything further Juliette waved her arms to stop them saying, "No! it's fine, Stefan won't hurt me. We know him quite well."

Philip stepped back and Jimmy lowered his gun, "How on earth do you know him?"

"Well he's been stationed around here for at least the last two years and he's been here several times. He wouldn't harm my father or any of us." She turned to Jimmy, "So put that gun away, soldier." She stopped crying and taking her father's arm, asked him, "Please save Edward, Papa."

Raoul merely said, "I'll do my best," and started attending to Edward.

Philip turned to Jimmy Turnbull and after making sure he had all the necessary information about the night's reconnoitre told him to, "Get back to camp as quickly as you can and report all that to the Colonel. Tell him I'll be along as soon as I know the Lieutenant is OK and then you'd better go and get that arm seen to."

"But what about the prisoner, Sir? Should I take him back with me?"

Philip looked across at Stefan who, on Raoul's instructions, was holding Edward's now naked leg steady as Raoul cut into the flesh to get to the damaged artery, "No, he'll be fine here with us. I'll bring him with me when I come and anyway you'll be quicker if you haven't got him in tow."

Juliette left to show Jimmy out and a little later came back with piping hot coffee for everyone but Raoul was far too busy and Stefan was standing by to help as much as he could so only she and Philip took a cup.

They sat on the stone floor and Philip took a long, lingering mouthful of the warm liquid; the tension in him easing as he drank it. He looked across at Raoul and was puzzled about the friendly relationship he seemed to have with this Stefan now helping him attend to Edward. Most of the French people he had met since landing in France disliked their German occupiers immensely and he had seen some examples of awful retribution taken against Frenchmen who had fraternised with them.

This was the first time he had seen Juliette since the holiday in the summer of 1938 and she was obviously worrying a great deal about Edward, but he needed to know more about Stefan before taking him back as his prisoner. He drank the last drop of coffee from his cup before asking the question, "How come you know Stefan so well?"

"That's a long story but I suppose you ought to know."

She suddenly turned her head and looked Philip directly in the eyes, "I know you have to take him with you as a prisoner but you will take care of him, won't you? Promise me you'll make sure no harm comes to him."

Philip was now even more puzzled and felt he must learn the whole story. "Of course I'll take care of him. I promise you, we take good care of prisoners. If he behaves himself and doesn't do anything stupid he'll be fine. In fact he'll probably be much safer as a prisoner than out there fighting in the battles yet to come."

Juliette pursed her lips and shook her head as if she was still not completely satisfied with the answer. She took a swig of her coffee, "He's a good man and he's lost enough already."

"So what's the story then? How do you know him and why are you so concerned about him?"

She took another mouthful of coffee before answering his questions, "His name is Stefan Reinke. Before the war he was a farrier and lived quite happily with his wife and two sons in a place called Freudenstadt in the Black Forest. He was conscripted into the army, and later so were both of his sons. The oldest was only about eighteen and I think the youngest was still only sixteen when they were both sent with the German 6th Army to the Russian front.

"Yes, but how do you know him so well?"

She smiled at Philip's impatience, "Give me time and I'll come to that."

She turned her head away to ask her father how things were going.

"Not now, sweetheart; let me just get on with it."

Tears appeared in her eyes at her father's rebuff and Philip wanted to comfort her, but decided against it.

She took another gulp of her coffee and wiped her eyes before continuing, "Stefan's commanding officer acquired a couple of horses for himself in no time at all after he came here. Just requisitioned them I think. He was always riding round on them, showing off as the great conqueror and occupier. It was all for show and he loved nothing more than riding into Thury-Harcourt market sending everyone scattering in all directions. He'd dig his spurs into the poor horse to make it rear up and woe betides anyone who got in his way, but he just laughed at the chaos he created."

She shook her head, "It was obvious he had no love for horses but he nevertheless needed someone to look after them and when he learned that Stefan was a farrier he transferred him to feed and groom the horses and have them ready for him every time he went on his jaunts. Stefan is wonderful around animals and seems to have an exceptional affinity with them, particularly the horses. He brought one of the horses here for Pa to look at after the commandant had been particularly vicious with his spurs. The poor animal was distressed as soon as Pa tried to approach the injury, but Stefan just stroked his head and spoke closely in the horse's ear and it immediately calmed down and let Pa treat the wound."

"So until a few weeks ago, that's what Stefan did and that's how we came to know him. Whenever there was a problem with the horses, he would bring them here for Pa to sort out, and if he had the time he'd help Pa with some of the other animals around."

She got up and went to have a closer look at what her father was doing, but she was soon back sitting with Philip, "So, that's it and when he learned that his youngest son had been killed at the battle for Stalingrad, he said we were the only ones he could talk to about it. And then less than a month later, he got the news that his eldest son had been killed at

Stalingrad as well. How can you hate anyone who's going through such heartache as that? Anyway that's it; that's all there is to it. He's a really nice fellow, hates the Nazis and what they've done to Germany and his family. We haven't seen him much in the last couple of months. I guess the Commandant had to get rid of the horses and do some real fighting after the invasion."

She took hold of Philip's hands and held them to her, "He did manage to come to see us a couple of weeks ago. The poor fellow was worried out of his mind as he hadn't heard anything from his wife in two months. She was always writing to him, so he was worried stiff about her. He kept saying that if anything had happened to her he'd have no-one left at all." She squeezed Philip's hands tightly, "So you will look after him won't you?"

"I'll do my best. I can't do any more than that."

All this time they had been watching Juliette's father as he carefully and precisely repaired the torn artery. He worked quickly and was soon releasing the tourniquet to see if his work was successful before stitching up the flesh around the wound.

He once again felt Edward's temperature, "He's still very cold. I've done all I can for now but I'm afraid that he may have lost far too much blood."

Philip interrupted, "But couldn't we give him some blood then; he can have some of mine. I've given blood several times. You could do that couldn't you, Monsieur Guilbert."

"I'm afraid we don't know his blood group and it would be dangerous to give him just any other sort of blood."

"No, Sir. The last time I gave blood I was told that I had group O blood with something called rhesus negative and it could be used for anyone no matter what blood group they are."

"Are you sure about that?"

"Well that's what I was told. They definitely told me that my blood could be used for anyone."

Raoul felt Edward's pulse, "He certainly is getting weaker, but I don't think we should risk it. And anyway, I'm not sure how to do it."

Juliette once more took her father's arm, "Do you think Eddy will be all right without any blood Pa?"

"That I don't know, sweetheart. He's in a really bad way but I guess he'd stand a much better chance if he has some."

"Then you must do it, Pa. You must do it."

He went to a cupboard and fetched out a bottle, a rubber tube and some syringes. "Maybe we could do it with these, but I'm not exactly sure how to go about it. I have no anticoagulant and the blood will just clot if we're not careful."

Philip went up to him and took the bottle from him, "Don't need this Monsieur. When I first gave blood they just fed the tube straight from me and into the recipient. Put me higher than Edward, feed the tube from my arm to Edward's and let my blood flow into his."

Luckily Raoul knew more about the technique than he had let on and although he had never actually done it before he soon had the blood flowing into Edward from Philip's arm. Unfortunately he had no idea how to measure the quantity of blood and was afraid he might take too much blood putting Philip in the same precarious position that Edward was. But after a while the flow of blood started to slow down and he realised that it was starting to coagulate in the needle in Philip's arm. So he stopped the procedure and just hoped that enough blood had trickled into Edward.

He removed the needles and tubes and got Stefan to hold a gauze pad on Edward's arm where the blood inlet had been made, "Fest drűcken, Stefan." He put a piece of gauze on Philip's arm and told him to hold it there for a while.

"You can get us all a cup of that coffee now, Juliette. Go and fetch the Calvados. We've done all we can for now and I'm sure we could all do with a little something to relax us." He looked at Philip's arm and put a bandage around the spot where he'd taken blood, "You can get up now but just sit down there for a while and have another drink"

He then removed Stefan's hand from the gauze to check Edward's arm.

He was about to bandage Edward's arm but as soon as Philip had got up from the table, Stefan rolled up the sleeve of his shirt and lay down in Philip's place, "Kann ich ihm jetzt mein Blut geben, Monsieur Guilbert?"

Raoul was somewhat taken aback by Stefan's offer to give his own blood and had some difficulty explaining that it could be very dangerous to give his blood to Edward. He hoped that finally he had convinced Stefan that it had nothing to do with race or nationality but was purely lack of knowledge of Edward's blood type or Stefan's.

When Monsieur Guilbert explained what the discussion had been about, Philip was quite touched at his enemy's wish to help the injured man who only a couple of hours ago had been trying to kill him. He determined to do all he could to look after Stefan.

By late morning medics had collected Edward from the Guilbert's house and he was now safely receiving further treatment.

And when Philip handed Stefan Reinke over as a prisoner of war, he stressed how he had helped save Edward's life and gave strict instructions that this man was to be treated with respect and kept safe, adding, "And if anything untoward happens to this prisoner, I'll have your guts for garters. Is that clear sergeant?" The sergeant merely nodded.

His own ankle was bandaged and as soon as darkness fell he was leading his men across the river at the point selected the previous night, and successfully surprising the remains of the enemy on the other side. Having crossed the river they turned southwards and by 0200 hours were in position and ready to cover the bridge repair operations at Le Bas.

Luckily the enemy bombardment to destroy the bridge had not been entirely successful with many of the mortar bombs and shells aimed at it falling many yards upstream.

Philip's unit was ordered to safeguard the bridge and the engineers working on it, and for most of the day were involved in dealing with ferocious attacks and counter attacks from the enemy. They nevertheless managed to hold their position allowing the sappers to build a causeway alongside the bridge for tracked vehicles and by the end of the afternoon complete the bridge improvements allowing all traffic to cross.

Just before eight o'clock that evening Philip's unit was trying to extend the safe area around the bridgehead when they again came under a vicious counter attack. It was during this attack that Jimmy Turnbull on Philip's right had a German soldier charging straight at him. Jimmy pointed his gun directly at the advancing German but to Philip's consternation he just froze and did not shoot. Seconds later Jimmy was dead having been bayoneted by his attacker and the German was lying dead on top of him; shot by Philip.

"You will look after my boys, won't you Mr Matthews?" had been the plea to Philip from Jimmy Turnbull's mother and now that same son was lying dead only feet away from him.

Why hadn't Jimmy shot him? "I'm not scared of dying," Jimmy had said only a couple of days ago, "but I am scared of killing another man."

Philip pulled the German off him and shouted at the top of his voice, "You silly bugger, none of us like all this killing but it's them or us and this time it's you. You silly bugger; what on earth am I going to say to your mother when I have to write to tell her?" but Philip's anger at this death was quickly left behind as he and his comrades continued to repulse the attack; an attack that was not without many more deaths.

Other units spread out along the river fared no better and also met fierce resistance, but steadily over the next four days the enemy was repulsed further and further back and by 10th August they had advanced sufficiently southwards to be ready to enter Thury-Harcourt.

It was a very tired and sleep-starved reformed fighting force that made their first attempt to take Thury-Harcourt. This was again strongly resisted by the enemy who were heavily concentrated in the town and it took a further four days of fighting, again with heavy casualties, before the town was finally taken.

The retreating Germans had however left behind numerous booby traps and to the disgust of the British troops had even mined the grand chateau at the edge of the town as an act of revenge. The once beautiful and historic building was now completely gutted; never to be restored but to remain a mere shell debarred of its former glory.

For Philip this was a particularly distressful day. He and Edward had enjoyed several days with Juliette and Madeleine here a few years previously, but the once beautiful town he remembered was no longer. The town hall where Juliette had arranged for them all to meet was now a mere shell. Its front and back wall were still standing and the clock on the top of the front wall was still intact, but all the windows were missing and the roof was no more. Inside everything had been destroyed leaving just a huge pile of rubble. Similarly, the ancient church next to the town hall was now roofless and windowless and it would be a long time before all the damage to it could be repaired.

It seemed that every building in the town had been destroyed, leaving strange structured brick edifices leaning precariously in all directions surrounding one at every turn. The former buildings reduced to absolute rubble littered every road with impassable mountains of bricks and masonry. How could such destruction be justified? How could such loss of life be justified?

CHAPTER SEVENTEEN

1946 - 1947

Juliette insisted on accompanying Edward to the field hospital following Raoul Guilbert's surgery on his leg, but by the time they reached the hospital Edward had become feverish and delirious. The place was awash with seriously wounded casualties being brought in from the battlefield and the overworked doctors suggested that the quick and easy option was to remove the leg. But Juliette argued against this and said she would give him the care and attention the otherwise busy nurses and doctors could not.

She spent every waking hour at his bedside, mopping his brow and gently massaging the leg to encourage the blood flow. Every day she begged for new dressings to clean and redress his wound and with all this attention, Edward had soon recovered and within a week was out of bed with Juliette helping him walk up and down the ward. Nevertheless, it was a full month before he was fit for active service again; a month in which he saw Juliette every day and it was obvious to both of them that their passionate feelings for each other had not changed.

For Philip, that month had been one of a constant round of battles, nights of lost sleep and even worse, more and more of his colleagues being killed and wounded, including the commanding officer who was killed when a lorry load of mines had exploded, whilst others were killed by an attack from their own aircraft when they were advancing towards Falaise, a town some sixteen or so miles south east of Thury-Harcourt. But before they were able to take this important town, news came through that because of the considerably diminished number of able fighting men in the regiment the 59th Division was to be disbanded and the remaining fit men transferred to other units.

Both Edward, now also promoted to Captain, and Philip spent the rest of the war gradually moving eastwards, finally ending up in Germany interviewing and interrogating captured German prisoners. Edward wrote to Juliette at every opportunity and before long he had decided to ask her to marry him when he next saw her. He somehow managed to do this by hitch-hiking across France to Thury-Harcourt when he was supposed to be making his way back to England to be demobbed in June 1946.

It had been a very long two years since he had last seen Juliette and as he neared the house with a kit bag in one hand and a holdall in the other, he wondered what to say to Monsieur or Madame Guilbert when they opened the door to him. But with still thirty or so yards to go, Juliette appeared at the gate looking up and down the road and when she saw Edward, she ran to him with outstretched arms. He dropped the bags and Juliette held him so tight he struggled for breath. They kissed and kissed again without saying a word until a tractor came along and the driver shouted for them to move and take the bags out of the road.

They quickly moved the bags but as soon as the tractor had passed they dropped them again and returned to hugging and kissing each other.

It must have been a good ten minutes before they released each other sufficiently for Edward to move to kneel beside her. He held her hands to his chest, looked directly into her eyes and the very first words he had spoken to her in almost two years were the ones he had been practising over and over since he had left the base in Germany.

"Je t'aime Juliette et tu m'as tant manquée. Veux tu m'épouser?"

"Oui. Oui. Of course I'll marry you," and they fell into each others arms again, but before they were able to say any more to each other, Juliette's mother was shouting from the house.

"Juliette, Juliette mais où en es tu? J'ai besoin de mettre la table pour le souper."

Juliette got to her feet and shouted back. "J'arrive maman. Je n'en ai pas pour longtemps."

Edward picked up his bags and with Juliette's arms linked tightly into his, they started towards the house.

"How come you came out of the gate just as I was turning the corner?" he asked.

She reached up and kissed him once more on the cheek, "I have no idea, I just felt a need to go outside, and there you were. Perhaps I'm psychic or maybe you were just willing me to come out."

They kissed again before continuing to the house but after only a few yards, Juliette pulled up with a jerk, "What are we going to say to mother and father? We can't just drop it out that we're going to get married. Or can we?"

"They're your parents. You know them best. What do you think we should do?"

"Just don't say anything straight away. I don't think Pa will take too kindly to having it just dropped on him. Maybe I'll be able to talk to Ma and get her to soften him up over the next few days." She suddenly realised that she had no idea how long Edward intended to stay, but he answered the question before she had asked it.

"I don't have a few days. I'm supposed to be on my way back to England to get demobbed. I really should be back in England by tomorrow night at the very latest. Really I ought to be on my way tonight, otherwise I could end up being charged with absent without leave."

Juliette started sobbing and held him tight, "Can I come with you? I don't want to be without you again."

"A few weeks that's all it'll be. As soon as I get demobbed, I'll come straight back here and we'll get married as soon as you like."

"But couldn't I just come with you now? It won't take me a few minutes to throw some clothes into a bag and we can be on our way."

"You can't just run out on your parents. I'll talk to them tonight and I promise I'll be back as soon as I can. Maybe a few more weeks will be more easily coped with than the last seven or eight years of being apart. At least we know now that we'll soon be together at last."

She reached up and gave him a long lingering kiss full on his lips before releasing him and reluctantly admitting he was probably right. "But I'll expect you to write to me every day and please, please don't be too long coming back to me."

Edward waited until they were all sat around the supper table before mentioning his wish to marry Juliette. The utter silence that followed made it obvious that neither of Juliette's parents were prepared for the suddenness of the proposal.

It was Juliette's father who spoke first, "Don't you think you should give this a bit more time? You hardly know each other. How often have you seen each other? It can't be more than a dozen times spread over almost as many years. No. I don't think you have thought this through properly. Why don't you go back to England Edward, settle yourself in a career and both get on with your lives. Now this blasted war is over, I thought Juliette had finally decided to do what she should have done years ago."

He turned to Juliette who already had tears in her eyes, "You've wasted enough years messing about instead of going to University. I know the damned war has made it difficult for you. God only knows, it's been difficult for all of us, but just when you've finally been offered a place for veterinary training you turn round and, out of the blue, decide you're going to abandon it all to get married to someone you hardly know."

Edward could see the tears forming in Juliette's eyes and wanted to say something but Raoul continued talking, "Madeleine's already finished her training and I'd hoped that both of you could become my partners here and take over the business in due course."

Juliette was now distraught and floods of tears streamed down her face.

Poor Edward was at a loss to know how to deal with the situation.

It was Madeleine, who had sat throughout the whole episode without saying a word, who came to the rescue and ignoring everything that her father had been saying, turned to Juliette and said, "So dear sister you're getting married; about time too. You've been pining for poor Edward long enough." She turned and looked towards her father, "Actually Pa, I think it's wonderful news. It's the best thing that's happened around here for years."

She turned to Juliette, "Can I be your bridesmaid?" Without waiting for an answer she got out of her seat and went and stood behind her father. She put her arms round his neck and kissed his cheek, "You wouldn't deprive me of being a bridesmaid would you Pa? I've never been a bridesmaid before."

She held her arms around his neck and kissed him again on the cheek, "It's been obvious for years that Juliette is besotted with Edward. She's never bothered about any other boy since she first met him." She kissed her father's cheek yet again, "You and Ma haven't seen her crying for him at night, and worrying about where he is and whether he's safe or not."

She let go of her father and put her arms around her mother, "You think it's a good idea for them to get married, Ma, don't you? You know how much she's yearned for him all these years. For goodness sake they're grown ups and know their own minds. Anyway, if they don't know what they want by now, they never will."

This action had the desired effect and although things were still not settled by the time Edward had been shown to the guest room and the rest of them had retired to bed, at least they were talking sensibly to each other and Raoul was no longer showing any signs of anger.

Very early the next morning Juliette was kissing Edward goodbye at the door, when her father came down the stairs and shook Edward's hand. "Hope everything goes well back home for you and we hope to see you again in a few weeks. We'll talk about wedding plans then."

Juliette's mother now came down the stairs and on hearing her husband's last remark said, "Well that's assuming that Juliette and I haven't sorted it all out before then."

They all relaxed at this and Raoul put his arm around his wife's waist and laughingly suggested, "It's about time we had this house to ourselves again Hilda. If Madeleine sorts out that Maurice she's been seeing for the last eighteen months perhaps we can have a double wedding. Save me having to pay for two weddings and we'll get shut of both of them at the same time."

Hilda dug her fist into his ribs, "That's not funny, my sweet." But they all laughed anyway.

Philip had been demobbed a couple of months earlier and was already settled back into Civvy Street. He had immediately become involved in the family business and was able very quickly to take some of the load off his Uncle Tom and Lucy. However he had been far more help to his mother, who was finding it increasingly difficult since the war to keep her shops stocked with the radios and other equipment being demanded by the public.

The first thing he did on the day after arriving home had been to visit Mrs Turnbull. He'd been dreading having to face her about the death of her son, and was surprised to find her far more composed about it than he had expected. He was even more surprised when she said, "Thank you so much for the letter you sent me. It helped me enormously to know that he was a hero and died saving the lives of his comrades at the end."

Philip had deliberately not revealed the real details of her son's death; how he had been unable to kill the German charging him and had ended up dead himself instead. He knew he had said that her son had died defending their position and the men repairing the bridge from an enemy attack, but he didn't remember writing anything about her son being a hero. *'No point telling her otherwise now though,'* he thought, *'If it comforts her to think of her son in that way who am I to tell her anything different now?'*

He tried to leave as soon as possible, but Mrs Turnbull insisted that she couldn't let him go without having a cup of tea and one of her lemon cakes, and so poor Philip had to stay for another two hours whilst she talked non stop about anything and everything. She seemed quite proud when she told Philip how well Leonard had done in the army since his injury at Caen.

"He's been promoted to sergeant you know and is now training National Servicemen. Doing really well and says he might be made up to Sergeant Major soon."

He did not know how to judge her real feelings in this matter. Did she really want her son to stay in the Army after what had happened to Jimmy?

By the time he finally managed to refuse any more tea and cakes and stand up ready to go, he had decided that this was a very lonely woman, who was afraid of losing her other son. Talking non-stop about this and anything else was the only way she could shut the fear out for a few moments. He left, wondering how many other mothers up and down the country were in a similar position.

He had been home over a month when his mother said he was spending too many evenings at home, "It's about time you went out and enjoyed yourself. You can you know. The war's over, so go and find yourself a nice girl instead of staying here with me. I've managed well enough since your father died and I can manage on my own without you fussing over me every evening."

After listening to these moans from his mother for the next three evenings he thought that maybe she was right. It was about time he went out and enjoyed himself but with whom? Edward was still in Germany and he didn't think contacting other old chums was a good idea. He didn't know whether any of them were still around and didn't want to talk to grieving wives or mothers if they were not, so his next thought was Teresa Hunter.

He hadn't bothered to write to her or contact her since his father's death, and had not even acknowledged the few letters she had written to him. He therefore knew nothing about where she was or what she was doing now. As far as he knew she could be married with a couple of kids and getting in touch with her would then turn out to be a bigger mistake than contacting his old school friends. So one evening when Aunt Alice was at home he casually asked if Teresa was still working at the hospital.

"Do you mean Teresa Hunter, the girl you took out a few times?"

Philip nodded and Alice smiled a knowing smile. "Yes, in fact she's now the sister on the ward next to mine." Her smile broadened as she added, "She's still single, and as far as I know she doesn't have a boyfriend."

Philip tried to keep the conversation as casual as possible and as soon as he found out from Alice what shift Teresa was on he quickly changed the subject. Nevertheless, the very next evening a very apprehensive Philip was outside the hospital hoping to catch Teresa as she finished work.

She recognised him straight away, which pleased Philip, because if she had not waved and walked towards him he may not have recognised her. This woman was far more beautiful than the pretty girl he remembered.

She was obviously thrilled to see him again and there was none of the incriminations about not answering her letters that he had expected. As they chatted he started to relax. Somehow she seemed a much less selfish person; no longer totally wrapped up in what she wanted and was certainly much more interesting than he remembered. Nevertheless he surprised himself when he suddenly said, "I've got the car round the corner. Can I drive you home?"

He was reminded of the old Teresa as she instantly took his arm, "Of course you can," but even so, by the time they arrived at her home he'd made up his mind to see her again and as he helped her out of the car he asked if she would like to meet up again one evening.

She jumped at the invitation, "It's my weekend off this weekend, so perhaps we could spend Saturday or Sunday together." She looked closely into Philip's eyes trying to gauge his reaction before adding, "Or perhaps both Saturday and Sunday if you like."

Philip was taken aback; this was again more like the old Teresa always wanting to push the relationship along faster than he did.

Nevertheless he thought, *"What the hell, I haven't been out with a girl in years, so maybe I should go along with her this time,"* so without any further thought about the matter he said, "Yes Saturday would be fine," and before she could say anything else, he added, "Why don't I pick you up at say ten o'clock? Bring some walking shoes with you and we can go to Cannock Chase and take in some of the fresh air."

Fresh air and walking on Cannock Chase was not exactly what Teresa had in mind, but she was not going to ruin seeing Philip again by objecting, so she merely said, "Yes, that would nice. I'll put up a picnic lunch for us."

Saturday was a gloriously sunny summer day and for Teresa it turned out to be a far more successful outing than she had anticipated.

Philip drove on to the Chase and pulled off the road near to the Military Cemetery and suggested that Teresa should change out of her high heeled shoes so they could go walking. He leaned over his seat and took the flat shoes out of Teresa's bag he had put on the back seat along with the picnic she had prepared. When he turned back to give them to her she had already slipped off her shoes and was unclipping her stocking from her suspender.

Philip reddened at the sight of her exposed thigh, "Oops, sorry; I'll leave you to it," and with that he dropped the shoes in her lap and went to get out of the car.

She turned round and grasped his arm, "No need to go, I'm sure you've seen a girl's legs before and I have no intention of spoiling these stockings on the bracken out there. Anyway I need you to pass me my socks. They're in the same bag as the shoes."

He found the white ankle socks and handed them to her, "I'll just check the ground is firm enough to leave the car here." She smiled at his embarrassment as he got out of the car but was sensible enough not to let him see it.

When she got out of the car, Philip pointed to the cemetery, "Can we just have a look over there first? It won't take long."

They moved along the graves of the New Zealand soldiers who had died at the nearby camp in the First World War. And then they moved further into the cemetery and started looking at the headstones of German prisoners of war.

Quite suddenly and unexpectedly Philip let out a cry as he pointed to one of the headstones, "I know this man, or at least I think I do. I'm sure Juliette said the German who carried Edward when he was injured was called Stefan Reinke." He read the markings on the stone, "Stefan Reike. 19.10.1903. 20.8.1945. That would make him nearly forty-two when he died. Yes, I guess that's about right and when we took him prisoner I suppose he could have been brought to the camp here."

Philip's hand moved to cover his mouth as the reality of what he had just said hit him. "I promised Juliette I'd make sure he was OK. If it's the same man, why the hell did he have to die?"

Teresa wanted to ask him more about it but when she saw the tears streaming down his face she instead merely took his arm without speaking and left him to his thoughts. It was some time before Philip moved from the spot, but when he did, he took out his handkerchief and wiped his brow. "Phew, it's going to be a hot one today isn't it?" was all he said, but Teresa could not help but notice that he was also wiping the tears from his eyes as he tried to control his composure.

Philip moved Teresa's arm from his and led her to the gates of the cemetery, "Just stay here, I won't be a minute." He went to the car and when he came back with the picnic basket they started to walk along the path towards the copse at the bottom of the hill. They had walked some way without saying anything to each other before Philip finally broke the silence. "I'm sorry about that back there. I've seen too many dead men over the last few years. Too many of them were my friends killed right next to me and I saw too many dead Germans as well." He stopped and turned to Teresa, "I had that man in my sights and almost killed him, but I was so pleased that I didn't." Teresa detected the faltering in his voice as he continued, "My God what was it all for? I had thought he was at least one German who'd get back to his wife. He'd lost both of his sons to the bloody war. Why the hell did he have to die as well?"

They continued walking in silence for some time before he spoke again, "I'm sorry I shouldn't have taken you in there. It just brings it all back and that isn't what I intended for today."

The tears were once more streaming down his face, and Teresa gently guided him to a grassy patch at the side of the path and sat him down before sitting beside him. Without any encouragement from Teresa, Philip carried on talking, "As we fought our way South, in town after town, there was utter devastation. We may have been successful in driving the

Germans that were still able to move from the town, but there were still far too many dead and dying bodies lying all over the place."

He took a handkerchief from his pocket and this time he unashamedly wiped the tears from his eyes, "And they weren't just dead Germans either, but sometimes they were the bodies of the local men, women and children, torn to pieces, just lying there where they'd been killed."

He wiped the tears from his eyes again, "And you know what was even worse? We just had to leave them there and get on with the fighting; all the time pushing forward to kill as many more Germans as we could. And if more of the locals were killed well that's just what happens in war, isn't it? Or, at least that's what we were told. They were just the casualties of war."

This was the first time that Philip had talked to anyone about his war experiences and he did not know why he was doing it now. But the memories were too much for him and he broke down completely, sobbing his heart out. Teresa took him in her arms and held him tight, allowing his tears to soak the shoulder of her blouse. She too was crying now, not only at Philip's pain but also at these vivid images of war that she had never really thought about before; her own tears eventually running into Philip's hair as she caressed his head.

They stayed locked together for a long time until Philip became less distressed and was able to move away to wipe the moisture from his face. He looked at Teresa, saw the tears running down her face, and leaned forward to kiss them away. She immediately responded by kissing him long and hard on his lips. They fell back together on to the grass and held each other tightly, their legs wrapped around each other as they each felt the warmth and full contours of the other's body pushed against them. For the first time ever, Philip felt the insatiable need to take Teresa to him and he had great difficulty stopping himself from doing so.

He could feel Teresa pushing her womanhood harder against him, and as she moved slowly from side to side against him, he grew more and more excited. He moved his hand downwards, feeling the smoothness and urgency in her body as he did so. His hand moved further, feeling the softness of her thighs through the thinness of her skirt. Teresa continued to hold him even tighter as his hand slid over the material until he suddenly felt the warm bare flesh of her naked leg beneath his hand. The shock made him realise that he would soon pass the point of no return and he quickly pulled back and rolled away from her.

He looked into Teresa's face, now contorted with apprehension as she awaited Philip's reaction to what had just taken place. They were both breathing heavily and deeply and Philip felt certain that Teresa wanted him to re-engage with her just as much as his body was urging him to do so, but he knew he would regret such action later and so he just lay there, without moving and without touching her.

It was some time before either of them had gained their composure and Philip was able to speak, "I'm sorry about that. I shouldn't have taken advantage of the situation like that."

Teresa had thought a lot about Philip during the years since she had last seen him and thought she now understood his complex and sensitive self. She had come to realise that Philip was a man who needed to commit himself emotionally to a woman before he could commit himself physically to her. She wanted to go back to where they had been only minutes previously, but the grown up Teresa knew perfectly well that that would bring about a sudden, and for her, a disastrous end to the relationship she so desperately wanted, before it had even started.

She held back, unsure how to react to Philip's apology, but eventually diffidently and almost reluctantly reached out and touched his cheek, "There's no need to be sorry." She hesitated as she tried to make up her mind whether to say what she wanted to say, but quickly decided to say it anyway, before she lost the chance, "I'm not sorry, and you shouldn't be either." She smiled as she gave Philip the excuse he needed for what had happened, "We both needed a little comfort for a few minutes and that's all it was, wasn't it?"

She stroked Philip's cheek and even though she still found it difficult not to give in to the urge to return into his arms, she held back and said what she knew he was waiting to hear, "But you were right to move away and I'm glad we didn't go any further."

That said, they just lay there side by side, the only contact being Teresa's hand still resting against his cheek. Eventually Philip took her hand and moving it to his lips, gently kissed her fingers. Neither moved for the next ten minutes as they just lay there looking at the deep blue, cloudless sky.

For Philip, this was the first time he had seen Teresa as anything other than a girl whose company he enjoyed and one whom he could spend a pleasant and enjoyable time with. Teresa instinctively seemed to understand this and not wanting to lose him again, vowed to herself that she would let Philip do all the running from now on.

They eventually sat up and devoured their lunch and quenched their sudden thirst with the bottled beer now warm from the overhead sun, before moving to sit under the shade of a nearby tree to protect themselves from the blazing heat. They had both relaxed whilst eating and with the earlier embarrassing events behind them, Philip was able to talk at length about his wartime experiences. Teresa just let him talk, knowing that this was the best and most cathartic way for him to rid himself of his nightmares.

By the time they left the cinema, arm in arm late that evening, they had become a man and woman out together like every other courting couple around.

The next few months for Edward were quite different than for Philip.

Edward's life was a hectic round of fitting in weekend visits to France whenever he could, whilst at the same time trying to cope with studying for his solicitor's exams. He had joined the local firm of Hastings and Hepplewhite, and although he had gained his law degree before joining the army, he still needed to complete the professional examinations before he could call himself a solicitor. He wanted to finish them as quickly as possible so that he could show Juliette's father of his intention to give Juliette a good life in England.

Tom and Mary had been shocked when the first thing their son had told them on returning home from being demobbed was that he was getting married to some French girl that they had never met. They were even more shocked when he told them of their intention to get married before Christmas if it could be arranged.

Juliette's family visited England at the end of September and after spending a few days with Hilda's mother had been invited to spend a long weekend with Edward's parents. The visit was a complete success. Tom took to Juliette straight away and although Mary had been very wary at first, she relented as soon as she realised that this girl was as besotted with her son as he was with her.

The conversation soon turned to the subject of the proposed wedding with both sets of parents trying to convince Edward and Juliette to delay the marriage at least until Edward had qualified.

The lovers sat quietly together whilst all this was going on, but eventually Edward had heard enough, "There's nothing you can say that will put us off. We've been apart for far too many years already, and of course we'd like your blessing to the arrangements, nevertheless we both feel that two people in their mid twenties like us are old enough to go ahead without their parent's consent if necessary." He turned and looked at Juliette to check that she was in agreement with him, before adding, "We want you all to be there and share the day with us, but if you're not." He paused before adding, "Then we'll get married anyway."

Both Raoul and Tom reacted forcefully against this implied threat, and it took Madeleine once again to bring order to the conversation before it got totally out of hand. Soon Madeleine had won over both mothers who now joined Madeleine in supporting the lovers. After much more discussion, it was finally agreed that the wedding would take place in France on Juliette's twenty-sixth birthday on New Year's Eve with the Guilberts making all the necessary arrangements, including finding accommodation for Edward, his family and any friends he wanted at the wedding.

In the event, the only ones who travelled from England for the wedding with Edward were his mother; father; his Grandma Hadley; Philip, who had been pleased to be asked to be Edward's best man, and Philip's mother.

For Juliette and Edward it was the happiest day of their life and it was again obvious to everyone how much in love they both were. The happiness of the wedding was only marginally happier than the two day's honeymooning they spent in Paris before they returned to England to start married life together.

Edward finished work at lunchtime on the Thursday before the Whitsunday bank holiday, as arranged. The idea was that as soon as he had packed the car and they had some lunch, he and Juliette would drive to Portsmouth to catch the overnight ferry to France for their first visit to Juliette's parents since their marriage. But when he arrived home, he was perturbed to find that Juliette was not in. Instead he found a note from her on the hall table where he always dropped his house keys.

He quickly opened the note.

'Darling
I've had to pop into town but should not be long.
May even be back before you see this note.
All my love, J.'

The note ended with a complete line of *xxxxx's.*

He could not think of any reason why she would have wanted to go into town. She had been excited for the last month about this trip and he was sure that all they needed for the visit was in the packed cases sitting in the hall. They had even bought small gifts for Madeleine and her parents. So why on earth did she need to go into town?

He decided to start packing the car, but looking at his watch he realised that the next bus was due at any moment. He dropped the case by the door and went to the gate arriving just as the bus passed the house. To his relief the bus stopped at the stop fifty yards up the road. He waited with baited breath, as the conductor helped old Mrs Wilson from the other side of the road off the bus. He thought the conductor was going to jump back on the bus, but in fact, he held his hand to help Juliette off. As soon as she saw Edward, she beamed her usual broad and glorious smile. He walked towards her, surprised to notice that she only had her handbag with her. No shopping, what had she needed to go to town for?

"Wait until we get into the house. I'll tell you soon enough."

Inside the house she walked straight into the kitchen, took off her coat and handed it to Edward, before sitting in the fireside chair.

Edward rushed back from hanging up her coat, "Well? What did you need from town? Surely we could have picked up anything you need on our way?"

She smiled and took his hands in hers. She guided them to her stomach and held them there, "Not this we couldn't!"

It took Edward a full ten seconds for the penny to drop, by which time Juliette had started to tell him in more detail where she had been.

"I missed my period last month. I'm sorry I didn't say anything in case it was just one of those things, but I should have had another period by now, so I thought I should go to see the doctor."

Edward was speechless; he just lifted her from the chair and held her to him. He kissed her on the cheek before asking, "And are you?"

"Well Doctor Stokes thinks so, but he wants me to go back to see him in another month to make sure."

Edward spent the next quarter of an hour fussing over Juliette, constantly talking and asking questions, "Shall we go and see Mom and Dad and tell them before we go?" Juliette shook her head from side to side. Edward shook his head in unison, "No. You don't want to tell them yet do you?"

She shook her head again, "Not just yet. Let's just get the things in the car and we can talk about it on the way."

Edward had almost forgotten about the trip but suddenly became quite agitated, "Do you think we should call it off? What if it's a bad crossing and you get sick? No. I think we should stay here."

It was now Juliette's turn to fuss over Edward. She held her arm out, pulling him to the seat beside her, "Now don't be silly. I'm having a baby. It's something women do you know. It's perfectly normal and although you don't seem to have noticed, I've felt sick almost every morning for the last couple of weeks anyway. So if I'm sick on the boat, it probably won't be the waves causing the problem."

She took his hands into hers, “Look, let’s have some lunch; we can talk about everything on the way. We don’t want to miss the boat, do we?” She laughed as she gave him a quick peck on the lips, “And I’m sorry that I didn’t say anything before. Do you forgive me?”

He just nodded his head with a broad smile across his face, “Of course; I could forgive you anything.”

“So you won’t mind if we tell Ma and Pa when we see them then, even though we haven’t said anything to your parents? It’s just that I would like to tell them face to face now and not in a letter in a few weeks?”

“And when will we tell my parents then?”

“Can we wait until next month to make absolutely certain that everything’s OK?”

Edward was so happy that he readily agreed.

Juliette was so anxious to tell her parents the news that no sooner had they sat down after their arrival, she announced her pregnancy to them. Her parents did not immediately show the pleasure that she had expected. Edward could tell that she was hurt at this lack of enthusiasm.

Madeleine, who was overjoyed at the news, had obviously sensed this as well and once again came to the rescue. She jumped out of her seat and came and gave Juliette a hug, “You clever girl, that’s wonderful news.” She turned and gave Edward a hug, before returning to hug Juliette again, “So when exactly am I going to have a nephew or niece?

Probably the end of January, beginning of February, but I’ve a long time to go yet and anything could happen.”

“You’ll be fine, won’t she Edward?”

“Well I’ll do my best to look after her.”

But Madeleine was not listening to his answer and was asking more questions before Edward had finished, “Do you want a boy or a girl? And have you thought of any names yet?”

Gradually Madeleine’s enthusiasm brought her parents round and they too were asking questions about the plans for the pregnancy and the baby.

“What did the doctor say?” “Is he sure the baby is all right?” “What did he say about looking after yourself?”

Juliette tried to answer as many of the questions as she could, but when asked, “And will you be coming back here to have the baby?” she was rather stumped for an answer, as it was something she and Edward had not spoken about on the journey.

She looked across at Edward for help because she knew that to say she was going to have the baby in England would probably upset her mother.

“We haven’t yet decided Madame Guilbert but I think it would be best if

Juliette didn't travel in the last week or so."

Juliette's mother was about to say something, but before she could Edward continued speaking, "Why don't you visit just before the baby is due and if you stayed until after the birth, I'm sure Juliette would love to have your help?"

"Well I could probably stay for a few weeks, couldn't I, Raoul?"

Edward now wished he hadn't made the offer, a few weeks was certainly not what he had in mind, but it was too late to withdraw the offer now.

Madeleine came to the rescue, yet again, "What if I go over with you, Ma? We could travel together and I'm sure I could manage to get away for maybe a week or even ten days."

The questions and the arrangements that needed to be made about the forthcoming birth were the main topic of conversation for the whole of the weekend, and, at times, Juliette almost wished her mother would change the subject. She was pleased that her mother was now showing enthusiasm about the baby, but she also wished that she and Edward had sorted out more between themselves before she had mentioned it at home. So, on their way back to England, they talked at length about what they each really wanted, and determined to sort out all their answers ready for the next time they visited.

However, Juliette did not have an easy pregnancy and although her mother had been to England and spent a week with Juliette in the summer, the next time Juliette and Edward visited her parents in France was over the following Christmas holiday.

They arrived on the day before Christmas Eve and were staying until the day after Boxing Day. Juliette had felt much better for the last two months, and although the boat crossing had been a bit rough, by the time they arrived at her parent's home she was feeling better than she had done in a long time and looked the picture of health. Or at least as much as a blossoming and large pregnant woman could. The questions flowed thick and fast again, but this time, all the plans for the birth were in hand and Juliette had all her answers ready.

"I'm going to have the baby in the maternity hospital in Bloxwich, and even if Edward is at work when I start, he should be able to get home and get me to the hospital in just over half an hour. So everything will be fine."

"And what if Edward is out on business when you call him?" interrupted her mother, ever the worrier.

"Oh, that's fine, I have a long list of people I can call on to take me. His mother and father are only on the other end of a telephone and could be with me in no time, and there are loads of others who've offered to help, so there's absolutely no need to worry, Ma. I'm sure we've thought of everything."

Juliette had only eaten half of her lunch on Boxing Day when she asked to be excused, saying she wanted to go and lie down, "I've probably been doing too much, and I've certainly been eating too much."

Edward got up out of his chair and took her arm, "I'll help you up the stairs but are you sure you're all right? You're looking a little pale."

"No I'm fine, just an upset tummy and I need a little sleep." She took Edward's hand from her arm, "I can manage on my own. You sit down and finish your lunch. I'll be just fine when I've had a sleep."

After lunch, the four of them played cards. Whist was not Edward's game, and he and Madeleine lost all the games in the first rubber, but after losing the first game in the second rubber went on to win it. In the third rubber they managed to win the second game, "Everything rests on this game, Madeleine. Do you think we can win?"

Hilda collected all the cards together and shuffled them, but instead of dealing them, she got up from her chair and handed them to Edward, "Just hold on to these for a minute Edward. I think I just heard Juliette moaning up stairs. I'll just go and check."

"Are you sure?" Raoul asked, "I didn't hear anything."

"Maybe it was nothing, but I'll check anyway," and with that she left.

Raoul reached for the whisky bottle, "Can I pour anyone another drink?" but before anyone had time to answer Hilda was calling from the top of the stairs.

"Edward, can you come up here, we need your help?"

Edward bounded up the stairs as fast as he could. Juliette was sitting on the bed, her arms wrapped around her bulging stomach. Her mother had her arms around her and was stroking her hair.

A very worried Edward asked, "What's the matter, sweetheart? Are you all right?"

It was Hilda who answered, "No I don't think she is. She says she's been having pains."

He moved to the other side of the bed and sat on it, "What pains sweetheart? Where are they?"

Again it was Hilda who answered, "Well the way Juliette described them, they sound very much like labour pains to me." She turned and looked at Juliette; her face now only inches from her daughter's, "Are you sure you've got your dates right, Juliette. I thought you had a good month to go yet."

"Yes I'm sure." She took her mother's arm from her shoulders and lay back on the bed, "Anyway I'm OK now. I haven't had any more pain since you came up, Ma. So like I said before I came up, I've probably been eating too much."

"Edward leaned over and kissed her on the forehead, "You go back to sleep, sweetheart."

He turned to his mother-in-law, "Why don't you go back down stairs? I'll stay here with Juliette and I'll give you a call if she gets any more pain."

"I think I'll stay here as well for a bit. Just too make sure."

Edward knew there was no point arguing with her on this matter, and they both sat on the bed, one each side of Juliette, without speaking.

Ten minutes later, Juliette opened her eyes, and rolled her legs upwards and grimaced as the pain returned.

Juliette turned for comfort from Edward, but her mother immediately asked her daughter to describe the nature of the pain. "That certainly sounds like labour pains to me, but whatever it is, I think we'd better get it checked out as soon as possible."

"Where do you suggest we take her?" was Edward's immediate response. He tried to keep the panic from his voice as he said, "It's Boxing Day, is there anyone we can get to help? Is there a doctor we can call?"

"I'll go and ask Raoul, but I think the best thing to do would be to take her to the cottage hospital. It's run by nuns and some of them are trained in midwifery. I know they have maternity facilities there, so that's probably the best place for us to go."

She got up to go, but stopped at the door, turned round and spoke to Edward, "Get a few of Juliette's things together Edward, just in case it is the baby coming," and as she left the room, she muttered to herself, but sufficiently loud for Juliette to hear, "You must have your dates wrong."

Juliette had tears in eyes as she shook her head and whispered to Edward, "I'm sure I haven't. I've always been so careful to note my periods in my diary."

Edward hugged her, "It doesn't matter now, sweetheart. We just need to sort this out, and if it is the baby coming early, then you need to just try and relax." He kissed her on each cheek as he helped her up from the bed, "I'm sure everything will be OK, so stop worrying. At least it's better to sort it out today rather than have problems on the boat tomorrow."

"But I'm sure my dates are right!"

"I'm sure they are. Like you say, it's probably just something you've eaten. But your mother's right. We should get it sorted."

Just as they were about to go, Juliette had another bout of pain and she had to rest again before leaving the house. On seeing his daughter doubled up for the first time, Raoul decided to telephone the cottage hospital before they left to ask if they could make sure a doctor was in attendance when they arrived and when he put down the phone he told the others what had been said.

"The Sister I spoke to said that the doctor they usually called on is away for the holiday break, but that Mother Superior was medically trained and two of the Sisters were qualified midwifes so that between them they'll be able to sort out any problem. She was going to let Mother Superior know we're on our way, so not to worry as they'll be ready to check Juliette over as soon as we arrive."

"Are you sure they can't get in touch with another doctor?" Hilda asked.

"The Sister didn't really answer the question when I asked. She just said she didn't think it was necessary. She's sure the Sisters will manage perfectly well."

By the time they reached the hospital some half an hour later, Juliette was again experiencing another bout of pain. As soon as she entered the building a nun took charge of her, "Venez avec moi ma chère, l'infirmièse va vous examiner."

Both Edward and Hilda started to follow. The nun stopped their progress. "Je vous demande de vous mettre là. Je ne pense que pas cela prenne longtemps et si tōt que j'ai des nouvelles je vous le ferai savoir."

Although the sister had merely 'suggested' that they sit and wait, it was spoken in such a way as to clearly indicate it was an order.

"I caught the first bit about sitting and waiting," Edward said as soon as they had sat down, "But what was the rest? She spoke too quickly for me to catch it."

Hilda took his hand and squeezed it, "She just said to wait here and she'd let us know as soon as they know anything themselves."

It was at least half an hour before a different Sister came out to talk to them. She stood directly in front of Edward and spoke with what he detected was a distinct American accent, "Juliette tells me you are English Mr Richards, and has asked me to make sure that you know what is going on, so I will speak in English."

She then looked at Raoul and Hilda, "On en discutera une fois que j'aurai parlé à Monsieur Richards."

"That will not be necessary, Sister. We both speak English."

"Ah, bon. That will save me saying it twice." She turned her attention back to Edward, "I am Sister Beatrice and I have checked Juliette over thoroughly. She says she's not due for another month, but I am certain that the pains she has been feeling are contractions. I have listened to the baby's heart, and it seems fine at the moment and I cannot find anything untoward or anything to worry about."

Edward listened carefully but was nevertheless concerned. He knew that Juliette had not made any mistakes over the date, "But she is only eight months, isn't that going to cause a problem?"

"I shouldn't think so. It will probably be a smallish baby, but nine months is not an exact timescale you know. Plenty of women have early babies and everything is fine."

"Can I go and see her now?" Edward asked.

She did not answer immediately but asked, "Do you mind if I sit down with you for a while?"

Edward stood and moved to the next chair so that she could sit between him and Hilda. Once seated, she spoke to Hilda, "I think it would be best if we let her rest for now, don't you Madame Guilbert? She's in the very early stages and it will be a long time before things start moving. I'm sure you know Madame Guilbert that a first baby can take hours to be born."

She then turned and spoke to Raoul, "I take it you have a telephone at home, Monsieur Guilbert." Raoul nodded. "Well why don't you all go home, have something to eat and have a rest, and I'll give you a call as soon as anything starts happening."

Again the suggestion was said in such a way that it seemed like an order to Edward. *"Are all these nuns as bossy as this?"* he thought to himself.

It was almost as though Sister Beatrice had read his mind, because she immediately looked him directly in the eye, "We only want to do what is best for Juliette. Mr Richards, and right now, I'm sure Juliette would like to get some rest." She stood up, once more facing them all, "So why don't you just pop in and say goodbye and tell her you'll be back in the morning." She looked at Edward, "You could well be a father by then, Monsieur Richards," and then looking at Hilda and Raoul in turn added, "And you could be a grand-mère and grand-père by then." She held out her hand to shake each of theirs in turn, "So just pop in for two minutes and we'll see you in the morning. I'll call you if I feel it is necessary before them," and with that she went to walk away.

Edward immediately touched the Sister on her arm. She turned to look at Edward but just continued walking, "This is the way to your wife, Mr Richards. You must only stay a minute though. She needs her rest."

"No. I'm sorry but I'm going to stay with her."

Sister Beatrice stopped and gazed at Edward in obvious incredulity, "That is not necessary. We will look after her."

She turned to walk away believing that was the end of the matter, but Edward once again caught her arm, "I'm sure you will look after her fine, and I thank you for that, but I'm staying here. Juliette and I have agreed that I should be with her when she gives birth."

This time the Sister's reaction was even more unmistakable. She glared aggressively at Edward, "I don't think so, Mr Richards. We don't have any of that nonsense here. Husbands are not required at the birth. It is most certainly not their place to be present."

Edward was not prepared to be put off, "But that is exactly what Juliette wants. She is the one giving birth, not anyone else. So ask her. I'm sure it's what she wants."

The Sister was now becoming belligerent, "And what has that got to do with anything, may I ask? I am in charge here and we certainly don't want men around getting in our way."

Edward was about to say more but Hilda stood between them facing Edward. She put her finger to her mouth as an indication for Edward to calm down before turning to face the Sister. "I do know that is what Juliette wants. She has spoken about it many times, but just let me have a chat with Edward and perhaps we can pop and see you after we've seen Juliette?"

Hilda's intervention had the desired effect of calming down both Sister Beatrice and Edward. The Sister merely nodded her head and went on her way, and the three of them returned to the seats and sat down.

As soon as they were seated Edward protested to Hilda, "I am staying here, even if they chuck me out of the room when the baby is coming. I can't go home with you and just sit around wondering what's happening all the while."

Hilda was now more tender towards Edward than he had ever known her. She took his head in her hands and kissed his forehead before speaking, "I know my sweet. I know it isn't what either of you wanted. I know the maternity hospital back home had agreed you could be there, but unfortunately things haven't worked out as you expected have they?" She pressed her hands into his cheeks and shook her head before continuing, "None of us wanted it this way. We're all in shock about it, but the one we should really think about is darling Juliette in there. She needs the Sisters to look after her now and if we keep antagonising them, it will be poor Juliette who'll suffer." She mover her head closer to Edward's and stared directly in his eyes, "And we all want what's best for her, don't we?"

Edward, tears now running down his face, nodded in agreement.

Hilda smiled and continued, "So why don't I go and see the Sister;

explain how you want to stay here and just keep Juliette company for a while. I'm sure she will agree to that if I also tell her that when they want to check on Juliette, or when the baby is finally coming, you will leave the room as soon as they ask you too."

Edward merely nodded his head without saying anything.

Hilda took a handkerchief from her handbag and wiped his eyes, "And when the baby is born, you can be right here to go in as soon as they've tidied things up. I'm sure the Sister won't mind that."

Hilda later came out of the Sister's office smiling. Everything had been agreed.

The rising winter sunlight was streaming directly through the window at daybreak the next morning. Edward had been with Juliette all night, gently talking to her between the contractions and holding her hand tightly through them. He woke with a start, annoyed with himself for having fallen asleep.

"I'm sorry, sweetheart. How long have I been asleep?"

Juliette was lying there smiling at him and about to answer, when she winced at the next contraction.

At that moment, Sister Beatrice entered the room, "If you just pop out now Mr Richards, I can check everything is OK."

Edward did as he was bid, but was allowed back into the room five minutes later. "We're getting there but very slowly I'm afraid. A few hours to go yet I think," was all the Sister said.

And so the pattern repeated itself throughout the day. Contraction followed contraction, but they did not seem to be getting any closer. Sister Beatrice came in at regular intervals, and after sending Edward out of the room would examine Juliette and announce, "Not yet, I'm afraid. But don't worry; it can go on for a couple of days sometimes."

Edward was let back into the room. Cups of tea, coffee and even sandwiches were brought in by the other Sisters. Hilda, Madeleine and Raoul visited in the afternoon but were only allowed to stay for five minutes. By eight o'clock that evening when Sister Beatrice came to check on Juliette, both Juliette and Edward were exceptionally tired and exhausted and beginning to wonder whether their baby would ever be born.

Edward had been timing the contractions and for the last hour they had been coming more often, but he was also becoming increasingly concerned about Juliette. She was definitely becoming more and more pallid and seemed unable to keep her eyes open. She was now rarely smiling at him and when he squeezed her hand she seemed unable to squeeze his back.

He mentioned all of this to Sister Beatrice when she came out of the room after examining Juliette.

"Yes I know, but she hasn't had any sleep in the last two days so one would expect her to be somewhat exhausted. But the good news is I believe the baby will put in an appearance soon, so with a bit of luck she should be able to have a night's sleep tonight."

At the next examination, Edward was sent out of the room permanently and he had to sit in the corridor waiting.

He tried to keep his eyes open but was awoken some time later by the banging of doors. Everyone seemed to be rushing in and out of the room, fetching towels, bandages and all sorts of weird instruments. He could hear Sister Beatrice giving orders in the room, but she was speaking in French too quickly for him to catch what she was saying. It did however seem to him, that gradually the instructions became more and more tense and volatile.

A young novice came running out of the room, went straight past Edward without even glancing at him, and ran out of the front entrance. She didn't even bother to shut the door behind her but left it wide open; the cold winter wind blowing on to Edward's face. Five minutes later she returned with a priest in tow, and both ignored Edward, neither of them looking at him or acknowledging him as they hurried along.

Edward was now distraught and shouted after them, "What on earth is going on?" but they did not stop or answer him. He got up and followed them to the delivery room. His way was barred at the door by the novice. He went to push past her, but stopped frozen when he saw the sight in front of him. The sheet covering Juliette was covered in blood. Sister Beatrice was kneeling at her feet trying to stop the flow of blood streaming to the floor and the priest was now standing at Juliette's side giving her the last rites.

Edward was violently sick before he passed out.

Four days later, on Juliette's twenty-seventh birthday, the same congregation were gathered in the same church as were there exactly twelve months earlier. All the attention was again on Juliette, but this time, she was not the gloriously beautiful and radiant bride, but was hidden in the wooden box in front of the priest, who was tediously and unemotionally working his way through the Requiem Mass in monotone Latin.

Edward had not had any proper sleep since the last time he had slept with Juliette at his side on Christmas night. As he now stood, sat, and kneeled in unison with everyone else, he became overwhelmed with anger at the events of four days earlier. He had been too distraught with the loss of the love of his life to think of anything else until now, but why hadn't the Sisters saved his wife instead of the baby? He determined there and then that his brief twelve month encounter with Catholicism was over. He had questioned the existence of God, over and over again as he witnessed the death and destruction during the war, but since marrying Juliette he had for her sake tried to put all his doubts behind him. He had tried to forgive this God for everything he had seen in the war, but no longer. How could any God do this to Juliette and take her away from him?

The tedious Latin ritual stopped and he sat down when everyone else did. The priest now went to the pulpit and gabbled away in French. Edward tried to concentrate but found it almost physically impossible to do so. Every now and then he heard the odd word.

How dare this damn priest talk about Juliette like this? She wasn't in the arms of Jesus. She was in that coffin, dead and lost to him for ever. How dare he suggest that it was anyone's will that Juliette should die so that the child should live? He wanted to shout out with rage and tell the priest to shut up. Instead he broke down in uncontrollable distress, shaking and shedding the tears that he had been too much in shock to shed previously.

He continued to shake and weep for the rest of the service, nothing around had any meaning whatsoever to him any more. As the coffin passed him on the way out of the church, he wished he was in there with Juliette or better still was in there instead of her. Everyone was waiting for Edward to follow the coffin out of the church, but he just stood there, motionless. Philip came forward from two rows behind and took his arm. Madeleine moved to the other side of him and together one on each side of him, they helped and guided him along behind the coffin. They stayed at his side steadying him for the journey to the cemetery and at the graveside.

Madeleine took his hand and guided it to the box so that Edward could be the first to throw soil onto the coffin now resting six feet below at the bottom of the grave.

His eyes never left the coffin for the whole of the proceedings at the graveside; everything done and everything said to him had been a total blur.

His mind was in a complete whirl, but as he was helped away from the graveside, he vowed to himself that he would never again enter a church or have any dealings with their cruel, merciless and heartless God.

Edward had left the Guilbert's house early on New Year's Day; the day after the funeral; intending to get away before he had to talk to anyone about anything and without ever seeing his new born son. He knew he should feel something toward the child, but in his present angry state at what at happened, he knew that to see his son or talk about him to anyone would cause him to erupt into an uncontrollable rage in which anything could happen. At heart he knew that Juliette's death was not the child's fault, but right now he blamed everyone including the child and himself. But most of all he blamed the nuns and their Catholic Church's principles. He could not forgive them even if he had wanted to; and right now he did not wish to. It was their church, whose dictates about God's will and demands they all believed in, that had caused them to suggest that Juliette's death at the expense of the new born child's life was God's will.

"How dare they suggest that my wife's death was anyone's will?"

Even before Juliette was cold and in her coffin, people had been telling him that he had to think of his son now; that was what Juliette would have wanted. Others had suggested that no one was to blame for her death; it was just one of things. But, Edward wanted to blame someone because he knew that, at that moment in time to absolve others of her death would mean that the only one left to blame was himself. And that was his nightmare; the terrifying reality of which was slowly driving him mad. In this state of mind he knew he was not emotionally capable of talking about, and even less of actually making, any arrangements for his son's care or upbringing.

His only release was to go and let others sort things out. He crept down the stairs and opened the front door as quietly as he could, but as he tried to pull it closed noiselessly behind him, it was held open by some other force.

"And where do you think you are going at this time in the morning?" It was Madeleine who was in bare feet and still pulling on her dressing gown.

Edward just looked at her, unable to say or do anything.

"Come into the kitchen a bit. I'll freeze out here dressed like this. It will be a bit warmer by the range in the kitchen."

She led Edward into the kitchen and after making coffee for them; they sat silently for quite a while before Edward finally opened up and spoke of his feelings for the first time.

As they spoke Edward realised that Madeleine not only understand his pain but gradually he came to understand that she and many others were in as great a pain as he was. He also realised that for Madeleine the pain was also mixed with some of the anger he was feeling. But none of it really helped. Half and hour later he was still as determined as ever that for him, he would have to go back home and suffer in solitude.

"What do you propose to do about the baby? Sister Beatrice said we could bring him home soon."

“I can’t think about that now. Will you sort it all for me?”

Madeleine just shrugged her shoulders and nodded her head without saying anything.

“I have to go Madeleine. If I don’t go right now, I know I’ll go mad trying to cope with everyone around.” He got up, picked up his bags, kissed Madeleine on the top of her head and left without a further word.

On returning home, he shut himself away, refusing to see any of his family and friends. His mother did call every day to bring him something to eat, but in the first few days he only ate any of it when she insisted that she was not going until he had eaten something. They sat in total silence as she watched him eat. Eventually, after a few days, they did manage to have brief conversations together, but at any mention of Juliette or the baby he would clam up and return to his usual silence.

This continued for most of January, but towards the end of the month Madeleine arrived unannounced. She refused Edward’s mother’s offer to put her up, insisting instead that she and Edward had a lot to talk about and so she would prefer to stay at Edward’s house.

Madeleine prepared supper and they each ate it sparingly, leaving most uneaten on the plate. Afterwards they sat in silence each with a glass of Edward’s whisky in their hand and the bottle on the coffee table ready for refills, but slowly after several whiskies they were able to talk. At first about things in general but then Edward mentioned Juliette’s name and gradually they reached a point where they shared the pain they felt. The tears flowed and flowed until there was no more left to shed and little by little that shared pain became slightly more bearable.

Edward had always found it easy to talk to Madeleine and eventually he opened up and started making some of the decisions he had previously avoided.

It was agreed that Edward was in no fit state to look after the baby and he readily accepted when Madeleine said that her mother was prepared to look after him for the time being.

This agreed, Madeleine moved on to the next question, “And what name do you want to give him?”

“I haven’t even thought about it. Juliette did not want us to definitely settle on any names until the baby arrived. I think she thought it would be bad luck if we did. Why don’t you choose? You knew Juliette as well as any one. What do you think she would have liked?”

“I don’t know but mother’s been calling him Julian. I think that’s because it’s the nearest boy’s name to Juliette, and that it somehow helps her to think of him as part of Juliette.”

It was not a name that Edward would ever have thought of, but nevertheless he did not even think any more about it before saying, "If that's what your mother wants then Julian it is."

Over the next few days they talked about all aspects of their lives. On the evening before Madeleine was due to return home, they were again drinking whisky together when Madeleine commented that Juliette's death had made her realise that nothing in life was certain. She took another swig of the whisky and said, "You know what?" and without waiting for an answer announced, "From now on I'm going to live my life for today and not put off anything until tomorrow." She took another drink and with a great smile on her face said, "And I've just decided that when I get home I'm going to tell Maurice that if he wants to marry me he better do so straight away before I change my mind. I shall tell him that I want to get married before the end of February or he'll have missed his chance."

She looked directly at Edward, "And as for you Mr Richards, you'd better sort yourself out, because I want you at my wedding as the number one guest. And I shall tell Maurice that the wedding is off if you don't agree. Oh and by the way bring Philip with you. He'll be company for you and anyway I would like him to come to my wedding as well."

Finally then, it was Madeleine who brought Edward back into the real world. He returned to work the day after Madeleine left and by the time of the wedding three weeks later, he was beginning to cope with life and all it had to throw at him.

He saw his son for the first time on Madeleine's wedding day but felt nothing towards him. He was just a baby, anybody's baby, and he made no attempt to hold him; and certainly made no attempt to bond in any way with him. He left the following day after putting fresh flowers on Juliette's grave, but without seeing his son again.

On the ferry trip back from the wedding, Philip tried to get Edward to talk about Juliette; a subject that had somehow always been avoided since the funeral. But Edward interrupted him as soon as he mentioned Juliette's name by saying that Juliette, her death and his son, were barred subjects and were not to be brought up by Philip on any occasion either then or in the future.

Following the initial total despair and antagonism towards everything and everyone, on his return from Madeleine's wedding, Edward relentlessly and unceasingly immersed himself in work in order to fill every second of every day to block out any thoughts of anything else.

He rarely saw Philip, and when he did, Juliette's name was never mentioned.

And that was how it was for the following six months until one evening, Edward phoned Philip and asked him to come over to see him. No sooner had they sat down than Edward said, "I really loved Juliette you know?"

Not knowing what was coming next, "Yes, I know," was all that Philip could say.

"I know we were only properly together for just a year, but it was the best twelve months of my life.

"Yes I know," was again all that Philip could say.

"And you know what Philip?" But he did not wait for an answer, "I wouldn't have wanted to miss that twelve months especially if I'd known it was all we were to get together. I just wish it hadn't happened that way though. She didn't deserve to die like that."

Philip put his hand on Edward's shoulder, and feeling that perhaps he was expected to make a comment, said, "I know she didn't. But it was obvious to everyone how you two felt about each other. She loved you to bits, you know. And I'm sure it was the best year of her life too."

"Do you really think so? Do you think she really loved me that much?

Philip nodded his agreement, "I know she did, and so did everyone else."

Tears suddenly appeared in Edward's eyes, "Yes, but would she have wanted to have had that particular twelve months if she'd known what was going to happen?

This was the question that Philip knew he could not answer; a catch 22 in which it was impossible to give an answer 'Yes' or 'No'. Perhaps Edward realised the dilemma he had put Philip in, because he did not wait for an answer but immediately asked, "Mother tells me you are seeing more of Teresa these days. Any chance of any wedding bells soon?"

"Whoa; slow down a bit. We're just good friends and I don't know that I feel that way about her."

"If you mean that you don't feel what I felt about Juliette, then maybe that's a good thing. If you love too much, then it just hurts all the more when it ends. I think you should do what I intend to do from now on. Live for the day. Marry the girl before it's all too late." But Philip had no intention of heeding Edward's advice. Not for now anyway.

In the following six years Edward only visited France and Juliette's grave four times and although he saw his son on each of the visits there was never any connection between the two of them. If it hadn't been for the fact that Madeleine wrote to him letting him know how Julian was getting on, he would never have known anything about his son.

CHAPTER EIGHTEEN

1953

By 1953, life had changed considerably for both Philip and Edward.

During Edward's marriage to Juliette the two friends rarely met and only saw each other on family occasions. Following Juliette's death, Philip had tried to be there for his friend, and whilst this had worked for a few months, they very soon started to drift apart again as they each became more and more involved in their new careers.

For Edward, life had changed in ways he almost certainly would never have chosen if Juliette was still alive. Initially he immersed himself in work and after qualifying as a solicitor was made a partner of the firm, now called Hastings, Hepplewhite and Richards but soon become bored with the routine of seeing clients about petty and minor issues.

His father Tom suggested he should become involved in local politics and perhaps stand for the local council. At first, he only agreed to do this as a means of filling his free time, hoping it would prevent him from being on his own and having to deal with his continued sadness. However, once elected he became totally involved in all manner of local affairs and was quickly recognised as the up and coming star of the local labour party. And when the local MP died suddenly of a heart attack at the end of April, Edward was selected as candidate and throughout the whole of June 1953 he was engrossed in canvassing and attending meetings arranged by his agent in various local schools and halls.

For Philip, life had moved on in a much more predictable way. After joining the family firm he had successfully settled into all aspects of the business. At first he was mainly involved in the manufacturing business where his Uncle Tom and Lucy Evans had been pleased to let him take some of the ever growing pressure away from them and had quickly become an indispensable decision maker, enabling the non military side of the business to steadily grow. His mother, who wanted to take things easier, had quickly recognised his management ability and with Tom and Lucy's approval had made him the Managing Director of her expanding retail business, and so Philip had to share his time between the two enterprises.

By 1953 business was still good on the manufacturing side, but for the shop outlets trade was booming. Under Philip's management more shops were opened and sales were increasing month on month. There had been a dip in sales in 1948, when the purchase tax on radios and televisions had been increased to over sixty-six per cent, but sales had picked up again since then, and had received a tremendous boost over the last few months.

The coronation of the young Queen Elizabeth was to be not only the biggest national event of celebration since the end of the war, but also the largest outside television broadcast ever. People in their thousands were buying television sets in readiness for the event, and Grace's foresight in realising years earlier that television was the entertainment media of the future by forging distribution contracts with the manufacturers, had given their high street shops a head start on most of their rivals.

In his personal life, Philip had decided on his thirtieth birthday that a man of that age ought to have a wife and so he had married Teresa in the autumn of 1950. He had settled comfortably into the role of husband, and was for the most part happy that he had taken the decision to wed. However, Teresa had wanted to have a baby as soon as they were married and was now getting increasingly distressed that, over two years after the wedding, she was still not pregnant. At first this had not caused a problem but gradually it started creating more and more stress between them.

The week before the coronation, Philip returned home to find Teresa in tears yet again. He had been greeted in this way at regular monthly intervals for almost a year. He tried to console his wife as best he could, but he knew that the usual, "These things sometimes take time," would no longer be sufficient.

"Why don't you go and see the doctor? Perhaps there's something physically preventing it."

"Oh, I see. It's my fault is it? I don't suppose you've ever thought that you could be the problem, have you?"

Philip was shocked at this comment as he had never considered it possible that he could be the reason that Teresa had not become pregnant. He sat there in silence wondering how to respond to the suggestion. Finally he said, "You're right, it could be me. So what I suggest is that if you're not pregnant by the time our wedding anniversary comes round, I think we should both go and see the doctor and see what he says."

Philip hoped that for the time being his answer had delayed the immediate problem; or at least he hoped that it had done so until the next month. He was expecting an immediate reaction from Teresa but before she could respond, the telephone started to ring.

"You'd better see who that is Philip. But if it's for me, you'll have to put them off because I can't speak to anyone right now."

"Oh, let it ring. It'll soon stop and they'll ring back if it is anything important," was Philip's response, but the phone did not stop ringing and he was eventually forced to get up and answer it.

It was Lucy Evans on the line and she sounded in a very distraught state. She did not go into her usual enquiries as to how he and Teresa were keeping, but immediately asked, "Can you spare me some time this evening if I come over? I think we have a problem that we need to talk about."

"What problem? Can't it wait until the morning? I was going to the new Liverpool store tomorrow, but I could put it off until the afternoon, so if you can be at the office a bit earlier, say seven thirty or quarter to eight, we can chat about it then."

"I don't think talking about it here at the factory is a good thing. I could be with you in less than half an hour and I really would like to talk to you tonight if possible. I shan't sleep if I have to wait until in the morning."

Philip, sensing the level of agitation in her voice, put his head in his free hand and thought to himself, *"And now I've two women's problems to sort out"*, but he knew Lucy wasn't the type to panic over nothing so he said, "Can you perhaps leave it for say an hour?" He looked at his watch; it was almost seven o'clock, "If you get here for say eight that would be fine."

He could sense the disappointment in her voice when she replied, "OK. See you about eight," and immediately put the phone down.

Philip had managed to calm Teresa by the time the bell rang at exactly eight o'clock and she was the perfectly calm and loving wife when she greeted Lucy at the door.

"Lovely to see you Lucy; how are things with you?" but Lucy merely replied with a polite, "Fine, thank you, and I trust you're keeping well?"

This was a question that Teresa did not wish to answer, so she replied with an equally polite, "Yes thank you," before excusing herself by saying, "I know you two have business to talk about and I have plenty to do, so if you don't mind I'll leave you to it." She was about to leave when she turned to Philip and said, "Let me know if you want me to make a drink," and without waiting for an answer she left the room.

"Would you like a cup of tea or coffee Lucy? Or would you like something stronger?"

"I think I need something stronger please."

Philip poured Lucy a sherry and a whisky for himself. "Now tell me what this is all about? What's so important that it can't wait 'til tomorrow?"

Lucy took a sip of her drink before replying. "Well as you know, we've been developing many new lines recently; particularly ones using the smaller valves and even some with the new printed circuits and we've had to use several new suppliers for parts. It's difficult to keep track of it all, but I do try to make sure that Tom has all the parts he needs in good time for production."

Philip nodded his head, "Yes I know all that, but please get to the point."

But Lucy would not be rushed and took another sip of sherry. "I was just packing up tonight, when Tom came to see me. He'd been sorting out from stores the parts he wanted for tomorrow's schedules, and when he came to give me the keys to the stores to lock away in the safe, he said he'd taken the last box of valves for the T27 model and would I order some more."

"So, where's the problem in that?"

"Patience please, Philip. I'm getting to that. I made a note of what he wanted and he left. I was about to put my coat on and lock up, when I remembered that I'd only signed a cheque to Bridges for a load of those same valves just three days ago. As you know we don't pay an invoice until we've received confirmation from stores that the goods have been received, so I got out the paperwork and sure enough a good's received note was pinned to the invoice with my signature on it showing that I'd issued the cheque."

"So what does that all mean? Perhaps Tom had just looked for them in the wrong rack or something."

"Well that's what I thought, but Tom had left by then and I was the only person in the building. So I took the stockroom key out of the safe and went to look for myself. I spent the next hour checking on every shelf and every box. They were nowhere to be found and I started to get a funny feeling about it all. I knew Tom and Mary were on some canvassing jaunt with Edward tonight, so that's when I phoned you."

"But I still don't see the panic. You'll probably be able to sort it all out with Tom in the morning. There's probably been some silly cock up somewhere."

"I don't know about that. Your Dad always taught me to trust my instincts and I have to tell you Philip, I've a really bad feeling about this."

"But why? I don't see it as a problem, just a silly mistake somehow."

Lucy stared directly at him, and smiled, "I knew that was what you'd say, so when you said you couldn't see me straight away, I decided to check when we had last ordered the same valves from Bridges." She finished her sherry and held her glass out to Philip for a refill. Whilst waiting she took a number of papers from her briefcase, and handed them to Philip in exchange for the refilled glass.

He looked over the papers. "These are all orders for valves from Bridges, but they all look all right to me. What am I supposed to see?"

She put her glass on the coffee table and took the papers from Philip. She flipped to the copy order sheet for two of the orders and held them out to Philip. "Those are the carbon copies of orders sent to the suppliers but we can't have used that many since then. And anyway, look at the signature."

Philip glanced at them, "So they both have my signature on them. The signature's a bit smudged through the carbon paper but I guess it was me who signed them."

"But look at the date on the last one and then check your diary. You weren't even at the factory on that date. So how could you have signed it?"

Philip knocked back the rest of his whisky with a gulp. "Well perhaps the wrong date was put on it."

"I hope it is as simple as that Philip, but I've got this real funny feeling about it and the more I think about it, the more I feel my instinct may be right. I sincerely hope not, but I can't get it out of my head that we have some sort of fiddle going on here. And right now, I've no idea what the fiddle is or who might be involved."

At that point Teresa came into the room with a tray of sandwiches. She had changed her dress and had put fresh make-up on her face. "There's a fresh pot of tea in the kitchen Philip. Can you fetch it please and bring in some cups with you? I should think Lucy is starving if she came straight here from work." She looked at Philip and then across at Lucy and said, "My word, you pair look mighty serious. Is it really that bad?"

Philip got up and as he left the room said, "I'll just fetch the tea and then perhaps we can all talk about it." On his return he looked at Lucy and asked, "Do you mind if we talk about this in front of Teresa?" He laughed as he added, "I'm pretty sure she can't have anything to do with it."

"Do with what?" Teresa looked from one to the other and back again waiting for a response.

Philip just shrugged his shoulders but it was Lucy who spoke, "I guess it won't do any harm to talk it through with Teresa. As an outsider she may even think of something we can't see."

And so Lucy went through it all again, and by the time she finished for the second time, Philip was convinced that they did indeed have a problem.

Initially he suggested that he and Lucy should get together with Tom first thing the next morning and go through all the paperwork; checking the stock against it all. It was Teresa who squashed that idea, "I reckon that if Lucy thinks someone, somewhere is fiddling the books then I would take the matter very seriously. If there is a fiddle going on and you start investigating it, you have absolutely no idea how or where it might lead. And since you have no idea who could be involved, wouldn't it better to try and get things checked when no one else is around? Otherwise, you could easily alert the person or persons involved and they could get rid of any evidence and then you really would have a problem to sort it out."

Lucy nodded her head, "Much as I don't want to leave this in the air for longer than necessary, I'm bound to agree that Teresa has a point. If someone is on the fiddle, then at the moment we have no idea whether it is someone in the office, or someone in stores, or even someone at Bridges, and we can't go around searching and asking questions of all and sundry until we at least know what we're dealing with."

They spent the next hour discussing several alternate plans of action and it was almost midnight by the time they had finally decided what route to take. They all agreed that Tom should be informed as soon as possible, and even though it was so late, it was decided that Philip should call his Uncle Tom at home and get his agreement to everything before they did anything more about it all.

It was a sleepy Tom who answered the phone, but he was soon wide awake when Philip had outlined the problem to him and readily agreed to the plan. Lucy would get to work a little earlier on the following morning and put all the papers back in their place before anyone else arrived. Tom would also arrive a little early and have a look in the storeroom to satisfy himself that the items had not just been missed. These days, arriving early was not unusual for either of them so that would not present a problem.

As soon as Philip arrived at the new Liverpool shop the next morning, he telephoned the company accountants and asked to speak to Mark Cartwright, the junior partner, who had been in the same school year as Philip at the grammar school. After quickly explaining the problem to Mark he asked if he had any advice about how to go about the checks they proposed to carry out at the factory on the following day, which being a Saturday would mean other staff would not be around.

"I think the best thing would be if I can get one of our people to come and give you a hand. I'd come myself but I've promised to take my wife and the children to my in-laws tomorrow and my life wouldn't be worth living if I tried to get out of that. I'll make sure I send someone who knows how to tackle it and I'll have a chat to them to make sure they go about it in the right way. I'll sort it all out this morning and I'll give you a call back and let you know who is coming."

"That'll be great Mark, but I'm in Liverpool today, so could you ring Lucy Evans at the factory and let her know. I'll ring her now and tell her to expect your call. You will make sure you only speak to Lucy though won't you?"

The next morning when Philip arrived at the factory, he found Lucy already at her desk pouring over the mountain of papers spread out in front of her. Normally Lucy was the epitome of decorum with an immaculate dress sense, but this morning her hair was all dishevelled, the usual pristine make-up was missing, and it appeared that she had not slept for days.

"Morning Lucy. How's it going? How long have you been here?"

Lucy looked up for the first time since Philip had entered the room, "Oh, hello Philip, I didn't hear you come in."

"Are you OK, Lucy? You look as if you've been at it all night."

"I just couldn't sleep last night so I got up and came in to look at things. I've been so worried about it all ever since we spoke on Thursday night and it was murder yesterday trying to act normally and not being able to check things out."

"Well we can sort it all out today. I'm sure it will be some sort of mistake and we'll soon get to the bottom of it."

"You don't actually believe that though, do you Philip? You wouldn't have phoned Mark Cartwright if that was all you thought was going on, would you?" Philip merely moved his head slightly as Lucy continued speaking, "Oh, by the way Mark did phone yesterday. He said he was sending Tony Morris and a Sam Prior to help us and that they'd be with us before nine o'clock."

Philip pulled up a chair, and sat opposite Lucy. "We've had Tony Morris here before haven't we? Isn't he the droopy one who never seems to know what he's doing?"

Lucy smiled; seeming to relax for the first time since he had arrived. "Yes, but he's also the good looking one that the girls downstairs always go gaga over. I've never heard of this Sam Prior before though." She stopped smiling and looked directly at Philip, "You didn't answer my question though. You don't actually believe all this is a mistake do you?"

Philip had been considering this issue for the last thirty-six hours and he could not see any way that the orders could be a mere mistake. He shook his head, "Unfortunately I don't, but hopefully it will be just the three Bridges' orders you showed to me."

"That's what I'd hoped Philip, but look at these." She scooped up a number of papers off her desk and passed them to Philip. "All of those are orders from Bridges over the last twelve months, and I'm sure we couldn't have used all those components in that time."

Before Philip was able to inspect the papers she picked up another paper and handed it to him, "That's a total of all those orders broken down into the different components ordered. If we'd used all those parts we'd have had to double the size of the production line by now."

Philip looked at the list and felt physically sick as he absorbed the detail on it, "You mean these are components actually ordered from Bridges. There's enough here to keep us going for months. When Uncle Tom arrives I'm sure he'll sort it all out. They must be in the stockroom somewhere."

Lucy looked askance at Philip, "Not if they never got to the stockroom."

"Never put in the stockroom? What do you mean? Haven't you checked these figures to the delivery forms?"

"Yes I have, but I now don't think that necessarily means they reached the stockroom."

"But I thought Uncle Tom had signed for the delivery of most of those items. Surely you don't mean that he's stolen the missing items?"

At this point they heard noises downstairs and Lucy put her finger to her mouth as a signal for them to be silent.

Two people, a man and a woman were talking as they made their way up the stairs to the offices. It was Tom who opened the door holding it open for a girl to enter in front of him. As she came through the door she looked directly at Philip and smiled. Philip wanted to smile back but he was transfixed by the freshness and beauty of the girl who walked straight up to him, holding out her hand to shake his, "Hi, I'm Sam Prior, Mr Matthews."

Philip jumped up from his seat, and shook her outstretched hand, managing a mere, "Hello." The girl's hand was smooth and warm in his, and he felt this unexplainable urge to grasp it with both hands and pull her closer to him. The girl's eyes moved and he became acutely aware that she was staring directly into his own eyes. However, as soon as she had his attention, her eyes fell to look at their clasped hands and he realised he'd been holding it longer than was socially necessary. He immediately let go of her hand and quickly dropped his own hand to his side with a jolt.

She smiled before turning towards Lucy, holding out her hand across the desk to shake Lucy's. "And you must be Mrs Evans. Mr Richards says this place couldn't run at all without you."

Philip stood to one side to let her shake Lucy's hand. He stood silent utterly confused by what had just happened and the way that a simple hand shake with this girl had disturbed him so much. Never before had the presence of any woman affected him in this way. He had no real recollection of how long he had been holding her hand, but hoped nothing untoward had been noticed by Tom or Lucy and that the girl had not seen it as being anything unusual either.

Lucy shook the girl's hand, "I'm sorry but who is this Mr Richards that has been talking about me?" As soon as she had said this she realised that she had been talking about Tom. She pointed to Tom "You mean this Mr Richards?"

"Yes this Mr Richards, Edward's father."

Tom stepped forward, "Perhaps I should explain? I can see you are both a little confused. But first why don't Sam and me go and make us all a nice cup of tea before we get started?"

Sam stepped forward to block his way to the door, "I'll go and do that Mr Richards, if you just tell me where everything is."

Lucy told Sam where the kitchen was and where everything was, and when she had left the room they all sat down.

The action of Sam leaving shook Philip out of his contemplations and back into the real world. For the first time since Tom had arrived with Sam, he managed to speak, "So she's the Sam Prior from the accountants. I thought Sam Prior was a man."

Lucy laughed, "So did I."

Tom joined in the laughter, "No, her name's Samantha but everyone calls her Sam."

Philip was still confused by his reaction to meeting this young woman but nevertheless wanted to know all about her, "And how do you know her then? She hasn't been here on an audit or anything before has she?"

Tom replied, "No, I don't think so."

"So how come she knows you and did she say she knows Edward as well?"

"Well, I've known her for years. Actually it's her father I know. I first met him when I became a local councillor and he was campaigning in a different ward. He helped me tremendously by showing me around in the early days and we've been friends ever since."

"But you said she knows Edward as well?"

"Yes. Edward met the family a long time ago, but Samantha was only a child then. He met her again about six months ago and things have just moved on from there."

"What do you mean by 'things have moved on'? Do you mean they are courting?"

"I'm not sure that's what I'd call it. She's been helping Edward a lot with his campaigning since he became the parliamentary candidate and so they do see each often, but I'm not sure whether it's any more serious than that she just wants to help out."

Tom went silent as he considered whether what he had just said was accurate or whether Samantha and Edward were much closer than he had imagined. For his part, Philip felt that perhaps he should let the subject drop and start dealing with the real task of the day, even though he had many more questions he wanted to ask about Samantha.

Tom however was still thinking about the issue and continued talking, "Actually, her Dad is Edward's agent in charge of his political campaign, so I guess she is just helping out." He obviously had not totally convinced himself that this was truly the case however, when he added almost to himself, "They do always seem to be together though and I don't think it's always on campaign business."

Philip was shocked and confused at his own feeling to this comment. How could he, a married man have any feelings or be bothered whether Edward was seeing this girl or not? He had only met her a couple of minutes ago and had simply touched her hand and said a mere single word to her. Nevertheless he desperately wanted to know how close she was to Edward and so he asked Tom, "So you think Edward has found himself someone at last? If he has I'm sure she would be good for him. He's been on his own far too long."

"Well, yes I guess he has and she is a really nice girl, but let's not jump to conclusions too quickly." Tom stopped for a moment as if considering things again and smiled with some level of satisfaction as he said. "Actually they do seem to have got very close over the last few weeks."

Philip's heart jumped at this but how could he feel jealous of poor Edward who had lost the love of his life in such tragic circumstances. It would be marvellous for Edward if he could find someone to help fill the gap that had been in his life for so many years.

Philip tried to dismiss his own feelings by changing the subject, "I've never heard about her from Mark Cartwright before. How long has she been working for them?"

"Only a couple of months, I think. She's a very clever girl is our Samantha. Qualified as a chartered accountant in no time at all and the firm she was working for didn't seem to want to pay her any more so she decided to move. I think it had something to do with the fact that she's a woman and the men in the office, particularly the unqualified ones, didn't like the idea of having her around. So when Mark Cartwright offered her a job she jumped at it."

At that moment there was a bang on the door and Sam spoke from the other side, "Can you open the door for me please, only I've got my hands full?"

Philip jumped up to open the door and almost knocked Tom over who being much nearer to the door had also got up from his seat. Philip graciously stood aside allowing Tom to actually open it. However as soon as Samantha entered the room he took the tray from her with a, "Let me take that for you," and placed it on Lucy's desk.

Tom pulled up another chair for Sam and they all sat down again.

Samantha was the first to speak, "Sorry, I forgot to mention that Mr Morris won't be coming." She passed a cup of tea to each in turn and as she gave Philip his added, "Mr Cartwright said to tell you that he's very sorry but just as we were leaving the office last evening, Tony suddenly remembered that he'd promised to take his mother shopping today and so he couldn't come. I do hope it won't cause a problem."

Philip was almost relieved that Tony Morris would not be coming. As soon as Lucy had mentioned his name, he had worried that based on the few times he had seen him he really did not think that he was up to the job, and certainly not the one today. He smiled at Sam and said, "I'm sure you'll be able to put us on the right track so perhaps we should get started."

He took a swig of his tea. "Now where were we Lucy? What were you saying about all these orders?"

Lucy picked up all the papers from her desk again and after sorting them into a sensible order, handed the summary sheet of orders to Tom. "I've looked at all the orders from Bridges for the last few months and this is a summary of them. What do you think, Tom? Do you reckon we've had all those items?"

Tom put down his cup, and put on his reading glasses before taking the list from Lucy. As he checked off the items, the shock was more and more evident in his face. He looked up at Lucy in disbelief. "These can't possibly be right. There's no way we could have ordered all this stuff. We wouldn't have needed half of this lot; no probably less than half of it."

He looked across at Lucy, "Are you sure these dates and volumes are correct?" He looked down at the list again, "There are three orders for these magic-eye tuning indicators in March, another two in April." His finger moved further down the list, "Oh, my God! There's another two orders here for this month. That's totally wrong; we wouldn't have needed more than one of these orders each month at the very most." He looked across at Lucy again, "You must have made a mistake, Lucy."

Philip took the list from Tom, and checked the items he had just referred to, "Are you sure these items couldn't just be sitting in the storeroom, Tom?"

There was a note of anger in Tom's voice as he responded to Philip's question, "No! Definitely not! I checked everything yesterday and there most certainly is not this quantity in the storeroom. I had a good look at everything and I'm sure there's nothing surplus to what I would have expected. So, no, to answer your question Philip, I'm sure they aren't sitting in the storeroom."

He once again turned to Lucy, "You say these are orders from Bridges, but we can't have delivery notes for them, because I'm sure they've never been delivered."

Lucy sorted through the papers in front of her and extracted some which she handed to Tom, "Here are the delivery notes for those items and except for the very last one we've paid Bridges for them all. I've checked the cheque stubs."

Sam had been sitting quietly behind Tom and Philip listening to the conversation. She leaned forward in her seat and reached between Tom and Philip to pick up the papers that Tom had put back on the desk. Philip had deliberately not looked at her since she had sat down but had nevertheless been intensely aware of her presence. With every breath he took he'd been deeply conscious of her heady perfume from the moment she had stepped into the room with Tom. But it was not merely this that was affecting him. Somehow her very presence was disturbing him in some unexplainable way and as she leaned forward he closed his eyes, took a deep breath, and for a brief moment basked in the pungent bouquet of her fragrance and the nearness of her.

She leaned back in her chair, turning over the papers, "If I've understood things properly, then you're saying that whilst at first glance all the orders look OK, and that delivery has been made and the goods paid for on each of the orders, no-one is quite certain at this stage, which, if any, of these orders, delivery, or payment is correct or not."

Lucy was the first to respond, "So what do you suggest we do?"

"I suggest we take say two or three of the most suspect items and follow it through from start to finish. We need to make a list of every person who was or could have been involved at every stage and gradually I'm sure we'll get to the bottom of it all."

Tom was the first to openly state what was on everyone's mind, "But the three of us are the ones who've signed the documents and as far as I can see it, we are the only ones who have free access and involvement in ordering, goods received and payment aspects of everything. So are you saying it could be something one of us has done?"

"Well at this stage Mr Richards what I am saying is that we need to determine who, including yourselves has been involved. For instance, I understand that Mr Matthews told Mr Cartwright yesterday that although it looked as if one of the orders had been signed by him, he had not been here on that particular day, so either the date is wrong or someone forged his signature. So that is one thing we have to check. Did he sign it or is it forged?"

Tom responded immediately, "So you think someone could be forging some of this stuff? Well I can tell you it isn't me, so let's clear that up straight away."

Philip looked at Tom and tried to reassure him, "I don't think Samantha is suggesting that any of us three is on the fiddle, but she is right, we have to eliminate that before we go any further."

He did not give Tom any opportunity to respond further but just continued, "We have to do what Samantha suggests and look at every one of these items and until that's done I guess we'll each be a suspect. So the sooner we sort it out the better. Personally I'm certain that the worst that any of us can possibly be guilty of is that we've made a genuine mistake about something and since this no longer looks like a mere mistake to me, I'm sure we'll be able to get that out of the way very quickly."

Even whilst he was saying this, he nevertheless feared that his Uncle would not be able to understand the need to check his actions, so he decided to take the heat out of the situation by allocating tasks for everyone to do.

"Uncle Tom, why don't you go down Lucy's list and cross off every one that you know is genuine? Any you're not sure about we can leave for a while and then we can all concentrate on the ones you feel are 'iffy'."

He turned to Lucy, "If you sort out the bank statements Lucy, we can cross off the payments made against the cheque stubs and at least then we'll know whether Bridges have had the money or not."

He was about to ask Samantha to make notes on everything as they dealt with it, when she interrupted him, "I've been thinking about that. What if the cheques were fraudulently made out to someone else?"

Lucy was at first bemused at this suggestion, but as she spoke her irritation at the suggestion became more and more obvious, "That couldn't have happened. Tom, or Philip, or me, sign every cheque and because they are usually busy on other things, I'm the one who nearly always signs them and I can tell you that I would only sign them against all the proper paperwork. Any bills for Bridges would only have been made out to

Bridges. They couldn't possibly have been made out to anyone else."

Philip sighed as he realised that Samantha had now unintentionally upset Lucy as well, "Calm down Lucy. No-one is suggesting that you've done anything wrong. Sam just didn't know what our systems are." He turned to Sam, "I'm with Lucy on this one, Sam. We can account for every cheque issued and anyway the bank only pays cheques signed by us."

Sam had however been gradually formulating a possible explanation for all of the unanswered questions in her mind and had become convinced that this was a well thought out and deliberate fraud. By whom, she had no idea, but she nevertheless felt certain that the actual cheque payments would hold the answer. "Have we got the paid cheques from the bank? We can soon eliminate that the paid cheques have nothing to do with anything then."

Lucy's anger had only abated slightly when she replied, "We don't have the paid cheques. The bank keeps those."

"But I'm sure the bank will let you have them if you ask for them." Samantha did not wait for any reaction to this before adding, "Why don't you give the bank a call now and ask them if they can sort out the paid cheques first thing on Monday and let us have them as soon as they can?"

Philip looked at his watch, "I know the bank is busy on a Saturday morning Lucy, but I suppose you could give them a call now and arrange it for Monday."

The rest of the morning was spent making lists and notes of suspect items. Tom continually kept going downstairs to the stores to check that items were not there. By lunchtime they were all exhausted; their lists still posing more questions than they had answered.

The answer became blindingly clear on Monday evening. Martins Bank had agreed to hand the paid cheques to Samantha last thing on Monday afternoon and once all the rest of the staff had left, Tom, Lucy and Philip were anxiously sitting around Lucy's desk waiting for her arrival.

As soon as she walked into the room, Philip became acutely aware once more of her perfume; the same perfume that she had worn two day's earlier. He had felt somewhat disheartened since Saturday; a feeling he couldn't really explain. However, when Sam entered the room and smiled, his melancholy lifted and he felt a new man.

Samantha passed the sealed packet of cheques to Lucy, who tore it open and started to thumb through the pile of cheques. She let out an ear-piercing cry of alarm as she took a cheque from out of the pile, "Oh my God! What have you done Michael?" By the time she handed the cheque to Philip tears were flooding down her face, "How could I have been so stupid?"

Lucy passed the cheque to Tom and continued thumbing through the rest of the bundle. She said nothing more as she looked at each cheque in turn, and although she took a cheque from the pile every so often and passed it across the table, she did not look up until she had reached the end of the pile. The tears were streaming down her face, as she held her hand across her mouth, shaking her head from side as she repeated over and over again, "I'm sorry. I'm so sorry."

Tom looked at the first cheque, a look of total disbelief on his face and without saying a word he passed the cheque to Philip.

The cheque was not made out to C. E. Bridge Ltd., as it should have been but was all written in capital letters. It now read Pay MICHAEL BURBRIDGE. Philip looked closely at the cheque. It was definitely signed by Lucy but it quickly dawned on him that when Michael Burbridge had made out the cheques for Lucy to sign, it had probably read C E BRIDGE with sufficient space between the letters for Michael to add the rest afterwards. All the other cheques were made out the same.

Philip's father Frank had first met Michael Burbridge when in hospital following the tragic accident which had resulted in him spending the rest of his life in a wheelchair. Michael had been in the next bed to Frank for about two weeks. He had skidded on his motorbike in wet weather and ended up with the bike on top of his right leg crushing it. Fortunately the doctors had managed to save his leg but he was left with a severe limp.

Frank had enjoyed having this intelligent young man to chat to and Michael was able to take Frank's mind off his own predicament as they talked about anything and everything. Michael visited Frank in hospital a couple of times after he himself had been discharged, but following his own discharge Frank had not seen him or heard anything of him until he saw him in town one day.

Frank and Grace had just had lunch at the George Hotel and as Frank was being carefully guided down the steps in his wheelchair he noticed the awkward step of a man walking in front of Sister Dora's statue. He immediately recognised it as being Michael Burbridge's gait and shouted across the square to him. They chatted for some time during which Frank learned that Michael was out of work and was looking for another job as a bookkeeper. Without any further thought Frank offered him a job in the office to help Lucy with her ever increasing workload.

Michael Burbridge had learned all the new tasks handed to him quickly and after Frank's death had been a tremendous help to Lucy and soon become an indispensable assistant.

Tom was looking at each cheque in turn before handing them on to Philip, "But I still don't understand it, what has happened to the ordered goods and the real payments to Bridges?"

Sam took a cheque from Tom and looked at it, "I hate to say this, Mr Richards, but there never were any real orders for these cheques. We'll probably never know why and how this started, but I'm pretty sure that this Michael Burbridge saw the opportunity one day when making out the cheques and then deliberately set out to make money out of it."

Tom looked puzzled, "But it's not just the cheques is it; what about the order forms and delivery notes?"

"Well there's a box full of order forms over there. They're not numbered, so anyone could take a few and make out a fictitious order. He just had to forge a signature; scrap the top copy that should have gone to Bridges; and file the carbon copy in your files."

Tom was still looking puzzled, "OK, but the delivery note is one of Bridges. We don't have those lying around."

"Well I can only assume he somehow got hold of a blank form from them and had some printed. I can't see any other explanation."

The next four hours were spent not only making a list of the altered cheques but also getting out previous years' orders and identifying further fraudulent documents.

Lucy added up the total of all the items and was almost weeping as she sat staring at the final figure in front of her, "That's more than four times his wages for that same period and that's assuming that what we've listed is everything. What on earth has he done with it all?"

"We'll probably never know the answer to that Lucy," said Philip, "But what we need to think about before we go home is what we're going to do about it all."

"Put the bastard in a prison cell and throw away the key," was Tom's immediate response.

Lucy shook her head as if to disagree, "So you think we should go to the police about this then. You don't mind that it'll be in the papers that we've allowed ourselves to be swindled?"

They took another hour to discuss the option of police or no police. Eventually it was Philip who wound up the discussion by saying he thought it could be more damaging in the long run if it got out that an employee had defrauded them out of so much money and they'd let him get away with it.

They all finally agreed that the police should be brought in and started to put away the papers ready to go home when Tom asked, "One last question, what are we going to do when bloody Michael turns up for work tomorrow? Are we just going to say nothing and let him carry on working 'til we manage to get the police here?"

They all sat down again, but Philip quickly sorted out the problem, "I suggest we all go home now and get some sleep or we won't be fit to do anything. I'll get here early tomorrow and be ready to see Michael as soon as he arrives." He turned to Tom, "Perhaps you or Lucy wouldn't mind seeing him with me and perhaps the other could go straight to the police station, explain the situation and bring the police back with them. They can then do what they need to do with him."

Tom volunteered to go the police, "I'd better be the one to go to the police and Lucy can sit in with you. If I see him, I'll want to give him a good slap for all this lot and then it'd be me the police would want as well."

For Edward, the next two months were extremely hectic. He won the by-election and became an MP. He wasted no time in finding a flat in London and spent all the time he could in the Parliament learning his new trade and getting to know as many of his fellow MP's as possible. However he started to miss Samantha and arranged to see her whenever he could get back to Walsall.

For Philip the two months following Michael Burbridge's arrest had been equally stressful and unsettling but for quite different reasons.

Firstly, Teresa had continually pestered him about their inability to start a baby and had insisted they should find out if either of them had a medical problem preventing her conception. Initially, Philip kept putting it off saying that the Michael Burbridge business had created so many problems at work that he couldn't spare the time, but he eventually succumbed to her pestering and agreed to see a consultant with her.

Secondly, he and Lucy had to sort out the books and paperwork to make sure they had identified all the necessary fraudulent documentation for the police in readiness for Michael Burbridge's prosecution. He had asked Mark Cartwright for some help in this and was quietly pleased when Mark suggested that since Samantha had been involved from the start it would be useful if she were to spend a couple of days a week on the task with them.

"It would be very helpful from our viewpoint as well," Mark had said. "As auditors we need to satisfy ourselves of the extent of the fraud anyway, so Sam will be able to deal with our auditing needs at the same time. That way we won't be charging twice for similar work."

Philip had insisted on being at the factory on the days set aside for Sam's visits. "I really want to keep on top of all this," he had said to Lucy when telling her of the arrangement, "And anyway, I'm sure we'll sort everything out much more quickly if the three of us work together."

Lucy had readily agreed but on many of the days Samantha and Philip were working on the documentation, she was only too happy to leave them sorting it out without her whilst she continued with her own work; work that had increased dramatically now that she no longer had an assistant.

Philip was never happier that when she left them to it. He enjoyed working with Samantha and always had a good feeling when she was sitting next to him. But when Samantha spoke about Edward in ways that suggested they were getting close, he struggled with his own feelings for her; feelings that he couldn't do anything about; after all he was a married man and Edward wasn't any more. So he just tried to enjoy the time she was near him, but as soon as it was time to go home, the pleasure he felt at having her near him would plummet and he would start to count the days until their next meeting.

By the end of July, Philip and Samantha had effectively completed all the work and a final meeting to advise the police of all their findings was arranged for August 4th. Philip was inwardly dreading that after that he would no longer be seeing Samantha on a regular basis. His feelings had to be ignored however and he had to act as naturally as he possibly could so he asked Tom, Lucy, Samantha and Mark Cartwright to attend the meeting arranged for two o'clock in the afternoon.

When he arrived home on the previous evening he had great difficulty controlling his anger when Teresa told him that she had arranged for their consultation for the following morning. "Why tomorrow? I can't possibly be there at such short notice. I've got a meeting with the police tomorrow, can't we do it another day?"

Teresa sensed the anger in his voice and had difficulty controlling the tears, "Mr Fielding, the consultant came to me today and said he'd had a cancellation for in the morning and if we see him then he won't charge us for the consultation as a special favour to me. So please can't we see him? I think the sooner we get things sorted the better don't you?"

Philip understood the stress Teresa was under about this whole baby thing. He stepped forward and put his arms around her, "What time do we need to see Mr Fielding and how long do you think it will take?"

She looked appealingly into his eyes, "I've said we'll be there at ten o'clock. I doubt if it'll take more than about half an hour, but if he wants to do examinations or tests it could take a little longer."

"OK, we'll go and see him, but perhaps I could leave if he decides to examine you. You won't want me there whilst he does that anyway will you?"

Teresa had deliberately not raised with Philip the probability that the consultant would want to examine him. Neither had she told him that he'd probably want Philip to provide a specimen of his sperm and she certainly wasn't going to tell him now and give him an excuse to change his mind after he'd agreed to go with her. "All right, but can I ring you at work if he has anything to tell us after examining me?"

Philip smiled and nodded his head in agreement. He had however been well aware all along of Teresa's reluctance to tell him that the doctor would wish to examine him and probably want a sample of his sperm. Much as he disliked the idea of producing a sample on request, he was nevertheless prepared for this, but had never discussed it with Teresa.

All the time he and Teresa were with the consultant Philip had difficulty concentrating on what was being said. He was thinking about the meeting that afternoon and the fact that after it, he would have no idea if, or when he might see Samantha again. Try as he may to think about other things, this thought kept coming back. He had asked Lucy to provide some sandwiches for lunch so that he could chat about the afternoon meeting with her and Tom before the police arrived and had casually mentioned that if she and Tom felt it would be useful she could ask Mark and Sam to join them for lunch as well. Lucy had said, "I'll ask Tom about that and let you know."

"No need, I'll just leave it to you. If they're there, that's fine; and if you and Tom decide not to invite them that's fine as well. They'll be with us at two for the meeting anyway." Nevertheless as Philip drove from the hospital to the factory, he was hoping that Lucy had taken up the suggestion and that Sam would be there.

When he got to Lucy's office, his spirits rose as he opened the door once again catching the aroma of the particular perfume he now recognised as Samantha's.

But as soon as Lucy spoke his pleasure at finding her there was immediately dashed. "Hi, Philip, Samantha was just showing me her engagement ring." She reached across her desk and lifted Samantha's left hand into view, "Look. It's gorgeous isn't it?"

Philip stepped forward hoping the shaking inside him was not obvious. He took hold of Samantha's hand and admired the ring; a large green emerald stone surrounded by a circle of small diamonds. He remembered the last time he had held her hand, the first time he had met her. Once again he did not want to let go of it but this time he had an excuse to hold on to it a little longer. In fact he took hold of her other hand, guiding her to her feet. "Congratulations. I'm very pleased for you," he even managed a smile as he added, "and Edward, I presume?"

She smiled back, one of her gorgeous broad smiles that affected him so much. The smile continued as she nodded her head and said, "Of course. Who else would it be?"

Philip ignored the rhetorical question, and asked, "And has this been planned for some time?"

It seemed to Philip that she had no wish to let go of his hands, nor to stop smiling, "No, it was a complete surprise. Edward took me out to dinner last evening and asked me right there in the restaurant."

Lucy interrupted before Philip was able to ask anything further, "It was her twenty-third birthday yesterday. Did you know that Philip?"

For the second time in as many minutes, Philip was again taken aback. First by the engagement and now by the fact that he had not known it was her birthday. But then what would he have done, or what could he have done about it even if he had known the date of her birthday? He determined that perhaps he had by now held her hand for as long as he ought, but he first asked, "And may I kiss the birthday girl and the bride to be? Or would Edward have something to say about that?"

She did not answer the question but merely leaned slightly forward and presented her cheek for him to kiss. He gave her an avuncular peck on her cheek and as he stepped back said, "I hope you'll be very happy together."

He let go of her hand but she immediately took hold of his again and mouthed a, "Thank you." As she did so their eyes met and she once again smiled for him, before leaning forward and giving him an equally perfunctory kiss on his left cheek. He would remember the time, the place, the smile and especially that kiss for the rest of his life.

CHAPTER NINETEEN

1955 - 1956

Two weeks after their meeting with the consultant, Teresa came home from the hospital and told Philip that Mr Fielding had seen her that morning and had suggested that Philip was responsible for her inability to conceive.

"But I thought doctors weren't supposed to discuss patient's details with someone else, so how come he didn't want to see me to tell me about this? Perhaps I should arrange to see him and ask if anything can be done."

Teresa broke into tears and said she did not want to see any doctors or consultants about their problems any more. Philip had consoled her and once the tears had stopped she said, "I think it'd be best if we just reconciled ourselves to never having children and getting on with our lives."

"Maybe, but I'd like to see him anyway and hear exactly what he's got to say about it for myself."

But she burst into tears again and asked him not to take it any further. The subject was dropped and never raised again.

When Michael Burbridge appeared before magistrates in early September 1953, he pleaded guilty to all the charges, but because of the seriousness of the charge he was to appear before a judge at the County Court for sentencing in November. He had consistently refused to say what he had spent the ill-gotten money on, although the police said they had strong reasons to believe it had been used for gambling. In his summing up, the Judge said that Michael had been in a position of trust which he had taken full advantage of in committing his crime and in taking this into account he felt that a prison sentence of three years was appropriate.

Michael was obviously shocked at the length of the sentence and when being taken down, pointed his finger at Philip and staring directly at him shouted, "I'll get you for this when I get out, so don't forget."

In the May 1955 General Election Edward held on to his seat with an increased majority. He was now well established at Westminster and when Hugh Gaitskell took over leadership of the party later that year, he was given a junior opposition ministerial post.

Following their engagement, much to Samantha's disappointment, Edward had kept putting off making plans for the wedding. However soon after regaining his seat he finally told Samantha to make the plans for the wedding and they were married in October 1955. Philip had once again been Edward's best man, but this time he found it very difficult to feel as enthusiastic in supporting Edward to marry Samantha as he had been when he had married Juliette.

Since Sam's engagement to Edward, Philip had realised that every time he was in her company, he had these warm feelings of contentment and he wanted the pleasure of the occasion to last. And every time they parted, he subconsciously started to count the days or weeks until their next meeting.

He tried to convince himself that they were merely two close friends who just happened to be people of different sex. After all she was Edward's girl and was going to marry him and he was married to Teresa so they could only ever be just friends and that was how it would always have to be. But when Edward had announced the actual wedding date and asked him to be best man, he knew that the despair he felt meant that these feelings were no such thing and for the first time he had to admit privately to himself that he was desperately in love with Samantha.

Philip had suggested to Teresa that they should invite Edward and Sam to supper, ostensibly to go over all the final plans for the wedding and give them the wedding gift they had purchased for them. The dinner party was arranged for the weekend before the wedding and once again Philip found himself mentally counting off the days until he would meet Sam again. His last thought each evening before going to sleep was of Samantha and that there was now one day less until he next saw her and each morning he started counting down the hours until he was able to knock another day off the waiting and by the time the day arrived, Philip was only too aware that Edward's announcement of the wedding date and the 'best man' request had disturbed him far more than he would have believed possible.

He spent the whole evening acutely aware of Samantha's presence next to him at the table, and when supper was finished he and Edward went into the lounge whilst the girls went to the kitchen to make coffee. When they returned he took the coffee tray off Teresa and poured everyone a coffee before going to sit down.

"Come and sit here between Teresa and me," said Samantha indicating the space on the settee on which she and Teresa were sitting. He sat down and was now even more aware of her closeness; a closeness he found almost unbearable as it was impossible for him to avoid their thighs and legs touching as they sat next to each other. The warmth and sensitivity from touching Samantha was so much more acute than he felt from the similar intimacy of his other leg next to Teresa.

He drank his coffee as quickly as possible and stood up. He placed his cup on the tray and turning to Teresa said, "Shall I fetch the wedding gift? Sam and Edward can open it now can't they?"

When he returned Teresa moved the coffee tray off the coffee table and placed it on the floor indicating that Philip should put the large package he was carrying on to the table. He turned to Edward, "May you be very happy together." He then turned to Samantha, "Teresa said it was what you wanted."

Samantha looked at Teresa, "Do we open it now?"

"Of course; I hope it's the one you wanted."

As she stood up, she turned to Edward, "Come on. This is for both of us so come and help me open it."

Sam removed the big red bow and carefully removed the coloured wedding wrapping paper. She opened the box and took out a dinner plate from the top of the Royal Doulton dinner service.

"Thank you. This is exactly the pattern I wanted." She gave the plate to Edward, "Look, Edward. It's beautiful, isn't it?"

She turned to Teresa and gave her a kiss on the cheek. "Thank you so much. This is very generous of you both."

As Sam stepped back, Edward gave the plate back to her and stepped to also kiss Teresa on each cheek, "Thank you both for the gift; it is lovely and I'm so pleased that Sam likes the pattern." He turned to Samantha, "We'll have to make sure that Teresa and Philip are the first dinner guests to use this; you'll have to make sure I put a date in my diary for it, dear."

But Samantha had moved to Philip and now had her back to Edward. She moved closer to Philip; gave him a hug and said, "Thank you so much. It's exactly what I wanted." Philip went to kiss her on the cheek but instead of offering her cheek she repositioned her face and kissed him lightly on the lips. It was only a peck, but it was on the lips. She released her arms from around him before turning to answer Edward. The whole episode was so quick that Philip was left wondering whether it had actually happened.

"That's a grand idea darling." She laughed and spoke directly to Teresa, "It's not easy to get a date in his diary these days but I'll make sure we make arrangements as soon as we come back from honeymoon."

However after their marriage, Edward spent so much of his time in London, not only during the week but often staying in his London flat at weekends as well that although Samantha made several dates for the dinner party, Edward always asked Samantha to cancel, often at the last minute, for some reason or other. In the end Samantha had to apologise to

Teresa so much that she stopped trying to make any arrangements, just hoping that Edward might have a fit of conscience about it and suggest a possible date for the dinner party himself. He never did.

Around the time of Sam and Edward's wedding, Philip had noticed that Tom seemed to get out of breath quite quickly, particularly when climbing the stairs to the office or carrying parts for the girls on the production line. Tom dismissed Philip's concerns for several weeks but eventually agreed to see the doctor about it. He was diagnosed as having angina and advised to take total rest for several weeks and then to take things easy after that.

Lucy was now in turmoil as to how they would manage. They had replaced Michael Burbridge with a young married girl, who learned the job quite quickly but after only a few months had announced she was pregnant and would be leaving and left in the same week Tom received his diagnosis.

Philip suggested they should now employ a qualified accountant to look after thc books of both the manufacturing and retail businesses and casually suggested Samantha as a suitable candidate. Tom had readily agreed his new daughter-in-law would be ideal and could even represent him at board meetings if he was unable to attend.

"Why don't you have a word with her and offer her the job if she's interested, Uncle Tom. I leave it entirely up to you and Lucy to sort out what to pay her, but make it attractive enough to entice her away from Mark Cartwright. I know he thinks highly of her, so make it worth her while to come to us."

For Philip however, it meant a great deal more than solving a business problem, it meant that he would be able to work closely with Samantha once again. Suggesting that Tom and Lucy should sort out all the details was merely his way of not appearing too eager about it all.

Frank's old office was rebuilt on the side of the factory for Tom to work in so that he did not have to keep walking up the stairs. His existing office on the attic floor was then handed over to Sam to work in.

Philip deliberately arranged meetings at a number of shops on Samantha's first day at work as he wanted to continue the deception of not caring one way or the other whether she was around or not.

The reality was quite different though and by the time he arrived late at the factory the next morning, he could barely contain his anticipation of being able to see her. He'd found an excuse to pop into the Walsall shop first and all the time he was there he could not understand why he'd been so stupid as to arrange such an unnecessary sham and after he left the shop he found the time it took him to get to the factory almost unbearable.

He quickly climbed the stairs. The door to her office was wide open so he entered without knocking. There was a woman standing sorting papers in the filing cabinet with her back to him. His heart suddenly sank and all the anticipation and apprehension of waiting for this moment went. He did not recognise the girl standing at the cabinet. She had deep black shoulder length hair. Samantha had magnificent light brown hair which was always so carefully brushed and styled. This girl's hair was glistening in the sunlight and swung loosely across her face as she turned to face Philip.

"Hello, Philip, I didn't hear you come in."

The charming voice was Samantha's, the stunning figure was Samantha's, the exquisite legs showing beneath her business skirt were Samantha's and above all the beautiful face and sparkling blue eyes were Samantha's, but the hair belonged to someone else. As he walked towards her he became aware of a perfume that was not Samantha's either. It was a fragrance from somewhere in his past, but for now he could not remember when or where.

"You've changed your hair?"

"Yes." She swung her head so that the hair swung freely across her face once again. "Do you like it?"

He lied, "Yes it's lovely," but the words in his head were actually *"No, it's horrible. What the hell have you changed it for?"* Instead he asked a more polite, "Any special reason for changing the colour?"

Now it was Sam's turn to be untruthful, "Oh, you know us girls, always wanting to try something different."

"And does Edward like it?"

"Yes he loves it. Actually he encouraged me to try it."

"And you've changed your perfume?" He was annoyed with himself as soon as he said this. Now she would know that he had noticed her perfume before. What would she make of that?

She however acted as if nothing untoward had been said, "Yes. Edward gave it to me. Do you like it?"

Philip smiled as he once again spoke words different to those going around in his head, "It's lovely." It was indeed a pleasant and agreeable fragrance but it was not the aroma that had pervaded his senses every time he'd been in her company before. It was the loss of that sensation that he disliked.

Lucy joined them soon after Philip's arrival and the three of them spent most of the day together talking about the business and the things they wanted Samantha to take responsibility for. Every time Philip caught a whiff of the new perfume he tried to recall where he had encountered it before. The only fragrance he had ever instantly recognised was the one that Samantha usually wore, but somehow this new scent had a familiar odour about it.

Late in the afternoon, Lucy stood up, “I’m parched again with all this talking; anyone for another cup of tea?”

As soon as Lucy left the room to make the tea, Samantha suddenly asked, “What do you remember about Juliette, Philip?”

“She was half French; half English; could speak both languages fluently and it was a tragedy that she died in that way.”

“Yes I know all that, but what was she really like?”

“I don’t know what you want me to say. What exactly do you want to know? And anyway wouldn’t it be better if you talked to Edward about her?”

She averted her eyes from Philip’s and looked down at the desk, “Well that would be fine if he’d talk about it.” She looked up and stared directly at him, “Can I say something just between the two of us?”

“Sure. Fire away.”

“You won’t say anything to anyone else will you; and especially not to Edward?” She hesitated for a moment, “Or Teresa?”

“Of course.”

She stared fixedly directly into his eyes as if trying to see right into his head, “Promise?”

Philip wondered what it was that she wanted to say. He smiled as reassuringly as he could and giving a three fingered scout salute said, “I promise. Scouts honour. Of course I won’t speak to anyone else about whatever it is if you don’t want me to, but if it’s that personal should you be telling even me?”

“You know Edward better than anyone else I know, so you’re the only one I can talk to about it. And more importantly I trust you not to gossip to anyone else about it.” She smiled as she added, “And I know you’d keep it to yourself even if I hadn’t made you promise.”

“So what is it that’s bothering you?”

“It’s difficult to explain really, but it’s all to do with Juliette and Edward. I know he was madly in love with her. Mary made a point of telling me that the very first time I went out on a proper date with him. But since then it’s as if it’s a forbidden subject. Whenever I’ve mentioned it again to Tom or Mary, they just say I should chat to Edward about it just as you’ve done. But when I have asked Edward about her, he just says that it’s all in the past and best left there.”

"Well perhaps if that's how he wants it, that's how you should leave it."

"But why should I? I know she existed and I know she's no longer here, but she was a part of his life; an important part that I want to know about."

Philip thought he detected a tear appearing in her eye as she continued, "And they had a child together for God's sake, a child he never sees and never seems to want to see. What's all that about?"

She wiped her eye with the back of her hand, "I've suggested that we invite Julian over to spend time with us, but he won't even talk about that. I even said I was going to write and say I would go over to fetch him and Edward went absolutely ballistic at that. For a minute I feared he was going to hit me, but he just turned away and went off to his study. I think he must have slept in there, because he certainly didn't come to bed, and when I got up the next morning he'd already gone back to London. He'd left a note on the kitchen table. All it said was 'Will call you when I have a minute, love Edward'. I didn't know whether he was still mad at me or not. And I didn't really know what I'd said that was wrong anyway. At least he'd put 'love Edward' so perhaps he wasn't still mad at me after all. What do you think?"

"I really don't know, Samantha. I used to think I knew all there was to know about Edward. I certainly thought that when we were children, but I think the war changed things for both of us and we haven't been as close since our time in France. For a while I thought that perhaps it was because I'd been promoted ahead of him but I don't really think it was that."

"So what do you think it is? Is it all Juliette? And how does she fit into whatever's going on his head?"

"Well I know he was constantly worried about her even before we landed in France, but once we were engaged in battle he was absolutely paranoid about her safety. It was the only thing he could talk about. The battle was moving closer and closer to where she lived and it was not just the soldiers that were getting killed. I feared for her family so I can only guess what poor Edward was going through."

"But you still aren't telling me about Juliette. How does she fit into all of it?"

Philip was thoughtful for a moment and was about to speak when they heard Lucy's footsteps outside the door.

Samantha put her finger to her mouth as a signal to stay quiet and as Lucy entered the room she got up from her seat to help Lucy with the tray. As she did so she merely said, "I'd welcome your comments on that some other time Philip."

And when they'd all sat down again she acted as if nothing out of the ordinary was going on. "Where were we Lucy? Oh yes, you were about to tell me about the workers tax and national insurance you want me to deal with."

Philip tried to keep his mind on the conversation but all the time he was thinking about what to say when next Samantha raised the subject.

He thought seriously about Juliette for the first time in years and he realised that what Samantha had said about Edward not wanting to talk about her was absolutely true. He had not really thought about it before but it was a fact that Edward had not even mentioned her name in a long, long time. He also recalled the way Edward had avoided giving any real answer when he or Teresa had asked about Julian. Was Edward just blanking it all out of his mind or was the whole matter still so painful that he could not bear to deal with any of it, including his son?

And then it struck him. The perfume? The hair? They were Juliette's.

He took a breath to take in the aroma of the perfume once more. Yes it was the perfume that Juliette had worn for her wedding; the perfume that Edward had specially bought her for the occasion.

He had insisted that Philip take a good whiff of it when Juliette and her father came up the aisle and reached them. He had whispered, "Cost me an absolute fortune." He had then dug his elbow into Philip's ribs as he quietly added, "But worth every penny don't you think?"

Philip looked across at Samantha. The hair! It was Juliette's or as near as damn it. My God he's trying to turn Samantha into Juliette! At this thought his mind went into overdrive as he tried to work out how he could talk to Samantha about Juliette without giving any indication of the conclusions he had just reached.

In the weeks that followed Sam settled well into her new job and was soon making a hell of a difference to the amount of work that both Lucy and Philip had previously had to deal with. The old happy and contented Lucy returned and within weeks it became obvious that a great weight had been lifted from her.

For Philip, Samantha's presence had a dual effect on him. Firstly, he was amazed at how she seemed to cope so effortlessly with matters that he had previously spent hours trying to master and deal with.

Every time there was a problem at one of the shops he had always rushed half way across the country to deal with it in situ. But Samantha invariably dealt with the problem on the telephone, and after a while Philip realised that she was not only superb at solving the problem quickly there and then, but also had this amazing knack of letting the shop manager think that the solution had been his all along.

His mother mentioned this after she had made one of her, now very infrequent shop visits. “I won’t tell you which branch it was because I don’t want you to embarrass the girls there about it, but they reckon it’s much better now that you don’t visit so often. They’re always stressed out when you’re about to visit; worried to death you’re going to complain about something or other. They say that Samantha is a real breath of fresh air and even the managers think she’s a real gem.”

Philip was pleased to hear this but was not quite so pleased when his mother continued, “I’d let Samantha sort things out in future and avoid visiting the shops yourself. You can come across as the army officer in charge of his troops sometimes you know.”

Even though Philip was shocked by his mother’s words he nevertheless took her advice. After all, not visiting the branches meant he could spend far more time at the factory and in Samantha’s company.

He expected Samantha to bring up the subject of Juliette and Edward again, but she did not do so, and after a few weeks he decided she had probably managed to sort things out with Edward.

Even so, every time he saw her with her black hair, he couldn’t get the thought that Edward wanted her to be a replacement Juliette out of his head. It seemed the old perfume had been dispatched to the bin and she was always wearing the ‘Juliette’ perfume. Edward must have bought her a continuous supply of it. He wished so much that he could ask her to go back to the old perfume.

But whatever Edward wanted of her she was nevertheless the same wonderful girl who brought joy to him. She was Samantha to him and not Juliette, the hair and perfume made no difference to that; and now that he saw her so often, he was able to continue to keep her presence with him even when they were apart.

Early one Monday morning, in the middle of July, Philip was talking to Lucy in her office when there was a knock on the door and without waiting to be asked in, Samantha opened the door and walked in. She had an enormous smile on her face.

“Sorry for barging in but I wanted to give you both these invitations to my birthday party in a couple of week’s time. Edward says he’s cleared his diary for the whole of the weekend.”

She gave an envelope to Lucy and smiled as she gave Philip his envelope, “You will come, won’t you?” and still smiling added, “It’s on the sixth of next month; the Saturday after my birthday on the third.”

Philip wondered whether the addition of *‘my birthday on the third’*, was a special reminder to him of her birth date. It was a date he already held in his head so he just smiled back and said, "We wouldn't miss it for the world, would we Lucy?" He did not wait for Lucy's response before adding, "I'll have to check with Teresa whether she can make it. I know she's down to work some weekends at the hospital."

Samantha looked directly at him as she pronounced, "Well she'll just have to change her shift that weekend won't she?" She turned and as she left the room she merely commented, "I guess you two have work to do, and so have I, so I'll see you later," and with that she dashed out of the office.

Whenever their work allowed them to, Teresa and Philip would get up late at the weekend and Teresa would cook a full fry up of bacon, eggs, sausages, mushrooms, baked beans and bread fried in the cooking fat, washed down with several cups of piping hot tea. The day of the party was such a day and Teresa and Philip were sitting in their kitchen, still in their dressing gowns tucking into their breakfast. The kitchen door and window had both been flung wide open to try to let some fresh air into the room. It had been a stiflingly hot summer night with the sizzling sun rising early giving the promise of yet another cloudless and swelteringly scorching day.

The telephone rang and Philip answered it. Teresa heard him say, "Just a minute, I'll get her for you," before he shouted, "It's the hospital for you, Teresa. Can you come and take it?"

Philip closed the door behind him to give Teresa more privacy on the phone, but she was obviously soon annoyed about something because he could still hear her raised voice from time to time. He heard her say, "I'll see what I can do and I'll get back to you." The phone was slammed down as she muttered aloud, "Damn. Damn. Damn. Why today of all days?"

She did not return to the kitchen but started to use the telephone again. Again the conversation ended with the phone being slammed down to be followed by another, "Damn. Damn. Damn," but this time there was a fourth and fifth "Damn. Damn."

Philip could hear her still muttering more 'damns' as she picked up the phone to make another call. This time the conversation was more controlled and he could not hear what was being said.

This call lasted about fifteen minutes and by the time Teresa had finished, Philip was thinking that maybe he should have put Teresa's breakfast back in the oven to keep warm. Teresa asked Philip for his handkerchief as soon as she entered the room. She wiped her eyes and sat down without saying another word.

“What’s the matter? Is there anything I can do?” Teresa did not answer him straight away but just shook her head. She blew her nose into his handkerchief, screwed it up and gave it back to him, “I’ve been looking forward to this party ever since you brought the invitation home. I’ve bought a new dress, and most of all I did double shifts last weekend so that I could have this weekend off, and now the Sister who was supposed to work has gone and got appendicitis.” She started picking at her cold meal. “Would you believe it?”

“So does that mean they want you to go in? You’ll be all right for the party tonight though won’t you?”

There was anger in Teresa’s voice as she answered, “No, I will not be all right for the party tonight. It’s the nightshift they want me to cover.”

Teresa took another mouthful of the food before putting her fork down and pushing the remains of her meal away. Philip reached forward and picked up the plate, “Do you want me to warm this for you?”

She angrily shouted at him, “No I don’t want you to warm it,” after which she looked up and smiled at him, “I’m sorry I shouldn’t take it out on you. You’ll just have to go to the party on your own.”

“Can’t anyone else do the shift? What about Auntie Alice? I’m sure she’d cover for you.”

“What do you think I’ve been doing for the last twenty minutes? I phoned your home and your mother answered. Apparently Alice is on today from eight ‘til eight and she’s due back tomorrow eight ‘til eight. So she can’t help, can she? The trouble is that as this is the holiday fortnight for most of the factories around, we are short staffed anyway, and the hospital says that I’m the only sister left that they can call on. Sorry but you’ll just have to go to the party on your own.”

“There’s no point me going on my own. I’ll give Edward a call and tell him we have to call off. There are plenty of others going and they probably won’t even miss us.”

“No you must go. It should be a good party and I’ll feel doubly guilty if you miss out on the fun as well.”

The sun was still shining in a clear sky as a solitary Philip walked up to the front door and rang the bell at Edward’s house later that evening. There was no breeze and the heat was still as oppressive as it had been all day.

Philip had dropped Teresa off at the hospital and was arriving later than the invitation stated and the party was in full swing when he arrived. A girl, whom he had never met before, opened the door but then he realised from the black skirt and white blouse she was wearing that she was someone they had hired in for the evening, probably to look after the food and drinks. The girl asked if she could take his briefcase off him and keep it safe during the party but Philip declined the invitation.

Sam came out into the hall and looked pleased to see him. She had on a black dress with a lace overlay at the top and a slightly flowing skirt which ended just below the knees. Her black shoes had high stiletto heels which accentuated her beautiful legs and the wide black belt around her narrow waist gave her the classic hour glass figure. The wide and low neck line of the dress exposed her smooth skin. A single row of pearls hung round her neck beneath which small beads of sweat on her skin shimmered in the sunlight. She had a deep red rose pinned into one side of her hair. It was still dyed black but its sheen seemed entirely natural and for once Philip forgot that this was not her natural colour.

She gave Philip a quick peck on the cheek before commenting, "I'm sorry that Teresa couldn't make it. It's such a shame she has to miss the party but I'm glad you decided to come."

He handed her the briefcase, "Teresa said you'd asked her to bring some records along for the party. They're all in there. I trust they're the ones you wanted?"

He then passed her the parcel he was holding and gave her a return peck on her cheek, "Happy birthday, I do hope you like it. Teresa chose it, so you best speak to her if it's not to your liking."

"I'm sure it'll be fine, Teresa always seems to pick the right things, but since she's not here I'll thank you for it. I'll open it later if you don't mind."

She put the parcel down on the telephone table, "Would you believe it but Edward isn't here yet? He phoned last night and said he wouldn't be coming back until today as Mr Gaitskell had asked him to sort out some problem or other and let him have the answers by Monday morning. He rang this morning and said he'd be here in plenty of time but I haven't heard from him since so I've no idea where he is."

She took hold of Philip's hand and led him into the sitting room where the sound of all the others chatting was coming from, "So until he arrives you can act as host for me, can't you?"

There were about a dozen people talking in the sitting room, but the French windows were wide open and there were many more guests out in the garden.

As they entered the room the talking seemed to stop and all heads turned towards them, "No, I'm sorry folks, it isn't Edward, but for those of you who don't know him this is our very good friend Philip."

She let go of Philip's hand and put the case down by the record player on which the Frank Sinatra ballad 'Embraceable You' was being played. Beckoning to a girl who was dressed similarly to the one who had opened the door, she said, "Mary, be a good girl and get Philip a drink please." She looked at Philip, "Whisky is it?" but before he could answer the telephone rang and she dashed out of the room to answer it.

Philip took the drink from Mary and merely nodding to the folks in the room made his way out into the garden. He said, "Hello" to his Uncle Tom, Aunt Mary and Samantha's mother and father who were all sitting together in garden chairs on the patio. Most of the other guests were standing in small groups on the lawn; the far end of which had been allocated to a clock golf game. Lucy was standing at one of the clock numbers concentrating on her next shot, but looked up as the ball went running way past the hole and she waved at Philip. He estimated that there were probably forty to fifty guests, some of whom he did not know and guessed they were probably Edward's political and legal friends.

It was a red faced Sam who came back into the garden a few minutes later and went straight up to Philip without saying a word to any of the other guests as she dashed past them. With a curt, "Excuse us a minute," to the couple he was chatting to, she took Philip's arm and pulled him away from them. "It's Edward on the phone. He wants to speak to you." She pushed him towards the door, "So you best go and speak to the master. We must all do his bidding mustn't we?"

Philip looked questioningly at Samantha, as if to ask if that was what she really wanted. She just pursed her lips in a half smile, "Yes, just go and speak to him," and then as if by an afterthought she added, "Please."

Philip worked his way back through the crowded sitting room carefully closing the door behind him. Picking up the phone he quietly said, "Hi Edward. What's the problem?"

"What has Sam said to you?"

"Nothing, why? She just said you wanted to speak to me."

"Well she's none too pleased with me. No, that's putting it mildly, she's bloody mad at me; and she's every right to be. But, honestly mate, it's not my fault." There was a short silence before he added, "Well it's not entirely my fault."

"What's not your fault? Are you hurt or something?"

"No I'm fine. Or at least I am 'til Sam gets her hands on me."

Philip was starting to wonder when Edward would get to the point and tell him what was going on, "Why don't you just tell me what you want? Do you want me to pick you up from the station or something?"

"I wish it was that easy mate, but I'm still stuck here at Euston station and it would take you all night to pick me up from here."

"What the hell are you still doing in London? Sam's been telling everyone you'd be back here any minute."

"I know and I should have been but I missed the bloody train. Honestly I ran as fast I could from the taxi, but by the time I'd got my ticket out for the collector, the damn train was pulling out of the station and he wouldn't let me through the barrier to get on it. I got on the next train and, you won't believe this, but an hour after it should have left the bloody thing hadn't moved. They finally came along and said there was something wrong with the engine and we'd have to get off and get the next train on another platform. So I'm still here and I thought I'd best telephone Sam."

There was a clicking on the line, and he heard Edward saying, "Damn, I've run out of coins for the phone. I'll have to ring you in a minute."

Philip put the phone down and snatched it up as soon as it rang a couple of minutes later. It was a woman's voice on the phone, "This is the operator. I have a request for a reverse charge call from a London number. Are you prepared to pay for the call?"

"Yes, of course, that will be fine," and without thinking of what it might sound like, added, "Just put me through as fast as you can."

The operator gave a curt, "Of course, Sir," but he thought he heard her say, probably with her hand over the mouthpiece, "There's no need for him to speak to me like that; I'm only doing my job."

There was another click and Edward was back on the line, "Thank God I've got you back. I've got absolutely no change left."

Philip thought it was about time he got Edward to say exactly what he was going to do, "So what are your plans now? What time can we expect you back?"

"Well that's the point. The next train is the mail train and that takes ages to get back to Birmingham and the party will be all over by then. So I thought it'd be best if I went back to the flat and checked over all this stuff I've been doing for Gaitskell again. Then I can catch the first train in the morning. I should be back before lunch and I thought I could take Sam, you and Teresa out for Sunday lunch somewhere to make up for all this trouble."

"Don't you think you should be making arrangements like this with Sam and not with me?"

"That's exactly what I was trying to do with Sam."

"And what did she say?"

"That's the point, she didn't say anything. She just said I should sort it out with you, and that's when she put the phone down and went off to find you."

Philip suddenly realised how he was being used as a piggy in the middle.

"So what do you want me to do?"

"Just go and sort it out with Sam, for me mate. Act as host at the party and try and make sure she enjoys herself and I'll see you tomorrow. I'll call you from the flat first thing in the morning and let you know what time the train gets in and if you could all pick me up at New Street station, we can have lunch in town somewhere."

"And what do I say to Sam now? She's got all these guests here and they all want to know where you are."

"I'll have to leave all that to you mate. I'm sure you'll say the right thing to everyone."

Philip wanted to ask more questions and also say that Teresa was not with him, but on balance felt more talking would achieve nothing, so he just said, "I'll do my best, but it won't be the same as your being here."

Edward merely said, "See you at the station tomorrow," and put down the phone.

Philip returned the phone to its cradle and went to find Samantha. When he found her she was in the garden, laughing and joking with two of her guests. The usually demure and composed Samantha, who never had more than two alcoholic drinks in an evening, had obviously had more than that in the time Philip had been on the telephone. She was usually quietly spoken and the perfect unpretentious and most unflappable of hostesses. Right now however, her voice was not only loud but was several tones higher than usual. She called across to Mary and as Mary moved towards her she downed the remains of her drink in one gulp, and took a fresh glass from Mary's tray as soon as she was able to reach it. Mary took her empty glass and went to turn away. Samantha stopped her and told her to wait where she was. She finished the new drink in three gulps without taking the glass from her lips, and as soon as the glass was empty, she put it on the tray and took another full glass, before continuing the conversation with the two now highly embarrassed guests.

Philip went up to her as quickly as he could and took her arm. "And what did Edward have to say to you?" she demanded.

"We'll talk about that in a moment but don't you think it would a good idea to let your guests have some food? I'm sure they're all starving. I know I am."

He turned to Mary, "Is the food in the dining room, Mary? Would you like people to help themselves in there, or do you want to bring it out here."

Mary, who was herself embarrassed at the hostess's actions meekly said, "Mrs Richards said the guests could help themselves. It's just a buffet and it's all laid out on the dining room table."

"Do you need to prepare anything or do you want them to come and get it right away?"

"Mrs Thompson's the one who's prepared all the food and she was going to warm a few bits and pieces in the kitchen, so I'll just check with her how long it'll take and let you know," and with that she whisked away before Samantha was able to give alternate instructions. She was back in two minutes with the information that Mrs Thompson was just taking the warm food out of the oven, so perhaps the guests would like to start getting the food as soon as they wanted to."

"Do you hear that folks?" shouted Philip, "Food is ready in the dining room so please go and help yourself as soon as you wish."

Nobody moved; everyone waiting for someone else to make the first move. Philip turned to the couple that Samantha was still talking to, "I'm sure you're ready for something to eat, aren't you?" They took the hint and without saying a word to Samantha turned and made their way to the dining room. Soon most of the others followed.

Samantha went to follow as well but Philip held her arm and stopped her movement. He spoke quietly but firmly, "I'll tell you about the call now, but why don't you come into the kitchen with me? It'll be quieter in there, away from all these inquisitive ears."

He did not wait for a reply, but took her drink off her and firmly taking her arm led her into the kitchen. Mrs Thompson was taking a tray of chicken legs out of the oven, "Is that the last one of those, Mrs Thompson?"

Mrs Thompson nodded. "Well can you take those into the dining room and stay there for a while? I just want a word with Mrs Richards." Mrs Thompson put the hot food on a plate and as she went out of the room Philip said, "We won't be more than a couple of minutes."

"What about the coffee? Mrs Richards said I was to make coffee for anyone who wanted it with their food."

"I'm sure they'll manage without coffee for a bit Mrs Thompson, and anyway we won't be long. So just give us a few minutes, please."

Philip closed the door behind Mrs Thompson and when he turned around, Samantha was sitting in a kitchen chair; her elbows on the table and her head held in her hands. She started to cry uncontrollably, "Why did he have to do this? And why today of all days? He promised me he'd be here."

Philip handed her his handkerchief, "He couldn't help it Samantha. Everything just seems to have gone wrong for him."

She looked up and dried her eyes, "That's what you really think, is it? I wish I could see it that way as well, but tell me, why does he always put his damn job before me? Am I really second best?"

Philip did not know what to say or do, "I'm sure that's not true, but there are times when things just get in the way for all of us. Take this business with Teresa for instance. She didn't want to go to work this weekend and had made specific plans not to, but in the end events took over and she just had to go in."

She started sobbing again, "But he promised me." She wiped her eyes again, her mascara and make-up coming off on to the handkerchief. "He swore he wouldn't miss this party and that he'd be here."

Philip told her about the telephone conversation and of Edward's remorse at not being able to make the party. "He said he'll catch the early train in the morning and take you out to lunch to make up for tonight. He suggested that Teresa and I join you but Teresa will be whacked after her night shift and will be in bed most of tomorrow, so we'll have to take a rain check on lunch, if you don't mind."

Samantha did not seem to be listening to him but merely wiped her eyes again, resulting in even more make-up going on to the handkerchief, "But he promised me he'd be here and I'm not going to forgive him that easily."

Philip sat down on the chair opposite her and neither of them spoke for several minutes. Suddenly Samantha took a deep breath, looked up at Philip, "Well damn him, let's go and enjoy this party Philip."

Philip smiled at her sudden change of spirit, "Not until you've had a large cup of coffee." He took the handkerchief out of her hand, opened it and displayed all the marks on it to Samantha, "And put on a new face."

She laughed, and for the first time that evening she was the Samantha of old that he loved so much. "You make the coffee then Philip while I nip upstairs and put on a new face. And then we'll go out there and knock 'em all dead, and if that has to be without my missing husband, then so be it."

She reached across the table and touched his hand, "And I know what that look means, so I promise to lay off the alcohol for the rest of the evening."

Philip merely said, "Good," before she got up and left the room.

Samantha looked prim and perfect again when she returned to the kitchen, where she drank the black coffee quickly before they both returned to the guests. She kept to her word about enjoying herself without alcohol, but mainly she made sure that everyone else enjoyed themselves and the rest of the evening was a huge success.

It was almost one o'clock before Philip made to go with the last of the guests but Samantha called him back saying he had forgotten all the records he had brought with him. The other guests left and Philip and Samantha re-entered the house.

"Come into the kitchen, Philip. I'll make us some more coffee and whilst I've got you on your own, I'd like to talk to you about the conversation we never finished weeks ago."

Philip had thought that Samantha had forgotten all about the unfinished conversation about Juliette and had been hoping that it wouldn't be brought up again. He'd thought about it several times, but had never reached a conclusion as to how best play it. Should he be absolutely honest with Sam and tell her he thought Edward was trying to turn her into a substitute Juliette, or should he play it down and pretend that Juliette was merely part of Edward's forgotten past?

At first however the conversation revolved around the party, the various guests and the various titbits of conversations that had taken place with people during the evening. Samantha made the coffee and as she gave Philip his cup she indicated he should sit at the kitchen table opposite her.

"So, are you going to tell me all about Juliette now?"

"What is it you want me to say?"

She shook her head from side to side, "If I knew that I wouldn't be asking the question would I? But why don't you start by telling me what you thought of their relationship. No-one's ever actually said it but I get the impression that she was the love of his life. Was she?"

A direct question demanding a direct answer! Philip decided to deal with everything perfectly straight and tell Samantha exactly how he had viewed the relationship at the time, "I guess you could say that. We first met Juliette and her sister on a beach in France in '38 and Edward was smitten with Juliette right from the moment he first saw her. And it seemed to me that she felt the same about him."

"And what about the other sister, Madeleine isn't it, were you smitten with her?"

Philip let out a laugh, "Madeleine was," he stopped to correct himself, "Madeleine is a lovely girl, but no, I wasn't smitten with her and I'm pretty sure that she did not see me in a romantic way either."

"But it was different for Edward and Juliette?"

"Absolutely, they wanted to spend every spare minute alone together."

"So what happened when the holiday ended?"

"We came home and Edward was as miserable as sin. He went back several times to see her in the following year, and I know they wrote to each other regularly, but the war put an end to the visits and after the Germans invaded France, they weren't even able to write to each other."

"But he didn't forget her?"

Philip wondered where all the questions were leading to and tried to short cut them, "You know all this, Sam. They met up again during the war and as soon as Edward was demobbed they were married. Twelve months later she had a child but she died giving birth, and after a while Edward got on with his life without her."

Another 'but' question followed, "But he hasn't got on with his life without her, has he?"

The first of the dreaded questions had finally been asked. "As far as I know he has. He doesn't talk about her much so I guess he is getting on with his life. He's married you, hasn't he, so that must say that he's moved on, doesn't it?" He immediately wished he hadn't added the 'doesn't it'.

"I wished I could be sure of that. Why does he stay in London so much? I wish he came home more often."

"I think you know the answer to that. He has to be in London, that's where Parliament is." Philip was still unsure where the conversation was going or what Samantha was really unhappy about. "I suppose Edward might say he doesn't know why you stay here and don't join him in London."

"He did suggest that when we first got married." She looked at Philip and tears came to her eyes again, "I suppose I should have given it a try, shouldn't I?"

"Maybe, but I'm guessing that the real question is more to do with the fact that you have all sorts of things going on in your head and you're not actually talking to Edward about them." He waited for a response but she said nothing. She just looked at him as if waiting for him to say more, but neither said anything for several minutes. They were looking straight into each other's eyes and Philip was beginning to find it very difficult to concentrate.

Eventually it was Samantha who broke the connection and spoke, "Look I know you're trying to say the right thing and I'm sorry to put you in this awkward position." She reached across and touched his hand very lightly. She squeezed it as she said, "But you're the only one I feel I can talk about it. I know you won't tell anyone else about my problems." She squeezed his hand again before questioning this, "You won't talk to anyone about this conversation will you?"

He shook his head, "Of course not if that's how you want it."

She pulled her hand back and mouthed a, "Thank you," and averted her eyes from his. "I want to talk to you about Juliette some more but first can I ask you about Julian."

Philip shrugged his shoulders, "Edward rarely talks about Julian so I know very little about him. So I doubt if I can help you much on the subject of Julian."

"But you've at least met the boy haven't you? That's more than I have."

"Only years ago when he was a baby; when I went to Madeleine's wedding just after he was born."

Samantha continued talking without seeming to take in any of this comment, "When I was at the London flat a while back I picked the post up one morning. One of the letters addressed to Edward had obviously come from France. I just gave it to him with all the rest, but when I asked him about it later he brushed it aside by saying it was a letter from Madeleine thanking him for the money he'd sent for Julian."

"Well I'm sure it was. He's never said anything about it to me but I'm sure he'd do the right thing financially for his son."

Sam looked directly at Philip again with questioning eyes, "But that's exactly it, he is his son. Why does he never visit him or want to see him?"

She kept looking at Philip waiting for his answer but Philip did not know how to answer the question and eventually said, "I'm sorry I don't know, you'll have to ask Edward about that, not me."

"I did ask when he got the letter. I asked him how Julian was and he just said that he was as well as could be expected." She repeated the statement, "As well as can be expected, what the hell does that mean? And when I suggested we should ask Julian to stay with us sometime, he just got annoyed by my questions and told me to drop the subject."

"So did you? Drop the subject I mean."

"Well yes. What else could I have done?"

"Well maybe you should have persevered and made him talk about it."

"Maybe I should have, but do you know what he meant by, as well as can be expected?"

Philip was surprised she did not seem to know anything about Julian, but it had been a 'none subject' for Edward and his parents for a long time. He nevertheless thought that Samantha should know and decided to tell her everything he knew. "Edward is not the only one who gets letters from Madeleine. She and I write to each other very occasionally, but I'm not sure that Edward knows about that. I've never felt the need to tell him."

Samantha was obviously becoming irritated and wanted him to come to the point, "And she tells you about Julian?"

"Sometimes, Yes."

She leaned forward and again looked directly into his eyes demanding details, "So?"

"Well you know it was giving birth to Julian that caused Juliette's death, but what no-one knew at the time was the problems during birth had also affected Julian."

Samantha put her hand to her mouth, "Oh, my God, what problems?"

"Well at first they all thought everything was normal. He was a little slow in learning to walk but the doctor said that was nothing unusual. But the big problem was that he was making no progress at all with talking and they noticed that he did not seem to respond to noises." He could still feel the questioning in her eyes as he added, "Julian is partially deaf."

She just stared unbelievingly at him, "Why on earth hasn't Edward told me that?"

"Edward's the only one who can answer that question but unfortunately deafness is not the poor lad's only problem."

"Why what on earth else is there?"

"Apparently he has some movement difficulties on his right side which make him seem a bit slow and awkward."

"But he's nine years old now, so how is he coping now?"

"To be honest I don't know. I think he can hear a bit and I gather he's learned sign language and has even started to lip read a bit. But of course he probably only understands French so it could be difficult for him if he came here and that may be why Edward doesn't want him to come."

"Well thank you for telling me and you're right I should force Edward to talk about him." She smiled, "And whilst we're talking about children can I ask you something personal?"

He laughed almost guessing what was coming next, "You can ask so long as I don't have to give you an answer."

OK. That's a deal."

"So what's the question?"

She hesitated for a moment before asking, "I've often wondered why you and Teresa have never had children. Don't you want children?"

He had never discussed this subject with anyone other than Teresa and knew that Teresa would not be pleased if she knew he was discussing it with Samantha. Nevertheless he felt he could talk to Samantha about anything, knowing perfectly well that she would never gossip to anyone else about it. That was the agreement they had about the things she had told him and he was absolutely certain that the confidentially would work the other way as well. And so he told her all about the problems he and Teresa had had trying to start a baby without success and how they'd had tests which showed he was the one with the problem.

"Don't answer if you don't want to, but how is Teresa about that?"

"Funny thing she seemed to accept it completely and moved from being desperate to have a child to letting the whole subject drop overnight. We never mention it now but she seems perfectly OK about the situation."

Samantha leaned forward and touched his hand again, this time not removing it straight away. She was looking directly into his eyes again as she said, "I'm so sorry. You'd make a great Dad."

Her hand was still touching his and the effect this was having on him was almost unbearable but he did not want it to end, "Thank you, but shall we change the subject now?"

She smiled, "Absolutely. I want you to tell me more about Juliette anyway." She moved her hand away from his and continued, "I don't expect Edward to forget her but do you really think he's got over her particularly losing her in the tragic way he did? The honest truth please."

Although Philip was no longer looking directly into her eyes he could still feel the warmth that it had given him throughout his body and he wondered whether she felt the same. Probably not, was his assessment of the situation.

She lightly touched his hand again, pulling it back immediately, "Well am I going to get an answer?"

He wanted to grab her hand and hold on to it, but did not wish to spoil the closeness of the moment by doing anything so stupid. He decided to be as honest as she had asked him to be, and just trust that whatever he said would not spoil their relationship. "No I don't think he's forgotten her and what they had. And honestly I don't think he ever will. But in fact I feel that is how it should be. His feelings for Juliette," he stopped for a second before adding forcefully, "And hers for him, were very special. They were madly in love, and one didn't have to be in their company for long before that became blindingly obvious." He looked soulfully at her. "I'm sorry if that isn't what you wanted to hear, but you did ask me to be honest."

She smiled, "Not at all. That's exactly what I expected you to say. I never really had any illusions about the relationship he had with Juliette, and I know I can never replace her for him." She leaned across the table closer to Philip and shook her head from side to side, "But that's the whole point, isn't it?" Her voice became quite determined and increased in volume, "I don't want to replace her. I don't want him to forget about her. I want him to talk about her. I want him to tell me about her." She stopped and looked as if she was about to cry, but she took a deep breath to stem the tears before she continued, "But most of all I want him to accept me for who I am. I know I'm not the love of his life but it would be nice to be told that I am the present love in his life."

Philip responded with, "You should be telling Edward all this," and without stopping to think what he was saying added, "And make sure he always sees the you and not the Juliette."

"What do you mean? How do I do that?"

Philip closed his eyes for a second and thought, *'How could I have said anything so stupid?'* and in the circumstances he just shrugged his shoulders.

"It's the hair isn't it?"

"Why on earth do you say that?"

"Oh, just something that Edward's mother said to me tonight before you came."

"And what was that?"

"She complemented me on how nice I looked but, like you've just said, she also said that I should be myself and go back to my own hair colour."

"And that's what started all this off again?"

"Yes I suppose so, but if Edward had been here then we wouldn't be talking like this, would we?" She ran her fingers through her hair and said, "This is her hair isn't it? I really didn't know when Edward first suggested it. He says he really likes it this colour so that's why I've kept it like this."

She put both hands to her head, one on each side, and rubbed it roughly, taking all semblance of style from it, "I've been quite stupid, haven't I?" She looked questioningly into his eyes, "The honest truth again, please."

"I would never say you're stupid but maybe the hair was a mistake for Edward as well."

"How do you mean?"

"Well, just suppose he didn't really give it a thought until you'd changed the colour, but afterwards, maybe, just maybe, it became a constant reminder to him that you weren't Juliette but he could no longer see you as you either."

She laughed out loud, and for the first time since they had sat down in the kitchen she seemed to relax, "I think we should leave it there." She continued laughing, "We don't really want to get into deep psychological stuff like that, do we?"

He laughed with her and was glad that the tension had finally been broken.

She reached out and touched the side of his face, "But thank you for that.

I think I know what I have to do, now."

"And what's that?"

"Well if you'll let me have Monday morning off, I'll go to the hairdressers and get my old colour back." She laughed out loud again, "That's if I can remember what colour it was."

"And you will talk to Edward?"

"Yes. I'll talk to Edward."

Philip stood up and reached into his pocket and took out a small packet wrapped in birthday paper. He handed it to Samantha, "This is for you, happy birthday."

"But I've already had a present from you."

"Well this one is just from me. Teresa doesn't know about it, and I've been in two minds whether I should give it to you anyway."

She looked at him quizzically, "Can I open it now?"

"Yes of course. Rightly or wrongly, I've given it to you now."

She unwrapped the paper and looked carefully at the box of perfume and then back at Philip. "Are you trying to tell me something here?"

"Only that you are a very special girl whom I'm very fond of." He hesitated slightly before continuing, "And that I always loved it when you wore that particular perfume."

She took the bottle out of the box and sprayed a little on to her neck, "I think if I am going to be the old me, then I should start to wear this again sometimes. Don't you think?"

She did not wait for answer but said, "Thank you very much," as she leaned forward to give him a kiss, but instead of the usual kiss on the cheek, she kissed him full on the lips and held it there for a several seconds. She pulled back and mouthed another, "Thank you." She put the bottle back in its box, "And we'll keep all of tonight's conversations to ourselves, yes?"

Philip leaned forward and kissed her again on the lips. She did not stop him and he wanted to put his arms around her and hold her to him, but instead eventually pulled back saying, "And should we keep that to ourselves as well?"

She smiled and looked into his eyes again, "I think it would be best, don't you?"

He nodded his head, "Probably."

She took his arm and led him out of the room, "And now it's time for you to go home, before we do anything really stupid."

She opened the front door for him to leave, but there was no goodnight kiss, not even the usual farewell peck on the cheek.

CHAPTER TWENTY

1957

Samantha was determined not to be a replacement Juliette for Edward and not only had her hair back to its natural colour but now wore her old perfume far more often than the perfume Edward had bought her. Edward accepted this return to the real Samantha without any comment whatsoever.

She also heeded Philip's advice and tried to get Edward to talk about the matters she had asked him about at the party. This was not anything like as successful and was always met with the usual, "That's all in the past and I don't want to talk about it," response whenever the subject of Juliette or Julian was raised. After such exchanges Edward would go into a gloomy mood for several hours or even days. It appeared that all of Samantha's efforts to clear the air on this subject were doomed to failure and that it would always be an insurmountable obstacle in their marriage.

During the months following her birthday party she often raised the subject again with Philip when no one else was in the office with them. Philip was unsure how he was meant to respond but time and again Samantha started the conversation by saying that Philip was a particular friend, whom she knew she could trust and confide in, without fear that her marriage problems would be talked about.

"I know I probably shouldn't say this, but I sometimes feel closer to you than I do to Edward." She looked a little embarrassed at saying this and tried to explain it away by declaring, "I find it so easy to talk to you Philip. I just wish Edward felt it as easy to talk to me about things." She reached forward and touched Philip's arm, "I feel so much better after you've listened to me babbling on." She laughed as she added, "And you are so much cheaper than a shrink."

During these conversations no direct reference was ever made of the time they spent chatting together late into the night at the party, and no mention was ever made of the kisses that had been exchanged between them.

Nevertheless, Philip now felt a new closeness to Samantha and even though she had said she felt close to him, he had no idea whether what she felt was anything like the feelings he had for her, or why she talked to him about matters that were really personal between her and Edward.

He so wanted to tell her his true feelings but desperately didn't want to lose her either, and in order to make sure that didn't happen he knew he had to keep things on a purely platonic level whatever his personal feelings were. He was convinced that to do otherwise would undoubtedly shock Samantha and this special relationship between them would be lost for ever.

On New Year's Eve as Edward and Samantha sat waiting to welcome in 1957, Edward was once again particularly melancholy. He was sitting in his armchair, drink in hand; a drink that he had not touched in the last half an hour. Samantha knew perfectly well the reason for his despondency and depression on this particular date, but on this occasion determined not to ignore the significance of the day as she had done in previous years.

"I know today has extremely painful memories for you Edward but please can you let me share them with you for once. I'm not stupid. I know how important Juliette was to you and I've never wished to take any of your memories or feelings about her away from you."

She got out of her own chair, moved towards him and kneeling on the floor put her arms around him. He looked at her with mournful eyes and she thought that he was about to push her away with the usual 'barred subject' comment. But he did not do so. He put his arms tightly around her and put his head on her shoulder and they just held each other without anything being said. After a little while his body started to shake and she could feel his tears against her cheek. She just held him tighter against her own body and inwardly rejoiced as she hoped that at last maybe the spell had been broken.

She was also crying before long and even though she found that reaching up to hold him whilst kneeling on the floor extremely uncomfortable she was not about to reposition herself unless Edward made some sort of move.

Eventually he moved his head slightly and lightly kissed her on the cheeks, "I'm so sorry. I'm so sorry."

"What is there to be sorry about? There's no need to be sorry about anything."

He released his hold on her. Her heart stopped as she feared what might be coming next, but instead of pushing her away as she half expected, he looked directly into her eyes and said, "I do love you." He gently touched her cheeks and smiled as he added, "I wouldn't have married you if I hadn't."

Samantha merely looked back into his eyes and mouthed the words, "I love you too."

He put his arms under her shoulders and lifted her from her kneeling position. She stood up unsure of what to do next, but Edward tapped his leg and said, "Just sit here for a while. It's been a long time since you sat on my lap."

She did as requested and as soon as she put her arm round his shoulders, he took her in his arms again and kissed her full on the lips. Although she loved this attention she did wonder whether this was merely his way of making sure she would drop the questions about Juliette, but to her surprise when he ended the kiss he immediately said, "It would have been Juliette's birthday today."

She merely pursed her lips and nodded her head unsure whether she was expected to give a spoken reply. Edward simply touched her cheek and continued, "She was born today. She got married today." He paused before continuing, "And she was buried today."

Samantha had wanted him to talk about Juliette for so long, but now that he was, she was unsure how to deal with the situation. With tears in her eyes, she nodded her head and said, "I know." She wiped a tear from her eye and added, "I'm so sorry."

Her uncertainty and fears about how to deal with the situation were however unnecessary because once Edward had started to talk about Juliette it was almost as if he could not stop. He had hardly mentioned her name to anyone in years but now that he had it was as if the lid on his feelings about his life with her suddenly exploded with all the emotion he'd clamped tightly away for so long.

He talked about how he had first met her, how besotted he was with her and how he had missed her so much during the war years. And then he moved on to the events surrounding her death. Samantha was somewhat shocked at the extent of his anger about this. He was so clearly outraged at the circumstances of her death; circumstances that he neither knew the full details of or the reason for them.

"They never told me why she had to die and they never told me what caused her death." He pulled Samantha towards him and held her clamped tightly against him, "Why did the bastards let her die? It would have been better if the baby had died and she had lived, but that isn't the way they do things is it?" He did not wait for an answer before continuing to vent his anger, "All they could say was 'it's the Lord's will.' Well if that's what the Lord wants then I don't want anything to do with their Lord."

After a while Edward picked up his drink and knocked it back in one gulp before asking Sam to replenish it for him. She poured a drink for herself as well and when she went to sit on his lap again he suggested that it would be more comfortable if she sat back in her own chair. Samantha thought that this meant the end of the conversation but instead Edward continued to talk not only about Juliette and Julian but about other things that had been closed subjects before, such as his war experiences. By the end of the evening Samantha felt that she now knew the real Edward better than she had ever done before. As the clock started to strike midnight, Edward stood up and moved towards Samantha glass in hand. She also stood up and Edward kissed her with a passion that had been missing from their relationship for some time.

He picked up Samantha's glass from the coffee table and gave it to her. "Here's to a New Year and a new start."

Samantha repeated the words, "To the New Year and a new start," and at that moment felt they were truly starting afresh and that she should forget all about the feelings she had felt for Philip over the last few years and leave them behind her.

At the same hour Philip was toasting in the New Year at a family party at his mother's house. The toast was followed by the usual round of hugs and kisses to everyone in the room. He returned to kiss Teresa a second time but his mind was miles away. He wanted to kiss the woman that at that very moment was being kissed so passionately by Edward.

On the first day back at work in the New Year, Philip told Tom, Lucy and his mother that he wanted to hold a board meeting as soon as possible to talk about the future direction that the two businesses should take.

Usually all matters were decided on an informal basis and everyone was puzzled as to why Philip wanted such a formal meeting. Their curiosity got the better of them and they agreed to meet that same afternoon and, well before the allotted time, they were all seated round the table in Lucy's office waiting for Philip to arrive.

As soon as he did and had sat down, Tom spoke, "You called this meeting Philip. So what's it all this about?"

Philip took a number of papers out of his briefcase and laid them on the table, "First these are some figures Sam collated for me last week." He passed a copy to each of them, "They're the figures of our own radio sales over the last few years and you'll see that most are being sold in our own shops."

"Well that's a good thing isn't it?" asked Tom.

"It could be, except that our shop managers tell us that many of the sales are only made because they have been told to push our products."

He passed a further set of papers round the table, "These are the sales of all the other wirelesses in the shops. You can see that we're selling far more of the cheaper models from Ever Ready, Bush, Ferranti, GEC and the rest, than we are of our models. It seems that the majority of people want to buy the new portable radios in all sorts of designs and fashions."

Tom interrupted again, "But we've spoken about this before and we've agreed that we can't compete with the big boys. Our strength is the quality of our goods not all these cheap bakelite models."

"Thank you Uncle Tom. You've brought us right to the point. Our strength is quality not mass production. And while we're on the subject, I think that's also the only reason we're still getting some military orders."

"Well the military know a good thing when they see it."

Philip did not answer but took another paper from the pile in front of him and passed it to Tom, "I received this in the post this morning."

Tom read the letter and passed it to Lucy, "We knew that would happen sooner or later. It just means we'll have to get someone else."

Philip's mother spoke for the first time, "What does it say, Lucy?"

"It's from Leonard Oakes. He says that Professor Rhodes is retiring at the end of the academic year and won't be able to give him any of the small amounts of help he's been giving since the war. And worse than that, Leonard said that he wants to retire at the same time."

"So what does that mean?" asked Grace.

Everyone looked at Philip for an answer but he turned to Lucy, "What do you think it means Lucy?"

Lucy looked a little lost in thought for a while but eventually spoke, "It probably means we'll soon be losing more of our military orders to the big boys. We've already noticed a downturn in their orders over the last couple of years."

Philip shuddered at the half expected sardonic response from Tom, "So what do you suggest we do about all this, Master Philip? After all you're the one who called us together."

But it was Lucy who spoke first, "I don't want to make things any worse, Philip, but over Christmas I've been thinking that it's about time I started to take it easy as well. I was going to chat to you and Tom about it over the next few days but I suppose I should throw it into the arena now." She lowered her head as she said, "Sorry, I don't want to make things any worse."

Tom threw up his arms in a mock gesture of despair, "Well that's it then. We might as well close shop right now. I take it that you'll be the one to break the good news to everyone on the shop floor, Philip, because I'm damned if I'm going to do it."

Grace came to Philip's rescue, "I don't think it'll be as bad as that Tom.

I'm sure Philip will be able to sort something out. Won't you Philip?"

"It's all right for you to say that, Grace, but it seems to me that your shops will be fine. After all you don't need our equipment to make sales. You can just sell everyone else's stuff and probably make more profit than you are already."

"I'm sorry you feel that way, Tom. You know perfectly well that we've always supported the factory and we'll continue to do so." She turned to Philip once again, "Won't we Philip?"

This time it was Lucy that came to Philip's rescue, "Can everyone just calm down and let's look at this situation coolly." She turned to Philip, "Do you have any ideas Philip?"

"Well yes, I do have one or two thoughts on the matter, but I'm not sure that any of them will give all the answers."

Tom put his hands on his head and leaned back in his chair, "So what are these thoughts of yours?"

"Firstly Uncle Tom, I think it's fair to say that we have to make changes, whether we want to or not. I'm as sad as anyone that this factory that's provided us all with such a good living for so long, looks likely to gradually lose out to all the big boys. We could try to compete with them, but that would mean investing a great deal in modernisation, many more lines and probably a much larger factory. I'm sure the bank would consider a loan request for the expansion, but I'm also sure that they'd expect us to invest much more of our own money in the venture. They'd probably want to take our houses as security and then what would happen if it all failed? I for one don't think we can take that gamble."

Tom leaned even further back in his chair and had to steady himself quickly to prevent the chair from toppling over. After he had settled himself he said, "Your father and I took the gamble way back and it paid off then, so why can't it do so again?"

Grace, who was sitting next to him, took his arm and spoke quietly to him, "But you and Frank were young men then, Tom. Do you still have the same drive to make it all happen again?"

Tom shook his head, "Of course you're right, Grace. My doctor keeps telling me to take things easy." He looked across the desk at Lucy, "And I should be thinking of retiring as well Lucy, but I'm worried about the effect it'll have on all the workers. Some of them have been with us for as long as I can remember and we owe them. If the factory closes, what will they do?"

He stared directly at Grace, "And what about your Johnny? He loves it here and he's turned into a great craftsman. Some of his specialist cabinets are superb." He turned to Philip, "You can't tell him that he's no longer needed Philip. It would destroy him."

"I know that Uncle Tom, and I don't think we have to, but I do think we have to change."

Tom leaned back in his chair again making sure this time that it was not too far, "OK. I give in. How do we have to change?"

"You've really already given all the answers, Uncle Tom. We can't compete on the mass production front. Our strength has always been quality. You and Dad always designed wirelesses as pieces of furniture and we still do. So why don't we concentrate on making quality furniture and fit wirelesses, televisions, record players and all that sort of things into the furniture. I know there'll only be a limited call for such stuff, but as long as it pays for a decent wage to all the workers and provides you and Lucy with a reasonable income in your retirement, do we really want anything else?"

"And you really think that would work?"

"I think we'd have to change our sales techniques, but yes, I think it could work."

The conversation went on for several more hours but eventually the decision was made to change direction. They all agreed that they were likely to lose the few military contracts they still had and also agreed that they should accept that as inevitable. Lucy and Tom agreed to stay on for another couple of years to help reorganise the changes, after which they would gradually do less and less hours until they finally wished to retire altogether.

That evening Philip had a meeting with his mother at which it was decided to extend the items sold in the shops to include even more of other manufacturer's goods and also to start a catalogue sales business.

The next day Philip was alone with Samantha explaining the new approach to her and together they drew up a timetable for the changes. After a while she asked if he would like a cup of tea and went to fetch one for them. As soon as she sat back down she started to tell Philip about her discussions with Edward on New Year's Eve.

She was clearly thrilled with the way things had turned out that evening and Philip was pleased that at last she and Edward had been able to clear the air about Juliette. He was nevertheless somewhat irritated that she spoke so excitedly about the evening particularly the fact that it was obvious that whatever had been said had clearly brought her and Edward closer. He also detected a change in the way she now spoke of Edward and suspected that it was not only talking that had occurred between them that night.

However over the next few weeks and months as he and Samantha worked very closely together to make the necessary business changes, he gradually sensed the old closeness and electricity between them returning. Or was it just wishful thinking on his part?

She continued to confide in him from time to time, and as summer approached she seemed to be becoming disillusioned again that Edward was spending more and more time, including their precious weekends, in London. But what made it worse was that he was no longer giving her any reason as to why he needed to stay there. At the start of the year Samantha had spent some weekends in London with Edward and when she possibly could, had spent the odd few days and nights in the London flat during the week as well, but gradually Edward seemed to find excuses why it wasn't worth the effort for her and her visits became less and less frequent.

Ever since Frank had set up the business with Tom he had always insisted that the two of them should visit all of the trade shows, and they had first exhibited their own products at the Wireless Exhibition at the Royal Albert Hall as early as 1924. They subsequently exhibited at every Radiolympia until the exhibitions had ceased for the duration of the war.

When Philip joined the firm after the war he suggested to Tom that they should consider exhibiting again at the National Radio Exhibition in 1947 and they had done so with some success. They had exhibited at every show since then, and part of the new business plans was to have their up market 'furniture' models available for the 1957 show at Earls Court in August.

But at the beginning of August Tom had another of his angina attacks and his doctor insisted that he should rest up again for at least three weeks. Tom suggested that Samantha should take his place at the exhibition saying that she would do a far better job than he could anyway. Samantha jumped at the opportunity, knowing that Edward had said he had to be in London at the end of August on Labour party business and she would be able to stay at the flat with him.

"You could stay at the flat as well Philip. It will save on hotel expenses. Actually why don't you ask Teresa to come as well?"

"I'm not sure about that, Sam. You and Edward won't want us around and I don't think Teresa could have the time off work anyway. No I think I'll just stay in the hotel as usual, but it would be nice if you and Edward had dinner with me one evening, my treat."

But Samantha insisted Philip should stay in the guest room at the flat and when she told Edward about them both staying she detected a definite hesitancy in his response that made her feel that once again her own proposed visit to London was perhaps not to his liking.

The exhibition was to open on Wednesday 28th August and Samantha made arrangements for herself and Philip to travel by train to London on the Monday morning with Edward, and Teresa managed to work her shifts so that she could join them on the following Saturday for a five day break.

But Edward once again thwarted Samantha's plans on the previous Friday by saying he had to return to London on Sunday. When Samantha said she would travel with him he rejected the suggestion with, "I've got to meet someone on Sunday evening so you'd only be on your own. No, you travel down with Philip on Monday as planned."

Samantha was still smarting from Edward's rejection when she met Philip at the railway station on Monday morning.

Philip took her case from her and placed it next to his own. He looked around for Edward, "Where's Edward?"

"He isn't coming. He went back yesterday. I've told him we'll see him this evening at the flat."

"I was going to suggest that I took you both out to dinner this evening. We may not have time later in the week when the exhibition is open."

"That would be nice." She then added rather sarcastically, "That's always assuming Edward is back before all the restaurants are closed of course."

Philip picked up both cases and they made their way to the London train. They found their seats and sat down.

The carriage soon filled up with other passengers all of whom looked like business men commuting to the capital and who, as soon as they were seated opened up their newspapers and disappeared behind them.

Sam was obviously amused at how they all looked and acted as if they were made from the same mould. She turned to Philip and smiled. He knew exactly what had amused her and smiled back.

As the train pulled away from the station and they both settled back for the journey, Philip very quickly became acutely aware of Samantha's presence next to him. At work they would sit at opposite sides of a desk, but now Samantha was sitting next to him and making absolutely no attempt to leave any space between them. Her leg was resting against his and, much as he tried, he could not dispel the effect this was having on his whole body.

He remained motionless, not wishing to move from her, but not daring to move any closer either. He feared that if he did so, she would immediately move away and that was the last thing he wanted.

Neither of them spoke and the only sound was of the train itself interrupted occasionally by the rustle of paper as the other passengers turned over the pages of their newspapers.

Half an hour into the journey and Philip and Samantha had not moved. He turned his head to look at her. She had closed her eyes and her head leaned to one side. He was unsure whether she was asleep or not, but believing that she was, a warmth flooded through him as he enjoyed the experience of her asleep next to him.

She made a very weak moan as she moved slightly in her seat. Her head fell further to the side and came to rest on his shoulder. He decided to close his own eyes and enjoy the sensation, but he was soon disturbed by the ticket collector asking for tickets.

He tried to find the tickets without unsettling Samantha. "Don't disturb your wife, Sir. I'll pop in for the tickets when I come back down the train."

But Samantha was awoken by the noise. She lifted her head and sat upright in her seat. Philip handed the tickets to the guard without saying a word, but in his head he was uttering a stream of *"damn, damn and damn,"* at the man.

Samantha smiled at Philip and he wondered whether she realised the effect she had on him. He smiled back, turned his head forward and re-entered his imaginations. He did not know how long he'd been smiling at the pleasant thoughts he was having or how long Samantha had been staring at him. It was probably mere seconds but to him it felt much longer. He could feel her eyes on him and wanted to turn and look into them, but was afraid to do so. She leaned forward and whispered in his ear, "A penny for your thoughts?"

This time he turned and looked at her, "Sorry, what did you say?"

She laughed before taking his arm and speaking into his ear again, "I was wondering what my husband was thinking and offered him a penny for his thoughts?" She leaned back and laughed again, ignoring all the stares of the other passengers. She moved closer to Philip and nodded her head towards the other passengers who quickly returned to their crosswords, before whispering, "Do you think we seem like a married couple to all of them as well?"

Philip let down his guard and answered without thinking, "Oh, I do hope so."

She held on to his arm and moved closer to him, her lips almost touching his cheek, "So what were you so wrapped up in thought about then?"

Philip was at a loss how to answer the question. He had wanted to tell her for so long about his feelings for her, but still dreaded the rejection he feared would result if he did so. And, in any case he did not want to talk about any of these things with an audience, even if they were pretending not to be listening, "I don't think this is the time or place, so maybe it would be best if my thoughts remained as just that, my thoughts."

"Now you do have me mystified and you can't leave it in the air just like that. I thought we were friends; friends that had no secrets between them."

He nodded his head slightly towards the others, "Not here, not now."

"Only if you promise to tell me later."

"Maybe and maybe not. We'll have to see."

He hoped that was the end of the conversation but Samantha persisted, "You seemed pleased with yourself when I was watching you, so just tell me, were they nice thoughts you were having?"

Again he answered before thinking, "Very nice thoughts."

"Then I'll only let you off the hook now if you promise to tell me later."

"We'll see."

She snuggled up to him and again whispered directly into his ear, "I shall insist."

When the train arrived in London they took a taxi, went straight to the exhibition hall and spent the day organising things around their stand where there were always so many people about that the train conversation was not raised by Samantha again.

They left Earls Court at around six o'clock and arrived at the flat half an hour later. Philip paid the taxi driver and carried both cases up the steps to the flat. Samantha opened the door expecting Edward to already be there, but he wasn't. She found a note from him on the telephone table in the hall. She snatched it up, opened the envelope and quickly read it.

"Damn the man! He's done it again."

Philip realised she was having difficulty holding back her tears. "What's the matter? What's he done?"

She said nothing but just handed him the note. He noticed that it was headed merely to *'Sam.'* It continued,

'Sorry about this evening but I have to attend a dinner in Brighton. It's some Union do that I hadn't put in my own diary and had forgotten all about until my secretary reminded me this morning. Waited as long as I could to see you but have to dash now to catch the train. Am booked into the hotel for tonight so I'll be staying in Brighton and I'll see you tomorrow evening. Have enclosed some cash for you and

Philip to have dinner somewhere nice.

Sorry love Edward

PS. Will try to ring you later before dinner if I can, but don't worry if you are out.

Philip handed the note back to her, "I'm sure it's just one of those things he couldn't get out of."

"Yes I know you're probably right but it's typical Edward anyway. I sometimes feel he does these things deliberately."

"I'm sure that isn't true. I'm sure it can't be helped, so why don't we get washed and brushed up and go and have something to eat, like he says?"

"Do you mind if we don't Philip? I really don't feel like going out now. I hadn't planned on us eating in tonight but I'm sure we'll find some food in the kitchen."

He followed her into the kitchen and watched as she looked for food. There was a piece of paper on the kitchen table with a pile of cash on it. "My, my, he actually remembered to get the food I asked him to."

She picked up the paper and laughed, "Or at least he's got the cleaning lady to get it for him."

She opened the refrigerator, "Let's see what he's got." She took out a plate on which was a pile of sausages and placed it on the table. A bottle of milk followed. She looked at the list, "If we can find the potatoes listed here we can have sausage and mash and we should find some tea somewhere." She reached into the cupboard and took out two bottles, "Or maybe, we can have something a bit stronger."

She handed one of the bottles to Philip and put the other on the table, "Why don't you open that for me? I think some of that is exactly what I need right now." She pointed to a cupboard, "You should find glasses up there and there should be a bottle opener in that drawer over there."

By the time Philip had opened the bottle and poured her a glass of wine, Samantha had found the potatoes and was busy peeling them at the sink.

He gave her the glass and took the potato peeler from her, "Why don't you take that drink with you and go and freshen up while I peel these potatoes?" He stopped her as she turned to do as he bid, "Are you sure you wouldn't rather go out to eat though?"

"What's the matter? Isn't sausage and mash good enough for you?" she mocked.

He smiled, "There's nothing better that I'd rather have to eat tonight."

He wanted to say *'especially if I can have it here with you,'* but decided against it. From the broad smile and look she gave him, he wondered whether she had read his mind.

They had almost finished their meal when the telephone rang and Samantha got up to answer it. She was soon back at the table. She sat down, pushed her almost empty plate away and took a swig from her glass without saying anything.

"Is everything OK?"

"Yes fine. That was Edward with another of his short and sweet conversations." She shrugged her shoulders as she tried to mimic Edward's end of the conversation, "Sorry about tonight. Must dash, they're calling us into dinner. Have a nice evening and I'll see you tomorrow."

She took another mouthful of her wine, emptying the glass before placing it back on the table. Philip went to open the second bottle to refill the glass but she took his arm and prevented him from doing so, "No. I think I've had quite enough for this evening. Why don't we put these dirty dishes in the kitchen and go and sit in the lounge where you can tell me all the things you wouldn't tell me on the train this morning instead?"

Philip got up and started to collect the plates together, "Let's just wash these up first."

"No leave them. I'm sure Edward's cleaning lady will wash them up in the morning."

But Philip insisted and she went to follow him into the kitchen. "No. You cooked the meal so I'll do the dishes. You just go and put your legs up and I'll join you as soon as I've finished."

Samantha gave a mock salute; a, "Yes Sir," and made her way to the lounge.

When Philip entered the room a little while later she was sitting on the settee and she signalled for him to sit next to her. As soon as he sat down she moved closer to him, cupped her arms in his and said, "And now you can tell me all about it."

"There's nothing to tell; nothing important anyway."

"Important or not I want to hear about it. You've listened to me babbling on often enough. I just want to return the favour for once. You know anything you say will stay just between the two of us and I'm sure that nothing you say will shock me."

Philip smiled, and not wishing to spoil the intimacy of the moment said, "I'm not so sure about that, so let's leave it please."

She pulled even closer to him, "You idiot! Do you really think I have no idea at all of what goes through your head when we're together?"

His heart started pounding as she continued, "I'm not oblivious to your feelings and do you really think that I've no feelings myself when we're together." She laughed and added, "In fact I quite liked it when the ticket collector referred to me as your wife, and I think you did too. Am I right or am I right?"

Philip merely nodded his head before saying, "But we are a husband and a wife, but not each other's husband and wife, and that's a hell of a big difference."

She let go of his arm and leaned back away from him, "Philip, we can try and ignore these feelings and just carry on in the same way we always have, but I don't think that will work in the long run unless we talk about it and decide what, if anything, we do about it."

She stared at him waiting for some sort of response but he just sat there totally unsure of how to deal with the situation. He wanted to kiss her and his whole body willed him to do so, but still he held back and merely asked, "And what do you suggest then?"

She thumped her chest with her fist, "In here I want to say one thing, but up here," she then touched her head, "I'm being given a different answer, and I need you to help me decide what's right. I don't think I can just ignore it all any more."

"And do you think I can help you decide, when I don't know how to deal with it myself?"

She took a deep breath before replying, "I know we're not married to each other, but that's the tragedy of it all isn't it? You shouldn't have married Teresa and I shouldn't have married Edward. I knew that almost as soon as I met you."

"But you still went ahead and married Edward anyway."

"Sorry, but you weren't available were you?" She saw how hurt he was at this and immediately added, "I'm not blaming you about anything. We've both made our choices and now we have to live with them." She took his hand and squeezed it, "I just wanted to hear you say you feel the same and I haven't been imagining things all these years."

He looked directly into her eyes and mouthed the words, "I love you," before clearly stating, "You haven't been imagining anything."

She returned his stare and said, "So what now? Keep our feelings hidden for ever I suppose?"

"Well just one kiss wouldn't hurt would it?" He leaned forward stopping inches from her face to ask, "Would it?" again.

She gave a brief smile and a brief shake of her head before closing the gap between them.

Ten minutes later Philip stood up and lifted her into his arms and carried her into the bedroom where they stood facing each other as they very, very slowly undressed each other. It was as if they each wanted to give the other the opportunity to stop the madness at any point, but each willing the other not to do so.

When every piece of clothing had been dispatched to the floor, they looked longingly at each other's naked body without touching. Neither of them had ever experienced such powerful emotions before and whilst they desperately wanted to wrap their body around the other, they also wanted to savour every second and etch every moment in their mind for fear that it would never happen again or worse still that it was all a dream from which they would soon awake.

Neither of them made any move for several minutes but just stood transfixed as they looked into each others eyes. Eventually, Philip mouthed the words, "I love you," and Samantha mouthed the same words in return. He reached forward and hesitantly touched her breast, his hand almost shaking as he did so. She shook as he moved his hand away but smiled as he stepped forward lifting her into his arms and carrying her to the bed; gently placing her on her back on it. He stepped away from the bed to once again take delight in looking at her beautiful body from head to toe and back from toe to her head. He smiled as he stared at her exquisite face. She smiled back at him, savouring the moment and the enormous pleasure that she knew she was giving him; almost instinctively knowing that no other woman had ever had this effect on him.

She took his hand and pulled him gently down until he was lying on his back next to her. Neither spoke or moved for several minutes but with heads turned towards each other they just stared at each other's face.

Eventually he reached forward and touched her cheek, "If you think this has gone far enough, please say so now, because I don't think I can bear not touching you for much longer."

"And do you think we should stop?"

He nodded his head in the affirmative but actually said, "But I don't want to."

"Then please don't." She leaned forward and gently and very lightly kissed him on his lips, "I would like to have at least this one night with you even if it is the only night we ever spend together."

And so, right or wrong, the decision was made and the point of no return had been reached. She took his hand and placed it on her breast, taking a deep breath as she did so, so that the breast gently rose in his open palm. Leaving his hand where it was, she placed her own hands either side of his face and carefully explored its contours. Over the next hour, hesitantly at first, they each slowly discovered the exquisite softness, the amazing smoothness, the unbelievable wetness and the unceasing hardness of every bit of the other's body.

Once they had experienced the joy and pleasure of touch with their finger tips, they explored it all again with their palms. They then rediscovered every part again with their lips, breathing in the incredible aroma of each other's sex as they did so, before he finally carefully and gently entered her.

His movement was slow and deliberate, knowing that they both wanted it never to end. He pushed as deep inside her as he could, and stopped. He looked deep into her eyes, now only inches away from his own, and felt at that moment that they were utterly and completely a single being. He hoped that she felt the same as she started to move her hips beneath him: slowly and steadily at first, but gradually ever faster until the final moment came for both of them almost together.

Samantha woke early the next morning and smiled smugly to herself and she snuggled even closer to Philip who was lying with his arm wrapped around her. She relived the events of the previous evening and was somewhat surprised that she felt absolutely no guilt at what had occurred. In fact, it was just the opposite, she was elated with the fact that she and Philip had slept together and that her lover was still beside her.

Philip roused, kissed her, and they made love again, eventually deciding that they had work to do and would soon need to be on their way to Earls Court. Samantha suggested that to save time they should bath together and Philip readily agreed but instead of saving time, the pleasure of soaping and washing each other was a paradise of joy that they possibly would never enjoy again and so they did not rush any part of the pleasure of exploring each other's body one last time.

They dried each other, constantly stopping to kiss, and afterwards watched each other dress before finally deciding they really must rush if they were going to go to the exhibition hall at all.

They dashed into the kitchen, Samantha making toast whilst Philip made the coffee, neither of them wanting to break the spell by actually talking about the future and what, if anything, they were going to do about their feelings for each other.

They were about to rush out of the door when Philip caught Samantha's arm and stopped her from opening it. He took her in his arms and kissed her for what he feared may be the last time.

He pulled her back as she went to open the door, "I don't want all this to end. I know there'll be enormous hurdles to jump over but I really would like us to be together. Is that what you want?"

"You know it is." She gave him a quick peck on the cheek before continuing with the 'but' that he knew would inevitably follow. "But, there are too many people who'll get hurt if we did; people who have done nothing to deserve it." She gave him another kiss, this time a long, lingering one on the lips before saying. "We need to think about this carefully." She saw the 'hurt boy' look on his face, "I will think seriously about it, I promise. But I need time." She touched his cheek, "And I think you should think carefully about it too." She opened the door, took his hand and led him outside as she said, "I promise I'll let you know soon."

The subject of the previous night's events was not mentioned again between them the whole of that day until the taxi had almost reached the flat that evening, when Samantha asked, "Do we try to act as if nothing extraordinary has happened or do you want me to say something to Edward?"

"Have you made up your mind about wanting to be with me then?"

"That isn't the question, my sweet. My mind was made up about that several months ago. The question is 'Can it happen?' and I'm sorry but the jury is still out on that one."

"So, why ask if you should say anything to Edward? Do you want too?"

She merely shook her head from side to side and so the decision was made, for today anyway.

Edward was already in the flat and after giving Samantha a cursory kiss and hug, he immediately urged them to get ready to go out again, "I'm going to take you to this super French restaurant I've found in the West End. You'll love it Philip."

Edward was having a drink of whisky in the lounge when Philip came out of his bedroom after dressing to go out. He called to Philip to join him, "In here Philip. Do you want a snifter before we go out?"

"No thanks. I think I'll wait 'til we get to the restaurant."

"Oh have one, I am. Knowing Sam, I'm sure she'll be ages yet. So what else are we expected to do while we wait?"

He got up from his chair and ignoring Philip's refusal poured a glass for him and refilled his own glass.

He passed the glass to Philip, who took it without comment and merely held it untouched whilst they waited for Samantha.

Samantha joined them just as Edward was refilling his glass again. Philip felt that she looked gorgeous and wanted to tell her how much she was affecting him at that moment, but he merely said, "You look very nice tonight, Sam. Doesn't she Edward?"

He responded with a, "Yes. Very nice," as he continued to pour his drink and without properly looking at her. After he had taken a sip from his glass he turned and faced her and said, "Yes, very nice. Do you want a drink before we go, love?"

She declined and stood waiting while Edward downed the drink he had just poured for himself in one gulp and put his glass next to the whisky decanter. Philip placed his only half empty glass next to it and as he followed Edward and Samantha out of the room he once again took in the powerful aroma of her perfume. He was, for the first time ever, now certain that she had tonight used this particular perfume for him and him alone.

Edward was about to lock the door when the telephone started to ring. He went to go back into the flat but changed his mind, slammed the door and locked it saying, "If it's important, they can ring back in the morning."

The restaurant was everything Edward had promised. The food, the wine, the presentation, the service and the place itself were superb. The only problem for Philip was that Edward was sitting on the other side of Samantha and he and Sam were not the only two at the table. On balance though, he decided he would rather be sitting at the table with the two of them than not be there at all.

He was at least close to Samantha even if he couldn't take advantage of the situation. But as soon as they had sat down she had moved her right foot towards him and it remained gently pressed against his own left foot for the whole evening. He knew this was the closest he would be to her tonight, for the foreseeable future, or maybe forever, but for now he accepted the situation and took joy in knowing what he had not known twenty-four hours earlier, namely that his own feelings for her were fully reciprocated.

Edward himself was in remarkable good form all evening, helped perhaps by the contents of the three bottles of wine he ordered, most of which he consumed himself. At times Philip felt as though they were eleven year old schoolboys again, laughing and joking about anything and everything. They talked about old times at school, at university and fleetingly about their time in the army. All the stories were of the good times and the humorous times they'd had together with no mention being made of the bad war memories that were best forgotten.

For most of the evening Samantha was an outsider; a mere passive listener, but she learned more about her husband and her lover in those few hours than she had learned from Edward in all the years she had known him.

It was almost midnight when their taxi pulled up outside the flat and as they walked up to the front door they could hear the phone ringing inside. It stopped before a very unsteady Edward managed to get the key in the lock.

As Edward stood back so that Samantha could open the door he asked, "Who the hell do you think could be ringing at this time of night?"

"I haven't a clue. Do you think it will be one of your political colleagues?"

"Well if it is, I'll tell them what for if they ring again."

Samantha took off her coat and hung it up, "Anyone for coffee? Or maybe cocoa, I'm sure I put some on the shopping list?"

Edward took off his dinner jacket and as he dropped it on the chair in the hall said, "I'm sure Philip would rather have a night cap wouldn't you old fellow?"

Philip turned to Samantha, "Actually Samantha I'd love a cup of cocoa, if you don't mind the trouble."

"No trouble at all. I think I'll join you. Are you sure you don't want one, Edward?"

"Damn sure, I'm having a night cap even if neither of you are joining me."

Just as Samantha came into the lounge carrying the tray on which were two mugs of steaming cocoa the telephone began to ring again.

"Who the hell is that?" asked Edward. "Can you get it, Sam? And if it's for me tell them I'm not here will you?"

Samantha put the tray on the coffee table and went to answer the phone in the hall. She was as white as a sheet when she came back, "It's your mother on the phone Edward. She wants to speak to you."

"What on earth does she want at this time of night?" but Samantha merely said, "She wouldn't tell me, she only wants to speak to you," to which Edward angrily demanded, "Why what's the matter? What's going on?"

Philip thought she was going to burst into tears at Edward's retort, but she held back her tears and said directly to Edward, "Just go and speak to your mother." She sat down, picked up her mug and, without saying a further word held it close to her, as if taking some comfort in its warmth.

As soon as Edward had left the room, Philip asked, "What's the matter? Is it Uncle Tom?"

Samantha who had been staring vacantly at the carpet looked up, "She wouldn't say. She was sobbing her heart out and all she would say was that she wanted to speak to Edward, but I guess that it must be something to do with Tom."

It was almost half an hour later when Edward came off the telephone and rejoined them in the lounge. He looked totally drained with all the colour gone from his face. His eyes were bloodshot and he was very unsteady on his feet. Both Samantha and Philip got up and helped him into his seat.

Samantha waited until he was seated before asking, "What has happened? Is it your father?"

At first Edward merely nodded his head and put his head in his hands.

Samantha sat down next to him and put her arm round his shoulder, "Has he had another turn? Is he going to be all right?"

This time Edward shook his head from side to side before lifting his head and looking directly at Samantha, "No. He's dead. Mother's been trying to get hold of me all evening. It must have been her ringing when we were going out. She's in a terrible state; says she didn't want to ring anyone else until she'd spoken to me, so she's been trying to get me ever since the doctor left. Wouldn't even ask the next door neighbour to come and sit with her."

He looked at Philip and then back to Samantha, "Dad's body is still in the house with her. The doctor said the undertakers will collect it in the morning." He suddenly got up from his seat saying, "I must go and be with her straight away." He looked at his watch, "Twenty to one, if I go now there won't be any traffic on the roads, and with a bit of luck, I should be back with her just after four."

Samantha stood up and prevented him from leaving the room, "Sit down a minute; you're in no fit state to drive anywhere tonight. You're far too upset and anyway you've had far too much to drink."

He went to get up again, "Must phone for a cab then and catch the next train back."

Samantha stopped him going to the phone, "Sit down, you're just not thinking straight. You need to get a rest before you do anything. And anyway I very much doubt if there's a train at this time of night."

Philip, who had been sitting quietly; an outsider to the conversation; interrupted, "Why don't I go and phone my mother and let her know what's happened? She could be with your mother in half an hour and I'm sure that if Auntie Alice is not on night shift, she'll go with her and help sort things out for your mother."

Edward settled back down next to Samantha. She moved closer to him and put her arms around him, kissing him lightly on the cheek as she did so. He did not answer Philip's question but just sat there with his head in his hands.

Samantha looked at Philip and gave him a brief smile, and realising he had not received an answer, lifted Edward's chin and said to him, "Philip is going to phone his mother and ask her to go and stay with your mother tonight, so why don't you go to bed now? You need to try and get some sleep before you go charging home. I'll put the alarm on and we can drive up to your mother's first thing in the morning. There isn't anything we can do tonight anyway."

Edward merely nodded his head and as Philip got up to make the call, Samantha spoke softly to Edward again, "I'll speak to your mother as soon as Philip has spoken to his mother, so you just get off to bed and I'll join you in a minute or two."

Fifteen minutes later, with all the arrangements made, Philip was lying in his bed reliving all that had happened in the previous forty-eight hours. He so wanted to talk to Samantha but knew it was unlikely they would be alone together again in the near future. He could hear Edward and Samantha talking in the next room and when the talking stopped he realised the noises he was now hearing was Edward making love to his wife. He lay frozen in his bed trying to ignore the sounds, but became more and more distressed during the short time before silence fell. However, even in the silence, he could not get the thought of Edward and Samantha making love out of his mind, and he had a very restless night with very little sleep.

Philip stayed in London for the next two weeks, spending all but one day at the exhibition and almost every night alone in Edward's flat. Teresa joined him at the weekend as previously arranged but she only stayed two nights as they had to be back for the funeral.

Philip constantly thought of Samantha and desperately wanted to see her. Several times he picked up the telephone to speak to her, but only actually rang the number twice. The first time, Edward answered and Philip spent the time talking to him about the funeral arrangements and how everyone was coping. The second time Samantha answered, but he realised Edward was with her, so he again merely spent the time asking how everyone was and on general chat about funeral plans and the exhibition.

At the funeral he desperately wanted to speak to Samantha, but there were always other people about and the only bit of intimacy that passed between them was when he gave Samantha a socially acceptable peck on the cheek immediately after giving his Aunt Mary a similar kiss.

During the following weeks at the office, things were so hectic trying to sort out new arrangements to keep the business ticking over now that Tom was no longer around, that Sam and Philip were rarely in the same place at the same time, and when they were, Lucy or someone else always seemed to be there as well.

As the weeks rolled on Samantha seemed to become more distant from Philip and he began to think she not only had regrets about the night they had spent together, but no longer wished to maintain the close friendship that existed before.

At the beginning of November he couldn't stand the constant fretfulness he felt, and the uncertainty of how to react to Samantha, any longer. He had to know what her feelings were even it meant their friendship was gone for ever, and so when he arranged a meeting with a potential Japanese supplier in London, he insisted that Samantha go with him to the meeting.

And so, almost three months after the last time he'd been alone on a train with her, he once again met her at the station early one Wednesday morning to catch the train for their ten-thirty meeting at the Oxford Street shop.

Philip had reserved seats in the first class dining car on a table for two and whilst breakfast was being served they only spoke about the forthcoming meeting with the Japanese suppliers.

But Philip had already decided that this train journey would be the best opportunity he would have to discuss his personal feelings with Samantha and so he finished eating the portion of sausage in his mouth, put down his knife and fork, and touched Samantha's hand, "Can we talk about us and what happened the last time we travelled to London?"

Samantha moved her hand away from his, and put down her own knife and fork, "And what is there to talk about? You are married. I am married. So I don't think there can be an us, can there?"

Philip was thrown by this comment. Was this the short sharp rebuff he had feared all these weeks? If it was, maybe he should let the whole thing drop before he said all the wrong things and just made the situation unrecoverable.

Or did the 'can there' mean that she still wanted the relationship to continue? Samantha was far too important to him to accept it as a direct rejection. He also knew that it was now or never, and that if he did not say the things he had been practicing in his head for the last week since arranging the trip, then he would regret it, maybe for the rest of his life.

He took a deep breath before reaching across the table and taking Samantha's hand into his again. This time she did not remove it but just looked up and smiled a sad and wistful smile.

"I do so hope there is an us. Whether we can be together or not is something we need to talk about, but even if you decide that it's not possible, it won't make any difference to the way I feel." He leaned forward and fixed his eyes on hers, "I love you Samantha. I always have and I always will."

She did not respond to his declaration, but Philip took some encouragement from her smile and the fact that she squeezed his hand.

"Please tell me what you're thinking Samantha. Please help me out here a little."

This time her smile almost became a laugh as she asked, "Why don't you tell me how I can help you?"

Philip had always felt close to her and before they had slept together had felt that they were truly soul mates who could talk about all things, even highly personal matters. But now, he did not understand what was happening. Was she teasing him? Did she have any idea at all about the discomfort and torment he was in? He wanted to tell her how much he wanted to be with her, but once again felt the unbearable pangs of anxiety at possible rejection that were constantly eating away at him. She had squeezed his hand again as she had asked the question. He decided to take encouragement from this and be totally honest about his feelings even if this meant a final rejection.

He leaned forward again and squeezed her hand back, "The night we spent together was not something I took lightly. You mean a great deal to me and much as I've always tried to brush my feelings for you aside, I just can't do it. I can't even explain it to myself. The feelings I have when you are around are something I've never felt for anyone before. I want to be with you, but I don't know what you want and it's driving me crazy. But most of all I don't want to lose you completely, and I'm afraid that saying things like this will just drive you away."

"And why do you think you will drive me away?"

"Because I have no idea what you want. After what happened the last time we were in London, I thought we might have some sort of future together, but now I'm not sure what you're feelings on the matter are. I know that someone else has always been around whenever we've met since, but now I'm not sure that isn't how you planned it."

Samantha lifted her finger to her mouth and quietly said, "Shh." She then spoke quite quietly, "You don't need to say any more. I'm sorry we haven't spoken before now. I've been desperate to talk to you as well, but I needed to be sure about things first."

"And are you sure now?"

"I'm sure about one thing but unfortunately knowing for certain poses more problems than it solves."

"I don't understand. If you're certain about us then can't we solve all the other problems by being together?"

"Actually I didn't say I was certain about us."

For Philip this reply was like a sudden kick in the groin. Was she saying that she wanted to stay with Edward? Was this the end of any sort of relationship between them? He had to know, "So have you decided you want to stay with Edward?"

"Please, please just stop for a moment. You; me; Edward; Teresa; my Mom; my Dad; your Mom and everybody else; they're the problems that are left."

She went to continue but Philip interrupted with, "So what are you certain of?"

She hesitated for several seconds before responding with, "The one thing I am now certain of is that I'm pregnant."

Philip's world fell apart at that moment and by the look of concern and apprehension on her face, it was obvious that Samantha knew it had.

"I've wanted to say something ever since I missed my first period, but I didn't know whether I'd just skipped a period because I was so churned up about you and me, and with all the stress of dealing with Tom's death. So I just worried for another month, but when I missed again, I couldn't decide whether I wanted the baby to be yours or Edward's. And what made it so much worse, was I had no idea how you'd feel about having a baby with me, and I certainly don't know whether Edward would want another child. Knowing how traumatised he's always been around Juliette's death and Julian's birth, I just didn't know whether he'd be able to cope with the fear of a similar thing happening to me, even if he did want a baby with me."

"And what has he said about the baby then?"

"Actually I haven't told him yet. I've been so confused. I didn't want to say anything that might upset him unnecessarily, particularly whilst he was trying to cope with Tom's death on top of all that had happened to Juliette."

She sat quietly for a few moments, as if thinking about what reaction she might have from Edward. "I've told him I want to stay at the London flat tonight so I plan to tell him then, but I wanted to tell you first, particularly as I'm not sure whether the baby is yours and not his."

She was silent again and just stared at Philip, willing him to speak. For his part, his head was in a whirl and he spoke without thinking, "But why do you think the baby might be mine?" He regretted saying such a stupid thing as soon as he had said it, but instantly realised that to try and put the matter right would only make things even worse.

However Samantha just laughed, seeming to be more amused than offended by the stupid question and merely said, “And why do you think I think it could be yours? Do you want me to draw you a diagram?”

Philip smiled at her comment and the huge tension left him and he started to think more clearly about the unexpected news. And suddenly he felt confident he was not going to lose Samantha, even though the two of them may never actually be together. However, he also realised that their being together would not solve Samantha’s immediate problems but probably make them worse. The resolution was not to pressurise her into leaving Edward. That way he may be able to keep her to him, even if it meant they would never actually be together physically. This was a situation he had to accept and one that may even last for the rest of their lives. Now all he had to do was to talk to her and let her reach her own conclusion.

He took both of her hands in his and desperately wanted to give her a big hug, “I would be the happiest man alive if the baby was mine, but you know that’s unlikely don’t you? I’ve had tests and the doctors tell me I can’t have children.”

As soon as Philip had admitted that the child could not possibly be his, he could almost see the angst fall away from her. He was absolutely certain that Samantha would never pretend the child was Edward’s if she thought it might not be. He also knew that he could not be party to such a lie either. The child was Edward’s and whatever his reaction was to that news, telling him that both Samantha and the child were leaving him at the same time would totally destroy him, particularly after the loss of Juliette.

Samantha nodded her head and said, “Yes, I suppose I know the child isn’t yours but I would have liked to have a child with you.”

She went to continue speaking but Philip prevented her from doing so by putting his finger to her lips. His mind was now perfectly clear about what he needed to say. He also knew that he had to say it all before Samantha had a chance to stop his train of thought.

“Before you say any more, let me say that I would love for us to have children together, but that will never be. But, you know what? I don’t actually mind that the baby isn’t mine. It doesn’t change the way I feel about you or the baby. It is your baby and if you want to be with me and let me bring up the child as mine, then I would like that very much. But if you choose otherwise and stay with Edward then I still want to be there for you.” He stopped momentarily before saying, “And the baby.”

There were other things he wanted to say, but at that moment he felt he should let Samantha give her thoughts on what he had already said before saying anything more.

At first she merely mouthed the words, "Thank you," and stared directly at him as if trying to read his mind. Eventually she said, "It would be nice if there was an easy solution, but there isn't is there? The trouble is that we are both married." She smiled as she added, "And unfortunately not to each other."

The 'unfortunately' made Philip wonder whether he had reached a decision about what to do too quickly. Was there still a chance that they could be together?

"But that is exactly what I want us to be. Married to each other I mean."

"And maybe that's what I would like too, but it isn't just you and me, is it? Edward doesn't make me unhappy and I don't think Teresa makes you unhappy either. But we would make them terribly unhappy and they don't really deserve that do they?"

Philip merely shook his head without saying anything and Samantha continued talking, "And it doesn't end there; it would affect so many other people; people that mean a lot to us both. My Mom and Dad, your Mom, and what about Mary? What would she feel losing her grandchild so soon after losing Tom? I don't think I can knowingly hurt so many people."

"So does that mean we have to be unhappy?"

Samantha gave Philip a weak smile before answering, "I don't know, does it mean that? It doesn't make me unhappy to know you feel the way you do about me. In fact I think I'm more able to deal with other things because of it. And I would like to think that my feeling the way I do about you is some consolation to you even if we cannot be together."

"So you do feel something for me?"

She shook her head from side to side, but it was not meant as a, 'No' to Philip's question but as unbelief that he needed to ask the question. She answered him anyway, "Of course I feel something for you and it's been driving me crazy almost since I first met you. But we can't hurt all these people, can we?" She paused for a moment before adding, "Especially not now anyway."

"So what do we do?"

Samantha wanted to be in some other place where she could put her arms around Philip as she answered this question. Her heart and body wanted one thing, but her head told her a completely different story.

"We've both made decisions in the past that mean we can't be together as a couple now. Things would be totally different if we hadn't made those decisions, but we did, so now we have to live with them. You were already married when I met you. I always felt strange and confused about my feelings for you, but it wasn't until I had married Edward, that I knew for certain what you actually meant to me and what those feelings were all about. But by then I was married to Edward. You were married to Teresa. Nobody forced us to make those decisions, and we didn't have to get married to them, did we?"

Philip smiled at being told that he didn't have to marry Teresa.

"You're right of course, but do you know how many years I consciously waited for the right girl to come along. In the end I thought such notions were just the thing of romance novels and were not part of real life. And when I met you and found out that it was possible to meet the 'love of one's life', it was too late. Wasn't it?"

Samantha returned the smile and said, "Yes, and in answer to your question, you are going to stay with Teresa and I'm going to stay with Edward."

"And that's the end of any relationship we might have had then?"

"That depends on you. You know how I feel about you and I know how you feel about me and no-one can take that away from us. If you mean is this the end of any physical relationship between us, then I think the answer to that must be 'Yes', don't you?"

Philip went to answer but Samantha spoke before he could say anything, "But I hope that it doesn't mean we won't have any sort of relationship, but just not an illicit sexual one. I want you as a dear friend and I hope I'll be able to chat to you as we've always done. I don't suppose for one minute that always playing the part of being only good friends and nothing more will be easy for either of us, but that's how it must be."

She held his hands tightly in hers and looked directly into his eyes, "But don't ever forget that I do love you even if I never say it again."

And so the decision was made, life was not to change for either of them in the way their emotions were pleading for them to change. Common sense had won the day, not their emotions and sensibilities. And common sense, and not emotion, was to rule their destiny.

Book Three

(1957 to 1982)

The Fruitful Grape

How long, how long, in infinite Pursuit
Of This and That endeavour and dispute?
Better be merry with the fruitful Grape
Than sadden after none, or bitter Fruit.

Rubáiyát of Omar Khayyám
as translated by Edward Fitzgerald

CHAPTER TWENTY– ONE

1957 - 1958

Samantha Richards woke with a start as she heard the newspaper being pushed through the letter box. She looked at the alarm clock and was surprised to see that it was just after eight o'clock. Why hadn't the alarm gone off at seven, like it was supposed to? And then she remembered it had gone off, but she must have dropped off again after the very disturbed night's sleep she had had. At first she couldn't get to sleep wondering why her husband hadn't telephoned the previous evening and then when she did doze off she was soon woken by an urgent need to use the toilet. That had happened several times and the last time she had been sick again.

Samantha had told Edward she was pregnant less than a month ago, and whenever he was in London he had telephoned her at least once a day since then to check that she was all right. Yesterday had been no exception. He had phoned from the House of Commons in the morning and told her, "I'm down to give a speech in the House tomorrow and I'll be working on it all evening. I don't want to be disturbed so don't ring me except in a real emergency, but don't worry I'll ring when I've got a minute to spare."

But he had not phoned her as promised, and as she climbed into bed at midnight she decided to call even though he told her not to. The phone had not been answered and she had eventually fallen asleep wondering why he hadn't answered.

She jumped out of bed, again wondering why he hadn't answered her call. *'He wouldn't have gone out, would he? Surely not at that time? Perhaps he'd fallen asleep working on his speech and hadn't heard the phone? Should I try him again now?'* but just as she picked up the phone to do so, she suddenly felt sick once more and had to dash to the bathroom yet again.

It was another twenty minutes before she felt well enough to try ringing him, but once more there was no answer. *'He would have gone to the House by now, probably to go through his speech with one of the other MPs. Yes that was it; he would have expected me to be on my way to work by now, so he's sure to phone me there a little later.'*

Although Samantha still felt a little queasy, she nevertheless wanted to get to work as soon as she could. She was certain Edward would call her there and she wanted to make sure she was there to receive it. She washed and dressed as quickly as she could hoping she had managed to wash away any lingering hint of being sick. She looked at her watch. The next bus was in ten minutes; just enough time to put on a bit of lipstick and splash on plenty of the perfume that she knew Philip liked, to help her feel a bit more human.

She put on her winter coat to protect her from the cold damp December morning, grabbed the paper off the hall floor and dashed out of the house. The smoky taste of fog still hung in the air but at least it was nothing like the choking fog of the previous evening. She was relieved to see a couple of people waiting at the bus stop; at least she hadn't missed it.

The bus arrived on time and as she got on she decided to ring Edward's secretary, Guinivere Isherwood, at the House of Commons as soon as she arrived at work. Who on earth called their daughter Guinivere these days? That was certainly not a name to be considered if her child was a girl! She smiled to herself at the thought of naming the baby after Guinivere's King if it was a boy. There was no way she would call her son Arthur, but then who in their right mind would call a girl Sam?

Samantha was anxious not to feel sick again whilst on the bus, so she sat downstairs at the back by the open doorway and settled down to read her newspaper. The lead story on the front page added to her discomfort.

The main headline read *'52 DIE IN LONDON FOG RAIL CRASH'*. She read on.

52 people were killed, 140 seriously injured and 56 slightly injured when two trains crashed in thick fog in London last night under a fly-over bridge on the mid Kent line, 200 yards on the Lewisham side of St John's Station. The accident happened in the rush hour.

Her immediate thought was *'thank goodness Edward walked from the House of Commons to the flat and did not need to catch a train'*. But then she thought of the poor dead and injured; their families; their wives and children; and she felt guilty that her first thought was of herself and her own family.

The bus conductor interrupted Samantha's concentration on the newspaper story with his, "Fares please Miss?"

Samantha took out her purse and gave him the exact fare. She put her purse back in her handbag and continued reading the article'

A fast steam train, bound from Cannon Street to Ramsgate, ran into the back of a stationary electric train, which was on the way to Hayes,

Kent, from Charing Cross. A carriage forced upwards by the impact, hit the bridge as a third train was about to pass over it. The bridge collapsed on the wrecked coaches underneath.

She began to feel physically sick again as she read the details, so she folded the paper, not wishing to read any more.

She suddenly reopened the paper and read this same paragraph again. The train was *'on its way to Hayes, Kent'*. Who was it that had told her recently that they lived in Hayes, Kent? It took her a little time to recall that it was Guinivere on the one and only occasion she had ever met her at a House of Commons drinks function that Edward had taken her to. Was it possible that Guinivere was on the train? Samantha went cold and shivered at the thought. She quickly scanned the rest of the article and all the other pages to see if there was any mention of the names of the killed or injured but could not find any. Too early for that level of detail yet! They would want to get in touch with their family before issuing names, wouldn't they? Samantha could not remember whether Guinivere had a family and she did not even know if she had a boyfriend. Edward had never talked about her.

She was still worrying about Guinivere when she arrived at work and decided against phoning her. No, it would be better to wait for Edward to phone her. A few weeks ago she wouldn't have expected Edward to call her on a daily basis, so why was she so upset by it now?

As she passed Philip's office on the way to her own she stopped outside the door. She touched her tummy and smiled at the thought of the child growing within her, and knew that she would feel much better if she spent a few minutes with Philip, so she knocked on his door, and was relieved to hear his immediate, "Come in."

She pushed open the door but was disappointed to see Lucy sitting opposite him with papers spread all over the desk.

"Sorry Philip. I didn't know that Lucy was with you, I'll call back later."

"That's OK Sam, I think we've nearly finished haven't we Lucy?"

"Well there are a couple of other things I want your view on, but they can wait if Samantha needs to see you straight away. I can always pop back later when you and Samantha are through."

Lucy was already standing and collecting her papers together before she turned to speak to Samantha, "How are you keeping, Samantha? Has all that morning sickness gone yet?"

Samantha knew that if she gave Lucy half a chance they could be talking about her condition and babies for the next ten minutes and that was the last thing she wanted at the moment, so she just said, "I'm keeping fine, thanks Lucy. Just wish it was a bit warmer though. But look, you finish off everything with Philip. What I wanted to ask him can wait."

She looked across at Philip, "You finish off with Lucy, Philip. Give me a shout when you're free and I'll pop back then. I'll probably have those figures you wanted finished by then anyway."

She turned to Lucy, "Perhaps you and I can catch up on things a little later Lucy," and with that she left the room.

Samantha sat in her office mulling over the figures, but her mind was not on her work. She kept looking at the telephone willing it to ring. She did not know whether she wanted it to be Edward checking that she was OK and explaining why he hadn't telephoned last night as he had promised, or Philip saying he was now alone and ready to see her. But the telephone was silent for the next forty minutes and when it did ring she jerked, almost shocked by the noise it made.

"Hi, Sam, I'm ready to see you now if you want to pop in."

"Fine, I'll be with you in a minute or so," and with that she replaced the hand piece without another word.

She sat down opposite Philip in his office and was about to speak when Lucy came barging in carrying two mugs on a tray, "I hope you're ready for another cup of tea, Philip? I was making one for myself and I know you never say no to one, and I bet you haven't made yourself one yet, have you Samantha?" She placed the tray on the desk, "Right, I'll leave you two to get on with it," and with that she left the room.

Sam took a mug and Philip merely said, "Thanks," as she handed it to him. He caught a whiff of her perfume and smiled one of his beautiful smiles; his fingers touched hers as he took the mug. He looked directly at her and she could feel the old emotions welling up inside her as their eyes met, "Are you all right, Samantha, you look a little bothered this morning?"

Samantha took her mug and placed it in front of her on the desk, wrapping her hands around it as if warming them up. She did not understand why she felt so down this morning, and found it difficult to hold back a tear. She so wanted Philip to come and give her a hug to make her feel better, but knew that was not part of the agreement. Philip bit his lower lip without averting his eyes from hers, and she knew instinctively that he was thinking the same thing. Maybe it helped just knowing he still felt the same about her.

Now that she had Philip's attention and he was waiting for her to say what she wanted to see him about, she felt a little silly for bothering. But when Philip reached across the table and held his hand around hers, she shuddered at his touch, and closed her eyes enjoying for a moment this small measure of intimacy between them. He reached across with his other hand and enclosed both of hers, "Are you sure you're OK, sweetheart? What is it that's bothering you?"

She opened her eyes, removed her hands from his, and gently stroking his hand said, "Well, for one thing not being able to do things like this more often." She took her hand completely away adding, "But we can't, we just can't!"

Philip moved his hands away, picked up his mug and took a drink from it. He just looked at her as he said, "So, what do we talk about then?" but before she could answer the telephone rang and Philip picked it up. He listened without saying anything and then passed the telephone to Samantha, "It's Mary. She wants to speak to you."

"Mary? Mary who?"

"Mary. Your mother-in-law Mary. My! You aren't quite with it this morning are you?"

"Oh, that Mary! What does she want?"

"I haven't a clue. Jane will put her through as soon as you take the call and then you can find out."

Samantha took the phone and asked Jane to put her mother-in-law through.

It was a very agitated Mary who spoke without even an 'hello' or 'how are you?' "Have you had a call from someone asking you if you are Edward's wife yet?"

"No. Why?"

"Well someone's just phoned me asking if I was Mrs Richards, Edward Richards' wife, and when I said 'No, I was his mother,' they just said did I know how they could get in touch with you. Wouldn't say who they were, what they wanted or anything. Said they'd rung your home number but couldn't get a reply. What's going on, Samantha? What do they want?"

"I have no idea what they want. Did you give them this number or anything? How did you leave it?"

It was now a very irritated mother-in-law on the telephone, "Of course, I gave them your work's number. That's what they asked for, a number where they could reach you, so of course I gave them the number. What's going on Samantha? Is Edward all right?"

"Well he was fine when I spoke to him yesterday."

She was about to say, "I haven't heard from him today," when Jane came rushing through the door without knocking and spoke without waiting for Samantha to stop speaking, "There's someone on the phone for you Mrs

Richards. I told them you were on the phone and I'd put them through as soon as you'd finished, but they said they couldn't wait and that I should interrupt your call."

The colour drained out of Samantha in a second and she felt that she was about to faint. She sat there open mouthed and seemingly unable to move.

Philip came round the desk, took the phone from her and spoke into it, "Samantha's needed on another line, Aunt Mary. I'll ring you back as soon as she's finished the call." He put the phone in the cradle without waiting for any response from his aunt.

"Go and put the call straight through here, Jane. Quick now! We don't want to leave them hanging on the line too long now, do we?"

Jane dashed out of the room even faster than she had come in and in no time at all the phone on Philip's desk was ringing again. Samantha just looked at it as Philip picked it up, "Hello, can I help you?"

A man's voice asked, "I'm sorry. I understood I was being put through to Mrs Richards. Mrs Edward Richards. Is she there? Can I speak to her?"

"Yes she's here, but she doesn't feel too well, can you tell me what this is about please?"

"I must speak to Mrs Richards. If she's there, please put her on."

Philip realised that no matter how many more questions he asked, he was not going to get anywhere with this man, so he handed the phone to Samantha, putting his hand on her shoulder as he did so, "I'm sorry, Sam, but he'll only speak to you."

All sorts of things had been going through Samantha's mind in the few seconds that Philip had been speaking and by the time she held the phone to her ear, she was shaking uncontrollably. Her voice was very quaky as she spoke, "Can I help you?"

"Is that Mrs Edward Richards?"

"Yes"

"The wife of Edward Richards, the MP?"

"Yes, of course I am. Who are you and what is this all about?"

"I'm sorry to bother you Mrs Richards, but I'm PC Arthur Danby and I'm phoning from Lewisham Police Station. Your husband was injured in the train crash last night." His voice became firmer as he said, "I'm told he'll be all right, but at the moment he is in St Alfege's Hospital in Greenwich."

Samantha froze in shock and dropped the phone. Philip picked it up and spoke into the phone, "What's going on, who are you and what have you just said to Mrs Richards?"

"I'm sorry, Sir. Can I speak to Mrs Richards again?"

"I don't know what you've said to her, but she is in no state to speak to you anymore, so can you just tell me what's going on?"

"I'm sorry Sir, if you can just put Mrs Richards back on for a second so she can give me permission to speak to you, I'll be able to tell you all you want to know."

Philip was sensible enough not to argue any more; he held the phone to Samantha's ear saying, "Just tell him it's OK for him to speak to me, Sam, and I'll take it from there."

Samantha spoke very quietly and shakily, "Are you sure my husband is all right?"

"Yes ma'am, he's alive and I'm told he will make a good recovery."

Samantha looked at Philip as she said "Thank goodness for that. Can you please explain to Philip where he is and what we need to do to come and see him, please?"

She did not hear him reply, "Yes ma'am," as Philip took back the phone and held it to his own ear.

After listening to the constable for a while, Philip reached for his pen and some paper and started taking down the details of where Edward was and how to find the hospital once they got to Greenwich. He finished with a "Well thank you constable." He was just about to put the phone down, when he asked, "Can you give me the telephone number of the hospital?" He wrote it down and then said, "And you'd better give me your number in case we need to get back to you." When he had written that down, he merely said, "Thanks," and put the phone down.

He knelt on the floor next to where Samantha was sitting, put his arms round her and allowed her to cry on his shoulder without saying anything.

Eventually, when she lifted her head he kissed her gently on the cheek. She turned her head and looked into his eyes, but he knew this was absolutely the wrong time to hold her any more, so he let her go and said, "PC Danby said Edward was going to be all right and his injuries weren't life threatening. So why don't I take you home to collect a few things together and then I'll take you to Greenwich so you can see how he is for yourself?"

Samantha nodded her head, but then smiled as she said, "Did that constable say his name was Arthur?"

"Yes I think so, why?"

She laughed at her thoughts, a moment of relief from her anxiety and worry, "Oh just something I was thinking about on the bus this morning. Remind me to tell you about it sometime?"

"Come on then, we ought to get going if you want to see Edward today. I'll take you to the hospital and then drop you back at your London flat before I come back. That way you'll be around to see Edward as much as you need over the next few days."

"But I haven't finished the figures you want yet."

He smiled and shook his head, "I think I'll manage without a few figures. Right now there are far more important things to do. So come on, let's get you home to collect a few clothes and anything else you may need and get on our way. I'll let Lucy know what's going on whilst you go and get your things from your office."

They were both leaving his office when the telephone rang again. They stopped and looked at each other apprehensively, "Just go and get your things and I'll take that," said Philip.

It was his Aunt Mary wanting to know what the man had said. Philip couldn't believe he had forgotten all about her. He told her the bare details of what had happened as quickly as he could, but she wanted to know everything and he had to repeat the details several times.

He tried to finish the conversation by saying, "Sorry Aunt but I must go. I'm taking Samantha to the hospital so we need to get on our way if we're to see Edward today. I'll ring you from the hospital as soon as we've seen him and let you know how he is."

"You won't need to do that because I'm coming with you," was the immediate reply. "It won't take me long to put a few things in a bag so you can pick me up as soon as you can get here."

Philip, who had begun to look forward to spending a few hours with Samantha, even if it was in these distressing circumstances, was taken aback by this demand. He was unsure how to respond to it. He was dragged out of his thoughts when his aunt said, "Are you still there Philip?"

"Yes, sorry, I'll see you in a bit then," was all that he could think to say. He went to put down the phone but she continued talking, "I presume we'll be staying at Edward's London flat, so make sure Samantha has the key with her?"

"Yes of course. I'll drop you and Samantha off at the flat after we've seen Edward and then I'll drive back later tonight."

"No you can't do that; you'll have to stay as well. We shall want you around to take us to the hospital tomorrow and possibly for a few days after that. You'll have to sleep on the settee or book yourself into a hotel for a couple of nights. So tell Teresa what you're doing and collect an overnight bag yourself."

Philip knew that when his aunt was in this sort of organising mode it was pointless arguing with her, so he just said, "Yes, OK I'll do that straight away and I'll pick you up as soon as I can."

As Philip drove Samantha home he told her what Edward's mother had arranged. She sighed and said, "Oh well, I suppose it's only natural for her to want to see Edward. I would want to see my son in similar circumstances." She touched his hand and added, "But I would appreciate you being around for a day or two as well if you can manage it."

Samantha was silent for a while and then suddenly said, "What I don't understand is why Edward was on one of those trains anyway. He was supposed to be staying at the flat working on his speech." She turned her head towards Philip, "What do you think he was doing on a train instead?"

"I have no idea, but he was, so there's nothing we can do about it now. The important thing is that he's alive and we need to make sure he gets better quickly. He was probably just going to one of his meetings somewhere, so perhaps you should let him tell you in his own good time. I wouldn't bother him with it just yet though and I certainly wouldn't ask him whilst Aunt Mary is around."

The subject was dropped and not raised again.

Half way to London the fog started to return and it was after four o'clock when they arrived at the hospital. Afternoon visiting had finished, but Philip managed to speak to the Ward Sister, who told them Edward was stable but was still sedated and waiting his turn to go into surgery so that the doctors could clean up his foot wound.

"Why what's the matter with his foot?" was Samantha's immediate response.

"I'm sorry, hasn't anyone explained to you? Your husband was trapped in the wreckage of the train. He has two broken ribs and a number of cuts and bruises on his body. They're not serious and should heal over the next few weeks, but the main problem is that he was trapped by his foot. A doctor from here had to crawl inside the smashed carriage to get to him and others. He administered morphine on the spot to those trapped whilst the other rescuers tried to get them out. But Mr Richards' foot was completely shattered and jammed under the seat and he had lost a lot of blood. The firemen said it would take some time to cut away the wrecked carriage and the seat to release his foot, but the doctor felt that even if they were able to do that quickly, he would nevertheless lose his foot. So he amputated the foot there in a very cramped and difficult situation."

"Oh my God, what's he going to do without a foot?" declared Mary.

"I know it sounds dreadful at the moment but look at this way. He's alive and I'm sure he'll recover. There were a lot of other people on those trains that didn't make it. In fact I understand that the woman sitting next to your husband and the two men sitting behind him were all dead when the doctor got to them."

Samantha put her arms around her mother-in-law, "Yes maybe we should look on the bright side. There are plenty of other families visiting their relatives in the morgue today."

Mary gave her a tight squeeze, "Yes of course you're right Samantha."

She then turned to the Sister, "I know it's not visiting time and that you are very busy, but could we just pop and see my son for a wee while?"

"Just for a few minutes then, but you'll find him very sleepy as we are keeping him sedated at least until after he's been to theatre."

Why is he going into theatre?" asked Samantha.

"Well as I said, the doctor had to deal with the foot in very difficult and awkward circumstances, so he needs to go into surgery to have it cleaned."

"And when are you going to do that?"

"Unfortunately I have no idea. There are so many other patients who need surgery far more urgently that Mr Richards. The doctors are working flat out but it could even be tomorrow before the surgeons get round to him."

Philip waited outside the ward whilst Samantha and his aunt went to see Edward. Half an hour later they came out both with a very worried look on their faces.

"How is he?" he asked.

Samantha was about to speak, but Mary took over, "He's in a very bad way. He did open his eyes and say hello but that was all we got out of him. The nurses have now sent us out so that they can redress his wounds."

"So what do we do, wait or shall we get something to eat and come back later?"

"The Sister said she'd rather we left it for today. We can ring later and find out how he is and then come back tomorrow. I think they are so busy at the moment that they want as few interruptions as possible."

Philip stayed in London with them for the next three days, ferrying the two women to and from the hospital and making sure they did not neglect themselves by not eating or drinking regularly.

He found it difficult to sleep knowing that Samantha was only a few feet away from him. Each night he lay awake on the uncomfortable settee reliving the events of the last time he and Samantha had been together in this flat. Perhaps it was just as well his aunt was around all the time, otherwise he may have found it impossible not to attempt to repeat the wonderful experience. However, even though he felt no remorse or guilt that they had slept together that one time, he knew things would be totally different for both of them if they repeated the experience now. Not only because Edward was lying injured in hospital but also because they had said they would not repeat it ever again for the sake of the baby.

A more difficult and gruelling thing for him to deal with however was the fact that he was not even able to snatch the odd minute when he and Samantha could speak without his aunt around.

Over breakfast on Sunday morning Philip said he intended to go home that evening after bringing Sam and his aunt back to the flat. He had been aware on each visit to Edward that Samantha had not spent any time alone with her husband, and so he asked his Aunt Mary if she wanted to go back home to Walsall with him.

"Why on earth would I want to do that? I shall stay here until Edward is able to come back home with us. And anyway, Samantha needs me here."

She turned to Samantha, "You don't want to be on your own, do you?"

Samantha knew that to argue would be pointless and almost suggested she should go back home herself with Philip, collect a few clean clothes and come back tomorrow on the train, but thought better of it and let the whole idea rest.

By the time they visited Edward on that Sunday afternoon, he was sitting up in bed and much more like his old self. He had even been out of bed that morning and had managed to hobble a few yards on crutches.

Mary had spent every moment of visiting time at Edward's bedside and as the Ward Sister ran a strict only two at the bed policy, it was Samantha who had to leave her husband so that Philip could see him for a few minutes. The same thing happened during Sunday afternoon visiting and it was Samantha who came out after half an hour to allow Philip to go and see his cousin.

Edward greeted Philip warmly and chatted away to him for the next ten minutes totally ignoring his mother, "You saved my leg once, Philip. Pity you couldn't do it again."

"I don't think I could have done anything for you even if I'd been with you this time. I wouldn't have been able to do what that doctor did. From what I hear, you were extremely lucky he was able to get to you in time. I hope you're not going to get yourself in these silly situations again. I would have thought that twice was enough for anyone."

Mary interrupted the conversation, "Twice is twice too much for anyone." She took hold of Edward's head and turned it towards her, "And you better promise me you won't do anything as stupid again."

"Oh Ma, there wasn't anything I could do about it. You can't keep me wrapped up in cotton wool for the rest of my life."

"We'll have to see about that," was her response.

It was now Philip's turn to interrupt before Edward said something that would hurt his mother, "Why don't you and I go and get a cup of tea Aunt and let Samantha come in and spend a bit of time on her own with Edward?"

"That's silly; what's the point of doing that? Two of us can be here so I might as well stay. You don't mind do you dear?"

Philip was astonished when Edward merely shook his head from side to side in agreement.

"I'll just go and let Sam come back then." As he went to leave he turned and moved towards Edward, "I'm off home tonight but I'll keep in touch with Sam and your mother to learn how you're doing, and if it's OK with you, I might come down next weekend with Teresa to see you."

He held out his hand and Edward shook it, "Come and see me as often you can."

Philip found Samantha sitting in the waiting area reading the newspapers that had been left there. She had tears in her eyes.

Philip sat down next to her and took her hand in his, "What's the matter, sweetheart? Edward is going to be fine. He's a survivor and he's already talking about getting an artificial foot. I'm sure he'll be fine then."

"I know he'll make a good recovery. I think it will take longer 'til he's able to walk without crutches than he does, but I'm sure he'll do it as quickly as anyone. No it's not Edward I'm upset about, it's this here." She passed Philip the newspaper and pointed to an article in it, "Look at the list of names there. That's the latest list of the known dead."

Philip merely glanced at the headline, *'Death toll now 92 in rail disaster. Seriously injured 110. Slightly injured 57.'* He looked at the list of dead without reading any of the names, "You shouldn't be upsetting yourself with a list of names you don't even know."

"But that's the point, I do." She took the paper back from Philip and pointed to one of the names on the list.

Philip read the name, Miss Guinivere Isherwood of Hayes, Kent. "Who is Guinivere Isherwood? And what's she to you? I've never heard of her or heard you mention her."

"She's Edward's secretary." Samantha looked directly at Philip, "They must have been on the train together. She might even have been the girl sitting next to Edward. The one the Sister said had died when we first spoke to her."

"Did you know her well?"

"No, not really, I've only met her once and spoken to her on the phone a few times. But that's not the point, is it?"

Philip squeezed her hand, "No I guess not. It's dreadful that anyone has died, but one thing I learned in the war was that if we allow ourselves to get too affected by all the death around, we'll be so traumatised that we forget to get on with living and enjoy being alive."

"Very profound, I'm sure." She took her hand from his, "What I don't understand is what they were doing on the same train? And if they were together, then why hasn't Edward mentioned her or asked if she's all right?"

She paused for a moment before asking, "Why do you think he was on that train Philip, and why a train going out of London that she was also on?"

Philip just looked at her trying to think of something sensible to say in answer to her questions, "Edward has said to me that he doesn't want to talk about the crash. It upsets him too much. So maybe he's already asked one of the nurses about her and learnt that she died. We learnt from bitter experience in the war that you shouldn't dwell on such things, and we deliberately didn't talk about the comrades we'd lost. So perhaps that's just what Edward is doing now; just trying to put it out of his mind."

He took her hand again, "And if they were on the train together, so what? They worked together for goodness sake, so it almost certainly had to do with work. So why don't you just ask him? I'm sure there's a simple and innocent explanation."

"I can't do that with his mother always around."

"Then you'll just have to wait 'til she isn't around. So stop worrying and go back to him. I'm sure he'd rather talk to you than anyone else. And he'll be wondering what's happened to you by now."

He gave her a quick peck on the cheek, "So dry those eyes and off you go. I'll see you back here in a short while."

Samantha got her answers the following afternoon, when fifteen minutes into visiting time, Edward insisted that his mother let him spend a little time alone with Samantha. She reluctantly left mumbling, "I'll go and get myself a cup of tea then."

As soon as she had gone, Edward took Samantha's hand and said, "Did you know my secretary died in that crash?"

She nodded her head, "Mm. I read it in the paper yesterday."

"And I guess you wondered why I was on the train with her?"

The sixty-four thousand dollar question! What should she say to that? She merely nodded her head without saying a word.

"She shouldn't have been on the train and neither should I. When the fog came down, I told her to go home early, but just as she was going we realised that some of the papers she'd been working on earlier in the week weren't in the pile. The silly girl had taken them home to work on and forgotten to bring them in that morning. I needed them for my speech, so she suggested that she'd collect them from home and bring them to the flat later. I didn't want her to do that, so I said I'd go with her, collect the papers and then I could work on them on my way back to the flat."

Edward now had tears in his eyes and she sensed the pain he was going through, "If she hadn't waited for me, she'd have been on an earlier train."

The tears were now streaming down his face and it was some time before he finally said, "So you see I killed her. How do I live with that?"

She got up from her seat and put her arms around her husband to try and comfort him in his pain. He winced as her arms caught his broken ribs. She released her tight hold and suddenly recalled a time almost twelve months earlier when she had comforted him in similar distress. That was the only time he'd talked openly about his feelings for his first wife Juliette; their wedding; and her death giving birth to their son; a son who lived in France with Juliette's parents and a son he never spoke about and never visited.

Now, she just repeated what she did then; she held him and let his tears flow; but not as tightly this time. But in the present situation, in hospital, unlike on last New Year's Eve when they were alone at home together, this was all the comfort she could give him.

He pulled away from her, wiping the wetness from his face as he did so, "I killed her, just like I killed Juliette, didn't I?"

"You haven't killed anyone, so stop talking like that. If she'd caught the earlier train and that had been the one in the crash, would that have been your fault. Of course not, and the fact that you were both on the later train wasn't your fault either." She wanted to change the subject but knew there were other things to settle before his mother returned, "Did she have a family and don't you think you should write to them?"

He reached across to the cupboard at the side of his bed and took two tissues from the box. He started to wipe his eyes with one of them and gave the other to Samantha, "You'd better wipe your eyes before Ma gets back." He smiled as he added, "And try not to spoil your makeup or mother will guess something's up."

He put the crumpled tissue back on the box, "And yes she did have a mother and father but I think they live in Oxfordshire somewhere. I'll have to get in touch with someone and try and find out their address. Or maybe I should phone them. What do you think?"

"If you can get to the phone, I think you should do both. Write to them and phone."

"And what about the funeral? I think I should go to that if I can. What do you think?"

Why don't you ask them when and where it will be when you phone? I'm sure we could get you there somehow if the doctors will allow it."

He leaned forward and kissed her just as his mother was coming back into the ward, "Thanks. I'll do what I can after you've gone. I'll let you know how I get on when you visit tonight." He kissed her again and whispered in her ear, "Let's not say anything about all of this to my mother. It will only give her something else to worry about."

Nothing more was said about Guinivere that afternoon, but as Samantha and Mary were leaving, the Sister caught Samantha's arm and invited her into her officc. Mary went to follow, but the Sister said, "I won't keep her a minute, Mrs Richards," and closed the door before she was able to enter.

Once inside she invited Samantha to sit and said, "I hope Mr Richards' mother doesn't get too upset at not being here, but your husband asked me to enquire of the doctors if it would be possible for him to transfer to the General Hospital back in your home town as soon as possible, and he didn't want his mother to know about his request in case the doctors said no. He thought she might be a bit belligerent with me or the doctors if they weren't happy about it. Has he spoken to you about it?"

"Well no. But we don't get much chance to chat without his mother being there."

"Yes, I've noticed that. What do you think about the idea? He said he had two relatives who were Sisters at the General and was sure they'd be able to sort out that end."

"Well yes, I think Teresa and Alice would only be too happy to do that, and I'm sure Edward would be much happier if we were all back home. So have the doctors said anything about it?"

"Yes. I've been able to ask Dr. Simkin this afternoon. He was quite keen on the idea. As you can see we're bursting to capacity with all the injured from the crash and, please don't take this wrong way, but we're desperate for any spare beds we can get for our other patients who still need treatment. So yes, he said he thought that your husband could possibly be moved later this week, say Thursday or Friday. He did make a couple of very big provisos though. Firstly, you'll have to do all the arranging with the General at Walsall, and secondly, he insists that he'll have to be moved in an ambulance with a nurse accompanying him. And most importantly you will have to pay for a private ambulance and the nurse."

She leaned forward in her seat and stared at Samantha, "So what do you think now?"

Samantha did not hesitate, "Yes, I'm sure we can arrange all that."

The Sister looked at her notes on her desk, "Oh dear, I nearly forgot. Dr. Simkin insists that he can only discharge Mr Richards from here if he has a letter from the General accepting full responsible for his continued treatment. I gather that your husband is the local MP so perhaps that won't prove too difficult for you."

Samantha wondered if it would be a problem, but felt almost certain that Teresa and Alice could sort everything out between them, so she said, "No, I'm sure we can arrange all that."

Samantha suddenly had another thought, "I don't know if you know but my husband's secretary was killed in the crash, and he'd like to go to the funeral if he can. Do you think that would be possible?"

A big smile spread across the Sister's face, "Oh dear! He does like to stretch things all the way, doesn't he?"

Samantha smiled back, "Perhaps that's the MP in him."

The Sister continued smiling, "Look I don't want to go back to Dr. Simkin with that. So what I suggest is that if we can arrange the transfer on the day of the funeral, then if you make sure there's a wheelchair on the ambulance and the nurse is with him all the time, then maybe he can go to the funeral on the way back to Walsall. What do you think?"

"Thank you. I'll do what I can. I'm sure Edward will appreciate that and I know he's grateful for everything else you are all doing for him."

"Can I ask that this funeral thing is just between you and your husband? If I'm asked I would like to say that I know nothing about it."

"That's fine. I understand, and thank you again."

Samantha held her hand across the table and shook the Sister's hand, "Thank you for everything."

She went to leave but the Sister stopped her, "Just one other thing Mrs Richards." She reached to the floor and produced a battered leather case. "I believe this is your husband's briefcase. It was found in the carriage of the train when they had made it safe enough to go in and search for people's belongings. It apparently has Mr Richards' papers in it. The police brought it over a little while ago. I was going to give it to your husband but I thought that maybe it would only encourage him to try and do some work before he's ready. So I 'd rather you take it away and give it to him when he gets home."

Samantha took the briefcase and once again thanked the Sister for everything she had done.

The next few days were the most hectic Samantha had experienced in a long time, but she managed to make all the necessary arrangements for Edward's transfer on the Friday of that week. Teresa managed to coerce doctors at the General Hospital to accept Edward as a patient, but she only managed to get the letter agreeing to this from the surgeon at the General minutes before she and Philip left Walsall on the Thursday afternoon. They went straight to St. Alfege's hospital and gave Dr Simkin the letter, which also described Teresa as a very experienced and capable nursing Sister who could accompany Edward on his transfer to Walsall.

And so, early on the Friday morning, Philip took Samantha and Teresa to the hospital to meet the ambulance. Much to Edward's annoyance, Dr Simkin insisted that he should lie down for the journey.

Philip returned to the flat and picked up his aunt to take her back home whilst the ambulance went as fast as it could to Abingdon, just south of Oxford, so that Edward and Samantha could attend Guinivere's funeral.

They just managed to find St. Helen's Church and manoeuvre Edward into the wheelchair and into the church by noon for the start of the service.

After the service the ambulance followed at the end of the cortège to the cemetery; the ambulance driver keeping as far back from the last car as he dared. Edward said he did not think an ambulance should be part of the procession of funeral cars, but the ambulance driver had no idea where the cemetery was and did not want to lose sight of the last car.

By the time the driver, Teresa and Samantha had managed to get Edward into the wheelchair and wheel him to the graveside, the vicar was already well into his ashes to ashes homily. Samantha held Edward's hand as the coffin was lowered and was somewhat surprised at how much he was shaking. She looked at him and was even more surprised to see the tears streaming down his face. Perhaps he was remembering his father's funeral just a few months earlier, or maybe he was thinking back to the burial of his first wife which had been so traumatic and devastating to him.

As everyone started to move away from the graveside, she gave Edward a handkerchief and went to move the wheelchair but he stopped her, "Can you just leave me here for a bit?"

She did not realise Edward had felt this close to Guinivere, and for a moment, once again wondered why they were on the train together. Earlier in the week Edward had given her a perfectly good explanation; an explanation she had accepted without question, but when she was trying to sort out the arrangements for attending this funeral and getting Edward back to Walsall, she had looked in his briefcase to find a telephone number from his address book and had taken out some of the documents that were in the case. On the top of the pile was a typed copy of the speech he was to give in the House the day after the accident. And the other papers were research data and notes that had almost certainly been written by Guinivere. So what were the papers he said were at Guinivere's house in Hayes? But she was being silly, they were probably a different set of notes he needed, and she should stop thinking such stupid things. She never raised the subject with Edward again.

Edward's healing progressed rapidly back at the Walsall General, particularly as he was on Alice's ward and she made sure he had all the treatment available. He returned home for Christmas, hobbling around on crutches and by the New Year was making plans to get back to Parliament.

He was nevertheless extremely frustrated that he had to wait for further strengthening in his stump before he could have a prosthetic foot fitted, but with his pestering and Alice's badgering of the appropriate people he was walking without crutches on his new foot by Easter. He'd had a limp ever since being shot in that leg in 1944 and the only noticeable effect of his new injury was that the limp was now slightly more pronounced.

He returned to Parliament at the beginning of May and although they still lived apart for most of the week, unlike previously when he often stayed in London on Friday night and sometimes for the whole weekend on party business or to attend some function or other, Edward now came home every Friday as soon as business in the House was over. Samantha took this change to be a sign of his concern about her and the baby.

He'd certainly became more and more attentive as her pregnancy progressed, insisting she saw the best (and most expensive) gynaecologist and had the best maternity care. Samantha nevertheless insisted that she wanted to have the baby in the NHS maternity wing in the hospital and did not want to go to a private nursing home to have the child.

Edward eventually agreed but as the time for the birth drew nearer he became almost paranoid about her welfare and she was constantly trying to convince him that everything was going to be all right and that what had happened to Juliette would not happen to her.

By the end of May, Edward was almost unbearable and Samantha was somewhat relieved that he was still in London when her contractions started early on Friday morning. Edward had insisted that for the last few weeks of her pregnancy she should stay with his mother whenever he was in London; an arrangement she was not terribly happy about but knew it was not sensible to be entirely on her own. She lay in bed for a while, timing the pains, and when she was certain they were real contractions she called her mother-in-law.

To Samantha's surprise, Mary was remarkably calm and business like about everything, to the point where she was even glad she was staying with her. She was even more astonished when Mary said, "I know Edward said I was to ring him when you started but I'll not bother him yet. You don't want him fussing over you until it's all over. You've got far more important things to do than cope with his paranoia and his panicking all round you."

Samantha had never heard Mary talk about her son like this before and did not know whether to agree with her or not, "But don't you think he'll be annoyed if you don't phone him?"

"Possibly, but I'll soon deal with that so don't you worry about it. Now I suggest you get yourself dressed as quick as you can, and then let's get you to the hospital."

Twenty minutes later, Samantha was in the delivery ward and by midday she was holding her beautiful baby daughter. Mary had been holding her hand throughout and Samantha felt a closeness to her mother-in-law that she had never experienced before.

She smiled at Samantha and asked, "Can I have a quick hug of my grand-daughter, and then I think I should go and phone Edward."

Samantha passed the baby to her, "Oh, my God, I'd forgotten you hadn't phoned him. You'd better do it quickly or else he'll be furious."

Mary held the child in one arm and stroked Samantha's forehead with her free hand, "Calm down, calm down! I've told you, I'll deal with Edward. He doesn't have to worry anymore does he? I can now tell him that you are perfectly well and that he has a wonderful baby daughter."

She held the baby close and kissed her on her head before handing the child back to her mother, "I suppose I'd better go and phone him then. It'll give you a bit of time to spend with your baby. And before I go what are you going to call her? I can't refer to her as baby all the time can I?"

"I'll have to talk to Edward about that first."

"What do you mean? Haven't you already sorted out a name?"

"Well Edward said it would be bad luck to decide on names before we knew the baby was safe and well."

"Goodness, he has been paranoid about it all hasn't he? But you must have thought about names, so what do you want to call her?"

Samantha wondered if she should answer this question without clearing it with Edward, but answered anyway, "I like Charlotte Louise. Charlotte was my grandmother's name and well, I've always liked the name Louise."

Mary let out another, "Goodness!" before adding, "You do like to give girls names that can be shortened into boy's names in your family don't you? First it's Sam and now it's Charley."

Samantha reddened at her mother-in-law's jibe. Mary saw how she had embarrassed her and immediately said, "I'm sorry. I shouldn't have said that. Actually I think Charlotte is a lovely name and that's what I'll always call her even if others do shorten it."

"Well, I was planning that we should call her Louise and not use the name Charlotte except on her birth certificate etcetera."

"So why not call her Louise Charlotte then?"

"Just because Charlotte Louise Richards sounds that much better than Louise Charlotte Richards."

Mary mumbled the two names over and over, "You're right, Charlotte Louise Richards has a nicer ring to it." She came to the bedside and touched the baby, "Welcome to the world Charlotte Louise Richards."

"But I haven't spoken to Edward about it yet."

"Oh he'll love it. And I shall be very happy to call my granddaughter Louise. Louise was my grandmother's name, so you've made a very good choice and I approve of it whole heartedly."

She went towards the door, "And now I'd better go and ring Edward. Do you want me to phone anyone else or do you want me to leave all that to Edward?"

"Could you just get in touch with my Mom and Dad please? But don't say anything about the name to them, or to Edward, until I've spoken to him. You won't will you?"

Mary muttered something as she went away. Sam thought it was "Of course not!" but was not sure.

The nurse came to the bedside to check on things as soon as Mary had left and suggested that Samantha should put the baby to the breast for a few minutes before she took her to her cot. "I know she probably won't get any milk yet but it'll help you both to get used to each other and enjoy the closeness of it. I know when I had my first child it was the most wonderful experience I'd ever felt."

Samantha did as she suggested. She bared her breast, unwrapped part of the blanket from around Louise's head and held her mouth to the nipple. The child immediately started a sucking motion but very quickly went back to sleep enjoying the warmth and comfort of her mother's body.

For the first time, Samantha was on her own with Louise and was able to privately inspect and enjoy every aspect of her baby. All her fingers and toes were there and even a tiny fragile nail on each one of them. She looked closely at the face, trying to work out who she took after, but the features were difficult to determine as the face was still puckered from the birth.

She wanted the baby to open her eyes so that she could check their colour. She thought they were blue, the same as her own and Edward's, but was not absolutely sure. "Open your eyes little one so I can check," but then quietly said to the sleeping child, "Stay asleep sweetheart; it doesn't matter, Philip has blue eyes as well so blue eyes won't prove anything."

She brushed her hand over the baby's almost bald head and inspected the few wisps of fine hair that were glistening under the bright fluorescent lights shining down from the ceiling. She shook as she gently held the strands between her thumb and finger. They were the same deep red colour as Edward's hair. After carefully checking the remaining few strands, she closed her eyes and sighed, relieved in the knowledge that she would not have to deceive Edward over Louise's parentage any longer.

It wasn't that she wanted Edward's child and not Philip's, but that she didn't think she could successfully mislead all her family and friends and particularly this beautiful small baby cradled in her arms for the rest of the innocent child's life, by pretending that she was Edward's, if there was the slightest chance that she was really Philip's child.

She lay back on the pillow and relaxed and wondered how Philip would react when he saw Louise. He had said he would love the child and wanted to be part of its life merely because she was the mother. He had told her that tests had shown he couldn't father a child, but that made absolutely no difference to the feelings he already felt for the child, even before she was born. She was certain that Edward would not have taken the same view if he thought the child was not his.

She closed her eyes and pondered how Edward would react to the child. He had not been a real father in his son's life, but Samantha hoped now that both she and his daughter were here safe and well, he would react totally differently towards Louise and be a true father to her. If he did then Louise would have the best of both worlds. A biological father who would love and care for her as a true father, and a favourite uncle who would always be there for her. Her thoughts wandered between Edward and Philip and she became more and more drowsy.

She was awoken some time later by the baby's cries.

"I think she wants feeding." Edward was sitting on the chair at the side of the bed; a very large bunch of flowers resting in his lap. He had the biggest and widest smile that she had ever witnessed from him.

"How long have you been sitting there?"

The smile did not leave his face as he answered, "Probably about ten minutes. You and Louise looked so contented and peaceful together, I didn't want to spoil the pleasure of just sitting here and watching you both."

Samantha looked at the clock, "But it's only half past one, how on earth have you got here so quickly?"

"I phoned before I left for work this morning and there was no answer, so I kept trying for about ten minutes before deciding you'd probably started and Ma, being Ma, had brought you here without bothering to let me know what was going on, so I just caught the first train I could and here I am."

"I'm sorry she didn't phone, I did ask her to." She suddenly realised what he had said, "You called her Louise but we hadn't discussed her name."

"I know, but when I saw Ma before I came in, she said everything was fine and both you and baby Louise were fit and well and that I should stop worrying and enjoy being a very lucky father. So I just presumed you'd decided on that name."

"I'm sorry, I did tell her it was just a thought and I wanted to talk to you about her names first."

He leaned across and kissed her gently on the lips, "I know, she said." He kissed her again and added, "And anyway I like Charlotte Louise, so that's settled."

"So she did tell you then?"

He nodded and, as he handed her the flowers, just said, "And do I get to hold my daughter then?" He took her in his arms and as he did so, Samantha could tell from the way he was looking at the baby that he would be the real father she wanted him to be for Louise.

The nurse came and took Louise from him, saying Samantha should get some rest whilst she had the chance. "She won't get much chance when she goes back home, so why don't you leave her for a while and come back a little later?"

Samantha later enjoyed the attention she had from her mother and father, but it was short lived, for as soon as the nurse brought the baby back, all their attention was on their new grandchild and Samantha felt almost redundant. So when she saw Teresa coming into the ward, her heart jumped as she waited for Philip to follow her. But he did not.

"I hope you don't mind, but I've just finished my shift and I thought I'd pop and see you before going home." She was soon making all the same 'she's a beautiful baby' and 'isn't she lovely' and 'I'm so pleased that you are both well' and 'can I hold her a moment?' comments that Samantha's other visitors had made.

Samantha tried desperately to hide the enormous disappointment she felt that Philip was not with Teresa. She was sure she would feel differently if he was saying all these things to her. He had said he would love her child but she nevertheless wanted to see his reaction when he first saw Louise.

Even though she ached to ask Teresa whether Philip knew she'd had the baby, she didn't say anything as she didn't want to highlight the fact that she wanted to see him. But when Teresa was leaving and said, "I'll pop and see you again sometime," Samantha took the opportunity and replied, "Of course, but bring Philip with you next time."

"Yes. I'm sorry about that. I tried to phone and tell him about the baby, but he's away at the Edinburgh shop today, and he'd already left when I phoned, so he won't know until he gets home. I'm sure he'd have popped in if he were here."

Samantha did not want to show her real feelings on the matter so she merely said, "Oh don't worry him about it; there'll be plenty of time for you to bring him to meet Louise when I'm back home."

Samantha had a disturbed sleep all that night, not only with baby Louise, but also feeling the need to see Philip. She knew she should not feel that way but could not help her feelings.

The next morning she went and had a shower and was returning to her bed dressed in her nightgown and dressing gown, her hair still wet and dishevelled, when there was Philip at her bedside looking lost. He turned as she neared him and she saw by the look on his face that he was as pleased to see her as she was to see him.

If it had been anyone else, she would have worried about the state of her hair and the fact she was not properly groomed and dressed, but all that mattered now was that Philip was here and on his own!

Her instincts were to dash to him and throw her arms around him, but that was not possible; that would go against everything they'd agreed.

However as she reached him he put his hands on her upper arms, leaned forward and kissed her on the cheek. They both closed their eyes as he did so, and when she felt the tension as his hands squeezed her arms ever tighter, she realised that the struggle he was having to not take her in his arms, was as great as hers was not to throw her body tightly against his.

He suddenly let go of her and said, "Congratulations," but after a quick check to make sure no-one else in the ward was looking, mouthed the words, "I love you."

She mouthed the words back before saying aloud, "It's lovely to see you, but I must look a mess. I haven't even dried my hair yet."

He laughed as he lightly touched her hair, "I hadn't even noticed."

She laughed back, "Liar," and touching her tummy added, "At least, now Louise has been born, I'll be able to dress to kill when your John marries Jane next month." She jabbed him in the ribs with a, "And you'd better notice me then." She grabbed his hand saying, "Do you want to see Louise?"

"Of course, she is the second reason I'm here."

She smiled and asked, "And what's the first then?"

He merely smiled back and said, "Do you really need to ask that?"

She did not answer but held on to his hand and led him to the row of cots at the end of the ward. She stopped at the third one, squeezed his hand even tighter and leaning her shoulder against his, said, "Meet Charlotte Louise."

Philip looked at the wee child asleep in the cot. She was completely covered except for the tiny sweet face. Her eyes were tightly shut as she lay there virtually motionless, except for the almost imperceptible movement as she took her tiny breath in followed by her breath out. He was immediately filled with love for her; almost the same unexplainable feelings he had the first moment he had set eyes on Samantha. Samantha looked at his face and saw the wonder in his eyes as they filled with moisture. She knew instantly that the tears were tears of joy and happiness.

She gave him a quick peck on the cheek, saying in his ear, "I'm sorry, sweetheart, but the nurses don't like us taking babies out when they're sleeping like that, so you'll have to wait until some other time to hold her."

He looked at Samantha, wiping the dampness from his face as he did so, "Just seeing you both is more than I'd expected." He reached into his pocket and took out an envelope, "I was only supposed to give this to the nurse and ask her to let you have it, but I couldn't go without at least trying to see you."

"She held his hand tightly again, "I'm glad you did."

He gave the envelope to her saying, "I guess I'd better go now. Teresa's not working today and suggested we should pop and see you this afternoon, so maybe you can give Louise to me to hold for a minute then?"

He took a small paper bag from his pocket and gave it to her, "And this is from me." He laughed, "Just in case you have a spare minute and want something to read."

She did not want him to go but knew that was not an option if their feelings for each other were to remain just feelings; and more importantly feelings that no-one else ever suspected.

After he had gone she dried and brushed her hair, put on a little lipstick, and sat back on the bed before taking the thin leather bound book from the paper bag. It was a copy of Edward Fitzgerald's translation of the Rubáiyát of Omar Khayyám. She opened it at the page where the leather bookmark had been placed and read the verse on the right hand page,

Ah Love! could thou and I with Fate conspire
To grasp this Sorry Scheme of Things entire,
Would not we shatter it to bits - and then
Re-mould it nearer the Heart's Desire!

And she knew exactly why Philip had placed the bookmark at that particular page.

Shc tore open the envelope he had given her and read the card, but was a little disappointed, although not in the least surprised, to find it was written by Teresa. She went to throw the envelope away, but realised something else was in it. She looked and took out the small envelope within it. Inside was a single card with only the words 'Thank you' printed on it. She knew who that was from and no other words were necessary to say everything she had wanted to hear.

CHAPTER TWENTY- TWO

1965

"Edward, where are you? Can you look after Louise for a bit whilst I try and get everything ready for this party?"

Samantha had no reply, so she went to the bottom of the stairs and shouted again, "Edward, can you please leave what you're doing and keep Louise occupied for a bit?"

Edward came out of the small bedroom which had been furnished as an office for him and stood at the top of the stairs, "I'll be down in a minute when I've finished this telephone call."

"It's your daughter's seventh birthday today, so can't you leave work for just one day and spend some time with her. Everyone will be here soon and I haven't finished all the preparations yet."

"I'll be down in a minute," and with that he went back into his office.

Following Louise's birth, Edward had said he wanted Sam to be a full time mother and move permanently to London with him and only spend time in their Walsall home when constituency business demanded it. Samantha however, had not only assumed she would return to work when Louise was older, but also realised she would lose the family support network by such a move. Nevertheless she agreed and had spent several months at the London flat during that first year.

Although she saw Edward more often during these months, he never seemed to be with her for more than a few minutes. He did find time to fuss over Louise but otherwise would only be home long enough to grab a bite to eat or get changed before chasing out to some meeting or other. Often he retuned home so late that Samantha had already gone to bed, and the next morning he would dash out immediately after dressing without talking to her at all. She had never felt as lonely as she did during those months, and when the winter came with its dark mornings and even darker foggy nights, she was glad to return home to Walsall for the Christmas break. She did not return to London in the New Year and only returned there occasionally for the odd week or so, or when Edward specially asked her to attend a function with him.

When she was not in London it did seem that Edward missed her more than she had thought and came back home far more often than he had before her pregnancy. He often returned for one and sometimes two nights during the week; a thing he had never done in the past. And, as Louise grew into a little girl with her own personality, he always responded to her happy and smiling face, ready to play with her and read her stories at night whenever he could. For a while Edward was the father Samantha had wanted him to be, but gradually he returned home less frequently, and when Harold Wilson took over the leadership of the party in 1963 following the death of Hugh Gaitskell, Edward's midweek visits almost ceased completely. He said it was because he wanted to establish himself with the new party hierarchy, but Samantha felt that there was more to it than that.

In October 1964, the labour party won power with a mere five majority and Edward was given a junior ministerial post in the Foreign Office. After that his home visits became even less frequent and mostly only occurred when he had to deal with constituency matters and his constituency surgery.

When Louise was two, Samantha announced that she was thinking of returning to work. Neither, Edward nor his mother liked the idea and both said to Samantha, "Mothers should stay at home and look after their husbands and children,"

This infuriated Samantha, who most of the time felt she was the only one actually there for Louise. She had talked to Philip about it, but he admitted he had ulterior motives in wanting her to return to work. Officially, he said this was because he wanted to expand the retail side of the business and he and Lucy needed her expertise to help them do this. When they were alone however he admitted that the real reason was that he missed seeing her.

He still wanted their relationship to be far more than that of mere work colleagues, and they had even discussed the possibility again. In the end however, they each agreed that would now cause more pain and hurt for more people, including Louise, than it would have done when Sam had first told Philip she was pregnant.

Nevertheless, Samantha also knew in her heart that she may not have been so anxious to return to work if it had not involved seeing Philip more often. She thought long and hard before coming to a decision and only opted to return when Louise was old enough to go to a children's play group. At first this had been on a part time basis, but each year she gradually increased her working hours to coincide with the longer hours Louise was at nursery and then at school.

Grace Matthews, Philip's mother, announced in 1963 that she wanted to retire and no longer be involved in the retail business she had built up from nothing and she handed over total control of her business to Philip. Lucy, who had been saying she wanted to retire ever since Edward's father Tom had died suddenly the year before Louise had been born, decided to retire at the same time. John, Philip's younger brother, still worked designing and manufacturing bespoke furniture to contain televisions, radios, record players and such, but he was the first to admit that he was not a businessman and would not consider any managerial role.

Philip called all the family members together to discuss the long term future of the business at which Grace, Lucy, and Mary, each said that all they wanted was sufficient income from their shares to give them a reasonable standard of living. Edward said he did not have the time to be involved in the business and would leave everything to Philip, particularly now that Samantha was working almost full time and could keep an eye on the finances for him. Neither Philip nor Samantha quite knew how to take this comment but had let it drop.

It seemed to Philip that he was the only family member who now had any real concern about how the business was run and now for the first time ever he had to employ senior people who were not members of the family to run parts of the business and to help him keep some sort of overall control he started to make long term plans for the company.

The first step was the restructure of the three separate businesses of manufacture, high street shops and catalogue sales under one single group company in 1964, named MR Communications Group. A new group administration block was built next to the existing factory, but Philip kept the small set of offices in the old building so that he could work separately and quietly away from his team in the new offices next door.

His next step was to create a new company to try out a sales venture he had been contemplating for some time. The frugality of the immediate post war years was now over and large numbers of people had disposable income to spend on all sorts of electrical goods. He rented an out of town warehouse, filled it with TV's, fridges, washing machines, hi-fi, and all sorts of other electrical goods and sold them still in their unopened boxes on a cash and carry basis. In this way he was able to sell at prices lower than those of the high street shops. He was even surprised himself at the rapid success of the venture.

Ten minutes after Samantha had asked him to come and look after Louise, Edward was still in his office and she was finding it difficult to complete the party preparations whilst Louise was asking her to, "Look at this, Mommy," and, "When is everyone coming, Mommy?" and "Is it time yet, Mommy?"

Samantha answered all her questions but five minutes later Louise was back again asking, "Grandma will bring my doll that I left at her house last week won't she Mommy?"

"I'm sure she will sweetheart."

"But will you phone her and make sure?"

Sam left her preparations yet again and went into the hall to once more call on Edward to sort out his daughter, but instead she picked up the phone to speak to her mother and check about the doll herself. She put the receiver to her ear and heard Edward's voice instead of the dialling tone.

"I must go. I'll see you tomorrow."

She went to put the phone down but held on for a moment, only to hear a woman's seductive voice reply, "I can't wait, so get here as soon as you can."

Samantha returned the phone to its cradle as quickly and as quietly as she could. *"What did she mean by, 'I can't wait'?"* She rushed back into the kitchen trying to put the words out of her head; after all, it probably meant absolutely nothing.

No sooner had Edward come down stairs and started to play with Louise, than the door bell rang and the first of the children coming to the party arrived. After that, Samantha gave no more thought about what she heard on the telephone until the mothers and fathers had all collected their offspring some three hours later. The thoughts disturbing her once more as she sat down to enjoy a cup of tea before the grown ups arrived, but no sooner had she sat down than the door bell rang. Louise ran to the window to see who was at the door. She ran into the hall declaring, "It's Grandma and Grandpa, Mommy. Do you think they'll have a present for me?"

Reluctantly Samantha put her almost full cup of tea on the coffee table and got up to let her parents in. Ten minutes later, just as she sat down with her tea again, the door bell rang. This time it was Edward's mother. She was followed in quick succession by the rest of the family; each bearing gifts for the little girl who was the light of their life to all of them. Soon the lounge was littered with birthday paper as Louise tore open the wrapping from each gift.

Philip and Teresa were the last of the family to arrive and Samantha had begun to think that maybe something was wrong, but when the bell rang again and Louise announced from the window that, "It's Uncle Philip," with a big beam of delight on her face, Samantha started to relax and forgot all about the voice on the phone.

As soon as Samantha opened the door, Louise dashed to Philip, holding out her arms demanding to be picked up. Both Samantha and Teresa smiled as she did so, and both looked at Philip waiting for him to do her bidding. Immediately she was up in his arms, Louise was kissing him first on one cheek and then on the other, her long red hair flowing freely from side to side as she did so. “Come and see all my presents, Uncle Philip. Wait ‘til you see what Nanna Richards has bought me.” Philip winked at Samantha as he went past her carrying Louise in his arms into the lounge.

“Put your Uncle Philip down and let him get his coat off.” It was Edward making the demand and immediately Louise wriggled to be dropped to the floor as her father required. Philip said his ‘hellos’ to all the others present and Edward stood up and shook hands with him, adding, “She makes a bigger fuss of you than she does of me,”

Philip replied with, “That’s nonsense,” but nevertheless felt a gush of pride and pleasure that maybe it was true.

He had never intentionally set out to be more important in Louise’s life than her father, but Louise was so special to him, that he had no desire to take a back seat in her life either. Nevertheless, he always trod the very fine line between trying to be a part of both Louise’s and Samantha’s lives, without actually crossing over the line to become far more than an uncle to Louise, and a good friend to Samantha. He thought he managed the first well even though he found the second a constant strain on his emotions. Did Edward’s comment mean that he had taken his relationship too far?

But no sooner had he sat down than Louise was back grabbing his hand and demanding that he, “Come and see my new bike that Mommy and Daddy have given me.”

Philip shrugged his shoulders and pulled a face as if being asked to do something against his wishes, but nothing was further from the truth and Samantha smiled at him as if to say, “Go on, you know you want to,” as Louise kept pulling on his hand making it seem that he was only doing her bidding.

He turned to Louise and enquired, “Shall we ask everyone else to come and see it as well, Louise?”

Louise stopped momentarily to consider the question, but merely turned to Teresa and taking hold of her hand demanded, “You come as well, Auntie Teresa,” before leading the way outside into the garden.

“Why don’t you all go with them?” queried Samantha. “I’ll get the food sorted. I think it’s still warm enough for us to eat outside. What do you think, Edward?”

“Yes. I’m sure it is and Louise will be able to run around out there better than in here.”

An hour later Samantha went back into the house and returned with a birthday cake on which seven candles were burning. Louise jumped up and down when she saw it and grinned from ear to ear as everyone sang 'Happy birthday' for her. It was the third time that 'Happy birthday' had been sung to her that day and it was the second birthday cake she had been allowed to cut that afternoon.

Everyone was provided with a piece of the sponge cake loaded with icing sugar, which Louise insisted on carrying to them, but no sooner had it been eaten and Louise had been required to collect the empty plates from everyone and return them to the kitchen than Edward said, "And now Birthday girl, I think it's time you said goodnight to everyone and went off to bed."

"But it's my birthday, Daddy. Can't I stay up a bit longer?"

"No you can't. So say your goodnights and let's have you up those stairs."

Louise's face dropped as she sniffed back a tear, but she knew that whilst she might be able to bargain with her mother she dare not even try with her father.

Philip saw the moisture in her eyes as she turned to kiss each of them goodnight. When she reached him, he wanted to pick her up and kiss the tears from her cheeks but knew that he should not do any such thing. But Louise once more grabbed his hand and, turning to her father for approval asked, "Can Uncle Philip come and read me a story before I go to sleep?"

Edward laughed, and nodded his head saying, "I suppose so, as it's your birthday," before turning to Philip and stating, "I told you she's getting fonder of you than me, Philip."

Samantha took Louise by the hand saying, "Come on sweetheart, let's go and get you ready for bed. Uncle Philip will come up in a few minutes to read your story." She spoke to Philip as she led Louise away, "Come up in about five minutes, I'll have her in bed by then."

In exactly five minutes, Philip finished the rest of his drink and went upstairs to find Louise already in her bed, story book in hand and opened at the page she wanted reading to her.

Samantha was folding Louise's clothes as he entered the room, but as soon as he sat on the bed to read the story she put the clothes away and sat at the foot of the bed next to him. They smiled at each other briefly before he started reading. He was aware of Samantha's closeness and wanted to move even closer to her, but contented himself that he was alone with the two people he loved most, and savoured the few moments they had together.

As he read, Louise laid her head on the pillow and snuggled further into the blankets. Samantha moved closer to him and touched his free hand resting on the bed. He moved it slightly so that it was out of Louise's vision and Samantha stroked the back of it. He wanted to close his eyes so that he could relish the joy of being touched by her more vividly in his head, but continued reading and looking at Louise. Louise turned to him and smiled and his heart was totally lost in the emotion surging inside his chest. He took pleasure in the beauty of the child in front of him, her soft red hair flowing across the pillow; her sweet innocent face so incredibly and stunningly beautiful. He loved this child and knew that his love for her could not be any greater if she had been his own.

Gradually, Louise's eyes closed and she fell asleep as he quietly read. He closed the book; leaned forward to kiss her very lightly on the forehead and gave Samantha's hand one last squeeze before standing up.

Sam leaned over her daughter and kissed her on each cheek, and then took the book from Philip and placed it on the bedside table. He went to open the door as she switched off the light, but she stopped him from doing so and instead leaned forward and kissed him firmly but briefly on the lips. He wanted to take her in his arms and return the kiss for much longer, but that was not part of their contract and they both knew it, so he merely took hold of her hand and stroked it gently once more before letting it go to open the door; both knowing that the joy of those last few minutes together with Louise, would have to sustain them for many weeks before anything similar might happen.

Two weeks later Samantha was sitting in Philip's office discussing the latest sales figures with him when his telephone rang. She went to leave but he signalled for her to stay seated in the chair opposite him as he picked up the receiver and listened for a moment before speaking.

"Yes Mrs Richards is with me. Who wants to speak to her?" He waited for the response before adding, "Sorry, can you repeat that? Who did you say wants to speak to Mrs Richards?"

As he listened to the reply he wrote the name on his pad and read from the paper as he handed the phone to Sam, "A Mrs Holland wants to speak to you Sam."

Samantha shook her head from side to side saying, "I don't know a Mrs Holland. Who is she?"

Philip spoke again into the phone, "Jane. Did Mrs Holland say who she was or what she wants?"

As he waited for the response Samantha gasped and she put her hand to her mouth as she suddenly recognised the name, "It's Louise's head teacher. Something has happened to Louise. Oh, my God. What does she want?"

Samantha snatched the phone from Philip's grip and as soon as Jane put the call through started to frantically speak into it, "Hello Mrs Holland. This is Samantha Richards here. What's the problem? Is Louise all right?"

"Calm down Mrs Richards. Louise will be fine. She's had a slight accident and cut her leg. I don't think it's too serious but I've got the school secretary to take her to the General Hospital to have it checked out and I'm just letting you know so that you can go there yourself."

"But what has she done? How bad is it?"

"She fell on the grass and cut her knee on a piece of glass."

"What on earth was glass doing on the grass? Don't you check for things like that?"

"I understand your anger, Mrs Richards. The truth is we have no idea how glass got there but I think someone must have thrown a milk bottle over the school wall. But perhaps we can have the investigation into how it happened later. For now I think you should go to the hospital and I'll be happy to talk to you tomorrow once Louise has been seen to."

Samantha started to calm down and asked, "But Louise is all right? It's nothing serious?"

"Well I imagine she may need a stitch or two, but I'm sure she'll be fine."

Sam's anxiety level shot up again, "Stitches? You didn't say anything about stitches."

Before the head teacher could answer Philip beckoned to Sam to give him the phone. She did so without any protest.

"Mrs Holland this is Philip Matthews, a work colleague of Mrs Richards. I've only heard one side of the conversation but I gather that Louise has been injured and possibly needs stitches in a wound? Can you tell me where she is now and I'll take Mrs Richards to her straight away?"

Mrs Holland explained everything again to the much calmer Philip and by the time he put down the phone, Samantha had already scooped up all her papers and was standing by the door to hear what Philip had to say before leaving for the hospital.

Philip picked up the receiver again and spoke to Jane on the switchboard, "Jane, Mrs Richards and I are leaving now and possibly won't be back for the rest of the afternoon, so can you just make a note of any further calls for either of us and tell them we'll ring them back in the morning?"

He returned the phone to its cradle and stood up, "Go and fetch your coat Sam and I'll take you to the hospital straight away. Mrs Holland said the secretary had only just left so with a bit of luck we shouldn't be far behind them reaching the hospital."

"I should ring Edward and let him know what's happened. He may want to come to see her himself?"

Philip crossed the room and took her arm, leading her out of the office, "I think you should stop panicking right now. Let's get to the hospital, find out how Louise is and then you can phone Edward. Chances are she'll be fine, and there'll be no need for Edward to make a special journey back here."

Samantha merely nodded her head before collecting her things and following Philip to his car.

Louise did need two stitches in the cut just below her knee, but when it was all finished and the wound was wrapped in a bandage, she hobbled out of the treatment room holding tightly on to her mother's hand and still sniffing for effect. But as soon as she saw her Uncle Philip the sniffing stopped and was replaced with a big grin.

"I've had to have two stitches in my leg and a needle in my arm Uncle Philip, and the nurse said that I don't have to go to school tomorrow."

Samantha laughed, "That's not exactly true, Louise. The nurse said she thought you would be fine but to keep an eye on you and if you were feeling sick or woozy in the morning to keep you at home."

"That's what I said. I can stay at home tomorrow."

Philip smiled as he took hold of Louise's other hand. He looked across at Samantha, "I think you've already lost that battle, Sam. I don't think there's any point trying to talk her out of it. Come on, I'll take you both home and then your Mommy can phone Daddy and let him know what's happened."

"Can I phone him, Mommy. I want to tell him about my injection and stitches."

Sam looked at Philip and they both laughed, "I don't think she's seriously hurt, do you Uncle Philip?"

"No, but I do think she's going to milk the sympathy from everyone for as long as she can."

Once they had got Louise settled on the settee at home, Philip went into the kitchen to get Louise a drink and make a cup of tea for Samantha and himself, telling Sam to get Edward on the phone and let him know what had happened.

"He'll still be in the House probably until later tonight. He doesn't like me to phone him there unless it's a real emergency, and this isn't an emergency now is it? Perhaps I should leave it 'til he gets back to the flat?"

"No. It isn't an emergency but I still think you should phone him and anyway Louise is expecting to speak to him, isn't she?"

Samantha went to the phone and rang the House of Commons number asking to be put through to Edward's office. A female, whom she took to be his secretary answered, "I'm sorry Mrs Richards, but Mr Richards is in the chamber at the moment. Can I give him a message?"

Samantha shuddered as she recognised the voice, even though she had never spoken to this particular secretary before. This was surely the woman who had said she 'couldn't wait' to see her husband, on Louise's birthday. She'd forgotten about the call but hearing the woman's voice again made her wonder what the comment had signified. She nevertheless determined not to show her concern.

"Could you just ask him to give me a call, when he has a minute please?"

"Will it be all right if he rings later or do you need him to ring from here before he goes home?"

Samantha felt offended that she should ask such a question and wanted to say, *"Why on earth would I ring him at the House if I was happy to leave it until he got back to the flat?"* but thought better of it and merely said, "Please just ask him to ring as soon as he can?"

She was about to put down the phone when the girl asked, "And what shall I tell him if he asks what it's about?"

Samantha's blood pressure shot up even higher and she wanted to scream at the arrogance of the woman, but merely said as calmly as she could, "Just tell him his wife wishes to speak to him," before slamming down the phone.

She walked into the kitchen just as Philip was coming out carrying the tray with the drinks on it. She stood in his way muttering, "Who the hell does that woman think she is? I swear I would have slapped her face if I'd been near enough to her."

Philip backed into the kitchen, "Come and sit down in here a minute and tell me what this is all about? What woman? And more to the point what has she said to upset you like this."

They both sat at the kitchen table, "Oh, it's just me. I guess I'm over reacting. I suppose she was only doing her job. Edward has probably told her to find out all she can about what a caller may want, so he's prepared in advance of calling back. But I'm his wife for God's sake, I don't have to tell her all our business." She looked questioningly at Philip, "I don't do I?"

"Of course not, but there's more to it than that. You wouldn't normally get upset by something as silly as an over officious secretary, so what is it that's really upsetting you? You're not still worried about Louise, are you? There's no need to, she's going to be fine. A few weeks from now and there probably won't even be much of a scar left."

She put out her hand to touch his, "No, I know this probably sounds awful but I'm so mad I'd totally forgotten about Louise's problem. It's just me being silly and overreacting to something that happened on Louise's birthday. I've probably got it all wrong anyway." She rubbed the back of his hand as she added, "And I have no right to imagine any such thing about Edward anyway." She pulled a face and laughed, "You've absolutely no idea what I'm talking about, do you?"

Philip shook his head without speaking.

"Perhaps I'll talk to you about it some other time if I start getting paranoid again, but for now let's go and see Louise."

The subject would probably never have been brought up again by Samantha, but for another event that happened about a month later.

Samantha was in bed reading late one evening when she had a call from Edward's mother telling her that her mother, Edward's grandmother, had died. She was in her nineties and it was not unexpected but it nevertheless took Samantha some time to convince her that there was no need to go chasing down to Bewdley that night. She told Mary she would drive her down to sort everything out the following morning after dropping Louise off at school. She also said she would let Edward know as soon as she could get hold of him and that she was sure he would ring her in the morning. This seemed to satisfy Mary and the conversation ended.

Samantha wondered whether to leave ringing Edward until first thing in the morning but decided to do so straight away, even though he may already be asleep.

She picked up the phone and dialled the number of the flat. It was ringing for a long time and she was beginning to think it would not be answered. But Edward had spoken to her earlier that evening from the flat so she knew he was there, so she let the phone ring and ring.

It was quite some time before it was answered by a very grumpy Edward asking, "What do you want at this time of night?" without waiting to hear who it was.

Samantha was taken aback by this brusque riposte and did not speak for a few seconds during which she was sure she heard another voice, a woman's voice, in the distance.

"I'm sorry to ring you at this time of night Edward, but I've just had your mother on the phone."

Before she was able to continue Edward butted in with, "What's the matter? Is she ill or something?"

"No, it's your grandmother. She died tonight and your mother wanted me to let you know."

"Oh dear! I always liked Grandma Hadley, but it isn't unexpected is it?"

Samantha was about to answer when she was sure she heard a woman's voice again in the distance say, "Hurry up, Teddy, this bed is getting cold" and without thinking asked, "Who was that?"

"Who was what?"

"That woman. I heard a woman."

Edward was silent for the briefest of moments before responding with, "Oh that, I've been listening to the wireless. Just a minute I'll go and switch it off."

She heard the phone placed on the table and a door close. She listened as circumspectly as she could but was unable to hear anything else until Edward picked up the phone and spoke again, "Sorry about that. What else did mother say?"

Samantha was thrown by the casual way he dealt with the incident, but went along with what she was certain was his deception, "She wants you to phone her first thing in the morning. I've said I'll take her down to your Grandma's to help her sort things out in the morning, so can you phone her and let her know what your plans are before I get there?"

"Do you think I should phone her now?"

She could not help the note of sarcasm in her voice as she answered the question, "That's up to you but I shouldn't stay out of bed too long. It might get cold!" and before Edward could respond, she added, "Goodnight and perhaps you can let me know what your plans are as well," and with that she put down the phone and starting shaking.

She rushed back to her own bed and wrapped herself in the blankets, but could not stop the trembling. She did not feel cold and it was only when she pulled the pillow tightly over her head and started silently screaming into it, that the tension began to subside and the quivering in her body abated. She released the tension from the pillow so that she could take in deep breaths and immediately the tears started to flow. She could not decide whether she was angry, shocked, or just sorry for herself, as she tried to decide what, if anything, to do about what she knew she had just found out. Edward had another woman in his bed. So what, she had slept with Philip in that same bed. But that was only once and it was totally different, wasn't it? She finally fell asleep without reaching a resolution on that question, only to be shaken out of her fretful slumbers by the shrill of the alarm clock going off.

It was two days later that she knocked on the door of Philip's office and waited for his, "Come in," before entering.

She stopped when she saw that Philip had the phone in his hand, "I'm sorry I'll call back if you're busy."

Philip returned the phone to its cradle, "No that's fine. John said he wanted a word with me today and I was just about to tell him I could see him now, but I'm more than happy to see you first." He pointed to the chair opposite to him, "Have a seat."

"I wanted to speak to you about a private matter but I can leave it until later if John is coming to see you."

"No, that's fine. Sit down." He picked up an envelope from his desk, "I wanted to have a word with you about this sometime anyway." He put the envelope back on the desk, "How did it go the last couple of days? Did you and Aunt Mary manage to sort everything out?"

"Yes. Fine. Edward was with us yesterday and he managed to make all the funeral arrangements. It's been arranged for next Monday, eleven o'clock." She shifted in her seat looking at the envelope on this desk, "What's that about?"

"That can wait 'til later, but first you can tell what it is that's bothering you. I recognise that worried look, so what is it?"

"Well I hope you're going to tell me that I'm being unnecessarily suspicious but I don't think I am."

"Suspicious about what? What has Aunt Mary been saying to you now?"

"Oh, no, it's nothing to do with Mary. It's Edward."

"And what has Edward done?"

"Well that's it. I'm not certain that he has 'done' anything, but it doesn't seem that way."

Philip stared intently at her without saying anything as if willing her to go on.

She smiled understanding the look perfectly and obediently continued, "Where do I begin?"

"At the beginning, I guess."

"The beginning? I think that was years ago, but best if I tell you what happened when I phoned Edward on Tuesday night to tell him about his grandmother."

She was silent for a moment and Philip gave her another one of his 'looks' waiting for her to continue.

"This is the difficult bit, because I felt sure I heard what I heard, but Edward said it was something else."

"And now you're talking in riddles, so why don't you just tell me in plain simple English what you think you heard?"

She took a deep breath before asking, "But you will tell me if you think I'm being stupid won't you?"

He smiled and nodded his head, "Of course. Now why don't you just tell me what it's all about?"

She took another deep breath, "Well I was sure I heard a woman's voice in the flat when I was speaking to Edward but he said it was the wireless he was listening to."

"And you don't believe it was the wireless?"

She pursed her lips and shook her head from side to side.

Philip knew the implications of what she had just said but nevertheless did not want to immediately concur with Sam's obvious conclusion.

"Perhaps it was the wireless, or maybe he was entertaining and she wasn't the only one there."

"Thank you for trying Philip, but it was after midnight and I'm sure that what I heard was a woman telling him to come back to bed."

"OK then, but when I asked you to start at the beginning you said it started years ago. Do you mean he's been seeing this woman for years?"

"Well no, of course not. Well not this woman anyway."

"And now you're losing me again. So start at the beginning and tell me everything that's on your mind."

Samantha spent the next fifteen minutes disclosing all the odd events that had concerned her over the years about Edward and other women.

She started with her concerns about Guinivere Isherwood and the Lewisham train crash and how affected Edward was at her graveside. She mentioned several other things Edward had said or done, that didn't quite add up. She told him about listening in to Edward's phone conversation on Louise's birthday and how she had later recognised the voice of the secretary. She ended by saying, "I can't be sure the voice I heard on Tuesday night was definitely his secretary's, but I think it was."

"And there could also be an innocent explanation for everything you've told me. It could have been the radio the other night, just like Edward said."

She laughed out loud relieved at last that she had shared her concerns with Philip, "But you don't believe that either do you?"

He said nothing but just shook his head negatively.

Neither of them spoke for some time, each waiting for the other to say something. Eventually it was Philip who broke the silence, "So what do you want to do about it?"

"I haven't a clue. What do you suggest?"

Philip looked at her long and hard before tentatively asking, "Do you want to think about leaving Edward and for us to be together?"

She shook her head quite violently from side to side, "That's just what I was hoping you wouldn't bring up right now. Our relationship has been bothering me ever since I spoke to Edward on Tuesday night."

"In what way?"

"Well here I am wondering what to do about a mere suspicion I have that Edward might have been unfaithful; a thing I have absolutely no proof of, when we both know that I am most certainly guilty of exactly the very same thing. So who am I to judge?"

Philip merely looked at her for quite a while pondering on what she had said. Eventually he shrugged his shoulders and said, "I'm sorry but I have absolutely no answer to that. And I'm sorry I mentioned us being together. I know we agreed to knock that idea on the head years ago and it was stupid of me to bring it up now."

"Perhaps, but it does sometimes help to know I'm not totally alone when Edward gives me cause to worry about what's going on in his life." She returned his stare before asking, "So what do you advise?"

"Well one of the main reasons you chose to stay with Edward when you first told me you were pregnant, was that you didn't want to deprive your child of a proper relationship with her father. Surely that's even more true after all these years, isn't it?"

"Yes, and for the most part, he's been a good father to Louise. I still don't understand why he seems totally unable to have any sort of relationship with Julian though."

"The only answer I can give you for that is that everything was far too painful for him when Julian was born. He couldn't deal with anything when Juliette died."

"And he still hasn't ever properly been able to deal with that, has he? I often think his whole life is a charade and everything he does is still clouded by the loss of her."

"I think you may be right about that. And as for this thing with Julian, well I can only say what I've said every other time you and I have talked about it, I just don't think he knows how to get close to him now even if wants to."

"So if we can't answer the Julian problem, can we solve this new problem?"

He again thought carefully before answering, "I don't think it's up to me to tell you what to do, but it seems to me that you first need to ask yourself if your suspicions are correct. You could find the answer to that by asking him face to face if he's having an affair. But if his answer is no, then you would have to decide whether you believed he was telling you the truth or not. So you may not be any better off than you are now. And if he said yes, you'd then have to decide what, if anything, you were going to do about it."

He waited for a while but Samantha did not respond so he continued, "Would you decide to forgive him and stay together? And if you couldn't forgive him what would you then do about it? And I'm not sure that right now you want to be faced with making those decisions, do you?"

She shook her head without responding.

"I think that by not answering any of those questions you've actually answered the question of what to do about it."

"Do nothing. Is that what you mean?"

"You have to decide that for yourself but it does seem to me that to do anything else right now could force you into a position I don't think you want to be in. Am I right?"

"I guess so." She put her hands to her face before continuing, "So I just try to stop thinking about it all, do I?"

Philip nodded.

"And if he is having an affair then I suppose I just have to hope that it doesn't become so serious that he wants to leave me and particularly Louise."

Philip merely pursed his lips with an, "Mm."

"So what was this letter you wanted to talk about?"

"I'm not sure it's appropriate right now, but knowing you, I imagine you'll pester me 'til I show it to you. I just hope it won't upset you even more."

"Why should it do that?"

He picked up the envelope and took a letter from it and handed it to Samantha, "It's a letter I had yesterday from Madeleine. It's about Julian. I take it that Edward still hasn't shown you any of the letters Madeleine has sent him?"

Samantha merely said, "No," as she took the letter and began to slowly read all five pages of it. Whilst she was doing so, Philip went out saying he was going to fetch them each a cup of tea. When he returned she was re-reading the letter a second time.

He passed a mug of tea to her and sat down before asking, "So what do you think?"

"I'm not sure what you want me to answer to that. You've told me before that he's a good artist but I didn't know he was that good."

"Well he's good enough to have won a scholarship to the École Nationale des Beaux-Arts in Paris. I guess that must be the premier art college in France." Philip picked up the envelope and took out three photographic slides from it and passed them Samantha, "These are photographs of some of his oil paintings. You really need a projector to see them properly and even then they probably still won't do justice to them, but if you hold them up to the light, you'll get some idea of his talent and style."

Samantha took the slides and moved to the window so that she could hold them up to the sunlight, "I can't see enough detail to judge anything from them." She handed them back to Philip, "Have you looked at them with a projector?"

"Yes, I looked at them at home last night. I wasn't certain you'd be in today else I'd have brought it here for you to see them. I'll bring it in next week if you like though."

Samantha sat down and continued drinking her tea, "Do you think Edward knows anything about this?"

"I can't be absolutely certain, but I think Madeleine still writes to Edward quite often. And I think he must still write to her."

He picked up the letter and turned to one of the pages, "Here look she says, 'It is good to hear that Louise is growing into a beautiful girl. I am so happy that Edward has such a good relationship with her'. I've never mentioned that in a letter. I haven't exactly avoided the subject but I've never mentioned Edward's relationship with Louise for fear of upsetting Madeleine and Julian, or her parents for that matter, because of Edward's non relationship with Julian. So I can only imagine that Edward's written about it in one of his letters to her. How else would she know?"

"So you think she would have written to Edward about Julian's scholarship, and sent him photos of his paintings as well?"

Philip shrugged his shoulders, not really wanting to answer the question, but Samantha gave him another one of her stares demanding an answer. He nevertheless paused before answering, "I guess so."

Samantha looked as if she was about to cry. Philip could not work out whether this was through anger or sorrow, when she blurted out in a raised voice, "Why the hell doesn't he tell me about these letters and what's in them. It's not as if I'm going to chastise or criticise him about Juliette or Julian, is it?"

"I have no idea why he keeps everything about Julian to himself, but I guess he's done it for so long that he has no idea how to change things now. So, maybe we should just leave things as they are?"

Samantha just nodded her head.

"And are you going to leave things as they are around your suspicions?"

"For now. I don't think I have any other choice."

"And what if your suspicions are proved right at some time in the future?"

"I'll just have to cross that bridge when it arrives." She finished drinking her tea, got up from her seat and was about to leave the room when she smiled back at Philip and added, "But maybe I should consider my options just in case."

Philip sat pondering on the things he and Samantha had been discussing. Was it possible that Edward was having an affair? He felt certain that it was highly possible, but he wasn't about to say that to Samantha.

He was annoyed with himself for asking if she wanted to be with him when she had first mentioned her suspicions. Why had he been so stupid to put any pressure on her like that? Much as he still wanted to be with her he knew that if it was ever to happen it would have to be her that made the decision. He promised himself not to ask her again hoping that one day she would raise the subject and make the suggestion to him.

He sat musing for half an hour, abandoning all the work he had to do whilst he did so. The telephone ringing woke him from his contemplations. It was Jane asking if he was free to see John yet as it would soon be his lunch hour and wondered if he should leave it until the afternoon, "No ask him to come straight up," he replied.

There was soon a knock on the door, but it was immediately opened before Philip gave his usual, "Come in." John and Jane walked in, hand in hand, both with a big beaming smile on their face. The holding of hands was not unusual, it was something they always seemed to be doing when they were together ever since they had first started courting, and it had not changed in all the years of their marriage. They were also always smiling when they were together, but somehow today's smile was bigger and grander than he had seen on their faces since the day of their wedding.

Philip beckoned them to sit down, adding, "You two look pleased about something."

John could not contain himself and before they had properly sat down he blurted out, "Yes. We're going to have a baby."

Philip got up from his seat and dashed round the desk to give his brother a great bear hug. He kissed him on the cheek, "I'm so pleased for you both. Congratulations."

He let go of John and turned his attention to Jane, "And can I give the mother to be a big kiss?"

She nodded and he gave her the same bear hug he had just given her husband, “Congratulations Jane. It’s great news.” Without letting go of Jane, he pulled John back into his arms and the three of them held each other with moisture appearing in all of their eyes.

After a while they all sat down. Philip was the first to speak, “And have you told Ma yet? She’ll be over the moon. Her first grandchild, she’ll be ecstatic.”

Both John and Jane went to answer but John deferred to his wife and allowed her to answer, “The doctor only confirmed it when I went to see him yesterday after work, and we went to see my Mom and Dad straight away and told them, and then we went to see your mother and Aunt Alice. John wanted to come and tell you and Teresa as well, but your mother kept us talking so long, it was a bit too late when we left. So we wanted to tell you first thing this morning before we told anyone else here.”

Philip looked at John and then at Jane, embarrassed he had kept them waiting to tell him for most of the morning, “I’m so sorry Jane. I shouldn’t have kept you waiting to see me for so long.”

“That’s all right. We knew you must be busy.”

Philip did not quite know how to respond. Jane had always been a rather shy girl who seemed to hold him in some awe. He had tried hard, particularly since she had married John, to put her at ease and did think he had had some success in this. Nevertheless at work, she always still treated him as the boss and never as a brother-in-law no matter how much he had tried to make her feel at ease. However, as he had got to know her better, he recognised more and more why his brother was so besotted with her. She not only had a simple beauty about her which had blossomed since marrying John, but had the most natural and pleasing nature that everyone warmed to. But after a few years of marriage, a sadness had seemed to gradually drift into both of them. It had been Aunt Alice who had confided in Philip that they were having difficulty conceiving the children they both longed for.

He had never discussed the matter with them but had always hoped that John did not have the same problem he had. That was one of the reasons he was so pleased for them both now. He knew that if he had loved Teresa as much as he loved Samantha then the thought of not having a child with her would have been unbearable. It was only bearable that he and Sam would never have a child together because he had been so easily able to dream of Louise as being his own child.

“You know Jane, even when I am busy, I should find the time for both of you. I’m so sorry I haven’t this morning.” Without waiting for any further response from them, he asked, "And what have the other's here said about the baby?"

This time it was John who answered, "We haven't told them yet. We wanted to tell you first. We didn't want you to hear it from anyone else."

Philip felt even worse now. He knew how difficult it would have been for them not to tell the others, "I'm surprised mother wasn't on the phone to me last night telling me about it. And I'm even more surprised she hasn't rung this morning."

Jane laughed out loud, "She has, three times, but I wouldn't put her through. I told her you were with an important client and couldn't be disturbed."

Philip was astounded that Jane had found the courage to stand up to his mother in this way. Perhaps pregnancy was going to sort out the fear she had of his mother. "Good for you, Jane. Keep it up."

They all laughed until the tears flowed.

CHAPTER TWENTY–THREE

1968

Edward looked at his watch as he stepped off the train at New Street Station. Almost eight o'clock. *'Too late to call Samantha and ask her to pick me up now'* he thought to himself. *'She'll be getting Louise ready for bed and anyway I'd rather talk to her at home when Louise is asleep'.*

He looked up the time of the next train to Walsall and decided to wait for that and get a taxi home from Walsall station.

Edward had been trying to work out what to say to Samantha all the way from Euston on the train, during which time he had consumed four whiskies from the refreshment bar to try to relax him. It hadn't worked, and he was no nearer now to knowing what to mention to her first, than he had been when getting on the train in London.

Everything had been going well for Edward at the end of April, when as a junior Foreign Office minister, he had spent a week in Zambia meeting with representatives of the Zimbabwe African National Union.

ZANU was the militant political organisation which Robert Mugabe had helped to establish as a separate organisation from Joshua Nkomo's ZAPU party, the Zimbabwe African Peoples Union. Both ZANU and ZAPU were opposed to the white rule in Rhodesia and its government controlled by Ian Smith's 'white supremacy' Rhodesian Front party. Britain's labour government's demand to Smith's government for an extension of political rights to black Africans had been rejected outright and instead Smith had unilaterally declared independence in 1965 in total opposition to Britain's demands, thus putting the foreign office in a very embarrassing position.

At the time of Edward's visit both Mugabe and Nkomo were languishing in a Rhodesian jail for their opposition to white rule. Arrangements had been made for Edward, along with two foreign office staff to have completely unofficial and very low key exploratory talks with some of the black freedom fighters who had fled to Zambia.

They were accompanied by Sophie Zumande, a Rhodesian woman whose own father was arrested just as the family had been fleeing Rhodesia because of their political views. She and her mother had travelled to England where she had been seconded to the foreign office as a liaison officer with ZANU. Her two brothers were now in Zambia working for ZANU and were two of the people included in the week's discussions.

By the end of the week Edward felt the visit had achieved nothing other than keeping the lines of communication with the freedom fighters open.

On a personal basis however, he deemed it a successful week. He had been attracted to Sophie the first time he had seen her and on the very first day of the trip he realised she found him equally attractive. She not only spent the first evening in the hotel bar almost exclusively at his side, but had kissed him outside her room before opening the door and leading him to her bed. She had slept with him every night of the trip; an arrangement that had been repeated several times after their return to London.

But things started to go wrong for Edward on the first Saturday evening following his return home and they went from bad to worse as the weeks progressed.

It started with the telephone call as soon as he had sat down after reading Louise a bedtime story. Samantha got up to answer it but was soon back in the lounge telling Edward the call was for him.

"Who is it at this time on a Saturday evening? Can't they leave me in peace just for one evening?"

"I have no idea. It's a woman and I didn't ask."

Edward was about to ask her why not but did not do so when he suddenly thought it could be Sophie or maybe his secretary Joanna Hurst with whom he'd been having an on and off affair for the last four years. But he hadn't given Sophie this number and he had always told Joanna not to call him when he was at home.

In the event it was neither of them, "Hello Edward, I know you only gave me this number for emergencies but I thought you would want to know as soon as possible."

He immediately recognised Madeleine's voice even though he had not spoken to her in years. Although they wrote to each other regularly about Julian, Edward had insisted that Madeleine's letters should only be sent to the London flat, and she had never phoned him before.

Panic suddenly welled up inside him, "What's the problem, Madeleine? What's the matter? Has something happened to Julian? Is he all right? Oh my God, he hasn't had an accident, has he?"

"Calm down Edward, it's nothing as serious as that, but yes, I am phoning about Julian."

All sorts of things started to flash through Edward's head, "Not serious? It must be serious or you wouldn't be ringing me. What on earth has happened?"

"Calm down, calm down! It's just that he's been arrested."

This statement did not help to calm Edward down one bit. He was still agitated as he started to imagine all the serious crimes that Julian may have committed, "What's he done? What's he been arrested for?"

"Well I'm hoping that it's just a case of him being in the wrong place at the wrong time."

Edward interrupted before Madeleine could continue, "What place? Where was he?"

The ever calm and sensible Madeleine responded by speaking to him like a mother, "Edward, just calm down. If you'll let me, I'll tell you everything, but you must calm down and let me finish."

Madeleine's quiet and soothing voice reminded him of the way she had spoken to him after Juliette had died. She had been the only one who had managed to reach him through his grief. He had felt that she understood his pain then and in a curious way had seemed to realise why he had just walked away from his son. She had not been critical of him then, nor had she ever rebuked him for not having direct contact with his son since. Instead she had kept in touch, written regularly about everything that was happening in Julian's life and acted as peacemaker whenever her mother and father had run Edward down for not being there for his son.

For his part, Edward had always financially supported Julian's upbringing, and unknown to his own wife and mother, had sent him birthday and Christmas presents, and in the last three years had sent money to Madeleine for Julian's living expenses in Paris; money that he asked Madeleine not to tell Julian where it came from.

"I'm sorry Madeleine, I will try to calm down, but please tell me what's going on quickly."

"Good. Now I presume you've heard about the student's protests that have been going on in Paris during the last few days?"

Edward interrupted yet again, "Julian wasn't amongst the rioting students, was he?" He did not wait for an answer before carrying on, "I've just been reading about it on the front page of today's paper." He recalled what the paper had said, "But the paper said it was left-wing agitators armed with iron bars and pick handles attacking the police. Julian isn't a left-wing agitator and he wouldn't arm himself to attack the police would he?"

"Edward you're doing it again. Just let me tell you what's happened."

Edward was suitably admonished and promised to keep quiet until she had finished.

"Well apparently he was amongst the students. Like you, I can't see him carrying any sort of weapon and anyway I understand he was with Nicole."

"Nicole? Who's Nicole?"

"Nicole is his girlfriend. I was just writing a letter telling you all about her when I had the phone call from the bursar at Julian's école telling me about his arrest. Her name is Nicole Broussard and she is a first year student studying art at the same school as Julian. But can I tell you the rest of the story?"

Edward apologised yet again before Madeleine continued, "Apparently Julian and Nicole were on the Boulevard St. Michael with all the other student demonstrators. I've no idea whether they were there just as onlookers or whether they were taking an active part in the protest march. Like you, I can't imagine Julian as a political agitator and I certainly can't believe he'd be armed with any sort of weapon or anything that could be used as a weapon. I do know that like many other students he was annoyed at all the petty regulations regarding the segregation of male and female students, particularly since he's been with Nicole. But all that's hardly the point, because for whatever reason both he and Nicole were arrested."

"But what have they been charged with?"

"I have no idea, in fact I don't even know if they've been officially charged with anything yet. All the news reports say over five hundred students have been arrested and some suggest that the number is well over six hundred, so I guess it'll take some time to process all of them."

Edward listened carefully as Madeleine filled him in on all she knew about Julian's and Nicole's arrest, but much of what she said was general information she had gleaned from newspaper and television reports; most of which seemed to suggest that the protest was only supported by a small number of agitators all of whom were intent of violent action. When she finished Edward asked her what if anything she suggested should be done.

"Well I'm not sure what I can do, or whether it will do any good, but I'm going to Paris tomorrow to see if I can visit Julian and find out exactly what happened. I'm really worried about him because of his hearing problem. If there is too much noise going on he won't be able to work out what the police are saying to him. They may read his response as arrogance or even contempt and that won't do him any good at all."

"Is there anything that you need me to do?"

"No. I just thought you should know what was going on."

Edward thought for only a moment before he said, "I'd really like to help in some way. Would it help if I tried to arrange a flight and meet you in Paris? I don't want to make anything worse for you or Julian, but I'll only be worrying all the time if I stay here."

Madeleine answered the question in her usual direct and honest way, "You know I'd love to see you anytime. I'm not really that sure about how to go about things so I'm sure you being there could help me personally, but I'm not sure how Julian would view your involvement. He doesn't really know you and it may not help for you to get directly involved with him in a matter like this."

Edward knew in his heart that she was right about Julian, but nevertheless wanted to do all he could for his son, "I'm sure you're right about Julian but I'd like to come anyway. I'll stay completely in the background and well clear of the police station so Julian needn't even know I'm there. But if I can help you at all, then I'd like to be around and at least I'll know what's happening first hand. What do you say?"

"Well if you're sure, I would welcome your advice."

Edward moved into his organising mode and they quickly sorted out that Madeleine would book a room for him at the hotel she was staying at, "I just hope I can get a flight tomorrow. I'll try and arrange that right now and ring you back."

No sooner had he finished talking to Madeleine than Edward was trying to book an airline ticket to Paris. It took him quite some time but eventually he managed to arrange a flight from Heathrow to Orly leaving at lunchtime .

He went back into the lounge and told Samantha all about Madeleine's phone call. She was somewhat surprised when he told her of his plans to go to Paris, and was even more surprised when he said he was leaving for London as soon as he'd packed a bag. "I'll stay in the London flat tonight so that I have plenty of time to get to Heathrow to catch the plane. I'll phone you when I get to the hotel and let you know what's going on."

"But John and Jane are having the boys christened tomorrow and we promised to go."

"I'm sure they won't miss me. You'll just have to apologise and tell them something more important turned up."

Samantha was annoyed at the way he had referred to something more important. She knew perfectly well that it was more important to Edward, but there was no way she would say that to John or Jane.

No matter how much Edward and Madeleine tried over the next few days, they weren't able to find out what charges had been laid against Julian, and to make matters worse, Madeleine was not even able to get to see him.

By Wednesday morning Edward felt he was wasting his time and no matter how long he stayed, they wouldn't be able to help and Julian would have to sort things out for himself, so he told Madeleine he had to return home for important government business. Whilst this was not entirely true, he nevertheless felt it was a good enough excuse in the circumstances and was a better reason than that he just felt it to be a waste of time to stay.

For Julian, his fate was decided not by anything that Madeleine did, or that Edward might have done, but by the turbulent and almost anarchic events that started in Paris and spread through the whole of France over the next few days and weeks. In the first week the number of student protestors grew each day and the police response became more confrontational and violent; so violent that Edward began to think Julian was probably better off in prison than taking part in these clashes with the police.

However, the protests that started as student's unrest gradually spread to broad dissatisfaction of the government by the general population. Soon, trade unions and other groups raised their own grievances by strike action and occupation of factories. Eventually the government had to give way to the demands, one of which was the release of all students arrested. So both Julian and Nicole were released with the charges against them dropped.

Edward had returned directly to London and did not return home until the following Saturday. He was clearly in a bad mood; a mood made worse when Samantha asked him about his visit to Paris and his son. Her questions were met with the same impenetrable lack of any proper response that always happened whenever she brought up the subject of Julian and, once again, she let the subject drop, but Edward's mood did not improve.

At first, she thought this was because Julian was still in prison and Edward had been unable to help in any way. Later, she thought it was because of the disastrous results for the labour party in the local elections, and the vicious attacks on Harold Wilson premiership demanding his resignation, which had coincided with Edward's return from Paris.

However, neither of these had anything to do with his depression. In fact he privately thought that if Wilson went, a seat in the cabinet may be possible under a different leader. But the party had rallied round Wilson and although Edward joined the party line in this, he nevertheless saw it as another missed opportunity, thus adding to his general gloominess.

The real reason for his melancholy was much more personal. He had become totally infatuated with Sophie. She was the main reason he had cut short his visit to France and on their first evening out together had tried to impress her with the London high life by taking her to a casino; a move he was later to regret bitterly.

In the last three years Edward had become a frequent patron at the Playboy club in Park Lane and Charlie Chester's casino in Soho, and had run up considerable gambling debts with both of them. So to save any further embarrassment he took Sophie out of London to the Room at the Top in Ilford on that first evening.

The burly doormen looked rather questioningly at Sophie, but reluctantly let Edward and his black partner in when Edward identified himself as a member of parliament. Sophie ignored the unspoken racial affront and wandered past them as if she owned the place. Inside she was equally dismissive of all the glares, knowing that for most of the men they were stares of lust. She also knew that most of the men probably assumed that such a glamorous black woman with a white man must be a call girl.

Edward tried to explain the rudiments of gambling to her, but she soon became highly excited as she used Edward's chips to bet on mostly losing single numbers. Edward tried to get her to make less risky bets by betting on 'rouge' or 'noir' and 'pair' and 'impair', but she would have none of it and kept putting chips on more and more single numbers. In that first evening Edward had lost more than he had ever done before.

When Edward met Sophie two evenings later, he suggested that they should go to a restaurant for a meal, but gave in when she asked to be taken to the Room at the Top again.

She took off her coat as soon as they entered the building and passed it to Edward to take to the cloakroom. She kissed him on the cheek and told him what drink to get her. She was wearing a very plain black cocktail dress which revealed far more of her bosom than Edward felt comfortable with in the mostly male dominated games room. He was nevertheless enchanted by her stunning beauty and as usual was willing to forgive her anything.

When Edward returned with the drinks, she was already placing a £5 chip on the table. He touched her on the shoulder, but she did not take her eyes off the roulette wheel until it stopped rotating and the ball dropped into number eleven. She jumped up and down with glee as the croupier pushed her chip and her winnings towards her.

She turned and threw her arms around Edward's neck almost knocking the drinks out of his hand, "It's going to be my lucky night tonight darling and I'm going to win loads and loads of money. Aren't I a clever girl then?"

He passed her drink to her. She knocked it back in one gulp and handed the glass back to Edward before asking the gentleman standing next to her, "What number shall I put it on now?"

He merely said, "That's entirely up to you my dear. You are the one who seems to have lady luck on your side." He turned to face Edward holding out his hand towards him, "I'm Roger Vaughan by the way."

Edward tried to juggle with the two glasses to shake his hand, but seeing his dilemma the man merely patted him on the shoulder, saying "Let's hope her luck holds for the rest of the night."

"Pleased to meet you Mr Vaughan. I'm Edward Richards."

"Oh don't be so formal Edward. I'm sure he'd prefer to be called Roger." Sophie turned to him, "That's right isn't it Roger?"

Suitably admonished Edward said, "Sorry," and smiling broadly added, "Very pleased to meet you Roger."

"Roger lent me the chip I've just won with." She turned and looked at her winnings and then back at Edward, "Does that mean I should give him my winnings, Edward?"

Roger immediately took her arm and declared, "No my dear, all the winnings are yours. I'm just glad you won."

Edward felt somewhat annoyed at the man's familiarity with Sophie and suggested that, "Perhaps you should give Roger his £5 chip back though, Sophie. After all he only lent it to you."

Sophie went to pick up the chip as Edward had suggested, but Roger stopped her doing so, "Not at all, Edward. It was well worth it to see such a pretty girl enjoy herself so much."

He picked up a number of chips from Sophie's pile and placed them in her hand, holding her hand for a moment between both of his own, "Why don't you see if your luck is still holding, Sophie? See if you can win again?"

Sophie turned to the table and started placing chips on several numbers. Edward tried to tell her that the chances of winning would be greater if she placed the chip at the corner of four numbers instead of a single number, but she became irritated with him saying that her winnings would be far less.

She had two more wins in the next ten minutes but this followed with a frenzy of bets when she placed chips on more and more numbers at each spin of the wheel. Soon the pile of chips in front of her had vanished and she was asking Edward to obtain more.

Roger was at their side all evening encouraging Sophie at every spin of the wheel and Edward was irritated by his presence until he also tried to discourage Sophie from being so wild with her bets. And when he stopped Edward getting more chips when Sophie's had almost vanished again and suggested they went to a nearby restaurant he knew of for something to eat, Edward jumped at the idea.

Sophie said, "But I'm not hungry and want to stay here."

Roger turned to Edward, "But you're ready for something to eat aren't you Edward? So let's go and if Sophie isn't hungry she can watch us eat?"

Edward was staggered when, instead of telling him to get lost, Sophie meekly picked up her handbag, dropped her remaining two chips in it and putting one arm in each of the men's arms said, "Come on then, maybe I'll be ready to eat when we get there."

Over dinner, Edward found he had a lot in common with Roger. They had both been to Birmingham University, but Roger was older than Edward and had graduated the year before Edward had started. He said he'd spent the war with the 7 Green Howards and had been part of their landing in Normandy on 6th June and had helped with the repatriation of German prisoners of war when the hostilities ended.

Sophie patiently listened to the two men recounting their war stories throughout the whole of the meal, but when she had knocked back the remains of her after dinner brandy, she interrupted their conversation and asked, "And what do you do now, Roger?"

He picked up his own brandy glass and drank the rest of it before replying, "I work for the old man in his manufacturing business. What do you do Edward?"

Edward did not want to admit to being an MP, so he said, "I'm a solicitor," and wanted to change the subject before being asked any more details said, "And what do you manufacture, Roger?"

It seemed that, for some reason, Roger did not want to give any details any more than Edward did, because instead of answering the question he looked at his watch and said, "Gracious, look at the time, I'm afraid I shall have to be going," and with that he turned and called the waiter and asked for the bill. He then twisted back to Edward and said, "Look I've really enjoyed this evening Edward. Why don't we do it again next week? I'll bring my wife along and we can make an evening of it."

Edward felt uncomfortable with the suggestion of meeting Roger's wife. She would undoubtedly guess that Sophie was not his wife, and if she found out he was an MP, then it could be really embarrassing. He was about to refuse the invitation but before he could say anything, Roger said, "Actually I don't think bringing the wife along is such a good idea. I'll tell you what, why don't I bring my secretary Helen instead?" He winked at Edward as he added, "And then we can really enjoy ourselves."

Edward was still desperately trying to think of a way to get out of it, but Sophie took hold of his arm declaring, "Yes, we must Edward," laughing out loud as she added, "I'd like to meet Roger's secretary."

Edward was still apprehensive at accepting the invitation and was about to give an excuse to get out of the arrangement when the waiter came back and presented the bill to Roger, so instead he said, "I'll see to that Roger if you want to get away." But his remark was ignored and Roger proceeded to pay the bill in spite of Edward's continued protests. The waiter thanked him for his generous tip before moving away. Roger immediately stood up and said, "Why don't we meet here next Tuesday at say seven-thirty. We'll have a nice meal and then we can go on to the casino for a couple of hours."

Edward still tried to avoid the invite, "I'm not sure I'll be able to make it particularly if something turns up at the last minute."

Roger took a card from his waistcoat pocket and handed it to him, "My number's on there. Give me a ring if it's a problem and we can meet up another evening."

On the following Tuesday, Edward had a three line whip for a vote expected to take place in the House sometime after eight o'clock that evening. He therefore had no alternative but to cancel the appointment, but Roger insisted they rearrange for the next evening. Sophie was not pleased when Edward told her of the cancellation and as soon as his call finished she phoned Roger and arranged to see him that evening anyway.

When Edward picked Sophie up in the taxi on the Wednesday evening she immediately started to excitedly tell him, "You missed a great time last night and Helen is really nice. And when I told Roger about our visit to meet my brothers and the others in Zambia he was really interested in what we're trying to do for the black opposition to Ian Smith and his white supremacy rule in Rhodesia."

"What on earth did you do that for? The visit was supposed to be confidential."

She grabbed hold of his arm and pulling him towards her, hugged him tightly, "Don't be silly darling. He isn't going to tell anyone, is he?"

"So you also told him that I'm an MP?"

She pulled him close again and kissed him on the cheek, "Of course, darling. What else should I have said?"

Edward was not happy about any of this and was even less so, when, almost as soon as they had finished ordering their meals in the restaurant, Roger starting asking him about the trip and what they were proposing to do to help the rebels.

"Nothing really, it was just a very low key exploratory meeting to hear their views. There was never any intention of actually doing anything. Find out what you can and report back, that was all I was expected to do."

He stared directly at Roger, "And now do you mind if we change the subject, Roger?" and turning to Helen, a charming girl in her mid twenties who, because of her demeanour and the way she referred to Roger, he began to think she actually was his secretary, and said, "Sophie tells me you enjoyed yourselves last night."

"Yes we had a great time when we were winning." The girls looked at each and started giggling when Helen turned to Roger and rather sheepishly said, "But we lost a bit too much in the end didn't we Roger?"

Once they had started giggling it was as if they didn't know how to stop, and for the next ten minutes both girls excitedly told of their winnings and losses at the roulette table. For Edward, the good thing about all this silly laughter was that the subject of the visit to Zambia was not mentioned again. Roger insisted on paying for the meal again and then insisted they go on to the casino.

For the first time ever, the thought of visiting a casino didn't seem a good idea to Edward and he began to wish he had found an excuse to cancel coming this evening as well. He wished this even more when Sophie was at the roulette table rapidly losing his money again.

Helen seemed to enjoy playing with the few chips Roger gave her, but Edward noticed how very careful she was, using only small value chips and not gambling at every spin of the wheel.

Sophie only had three wins all evening but even so as the croupier pushed the winning chips to her she jumped up and down screaming and giggling with delight, and as her pile of chips dwindled with her losses, she was equally vociferous in her cries of dismay. It seemed that everyone in the casino was looking at her antics.

Helen sensed Edward's embarrassment, "Are you all right, Edward? Would you rather not play?"

"Oh I think Sophie's doing enough for both of us, don't you? And anyway, I haven't had much luck at roulette lately either."

Roger heard the comment, "Perhaps we should go before Sophie loses even more for you. Perhaps we should go on to somewhere else?"

"Why? What do you suggest?"

"Have you ever played poker, Edward?"

"Sure. The Yanks taught me how to play when we were in Germany. Actually, I got quite good at it and even won money now and again."

"Well you're probably better at it than me then. I've only started to play with a few of the lads in the last couple of months, and I'd have been going to the weekly game tonight if I hadn't been coming out with you. Why don't I telephone them and see if they'll let us join them and you can win a few quid off us?"

Edward considered the offer tempting but nevertheless said, "Trouble is we can't just leave the girls can we? And we couldn't possibly play poker with someone like Sophie around. She's far too excitable. If I had a good hand she'd probably let the other players know about it just by the look on her face."

Roger leaned forward and whispered, "I doubt if she'd know what a good hand was, and anyway, we play in the back room of my local after closing time, and there are a couple of one-arm bandits in the bar to keep the girls happy." He laughed, "They only take two bob pieces so she can't lose too much on them can she?"

He took Helen by the arm and squeezed it, "You'll look after Sophie for Edward won't you my dear?"

He turned back to Edward without waiting for an answer, "She'll be fine with Helen and we'll give them plenty of two bobs to keep them going."

He laughed again as he took the two girls on his arms and led them away saying, "And I'm sure Helen will make sure she doesn't lose it all too quickly."

For the first hour Roger played reasonably well at the poker table. He hadn't won a great deal but unlike Edward he had at least not lost any. For Edward the opposite was the case. He was dealt some reasonable cards but someone else always seemed to have a better hand. The result was that not only had he lost all of the money he had cashed in from the chips, but had also got Roger to cash two cheques for him so that he could stay in the game and try to win back his losses. If he didn't start winning soon he would have to try and get his bank to extend his overdraft yet again.

But then he was dealt the hand he'd been waiting for; a straight flush, the nine of diamonds thru to the King. The bets got larger and larger with each round. Roger folded on the fourth round, leaving just three players remaining. One was the landlord who Edward felt had been playing rather recklessly and didn't seem to understand the game properly. He was still raising the bet at each call and had raised yet again. The other player folded, leaving only the two players. Edward checked his remaining cash. He did not have enough to call.

There was now about £1,800 in the pot and Edward looked at his cards again before asking, "Can I write a cheque to make up the difference?"

"Cash only, mate," said the landlord now the only other remaining player. "If Roger wants to cash another cheque for you then I'll wait, otherwise you'll have to fold."

Roger immediately took his arm and asked how much he wanted and as soon as the transaction was complete Edward sighed a sigh of relief, counted off enough cash to meet the raise, and raised again.

The other player looked at his cards and counted his remaining cash. Edward was sweating as he thought he might raise again, but after a long time he met Edward's raise and called.

Edward spent a long time considering whether to raise again before eventually laying his cards face up in front of him, his heart pounding as he anticipated scooping all the cash towards him.

But instead of throwing in his cards as he had expected, the other player laid his five cards, one at a time, on the table. Edward thought he was going to have a heart attack as the royal flush eventually was plain to see. Poor Edward smiled as best he could as he excused himself from the table saying, "Sorry gentlemen but that's me finished for the evening."

"You don't mind if I stay a little longer do you Edward?" said Roger.

Edward tried to make his reply sound as cheerful as he could, but did not think he was being too successful, "No, I'll go and check that the girls are OK," and without another word walked away from the table back to the girls still playing on the one-arm bandits in the bar.

He was surprised to find that Sophie had cash left and was still playing. She wasn't winning much money but she was at least winning more often than he had been. She stopped playing when he touched her on the shoulder and turned round to face him, giving him a kiss before asking, "Hello, sweetheart. Have you won loads of money?"

He merely replied, "Not much. I think we should be going soon."

She showed him the coins in her hand adding, "See, I haven't lost all your money tonight."

He smiled, "Well perhaps we should go before you do."

She shook her head from side to side and passed him her glass, "Why don't you see if the landlord will let us have another drink, and we'll go when we've finished that?"

He did as she asked and when he came back with the drinks he pointed to a nearby chair and said, "I'm whacked, so I'm just going to sit down over there if you don't mind."

Helen took her drink from him saying, "And I'll join you if that's OK."

She turned to Sophie and asked, "You don't mind do you Sophie? I could do with resting my legs as well."

They left Sophie still putting coins into the one-arm bandit and both sat down on either end of the small settee, and after sipping their drinks they both started to speak at the same time.

"I'm sorry," said Edward, "You first."

"No I was only going to say 'It's hot in here', so why don't you ask me what you were going to ask?"

Edward took another sip of his drink before speaking, "I was only going to ask how long you'd worked for Roger."

Helen said she had worked for him for about two years, and then, quite surprisingly suddenly said, "I've only accompanied him on these sorts of things for about the last six months though."

"I'm sorry Helen; I didn't mean to be inquisitive."

She smiled, "I know you weren't, but I wanted to tell you anyway. I really am his secretary and that's all I am." She then surprised Edward even more with her next remark, "He's not interested in me, or any other woman for that matter, so you don't have to worry about his flirting with Sophie in the restaurant. It's all part of the act. He's far more interested in the waiter than he could ever be in Sophie. Didn't you see him chatting to him when he went to pay the bill?"

She looked across to make sure Roger was nowhere within hearing distance before laughing out loud and adding, "That's probably why he insisted on eating in that particular restaurant and on paying the bill."

"So why do you come out with him then?"

She laughed out loud again, "And now you are being inquisitive."

Edward felt colour rising in his cheeks, "Yes, you're right. I'm sorry, I should mind my own business."

She laughed again, "No it's all right. It's rather odd as I usually keep such matters to myself, but for some peculiar reason I didn't want you to think the wrong things about me and I've been itching to tell you what it's all about." She pursed her lips and shrugged her shoulders, "Well first of all, he likes to have a pretty girl on his arm. Good for his image and it throws everyone else off the scent about his real nature."

"Yes but why do you do it?" Edward immediately said, "I'm sorry, that really is being too inquisitive so don't answer it."

"Well, I'd like to say I do it because his wife asked me to." She stopped for a moment and contemplated whether to continue, "Actually that's true, it was his wife who first asked me to accompany him on these outings of his, but I suppose the real truth is that he pays me and I need the money." She was thoughtful again, "So what does that make me?"

Edward touched her hand, "Well from what I can see, a very nice and sensitive girl."

It was now Edward's turn to be thoughtful as he pondered whether to ask his next question. Seeing his dilemma she smiled again and said, "Go on ask me. I can always refuse to answer if I want to."

He hesitated for a moment before asking, "Did his wife really ask you to do it?"

"She most certainly did and told me all about his preferences. Said she couldn't stand his affairs and wanted to divorce him, but he begged her not to and so this was a sort of compromise to keep up appearances as much for her sake as his. At first I couldn't believe what she had said and almost gave in my notice, but then I thought, why should I lose my job for him, so when she raised the subject with me again, I went along with it."

"But he didn't have to bring you with him tonight though did he? There are plenty of men, including me, who go to casinos on their own."

Edward could see that she was visibly shaken at this question and she remained silence for some time. He thought he had better change the subject and was about to do so, when she shifted in her seat slightly so that she could see Roger's back clearly and said, "If Roger knew what I've already told you, I could well lose my job and I most certainly will if he ever finds out what I'm about to tell you."

It was now Edward's turn to check that Roger was out of hearing range, "Then perhaps you shouldn't say anything. Whatever it is, I don't want you to lose your job."

"No, I have to say something. It's been bothering me ever since he and Sophie were talking about your visit to Zambia in the restaurant."

Edward felt his heart beating faster as he wondered what was coming next, but, after a quick check on Roger, she asked, "Do you know the business that Roger is in?" When Edward shook his head negatively, she moved slightly closer to him and continued in a quieter tone, "He's an arms manufacturer." She paused for a moment to let the implications sink in to Edward, "He and Sophie were talking very specifically about how she could purchase guns and ammunition from Roger and get them out to her brothers in Zambia. She seemed to think you might be persuaded to oil the waters for them, and that was when Roger said he'd sort it out."

"He'd sort it out? What did he mean by that?"

But Helen did not get the chance to answer. Roger had left the poker table and was walking towards them, "And what are you two talking about?" he asked as soon he reached them.

"Oh just this and that," Edward replied, and before Roger could ask another awkward question, he said what had been bothering him for the last couple of hours, "Would you mind awfully Roger, if I asked you not to cash the cheques I've given you until next week. Need to move a bit of money around to meet them."

Roger touched his nose and almost with a sneer said, "No problem at all, old boy. I'll hang on to them as long as you like. And don't worry; I won't be chasing you up for payment." He laughed aloud as he added, "Well not just yet anyway."

Everything that Helen had said suddenly clicked into place and Edward was now a very worried man. Was this man going to blackmail him into helping to transfer arms to Zambia? He so wished he had enough money to meet the cheques, but he needed somehow to make sure the cheques he had issued to the casino would be met first and he had no idea how he would achieve that either.

As they were leaving the pub Sophie threw her arms around his neck and kissed him full on the lips. There was a sudden flash of light and Edward whipped round to see where it came from. His worries increased when he realised someone had taken flash photographs of Sophie kissing him.

Roger immediately told the photographer to "Bugger off," and Edward tried to grab the camera from him. Roger prevented him from doing so, by saying, "I know you want to punch him on the nose Edward, but you'll only make things worse if you do."

"Very sensible of you Mr Vaughan, you wouldn't want my article to show you and Mr Richards as hooligans as well would you?"

Roger stepped between Edward and the photographer, "Look I don't know what you think you're doing, or what sort of story you think you have, but we're just friends enjoying a night out, so bugger off and leave us alone."

"Oh, but I'm sure the public would love to hear about their MP spending time with a lovely young lady who is not his wife. And I'm sure his colleagues would like to know about his gambling, particularly his illegal gambling and after hours drinking in a pub." He took out business cards and handed one to Edward, "I'll call you tomorrow Mr Richards to arrange a meeting so that you can tell me your side of the story before I pass these photographs to the dailies. I'm sure your wife would be interested in seeing them, wouldn't she?" and without saying any more he walked away.

Edward looked at the card and was horrified as he read it. It gave his name as Bernard Scrivens, Freelance reporter. He turned to Roger, "How on earth does he know our names and how did he know to find us here?"

Helen shook her head as she wondered how much Roger had to do with all the mess Edward was in. She wanted to accuse her boss of deliberately arranging for the newspaperman to be there but thought better of it, and tried to take the heat out of the situation for Edward, "He must have followed us from the casino, but you haven't committed any crime or even done anything wrong, so I'd just stop worrying if I were you."

None of this helped Edward's anxiety. "He mentioned after hours drinking and what about the photograph? I can't afford to have that in the papers."

Roger took the card from Edward and looked at it. "Freelance reporter. The papers won't be interested in that photograph. You've just spent an evening at a casino with a few friends, so what? Like Helen said, it's not a crime is it? I wouldn't worry about it, he probably won't even be in touch."

Edward put Sophie in a taxi and sent her home saying it would only make things worse if she stayed with him at the flat. He couldn't sleep when he got to bed and tossed and turned all night worrying about what might happen the next day. "How did Scrivens know my name? And how is he going to get in touch with me, the number at the flat is ex-directory? Damn it, he knows I'm an MP. Does that mean he'll phone me at work?"

He thought about Helen's comments and soon convinced himself the whole thing had been set up by Roger to increase his hold over him.

"Good God, even the poker was probably rigged so that I lost more money to him."

He had meetings the next morning and did not get back to his office until midday. No sooner had he sat down than Joanna, his secretary, said that a Mr Scrivens was on the phone, "He says you'll know who he is and he does seem pretty anxious to speak to you. This is the third time he's phoned already."

Edward desperately wanted to ask Joanna to tell this Scrivens he wasn't around to take the call, but had second thoughts and decided to take it.

The reporter spoke as soon as Edward picked up his extension, "Hi Mr Richards, can we meet somewhere? I think it'd be in your interest to speak to me before I send in my story."

"And what story would that be?"

"Well, I'll tell you that when we meet, shall we say one o'clock?"

But by now, Edward had decided to brazen it out with him. If Scrivens was a genuine reporter he probably wouldn't be able to do anything to stop the story. If he was a blackmailer the best thing would be to keep his distance, and if he was working for Roger, then again it would be best not to be compromised any further, at least for the time being.

"I think I'll pass on that. I don't think you'll have anything to say to interest me, Mr Scrivens. After all, the only thing you have is a photograph of me and a couple of friends at the end of a pleasant evening out."

"Well if you think it's OK for a foreign office minister to have friends like an arms manufacturer and a Rhodesian freedom fighter then we'll have to see what your political colleagues and the public think about that. I wish I had a female friend who was as passionate with me as this photograph shows your friend is with you. And what about this other friend? The one who pays your gambling debts for you. I wish I had a friend like that."

Edward started to shake and was glad that this man could not see him at that moment. He laughed out loud, hoping to put him off, "Mr Scrivens, you have no idea what you're talking about and I suggest you should be very careful about passing scurrilous and unsubstantiated stories full of lies to the national press. Why don't you look for a story of worth somewhere else, because there certainly isn't one with me and my friends?"

"Well if that's the way you want to play it Mr Richards, so be it, but don't say I didn't give you the opportunity to have your say."

Edward took a deep breath and replied as positively and strongly as he could, "As you say, Mr Scrivens, so be it. If you want to write a story about how I spent a pleasant evening with a few friends, then that's fine, but if you choose to make up other rubbish and lies about me or other people, just to sell a totally innocent photograph to the papers, then don't say I haven't warned you of the consequences."

He did not give the reporter a chance to add anything more before he finished the conversation, "I look forward to seeing what you have to say in the papers. I'm sure that anything honestly reported can only be good for me, so, good day, Mr Scrivens," and with that he put down the phone.

Joanna looked across at him and said, "Are you all right Edward, you look as white as a ghost?"

"No I'm fine Joanna. Just that bloody man trying to upset me."

She got up from her seat, walked up to him and put her arm around his shoulder, "Anything I can help you with?"

He touched her hand for a moment before removing it from his shoulder, "I don't think so. I just hope he's taken the hint and leaves it all alone now." He got up from his seat preventing her from putting her arm back and asked, "Is there anything in the diary I must attend to today or tomorrow? If not, I think I'll go home before whatever I'm coming down with gets any worse."

She went to her desk and checked the diary, "No there isn't anything I can't put off 'til next week." She went to walk back towards him, "Would you like me to come round later and get you something to eat? I haven't seen much of you outside of the office lately?"

At times like this Edward wished he had kept his philandering away from his secretaries. It had caused problems before with Guinevere and now it was causing problems with Joanna. "Actually Joanna, I didn't mean home to the flat, I meant I was going home to Walsall."

She looked disappointed and merely said, "Oh."

He still felt shaky inside and didn't want her around so he said, "What you could do before I go though is to fetch me a cup of tea," but as soon as she had left the room, he reached into his drawer and took out the whisky bottle, quickly taking a swig from it.

He didn't know whether his bluff with Scrivens had done the trick and was still worried about the photograph of him and Sophie in such a compromising clinch. It would certainly harm his career if it appeared in the press, particularly if the article made reference to a sexual relationship with Sophie. But at that moment he was more worried about Samantha seeing the photo in the paper before he had a chance to talk to her.

He took another swig from the bottle before returning it to his drawer and as he did so, he tried to work out what damage could be caused by Roger Vaughan. He didn't think there was anything that Scrivens could write about Roger and himself that would have any substance to it, but then he suddenly remembered what Scrivens had said on the phone about the friend who paid his gambling debts. *'What did he mean by that? Nobody had paid his gambling debts.'* He managed a weak smile as he thought, *'It's a pity though I could do with those vanishing.'* He started to shake violently again as he recalled his debt to Roger. *'How does Scrivens know about that? And what's even worse is how am I going to get Roger off my back now he's got those cheques?'*

He took the bottle from his drawer again and took another swig, but it didn't help. He wondered again whether this whole thing had been set up by Roger. If so, then surely Roger would contact him soon and make some sort of gesture to get this Scrivens guy off his back. *'Best if I get out of here as quickly as I can before he has any chance to get in touch with me.'* So when Joanna returned he drank the tea quickly before making the excuse that he needed to catch as early a train as he could.

He left his office giving instructions to Joanna that, if Mr Scrivens rang back or if a Mr Vaughan phoned, then she was not to tell either of them where he was, and she most certainly should not give them his home phone number.

As he left for the train, his mind was in total turmoil, but gradually the emphasis of the problem changed as he tried to work out what, and how much, he was going to tell Samantha when he got home. He had still not decided how or what to tell her when he opened the front door to his home.

"What on earth are you doing home? I wasn't expecting you until tomorrow night," Samantha asked as soon as he walked through the door.

"There are a few things I need to talk to you about, and I didn't want to wait 'til tomorrow."

Once he had sat down his first comment was, "I don't quite know where to start," and Samantha had given the standard answer to that comment, "Well they do say that at the beginning is as good a place as any."

He took a deep breath before admitting, "I've been rather foolish. I've had an affair," to which Samantha mockingly commented, "Only one?"

He was thrown by this remark. Did she know about Joanna? And had she guessed about Guinivere as well? If so perhaps he should tell her about that first, "Well yes I had an affair with Guinivere Isherwood but when you told me you were pregnant I tried to end it. That's what I was doing on the night of the accident. I was going with her to her flat, so that I could tell her it was over."

"You mean you just wanted one last fling with her?" Samantha asked indignantly.

"No, it wasn't like that. I wanted to end the affair when you told me about Louise but it wasn't easy working with her every day."

Samantha interrupted sarcastically, "No it wouldn't be, would it?"

Edward physically smarted at the retort, but tried to explain, "I didn't know how she'd react so I didn't want to tell her at the office or in any public place. And I didn't want to do it at the flat. If she turned awkward I didn't know how I'd get her out of the flat, so I thought it'd be easier to tell her at her home." He shook his head and added, "I promise you I wasn't going to stay with her that night, or ever again. I was just going to tell her and then leave her there."

He leaned forward and went to take Samantha's hand but she recoiled from his approach as he said, "And that's the truth, I promise."

"And that's meant to make me feel better is it? I saw you at her funeral, those were real tears."

He ignored the comment thinking it better to get other things said before he lost his nerve to do so, "And you are right, she wasn't the only one." He told her about his long relationship with Joanna and then told her all about Zambia and his affair with Sophie.

"And that's all of them is it?"

"Yes," and then he had second thoughts and decided to be completely honest, "Well unless you want to include two others that were only one nighters and didn't mean anything to either of us."

Samantha's mind flashed to her own one nighter; a night that meant more to her and her own lover than any other night of their lives.

If Edward was being totally honest about his affairs, should she tell all herself and admit to her relationship with Philip? Perhaps not, Edward's women were merely names to her whilst Philip was Edward's best and lifelong friend. What would it achieve to destroy that for everyone concerned? So instead she merely responded to the news of his one nighters with, "And that's what you've come home a day early to tell me is it? I think I'd rather not have known."

He looked at her intently and hesitated slightly before continuing, "No, there's worse to come yet."

Now she began to get really worried. She had guessed about the other women, even if she had never quite known for certain, but the look of almost despair on Edward's face, said a great deal more about his problems than his admissions so far warranted. She very nearly felt pity for the pathetic little boy in front of her, and was almost tempted to comfort him.

She resisted the temptation, knowing that to do so would break his need to confess whatever was troubling him, so she merely returned his stare and added, "And what the hell is worse than having several mistresses?"

He smarted at the question but merely replied with, "I've done a very stupid thing," his voice faltering as he continued, "Well I suppose it's two or three stupid things actually."

Samantha closed her eyes with all sorts of horrors flashing through her mind. *'One of them is pregnant?' 'Oh no! Two of them are pregnant?' 'Three stupid things? There can't possibly be three of them pregnant, can there?'*

She was almost relieved when he said, "I'm sorry but I've run up a few debts and some newspaper man took a picture of me with Sophie last night."

"But we can sort out a bit of debt and what's anyone going to do with a photo of you with some girl?"

"It wasn't just any photo though. Sophie was kissing me at the time."

"You bloody idiot. How did anybody get a photo like that?"

"I don't know, when we came out of this pub, Sophie just threw her arms round me and kissed me. And that's when the camera flashes went off." He put his head in his hands and ran them through his hair before continuing, "Then there's this other guy."

Samantha said nothing as she waited for whatever was coming next.

"I've only met him a couple of times but it now turns out he's an arms manufacturer. And what's worse is that I'm pretty sure he and Sophie were setting me up to get approval for them to ship guns and stuff out to Zambia for the people opposing Smith and his cronies in Rhodesia."

"But you haven't done anything about it have you?" Edward shook his head. "So just walk away and keep your nose clean. I really don't see what you're worrying about."

"The problem is that I can't just walk away. I stupidly let this guy lend me some money and we haven't got the money to pay him back."

Alarm bells started to ring for Samantha, "What the hell do you mean by WE haven't got the money to pay him back? You've still got the money your mother left you in her will last year."

"But she left all the money from the sale of the house to be put in trust for Louise, and," he hesitated trying to work out what to say next, "And there was death duty to pay on the rest…"

"I know all that," she interrupted, "But what about the rest of the money you did have?"

All the colour drained out of Edward's face and the look of total despair returned. He shook his head from side to side, "I'm sorry but all of that went months ago."

Her despair at his admissions now turned to anger as she almost screamed out, "Went? Went where?"

"Well I sent some of it out to Madeleine for Julian's school and lodging fees."

"But you couldn't have sent all of it. Or did you?"

He put his hands to his face again, knowing there was now no escape but to admit the whole mess to his wife, "No." He stopped and wiped the moisture from his eyes before admitting the inevitable, "Most of the rest of it went on my gambling."

"You mean it's all gone?"

He merely nodded his head.

Samantha was speechless and diverted her eyes from his gaze. She looked across at the line of family photographs on the table beneath the bay window, and stared at the two photographs his mother had given to her just before she died. The first was a studio photograph of Edward's father and Philip's father standing behind their respective wives. Edward's mother had the baby Edward in her arms and Philip's mother had Philip in hers. The other was a double photo frame, Edward's Uncle Joe in his army uniform in one half, whilst the other held his Military Medal and the citation.

When Edward's mother had given them to Samantha she'd asked her to keep them safe and had laughingly asked her not to let Edward sell the military medal. It suddenly dawned on Samantha why she'd said that, and why she'd changed her will just before she died; leaving much of it in a trust fund for Louise instead of everything to Edward.

She turned her head and spoke her thoughts quite forcefully, "You borrowed money off your mother didn't you?"

He nodded his head again, hardly managing to express the, "Yes."

She was astounded at what she had just ascertained, but she was even more irritated at the realisation that his mother had obviously known, or at least worked out, that her son had been gambling and not told her about it.

She then had another thought, "She didn't trust you with money after that, did she? And that's why she made Philip and me the trustees on Louise's trust instead of you, isn't it?"

She didn't wait for or want his response. She knew she was correct in her assumption. Why hadn't she worked it out or known about it a long time ago? Did his mother really know him that much better than she, his wife, did? She felt herself visibly shake as she tried to bring her mind back to the current situation, "So how much do you owe this….." she struggled to find an appropriate word to call the man who had deceived her husband, "This, this, arms dealer?"

"Just over two thousand." He paused for only a second before then admitting, "Well no, it's nearer three thousand. But it's not just him. I owe some money to a couple of casinos as well."

This was going from bad to worse for Samantha. All concerns about his affairs had long vanished from her mind. Why had she always trusted Edward to look after their finances? How could she have been so stupid and naive? After all she was the accountant in the family. She'd guessed about the women, so why hadn't she, the accountant, known about the money?

But now the accountant in her wanted to know all the dreadful details. "So how much are we talking about? How much do WE owe this man, and how much do WE owe the casinos?" The WE's were deliberately emphasised to cause extra discomfort to her wayward husband.

Edward suddenly realised that to give Samantha the total figure would be a bigger shock to her than anything else he had said so far. He had worried about confessing about Sophie, Joanna and the others, about Roger Vaughan and about Zambia, but he hadn't yet told her everything about Scrivens, and stupidly, until now, he hadn't really considered the need to tell Samantha about all the debts. He had only ever considered each debt as a separate issue when the demand to pay came and so had avoided ever worrying about the grand total. Now that the crunch had come and he was mentally adding up all the figures in his head, he was totally shocked at the result.

His heart jumped a beat as he contemplated Samantha's reaction. He could not bring himself to say the figure out aloud.

She became more and more angry as she waited for his response; anger that was evident in her eyes as she looked directly at him and demanded again, "I asked you how much do WE owe?" The WE was still being emphasised above all else.

Finally, knowing that to delay any further would only anger her more he plucked up the courage to tell her, "Probably about ten thousand."

Samantha's mouth dropped wide open as the figure sank in. She just stared at him, and it was some time before she finally closed her mouth. She shook her head and unbelievably asked, "Did you say, ten thousand pounds?"

He nodded his head slowly, the whole of his upper torso moving in unison with his head, "Maybe a bit more, say twelve."

"Twelve? How the hell has it got that bad? What have you spent it all on? You certainly haven't spent that sort of money on me or Louise."

He was shocked by what she had just said, and for the first time ever, he woke up to the reality of the complete mess he had made of everything. Nevertheless, he still found it difficult to admit out loud where the money had all gone. They both sat in silence as Samantha waited for a reply to her question and by the time he eventually managed to find the nerve to answer it honestly, he was sweating profusely and his heart was beating faster than it had all day, "I've gambled it away."

Samantha remained voiceless hoping for a better explanation. When it came, she tried to listen sympathetically and for a moment almost found herself feeling sorry for him. "I know you probably hate me right now, but you can't hate me more than I hate myself. The truth is that once I'd started gambling, it just got worse. I stupidly thought I could win back what I'd lost." He stopped and thought for a moment as the reality hit him, "But nobody ever does, do they? Win it back I mean. How could I be so stupid? I'm sorry. I'm so sorry."

But Samantha immediately shook her head, determined not to accept his reasons and certainly not to show him any compassion. She was still trying to absorb the enormity of the debt and chose to totally ignore what he had just said, "And how do you propose we repay the money?" The 'we' much less pronounced than before.

He did not reply but merely shrugged his shoulders and Samantha knew that shrug meant there was no cash left anywhere and that they had no means of paying off the debt. The practical accountant in her started to take over as she said, "I suppose we could take out a mortgage on the house, but the house isn't worth anything like twelve thousand. We could raise maybe six thousand on the house, perhaps seven if we're lucky, and we could try the bank for a loan for some of the rest."

Edward looked sheepish yet again and moved his head from side to side as he spoke, "I don't think the bank will lend us any more. We're already way over our overdraft limit."

Samantha stood up and went to leave the room, screaming as she did so, "We owe the bank as well? I don't think I can take any more of this. I'm going to make a drink and get to bed. We'll talk about it in the morning."

Edward jumped up and grabbed her arm, "Please don't go yet. Sit down again and let me finish all I have to tell you."

The tears that Samantha had been desperately trying to hold back could not be suppressed any longer and she cried uncontrollably as she sat down. She spoke through the tears, "Are you telling me there's even more?"

Edward nodded his head with a, "I'm sorry but yes there's something else I have to tell you."

"For God's sake, what else can there be?" She looked intently at him and he could feel the disgust from her eyes. "You better tell me everything else quickly. I don't think I can take much more." She continued staring at him whilst trying to dry her eyes on the back of her hand at the same time, "You'd better tell me the rest before I break down altogether."

Edward slowly told her about how Roger Vaughan had almost casually lent him money and then said that they could sort it out somehow later. "I now think he gave me the money so that he had some sort of hold over me with this arms business. But the worst is the bloke who took the photograph outside and what he said to me on the phone." He waited for some response from Samantha but she just sat there waiting for him to go on, so he continued, "He seemed to know that I had debts and suggested I was in league with this Roger chap and Sophie."

Fearing that there could be a morsel of truth in this, she suddenly spoke and said, "But you're not in league with anyone," then quite forcefully she added, "Are you?"

"Of course not! Of course not! But he's threatening to get the photo published in a national newspaper and tell the story anyway. I don't know whether he really means it, or whether he wants to blackmail me, or even whether he's in league with Roger and it's just another way of getting me to do whatever Roger really wants from me."

Again she did not say anything, but waited to see if there was anything more he had to say, but he merely added, "And I promise that really is everything."

"So where do we go from here?"

"Well if he really is a journalist then I fully expect the photo to be in at least one of tomorrow's papers and God only knows what the story will be that accompanies it."

Edward sat silently waiting for Samantha to respond but it was some time before she eventually got up again and said, "Well we can't do anything about that now, can we? It will either be published or it won't be. There's nothing I can do to change that, so you'll just have to deal with whatever comes."

She walked towards the door, "And now I really am going to make that drink and go to bed. We'll talk about everything in the morning after I've slept on it all." As she opened the door she said, "Oh and by the way, I don't want you in my bed tonight, so you can sleep somewhere else. The bed in the spare room isn't made up so you'll just have to make do with the couch."

The next morning she awoke feeling surprisingly refreshed. She was so exhausted after all the revelations of the previous evening that she had fallen asleep remarkably quickly. Edward however had had another fretful night and had slept little before getting up at six and trooping off to the newsagents to buy copies of every paper as soon as the shop had opened. He was sitting at the kitchen table carefully inspecting every page when Samantha walked into the kitchen and switched on the kettle.

She made the coffee without speaking, poured a single cup for herself, and sat down at the table opposite Edward. He sat looking at her wondering what, if anything, she would have to say this morning. She cupped the coffee in both hands warming them on its heat, and took several sips before speaking, "There's coffee in the pot if you want to pour yourself a cup." She then, quite sarcastically said, "Anything interesting in the papers?"

"Robert Kennedy died last night and all the papers are full of it. I can't find anything about me in any of them."

Kennedy had been shot twenty-four hours earlier and had been fighting for his life in hospital, so for Samantha her immediate reaction was not of shock at his death but one of some relief and she almost said, "So you've been saved by Robert Kennedy's assassination. How lucky?" But she quickly realised how totally crass that would sound and stopped herself before uttering any of it. She wondered whether Edward had had the same thought. Instead she took another sip of coffee before stating, "So we have another day to work out what to do then?"

She drank the rest of her coffee in one gulp and got up from her seat, "Louise is getting washed and dressed and when she's ready you can take her to school. I'm going to ring Philip to tell him I won't be in for a couple of hours so we can try and sort out this mess." She stopped and put her hand on Edward's shoulder, squeezing it tightly, almost hoping it would cause him pain, "Actually I think I'll ask him if he can spare the time to come over and help us sort it out."

"You can't do that. I don't want anyone to know about it."

She did not know whether to laugh or cry but chose the former, "Don't want anyone to know about it! It's going to be in the damned national newspapers. How the hell do you think people aren't going know about it?"

She almost felt sorry for the pathetic little boy who did not know how to respond, but instead continued with her onslaught, "He's your best friend. Who else do you suggest we ask to help us sort it out? I'm damn sure we're not going to do it without someone's help." She raised her voice again; the anger perfectly clear, "Or would you prefer I just left you to sort it out on your own?"

Edward was mortified by her words and knew that if he was to survive the total can of worms he had created, he needed someone's help. He trusted Philip and knew he wouldn't judge him or get mad at him as Samantha was increasingly doing.

"Maybe, you're right. Perhaps Philip will be able to come up with something, but I don't know what."

And so two hours later, a much more sanguine Samantha was sitting next to Edward at the kitchen table. Philip was sitting opposite them, coat off and his shirt sleeves rolled up, as he poured over the scribbles and figures that Sam and Edward had compiled whilst waiting for him to arrive.

Samantha had made a 'to do' list on which she had written in bold capitals items that needed to be dealt with immediately. On a second sheet she had listed other matters and had placed huge numbers in circles against each one, signifying the order in which the items needed to be dealt with after completion of sheet one. A third sheet listed each of the debts and to whom it was owed. Philip recognised the lists as being the sort of thing that the accountant Samantha regularly placed in front of him at work whenever any new problem needed tackling. It was carrying out this exercise that had concentrated her mind and away from the anger she felt towards Edward for the last two hours.

There was a fourth list that she had placed in front of Edward before Philip's arrival, on which she had written, again in bold letters.

1. STOP GAMBLING AND DON'T EVER DO IT AGAIN!!!

2. GET RID OF SOPHIE!!!
3. EITHER GET RID OF JOANNA OR STOP SEEING HER OUTSIDE OF WORK!!!
4. GIVE ME ALL THE CHEQUE BOOKS!!!
5. KEEP OFF ALL OTHER WOMEN!!!

And finally she had written,

6. AND I'M IN TOTAL CHARGE OF FINANCES FROM NOW ON!!!!!!

She told Edward in no uncertain terms, that the items on the list were non-negotiable and that their marriage was over if any of these conditions were ever broken again, even if that meant breaking Louise's heart in the process.

Edward readily agreed to all the points and the list was now tucked safely away in his pocket. Samantha was worried at how quickly he had agreed all the points and doubted that all would be adhered to. For now however, she had far more urgent things to worry about.

The most urgent thing on the list in front of Philip was to make sure that the cheques Edward had written in the last couple of days at the casino would be honoured by the bank. He had immediately offered to transfer money from his own account to meet them and suggested that his own name should now replace that of the casino on the list as the person to whom the money was owed. He also suggested that this new debt to him could be relegated to further down the list as being no longer urgent.

Next was the sum owing to Roger Vaughan. Philip suggested that he would do the same thing here, but Samantha immediately said, "No, I don't think that'll work."

Edward who had been silent up until now said, "Why won't it work, I thought we'd agreed we needed to get him off my back as quickly as possible?"

"Get him off your back, totally and finally," she said, "That's exactly the reason it may not work."

"I don't get your point either," said Philip, "Surely if Edward tells him to now cash the cheques he won't have any further hold over Edward? So why won't it work?"

"Why?" she replied indignantly, "I'll tell you why. Suppose he chooses not to cash the cheques but merely holds on to them as proof of the debt. If I understand what Edward's said correctly then at the moment he doesn't have any other sort of proof that Edward even borrowed money from him. But the cheques prove he has, and that's why we have to think of another way to make sure he cashes the cheques and acknowledges that no further debt is outstanding."

"And how do you propose we do that?" asked Edward.

Philip immediately jumped in with the answer, "You may not like this as a suggestion but I think we should provide your solicitor with the necessary funds so that he can issue a cheque on his clients' account. The solicitor then sends his cheque to this Roger Vaughan saying that it replaces your original cheques which have been stopped at the bank. At the same time, his letter can make the correct legal noises about the total cessation of all further contact and claims on you. I would think that whether he then cashes the solicitor's cheque or not, it can be shown you met your obligations to him and were no longer indebted to him."

Although reluctant at first to tell anyone else about his debts, Edward did finally agree to go and see Trevor Hepplewhite, his old solicitor partner at Hastings and Hepplewhite, and talk through Philip's suggestion with him.

The next item on the list was the payment of all the outstanding debts, which now included the debts to Philip that had replaced the ones to the casinos and Vaughan. "Samantha thinks we should perhaps take out a mortgage on the house, but she doesn't think we could raise enough to pay all the debts that way. What do you think, Philip?"

Samantha interrupted before Philip could answer, "I've been thinking about that, and I'd like us to think about an alternative first." She looked at Edward and then at Philip, "Neither of you may like my suggestion but I'd like to know what you think anyway."

Edward looked at her and merely said, "So, what is it you want us to consider?"

She now concentrated her reply at Edward, "You inherited your parent's share of the manufacturing business when your mother died." A sudden fear rose within her, which she immediately expressed, "I take it you do still have the shares? You haven't got rid of them or given them as security or anything, have you?"

"Of course not! You know perfectly well I can't do such a thing without the consent of the directors." Whilst Edward's reply showed that her sudden fear was unfounded, she nevertheless read into it that he had indeed considered it at sometime in the past. *'Thank God for the terms of the Articles,'* she thought, but did not express it.

She merely said, "Good," and then turned her attention to Philip, "Do you think you and the other directors would be prepared or able to buy

Edward's shares?"

Philip thought for a moment, "I guess Edward, as the solicitor, is better able to say whether and how it could be achieved under the Articles, but as far as I understand it, the directors by proper resolutions etc, can approve the sale by Edward provided they can also agree on the person who buys them. As to whether the other directors would wish to buy him out, well we'd just have to ask them. I personally would certainly consider it, but Edward has to want to dispose of them first."

"So you think it's a possibility?"

"If that's what Edward wants." He turned to Edward, "What do you want Edward?"

"Well actually I hate the idea. In all the mess I've created for myself, I did think I'd at least be able to leave my part of the business to Louise. Now you want me to deny her that. What sort of caddish father does that make me?"

Samantha quietly muttered to herself, but even though she didn't want the question answered, she knew that Edward was close enough to hear, "Do you really want us to answer that?"

She saw Edward flinch at the comment, before he turned to face Philip, "If I'm honest I don't really want your mother, or Lucy or your John to know I need to sell my share of the business."

Philip thought for a moment before responding, "I suppose you could say that as you don't have a personal interest in the business you wanted to take advantage of some of other business opportunity that had presented itself to you."

Edward did not comment and once again saw the animosity in Samantha's eyes as she answered for him, "I don't believe you've any option if you want to get out of the mess you've created for yourself."

She then looked back at Philip completely ignoring any possible further comment from Edward, "Do you think it might be possible for them to be bought by Louise's trust? At least that way they would be kept in the family."

"Again I think Edward or another solicitor would be better able to answer that, but I think that under the general terms of the trust's investment criteria, it might well be considered to be too risky an investment."

The discussion moved to and fro on the subject for some time, but eventually they all agreed that Edward's share in the business might be worth just about enough to clear his debts and subject to a proper valuation, Edward agreed to sell his shares.

The problem of the debts for the time being solved, the only thing left on the list was the threat of the newspaper report. Edward still thought he could avoid having to let Philip know about his sexual indiscretions but Samantha took away that choice when she said, "Right, now what about Sophie and this newspaper business."

Edward realised that if he didn't speak she was going to tell everything, including all about his affairs, but pre-empted this with, "What the hell, Philip knows most of the mess I'm in, so I might as well tell him everything else," and repeated everything he had told Samantha the previous evening; the Zambian trip, the affairs, the photograph with Sophie, the telephone call from Scrivens, the threatened newspaper report, the probable effect on his political career whether they were true of not, and finally said, "Clearly with the financial mess I'm in, I wouldn't be able to afford to sue for defamation, even if the accusations were totally untrue. You know what they say Philip, mud sticks, and whether the mud is the genuine article or not, it hardly ever matters in politics."

"I have no idea how these things work in government," said Philip, "And I certainly have no idea how you should really play it, but as I understood what you've said, other than being stupid…" He stopped here regretting that he had used the word stupid to describe his best friend.

Edward merely laughed, "Carry on mate, you're absolutely right, I am stupid, but it would be nice if I'm not reminded too often of the fact after this morning. I feel as though I've been kicked…" He turned to Samantha, "rightly kicked… last night and this morning by Sam, enough to last me a lifetime. I know I've been stupid and I deserve all your criticism, but even so it would be nice to be left with a bit of dignity and not reminded of how stupid I've been after this morning." He laughed as he looked at Philip and then at Samantha, "Or at least not too often."

Samantha was about to say he didn't deserve such consideration but though better of it. She had no desire to destroy her husband totally.

Philip returned Edward's laughter, "All right, I promise I'll only call you stupid this one last time and then I'll refrain from using it again."

Samantha could not stop herself from interjecting and emphasising the last two words, "That's unless you are stupid, YET AGAIN." She noticed Edward wince at the jibe and quickly added, "But otherwise, I promise I'll stop getting at you any more as well."

Edward smiled a grateful smile to each of them before asking Philip to continue what he was about to say before being interrupted.

Philip laughed again as he started with the barbed words he had promised he was using for the last time, "As I was saying, if everything you've said is true, then other than your being stupid, you haven't done anything illegal or, to date, anything that has irreversibly compromised you. But you are absolutely right, mud does stick and you'll have to suffer that one. I know I can't exactly put myself in your shoes and you have to decide how to deal with it yourself, but I've always found that the best way to get out of a mess is to admit that you're in it." Edward went to say something but Philip continued, "Yes, I know you've admitted everything to Samantha and now to me, but I really think you should perhaps admit it to whoever is your boss at Westminster. At least that way you'll have got your side of the story in first and if you do that you can't then be accused of taking an underhand bribe, can you? What's the worse that could happen if you came clean?"

"I'll be asked to resign my post at the foreign office and get booted back to the back benches, I suppose."

"And if you don't tell whoever it is before some scurrilous rubbish is printed in the paper, what's likely to happen then?"

Edward laughed, almost astonished at the simplicity of Philip's approach, "I'll probably get officially sacked from the ministry and get booted to the back benches even more quickly."

Philip threw up his hands and they both laughed as he said, "So."

Edward could not believe how relaxed he suddenly became and how quickly the weight fell from his shoulders, "So, I get on the phone now and tell the Foreign Minister my side of the story before anything is published. And then I talk to Trevor Hepplewhite and with your financial help we get bloody Vaughan and the other casinos off my back."

Edward was up at the crack of dawn on both Saturday and Sunday morning to fetch copies of all the papers from the newsagents. They were all filled with pages and pages of articles on the death of Robert Kennedy; comparisons with the assignation of JFK his elder brother, his family; his career; what was likely to happen politically in the US with his demise, and every other aspect of the Kennedy family that one could possibly imagine, but no picture of Edward and not the slightest mention of him in any article.

Samantha found him still pouring over the pages of the newspapers with tears in his eyes late on Sunday afternoon. She was so relieved that things were starting to fall into place and that there was nothing about Edward in the press, that she had even started to forgive some of his actions. She put her arm round his shoulders, "Why are you upset? It looks as if everything is going to be all right now, doesn't it?"

He grabbed her tightly around her waist, nudging his head into her stomach. She could feel him shaking as the tears flowed. It was some time before he spoke, "I am pleased at the way things seem to be turning out and I am grateful that you and Philip have helped so much. I also know that I shouldn't really be expressing any joy that there's nothing in the papers about me when it is perfectly obvious that it's probably only because of the death of a good man like Kennedy that's kept me off the pages. I was already ashamed at the troubles I brought on you, but I now feel enormous guilt and shame that the probable resolution to part of my problem has only occurred because of that poor man's death."

Nothing did appear in the papers and Edward felt that telling his story to the powers that be at Westminster may have had something to do with that. He resigned his post and returned to the back benches and after some negotiation Philip purchased all of his shares and all debts were cleared.

Philip confidentially told Samantha not to worry about the fact that they could not be purchased for the benefit of Louise through the trust, as he had made a codicil to his own will leaving the shares to Louise anyway; a fact that he had not bothered to tell Teresa about.

It was only four months later when Edward was promoted to the Whips' office and six months after that he was given another junior post, this time in Employment. At about the same time he rekindled his affair with Joanna. Samantha quite quickly became suspicious of this but decided to ignore it as all trust between them had been lost anyway and they no longer shared a bed.

CHAPTER TWENTY- FOUR

1972

Louise rushed into the house, dropped her sports bag and school bag in the hall, dashed up the stairs into her bedroom and threw off all her school clothes into an untidy heap on the carpet. Wrapping her dressing gown around her she charged into the bathroom, ran the water in the shower until it was piping hot, took off her dressing gown and let it fall to the floor before stepping into the steaming shower to get rid of all the sweat and odours of playing hockey.

She hated playing the game, especially on a freezing cold and windy day like today, and the previous night's rain had made things far worse by turning the ground into a sodden muddy quagmire. But this was the first time she had played for the school's under 15's team, and she had totally forgotten the weather and started to thoroughly enjoy the game after scoring an early goal. Things got even better after that, as she successfully ran rings around her opponents every time the ball was passed to her and scored two more goals. Her team won 5-1 and she left the field feeling exhilarated as several of her team mates patted her on the back and told her how well she had played. Perhaps hockey wasn't such a bad game after all?

She washed her hair and body, enjoying the feel of the warm water and lashings of soap suds cascading over her skin. She only got out when the water temperature started to fall, muttering to herself as she did so, "I bet Mom will moan again about all the hot water I've used." She stepped out of the shower and stood on her dressing gown, saying to herself, "With a bit of luck it'll have heated up again by the time she gets home."

She turned and looked at herself in the full length mirror on the wall. The water dripped from her body soaking the dressing gown as she inspected herself from head to toe. She had grown into a woman in the last year and she cupped her breasts, one in each hand, to admire the shape, texture and feel of them. She had been scared when she had experienced her first period, but now she was pleased with the further results of that experience. She examined the triangle of thickening hair below, the same deep red colour as the tresses on her head, and the same colour as her father's hair, or what he had left of it! She tried to imagine what her mother looked like down there. "I bet her light brown hair looks much better than this does!" She laughed to herself as she wondered whether her Grandma's had turned white at the same time that the hair on her head had.

She stretched her arms up to check that there was no unwanted hair under her arms, pleased that her mother had given her a razor a couple of weeks ago to get rid of it from time to time. She inspected her chin, and face, "Thank goodness I'm not a boy; I'd hate red hair growing all over my chin and under my nose." She then turned slightly to check on her buttocks and legs and was satisfied with what she saw. "It must be awful to have a big backside, fat legs and great big boobs like Perfect Pauline."

Contented with her review, she grabbed the big towel and dried herself as quickly as she could, before picking up her soaking dressing gown and running naked to her bedroom. She was sitting at her dressing table drying her hair; clad only in the new bra and matching pants her mother had bought her the previous weekend, when she heard the front door open and her mother shout, "I'm home Louise." A few moments later she was back at the bottom of the stairs shouting again, "Are you up there, Louise? You haven't forgotten we're all going to Uncle Philip's this evening have you?"

Louise switched off the hair drier and shouted back, "No of course not, but do I have to go? I'd rather stay here and watch TV or something."

"You know how much Teresa and Philip love to see you and anyway, Aunt Teresa is cooking us a meal. She'll probably have cooked something special for you now that you've turned vegetarian, so it'd be unfair for you to let the food go to waste by not turning up." She heard her mother move back towards the kitchen, but she was soon at the bottom of the stairs again, "What are you doing anyway? Have you done your homework yet?"

"Mother! Give it a rest will you? It's Friday night, I have all weekend to do my homework."

Samantha knew that to carry on the conversation any more was just going to cause more friction. She walked back into the kitchen, thinking to herself how quickly her daughter had grown up physically, but growing up had brought with it a much more argumentative, awkward and annoying teenager. She recalled herself at that same age and even after all these years still felt slightly ashamed at some of the things she had said to her own mother. *'Best to just let it be and give Louise her own space; that's the only way to deal with children of her age,'* she thought as she went to make a drink for herself before starting to get ready. She looked at the clock hoping that Edward would arrive from London soon.

She had expected Edward would spend more time at home when his party had lost power to the conservatives in the 1970 general election, and he had once again become a mere back bench opposition MP. But it wasn't to be and he still only came home when he had a function or constituency business to attend to back in Walsall.

He had promised he would make Teresa's dinner party tonight though, and Samantha hoped he would keep his word and not let everyone down, including Louise who had only agreed to go when her father had asked her to go for him. Samantha would find it almost impossible to forgive her husband if he let their daughter down.

She sat drinking the tea, worrying that she wasn't dealing with her daughter's transition from girl to woman particularly well but consoled herself by the fact that she was now the best of friends with her own mother. *'Perhaps Louise will be the best of friends with me in a couple of year's time'*, she thought. She shuddered that she might have to suffer Louise's tantrums for that long and said out loud, "Please God don't let it be longer than that."

Louise sat looking at her face in the mirror, "Why won't mother let me have my ears pierced? All the other girls in my class have had it done."

This was not true of course, but that wasn't the way an almost fourteen year old girl saw things. "And why can't I wear lipstick and eye makeup like everyone else? I hate my mother," she said out aloud, but not loud enough for her mother to hear.

She continued her mumblings, "I bet if I lived with Grandma and Grandpa Prior they'd let me have my ears pierced and let me wear makeup." She smiled to herself as she muttered, "I bet Uncle Philip would let me as well. I'll ask him tonight. That'll send you into a tizzy if he says yes, won't it mother?"

Her hair now dry, she picked up the brush and began to stroke the shoulder length locks into place. She grabbed her hair at the back so that it was held tightly against her skull, "I think I'll tell Mom I want it cut short when we next go to the hairdressers." She laughed as she spoke to herself in the mirror, "That'll annoy her. It'll serve her right for not letting me wear makeup." She pulled the hair even tighter and decided that actually she didn't like it, so she let it go and continued to brush it on to her shoulders.

She pulled a face at her reflection, "You know what you should do, Louise? You should go and live with your Grandma. She'd let you do everything you wanted to." She pointed a finger at the face in front of her, "You should go and see her tomorrow afternoon and ask her. Mother would have a fit if you moved out and lived with Grandma and Grandpa."

In actual fact, Samantha's mother was no different in her views than Sam was, but like all doting grandparents she allowed her grandchild much more freedom in the few hours they spent together than she would if she had sole responsibility for her upkeep and upbringing.

Louise had spent many weekends at her grandparents as she grew up, and always stayed there whenever her mother had gone away to attend some official political function or other with her husband.

Grandma and Grandpa Prior still lived in the same terraced house in North Walsall that Louise's mother had been born in. They had installed some gas fires in rooms a few years ago instead of the old coal fires but other than that the house was still as old fashioned as it had ever been. Grandma gave her two hot water bottles and covered her with a second eiderdown whenever Louise slept in her mother's old room at the back of the house. Even so, in mid-winter, she had to wrap all the blankets closely around her to keep warm at night.

None of this mattered to Louise however, for no matter how cold things were, the warmth of the love and affection she felt as soon as she entered the house more than compensated for the cold. She sometimes felt that for all the comforts of their own home, with its central heating, hot running water and inside toilets, it lacked the warmth of two people like her grandparents, who were so obviously devoted to each other. They were always smiling at each other, touching each other and sharing a joke together. How was it that two people could live together for as long as they had and still be doing the same affectionate, tender and caring things for and with each other, that you only expect from newly married couples?

Her own parents were never like that, in fact the only other married couple she ever saw acting like that was Uncle Philip's brother John and his wife Jane. It was so obvious they were besotted with each other, "I shall only marry someone who treats me like John treats Jane!"

Grandma had taught Louise to cook and sew long before her mother had allowed her to cook at home and even though Grandpa had left school at fourteen and hadn't had any formal education since, he was the most learned and knowledgeable man Louise knew.

She wished her own schoolteachers knew half the things he knew about history, geography, the universe, and even maths and Shakespeare. Her teachers were the ones who had been to University and were supposed to be experts. "Some expert when compared to my Grandpa."

He always seemed able to help with her schoolwork. On the few occasions he couldn't, he would admit it straight away and the next time she visited he would have several library books on the subject waiting for her. He would have read all of them and would go over the problem with her, explaining everything she needed to know much more clearly than her teachers did.

Lately however, her Grandpa had not always directly answered some of the questions she had asked, but had instead entered into discussion and forced her to consider many different aspects of the subject. This had been particularly so when discussing religion, politics, the nature of the universe and especially one's regard for other races and people of different cultures. Often she did not know what his own views on these matters were, but gradually as the arguments became deeper and more profound, she began to realise that he was not only a very knowledgeable man, but was the most understanding and compassionate of men.

Only last weekend after discussing politics and religion for over two hours, she had asked him whether he was a labour party supporter because he didn't like conservatives, and never went to church because he was against Christianity. She had never seen such a violent reaction from him as she had to that question.

"I thought you'd been listening to me. Obviously not! The issue is not whether I agree with anyone else's view or not, or whether I even think they are right or not, but whether they have genuinely come to that view by their own reasoned argument. And providing they don't condemn, oppose or persecute others for having a different view, I'll defend their right to hold that view whether I agree with them or not."

Louise was still trying to come to terms with and understand his statement and had only just started to realise its full significance after several very restless nights thinking about it.

"I'll pop and see him tomorrow, and let him know I think I've worked out what he was talking about and if I'm lucky Grandma will have baked her Saturday lunchtime meal of cottage pie brim full of steak and vegetables with crispy browned potato covering it." She thought for a moment, imagining the taste of the pie covered with lashings of Grandma's thick luscious gravy, and then admitted to herself that it was about time she told her mother and her Aunt Teresa that she wasn't really a vegetarian!

"That was a lovely meal, Auntie Teresa. I really enjoyed it, but maybe next time I'll have the same as everyone else and save you the bother of cooking a separate meal for me."

"I'm glad you enjoyed it Louise. It was a new recipe I found in one of my women's magazines."

"Does that mean you are no longer vegetarian Louise?" her father asked.

Samantha decided to jump in before the nice remark Louise had made about the meal turned into another argument with her father, “Yes that was a really nice meal, Teresa. I’ll clear away the things for you. You’ll give me a hand, won’t you Louise.”

Louise nodded her head and started to collect the plates together, but Teresa took them from her saying, “That’s all right Louise, your mother and I will do it. Why don’t you pour the coffee and then get your Dad and Uncle a brandy from over there? Don’t bother pouring coffee for your Mom and me. We’ll get ours later.”

As soon as she and Samantha had reached the kitchen, Teresa closed the door so the others couldn’t hear, “I wanted to have a chat with you, Sam. I’ve been a bit worried lately and I’d like your opinion. I suppose I should talk to someone at work but I don’t want them to think I’m wasting their time.”

“This sounds very intriguing. What’s the matter?”

“You won’t say anything about what I’m going to say to Edward or Philip, will you?”

“Now you do have me worried, but of course I won’t say anything if you don’t want me to.”

Teresa put the dirty crockery in the sink and sat down, “I’ve had this rash on my breasts for some time now. I thought it was a bit of eczema so I just kept putting cream on it.” She rubbed her hand across her face. “It didn’t do any good, in fact it’s got worse and I now don’t think it is eczema.”

“But if it isn’t some sort of eczema, what do you think it is?”

“I don’t know, but as I didn’t have it anywhere other than around my nipples, I suppose I should have had it checked out.”

“So have it checked out, and get it sorted.”

“It’s not as simple as that.”

“Of course it’s as simple as that. Go and get it checked out.”

“But it’s got worse.”

“How worse?”

“I’ve found these lumps.”

“Where?”

She pointed to her left breast, “A few weeks ago I found one here.”

“Teresa, what on earth are you saying? If you found a lump a few weeks ago, why haven’t you already had it checked out? You’re a nurse, for goodness sake. You know the right people to see.”

Teresa began to cry, “Please don’t be mad at me. I know I should have seen someone but I’m scared of what they might have to tell me.”

Samantha regretted her harsh words and put her arms around Teresa, “But you must go and see someone and I’ll come with you if that’ll help.

You know I will."

Teresa now began to cry uncontrollably and it was several minutes before she could speak again. "I found more lumps today; one in my other breast and one here under my arm." Samantha held her tight until she stopped crying and said to Samantha, "And you know what that means don't you?"

Samantha knelt on the floor beside Teresa and hugged her, both women were now crying. "You don't know anything until it's checked. It could be all sorts of things couldn't it?"

Teresa took Samantha's head in her hands and looked directly into her eyes, "But we both know what the chances are of it being something else, don't we?" Teresa even managed a smile as she added, "Zilch."

Samantha now took Teresa's head in her hands, "We'll go and sort it out tomorrow. Not next week and not even the day after tomorrow."

Teresa smiled, "Sorry Samantha but it can't be tomorrow or the day after. It's the weekend so I guess I can't do anything 'til Monday."

"Well you know who the best consultant to see is, don't you?"

"Mr Oldfield. I'll get in touch with his secretary on Monday." She looked at Samantha beseechingly, "You will come with me, won't you?" She bit her lip and added, "I'm really scared."

Samantha hugged her again, "I know, I know, but don't you know someone at the hospital who could give you his home number? You could then get him at home in the morning and see if he'll see you at his home tomorrow."

"I'm not sure that's possible."

"But you will try?"

Teresa nodded and stood up, "And now we both should tidy our faces and get back to the others."

Samantha gripped her arm, "Don't you think you should say something to Philip?"

Teresa pulled Samantha to her and hugged her again, "Not until after I've seen Mr Oldfield."

A week later Teresa was in the operating room having major breast surgery and three days later Philip was sitting at her bedside waiting for Michael Oldfield to come and give them the results of the surgery and the biopsy on the lumps removed.

He arrived with his registrar and shook Philip's hand before turning to collect a chair from the next bed and asking his registrar to close the curtains. He placed the chair at the side of the bed opposite to where Philip was sitting.

Philip was holding Teresa's hand and the doctor took the other, "And how are you feeling today, Teresa? Is the soreness getting any easier?"

"Not much, Mr Oldfield."

"It should start to feel easier in a few days."

Teresa forced a smile as she asked, "And what about the long term?"

He took a deep breath and looked from Teresa to Philip and back again before answering, "Well we had to take away most of both breasts as you know. Normally I would expect that to solve the problem."

Teresa closed her eyes and gripped Philip's hand so tightly that he winced with pain. She opened her eyes and looked at the doctor, trying to hold back the tears as she spoke, "Normally? What do you mean by normally?"

He looked at both of them again, trying to choose the right words, but Teresa spoke for him, "The lump under my arm and the biopsies, not good news is it?"

He squeezed her hand slightly. Teresa thought she saw a glint of a tear in his eye as he spoke, "I'm sorry Teresa, but all the biopsies were malignant, even the one from under your arm."

Again Teresa spoke before he was able to continue, "And that means it's probably already spread elsewhere?"

"I can't be certain. We'll take some more x-rays and see what, if anything, we find."

"But it doesn't look good?"

"Let's do the tests first."

She now turned over her hand and squashed his hand in hers, "The truth please, doctor? I'm a nurse remember. Tests or no tests you don't think you'll be able to cure me do you?"

"I'd like to say of course I can, but I know you too well to lie, so, no, I'm not hopeful."

"And how long does that give me?"

This time she was certain that there was a tear in his eye, "You know I'm not able to answer that with any sort of certainty, Teresa. You know as well as I do, that for some it can be quite some time and for others..." He merely shrugged his shoulders not able to speak the words.

Philip now spoke for the first time, "But what is your best guess, doctor?"

"I can't answer that, Philip. Not because I don't want to, but because it really does depend on so many things. We don't know for certain that it has even spread any further at all. And as Teresa knows a lot depends on the patient's attitude and how positive they can be."

Philip was about to speak again but Teresa put her hand to his mouth and stopped him. She turned to the doctor saying, "Thank you for being so honest, Mr Oldfield. And now if you don't mind I'd like to spend a little time talking to Philip."

He got up from his chair, "Of course, of course. I'll pop and see you later to make sure the drugs are keeping the pain at bay. I'll arrange for those x-rays as soon as possible and you know I'm available anytime you want to ask me more questions, or even just to chat about things." He held out his hand to shake Philip's. "And anytime you want to chat or ask me questions Philip, then my door's always open for you."

"Thank you Mr Oldfield."

"He held on to Philip's hand whilst he said, "Please call me Michael. Mr Oldfield's a bit too formal for this situation, don't you think?"

"Thank you, Michael," was all Philip could think to add.

Philip prevented the nurse from opening the curtain after the doctor had gone and for the next ten minutes he held Teresa as best he could, without either of them saying a word.

It was Teresa who finally broke the silence, "As soon as these wounds are healed Philip, I'm going to get out of here and I'm going to make the best of whatever time I have left." She touched his cheek and turned his head so that he was looking at her, "And don't worry we all die sometime, it just looks as though for me it might be sooner than I thought."

Philip felt a warmth and tenderness for Teresa that he had not felt in many years. He had never loved her with a passion and he still thought that marrying her had been a mistake, but she had always been there for him and had never given him cause for complaint, so now that she needed him he vowed to himself that he would devote all his energies to meeting whatever she needed with what time she had left. He smiled and hoped she realised that he meant what he was saying, "I promise I'll do whatever you want." He then repeated the, "I promise."

She put her hand over his mouth again, "No promises, you have no idea what it might be like before this is over, but it would be nice for us to spend a bit more time together as soon as I'm on my feet again."

The next few months were spent in a frenzy of activity during which Teresa made plans for a trip to see the natural wonders of North America. Philip argued against it and suggested they ask Michael Oldfield his view on the matter. He had responded with, "I agree with Philip, such a trip will be far too stressful for you. Perhaps you should do something less demanding."

"Maybe that's true but I've always wanted to go to America and I don't have much choice of when I can go do I?" She didn't wait for his answer but continued with, "And if I don't go what difference will it make? A few weeks? I'd rather spend what I've got left doing what I want." She turned to Philip, "Please don't try to talk me out of it either Philip. I want us to go now whilst we can. I'm not going to have another chance, am I?"

Philip had no answer to that so the plane tickets were bought. The return flight being an open ticket so that they could return as soon or as late as Teresa's health demanded. After spending a few days in New York, they bought a second hand car and spent the next five weeks journeying through the northern states from east to west, before crossing the Rockies from Salt Lake City to San Francisco. They then visited the sights in California and were in Las Vegas when Teresa finally admitted she could take no more and wanted to return home. Philip sold the car, (for half what he had paid for it) and purchased plane tickets back to New York from where they returned back to England.

Teresa was in a dreadful state by the time they reached home and was only too glad to be back in hospital receiving more relief for the ever increasing pain she had been experiencing for the last few weeks; pain she had not admitted to Philip until they were on their way home.

She spent the next three weeks in hospital with Philip becoming more and more distressed each time he visited. Each day she seemed to have lost more weight, her cheeks were more sunken and her eyes darker and strained with the increasing pain. He went to see Michael Oldfield, demanding he do something more to help her.

"I'm sorry Philip but there's nothing I can do that's not already being done. The cancer has spread to her vital organs and they are gradually ceasing to function. We're controlling the pain as much as we can, but that's about all we can do. I'm afraid it's just a matter of time before they cease altogether."

"So what does that mean?"

He stared at Philip almost disbelieving he needed to ask such a question, "I'm sorry Philip, but it means only one thing. She will die." Philip remained silent and did not ask the expected question. He answered it anyway, "I doubt she will live for more than another couple of months, and probably less. I should steel yourself for the end, it could come anytime."

Philip went back to Teresa's bedside and found Samantha sitting there. She was holding Teresa's hand and talking to her. She glanced across at Philip as he approached the bed and managed a weak smile before returning her attention to Teresa.

He had seen very little of Samantha in the last four months and wanted to run over to her and kiss her but instead he sat down on the opposite side of the bed and took hold of Teresa's other hand. For a moment he enjoyed the feeling he got from Samantha's presence, but immediately felt enormous guilt when he looked at his own dying wife between them, her pathetic frail, deathly white and wizened face on the pillow. How could she have become so thin and old in such a short time?

The three of them talked together for the next ten minutes, but Teresa suddenly said she felt tired and asked if Samantha would mind leaving.

"Of course not. I'll pop and see you again tomorrow." She bent over and kissed Teresa's forehead as she said this and then turned to go, but Teresa held on to her hand saying, "I want you to promise me that you'll look after Philip when I'm gone, Samantha." She then placed Samantha's hand in Philip's, "And I want you to look after Sam for me as well, Philip." There were tears in her eyes as she added, "I want you both to promise. Give me a decent funeral and then get on with your own lives. I want both of you to be happy and for both of you to havc what you want for yourselves." She looked at each of them in turn and smiled, "Life is too short to do anything else. I'm the living proof of that." She laughed to herself as she added, "Or should I say; the dying proof of that?"

Neither of them knew how to react, puzzled at why she had spoken in this particular way and asked such specific promises of them. Did she know how they felt about each other and this was Teresa giving her permission for them to be together? But neither of them questioned it and merely nodded their heads as agreement to the promises she had asked for.

"I won't keep Philip long Samantha, so why don't you wait for him downstairs? Have a cup of tea and get one for Philip. I'm sure he could do with a drink." Without waiting for any response, she continued, "He'll be with you in no time and you can both catch up with all the news."

As soon as Samantha had gone, Teresa asked Philip to sit closer to her, "I want you to go and see Mr Oldfield and tell him you're taking me home. Ask him to let you have the drugs I need to keep the pain down. Don't let him talk you out of it."

"But I'm sure they can look after you better than I can. Wouldn't it be better if you stayed here?"

She called up all the strength she could and held on to Philip's hand as tightly as her failing body would allow, "I've spent too much of my life in this place and I don't want to spend what little is left of it here. I want to go home. I want to die at home, not here."

Philip did not know how to respond, but knew from the tone in her voice that she was not going to take a 'No' as an answer, so he said, "I'll be off and catch Michael before he goes home then."

She held on to his hand and pulled him even closer to her, so that she could speak without anyone else hearing, "You know when, just after my op, you said you would do anything I asked of you?"

"Yes, of course. I'll go and see him now."

"No. it's not just that. I want you to make sure he gives you plenty of morphine." She pulled him even closer until she was speaking directly in to his ear, "I can't take any more, Philip. I've had enough; I don't want to go on. I want to die in my own bed and I want us to decide when that is."

He stood back and shook his head, not wanting to believe what he thought she implied in what she had just said.

She pulled him back to her again, "You promised you'd do anything I asked and that is what I want." She pushed him away slightly so that she could look into his eyes, "You go and see Michael Oldfield and then we can talk about it when we get home." She dropped his hand and waved him away, "Now go, sort it out with the doctor and then go and spend a bit of time with Samantha."

He kissed her on each cheek and was about to speak when she flipped her hand at him again, "Go. Go. And let me get some sleep."

He stood there for a few moments deciding whether to do as she bid, but she closed her eyes and turned her head away from him; the final signal that he should indeed go.

He found Samantha sitting in the canteen, a cup of now cold tea, waiting for him. As soon as she saw him, she got up and said she would fetch him a new cup. He stopped her from doing so and they sat down. This was the first time they had been alone together in months and he wanted to reach out and hug her to him, but he was stopped by his thoughts of Teresa and could do no more than just give her a perfunctory kiss on the cheek. Even so he could not prevent himself from saying, "I've missed you so much."

She smiled and touched his cheek slightly as she said, "I've missed you too," before picking up the cup again and adding, "And now I'll go and fetch that fresh cup of tea before we say too much more."

A hospital porter, who was sitting at the next table, moved his chair slightly to allow her to pass him. He had recognised her as soon as she had arrived and had immediately recognised the man who had joined her. He could hardly contain the hatred he felt for both of them. He wondered if either of them would recognise him after all this time. Probably not! He was, of course, much older, had lost weight and had allowed his now white hair to grow long enough to wear it in a ponytail. He also sported a white bushy beard and a gold earring in his left ear, all of which had changed his appearance considerably since he had last seen these two people.

Samantha returned with fresh tea and a piece of fruit cake for each of them. She thanked the porter for allowing her to pass again and sat down next to Philip without a second thought of the man or who he was.

Philip took her hand as soon as she sat down, "It's so good to see you. I really have missed you even more than I thought I would."

"I know, but you should be thinking about Teresa now. She's the one who needs you right now."

"It's thinking about Teresa that makes everything worse. I'd give anything for all this not to be happening to her but I can't; can I? I didn't think going on the trip was a good idea and seeing her now and the state she's in, I'm even more certain we shouldn't have gone. She'd have been much better with Mr Oldfield looking after her, wouldn't she?"

"Stop punishing yourself. She wanted to go and she wanted you to take her. I know what I'd want in similar circumstances and it most certainly wouldn't be spending my last few months in hospital."

"The trip did seem to go well at first and I thought she was right in wanting to go, but seeing her now I'm not so sure. She was really happy when we were in the States. It wasn't 'til I got her home that I realised how much she had deteriorated. She seemed so well and then suddenly she said she'd had enough. Perhaps we should have come home earlier? I kept asking her if she was OK, but she kept saying she was fine and wanted to continue."

"So you've given her what she wanted. Stop beating yourself up about it. She's in the best place now, so stop worrying."

"But she doesn't want to be here. She wants to go home. She's made me go and arrange it with Michael Oldfield. That's where I've been whilst my tea was getting cold."

"And what did he say?"

"He wasn't at all happy about it. He said she would only get worse and the pain could increase quite quickly. He also said she needed considerable nursing care, and that it wouldn't be easy at home dealing with her pain. He even warned me that she was no longer able to control her bladder and other functions. He suggested that I would have to get a nurse in to sort all that out, and the soiled bed linen etcetera."

"So, get a nurse. I know your Aunt Alice is retired now but I'm sure she'll still know enough medical people to sort someone out for you."

Philip took a swig of his tea, and said nothing.

Having received no response, Samantha spoke again, "Well I'm sure Mr

Oldfield is right when he says you'll need considerable help. You know I'll do what I can, but a proper nurse would be better. So ask Aunt Alice to find someone for you for the next few weeks."

He looked at her, carefully considering whether he should say what was on his mind. He hesitated before speaking, eventually plucking up the courage to say the thing that had been bothering him ever since he had left Teresa, "If Teresa has her way I don't think it'll come to that."

"Why? What do you mean?"

Again Philip hesitated to answer.

The porter squashed the remains of his cigarette in his saucer and in a yawning and stretching movement leaned back in his seat and moved even closer so that he could hear their conversation better.

Both Philip and Samantha were too wrapped up in themselves to even notice and Philip continued speaking, totally oblivious to the fact that there was anyone listening to them, "She's had enough and wants it all to end."

Samantha sat back in her seat, almost touching the man behind her. She looked hard at Philip as she tried to determine whether he was actually suggesting what he seemed to be. She leaned forward again and asked almost in a whisper, "Are you saying what I think you're saying?" By the look on Philip's face she knew that he was, "And that's why she wants to go home?"

He nodded his head, "But that isn't all."

Once again she said, "Why? What do you mean?"

Without hesitation this time, he admitted his real fear, "I think she wants me to help her."

Samantha put her hand to her mouth as she expressed a, "My God." She removed her hand and said, "Is that what she said?"

He nodded his head again, "More or less." He took her hand and asked, "What do you think I should do?"

Samantha thought long and hard before answering, "You want the truth?" He nodded his head and she continued, "The first time I saw her after you came back from the States, she'd deteriorated so much I hardly recognised her. I'm sure she puts on a brave face whenever you are with her, but every time I've seen her she's been in more and more distress with the pain. Almost straight away this afternoon, she told me she was in considerable pain and didn't think she could take much more. She also told me she didn't want to live any longer. I told her not to be silly, but she said there was nothing else left for her and it was the most rational thing that could happen and that I was to help you through it."

It suddenly dawned on Samantha exactly what Teresa had been saying and she let out another, “My God,” before continuing, “She was saying exactly the same thing to me wasn’t she? That’s what she meant and I didn’t see it at the time.”

“So what do you think I should do?”

She looked at Philip, feeling the pain he was suffering as he tried to sort out what to do. She wanted to take him in her arms and comfort him, but knew to do so would not help his dilemma, “You must talk to Teresa again, but in the end you must only do what feels right for you.” She leaned forward and kissed him on the cheek, “But don’t do anything silly and get yourself into trouble. Teresa wouldn’t want that either.”

“But I don’t know what feels right. I hate seeing her in all that pain and I want it to end for her as much as she does. I don’t know if I can do what she’s asking though.”

“I know, but talk to her again when you get home. I’m sure it’ll be easier to work things out with her and make the right decision there.”

“And will you stand by me, whatever that decision is?”

She leaned forward and kissed him on the cheek, “You know I will.”

“Thank you,” were the only words he could muster through his own pain.

She smiled and took his hand, “Now come on and get home. Get some sleep and see what tomorrow brings.”

Two days later Philip was at Teresa’s hospital bedside waiting to take her home. The hospital porter was holding the wheelchair ready to wheel her to Philip’s car. Jane had come with Philip to help sort out things for Teresa and together they helped Teresa out of bed and into the wheelchair. She screamed with pain as they moved her to the waiting chair. Philip told Jane to stop and asked Teresa if she really wanted to go home.

“You know I do, I’m not going to get what I want here am I?” She turned to Jane, “You understand why I want to go home don’t you Jane?”

Jane merely nodded her head, hoping that agreeing with Teresa would not annoy Philip. Teresa turned to Philip, “You have got my medicine haven’t you? I won’t be able to manage anything without it.”

Philip shuddered at the thought of what she was saying but nevertheless picked up the bag with all her bits and pieces from her locker and took the bottle from it so that she could see it.

The porter smiled to himself, knowing that they hadn’t a clue who he was. Jane walked behind the porter as he pushed Teresa to the door and became transfixed on the way he limped and dragged one leg behind the other; a limp that had got much worse by his years in prison. Philip was thinking far too much of other things to even notice.

Samantha and Alice were waiting for them when they arrived home and

Philip needed the help of both Jane and Samantha to lift Teresa out of the car and into the safety of his arms. He could not believe how light she was. How could she have lost this much weight in so little time?

He carried her to the bed that had been set up in the lounge and Alice helped to settle her into it. As soon as all the fussing had stopped, Teresa asked if they would mind leaving as she was very tired and needed to rest. But as soon as Jane, Sam and Alice had left she called Philip and asked him to lie on the bed next to her saying, "I want you near me for a bit. There are some things I need to tell you before I go."

"Why don't you rest for a bit? We'll have plenty of time to talk over the next few days. Lucy has been helping Sam with things at work, so I'm not going anywhere."

"I don't want to rest, I want to talk for a bit and then you can help me with the morphine." She turned and stared at the bedside table and a look of distress fell across her face, "Where is it? You did bring it from the hospital, didn't you?"

Philip took her hand and asked, "Are you in pain? Do you need some right now?"

She nodded her head, "I'm in constant pain but I'll manage for now. I just need to know you have it. You have, haven't you?"

He leaned forward and kissed her on her forehead, "Yes, of course, it's in the kitchen. I'll fetch it when you need it."

Teresa took a deep breath and bit her lip as she tried to control the pain in her stomach, "I just need to know it's there when the time comes." She patted the bed beside her, "Now lie down here and hold my hand whilst I talk to you."

Philip took off his shoes and jacket before loosening his tie and very carefully and gently lay on the bed, trying not to cause her more pain in the process. He lifted his head on to his hand so that he could see Teresa's face more clearly. He felt more emotion towards her at that moment than he had in all their married life and wondered what life would have been like if he had been the husband that she had always wanted him to be. He wished that for once and, at least for the time Teresa had left, that he could dismiss from his mind all thoughts about Samantha. It wasn't until he met Samantha that he realised that he had married Teresa for the wrong reasons and for the first time ever a wave of shame about his feeling for Samantha flooded over him.

As a young man he had always believed he would meet someone he would recognise straight away as being his soul mate in the same way that Edward had when he met and fell in love with Juliette. Why had he thrown away that belief and married Teresa? Looking at her now and seeing the pain she was in, made him regret that he was unable to love her in the way she had wanted and deserved. It wasn't her fault that he had made the mistake and now it was too late to do anything for her other than be with her in her last days.

He was awoken out of his musings when Teresa spoke to him, "Don't look so sad, all this isn't your fault. I'm dying and that's the end to it. It happens to everyone sometime and there's nothing either of us can do to stop it happening to me."

She looked at him and managed a smile, "I just don't want this pain and suffering to go on. I've seen too many suffer a lingering, painful and awful death and as the end often comes in the middle of the night, they often die on their own without any family with them." The smile left her face and Philip thought he saw a tear in her eye as she added, "And often there isn't even a nurse with them. We always seem to be too busy and always somewhere else." She took his hand, "I don't want that to happen to me. I want to choose when I go. I want you with me and I'll need you to help me choose when it happens."

Philip wanted desperately to say, *"I can't help you, if for no other reason than what you're asking is against the law,"* but knew he could not say any such thing at that moment, and chose to try to change the subject, "I'm sure there are more important things to talk about right now, so can we stop being so morbid and talk about other things?"

She gave him an unexpected smile, "I know you're not happy about what I'm asking, and I'm scared that you'll try to talk me out of it. You won't though will you?" and before he could answer she added, "Please don't. I've thought long and hard about this ever since I was first diagnosed. I know it's a lot to ask of you but I can't do it myself and leave you wondering why I had left you so cruelly. I need you to know it's what I want and I need you to help me. It's the last thing I'm going to ask of you, so please don't make it difficult. I can't do it without you."

Philip did not know what to say and they both lay staring at each other for some time before Teresa broke the silence, "And now I'll tell you all the other things I have to get off my chest before I go. I haven't been looking forward to this bit, but I need for you to understand a few things."

"What is there to understand? You've always been there for me and I've never doubted that you loved me."

"And I've never doubted that you loved me in your own way." She stopped and stared directly into his eyes before continuing, "But let's be honest, it was never the passionate love that we saw in Juliette and Edward was it? I always wanted to be the woman you were looking for, but I knew when we got married that I wasn't and I am sorry for that."

"I don't know what to say, but..."

She put her hand to his lips and stopped him continuing, "I don't want you to say anything. What I'm saying is not meant as a criticism and I don't want you to feel bad about it. You've been a good man and I'm grateful for the life you've given me. All I'm trying to say is that I'm sorry I couldn't make things better for you."

"But you have nothing to be sorry for. You know what they say 'It takes two to tango'? So you don't have to be sorry for anything."

She put her hand to his mouth again, "I've spent the last couple of weeks thinking about nothing else but what I wanted to say to you before I go. I know it's very selfish, but I just have to explain a few things about me. What I have to say is all about me, not you. So please let me just get on with it and please don't make things difficult for me by trying to give me excuses. I should have talked to you years ago, so please let me do so now. And above all else, none of what I have to say is a criticism against you so please don't assume it is." She looked at him and asked, "So can I get on with it?"

Once again Philip did not know how to react, so he stayed silent and let her speak. She however held her hand firmly on his mouth making it clear that she did not want him to say anything about what she was going to say.

"First of all, I want to say I'm sorry I couldn't give you the children you wanted." She held her hand tightly on his mouth as she continued, "I feel so guilty about that and what makes it worse is that I was pregnant once."

He forced her hand away from his mouth but she almost shouted at him, "Please don't say anything, just listen." Seeing how distressed she was he stayed silent other than to say, "OK."

"It happened when you were away in the army during the war. You know that I lived with my Mom and her brother, Uncle Arnold, and that when mother died I moved out very soon after her funeral don't you?" Philip nodded and let her continue, "Well what I've never told you is why I moved out so quickly."

Philip had never seen her look so distressed and wanted to ask her to stop, but somehow he knew that to do so would cause her even more anguish. She winced with the pain again.

"Do you want me to get the pain relief for you?"

"Not yet, let me finish this and then you can get it."

She started to heave with long and noisy breaths as she tried to get air into her lungs. "Often when my mother was out and had left Uncle Arnold to look after me he'd come into my room when I went to bed and touch me, and then later he made me touch him. I hated it and I hated him. At times I hated my mother as well, because when I tried to tell her she didn't believe me and told me to stop lying."

Philip found it difficult to believe what he was being told but, unlike her mother, he nevertheless did believe her and wanted to tell her so. She once more prevented him from saying anything as she continued, "When I was older, I threatened to go to the police if he didn't leave me alone and it stopped. But then after Mom's funeral and after everyone else had gone home, I went to bed leaving him drinking downstairs. He was drunk even before I went to bed and I guess he must have fallen asleep in the chair downstairs, because it was already starting to get light when I awoke to find him lying naked on my bed. He had pulled the blankets off me and well, I don't want to go into detail, but he raped me."

Philip had listened long enough, "And what did the police say?"

"I didn't go to the police. I just moved out the very next day."

Philip wanted to ask why she hadn't gone to the police. He also wanted to tell her that what happened was in no way her fault, but he knew that nothing he said would be helpful to her so he chose to say nothing. He sensed that there was more to come so instead he just remained silent, allowing her to dictate events.

As he waited for her to speak, she winced and her face become contorted by the obvious discomfort and agony she was experiencing, and it took several minutes before she was able to talk again through the pain.

When she did speak it was through gritted teeth as she tried to bear her distress and discomfort, "I became frantic when I missed my period. I was scared to death that I could be pregnant but I had no one to talk to and I couldn't go and see a doctor, could I?"

Philip merely shook his head and let her continue, "Anyway I couldn't believe it when I missed my next period as well. I'd never had sex with anyone, and when he raped me, I was fighting against it all the way, so how could I possibly be pregnant?" She stopped to take a deep breath and gain her composure again, "But it was fairly evident that I was, and that's when one of the other nurses found me crying my eyes out in the ladies toilet."

Tears were now streaming from Teresa's eyes and were flowing in great floods down her cheeks as she tried to muster up the courage and strength to continue. Philip could stand Teresa's anguish no longer. He wanted to comfort her and say the right thing to her, but what was the right thing? He wanted to know about the baby. Was it a boy or a girl? Had it been adopted? What had happened to it? He was torn between wanting the answer to all these questions and wanting to stop her obvious suffering and agony as she related events to him. How did any girl cope as an unmarried pregnant girl with all the prejudice that always automatically followed any girl in that position? Things may have been better if the father was a boy friend whom she could marry, but how did any woman cope with the trauma of becoming pregnant in those awful and terrible circumstances; a lone woman with no one to help her and then having to give away the child after carrying it for nine months. His mind was in turmoil as he tried to work out what to say and do, but all of his deliberations were of nothing to what she said next.

"She seemed to understand straight away and she told me she would help me sort it all out. She knew someone who could help me get rid of the baby. My only problem was going to be finding the money to pay for it."

Philip hoped she hadn't noticed his gasp of disbelief as she told him, "But I did manage to find the money and that was the end of the baby." A new flow of tears were now cascading down her cheeks, "And I've felt the guilt of that every day since."

Philip was quickly able to dismiss his shock. He understood that in her position he probably would have done exactly the same thing even though it was against the law. For the first time since she had started the tale he was able to understand and empathise with her plight, and he now felt he was ready to maybe say the right thing; or at least not the wrong thing.

"You shouldn't have kept this to yourself for so long, and you certainly shouldn't still be beating yourself up over it. You haven't got anything to feel guilty about. In fact you never did. You were the victim, and if society was more understanding about such matters then you'd have been properly supported and wouldn't have had to deal with it all alone."

Teresa did not react to what he had just said, but immediately curled up in obvious extreme pain. She let out a squeal that would have been a piercing shriek if she had had the strength to do so.

"Is the pain getting too much for you? Do you want me to fetch the morphine and give you a dose?"

She gave a very frail nod of her head in response.

She heaved as he gave her the measured dose of morphine. It was another fifteen minutes before it had enough effect for Teresa to talk again, and in all that time Philip could not get out of his head the dreadful thought that no-one would let an animal continue in such obvious remorseless and cruel agony. For the first time since Teresa had raised the subject, he began to feel that maybe what she was asking of him was the right thing to do.

Teresa opened her eyes and managed a weak smile as she said, "Thank you. It's getting a bit better now."

"Shall I leave you then and let you get some rest?"

She patted the bed beside her, "No, I want you to lie down here next to me again. I want to finish everything I have to say whilst I still have the energy."

He carefully leaned forward and gently kissed her on her lips, "I understand perfectly why you did what you did, so there's nothing more you need to say."

She managed another fragile smile, "I'm sorry sweetheart, but there is more I need to say; things I should have told you a long time ago."

He kissed her again and gave her a return smile, "And I take it you want me to stay silent whilst you tell me."

"Yes please. It's difficult enough without you interrupting."

"So what's it all about then?" He gave a gentle laugh as he drew his finger across his mouth from left to right, "Sorry, I'll zip this up and let you talk."

He did not know whether the strained look on her face was from further pain or from what she said. "I always regretted getting rid of my baby, and when we got married I thought that if we had a child, things would be OK. I started to panic when, month after month, I didn't get pregnant. I had become pregnant so easily when I didn't want to, so why couldn't I become pregnant when I wanted to? If I'd become pregnant that easily once, then I was sure that if I wasn't becoming pregnant now the problem must be with you. It couldn't possibly be me, could it? But I couldn't tell you about my baby and I couldn't come straight out and tell you the problem was you. Instead I suggested that we both have tests. So that's why I put you through all those tests and everything else. I'm sorry but I shouldn't have done that."

"It doesn't matter. The problem was with me, so that's OK. I was a little surprised that you took it so well though."

The tears began to trickle down her cheeks again, "But the truth is that I still don't actually know why I never became pregnant."

A deep frown appeared across Philip's brow, "Of course you do, that consultant told you that I couldn't give you a child."

The tears were now flowing freely and she had to gulp hard to get enough breath in her lungs to overcome her sobs before she could continue, "That isn't exactly what he said."

Philip tried hard to keep any semblance of anger from his voice as he asked, "So what did he say?"

"When he saw me on the ward one day he told me he had all the test results and I should contact his secretary to make appointments for both of us to see him." She took another deep breath, "Well that's not exactly true. What he actually said was that it would probably be best if he saw each of us on our own, so I was to ask his secretary to make two appointments and then he would see us together after that if I wanted him to."

She stopped as she tried to control her sobs. Philip chose not to say anything but just waited for her to get control. "It suddenly struck me that the way he said that he could see us together if I wanted him to, meant that he'd realised that I'd had an abortion. I just panicked and asked him why he couldn't just tell me there and then. He said it was highly unlikely that we could ever have children but he wasn't prepared to say more than that except to each of us privately. He repeated that he'd need to see us separately as he didn't wish to discuss either me with you or you with me before he'd told us our individual results, and then got our permission to speak in front of the other."

"But you did go to see him and he did tell you about my problem?"

"No I didn't. I never made the appointments. I'm so sorry but I was so scared that if he knew about the abortion all sorts of things might happen. He might get me sacked or even worse contact the police. I think I could have coped with either of those, but I couldn't chance you finding out."

"So is there anything wrong with me or not?"

The tears continued to flow, "I really don't know. All I do know is that when he saw me on the ward a week or so later he asked why we hadn't been to see him. I told him we'd talked and decided that if we couldn't have children, then we didn't want to know which one had the problem. He gave me an odd look and I couldn't work out what it meant when he said that he really thought it would be useful to go through our test results with each of us independently of the other." She shook her head, "I'm sorry, I took that to mean that we could both have some sort of problem, so that's when I came home and told you that the problem was with you. I still couldn't accept that it wasn't you and I still couldn't accept that it could be me. I had already been pregnant."

Teresa totally broke down and she reached out to pull Philip to her. His mind was in turmoil and total confusion, but he knew that he could not express any of his concern and dismay to his dying wife, who was so visibly distraught and troubled by everything she had said. He took out his handkerchief and wiped the tears from her eyes and face as he tried to be as compassionate as he could, "Don't worry about it any more, sweetheart.

We couldn't have a child and whether that was my fault or yours or both of us it really doesn't matter. So just stop crying and get some rest."

He moved closer to her and carefully put his arms around her, "Why don't you try and get some sleep? I'll stay here with you."

"No, I don't want to go to sleep just yet. I'm content now that I've got all that off my chest, and I want to enjoy you next to me for a while." She took a deep gasp of air as the pain began to increase again, "I don't want this to go on any more. I want the next time I go to sleep to be last time."

He shuddered at the thought and hoped she had not felt his movement. After a while she snuggled even closer to him and turned her head towards him as she spoke, "Stay next to me for a little while; at least until I can't take the pain any more." She looked directly into his eyes, "I don't want to wake up in the morning to more of this."

This time she clearly felt his shaking. She put her hand to his cheek and then moved her fingers across his lips in a gentle and loving caress, "I don't think I can take enough of that morphine on its own though. I thought I was going to throw up the last time you gave me a single dose, and I don't want to make a mess of it."

He did not know how to respond and merely asked, "So what do you want to do?"

"Perhaps you could put it in something; something that will take the taste away."

Philip did not like the way the conversation was going. He had not thought she would be making plans so soon, or in such an almost offhand way. He dreaded the thought of her death but dreaded the thought of her suffering getting worse even more. He had seen enough in the last few hours to know that all she wanted now was a dignified and peaceful death and that, much as he hated the idea, he must help her achieve it.

"I bought some tins of soup. I thought they were something you could eat. I got your favourite chicken soup. I could warm some of that for you if you like."

"That'll be fine but stay here and I'll tell you when to go and warm it."

They lay together in each other's arms for the next hour, during which time Philip tried to say all the right things about their life together. He even managed to make her laugh two or three times, but eventually the pain became too great for her to bear any more and she asked him to go and prepare the soup, "And don't forget to put plenty of the medicine in it. I don't want us to have to go through it all again."

Philip went to the kitchen taking the medicine bottle with him. He opened a tin of chicken soup and warmed it on the gas hob. He almost brought it to the boil, thinking that the morphine would lower its temperature sufficient to give to Teresa. He put the soup into a bowl, opened the bottle and added the mixture.

Teresa asked him to help her sit up when he took the soup to her. Once he had done this she asked him to fetch the bottle so that she could see how much he had added. He fetched the bottle which was now only half full and put it on the bedside table.

Teresa took every mouthful that he gave to her but often heaved as she desperately tried to swallow all of each spoonful. It was a slow process with each additional small portion taking longer and longer to swallow. She looked at the amount left in the dish and stopped Philip giving her any more, "I think that should do the trick. If I try to eat any more, I think I'll bring it all back."

She mouthed a, "Thank you," but as he tried to put the bowl and spoon back on the tray she coughed and he spilled some of the remaining liquid on the bedclothes. He quickly mopped it up with tissues and took out his handkerchief and wiped Teresa's lips. She managed a weak smile and said, "Now you can help me lie down again and then I want you to lie down next to me whilst I go to sleep."

He grabbed the spare blanket off the chair and threw it over himself as he snuggled up against her. She found the strength to lean forward to kiss him full on the lips, and gave him another, "Thank you," before closing her eyes and falling asleep.

When Philip awoke, a thin shaft of morning sunlight was shining through the wee gap in the curtains where they had not been fully closed. The beam cut its way across the otherwise dark room and came to rest upon his dead wife's peaceful face; at last free of all her suffering.

CHAPTER TWENTY– FIVE

1972

Philip looked through his bedroom window and was pleased the day had turned out to be the warm and clear 'Indian summer' October day he had been hoping for. *'There's nothing worse than having to attend a funeral on a damp rainy day; a funeral is bad enough without having to get soaked in the process,'* he thought as he tried to summon up enough courage to go downstairs and speak to members of his family who were patiently waiting in the lounge for the funeral cars to arrive. He knew he should go and make small talk with them, but right now that was the last thing he wanted to do. He had listened every time the door bell rang hoping it was Samantha, but she hadn't arrived yet.

He felt he had hidden in his bedroom long enough and ventured downstairs. However, instead of going into the lounge where the others were waiting, he went into the dining room to check that everything was ready for the guests when they returned from church. His sister-in-law Jane was in the dining room with her husband John. They were putting the finishing touches to the food on the table and making sure it was all properly covered.

Jane had been a tower of strength since Teresa had died. She had insisted on arranging all the catering and John had said he would sort out all the drinks. "You've got far more important things to worry about, so just leave all that to us," was Jane's immediate offer when they called on him the day after Teresa's death.

Jane had been true to her word and there was a veritable feast now laid out on the table, "I just hope it doesn't all dry up whilst we're at the church," was Jane's response when Philip kissed her and thanked her for all she had done.

He was on his way to the lounge when the front door bell rang, giving him an excuse not to join the others yet. Instead he went to open the door, hoping it would be Samantha at last.

Ever since he had discovered Teresa's dead body beside him, he had wanted to talk to someone he trusted about everything Teresa had told him. But in his heart he knew that what Teresa had admitted on that last day together was in effect her last confession and although she had not asked him to keep what she told him to himself, he nevertheless knew he could never destroy the sacredness of that confession to anyone, not even Samantha.

But neither could he get the things she had spoken of out of his head. Why hadn't she become pregnant a second time? Was the no children problem really his or not? Could the problem have been with Teresa? If it was, did that mean that Louise could be his? He had always wanted Louise to be his child and now what Teresa had said made it a bit more difficult to accept she wasn't.

He was totally obsessed with these unanswered questions until Sam and Edward came with Louise on the Sunday afternoon to see him, and the answer was once more abundantly clear. Louise was rapidly developing into a woman so like Samantha the first time he had seen her, except for one thing. The colour of her hair was so obviously Edward's and not his.

He had not seen Samantha on her own since the day at the hospital and he desperately wanted to just hold her hand for a minute and know that he wasn't really so much alone as he felt. His heart began to pound and he took a deep breath as he opened the door, knowing full well that it would not happen today; and neither should it on the day of Teresa's funeral.

Edward was the first through the door and he gave Philip a bear hug, almost kissing him on the cheek as he did so, "How are you today Philip?" but he did not wait for an answer before continuing, "I know it's no real comfort, old buddy, but we are all here for you whenever you need us." He did not let go of Philip, but held on to him for several seconds to show his real concern for his friend. Philip had not felt such warmth from his life long pal in a long time.

Louise followed her father's example and stepped up to Philip and put her arms round him, giving him a quick kiss on his cheek before releasing him.

Philip leaned forward and kissed her on her forehead. He wanted to make some comment about what a beautiful woman she had grown into, so like her mother, but thought better of it and merely said, "It's good to see you, Louise. Thank you for coming."

As soon as Louise stepped away, Samantha walked through the door and immediately put her arms around him. For years their normal greeting in such situations had been a mild hug and a kiss on the cheek, but encouraged by Edward's enthusiastic embrace of Philip, she too put her arms fully round his waist, and pressed her body against him as she kissed his cheek, holding her lips against his face for several seconds.

Philip returned the greeting by kissing her on her cheek. He wanted to hold on to her as he was taking great comfort in the embrace, but he nevertheless only held on to her for what he hoped was a socially accepted period of time bearing in mind the exceptional nature of the occasion. As soon as they parted he immediately turned to Edward, "My mother and Aunt Alice are in the lounge with the others. Do you think you and Samantha could chat to them 'til the cars arrive, only I just don't feel up to it right now?"

Edward patted him on the back, "Sure, no problem. Is there anything else we can help with?"

Philip shook his head, "No thanks. Maybe I'll be a bit more sociable when we've got the funeral over with." He looked at his watch, "The cars won't be here for another fifteen minutes yet, do you want me to ask Jane to make you a cup of tea before they arrive? Or would you like something a little stronger?"

Samantha interrupted before Edward could answer, "No, he would not, at least not until we get back." She looked at Edward, "But I'll get you a cup of tea if you want one whilst you go and chat to your Auntie Grace."

Edward replied with a, "No thanks, I'll be fine," before turning to Philip and adding, "Must do as the boss says Philip."

Samantha ignored the jibe and made her way into the lounge, touching Philip's arm lightly as she passed him.

Exactly ten minutes later Louise came into the kitchen and found Philip sitting at the table, cup of tea in his hand, none of which had been drunk, "Mom said to come and tell you that the cars have just arrived, Uncle Philip." He put down the cup and merely said, "Thank you."

To Philip's surprise she sat on the seat opposite him and cupped her hands around his. She leaned her head forward so that she could look closely into his eyes, "Are you all right, Uncle Philip? You look so sad."

"I'll be fine, Louise, but thank you for asking." He released his hands from her grasp but immediately cupped them around hers, "Your Aunt Teresa always had a soft spot for you, you know." He smiled and let go of her hands, "Come on, we best go and get this over with."

After the vicar had given the final prayer at the end of Teresa's funeral service, the organist started to play Bach's Toccata and Fugue in D minor, and for a while Philip did not know what he was now expected to do. The funeral director came to the front with his staff and they turned the coffin round and when they started to move, the director signalled to Philip to follow the coffin out of the church. Louise who was sitting two rows behind Philip thought he looked dreadfully lonely and sad as he slowly walked behind the coffin on his own and suddenly had an impulse to do something for him. She stepped out as he was about to pass her and took hold of his arm and slowly walked in step beside him. This simple action by Louise was more overwhelming to him than any part of the service, and for the first time since Teresa's death the tears started to stream down his face. Louise held on to his arm even tighter when she saw this and her own eyes filled with moisture, not for Teresa but for her unhappy uncle.

The rest of the funeral party moved slowly behind them but as the coffin reached the end of the aisle and turned left to the south door, two men who had been standing at the rear of the church stepped forward and halted the progress of the coffin. They spoke to the coffin bearers and pointed outside the church, and the coffin again began to be moved out of the church.

When Philip reached them the younger of the two men stopped his progress and asked if he was Philip Matthews, the husband of the deceased.

Philip was totally confused by the man's action and wiping the moisture from his eyes spoke quite angrily to him, "Yes, of course I am, but what's this all about? Are you blind or something? Can't you see we're in the middle of a funeral? Surely whatever you want can wait, can't it?"

"I'm afraid not Sir. In fact it can't wait at all."

"What can't wait and who the hell are you anyway?" Philip did not wait for an answer but quickly looked at his watch before adding, "We have a service arranged at Ryecroft Crematorium in half an hour so whatever it is will have to wait until after that. Whatever you want can't possibly be more important than that, so please go away and come and see me tomorrow."

The man was now clearly irritated by Philip's reaction and spoke quite firmly, "I'm Detective Sergeant Moore." He pulled a wallet from his waistcoat pocket and showed his warrant card to Philip before pointing to the man next to him and adding, "And this is DC Onions." He put his warrant card away and took hold of Philip's arm saying, "I know this is awkward for you Sir, and we have waited until the service is finished, but we'd like you to accompany us to the police station and answer a few questions for us."

The organist stumbled over his music as he tried to look in his mirror to see why the procession had stopped moving but he quickly found his place again and continued playing.

Philip took Louise's arm out of his own and stepped aside so that he could confront the man better. He took his pen from his pocket and picking up a spare order of service sheet, started to write his address and telephone number on it, "If this is something to do with the business or one of the shops then I'll be very happy to talk to you as much as you want later but, as I've said, we haven't finished my wife's funeral yet. Here's my address and telephone number, so please contact me later and we can sort everything out then."

He handed the policeman the paper and went to continue after the coffin. The policeman once again stopped him, "I'm sorry Sir, but there won't be any service at the crematorium today, and I would like you to come with us. Perhaps one of your friends could look after all your guests?"

"For God's sake, what's all this about? Surely it can't be so important that it can't wait a couple of hours."

Edward had now joined Philip and asked what was going on before DS Moore could answer.

"This man is a policeman and apparently he wants to ask me some questions about something or other. I've told him I'll help him in whatever it is later but he doesn't seem content with that. Can you talk some sense into him, Edward?"

It was now DS Moore who showed his irritation, "I'm sorry Sir, but I have tried to do this as quietly as I can, but I'm afraid you now leave me no option." He took hold of Philip's arm and said quite firmly, "Philip Matthews, I am arresting you on suspicion of the murder of your wife Teresa Matthews." He pulled on Philip's arm quite firmly and passed him over to the other policemen, "Now you don't want me to have to put cuffs on you, do you Sir? Not in front of all your family, so just go with DC Onions and I'm sure we can sort all this out peacefully at the station." He turned and spoke to the other detective, "Take him away, Robby and make sure you read him his rights before you stick him in the car."

He then turned to Edward, "And now Sir, if you'd be so kind, perhaps you can tell the others that there'll be no service at the Crematorium. Not today anyway. Oh, and perhaps you can point out which lady is Samantha Prior for me?"

"Samantha Richards you mean. She's my wife. What on earth do you want with her?"

"Well Sir, for the time being I just want to ask her a few questions. Before we interview Mr Matthews that is."

"Look I don't know where you've got this stupid notion that Mrs Matthews was murdered, but it's absolute nonsense. She died of terminal cancer. You've only got to ask her consultant at the hospital. She died of cancer and that's all there is to it."

"That may be so, but we have a statement from someone who says it's otherwise. So you see Sir, I have to investigate the matter and satisfy myself one way or the other. So until then, perhaps you'll let me get on with my job and tell me which lady is your wife?"

It was now Edward's turn to try and control the situation. He took hold of the detective's arm and tried to lead him out of the church, "Look, I guess you don't know who I am, but I'm Edward Richards, the local MP, so perhaps we can just go outside and you can tell me what all this is about?"

"Yes Sir, I'm well aware who you are, but surely you can see that I have to investigate an allegation as serious as this. And bearing in mind what our witness has said, I'm afraid we shall have to have a post mortem on Mrs Matthews. So you see I had to stop the funeral before the body goes to the Crematorium. I've been here some time, but out of consideration for you all, I deliberately left all this until the service was finished. Surely, you of all people can see that I couldn't leave it any longer." He shook his head, "I also know you are a solicitor by profession, Mr Richards, so I'm sure you realise better than most that I couldn't let you take the body to be burned. Now could I?"

Edward knew he was right and as a solicitor, sympathised with his predicament. He also knew that it was absolute nonsense to suggest that Philip had killed Teresa, and he certainly couldn't work out why anyone would make such a stupid suggestion to the police.

"And why do you want to talk to my wife?"

"I need to hear her side of the story Sir. I take no pleasure in all of this but please let me get on with my job and hopefully we can have it all sorted out quickly. Now can you ask your wife to come with me, Sir?"

"You want her to go to the police station as well?"

"It would be best if she would."

"And are you going to arrest her?"

"Well I hope not."

Edward did not know how to take this remark, but decided to leave the matter and talk to the rest of the guests, "If you'll just wait outside officer, I'll talk to all these people and sort things out with them, then I'll bring my wife to you and we can all get down to the station and sort this mess out."

Edward however did not wait to see whether the officer agreed with his last comment but turned and spoke to John instead.

The organist had come to the end of the Toccata and Fugue, but seeing that the congregation were still in the church and many of them still standing in their pew, he shrugged his shoulders and restarted the piece at the beginning again.

Edward now turned to try to speak to all the others present above the noise of the organ, "Ladies and Gentlemen, there has been a bit of a problem and so the service at the Crematorium has been cancelled. So if you'd like to make your way back to Philip's house, John and his wife Jane will look after you all there. I'll be along a bit later with Philip and Sam."

He did not bother to give any more explanation, but took hold of Sam's arm and the two of them marched out of the church, leaving the rest open mouthed and chattering to each other. The organist had stopped playing mid stream when he realised that Edward had started to speak. He scratched his ear and looked quite bemused as to what to do next. After a second's thought he shrugged his shoulders, collected his music together and left.

As soon as they arrived at the police station, Edward announced that he wanted to talk to his clients before anyone else spoke to either of them, "I also want to see this statement you say you have. I want to know what he is saying. I take it is a 'he'?"

"Well, I hope you don't mind Mr Richards but I would like to talk to your wife before I disclose what's in the statement. I will of course show it to you later, but bearing in mind your relationship with Mrs Richards, I'd like to interview her before you know of its contents. Perhaps in the circumstances it may be better if someone else represents your wife, don't you think?"

"No I do not! What are you inferring? Are you suggesting that I may not act properly?"

"Please Mr Richards I'm only trying to do my job as best as I can. I don't want to make any mistakes here, and you must admit it is rather unusual to say the least, for a husband to be representing his wife. In fact I'm not even sure that it's legal, let alone ethical." He held up his hand to prevent Edward from speaking before continuing, "But this whole situation is awkward for all of us, so what would you say if I allow you to speak to your wife, then I'll interview her with you present if that's what she wants, and with a bit of luck, I'd like to think I should be able to let her go after that."

"And what about Mr Matthews? Can I see him?"

"Of course I'll let you speak to Mr Matthews before I speak to him. That's assuming he wants you to act for him, but let's sort things out with your wife first."

Edward wanted to take him to task, but recognised that he was trying to do his best and decided not to antagonise him but try and get him on his side, "Thank you Sergeant, yes let's do that and I'll see the statement later as you suggest. Now perhaps you can show me to a room where I can talk to my wife before you speak to her?"

"Yes of course, but after I've spoken to your wife it may be some time before we are ready to speak to Mr Matthews. I need to speak to Mrs Matthews's consultant at the hospital first and his secretary says he is operating and won't be available for another couple of hours at least. She's going to phone me when he's out of theatre, so if we haven't finished with your wife by then, I'm afraid I'll have to postpone the interview 'til I get back from speaking to him. Now if you'll follow me I'll show you to a room you can use."

The room was a small plain interview room with just a table and a few plastic chairs placed either side of it. A glass jug of water and a few paper cups were the only things on the table. Samantha sat at the table but Edward stayed standing without saying a word until DS Moore had closed the door behind him as he left the room. As soon as the door closed Sam was able to speak to Edward for the first time since the funeral service, "What's all this about Edward? Why have they arrested Philip?"

"Well someone has apparently accused him of murdering Teresa, but I was hoping you could throw a bit of light on why someone would do that. They want to talk to you first, so what can you tell me?" was all he could say in response.

"Why on earth do they want to talk to me? I can't tell them anything other than it's ridiculous to think that Philip could do such a thing."

"Well they obviously think you know something. Why do you think that is? They haven't just picked you out at random, so they must have reason to think you know something." He sat down in the chair on the opposite side of the table, "You'd better tell me everything you know so that we can work out how serious this thing is for Philip."

"I have no idea what you're talking about. I don't know anything about a murder. Philip wouldn't kill anyone. And anyway we all know that Teresa was dying so why would he want to murder her? Just tell me why he would want to do that?"

"I've been thinking about that. She was in an awful lot of pain in the end wasn't she? Perhaps he wanted to help her out of the pain."

Samantha let out a cry and put her hands to her face, "Oh, my God, he didn't, did he?"

Edward's face dropped with horror at her reaction, "Didn't what?"

Tears started to stream down her face as she pleaded with Edward, "If I tell you something you don't have to tell the police do you?"

Edward suddenly wondered whether he had been right to act for Sam. *'Where was this leading?'* he thought to himself. *'Maybe it would have been better if someone else was here?'*

He put the thoughts aside and asked, "Just tell me everything you know then we'll worry about what we do about it." He continued before she could answer, "But I have to warn you that in my experience it only makes things worse in the end if we try to hide anything." He laughed as he added, "I'm sure that whatever it is can't be anywhere as dreadful as all the things I had to confess to you a few years ago."

"I just don't want to make things worse for Philip."

"I'm sure that the only way either of us can help Philip is by telling the truth. If Philip does the same thing, then the police can't play one of you off against the other, can they?"

Samantha thought long and hard before she answered, but once started she told Edward about everything that she and Philip had said in the canteen at the hospital. She finished by stressing, "But he was just telling me what Teresa had said to him and what Teresa wanted. When I was with her before Philip arrived she'd told me she couldn't stand the pain much more and although she didn't exactly say it, I'm sure she didn't want to go on any longer."

"And Philip didn't say he was going to assist her to die?"

"Well not exactly."

Up to this point Edward had thought the whole thing was rubbish and would be cleared up quickly, but this last remark by Samantha suddenly made him sit up and view the whole thing differently, "What do you mean by 'not exactly'?"

"I don't know what I mean by it. It's just that I don't think Philip had totally dismissed the idea."

Edward closed his eyes and let out a, "Shit" through clenched teeth. He opened his eyes, looked at Samantha and merely asked, "Why do you say that?"

Again Samantha took some time before answering, "Well I'm pretty sure Teresa would have brought the subject up as soon as they were alone together at home and I don't think Philip had decided definitely one way or the other whether he would try to talk her out of it."

"Well, for his sake, don't say anything like that again to anyone else, and preferably not to me again either. I'll try and forget you said it, but for God's sake don't say anything like it in front of the coppers."

"So what do we do now? Do you think I shouldn't tell the police anything about what was said at the hospital?"

"Before I answer that can I ask if you have ever talked to Philip, or anyone else for that matter, about this on any other occasion; maybe on the phone or at work?"

Sam did not need to think about her answer and immediately gave a very positive, "No. Never. Not to anyone."

"So, who is this person who's given the police a statement suggesting that he murdered Teresa? It must be someone that Philip has spoken to. I'll obviously have to ask him, but do you think he could have discussed this with anyone else?"

Again Sam did not need to think about it, but didn't want to give any reason for Edward to learn why she was so certain that she was the only person Philip would talk to about anything so personal, so all she said was, "I wouldn't have thought so."

They were both silent for a while; each trying to work out what was likely to happen now. The reasoning of each of them was however quite different from the other's. For Edward it was a case of trying to determine what was the best way to proceed in the best interests of Philip, guilty or not.

For Samantha it was a case of regret that she hadn't talked Philip out of even contemplating such a thing. Why had they been so concerned about Teresa's feelings and wishes? She wanted to turn the clock back and talk him out of even taking Teresa home. Why hadn't she talked him out of it?

She wanted to scream with guilt and anger at herself for not doing the right thing for Philip as all sorts of thoughts went through her mind. *'Why have we always worried about doing the right thing for Teresa and Edward? Why didn't we think about ourselves for once and realise that the idea of helping Teresa was bound to backfire? Why were we so stupid?'* And for the first time ever she felt anger against Teresa.

Ever since she first met Philip and fallen in love with him, she had regarded Teresa as a totally innocent party, and one who had never deserved to have her husband fall in love with someone else. At first she had felt the same way about Edward, but, as far as she was concerned he had relinquished that right a long time ago. She had stayed with him for Louise's sake, but also because she did not want to create problems for Teresa. But now all the sympathy and compassion for Teresa deserted her and she could only feel contempt for her. She wanted to shout out, *'How dare you have put the man I love in this position?'* Her head was throbbing and she had to try desperately hard to stop herself from declaring out loud, *'I hate you. I hate you for doing this to him.'*

It was Edward who roused her from her thoughts and the anger that was starting to consume her, "As I see it, no matter what happened and no matter what Philip said or didn't say, we have to convince the police one or two things. Firstly that Teresa died naturally. That's if anyone can say that dying in the pain she was in was natural. We know the consultant will say that she was going to die at any time and that her death was totally expected. On the other hand if the autopsy…," he stopped and looked directly at Samantha before continuing, "If the autopsy shows a different story, then we have to try to convince them that she took her own life and that Philip had nothing to do with it."

Samantha suddenly brightened, and for the first time in years wanted to hug her husband for giving her a glimpse of hope that he may be able to get Philip out of here without being charged, "And do you think you could do that?"

Edward smiled and gently touched his wife's hand, "Well we can only try, can't we?"

She shuddered as a sudden thought crossed her mind, "But I don't think Philip would want people to think that Teresa committed suicide."

Edward took her hands in his, looked directly at her and replied, "Well if it turns out that there's a problem with the autopsy, I'll just have to convince him otherwise, won't I? Suicide hasn't been a criminal matter for the last ten years, so the police won't be interested if we can convince them that's what happened." He squeezed her hand tighter, "But it'll be a totally different matter if they think Philip had anything to do with it. Assisting someone commit suicide is still a very serious criminal matter, and from what you've said, I guess that's what the police think may have happened."

"Oh my God, so you think he could be in trouble?"

"Look let's take this thing a step at a time shall we? If the autopsy throws up nothing out of the ordinary then I'm sure I can get Philip home in no time."

"And if it does?"

"Then we'll have to deal with it, won't we?"

Meanwhile Philip was lying on the bed in a cell trying to work out what was going on. His head had been throbbing ever since the incident in the church and what had started as a dull ache at the back of his skull had now developed into a constantly pulsating pain. He had never before suffered from headaches, but then he had never before been accused of murder either! Question after question had been racing through his mind without any answers being provided. *'How on earth have I ended up here? Who's given them a statement and what does it say? What do the police know? Why have they brought Sam in for questioning? What do they think she can tell them?'*

It was these last two questions that made him sit up with determination; a determination to make sure that Samantha wasn't dragged into this mess. Whatever was going to happen to him, he had to protect her all costs.

'Now think this out carefully, Philip Matthews. You are in a mess and the sooner you work out how to get out of it the better.'

He thought of Samantha's approach to any problem. Make a list of the difficulties; make a list of possible solutions; then make a final list of the preferred resolution and stick to it. *'No pen and paper, so I'll just have to do it in my head.'* He laughed out aloud as he realised that to do it on paper would be absolutely no solution if the police found it. *'Better in my head anyway. I wish Sam was here. It's so much easier to work out rational and logical answers to problems when we're doing it together.'*

For the first time since he had been put in this cell he spoke out aloud, "Where are you Samantha?" The thought of what she was going through at that moment increased the pain at the back of his head, which now felt as if someone had thumped him with a baseball bat. "I'm sorry sweetheart. What have I done to you?"

His concentration on Samantha nevertheless seemed to make his own predicament less important and he determined to get both of them out of the mess they were in. In an effort to stop thinking of where she was and the interrogation that the police were putting her through, he imagined that Samantha was in front of him helping him with the problem, and he started to put the questions to her so that they could collectively solve them.

"First, who is it that's accused me of murder and given them a statement? And why on earth do the police want to talk to you Samantha? I've never talked to you about what happened after Teresa came home, so there's nothing you can tell them is there?"

'But we did chat at the hospital about what Teresa wanted.'

"Yes that's true, but I didn't say what I was going to do. I was still very confused about what was right for Teresa."

He smiled and pointed his finger to the imaginary Samantha as question one was immediately answered for him. "But that's where this witness was, wasn't it? It's the only time I've spoken to anyone about what Teresa wanted."

He immediately imagined Samantha back in the interview room and with all the love he could muster he willed her to tell them exactly as it had happened. "Don't lie to them Sam. If you do, they'll only play one of us off against the other. We can't possibly tell them the same lies, so just tell them the truth that Teresa wanted to come home to die and I'll sort the rest out." He smiled to himself, knowing that if she told things as they were, then problem one was solved, "If we both just say that, then it's the word of two of us against what one other person thinks they did or did not hear."

He desperately wanted to be in the interview room with her and just hold her to him for a few minutes. He repeated over and over in his head for her to tell the truth, but eventually felt that she had responded positively to him and she was back in front of him saying, *'So what's the next problem.'*

"Finding out who's dropped us in this mess."

'Can't do that yet, so don't worry about it; go on to the next problem.'

"OK. Now what do I say about what actually happened at home?"

'Can't you tell them exactly what happened at home?'

Philip drew a deep breath as he tried to work out how sensible it was to do this, "Not a good idea in the circumstances."

'What circumstances?'

"I'll tell you exactly what happened when we're alone together. I was going to do that anyway when I could, but first there are a couple of other problems we need to deal with."

'What problems?'

"The post mortem and what happened to the drugs."

'Well, what will the post mortem find?'

"That she was dying of cancer and that she'd taken morphine for the pain."

'And is that all?'

"I'd have thought that was enough isn't it? She's dead, and she wouldn't be if she hadn't had cancer eating away at everything inside her, so let's just leave it. They'll find what they find and that's that."

'You don't want to talk about it?'

"No. I'll tell you everything later, but whatever the pathologist says I still have to explain the missing medicine."

'But the police won't know about that if you don't tell them.'

"They will when they find the bottle."

'You mean you didn't get rid of it?'

"No. After she died I just put the bottle in the kitchen cupboard with all the other medicines. It's still there."

'So, just don't tell the police it's there.'

"But they're sure to ask me and if I lie about it and then they get a warrant to search for it, I'll be in a deeper mess if I haven't told them where it is."

'So you have to tell them if they ask?'

"Absolutely, and that leads us to the next question. How do I explain the missing morphine? They'll know she shouldn't have had that much between leaving hospital and when she died."

'And you can't tell them?'

"I could, but that would only give me more grief and they wouldn't let me go that easily."

'So what are you going to say?'

Philip sat back and thought about this long and hard before replying, "I'll have to lie. There's no other way."

'Not a good idea to lie. If they think you're lying they won't let it go and it'll come back to haunt you.'

"But I can't tell them what really happened. That'll just prove I had wanted her to die and they'll never let that go, will they?"

'So what will you say?'

Philip sat back and pondered about this over and over. It was a full twenty minutes before he'd worked out the full answer he was going to give to the last question. It was another half an hour before he had determined all the answers to all the other questions he felt certain he was going to be asked.

"And so Mrs Richards, before we start this interview can I just make sure that you want your husband to act for you? Are you sure you wouldn't rather have a different solicitor here?"

Edward interrupted before Samantha could answer, "Why on earth would my wife want another solicitor here Sergeant? I think it would be better if you just got on with the interview. My wife has no idea what you want to ask her about, so the sooner we start the sooner this nonsense will be over."

DS Moore ignored his remarked and looked directly at Sam and asked, "And do you want your husband here Mrs Richards? We can get another solicitor for you if you would rather."

Edward went to speak again but the DS held his hand up to stop him speaking, "I'd like Mrs Richards to answer the question please. I may have to ask some questions that she'd rather not answer with you here."

Edward got to his feet and leaned forward until his face was only inches from the sergeant's, "And what questions would they be?"

"Please Mr Richards, it's precisely because you are obviously emotionally involved in this matter that I'm asking Mrs Richards the question." He turned to Sam again, "So Mrs Richards do you want a different solicitor here?"

Sam held out her arm pushing Edward back into his seat before answering, "I'm fine with my husband being here, so can we just get this whole thing over with please?"

"Fine if that's what you want. Can I start then by asking what your relationship is with Mr Matthews?"

"He's my husband's cousin and best friend and since I married Edward he's become a good friend to me as well."

"And that's all he is; just a friend?"

"Well no he's also my boss. I work for him. I'm his chief accountant."

"And that's all?"

"Yes that's all. He's my boss and a good friend. What else do you want me to say?"

"I just want you to tell me the truth."

Edward leaned forward in his seat, "My wife has answered your question so can we just get on with it?"

"Fine, let's do that." He looked in the folder he had brought into the room with him and read from a paper from within it before turning to face Sam again, "Can you tell me, Mrs Richards, what happened when Mr Matthews met you in the canteen at the hospital a week last Wednesday?"

"You mean the Wednesday before Teresa died?"

"Yes the Wednesday before she came out of hospital."

"Well nothing happened. We had a cup of tea and a piece of cake and we sat and chatted whilst we drank the tea."

"But what did Mr Matthews do before he sat down?"

"He didn't do anything. He sat down and I went to fetch him a cup of tea."

"He didn't kiss you?"

"I can't remember whether he did or he didn't."

"So he kisses you so often that you can't remember when it happens?"

Edward leaned forward in his chair again and almost spat his words at the detective, "What the hell are you getting at? We've already told you that Philip is our best friend. Good male friends often give a female friend a kiss on the cheek when they meet. I do it all the time, don't you? If he did kiss her then that's all that happened." He turned to Sam, "That's what happened, isn't it Sam?"

DS Moore was not fazed in the least by Edward's outburst and spoke very firmly to him in response, "Please don't try and put words into your wife's mouth, Mr Richards. Please remember you are here as her solicitor, and not her husband. If you want to act the husband bit then I shall have to ask you to leave and we'll get another solicitor for your wife as I suggested in the first place."

Edward was suitably admonished and decided, difficult though it was, to only act the solicitor part from now on, and try as best he could to keep all emotion out of the proceedings. He responded to the detective with a mere, "OK."

"Right then Mrs Richards, did Mr Matthews kiss you when he came to the table?"

"I suppose he may have done, but like my husband said, if he did it was only the sort of kiss on the cheek he often gives me when we meet or part."

He looked at the paper in his folder again, "So what would you say if I told you that I have a witness statement here claiming that he hugged you and gave you a passionate kiss?"

Samantha wanted to say, *'Then he must have been reading our minds,'* but avoided doing so and stated truthfully, "I'd say categorically that he was lying."

The sergeant stayed totally expressionless by this reply and Samantha could not tell whether he believed her or not. "So tell me Mrs Richards, what did you talk about?"

"We talked about Teresa. What else would we talk about?"

"I'll ask the questions if you don't mind Mrs Richards."

Samantha had decided before the interview started that she would not let the police put her down or act in anyway superior to her, so ignoring his jibe, she looked directly at him, and said, "What's your name Sergeant?"

"I've already told you. I'm DS Moore."

"Yes I know that but what's your Christian name?"

"What on earth do you need to know that for?"

"Well my name is Samantha and that's what I'd like you to address me as, instead of this Mrs Richards all the time. Or Sam will be fine if you prefer it. Now what do I call you? After all, as you said, I'm only here to help you with your enquiries, and as neither of us has anything to hide, let's be a bit less formal about it all. So what do I call you? Your Christian name I mean?"

His head was telling him to ignore her remarks and keep referring to her as Mrs Richards, but maybe if he got her to relax she might slip up and say more than she wanted to, so he told her his name, "It's Martin."

Sam immediately turned to the other policeman, "And what's your name, DC Onions?"

He almost spluttered at being asked the question but answered anyway. "Robert. Robert Onions. But you can call me Robbie if you want to, everyone else does."

"Robbie that's a nice name." She immediately turned to the Sergeant, "So Martin, what was it you wanted to know?"

He turned to his folder again, but this time it was more of a diversionary tactic rather than to read from the document and it was several seconds before he spoke.

'Success! I've won that round. Now all I have to do is win the contest,' Samantha thought as she waited for him to speak, *'Don't worry Philip I'm not going to let you down. They think I've started to relax but I'll not say anything stupid. I promise you.'*

"Mrs Rich….," he stopped himself mid word and started again, "Samantha. Can you tell me precisely what you spoke about?"

"We talked about Teresa."

"Yes, but what did you say about her precisely?"

"I can't remember word for word, but we obviously talked about how ill she was."

"And what did Mr Matthews say about that?"

"What was there to say? She was dying. She knew that. We knew that. In fact everyone knew that. It wasn't a case of was she going to die, it was simply a question of when and where."

"And Mr Matthews wanted to help that along?"

Edward leaned forward and Samantha knew he was about to explode again, but she held out her hand to stop him speaking, "It's all right Edward; I'll answer his question for him."

She then turned back to face her inquisitor, and trying to keep as calm and composed as she could said, "He knew she was in great pain and that she wanted to be able to die in her own home with her husband at her bedside. He didn't want her to die, but he knew he couldn't do anything at all to stop it. So he was going to do as she asked and take her home to die. And that's it; that's what we talked about and all I did was listen to him and try to comfort him in his own pain."

"And did that include discussing helping her on her way?"

The question she had been dreading had finally been put!! Samantha had already determined her answer to this question; the same answer that she felt certain Philip would give when he was asked the same question, "I don't know what you are implying Martin, but I've told you all that was said. Philip was taking her home to die, in what I suppose a religious person would say was the time chosen by God."

"And are you religious?"

"Not in that sense. But I can assure you that no other person determined when she was going to die."

"Not even Mrs Matthews herself?"

"Don't let's get into philosophical questions like that Martin. She was dying. She knew she was dying and I think any strength she may have had to fight against it had gone. So if that means she gave up and died in her own time then I couldn't argue against that."

Now it was Martin's turn to have unspoken questions in his head. *'How the hell did we get here? She's telling me that the woman just decided she wanted to die, so she just died. Get your act together, Martin Moore before this woman makes a fool of you.'*

He fumbled with his papers again pretending to read from one of the documents, "So what would you say if I told you that I have a statement here that claims that you and Mr Matthews discussed ways of, shall we say, assisting Mrs Matthews on her way?"

Samantha again spoke before Edward could stop her and ask to see the document he kept referring to. "I'd say he was lying."

"And that's it? He's a liar?"

Samantha summoned up all the strength she could to make sure she gave a composed and unhesitating answer, "Yes. I have no idea why he'd say such a thing but whoever he is, he's a liar."

Before the DS could say any more, Edward firmly said, "I think Mrs Richards has answered all your questions and told you all she has to say on the matter. This witness you say you have is at the very least, exaggerating the facts. I'm sure Mr Matthews will say the same thing as Mrs Richards, so unless you are going to show me this statement I suggest you let Mrs Richards go."

The detective was about to speak when there was a knock on the door. A very annoyed DS Moore shouted, "Come in." A uniformed policeman entered and gave him a note. He read the note, before handing it to his colleague to read. "Fine Mr Richards, you can take your wife home now, but I would ask that neither of you discusses this matter with anyone; well at least until after we've interviewed Mr Matthews." He looked at his watch before continuing, "I make it ten minutes to two now and Mr Oldfield, the consultant, has agreed to see us at quarter past, so we'd better get on our way if we aren't going to keep him waiting." He collected his papers together, got out of his seat, and was still talking as he made his way to the door, "I shouldn't think we'll be very long with him, so why don't you take your wife home and get back here for say quarter past three and we can interview Mr Matthews straight away when we get back?"

Edward jumped out of his seat, and ignoring Samantha followed him into the corridor, "And I'll have a chat with Mr Matthews whilst you're away."

"I'll speak to the desk sergeant as soon as I get back to arrange that."

"Wouldn't it be easier if I spoke to him whilst you are away?"

The DS stopped abruptly, turned round and spoke firmly to Edward, "No it would not Mr Richards, now if you'll let me get on my way, I'll see you around three-fifteen and you can speak to him then," and with that he whipped round and strode rapidly out of the station.

Edward walked back into the station at exactly three-fifteen to find DS Moore and DC Onions standing at the desk waiting for him. Moore looked at his watch and smirked, "Good timing Mr Richards. Now let's get on with interviewing Mr Matthews shall we?"

"Not until I've spoken to my client."

"Well of course you can see Mr Matthews but the desk sergeant here has already asked him about that and apparently he said he doesn't need to chat to you about anything before we interview him."

Edward took a step closer to DS Moore and looked at him as aggressively as he could, "I shall need to hear that from Mr Matthews himself."

"Of course Mr Richards; you can ask him in the interview room and if he wants to then we'll just leave you to it."

Edward was shown back to the same interview room and he sat patiently and silently opposite the two detectives whilst they waited for Philip. As soon as Philip entered the room, Edward got up and gave him a bear hug before the uniformed policeman who had brought him into the room could stop him. "Don't worry Philip I'm sure we'll get this sorted out in no time."

Philip stood back and smiled, "I'm not worried, Edward. I've done nothing wrong."

"Good. Good. Then let's have a chat before these officers interview you. I need to get a few things sorted with you before you're interviewed."

Philip had already decided that he did not want the police to think he and Edward were cooking up some story together. If nothing else, he didn't want to draw Edward into the deception he'd worked out ready for the interview. It was bad enough that Sam had been dragged into this mess, without making it worse by involving Edward unnecessarily.

He spoke firmly and loud enough to make sure that the seated policemen could hear, "There's only one thing you need to know Edward, and that's that I didn't kill Teresa, and neither the police nor anyone else can prove otherwise, because it didn't happen."

DC Moore gently clapped his hands together and smiled as he sarcastically said, "Well done, Mr Matthews, now if you sit down we'll see how true that is, shall we?"

Philip bit his lip and wondered whether he had been wrong in making the protestation so quickly, but he heard Samantha in his head telling him to *'Calm down, Philip. He's only trying to get you riled. He's got no proof of anything so don't let him get to you,'* and with that he said again quite firmly, "I'm sure we shall, officer. I'm sure we shall."

"OK Mr Matthews let's get started." But the officer's first question was not one that had even crossed his mind, "Tell me Mr Matthews are you having an affair with Mrs Richards?"

Philip blinked and threw his head back at this unforeseen question, but nevertheless quickly answered, "I beg your pardon?"

"It's a simple question requiring a simple 'yes' or 'no' answer, Mr Matthews. Are you having an affair with Mrs Richards?"

This time Philip answered with a firm, "No I am not," thankful that the question had been put in the present tense. If he had asked, "Have you ever been lovers?" no matter how much he may have wanted to say 'No' he did not think that he could have denied his feelings for Samantha by lying.

DS Moore was not in the least surprised at the answer. He had never expected him to admit to it even if it was true. Not in front of the woman's husband, anyway. But at least the way the question had been answered so positively and unflinchingly had shown him that the man in front of him was not going to be a pushover. It also confirmed his view that it would be a waste of time to go over the same questions he'd asked Mrs Richards. He would undoubtedly get the same answers he had from Samantha, so he moved on to something else that he hoped might throw him.

The next question was again unexpected by Philip, "Tell me, Mr Matthews, why did you kill your wife?"

Edward was about to object to the question but Philip stopped him speaking, "It's all right Edward, I don't mind answering the question." He turned his head to face his inquisitors and said unhesitatingly, "I haven't killed anyone." He then looked at Edward and smiled before turning back to face the DS, "No, unfortunately that's not true. Regrettably I have to admit that I did kill during the war." He leaned forward and looked straight into the officer's eyes, "But I did not kill my wife."

The officer was unmoved by the remark and immediately came back with his next, and again unexpected, question, "You sure about that, Sir? Are you telling me that your wife didn't ask you to?"

Philip leaned forward again, "I'm telling you that I did not kill my wife. End of story."

"I would prefer it if you would answer the question I actually asked you, Sir?" But this time Edward did manage to speak before Philip, "My client has answered the question, Sergeant, so can we move on and get all this baloney over with. Mr Matthews has told you that he did not kill his wife, so unless you have something to suggest otherwise, can we all just go home."

Philip flinched at Edward even suggesting that there may be something else. He wondered if it would not have been better if he wasn't there, but, on balance, he was pleased not to be totally on his own.

"OK Mr Richards, then let's move on shall we?" He took a copy of the Walsall Observer from under his folder and opened it at the Notices of Deaths page. "Tell me Mr Matthews, when exactly did you fetch your wife out of hospital?"

"Last Friday. Why?"

"Yes I know that, but what time exactly?"

"I collected her after lunch."

"And what time did you get home?"

I don't know about three o'clock or maybe just after. I had more important things to deal with than looking at the clock."

"Like how to assist your wife to die, do you mean?"

Philip just peered directly at him and smiled, without speaking.

"You aren't going to answer that question, are you?"

Philip could hear Samantha telling him clearly, *'You'll have to be very careful what you say to this one Philip. If you're not careful he'll lead you into a 'catch 22' situation and you don't want to let him draw you into that trap,'* so he again said nothing but merely smiled.

DS Moore smiled back. He felt certain that the subject of speeding up her death had been discussed between this man and his wife, but he was rapidly beginning to realise that it wasn't going to be easy to get him to admit to it. "So you got home at shall we say three o'clock?"

"It was probably a bit later than that."

"Never mind let's leave it at three. Was there only you there with your wife when you got home?"

"No. Well my sister-in-law Jane had helped me fetch my wife from the hospital, so she was there of course. And Mrs Richards and my Aunt Alice were already at the house. They'd been getting the room ready for Teresa."

"The bedroom, you mean?"

"No, we'd put the bed in the lounge. It's at the back of the house, so Teresa could see the garden through the French windows."

Philip detected a hint of cynicism in his, "That's nice," before Moore continued his questions, "And what time did they leave?"

"Oh, I don't know. Maybe half past four, or it may have been nearer five."

Edward interrupted, "Where is all this leading us? What does it matter when people came and went?"

The detective held up his hand, "I'm coming to that in a minute, Sir. Just let Mr Matthews answer the questions will you please?" He then picked up the newspaper and passed it across to Philip, pointing to an item that he had encircled in red, "This is this morning's Walsall Observer, Mr Matthews. Do you mind telling me what that is?"

Philip was now totally flummoxed by the line of questioning. There was hardly a question that had been asked that he had worked out the answer to in his cell, "It's the notice I put in the paper about my wife's death and the funeral."

"And what does it say about her death?

Philip furrowed his brow in disbelief at the line of questioning, as he read the start of the insert, "It says, 'Teresa Matthews, nee Hunter, wife of Philip Matthews, died peacefully in her sleep during the night of October 13th." He went to read on, but the officer stopped him.

"That's fine Mr Matthews; you can leave it there for the time being. So your wife died last Friday? Friday the thirteenth in fact; unlucky choice of day, Friday thirteenth, don't you think?"

Edward could not let the jibe go unchecked, "That's a totally uncalled for comment, Sergeant. Someone's death is not a thing to be joked about. So please keep such unnecessary observations to yourself, and get to the point." He raised his voice, to make his own point, "If there is one!"

"Oh, there's a point all right, Mr Richards."

"Then please get on with it."

DS Moore ignored the comment and asked his next question of Philip, "So what time did your wife die then?"

"I have no idea, during the night sometime. I found her dead when I awoke the next morning."

"But she went to sleep at what time?"

"I don't know, maybe ten or ten-thirty. Something like that anyway."

"And whilst your wife was asleep downstairs where were you?"

"Asleep on the bed with her."

"In the same bed?"

"No, I said, 'ON' the bed. I was lying on the bed holding her and I fell asleep when I knew she was asleep."

DS Moore fumbled with his papers, trying to determine whether he would get away with asking if Philip had stayed with her to make sure that whatever he had done was working, but decided against it. "So, Mr Matthews you got home from the hospital at three, three-thirty, and your wife goes to sleep say seven hours later and doesn't wake up. How do you explain that?"

"She died of cancer. Do you want to see the death certificate?"

The officer again ignored his remark and continued as if nothing had been said, "Do you know where I've just been Mr Matthews?"

"No, but I'm sure you're going to tell me."

"I've been to see your wife's consultant, Michael Oldfield, and do you know what he said when I told him that your wife was dead within hours of getting home?" Philip merely shrugged his shoulders and DS Moore continued without waiting for an answer. He took what appeared to be a statement from his folder and read from it, "His exact words were, 'I'm surprised she died that quickly'. What do you say to that Mr Matthews?"

Edward prevented Philip from answering by holding out his hand and asked to see the statement, "I'm sure that isn't all he said, so can I see what else is in his statement?"

DS Moore quickly put the paper back in his folder without allowing Edward to see it, "You can read it later Mr Richards, but for now let's move on shall we?" He ignored Edward's protestations at this action and proceeded with his next line of questions, "Tell me Mr Matthews, I understand that your wife was in a great deal of pain. Did the hospital give you anything to help her with that?"

"Yes, they gave her morphine."

"You mean they gave YOU the morphine to give to her as prescribed."

"Yes, they gave it to me."

"I understand that she had a dose immediately before leaving hospital so how many more doses did you give her before she went to sleep?"

"Two"

"And I take it the rest is still in the bottle?"

'The sixty-four thousand dollar question at last!!' "Yes, what's left of it. It's in the medicine cupboard in the kitchen at home."

"And we can collect that later, can we?"

"If you want to, yes of course. I was wondering what I should do with it anyway."

"And we'll find a full bottle less a couple of doses?"

'This is it Philip. Make sure you get this right and don't let him flummox you now.' "You'll find what's left, but we spilled some of it so there's more missing than the two doses I gave her."

The two officers looked at each other and grinned. Philip could almost read their unspoken words of 'we've got him now.'

"So, how did that happen, Mr Matthews?"

"I was giving Teresa her second dose, when she coughed and knocked the bottle out of my hand. I grabbed it as quickly as I could but some of it had spilled on the bed."

The two men looked at each other again and this time the grin turned into a great smirk of delight and the DS said, "Very convenient Mr Matthews. Very convenient."

But this was the conversation and the questions that Philip had fully expected and so his responses were now almost on auto pilot, "Not convenient at all. It made Teresa very distressed and I had to try and clean up the mess as quickly as I could without making her pain worse."

"And how did you do that?"

"How did I clean up the mess? I mopped it up with tissues."

"But the bedclothes will still be marked won't they?"

'Exactly the next expected question.' "I guess so, but I burned all the bedclothes."

Edward put his head in his hands. He could not believe what Philip was admitting to. It sounded so implausible to him and he was sure that neither of the men opposite believed a word of it either. He wanted to drag Philip out of the room and advise him not to answer any more questions, but his friend was not in the least bit perturbed, and in fact seemed to be enjoying himself, so he did nothing. For their part, neither officer could contain their delight at the way this was going any longer, and both of them simultaneously let out a guffaw of laughter. It took DS Moore several seconds to compose himself sufficiently to continue, "As I said Mr Matthews all very convenient, isn't it?"

It was now time for Philip to put forward his final piece of bluff. He just hoped his histrionic ability would not let him down. He put his hand to his mouth and let out an, "Oh, my God," before taking his hand away from his face and pointing a finger at the two men opposite and adding, "You both think I gave my wife an overdose, don't you? And that's why you've arrested me, isn't it?" This time he joined in their laughter, but nevertheless crossed his fingers under the table before continuing, "Well let me tell you that that's rubbish and the post mortem will prove it."

"We shall see, Mr Matthews, we shall see."

The interview continued for another hour covering all the same ground over and over again, but Philip kept exactly to his plans and they failed to get him to admit to anything other than spilling the medicine and burning the bedclothes. It was true that he had burned all of the bedclothes, but not because of a spill but because they had been covering Teresa when she died and were soiled. The burned remains were still in the incinerator at the bottom of the garden if the police wanted to check. Eventually, DS Moore realised he would not get any different answers no matter how many times he went over things and decided to talk about Philip's meeting with Samantha in the hospital canteen, and was not in the least surprised that Philip's answers were similar to hers.

Edward was certain that Philip was holding something back but, by the way he was dealing with all of the questions, he gradually became certain that whatever it was, neither he nor anyone else was ever going to find out his secret. His friend seemed so relaxed about it all, that he had to accept he knew what he was doing and so, for most of the time, he just sat back and let the bantering between the contenders continue unchecked.

Finally however he'd had enough of this policeman and decided it was time to get his own way at last, "I think my client has answered all your questions adequately, and as far as I can see you have absolutely no cause to continue questioning him. And you certainly have nothing to justify keeping him here. So unless you are going to present us with some evidence, I suggest it's time to let us go home."

"I've got statements here that throw doubt on what your client is saying and we'll have the results of the autopsy by mid-day on Monday."

"Fine, then show me the statements now, or we're going home."

Reluctantly DS Moore took the statements from his folder and handed them to Edward.

He read the one from the consultant first but, as he had expected, it clearly said that Teresa had a terminal illness and that he expected her to die within days. Although it did say he had not expected her to die quite so soon, he had also said that no-one could determine at her stage of the illness whether she would last weeks, days, or even hours. He even said that in his experience the patient often died at the time they chose and he knew that Teresa had wanted to die at home with her husband there and felt that was exactly what had happened. He passed the statement back to the officer, "That gives you absolutely nothing, sergeant and you know it."

He then turned to the other lengthier statement and read, *'I read in this morning's Walsall Observer that Mrs Teresa Matthews, an ex-patient at the hospital where I work died last Friday. I was shocked when I read this because I had heard her husband Philip Matthews and Samantha Prior talking about taking her home so that they could assist her to die.'*

Before he was able to get any further, Philip, who had leaned across to also read the document, suddenly snatched it from Edward. He waved it in front of the policemen, "I take it that you've checked if I have a criminal record?"

"Yes, that is the usual practice when we arrest someone."

He continued waving the paper, "And is it your practice to check the criminal record of so called witnesses?"

Edward took Philip's arm and lowered it to the table, "Of course they don't. Why are you asking?"

"Look at this here. Michael Burbridge gave them this statement."

Both policemen looked quite bemused, "So what?" piped up DC Onions.

"So what?" He waved the statement in their faces again, "Well Michael Burbridge used to work for me and he defrauded my company out of thousands of pounds. He got sent down for three years and when they were taking him down he threatened to get me and Samantha for it. Don't you think you ought to consider that and then decide how reliable his accusation is?" And with that, he dropped the paper on the table and sat back waiting for their response.

DS Moore scratched his head, saying, "We'll do that Mr Matthews and now I'll arrange for your bail. I'll want you back here at four o'clock on Monday afternoon. I'll have the autopsy result by then and we may have plenty more questions to ask."

Both Edward and Philip stood up and made their way to the door without saying another word, but DS Moore stopped them, "You don't mind if DC Onions comes with you and collects that bottle and the remains of your incinerator now though, do you?"

Philip smiled and said, almost with a gleam on his face, "Not at all, officer. Be my guest."

Philip entered his office at eight-thirty on the following Tuesday morning to find Samantha sitting waiting for him. As soon as the door had closed behind him, she got up from her seat and threw her arms around him, "I'm so glad that everything's been sorted out and you're not going to spend the next few years in prison."

The tensions and anxieties of the last few days had taken their toll on both of them. Neither had been concerned for their own jeopardy, but the stress of not knowing what the other was going through had been unbearable for each of them. They had both been aching for this moment ever since the police had arrested Philip at the funeral. Philip pulled Samantha closer to him, closing his eyes to fully savour the luxury and warmth of her body against his. He had not held her this close for such a long time and he did not want the pleasure of the moment to end. He wanted to kiss her but knew that a single kiss would never be sufficient and, much as his body was willing him to act differently, he gave her one last squeeze and gently pulled away from her.

"I think we should sit down," he said before smiling and adding, "And perhaps it would be better if we didn't sit on the same chair."

She stood unmoving, waiting and aching for him to take her in his arms again, but she knew from the look in his eyes, that to do so would be a step too far; a step beyond which neither of them would be satisfied until their need for each other had been satiated. She sat down and waited for Philip to sit in his chair on the opposite side of the desk. Neither of them spoke for several minutes but just stared across the table at each other, taking deep breaths in an attempt to take control of their own desires and return the situation to the acceptable moral position demanded by society from a married man and a married woman who were not wedded to each other.

It was Samantha who eventually spoke, "I'm so relieved that you're here. I've been so worried."

Philip smiled and gripped the sides of his chair to prevent himself from getting up and kissing her, "I was really worried when they took you to the police station and at first I thought they'd arrested you as well. I was going out of mind but, thank God, I managed to clear my head enough to sort out what I was going to tell them."

"Edward has told me everything you told the police but there are still a few things I don't understand."

"Such as?"

"Such as, did everything happen as you told them? I was so scared that you might have to lie to them."

"Well I didn't have to exactly lie, but I wasn't able to tell them 'the truth, the whole truth and nothing but the truth' either. But you know don't you, that I could never admit that to anyone but you?"

She threw him a kiss as she said, "Thank you," and then said, "On second thoughts it's probably best if you don't tell me either."

This time he did get up from his chair and went round the table to give her the kiss he had wanted to give her ever since he entered the room. It was a long, gentle kiss that fully expressed the depth of his love for her, but was undemanding of anything greater at that moment. He returned to his seat without either of them touching the other in any other way, "But I do have to tell you what went on. I'm not proud of what I did and I've been terribly confused by the whole thing ever since I woke to find Teresa dead at my side. I just hope you'll understand and not feel too badly of me."

She said, "I could never do that." as she lifted herself from her chair and began to go towards Philip, but he held up his hand and shook his head from side to side, showing that to do so was not a good idea.

She sat down, "I only want you to tell me if it feels right for you. For me that kiss said everything I need to know and the rest doesn't matter any more."

He smiled again and reached out across the table so that he could touch her hand, "But I have to tell you. You mean far too much to me and I don't want there to be any secrets between us."

There was a knock on the door and he released her hand before calling "Come in." Philip was surprised that it was Jane carrying a tray with mugs of steaming tea on it, "What on earth are you doing here? Have you decided to come back to work now that all the children are at school?"

She looked a little embarrassed as she answered, "Oh, no! It's half term and my mother's looking after them today. John is supposed to be taking me out for the day, but he had to come here and sort something out first. I saw you both arrive," she said as she placed the tray on the desk, "And I thought you could both probably do with a cup of tea." She went to Philip's side of the desk and kissed him on the cheek, a thing she had never done at work before, "I'm so glad you are back with us, Philip, we've been so worried about you all weekend. John said that it was that porter at the hospital who told all those lies about you. Why on earth would he want to get you into trouble like that?"

"It's a long story Jane. I'll tell you all about it when I next come to see you."

Jane touched his arm as she moved away, "And don't forget if there's anything John or I can do for you then please let us know. We both knew that all the stuff he told the police was absolute rubbish."

Philip knew that all she said was honestly and sincerely meant; it was impossible for Jane to do otherwise. He caught her hand as she moved away, "Thank you Jane that means a lot to me. And tell that brother of mine to pack in whatever he's doing and take his wife out for a treat. I'll pop over and see you both later in the week and tell you everything that went on at the police station." She gave him another one of her embarrassed smiles and as she rushed to the door, Philip called after her, "I want to thank you both properly for everything you've done for me lately anyway. I couldn't have managed without you over the last few weeks."

She quickly opened the door and left without looking back at him. He knew that her face would be bright red at such the compliment.

He immediately returned his attention to Samantha, "Right, where do I start? As soon as you and Aunt Alice had left on the day Teresa came out of hospital, she talked to me about lots of things; things she'd never spoken of before. What she actually said really isn't important right now, but what is important is the way she said it to me and only to me. It was as though she had to unload it all before she died and it felt as if she needed me to know these things, not as her husband, but as the one person she trusted; almost as her final confessor. Whether I'm right in thinking that or not doesn't matter, but what does matter is that I know she trusted me to keep those things to myself and not repeat them to others. All of it was about Teresa herself, and much as I'd like to talk to you about what she said, right now I feel that to do so would be totally wrong. But what is relevant is that I need you to understand the effect it had on me."

Samantha looked puzzled, "I don't understand what you mean. How did it have an effect on you?"

He took a swig of his tea before continuing, "Well, somehow it made me feel close to her. I can't explain it, but I think I felt closer to her as I lay there listening to her than I've ever felt, even before I met you. And what's more I think she knew it."

Samantha took her mug from off the table and drank from it as she waited silently for Philip to continue.

"Anyway I needed you to know that, because I think it determined everything I did that day from thereon." He looked across the table and waited until she had finished her drink so that they were again making eye contact with each other, "Actually I'm still a little confused by it all. The feelings I had then just haven't gone away. It's as if she needs me to mourn for her because she was afraid that nobody else would miss her."

"That's nonsense. We all miss her."

He was silent and thoughtful for a moment, "Maybe; maybe, but I'd best move on or else we'll be here all morning."

"So what happened after that?"

"Well we talked about how she wanted it all to end and she said she didn't want to wait any longer."

Samantha merely looked at him as he tried to form the right words to carry on. He sat back in his chair and sighed, "She said she didn't think she'd be able to swallow enough of the stuff on its own and so I went into the kitchen, heated up a tin of chicken soup and poured maybe half the bottle of morphine into the soup." He downed the last drops of tea from his mug, "And that's the bit I couldn't tell the police. If I'd told them I'd done that they would never have let me go, would they?"

"But the autopsy report didn't say anything about finding unexpected quantities of the morphine."

"Exactly, because when I'd done it I just froze. My head was spinning, my stomach was churning and the way I felt for her at that moment completely overwhelmed me. I didn't want to lose her and I couldn't do it."

"I don't understand. Edward said the autopsy showed that the last thing she had eaten was the chicken soup."

"She did, but not the soup with the morphine in it."

"So you decided you couldn't do it?"

"Well, yes and no. I was in two minds about giving it to her, but what really made up my mind, was the fact that it didn't look anything like chicken soup when I'd mixed all the morphine into it. So I threw that soup down the sink; got out another can, heated that up and put just a single dose of the morphine into it, and that's what she ate."

"So you lied about spilling the morphine on the bedclothes to explain away the medicine missing from the bottle?"

"Well yes and no. That's where I didn't tell the whole truth again. Teresa couldn't eat all the soup and when I moved the dish away, somehow it got tipped over and I had to clean it up with tissues, just as I told them, except it was soup and not the morphine." He laughed as he added, "But there was a bit of the morphine in the soup wasn't there, so it wasn't a total lie?"

"So you knew all along that they wouldn't find anything against you, because you didn't help Teresa to die, did you?"

"I wish it was as simple as that, but it isn't. Teresa thought the morphine was in the soup and with the way I feel right now, I don't think I'll ever be able to forgive myself for that." A tear appeared in his eye, "She trusted me, Samantha. She thought she could trust me and I let her down. I deceived her and I shouldn't have done that."

"You shouldn't blame yourself. She wouldn't have wanted you to end up in prison, and that's what would have happened if you'd done as she wanted."

"That's not the point Sam. You see I was shocked the next morning when I found her dead. I wasn't expecting that. She should have still been alive and I would have been able to tell her why and asked her forgiveness, but she was dead. And you know what? I'm convinced that she died because as far as she was concerned, I'd given her the overdose she wanted. She didn't die only of the cancer because if she'd known about the soup, I'm convinced she'd have awoken the next morning. So you see, I did kill her or at least I assisted her to die, and the fact that the police can't charge me with anything doesn't change that."

Samantha suddenly understood all of what Philip had said and in an odd sort of way, it made perfect sense to her. She now understood why Philip had been so melancholic and uncommunicative since Teresa's death. He would have been able to accept anything thrown at him if he had done what Teresa had requested. He would also have been able to live with himself if he had been honest with Teresa about the soup, but whilst she had absolved herself of everything to Philip before her death, he had done completely the opposite and had deceived her, and now could not put that right.

Samantha put her mug down, got up from her seat, walked around the desk, and took Philip's head in her arms and pressed it against her stomach. They both remained like that for some time before Samantha said, "I do understand sweetheart, or at least I think I do."

She let go of his head, knelt on the floor next to him and again took his head in her hands. She kissed him full on the lips, with the same love and tenderness that he had earlier kissed her, before stating, "I'm here for you any time you need me." She kissed him lightly on the lips again, "I know that this isn't the right time to say what I'm going to, but I have to say it whilst I've got the nerve to do so." She hesitated as if questioning it herself before finally saying, "I still love you and maybe we shouldn't keep holding back on our feelings. I don't care when that happens. Next week, next year or five or six years down the line, I'll be waiting for you."

CHAPTER TWENTY- SIX

JULY 1976

Philip initially tried to overcome the tragedy of Teresa's death by immersing himself energetically and almost pathologically in work. In doing so he successfully and substantially increased the number of cash and carry out of town electrical retail warehouses, where the pile 'em high and sell 'em cheap philosophy was highly cost-effective and profitable. He also expanded the range of goods in the high street shops and these were now more profitable than they had ever been.

However this business success did not bring Philip any real satisfaction and he was now, at aged fifty-six, beginning to think seriously about retiring from the increasingly competitive rat race. The satisfaction and pleasure he had experienced when building up the business after the war had long gone. He no longer had the incentive to drive himself, and everyone else, merely to create a bigger and bigger company. The thing he had most wanted for the last twenty-three years of his life was not money and power, but to be with the woman he had loved from the moment he had met her. A move that would not only have meant losing his best friend but more importantly could have meant both him and Samantha losing the affection and trust of Louise and neither of them dared risk that.

He often thought about Samantha's comment after being released by the police but although he longed to take up her offer, it had never been mentioned again by either of them.

The one part of the business that was no longer successful was the manufacturing of radio equipment which had eventually ceased altogether some years earlier. The firm could no longer compete with the big manufacturers, particularly those in the Far East, and the whole of the old factory space was now exclusively John's domain.

After John had married Jane, he had made all the dining room furniture and all the kitchen cabinets for their home, and when two of the customers for whom John had made hi-fi cabinets, saw the furniture in the workroom, they had asked if he would make other pieces for them. Soon John had a full order book and had developed a design style which quickly became a recognised 'classic', and expensive, line of dining room furniture.

When he made his own furniture he had carved a ladybird on a small unopened rosebud somewhere on each piece. He had done this, hoping that it would amuse Jane when she found them. It was Jane who insisted he should do the same on every piece of furniture he produced, and the 'rose and ladybird' quickly became his exclusive trademark. By 1976, John had a staff of eight craftsmen, all of whom he had trained himself and the workshop was now, not only busy with an order book of over eighteen months, but was also the happiest workplace Philip had ever been in.

Louise had spent every available moment in the last few months studying hard to get the grades needed to ensure the place she had been conditionally given at Edinburgh University to study medicine and was at last enjoying the freedom of having just finished the last of her 'A level' exams.

Her father as the local MP was opening a school fête and had originally insisted that Louise should accompany him and her mother to it, but after another argument, Samantha had stepped in and told him it was only fair to let Louise relax a bit after all the work she had put in studying for her exams.

Louise had matured considerably over the last few years and not just physically. She was indeed no longer a little girl but a grown woman, who still occasionally made her mother's life hell. But more importantly, Louise's whole outlook on life had matured and, probably because of her Grandpa's influence, she now had well thought out and very well developed views on most of the real 'life issues' far beyond her years.

In her final year at school she had thought she might be made school captain but it was not to be. Louise would have been a popular choice with the other girls, but the headmistress, who had the final say, had chosen 'Perfect Pauline' instead. This was the nickname the girls had given Pauline Downing way back in their first year at the school. Although Pauline was perhaps the brightest girl in her year, even though Louise surpassed her in the sciences, Louise's downfall in the eyes of the headmistress was that she was always confronting and arguing with teachers, often with questions they could not answer; a trait she had picked up from her Grandpa Prior. Pauline on the other hand, had always been the perfect and deferential pupil that the school and teachers seemed to prefer.

Louise had soon got over her disappointment however and had immersed herself in her studies determined to get as good as, if not better, A level grades than 'Perfect Pauline'.

Having won the battle with her father not to go to the fête, she had spent the last couple of hours on her own, lying on the settee in the lounge, watching Chris Evert beat Evonne Cawley in the women's final at Wimbledon, and was anxiously looking forward to watching the twenty year old Bjorn Borg play against Ilie Nastase in the men's final, when the door bell rang.

She immediately got up from the settee to turn the sound down on the TV in the hope the visitor would go away and leave her in peace, but just then Bjorn Borg stepped on to the centre court for his match, and all the girls in the crowd went wild at their new idol. Even Louise could not help letting out a little scream as the handsome Swede, his long blond hair held off his face by the usual headband, looked towards the camera and smiled.

The doorbell rang again as Louise went to adjust the sound. "Oh just go away," she muttered under her breath, but the caller was persistent and the bell rang a third time.

Louise had been looking forward to watching the gorgeous athletic Bjorn in this match all day and now that it was about to start, she did not want some uninvited visitor spoiling her afternoon, so she decided to just ignore whoever was at the door, hoping they would leave her in peace.

She lay back on the sofa and curled herself into a tight ball. The doorbell did not ring a fourth time, "Thank goodness they've gone. Now I can enjoy this match I peace."

But no sooner had she got herself comfortable again, there was a loud knocking at the window. She tried to curl up into a tighter ball hoping the visitor could not see her, but the knocking got even louder and more persistent. Eventually she gave in and looked towards the window. Sally-Anne Hamilton was peering through the window, her face right up against the glass as she continued her rat-tat-tatting on the pane and as soon as Louise looked up, she started waving her arms about and pointing towards the front door demanding to be let in.

Sally-Anne was the same age as Louise and had been in the same 6th form class as Louise at the Grammar School. She had moved to the area from London with her family two years earlier when her father, Eric, had been recruited by Louise's Uncle Philip to head up the expanding warehouse chain. At first Louise had willingly spent some time with Sally-Anne, showing her around and making sure she settled in at school and they had become quite good friends. Recently however, Sally-Anne had spent all the time she could with her boyfriend Steve, and the two girls had seen less of each other.

Louise reluctantly got up from the sofa and went to the door to let Sally-Anne in. She opened the door, said, "Hello," and "Come in," and without even looking at Sally-Anne immediately rushed back into the lounge, dived back on to the settee with her attention once again focused only on the dazzling Bjorn as he warmed up on court for his first ever Wimbledon finals match.

"Sit yourself down, Sally-Anne. I want to watch this. There's some orange squash in the fridge if you want it. Go and help yourself."

"Well I only popped in to ask if you wanted to go to London for a couple of days on Monday. My cousin said he can get some tickets for a concert on Monday evening and he said we can stay there at my uncle and aunt's for a couple of nights if we want to. What do you say? Shall we go?"

The warming up session had finished and the match was about to start. "Sounds great, but can we talk about it when this match has finished?"

"I've got to let Bruce know about the tickets though. I said I'd call him straight back after I'd spoken to you."

Louise was frustrated that her peaceful afternoon was being interrupted but didn't want to upset Sally-Anne. "I'm sure it'll be great, but can we talk about it later?" She sat up and looked at Sally-Anne for the first time, "I'll tell you what. Why don't you go and tell him we'll go? We can sort out all the details later. Use the phone in the hall." She picked up her glass and proffered it towards Sally-Anne, "And if you're getting yourself some squash afterwards, can you fill my glass again?"

Sally-Anne took the glass and went to phone her cousin. Louise turned her attention back to the TV screen.

She had met Sally-Anne's cousin Bruce at Easter when his family had visited the Hamilton's for the holiday break. Louise had agreed to go to the cinema with Sally-Anne, her boyfriend Steve, and Bruce and had quite enjoyed the evening with Bruce. She looked at Bjorn as he served one of his aces and jumped with delight. It would be nice to meet Bruce again. He was reasonably good looking for a twenty year old undergraduate but he wasn't a patch on Bjorn!

Sally-Anne returned with the squash and handed Louise her glass, "All sorted then. Steve is coming as well so he'll be able to drive us down there and we don't have to worry about train fare or accommodation. We can all stay at my aunt's."

Louise was too engrossed in the TV to take much notice of what was being said but she was shaken from her musing when Sally-Anne said, "Your Mom and Dad will be OK about us staying 'til Wednesday, won't they. Take some money and we can spend Tuesday in Oxford Street. It'll be great to have some fun for a change after all those exams, won't it?"

Louise suddenly became aware at what she had committed herself to before asking her parents, and felt certain her father wouldn't be happy about it. Nevertheless she did not want to let Sally-Anne see her concern, "Oh they're out all day today. I'll sort it out with them in the morning but it'll be fine. Now can we just watch this match and talk about it when it's over?"

From then on however, she could not relax as much as she had been previously, and even though Bjorn was slaughtering Ilie and finally won the title in three straight sets, her joy at this was overshadowed by her constant thoughts as to how to raise things with her father the next morning.

For much of her life, Louise had seen little of her father during the week and often saw little of him at weekends either, and in the last couple of years she had seen even less of him. She assumed the reason for this was parliamentary business, but the real reason was that Edward now spent more time in London to be with his secretary Joanna Hurst. Joanna had been Edward's mistress long before he had admitted it to Samantha at the same time as he had admitted to his gambling and his cash problems. At first Sam had insisted he should stop seeing her but had closed her eyes to it when she realised the affair had continued. She had been far more concerned about the gambling, and once she had taken total control of their finances and knew that the gambling had ceased, she managed to cope with this other addiction.

But for Edward, almost every thing he had done since the loss of Juliette almost thirty years previously had been an attempt to drive away and dispel the pain he still constantly felt at that loss. Pushing himself in his career; being with a woman or gambling had only ever been the drug, the soporific effect of which had temporarily taken that pain away.

Louise climbed into bed that night before her mother and father returned and tossed and turned until well after midnight trying to work out how to get them to agree to the London trip. She kept repeating to herself, "I'll tell them I'm a grown woman and old enough to sort out my own life," but had finally fallen asleep without reaching any conclusions.

The next morning she jumped out of bed as soon as she heard her mother moving about. She slipped on her dressing gown and joined her in the kitchen. "Did you enjoy your day yesterday, Mom?"

Her mother pursed her lips, "It was OK I suppose, but I could have done without having to spend the evening with the mayor and his wife. Usually they're good company, but what with walking round the fête all afternoon and trying to say the right thing to everyone, I'd had enough by the time we all arrived at the mayor's house for supper. How was your day? I heard that Bjorn Borg won. Was it a good match?"

"Yes, you should have seen it. He was brilliant." Louise smiled, "And good looking with it."

Samantha smiled back, amused at her daughter's comment, "And what do you have planned for today?"

"I'm going round to Sally-Anne's later to sort out about our trip tomorrow."

Samantha was busy making coffee ready for when Edward came down. "And what trip is that dear?"

'It's now or never' thought Louise. "Sally-Anne's aunt and uncle, you know the ones who live in London, have invited Sally-Anne to visit them for a couple of days and Sally-Anne's asked me to go with her."

"That's nice dear; it'll do you good to enjoy yourself for a few days. Do you plan to do anything special whilst you're down there?"

"Well we thought we might spend a bit of time shopping in Oxford Street and Sally-Anne's cousin has got some tickets for a concert tomorrow night. It should be good. I'm looking forward to it."

Samantha continued with the breakfast preparations and hardly seemed to be taking in anything Louise was saying, but nevertheless continued the conversation, "What sort of concert is that dear?"

"It's a new pop group from New York. They're called the Ramones apparently. I've never heard of them but Sally-Anne's cousin Bruce says they're great. So it should be good."

"Bit like the Beatles, are they? I've always liked them."

Although Louise had never heard of The Ramones before, she didn't think they were quite like the Beatles. She guessed they were more like the Rolling Stones but she nevertheless smiled to herself at her mother's assumption and merely said, "Something like that. So it's all right if I go then, is it?"

"Of course dear; remind me later and I'll give you some money to treat yourself in Oxford Street."

Louise was staggered that permission had been given so easily and with the minimum of questions, but at that moment Edward came into the kitchen and she worried that things might turn out differently when he knew about the trip. He gave both girls a peck on the cheek as he said good morning to each of them in turn. He switched on the radio before sitting at the table and picking up the morning paper to read. Samantha gave him a cup of coffee and he immediately started to unwrap his first cigar of the day.

"Do you have to smoke that thing whilst we're about to eat breakfast, dear?"

Edward looked at his wife and said nothing but nevertheless put the cigar unlit on the table and took a swig of his coffee. Louise wondered what had happened the previous day between her mother and father to make him so easily submissive. She merely smiled to herself; she did not want to know.

Her mother sat down and started to sip her own coffee, "Louise is going to London tomorrow for a few days. She's going with Sally-Anne and staying at her aunt's house. She deserves the break after her exams doesn't she?"

Edward briefly said, "That'll be nice for you. Have a good time," before turning to Samantha and adding, "I have an early start in London tomorrow so I'll be off about three o'clock this afternoon. Do you think you could give me a lift to the station?" He instantly turned back to his newspaper without waiting for an answer.

Samantha closed her eyes for a second and when she opened them she shook her head from side to side, which Louise took as another sign of her mother's current coldness towards her father. What had gone on between them yesterday? "Fine! I take it you've got enough clean shirts because I haven't washed the ones you brought back on Friday yet." This was more a statement than a question, because she didn't wait for an answer either, but quite firmly said, "Is what's in that paper more important than your daughter? Haven't you got anything to talk to her about? Wouldn't you like to know how her exams went?"

Edward put his paper down, almost looking sheepish at this rebuke.

For the next ten minutes he tried to carry on a conversation with Louise but it seemed to Louise that he was listening more intently to the news on the radio than he was to anything she was saying. And after a while he stopped listening to her altogether, as the newscaster reported how Israeli commandos had carried out a raid at Entebbe airport in Uganda and had rescued the hostages taken in the Air France Airbus hijacking some days earlier. Soon all three of them were listening intently to the news that all but three of the hundred or so hostages had been rescued alive and were now safely on their way back to Israel. When the news item finished the conversation was about the rescue and they didn't return to discussing more personal matters. Not that day at least.

Samantha dropped Louise off at Sally-Anne's on her way to work the next morning and thought no more about the trip until she saw Eric Hamilton at work later in the afternoon.

"We weren't going to let Sally-Anne go, and certainly not with that boyfriend of hers tagging along, until she told us that you and Edward were happy to let Louise go. Your Louise is such a sensible girl, and I'm sure

Sally-Anne won't do anything silly with her around."

Until this remark Samantha knew nothing about Sally-Anne's boyfriend Steve going, and it was from that moment that she started to worry!

She would have worried even more if she had known that Sally-Anne's uncle and aunt were away on holiday with their daughter, and that the only ones staying in the house were the two girls, Sally-Anne's boyfriend and her cousin, Bruce.

Louise herself was also shocked when she found this out, and was somewhat relieved when Bruce showed them the guest room with two single beds and said that Louise and Sally-Anne could have that room and Steve could have his sister's room.

The girls quickly decided who was having which bed and spent the next hour sorting out which dress they were each going to wear; carefully putting on their makeup and fussing with their hair in an effort to look as beautiful as they could for the evening out. By the time Bruce called from downstairs to say he had prepared some tea for them all before they left for the gig, Louise had relaxed and was beginning to look forward to attending her first pop concert. But as soon as they entered the kitchen to find the boys both dressed in scruffy jeans and T-shirts, Bruce let out a guffaw, "You're not going dressed like that are you?"

"Why what's the matter?"

"It's not a classical concert or opera we're going to you know. It's the Ramones."

"I know that, so what?" said Sally-Anne.

"Do you know what sort of group the Ramones are?"

Sally-Anne's face coloured as she admitted, "Not really, I'd never heard of them before you phoned me up about getting tickets."

Steve let out a laugh at this comment and she looked daggers at him as she angrily said, "And what are you laughing at?"

He got up and put his arm around her, "I'm sorry but it's so funny. No-one will be dressed like that. Even your make-up's wrong."

She shrugged him off with, "And what's wrong with my make-up? You've always liked me like this before."

He tried to put his arm around her again, but she would have none of it. She pushed him away and gave him a sharp punch in the ribs as she said, "What the f*** are we supposed to wear then?"

Louise shuddered at the vehemence in this remark by her friend. She had never heard her use the 'f' word before. It was also obvious that Steve was taken aback. He stood opened mouthed as Bruce came to the rescue, "I'm sorry Sally-Anne, I presumed you knew that they're a punk rock group."

Louise shook her head and before she had even thought that she may be laughed at for asking the question said, "So what! I know plenty of girls who've been to rock concerts dressed like this. So what's so different with these Ramones?"

Steve put his hand to his mouth to stifle any more laughter and Bruce just managed to control his amusement as he said, "I think it best if we just go to the concert and you find out for yourselves, but in the meantime I suggest you put on some jeans and a jumper if you've got them. I'm sure you'll feel much more comfortable when we get there if you do."

Sally-Anne was still seething, "And what about our make-up? You still haven't said what's wrong with that."

Bruce smiled and shook his head, "I'm sure if you just change your clothes, the make-up will be fine and you won't feel out of place."

Louise felt uneasy as she climbed the stairs with Sally-Anne to change, and was almost wishing she hadn't agreed to come on this trip. Nothing was turning out as she had envisioned it.

As soon as the door was closed behind them Sally-Anne shook with the rage she felt within her, "I could strangle bloody Bruce for not warning me about what to wear. I still don't know what's so different with this band anyway. What did he call them?"

"I think he said they were a punk rock band. What's 'punk' anyway?"

Both girls laughed at their ignorance and Louise finally said, "Like Bruce said, we're about to find out soon."

They each fell back on to their beds in a total fit of laughter and by the time they returned downstairs dressed in what they hoped was now more appropriate attire, the boys were both becoming agitated about the time, and as the girls sat down to eat the sandwiches Bruce had prepared, Steve asked, "Do you think you could eat that on our way? We were hoping to have a pint or two before we go to the Roundhouse."

Not wishing to cause any more trouble, each girl picked up a sandwich and as they stood up Sally-Anne turned aggressively to Steve, "Come on then, wouldn't want to take away your drinking time would we?"

The atmosphere relaxed somewhat as they walked to the underground and they were all laughing together as Bruce tried to explain what 'punk' meant, but the more he tried to sensibly give a description, the more the girls interrupted with wilder and wilder imaginary descriptions of their own until, by the time they came out of the tube station 'punk' had taken on a meaning even more outlandish and perverse than the real thing.

After about a hundred yards Bruce stopped outside a pub and, looking at his watch, put his arms out to stop the rest of them in their tracks, "Come on we've got a good half an hour before the show starts, just enough time for a couple of drinks," and without waiting for any agreement or disagreement from them he strode straight through the doors and into the bar. The others followed into the hazy atmosphere thick with tobacco smoke, where Sally-Anne immediately started to cough as the bitter air hit the back of her throat, but the boys took no notice at her discomfort.

"Right, what are you girls drinking?" Bruce asked without breaking his stride towards the bar.

Louise asked for a lemonade and Sally-Anne was still coughing as she asked for a glass of water, "You need something a bit stronger than water," said Steve as he followed behind Bruce, "I'll get you something a bit better than water for your cough."

Louise took Sally-Anne's arm and led her to a table in the corner near an open window and away from the worst of the smoke. "I hope the lads aren't going to spend the rest of the night drinking after the concert," Sally-Anne said as they sat down.

"Don't worry, if they do, we'll leave them to it and go back on our own."

Sally-Anne pulled a face, "But I'm not sure I know the way back to auntie's house without Bruce."

"Then we'll just have to ask the lad's for some money and take a taxi. The driver should know the way." Both girls laughed at the thought of a taxi back instead of the trudge on the underground.

"What have you girls found so funny then?" asked Steve as he placed their drinks in front of them. He gave Sally-Anne a kiss on the cheek, "Get that down you. It'll do you a power of good."

Bruce gave Steve his pint of bitter and took a sip from his own pint glass as he sat down. Once both men were seated they clinked their glasses saying, "Cheers," and then proceeded to race each other to see who could down their drink fastest. As soon as Bruce had plonked his empty glass on the table, Steve picked it up saying, "Same again?" and without waiting for a reply started to make his way back to the bar to get a refill.

The second pint went down their throats almost as fast as the first, but at least they didn't immediately get up for another refill.

Louise sipped at her drink and guessed it was a G and T. By the size of the glass she supposed it was at least a double. She looked at Sally-Anne and was surprised that her glass was already empty, "Steady on Sally-Anne we don't want to let the lads get us drunk."

Bruce grinned at her remark and took the empty glass and passed it to Steve, "I think your girlfriend would like another one of these." He reached out to take Louise's glass, but realising very little had been drunk from it, pulled his hand back and said, "You better get Louise's drink in a new glass, she hasn't finished the first yet."

Louise lifted her glass saying, "Not for me thank you. This is plenty for me."

"And I think I'd rather have that water now anyway," said Sally-Anne.

Nevertheless Steve returned a few minutes later with two more G and T's and placed one in front of each girl before fetching two further pints from the bar.

Louise wondered again whether the lads were trying to get them drunk and determined not to drink more than she ought even it meant offending them by leaving full glasses sitting on the table.

The third pints went down more sedately than the first two and when Bruce's glass was once more empty he looked at his watch saying, "Drink up girls, we'd better be on our way."

Sally-Anne drank the rest of her drink, but Louise, who had not yet emptied her first drink placed the glass on the table and stood up, "Right, let's get going then."

Steve finished his drink and pointing to Louise's full glass and then the half full glass, said, "Aren't you going to drink those, Louise?" To which she merely shook her head.

Bruce picked up the glasses, "Can't let good booze go to waste," and emptied the contents of each glass down his throat in one gulp. Louise thought he was already unsteady on his feet as he led them out of the pub.

When they reached The Roundhouse five minutes later, Louise was quite taken aback by the large crowd of punk rock followers pushing to get into the building before the show started. Although there was a couple of well dressed girls in the crowd Louise was nevertheless pleased she had changed into jeans and sweater. At least she was not so out of place from the rest of the crowd, even if she did not sport the chains and tattered clothing most of the others were wearing.

Inside they were pushed and shoved in all directions as people tried to get to the front but this changed as the crowd started screaming and jumping up and down in wild excitement as 'The Flaming Groovies' took to the stage. The same mayhem continued non-stop for the 'The Stranglers' and things got even worse when the main act, 'The Ramones' came on stage shouting their trademark slogan 'gobba gobba hey'.

At first Louise had wondered whether this was supposed to be a comic act as the young spotty lads in their torn denim jeans and leather jackets pranced and strutted across the stage, peevishly grunting into their microphones words that were totally indecipherable to Louise. They strummed and bashed out their so called music at a furiously fast pace as if they were trying to finish the session before anyone was able to complain about the racket they were making.

She couldn't help smiling to herself at their pathetic antics as they swaggered across the stage in ever increasingly ridiculous wide legged and knee bending poses. There was not a flicker from any of their gaunt unsmiling faces to reveal any emotion in their storm of incomprehensible gobbledegook and angry music so fiercely strummed on guitars and drums.

Louise's would have burst into a fit of laughter at the stupidity of it all, but for the fact that her head was now throbbing and her ears were hurting from the incessant beat from the drums and the discordant twanging from the guitars being blasted out from the amplifiers at full power.

Louise turned to Bruce intending to say, (or more precisely, shout to make herself heard above the screaming and screeching from the crowd) how ridiculous she thought it all was, but was amazed to see the total fascination and gob smacked concentration on his face as he rocked his head and shook his whole body in an attempt to express the beat and words that blurred into one another. He was obviously completely mesmerised by the complete cacophony of discordant sight and sounds on the stage.

She looked across at Sally-Anne and Steve and was again surprised to see that they too were caught up in the astonishing and breathtaking event.

She couldn't believe the noise and antics of all the people around her who seemed intent on competing with the players on the stage to see who could make the most dissonant racket. She started to feel a total outsider and probably the only one not completely enthralled and captivated by what everyone else clearly considered to be a magical performance. Was she really such a prude and what would she say to the boys if they asked if she had enjoyed it?

She decided to keep her real feelings to herself and perhaps just say it had been a refreshingly unique occasion if asked. Nevertheless she was thankful when the cast of four walked off the stage after a mere thirty minutes, but the screaming and chorus of cheers from the intoxicated crowd continued long after that and, for Louise, the humming in her ears did not cease until she fell asleep several hours later.

The crowd of spectators were still hyped up and cheering as they left The Roundhouse and Bruce moved to Louise's side and firmly clasped his arm around her waist as they pushed and jostled their way into the street and through the throng to the pub. She removed his arm as they entered the smoky atmosphere again, but he resisted her actions until she turned to him and firmly said, "Please not in here." She immediately rued saying the 'not in here' hoping he wouldn't interpret it as giving him permission to act in a similar familiar and intimate way later. She decided to leave it however; she would deal with any further unwanted familiarity from him when and if it happened.

Steve and Sally-Anne followed them to a table but without saying a word, Steve sat on a vacant chair and Sally-Anne plonked herself on his lap, from where she immediately hugged and kissed him oblivious to all around them.

Bruce put his hand out and separated the pair with a, "Can you stop that for a minute and tell me what you want to drink?"

Neither Steve nor Sally-Anne averted their eyes from the other's gaze as Steve muttered, "Same as we had before," before moving to kiss Sally-Anne again. More and more of the concert goers flooded into the pub and by the time Bruce returned with the drinks on a small tray, he had difficulty preventing his consignment from being splashed all over members of the bustling swarm.

He put the drinks on the table and squeezed up against Louise on the window bench which was only meant for one. He put his arm around her and went to pick up his glass, but Louise lifted his hand from her shoulder and quite deliberately moved it back to his side. She did not look at his reaction but could almost feel the tension and irritation in his voice as he forcefully demanded, "Can't you pair leave your snogging 'til later and get these drinks down you now I've struggled to get them?"

Sally-Anne pulled away from Steve and tried to hide her embarrassment at being reprimanded, by immediately picking up her glass to cover her burning cheeks. Steve just grinned as he picked up his glass and drank half of the contents in one fell swoop, before asking, "What did you think of the group, Louise? Weren't they great?"

"Well they were different anyway," and because she had nothing positive to say, she turned to Sally-Anne and asked, "Did you like them Sally-Anne?"

Sally-Anne looked across at Bruce and then at Steve before bursting into a fit of laughter as she said, "Like you said, they were different." She got up off Steve's lap and a reluctant Bruce moved to stand next to Steve, drink in hand, when she said she wanted to sit next to Louise so that they could talk more easily.

Louise willingly made room for Sally-Anne and, guessing that her friend's reaction undoubtedly meant that Sally-Anne had been as impressed with the group's musical talent as much as she had been, she also burst into a fit of laughter. The giggling continued with ever increasing animation and fervency as they demolished every aspect of the performance of the provocative prancing of the ill-clad four lads who had 'performed' for them earlier. Nothing escaped their critical onslaught; their long unkempt hair; their cheap old plimsolls; their tattered jeans; their ill fitting leather jackets; their eccentric posturing and pretentiousness; their bizarre musical bent and their extraordinary lyrics, all became available fodder for their amusement.

Every successive observation become more and more derogatory, as they tried to outdo each other with progressively ever more outlandish remarks about every facet of the performance and music of the four Ramones.

Fortunately for Sally-Anne and Louise, the bar was now bustling with a mass of equally noisy revellers all trying to make themselves heard over the beat and throbbing coming from the in-house stereo equipment, and no-one, not even the many punk rock aficionados, were taking any notice of what the girls were talking about.

Even Steve and Bruce were more concerned with refilling their glasses than what the girls were finding so amusing. Louise put her hand over her glass as Steve stood up to buy the next round, "No thanks, Steve. I think I've already had enough."

Sally-Anne picked up her glass and drank the little that was left, and was about to hand the glass to Steve for her umpteenth refill, but instead she took the glass back saying, "Actually, I think I've had enough as well and I'd rather have something to eat. Do you think we could go now? We can get some fish and chips on the way back."

Steve looked at Bruce who shrugged his shoulders saying, "Let's just have one more for the road before we go," and so it was another half an hour before they left the pub and another twenty minutes after that before they found the fish and chip shop. And it was just after midnight when both Sally-Anne and Steve were bringing up the contents of their stomachs and depositing it all over the gate outside Bruce's next door neighbour's house.

At the same time that Louise's friends were regurgitating their fish supper, Edward was opening the door to his flat after a very disturbing previous twenty four hours. It had started on the train back to London when he couldn't stop thinking about how fragile his relationship with his wife and his daughter had now become.

When he had first met Samantha she had recreated some of the feelings he felt in the early days with Juliette and when he married her he truly believed being with her would be as good as it had been with Juliette. But that was not to be. He did love Samantha but soon realised he was not 'in love' with her; certainly not in the same way he'd been 'in love' with Juliette.

During his marriage he had embarked on several affairs but these had always been simply reckless attempts to relive the euphoria he had always felt with Juliette; but it had never worked. Every time he took a woman to bed he mistakenly believed it would be the same as it was with Juliette, but it only ever turned out to be mere sex, and it had never been just 'sex' with Juliette. He regretted letting Samantha down so badly, but by the time he realised his relentless pursuit of happiness was futile and affected every one of his relationships, the damage had been done and he no longer knew how to even attempt to put things right.

His marriage failure was bad enough but his failure as a father was worse. He constantly rued the day he had abandoned his son and although he knew he should have put things right with Julian long ago, he had never been able to pluck up the courage to do so.

When Louise was born he vowed he would be the perfect father to her that he had not been to Julian, and at first he genuinely believed he was being the loving father she deserved him to be. But the love Louise gave to him in return was that of a child; sometimes overtly and freely given and at other times withheld for reasons he did not understand. In this she was no different to other children; often jumping into his arms and making a fuss of him as soon as he entered the room, and on other occasions ignoring his presence completely. He revelled in the love she showed him when she felt like it, but felt rejected on those occasions she ignored him.

Eventually he did come to understand the nature of a child's love for a parent and realise that when Louise did not give him any attention she just had more important things to do, but by then he also realised that no matter how much affection Louise showed him, it could never permanently take away his constant aching for Juliette, and in the last few years as Louise had matured into a woman, she too had grown away from him.

All of these years of unhappiness over Juliette's death had not only affected his relationships, but had finally started to have an effect on his health. He had been a heavy smoker since his University days and on entering parliament had started what Philip joked as being the 'Churchill' effect and smoke large cigars. He had also turned increasingly to the bottle, particularly when stressed and alone.

His unhappiness and lifestyle had aged him beyond his years and no matter how much he tried to think positively about other things, the more the nagging pain he had experienced in his chest more and more frequently for the last two years had increased.

He never admitted having the pains to anyone, always passing off any shortage of breath as too much smoking. But today, when the Whips office issued a three line whip on a bill he secretly did not agree with his pains gradually grew far worse. Joanna, his secretary, became more and more concerned about him as the day wore on but her attempts to get him to take things easy merely acted as a catalyst increasing his malaise, and when she suggested he should go home and get some rest, saying she would give him a call in plenty of time for the vote, he stormed out. When he returned to his office after the vote Joanna had already gone, so he collected the bottle of whisky he kept in his desk, deciding to drink away his pain and troubles when he got home.

He was well down the bottle by the time the taxi dropped him off at the flat and had begun to feel less agitated and stressed, but all that changed when he found Joanna sitting in the lounge waiting for him.

His reaction left Joanna in no doubt at how much he resented her presence as he opened the lounge door. "What the bloody hell are you doing here?" was the hostile greeting he uttered as soon as he saw her.

For a moment she was thrown by the rancour in his remark but quickly put it aside, determined to do what she had intended, "I wanted to talk to you and I was hoping you would listen to me for once."

He was not in the mood for cosy chats and let her know so immediately, "Be a good girl and just leave me alone. I've had a bloody awful day, so why don't you just go home?" She did not move, so he whipped the whisky bottle from his overcoat pocket and waved it in front of her face, "Well, if you have to stay here, then I'd be obliged if you'd just go to bed and let me relax with this."

But she was determined not to be put off by his outburst no matter how obnoxious he became, and passively said, "Let me hang your coat up and fetch a couple of glasses and I'll join you. I could do with some of that myself before I go to bed."

She took the bottle from him and put it on the table, giving it back to him after she had helped him out of his coat. "Just go and sit down and I'll get the glasses. Do you want something to eat?"

Early in their relationship she had done everything to please him but that had changed after the first flush of excitement had passed. Now she never reacted to his outbursts but just continued as if nothing untoward had happened. For Edward the ephemeral relief that sleeping with her had previously momentarily given him, was no longer present when they slept together. Maybe she had realised this and that he didn't love her in the way she seemed to love him. Perhaps she now felt the same and wanted to tell him it was over. *'At least that will save me the trouble,'* was the thought going through his head as he calmly did her bidding and went to sit down.

She returned and poured each of them a whisky before sitting on the chair opposite to him. He took a long swig from his glass and emptied its contents before passing the glass to her for a refill, "Fill the glass this time. It'll save you having to keep getting up."

She took the glass but he immediately clutched his chest and let out a yelp. He brushed off her attempt to help him, "Just get me the drink. That'll do the trick better than all your fussing."

She did not get the drink but sat down next to him instead, "This is exactly what I wanted to talk to you about. You can't go on ignoring all these pains you're getting."

"Stop fussing, woman. I've told you I'll see a doctor when I'm good and ready." The truth was however that Edward was scared to do so. He had seen his father with similar pains and look what had happened to him!

He jumped up, about to tell her to leave him and go, but the pain hit again even more sharply and he fell back into the seat.

"That's it. I've had enough of seeing you like this and I'm fed up of waiting for you to do something about it. I'd already arranged a doctor's appointment for you tomorrow at ten o'clock, and that's what I came here to tell you. I was going to stay tonight and take you there myself, but I'm not going to wait for that, I'm sending for an ambulance now."

Edward wanted to tell her to cancel the doctor's appointment and forget about the ambulance, but he was now in so much pain, that he was actually relieved something was at last going to be done about it.

Louise was the first to wake the next morning and she felt relieved that she had the bathroom to herself whilst the others were sleeping off their hangovers. She was dressed and had already eaten breakfast by the time Bruce, bleary eyed and still smelling of the previous night's beer came down the stairs.

"I hope you don't mind," said Louise, "But I've helped myself to tea and cereal?"

"Fine, help yourself to whatever you want." He burped as he sat down. "You couldn't make me a cup of coffee could you? I'm parched."

"Sure. No problem. Do you want anything to eat?"

"Just coffee for now, I might have something to eat later."

Louise put coffee in front of Bruce just as the other two dawdled groggily into the kitchen and being the only one fully awake and in control of her faculties, she became the chief cook and bottle washer, providing each of them with drink and sustenance until they slowly began to shake off the excesses of the previous night.

It was mid afternoon when Louise and Sally-Anne finally arrived in Oxford Street, where Sally-Anne made straight for Boots saying, "Hang on a minute, Louise, I want to get some aspirin, my head's throbbing something awful." And when she came back out of the shop added, "Can we go and get a coffee? I need a drink to wash down these pills."

Sally-Anne was feeling much better when they arrived back at the house, but Louise was seething inside. For her the day had been a total disaster.

The morning had been spent attending to the others and then waiting for Sally-Anne to get ready to go out. The afternoon had been no better. Sally-Anne had shown no enthusiasm for shopping and had made Louise feel like a mother dragging her rebellious child behind her.

She just hoped the evening would not be a similar calamity and was agreeably surprised when she saw that the boys had not only hosed off the mess from the next door neighbours gate and had generally tidied up in the house, but had laid the dining room table with plates and the best glasses and had placed a large candle ready to light in the centre.

"Right if you girls would like to go and get yourselves freshened up, I'll put this wine with the other in the fridge to cool, and then Steve and me will go and get something to eat from the Chinese takeaway."

Bruce gave the bottle to Steve saying, "Put that in the fridge, Steve," before picking the Chinese takeaway menu from the table and handing it to Louise. "Is there anything on there that you particularly fancy?"

"Whatever you get will be fine by me." She handed the menu to Sally-Anne, "How about you Sally-Anne?"

Sally-Anne shrugged her shoulders and handed the menu back to Bruce, "Yes whatever you get will be OK with me as well."

"Right we'll be off then. See you in a bit."

Louise ran after him, "Let me give you some money towards the meal."

Bruce shook his head violently from side to side, "No, this is my treat to make up for being such a berk last night. I promise not to get drunk tonight."

Louise smiled to herself and was even surprised at how she suddenly felt drawn towards this well dressed, well groomed and remarkably pleasant young man.

The evening made up for her awful day. The meal was well cooked and Bruce had excelled in the number and variety of dishes he had bought, which he insisted should all be emptied out of their silver foil containers and placed in proper bowls on the table. He had been out especially that afternoon to purchase chopsticks and these caused enormous excitement and laughter as they each tried to master the art of using them. By the time the meal and the bottles of wine were finished, the humour; the conversation; the company and the companionship had made Louise more relaxed and content than she had been in a long time and as they made their way to bed she was happy to briefly return Bruce's goodnight kiss before she entered her bedroom.

Louise got herself ready for sleep and lay in bed with the light on waiting for Sally-Anne to finish saying goodnight to Steve. She listened to them come up the stairs and for a short while could hear their canoodling on the landing but then she heard them laughing and soon after heard the bang as they both fell on to Steve's bed in the next room. *'Now what do I do?'* she thought to herself, *'Do I go and say something to Sally-Anne before she does something really stupid or do I just do nothing?'* She decided on the latter thinking, *'After all she is eighteen and it's up to her what she does,'* so she got out of bed and switched off the light, got back into bed and tried to ignore the noises coming from next door.

She was just dozing off when she became aware of someone coming into the room. "Are you OK Sally-Anne?" but there was no reply and as the steps got closer she turned and switched on the bedside lamp.

"My God, what are you doing here?"

Bruce was standing next to her bed, dressed only in his underpants. He moved closer to the bed and went to pull back the sheets.

"What the hell are you doing? Get out of here."

But he ignored her demands and continued tugging at the sheets, which Louise was now struggling to hold tightly up to her neck.

"Don't be silly, this is what you came down here for isn't it?"

Louise lay there open mouthed as she struggled to keep herself covered. She could not believe what he was saying as he continued, "I know it's what you and Sally-Anne wanted. Sally-Anne would have gone to Steve last night but she was too drunk. But none of us are drunk tonight, so stop being a silly girl and move over."

Louise tried to sound insistent as she spoke as forcefully as her dry mouth would allow, "Jesus! Why don't you just bugger off and get out of here and then we can forget all about this?"

"Oh for goodness sake stop teasing. It was obvious you wanted it when you kissed me and I'm beginning to feel cold standing here, so just be a good girl and let me get in." He laughed as he added, "I'm sure it won't take long for you to warm me up."

By now, Louise was really scared. She had only given him a goodnight peck. It meant absolutely nothing. So why was he behaving so obnoxiously? What had Sally-Anne said to make him think she wanted this? The only thing she wanted was for him to go.

She tried shouting as loud as she could through her parched lips but the croaky and husky words that came out where nothing like the volume her head was demanding, "Just go away before you do something really stupid. I don't want you here and I've never wanted you here. So go away now."

Momentarily he was thrown by this remark but almost as suddenly his expression changed and she could sense the anger radiating from him. "You stupid bitch! Why do you think I arranged all this and invited Sally-Anne to bring you down here? Why do you think I went to all the trouble to get the tickets for last night and why do you think I've spent all that money on the meal tonight? Now stop pretending to be such a prude and let me get in bed before I freeze to death."

He slipped off his pants and furiously yanked and pulled at the sheets until he finally managed to wrench them out of Louise's hands. As he pulled the sheets from her, she found the strength to let out an ear piercing scream that set the whole room shaking.

For Edward the last twenty four hours had been quite different. He had been admitted to hospital straight away, and whether it was the drugs he'd been given or merely the fact that something was at last being done about his pains, he was surprised how quickly he felt more comfortable.

Later that same afternoon Joanna was sitting by the bed when the specialist came to discuss the results of the tests and x-rays Edward had had that morning. The nurse pulled the curtain around the bed and suggested that Joanna should wait outside whilst the consultant spoke to Edward, but Edward was afraid of what was coming and wanted to have someone with him, and since Joanna was the one there then she would have to do.

"If it's all right with you doc, I'd rather she stayed."

The doctor merely said, "That's fine," before moving a chair so that he could sit next to Edward's bed. "Well Mr Richards, the news is not good I'm afraid." Edward looked at Joanna and she sensed the fear behind his eyes. They looked at each other for a few moments without saying anything before both turning back to the consultant.

"Shall I go on?" Edward nodded and the doctor fumbled through the papers he had laid on the bed before continuing, "How long have you been a smoker, Mr Richards?"

"I had my first cigarette when I was about thirteen, but I suppose I started smoking regularly when I went to University."

"I see and how many do you smoke a day now?"

Edward pointed to his cigar case on the bedside table, "I smoke cigars mainly, probably four or five of those each day," and when the doctor said nothing but merely looked at him, he added, "Yes, OK, maybe more than that."

The doctor looked at the size of the cigars, "So I guess you must be puffing away most of the time?"

The doctor moved on to the next item without further comment or waiting for an answer, "I see from these notes that your father suffered from angina and died from a heart attack." Edward merely nodded. "And I take it he was a smoker?" Again Edward nodded and mumbled, "Mm."

"Well, like I said Mr Richards, the news is not good. The tests and x-rays show that your heart is, well to put it bluntly, it's knackered. I'm actually surprised you've been able to do all the things you say you do. I'm sure we'll be able to sort out some help for you, but I'd suggest the first thing is something you should do for yourself."

Edward answered before being told, "I should stop smoking?"

"Sure unless you've got a death wish."

"And what can you do for me?"

The consultant looked directly at Edward and smiled a questioning smile. "Ideally you could do with a different heart," but before he could continue a very anxious Edward jumped in with, "And is that what you want to do?"

The doctor smiled, "Unfortunately Mr Richards, even though we are learning more about heart transplant surgery all the time, such surgery is still in its infancy; is a very risky business and the success rate is low."

Joanna took Edward's hand and asked, "So are you suggesting he needs a new heart or not? Or are you just ruling it out because it's too risky?"

He smiled a nervous embarrassed smile, "I'm sorry if you think I sounded flippant, I didn't mean to be. It's never easy giving bad news to patients." His smile spread across his face, "But actually….."

Before he could continue Joanna butted in, "Do I take it from the smile that there is something else you can do?"

He smiled and dipped his head, "Maybe, but I'm one of those doctors who try to tell things as they really are and not pussy foot about trying to make it sound OK when it isn't. So I don't want to give you false expectations at this stage, Mrs Richards. If I could just get a new heart off the shelf every time I needed one, and we had perfected the surgery and all the problems surrounding it, then in an ideal world, a new heart could well be the best choice. But it isn't a perfect world, so I wouldn't want to give the impression that we can cure your husband, but I'm sure there are things we can do to make things easier for him. But before I decide on exactly what let me arrange a few more tests and then I'll have a much better idea what other courses of action are possible."

Edward gripped Joanna's hand tightly, "Actually doctor this is my secretary. She's here because my wife is in Walsall. I somehow guessed the news would not be good and wanted someone with me."

The consultant ignored the comment and said, "I'll tell you what I propose we do. First I'm going to get some equipment rigged up so that we can monitor your heart over a longer period. Secondly I want your smoking to stop right now so your secretary's going to take those cigars away with her. And thirdly I'll try and explain more clearly what I think the problem is and what I'm pretty sure the further tests will confirm for us."

He waited for a response but there was none so he picked up a picture of the heart from his papers and used it to explain the problem as simply as he could before ending with, "So all that's what we'll need to try and sort out."

"By surgery do you mean?" asked Edward.

"Again the answer to that is a maybe, but I don't want to actually suggest anything until we see the results of the tests over the next few days." He touched Edward on the shoulder, "So I'll come and answer that question when I've got the results." He turned to Joanna, "Don't look quite so worried, I'm sure we can do something to help." He turned and spoke to the nurse about the tests he wanted before asking Edward and then Joanna, "Anything you want to ask me before I go?" and was off on his way as soon as they each shook their head. "See you later then Mr Richards."

Edward lay back and considered everything the doctor had told him. All the symptoms he had mentioned were ones he had been experiencing increasingly over the last two years; the breathlessness, having to walk more slowly, always taking the lift to avoid having to use stairs, and the tiredness. He had even fallen asleep a couple of times in the chamber and had only woken when the noise level had increased because some member had made an amusing remark or the opposing members had roared their disapproval at something said by the member speaking at that time. He also now realised how his illness had been the reason for his falling libido.

Even though nothing the doctor said had come as a great shock, being told the true bare facts about his health had nevertheless come as something of a wake up call to him. He had been worrying for a long time that he may drop dead at any time, but had always consoled himself with thoughts that perhaps it was indigestion. He knew he needed to exercise more and had considered giving up smoking for a long time, but actually doing something about either was a different matter altogether.

Later that evening, Edward was lying on his bed dying for a smoke and thinking about phoning Samantha to let her know what was going on. He knew he should have asked someone to do it before now but had just decided to ask a nurse when Joanna came for evening visiting.

She sat down and asked how he felt. He replied with, "Actually I'm pretty tired and could do with some rest," so she left almost immediately. He lay back in his bed and fell fast asleep without giving the phone call a second thought.

At first when Louise screamed nothing came out, but suddenly the air was vibrating with a full powered, earth-shattering blast that screeched from her lungs. Bruce's reaction was immediate and would have been comical if the situation had not been so serious. He struggled to pull his pants on with one hand whilst at the same time trying to place his other hand over Louise's mouth to stop the continuous series of shrieks that hit him one after the other, separated only by sufficient time for Louise to refill her lungs before letting go again. Finally he gave up trying to silence her and ran towards the door still tugging at his pants. The door knocked him flying as it was sharply opened by Sally-Anne shouting, "What on earth's the matter?"

Louise pulled the blanket tighter around her body and managed a smile when she saw Bruce trying to stem the blood that was now flowing from his shattered nose on to the carpet. He rushed passed Sally-Anne leaving a trail of blood spots along his path.

Sally-Anne rushed to the bed and put her arms around Louise as she repeated her question, "What on earth's happened? What's he done to you?"

Steve came to the door still pulling his T-shirt over his shoulders and trying to stop his unfastened jeans from falling down.

"Go away Steve. We don't need you here." He looked totally bemused as he left the room saying, "Rightyoh, just give me a shout if there's anything you want."

Sally-Anne took the corner of the sheet and tried to dry the tears that were now streaming down Louise's cheeks, "What's going on, Louise? What was all the screaming about?"

Louise sniffed and ran her hand across her eyes to try to remove the remaining wetness from them, "I thought he was going to rape me."

"Don't be silly. Bruce isn't like that."

Louise's whole body jerked rigid into a tense ball as the anger rose within her, "You weren't here Sally-Anne." She looked directly into Sally-Anne's eyes, "When I told him to clear off he just wouldn't and tried to get in bed with me."

"OK. OK. But he hasn't done anything to you has he?"

Louise was unsure whether this was a caring question or whether it was a statement made to defend her cousin. She decided to treat it as a concern for her welfare and answered accordingly, "No. I'm all right. He didn't actually touch me but I was sure he was going to. He just wouldn't take no for an answer."

The tears flowed again as Sally-Anne held her tight and tried to comfort her.

After a while Louise started to relax and even managed a smile when the blanket around Sally-Anne finally fell to the floor exposing her nakedness. Sally-Anne smiled back and held Louise even tighter, taking no action at all to re-cover herself.

Neither girl said anything for several minutes until eventually Louise, sniffing several times and picking up the blanket to wrap back around Sally-Anne, said, "I can't stay here, Sally-Anne. What if he comes back? I have to get out of here."

"He won't come back and anyway I'll stay here with you. I dare say Steve won't like it but he'll have to lump it won't he?"

But once Louise had said she couldn't stay her mind was made up. She was going to get out of the house as quickly as she could. "I'm sorry Sally-Anne, but I have to go. You can come with me if you want."

"But where will you go at this time of night? It's after midnight."

"I'll go to my Dad's flat. I can stay there and go home in the morning."

Sally-Anne spent all the time Louise was dressing and throwing her things into her bag to try and convince her stay but Louise would not listen. She was still shaking from the experience and wanted to be away from this house as soon as she could.

"But what are you going to tell your Dad? If Bruce didn't actually do anything to you, you aren't going to get him into trouble are you?"

"I don't want to get anyone into trouble but why did he think it was OK to come into my bedroom like that?"

"I guess he thought you liked him. I suppose we all did."

Louise wanted to scream at Sally-Anne, '*How much had she encouraged*

Bruce and schemed with him to get her here?' but when Sally-Anne, with tears streaming from her eyes, asked, "What are you going to tell your Dad?" she knew that she was genuinely worried for her cousin.

"I'll have to think about it, Sally-Anne, but I have to go. I'll speak to you again sometime." She leaned forward and gave her a hug, "Are you sure you won't come with me?"

"No, I'll be fine." She laughed out loud, "And if it's any consolation, I've decided I'm going to sleep in here tonight and tell Steve he'd better stay in his own room, or there'll be trouble."

Both girls hugged again. "Look why don't you let me get Steve to run you round to your Dad's?"

Louise looked questionably at her friend and smiled, "No I don't think so. I'd rather get a taxi."

Sally-Anne smiled back, "I understand but come straight back if you don't find a taxi."

Half an hour later, as Louise climbed the steps to her father's flat, she began to wonder if she had done the right thing by leaving and coming here. She had not yet worked out what she was going to say about why she was on his doorstep at this time of night, and even considered chasing after the taxi and going back to Bruce's house. She shuddered at the thought at having to face Bruce again and rang the doorbell. There was no immediate response and she stood there contemplating what to do now. *'Stupid girl! You should have phoned to make sure he was here before you came all this way.'* She rang the bell again and this time held her finger on it until she was sure she heard it ringing inside. *'If I'd phoned he would only have wanted to know what was going on, and I couldn't tell him on the phone, could I?"*

She was about to ring the bell again when she thought she heard a noise from inside. A woman's voice asked, "Who's there? What do you want at this time of night?"

Louise started to panic. *'Who was this woman? And what was she doing here? Where was her Dad?'*

Too late now to run away! "It's Louise. I wanted to see my Dad."

"Just a minute." Everything went quiet for a while and it seemed an age before she heard the bolts on the door being jerked back.

"You'd better come in, Louise," the lady said as she opened the door.

Louise wanted to ask, *'Who the hell are you? And what are you doing here in your night attire and wearing Dad's dressing gown?"* but kept her cool and merely said, "Where's my Dad? Is he in?"

"No Louise, he isn't," was all she said as she took Louise's bag and led the way into the lounge.

She plopped the bag on the floor and sat down, indicating to Louise to also sit down.

"What brings you here, Louise? Is anything the matter?"

Louise had had enough of dealing with unsavoury situations for one night and was determined to ignore the woman's questions and ask her own, "Who are you and what are you doing here?"

She wanted to disbelieve what her head was telling her about this woman, but she nevertheless wanted to know what was going on, "Have you left my Dad in bed? Is he too embarrassed to come and see me?"

The woman smiled, "No he isn't here. Actually he's in hospital, but don't worry he's being well looked after."

Louise immediately jumped in with, "What's the matter with him? When did he go to hospital? Does Mom know he's there?"

"Calm down, Louise. He had some pains and we sent for the ambulance. He's in the best place and when I left him tonight the pain was much easier. I told him to ring your mother, but I don't know whether he has yet."

She held out her hand to Louise inviting her to shake it, "I'm Joanna, your Dad's secretary by the way." Louise kept her hands to herself preferring not shake the hand extended out to her. Joanna got the message and took her hand back.

Louise was, by now, convinced that this Joanna was more than a secretary and was determined not to let her off the hook. Secretaries don't stay in their bosses' houses, and they certainly don't casually use their boss's dressing gown, "So what are you doing here or is that an awkward question for you to answer?"

Joanna ignored the bitterness she detected in the remark, "I've been to see your Dad in hospital and he asked me to come here and get some things he needs first thing in the morning, so to save time I thought I'd stay here rather than going all the way home only to come back again."

Louise couldn't help muttering, "Pull the other one," under her breath and didn't care if Joanna did hear the remark.

In fact Joanna had heard but determined to brazen it out, "It's a good job I did stay otherwise there wouldn't have been anyone here to let you in."

"At least I wouldn't have known about Dad and his so called secretary then though would I?" The word secretary had been pointedly emphasised.

Joanna sat back trying to decide how to continue this conversation and finally came to the conclusion that, given the current circumstances, honesty would probably be the best policy, "You're right Louise, there is more to it." She smiled as she said, "But I really am his secretary," and before Louise could respond again she said, "Look why don't I go and make us a cup of tea and then can we start this conversation all over again."

She got up from her seat and went towards the kitchen, stopping at the door to add, "And when I've finished telling you about me and your father, perhaps you'll let me know why you've arrived here at this time of night?"

An hour later, Louise was staggered that no matter how much she had tried to despise this woman for being in her father's flat and being her father's mistress, she had actually warmed to her and found herself actually liking her. She really was a nice lady and it was obvious that she cared a great deal for her father. So much so, that she obviously knew much more about her father and what made him tick than she knew herself. Half way through Joanna telling her how long she and her father had been lovers, it also dawned on Louise that her own mother probably knew all about it. *'And that's why they sleep in separate beds,'* she thought, but did not speak her conclusion out loud.

Eventually Louise felt sufficiently relaxed with Joanna to tell her what had happened and why she had turned up at her father's door so late at night even though reliving the trauma quickly brought back all the terror and fear of the distressing experience. Joanna at first took Louise's hand and gently stroked it, but when Louise tried to repeat the awful words Bruce had used, she broke down and Joanna moved to sit at her side and put her arms around her, "Shush now, you've gone through enough for one night."

Louise clung to Joanna and sobbed her heart out on her shoulder. Nothing was said by either of them as Louise's tears soaked into her father's dressing gown. Slowly the shaking eased, the weeping ceased, the heart beat slowed, and Louise began to feel at peace with herself.

"It wasn't my fault, was it? One kiss didn't really mean that I wanted him in my bed, did it?"

Joanna put her hands on either side of Louise's face and gently held her away so that they were looking into each other's eyes a mere few inches apart, "One kiss means one kiss and any man worth bothering about would know that." She smiled and Louise managed a weak smile back. "Take it from me, none of what happened was your fault, and inside you know that, so stop beating yourself up about it."

She suddenly laughed out loud, "I'm sorry Louise, but I just pictured him trying to get out the room with his pants round his ankles and Sally-Anne smashing his nose with the door. Serves the bastard right, I hope it's broken."

Louise joined in the laughter and they each started to take the mickey out of Bruce by embellishing his reaction after Louise had screamed, making ever more outlandish comments about Bruce's attempts to cover himself up and get out of the room.

Edward was woken early the next morning by a nurse with a cup of tea after the best night's sleep he'd had in a long time. He ignored the tea and lay back on his pillow trying to make some sense of his predicament. Yesterday, the doctor told him he'd need to take complete rest for at least two months and longer if it was decided that surgery was needed.

How on earth had he allowed things to get to this state? What had he achieved in his life? Nothing! So what was he going to do about it?

His initial answer was again that there was nothing he could do, but as he lay there considering things he started to worry about the future. '*What will I be able to do or not do when I get out of this hospital bed? That's assuming I live long enough of course.*'

He called the nurse back saying he needed to go to the bathroom to have a wash and use the toilet, but instead she pulled the curtains around him and he had the indignity of having to use the bed pan once more. She then hooked him on to a number of machines making it impossible for him to get out of bed and by lunchtime he was frantic for a smoke and still hadn't spoken to Samantha but at least he'd reached a conclusion on a number of life changing issues.

Firstly he was going to resign his seat. He was going to be out of action for months anyway, but more importantly, he had finally come to realise that he was probably never going to get a seat in the cabinet and so he decided he didn't want to stay in politics if that plum was not to be achieved. Being a solicitor again may not be all that bad? Perhaps his old firm would take him back?

Resigning his seat would also be the catalyst for him to finish with Joanna. After all, the excitement of the liaison had vanished a long time ago and if Joanna was honest, she'd probably agree that they were only still together because they'd been too lazy to do anything about it. He laughed as he considered this; he no longer had a wife and a mistress, or even two wives, but two women neither who was a true lover anymore, but both of whom now merely cared for his welfare like a mother.

Louise and Joanna talked until well after four that morning before going to their beds. Louise had fallen asleep immediately, exhausted from all the tension of the previous few hours. She slept soundly until she was woken by Joanna at eleven o'clock, and although she still didn't know what, if anything, she was going to do about her harrowing experiences of the previous evening, or about the newly acquired knowledge about her father's mistress, she at least felt more at ease with herself and more ready to face the new day.

Joanna was already washed and dressed ready for work. She handed a cup of tea to Louise, "There should be plenty of hot water for you to have a bath if you want one."

Louise looked at her watch, "Good Heavens! Look at the time. Shouldn't you have been at work ages ago? I'm sorry I shouldn't have kept you up so late last night. You just get off if you have to, I can sort myself out."

Joanna sat on the bed, "I think we need to talk a bit more before I go, don't you?"

"What about? I thought we said everything last night."

She touched Louise on the shoulder and smiled, "I just think you and I ought to get our stories straight before we leave here. I have to take your father the things he asked me to collect for him and I wouldn't want to say anything to him that you want kept to yourself. You may not realise it but he's very proud and protective of you, and in his present condition I'm not sure that hearing about what happened last night would do him any good."

She puckered her lips and pondered for a moment, "And whilst what I have with your father is very special to me, I have no wish to hurt your mother." She shook her head as she continued, "Right now it may not seem so to you, but I actually think your father is far fonder of your mother than he is of me, but that's my problem not yours." She laughed adding, "So what are we going to say to your mother and father?"

Louise had not given any thought to the possible full ramifications of telling them about Bruce and her meeting Joanna, but knew that Joanna was right if more harm was to be avoided. And so, the two woman worked out what they would do and say, and whilst they were not going to lie, a truce was drawn between them and agreements reached on what they wouldn't be saying about the last twenty-four hours, including doing nothing and saying nothing about Bruce's antics or Louise's newly acquired knowledge about Joanna being more than a secretary.

Six months later, Edward was no longer an MP but was working part time at Hastings and Hepplewhite again after having had a new heart valve fitted. Louise had got straight 'A's' in all her A levels and had commenced her course at Edinburgh. She had not only been surprised at how easy it had been to say nothing to her mother or father about Bruce or Joanna's real relationship with her father, but was astounded how both experiences had made her a much stronger and worldly wise woman.

CHAPTER TWENTY- SEVEN

LATE SUMMER 1978

"I'm afraid your heart has deteriorated since you last came to see me Mr Richards, and unfortunately I don't think you could stand another operation even if we were able to repair things again."

Edward was sitting in the consultancy room of the same consultant who had first told him of the seriousness of his heart problems over two years previously, "I guessed as much. I haven't been feeling at all well these last few months." He sat back in the chair and asked, "So what's the prognosis?" even though he was dreading the answer.

"I know it's not what you want to hear but you could just as easily ask how long is a piece of string. Worse scenario; your heart could give out at any time. On the other hand you could well be coming to see me again in a couple of years time; maybe even longer."

Edward's face told it all. "But you really don't think I'll last that long do you?"

He did not answer immediately but looked at the papers in front of him before looking up and speaking to Edward, "Probably not. Maybe you should warn your wife and family and prepare them for the inevitable. If you take it easy and we can ward off a heart attack then it's anyone's guess; but another heart attack may well be your last."

Edward tried to put on a brave face and smiled, "So I should put my house in order?"

The consultant merely curled up his lips and shrugged his shoulders; an action that said everything Edward needed to know.

"And that's how it is," he said to Philip two days later, "You won't say anything to Sam, will you? And please don't say anything to Louise. I'll tell them both in my own good time but there are a few things I want to do first."

Philip wanted to give his friend a hug as being the best way he knew to show his feelings but Edward had waited until they were sitting in the lounge bar of the Broadway pub before he had said anything about his condition. Philip tried to think of the right words to say but Edward saved him from his embarrassment, "You don't have to say anything, Phil; I haven't asked you to have lunch with me to get your sympathy, although my reason is selfish nevertheless."

The barman called out their number and Philip fetched their ploughman's from the bar. Almost as soon as he'd sat down again Edward said, "There's something I'd like you to do for me Philip. Well actually it's something I'd like you to do with me."

Philip, who was putting the butter on his French bread, put down his knife and said, "Fire away. I'll do anything you want me to."

"I'll like you to take me to France, don't think I could manage all the driving myself, and I certainly couldn't manage to travel by train or coach. What I'd like to do is visit some of the places we went together on the old motorbike before the war. Maybe go and visit the war cemeteries where our mates are buried." He laughed as he added, "And I promise I won't fall madly in love this time."

"Actually I'd like to do that myself." Philip laughed as he realised what he had said, "No, I don't mean fall in love, I mean visit the cemeteries. I've always felt a bit guilty I've never been to any of the reunions. I just wanted to forget all that war stuff, but yes, I'd like to come with you. When were you thinking of going?"

Edward laughed again, "After what the doc said, I think the sooner the better, don't you?" He only waited a few seconds before adding, "How about next Monday, for say two weeks?"

Philip knew that to go so soon would cause an awful lot of arranging at work but he also knew he'd never forgive himself if a delay meant that Edward was too ill to go, so he replied, "Next Monday it is then. I'll get on to the ferry people this afternoon and arrange it all. I'm sure we'll be able to find plenty of hotels to stay in when we get there."

Unlike the first time they had used this ferry crossing and had a very fretful night's rest on benches on the open deck, when Philip drove his car off the overnight ferry on the next Tuesday morning, both he and Edward were refreshed by a goodnight's sleep in the best cabins on board. They stopped at the first café they came to and enjoyed a petit déjeuner before leaving Le Havre on the same route to Honfleur they had taken forty years earlier. They parked the car and walked slowly to the harbour, where the scene greeting them was almost the same as the one that had welcomed them all those years before.

The fishing boats still puttered in and out of the harbour; the fisherman still sat in the sun mending their nets before hanging them on the harbour wall to dry; the mishmash of half timber and stone buildings still bordered the inner harbour and the cafés decked out with their multi-coloured umbrellas, table cloths and seats still created the amazing vista often painted by professional and budding artists alike. But now the fishing boats were outnumbered by the private boats and sea going yachts moored in the inner harbour with their gloss white hulls shimmering in the sunlight.

Edward was already struggling to get his breath after the short walk from the car park, and so for the next hour, they sat on the harbour wall just enjoying the heat of the sun whilst watching the world go by. After which they again walked very slowly around the harbour until they reached the same café where they had had their first taste of French red wine at the tender age of eighteen. Edward immediately suggested that they have lunch at the café, "Perhaps we should treat ourselves to a better glass of wine this time," he insisted and they both laughed at the memory of the tumbler full of awful cheap red wine they had forced themselves to sip drop by drop until the glass was empty.

They chose seats half facing the marina at an empty table under a wonderful deep burgundy umbrella with white tassels protecting them from the late summer sun searing down from the pale blue sky. They were in no hurry to order as they relaxed and enjoyed their first real taste of the unhurried pavement café lifestyle and watched the activity in the dock and the sightseers slowly wending their way along the waterfront.

The waiter arrived in his burgundy and white striped apron carrying a white napkin over his arm and Edward was soon chatting away to him in his excellent French, only breaking into English to ask, "Do you mind if I order for the both of us, Philip?" and without waiting for an answer continued discussing each item on the menu with the waiter in French. He eventually decided to order the fruits de mer, before turning his attention to the wine list. He laughed as he suggested, "Shall we have this cheap house red?" but he did not wait for a reply and instead ordered a '76 Brouilly.

By the time they had gorged themselves from the massive dish crammed with lobster; crab; mussels; prawns and a variety of other shell fish; had downed most of their second bottle of wine and were drinking their coffee it was mid afternoon. Philip looked at his watch, "I guess we should think about finding a hotel before long, we don't want to have to spend too much time finding one with vacant rooms."

Edward smiled, "Don't worry so much Philip, I'm sure we'll find somewhere easily enough," but when the waiter came with the bill and to refill their coffee cups, Edward began asking him about nearby hotels in French again. Philip managed to follow the gist of the conversation and watched as the waiter pointed and gave Edward directions. After he had left the table Edward said, "He seems pretty sure we'll get rooms at that hotel. In fact he's going to phone ahead and check for us, so just relax and enjoy your coffee."

Philip went to pick up the bill but Edward stopped him, "No this is my treat. I intend to do all the things on this trip that we couldn't afford to do the first time we came to France." He took out his wallet and laughed as he held it in front of Philip, "And when I've spent all this cash and travellers cheques, then that'll be the time to go back home."

Philip thanked him for lunch but also wondered what 'things' Edward had in mind for this trip. They had not really discussed Edward's plans in the short time between Edward asking him to come to France and leaving England. "So what plans do you have? What things do you want to do this trip that we couldn't do last time?"

Edward just looked at him for a while before answering, "Not that much really, but the trouble is I'm not sure how much I'll be able to do. So if it's OK with you, can we just take it a day at a time? And if the waiter's found us rooms can we start by just taking a slow stroll to the hotel? I'd like to have a nap before we do anything else."

Philip was shocked at Edward's need to rest so much and now realised how ill he really was, "Fine, I'm happy to do whatever you want. We'll see how things look in the morning and decide then whether to move on or not."

"Oh but I know exactly what I want to do tomorrow. I want us to go to Trouville and spend the day on the beach." He laughed as he took another sip of his coffee, "Or do you think two old men like us will be arrested if we sit there waiting to see if there are any girls on the beach as pretty as Juliette and Madeleine?"

Philip did not answer but merely smiled at his friend's remark as he suddenly realised why Edward had suggested this trip. He wanted to recapture some of the magic of when he had first met and immediately fell madly in love with Juliette and rekindle memories and experiences, the loss of which he had lamented over for the past thirty years.

He mulled over the problem as Edward counted out the money for the meal and added a considerable tip for the waiter. *'How on earth can I make sure it doesn't turn into a journey down memory lane that quickly becomes unbearable and disastrous for Edward in his current state of health?'*

Nevertheless by the time the waiter came back to tell them he had arranged rooms for them at the hotel, Philip had determined to try as best he could, to make sure that the memories reawakened would be the good memories and not the tragic ones that had tormented his friend for so long.

Edward was awake early the next morning and was knocking on Philip's bedroom door before he had finished dressing. As soon as Philip let him into the room, Edward was demanding that he hurry up as he wanted to leave for Trouville as soon as they had eaten breakfast. "It's a beautiful morning Philip and we don't want to miss any of the sun do we?"

Philip did not understand his friend's impatience but, in accordance with the promise he had made to himself the previous day, he did as Edward demanded. By lunchtime they had driven to Trouville, booked into a hotel just outside the town, taken a taxi into town, and were sitting on the beach eating the pâté spread on the baguettes and drinking the bottle of wine that Edward had purchased that morning before knocking on Philip's door.

"Do you remember eating a meal like this the last time we were here Philip?"

"Yes, but I don't remember us buying as good a bottle of wine as this on that holiday."

They both laughed but Edward's face suddenly dropped, "Trying to relive old memories doesn't really work, does it Philip? There are plenty of pretty young ladies sunning themselves today, but it isn't the same as when we were eighteen is it?" He turned and looked directly at Philip, "I think I've had enough of reminiscing for today." Philip thought he detected tears in his eyes as he shook his head and quietly, almost to himself, continued, "I'm never going to get her back, am I?"

Edward took another bite of his lunch and another swig from the bottle of wine. "Perhaps we should start acting our age, Philip. Why don't we finish this and make our way back to the hotel? There was a lovely view from the terrace and we could perhaps have an afternoon nap, like people of our age should?" He laughed as he took another swig of wine before handing the bottle to Philip, "So what do you say, shall we find ourselves a taxi and make our way back?"

Philip was relieved that Edward seemed to have given up the search for his lost youth, "I'll tell you what, Edward, why don't we ask the taxi driver if he can recommend a decent restaurant and I'll treat you to a good French meal tonight?"

"Maybe another night, Philip. I thought we could have an early meal at the hotel tonight and then go to the casino. I haven't been in a casino in years."

Philip did not know how to react to this suggestion. Samantha would never forgive him if this meant that Edward was starting his gambling habit again. But almost as if he could read his mind, Edward laughed and said, "Don't worry, old boy, I'm not going to get myself in debt all over again." He took out his wallet and counted out 1000 francs, "This is the maximum amount I'm prepared to play with tonight. I'll give you all my other cash and travellers cheques and I give you permission to refuse to give me any more once this is gone." He laughed as he added, "But I have a good feeling about this and I don't intend to lose any of it."

"I'll tell you what we'll do, Edward. I'll take the same amount with me and we'll leave everything else in the hotel safe. So drinks and everything else has to come out of this. And don't forget, we'll need enough for the taxi back to the hotel." He pointed his finger at Edward, "And we do this just tonight. We don't go anywhere near a casino after tonight."

Edward laughed so much he almost choked on his bread. He went red in the face; turned his back towards Philip and pointed to it. Philip understood the signal, slapped hard on Edward's back several times before he spat out the offending bread and started to breath easily again. Philip picked up the bottle and passed it to him and Edward drank a hefty slug of the wine before starting to laugh again, "Trust you to make rules like that, Philip." He held up his hand and gave the scout's three fingered salute, "Scouts honour, I promise to be a good boy after tonight," and they both laughed more than they had laughed together in many years.

But Edward was far more circumspect in the gaming rooms than Philip had ever expected. He had not yet made a single bet and had not even finished the glass of wine Philip had got for him an hour earlier as he merely stood watching other gamblers at the tables.

"Can I get you a refill for that, Edward?"

Edward held up his glass, "No I'm fine, but let me go and get you one."

"No thanks, I think I've had enough for the time being. Why don't we sit down a bit? I'm not doing very well. I've already lost about 300 francs so I don't mind going back to the hotel if you want to."

Edward patted his jacket pocket, "When I've played with some of this."

"I don't understand. Why haven't you played yet?"

"To tell you the truth, Philip, I've no idea. I don't understand it myself, but for now, I'm enjoying watching all these others losing their money." He smiled as he added, "It's a mug's game really isn't it? I can't believe I was just as daft once. I must have been mad."

"So do you want to go then?"

He put his glass to his lips and knocked back all the remaining liquid. "Not on your nelly." He touched his pocket bulging with the unused chips again, "At least not until some of this has been used." He took Philip's empty glass from him, "Let me get you another one of these and then let's enjoy ourselves at the roulette table for a bit."

He returned with the drinks but instead of making his way to the roulette table he found an empty settee and sat down on it. He patted the seat beside him and beckoned Philip to join him, and looked at his watch before speaking, "Maybe we should make our way further west tomorrow. Perhaps visit the cemeteries and pay our respects to our comrades." He reached into his pocket and took out a piece of paper, "I got this from the regiment a couple of weeks ago. It names some of the lads and the cemeteries they're buried in."

Philip took the paper, opened it and silently read the names, "Are you sure you're up to this Edward? I don't think it'll be easy remembering all of that horror again."

Edward took the paper from him, folded it and put it back in his pocket, "You know I thought I was the luckiest guy alive when I came round after her father had saved my life and I realised that Juliette was not only still alive but hadn't forgotten me. And when she said she'd marry me at the end of the war, I was over the moon. I thought the day I married her was the luckiest day of my life, but when we buried her exactly twelve months later I thought it was the unluckiest day for everyone concerned. I couldn't help thinking that everyone would've been better off if her father hadn't saved my life. If I had died that night she'd still be alive now. She may have visited my grave in one of these cemeteries a couple of times before finding some other guy to marry and maybe by now she'd be a grandmother with a dozen grandkids running round her."

This was exactly the sort of discussion that Philip was hoping they wouldn't have and he was at a loss to know how to deal with it. He merely touched Edward's arm suggesting, "You don't really mean all that, do you? What about Louise; she wouldn't be here if you'd died." He almost added that Julian wouldn't be alive either, but in the present circumstances felt that was best left unsaid.

Edward gave the merest hint of a smile as he said, "That's true." The smile broadened and he winked at Philip, "Do you think that if I can keep going long enough until she is Doctor Louise, she'll be able to sort out this blasted heart of mine."

"I'm sure she will," was all that Philip could think of as a suitable reply.

But Edward looked at his watch and immediately changed the subject, "My goodness it's almost midnight and I guess I should use these chips." He raised his glass and tapped Philip's glass, "Thanks for coming with me, I really appreciate it." He clinked the glasses together again, "Here's to a lucky streak at the tables," and with that he downed the contents and made his way to the nearest roulette table.

Philip finished his drink and joined him expecting him to now start placing bets, but he didn't. Instead he just stood there watching the croupier intensely each time he spun the wheel, and each time the ball dropped into a numbered slot he shook his head as if it wasn't doing what it should. This continued for the next fifteen minutes but then suddenly he was smiling without shaking his head, as the croupier called out, "Douze rouge – twelve red," and started to scoop up the losing chips and paying on the winning ones.

Edward looked at his watch, edged his way to the rim of the table, took all the chips from his pocket and placed all 1000 francs on number thirty-one. Philip wanted to stop him making such a large bet on a single number but somehow knew that Edward had been waiting all evening for this one bet.

The croupier spun the wheel and demanded, "No more bets" as the ball was sent on its way. Philip's eyes were transfixed on the ball as it rolled and bounced round the rim. He was frightened to take a breath in case the very act of breathing caused the ball to roll further than it should, but when the wheel started to slow down he could not bear to watch any longer. He turned and looked at Edward and was surprised to see that he was smiling and was not watching the spinning of the wheel either. He winked when he saw Philip looking at him and the smile widened into a broad grin as the clicking of the ball stopped, and the croupier announced, "Noir, trente et un. Black, thirty-one."

Philip could not believe it. He turned to check where the ball was sitting in the wheel, before looking back and grinning at Edward, but Edward merely winked at him again and waited for the croupier to push his winnings across to him. His face was impassive as he scooped up his own 1000 franc stake and the extra 35,000 francs in chips the croupier passed to him. Philip fully expected him to continue playing but instead he dropped a pile of chips in Philip's hand and then collected up the rest from the table, "I've had enough Philip, shall we cash these in and go?"

When they were sitting in the back of the taxi on the way back to the hotel, Philip could not contain his curiosity any longer, "I don't understand it Edward. You said you wanted to spend an evening at the casino, but then you just watched others playing without placing a bet, and then suddenly you put everything you'd got on one single number. How on earth did you know it was going to come up?"

Edward let out an enormous laugh and Philip thought he detected a tear in his eye as he held his watch for him to look at.

Philip read the time, "It's twenty past one, so what."

"But what's the date?"

Philip looked closely at the date number showing on the watch, "The thirty-first! You mean you gambled almost a hundred and twenty pounds on the date?"

"If I answer that question you have to promise me that you won't mention all this to anyone else."

"Of course not, if that's how you want it."

Edward pursed his lips as if considering whether to continue. Eventually he said, "You know what I was saying earlier about the day I married Juliette?" Philip nodded as Edward continued, "Well I know you're going to think this is stupid, but I just couldn't stop thinking about the date and when the twelve came up, I just had to see whether Juliette wanted me know whether thirty-one was lucky or not."

Philip looked puzzled as he tried to work it out, but Edward came to his rescue, "It came up twelve and December is the twelfth month and I know this is August but today is the thirty-first. The thirty-first of December is her birthday; our wedding day and the day of her funeral. Lucky or unlucky? I had to find out. It's absolutely stupid I know, but it was a moment of madness that seemed to make sense to me at the time."

"And now?"

He laughed as he replied, "I must have been certifiable, but it worked didn't it? So maybe she wants me to treat the date as lucky and not fret about it any more."

"I'm sure she never wanted you to fret about things."

Edward shook his head. "And what do you think she would want me to do with all these winnings?"

"I've no idea," Philip said, but not wanting Edward to get too morose over Juliette decided to try and change the subject, "Did you see the look on the croupier's face when you won?"

They both laughed as they discussed the faces of all the people round the table and were still both doubled up with laughter when the taxi pulled up at the hotel.

It was a bright, warm September day as they sat outside the café in the square at Thury-Harcourt eating their way through a modest lunch of cheese and bread washed down with a cold beer. They had spent the last seven days visiting the old battle grounds and the war cemeteries where their fallen comrades were buried and had spent this particular morning going round the village inspecting the various memorials to the 59th Staffordshire Division and the liberation of the town in August 1944.

Neither Juliette's nor Julian's name had been mentioned by either of them since the casino incident, but as they sat eating their late lunch, Philip wanted to ask Edward if they could go and see Madeleine. He was sure she would make them more than welcome, but was also unsure of Edward's wishes in the matter and decided, for the time being at least, to continue avoiding the subject of Juliette or her family.

Unbeknown to Philip however, Edward had deliberately sat at this table so that he could see the entrance to the shop across the square with the names 'Julian et Nicole' above it. Philip had his back to the shop and had not seen the name or the paintings displayed in the window.

Edward had learned of the studio's existence from a letter he had from Madeleine some months previously and had intentionally led Philip to the square. He had been disappointed to see the 'Fermé' sign hanging on the door as they entered the square and had been glancing across every few minutes to see if anyone arrived to remove the sign. He was still waiting when they finished the meal and when Philip got up saying he would pay the bill, Edward stopped him, "Sorry but I'd like to rest here a bit longer. Why don't we have another beer?" He made the drink last as long as he could and was beginning to think that no-one was going to open the studio.

He heard the child's laughter before he saw the three year old girl turn the corner and run to the door of the shop where she stopped. A man and a woman holding hands ran round the corner and Edward had to take a deep breath to try to slow down the beating of his heart. He recognised Julian immediately; he was so obviously Juliette's son. He had the same shining black shoulder length hair, which he threw back as he reached the child and picked her up, his laughter so reminiscent of Juliette's laughter. Edward could hardly breathe as he looked at the little girl; the granddaughter he had never seen before and the daughter-in-law he'd never seen before either.

The woman remonstrated with the girl for running off on her own, but as soon as she had done so, kissed her on the head as if to show she wasn't really angry.

Philip noticed Edward's deep breathing and touched his hand, "Are you OK?"

Edward merely replied, "Yes I'm fine," as he continued looking across at his son, granddaughter and daughter-in-law Nicole.

For the first time Philip turned to see what Edward was staring at and just managed to see the group enter the premises. He saw the name painted above the window and realised its significance, "Did you know that Julian had his studio there?" The reason for the drawn out lunch suddenly dawned on him and he did not wait for an answer before asking, "Have we been waiting here for him to come back?"

Edward picked up his glass and drained the remainder of the beer from it, "Sorry Philip, I should have said something to you, but I didn't know if anyone would come and open up the studio."

"So are we going across there to speak to him?"

Edward took several more deep breaths before replying, "Do you mind if we just sit here for a bit? I need to calm down before I face him."

But they had only sat waiting for a couple of minutes when the door opened and Julian and the child came out. Nicole stood in the doorway as Julian turned and gave her a kiss. She then leaned down and gave the girl a kiss before Julian took hold of the child's hand and led her away. Edward kept his stare on father and child as they rounded the corner and vanished from sight. He looked back at Nicole, who was still standing in the doorway as if expecting them to return any moment. Even at this distance, Edward knew he would like Julian's wife as much as Madeleine had said he would. She was indeed a very attractive woman; not the overt glamour of celebrities in the magazines, but an eye-catching natural beauty who radiated contentment and happiness. She looked round the square and stared at the two men sitting at the café. It was not an inquisitive stare but was almost as if she was saying 'hello' to them with a kind welcoming smile that endorsed the unspoken greeting.

Edward returned the smile and gave her a wave as she re-entered through the door.

"Does she know who you are?" Philip asked.

"I shouldn't think so. Maybe it's just her way of encouraging strangers to look at the paintings."

"And are we going to?"

"Maybe in a minute or two, let's see if Julian comes back first."

The waiter came out and asked if they wanted anything else. Philip said not and gave him a hundred franc note to cover the bill; telling him to keep the change.

They had only been waiting for five minutes when Edward stood up and said, "Let's go and see these paintings then." He took Philip's arm as they started to walk across the square, "I hope you don't mind Philip but I'd rather we didn't say who we are, or more specifically who I am. I've never met her and I don't know how she'll react to me and the way I've abandoned Julian over all these years." Philip merely acknowledged the statement without comment.

The bell on the inside of the door clanged as soon as they opened it. Nicole was sitting behind the desk working on a tapestry. She looked up, smiled and said, 'Good afternoon," to them as soon as they entered.

"How do you know we're English, Madame," Edward quizzed.

"But you are English aren't you?" Her English was good but was spoken with the beautiful French lilt that gave away her own nationality.

"Yes, of course, but that doesn't explain how you knew before we spoke."

She put the tapestry on the table and smiled the same enchanting smile she had given them across the square. As she stood up to shake his hand, Edward noticed that she was obviously a few months pregnant. "Ah," she said as she moved forward to also shake Philip's hand, "But I've heard you speak. I saw you this morning outside the church looking at the war memorial and as I passed you I realised you were speaking English." She took Philip's hand and shook it, "I'll leave you to wander round and look at the artwork yourselves, but if there's anything you want to know just ask."

Philip thanked her and turned to look at the paintings but Edward continued talking to her, "I noticed the names 'Julian et Nicole' outside, are those the names of the artists?"

"Yes Julian is my husband's name, and most of the pieces are his but there a few of mine as well." She held out her hand and he shook it again, "And I'm Nicole."

"And I'm Edward and this is my friend Philip. I take it Julian is not your husband's surname then?"

"Mais non!" she said before reverting back to English, "It's a long story but he prefers to only use his Christian name on his work and when we married I also started to only use my first name as well."

Edward knew that although Julian's birth certificate gave his parents' name as Richards, he had always used his grandparents' name of Guilbert so he quickly dropped the subject of names and turned his attention to studying the works on display.

Meanwhile Philip was looking at an oil painting of a landscape, trying to remember where he had seen the scene before and asked Nicole, "Is this painting of anywhere in particular?"

"Yes, it's a view from the back of Julian's great uncle's house in Hèrouvillette, just outside Caen. The poppies and other wild flowers were so amazing that Julian just had to paint it."

Philip almost said, "Ah yes, I remember now," but quickly changed it to, "Ah yes… it's very beautiful," so that Nicole would not ask any awkward questions as to how he knew the spot.

He moved to look at other paintings and was soon transfixed by the next three much larger oil paintings. Close up they were each merely bold and heavy splashes of brilliant colours, but when he took several steps back and viewed them through half closed eyes, their true magic came alive. They were no longer merely a miscellany of coloured oils splattered on the canvas, but became different aspects of a gipsy dancer's breathtaking movement as she spun round at speed; the glow from the fire highlighting her body, her hair and her multicoloured skirt against the background of the setting sun.

He stepped forward to read their titles, Gitane 1 (1977), Gitane 2 (1977) and Gitane 3 (1977) underneath. He moved back to once more take in the mesmerising atmosphere of each again as the gipsy completely immersed her pulsating and spinning body to the beat and rhythm of the music.

Edward however was more interested in inspecting all of Julian's work and was soon fascinated by his son's obvious artistic talent in so many different styles and mediums and could not decide which of the paintings he liked best. The few paintings of Nicole's didn't have the same distinctive quality of Julian's work, but the opposite was true of her sculptures. The many small intricate pieces clearly showed where Nicole's real talents lay; as did the tapestries that somehow had a vibrant exuberance that transcended the mere design and colour in them.

After a while Nicole, unsure whether she was ever going to get a sale, nervously asked, "And have you found one you like?"

"It's a very difficult choice. There are several I've really taken a fancy to, but I can't take them all."

She laughed, "Well if you do want to buy all of them, I don't mind packing them up for you." She said this in such a casual way, it was almost as if she realised that was exactly what he would like to do.

"Would you like me to make you a cup of coffee whilst you make your choice?" she asked as Edward started to slowly inspect each of the paintings for a second time.

He gave her a big smile, "Yes we'd like that very much, thank you." His smile turned to laughter as he said, "But if I did buy them all, you wouldn't have anything left to show other people would you?"

"Oh, but there are other paintings upstairs in the studio and I'm sure Julian would be happy to paint more."

"There are more upstairs? Could we see them?"

"If Julian was here he would bring them down for you to see." She patted her stomach, "But he has forbid me to carry the paintings down the stairs in my condition."

"Could we perhaps go up and see them then? I really would like to see any other work you have before I make my choice."

She looked concerned at this request, but eventually said, "We don't usually have people in the studio, but I suppose you could go and have a look. I'll make you that coffee and be with you in a minute."

Edward said, "Thank you," and immediately moved towards the stairs.

She stepped in front of him before he reached the first step, "I hope you don't mind me saying this but some of the paintings are still wet, and some of my pieces are still being worked on, so do you mind not touching any of them until I come up. You'll be able to see most of them and I'll be up in a minute to show you any you can't see properly."

"Of course; I understand perfectly. I wouldn't want to be responsible for spoiling anything."

Philip followed Edward up the stairs which led to an open studio area taking up the whole of the top floor. The room was ablaze with sunlight streaking through enormous skylights making it obvious why this bright space had been chosen as a studio. The room reeked of the odours of oil paints, turpentine, linseed oil, clay, and all the other artist's mediums used in the studio by both Julian and Nicole.

On one wall were the first rough sketches and intricate detailed drawings of sections of Julian's paintings and in the middle of the room were two easels with partly completed oil paintings on them. On the opposite wall were full size outlines of Nicole's sculptures and tapestries and against this wall was a small work table on which stood something covered with a wet muslin cloth. Edward wanted to walk across and inspect what he assumed would be the partly completed clay model Nicole was currently working on, but took note of her warning and stopped himself from doing so.

He scanned the rest of the studio and turned round to see what was in the space behind him to the side of the stairs. He immediately began to physically shake and gasp for air as he pointed in front of him. Philip thought he was having a heart attack and ran to his friend's aid, but when he also turned he saw the cause of Edward's agitation. Hanging on the wall was a much larger oil painting in a totally different style to any they had seen downstairs. This canvas could have been a Monet or a Degas or any of the other impressionist painters but for the fact that the woman whose face was smiling at the onlookers was Juliette and she was clearly wearing a twentieth century dress. She was sitting under the apple tree in the corner of the family garden and was wearing the Sunday best blue dress she had worn the first time Edward and Philip had visited her home. But the image was not a simple painting; it was a vision that brought a living Juliette into the room and captured the true essence of her beauty and character.

Philip turned and looked at Edward. He was still shaking and the tears were spilling down his face in a continuous stream. He wiped his face on the sleeve of his jacket; took his wallet from his inside pocket and extracted a photograph from within it. He obviously knew exactly where the picture was in the wallet as he didn't take his eyes off the painting as he removed it and passed it to Philip. The picture had been handled a great deal over the years but was still recognisable as the same image depicted in the painting.

But the photograph was in black and white and the level of detail was nothing like that in the painting and none of the wild flowers growing in profusion around Juliette in Julian's work were present on the photograph.

Edward took out his handkerchief and wiped his face again. The shaking had stopped but the moisture around the eyes continued to flow, "I took that picture of Juliette that first summer and I've carried it with me ever since. I'd forgotten I'd given Juliette a copy, but Julian must have used it to paint that from it. But how on earth has he managed to capture her in more detail than in the photo? How did he know the exact colour of her hair, her skin, her lips, and how did he know the colour of the dress?"

Philip moved to his friend and put his arms around him, "Maybe he loves her as much as you do?" The two men clung to each other and only separated when they heard Nicole coming up the stairs.

Philip took the tray from her as she reached the top of the steps and they each took a cup of coffee from it before he placed the empty tray on the floor; the only available free surface. Edward was still staring at the painting. She took a sip from her cup before speaking, "I can see you like that one, but unfortunately that is the one of Julian's paintings that is not for sale."

Philip was surprised that Edward was clearly not prepared to let Nicole know that he knew who was in the painting, "That's a shame. It's a wonderful painting. Is the girl anyone special?"

"Yes it's his mother."

"She is a very beautiful woman."

"Yes she was. She died when Julian was born, so Julian never knew her. Even so, his grandmother says it is a very good likeness of her."

Edward was just about to say, "It's an unbelievable likeness of her," but managed to stop himself from saying it and said, "I'm sure it is," and, "Are you sure that it's not for sale? I would be very happy to pay whatever you ask for it," instead.

"No. I'm sorry, but Julian would not sell that particular painting at any price." She looked around the studio, "There must be something else that has taken your fancy."

Edward wanted the painting above all else but he knew he had to lose this Juliette to his son as quickly and as permanently as he had lost the living Juliette for him. The pain in his face was obvious to Philip, who knew he had to somehow divert Edward's attention from the painting.

He looked around the room and saw a group of sketches pinned on the wall nearest to the easel where the latest painting was being worked on. He walked towards them, saying, "Come and have a look at these, Edward. They must be the outlines for that painting." He turned and spoke to Nicole, "Would you be prepared to sell my friend these?"

Edward moved to the drawings and was immediately spellbound by the two pencil sketches of Juliette's face. Both had captured her beauty in exactly the same way as the oil painting had.

Nicole put down her cup and joined the two men studying the sketches, "Julian doesn't usually sell his outline sketches. I suppose I could ask him if he would sell these, but he has taken our daughter to Caen this afternoon to buy the art materials we need. He won't be back until this evening, so you'd have to come back tomorrow to find out if he'll let you have them."

Again, Philip could see the frustration in Edward's face at this further difficulty in buying something of Juliette and decided to try to reach a compromise for him, "Unfortunately we won't be here tomorrow but why don't we have a look at the other paintings here, and whilst we decide what to purchase, perhaps you could have a think about selling these drawings as well." He did not wait for her to respond before taking Edward's arm and leading him to a smaller oil painting leaning against the back wall, "Edward, here's the painting for you."

This painting was in the same 'impressionist' style as the Juliette canvas and was of a woman and child playing on a beach. Edward looked back at the two oil paintings of the same size on the easels and realised that they were to be of the same woman and child on the beach.

Nicole picked up the completed painting and put it on a spare easel, "My husband only finished varnishing it last week and as you see, we haven't had it framed yet."

"Edward studied the painting and then looked at Nicole, "This is you and your daughter, isn't it? Would your husband be prepared to sell this one?"

"Unfortunately we have to eat so he cannot keep all the things he likes. So yes, I'm sure it's for sale."

The likeness was again, not only extraordinary, but the sheer enjoyment on the faces of the participants brought alive the happiness and joyfulness of mother and child playing on the sand against azure sky and sunlit sea.

Edward was so overjoyed at the thought of having this picture of his granddaughter and daughter-in-law painted by his son, that all he was able to say was, "I'll take it."

"I'm sorry but my husband prices his work and I have no idea how much to ask for it. Are you sure you cannot come back tomorrow? Julian can sort everything out with you then. He could even price and sign one of the drawings for you if he agrees to let you have it."

"Unfortunately we're not staying in Thury-Harcourt tonight and we have to go somewhere else before we leave so I'd really appreciate it if you could come up with a price for the painting. I'll be more than happy to pay whatever you ask." He pointed to the larger of the two drawings of Juliette's head, "And perhaps you'll have a think about these drawings as well. I'd particularly like this one and I'll pay you whatever figure you come up with for this as well."

She was clearly thrown by the offer, and knew that Julian would want her to make sure of the sale, but she needed to come up with a figure that Julian would approve of, so she asked again, "Are you sure you can't come back later this evening, say eight o'clock, when my husband gets back?"

"No I'm sorry. We just have one other place to go in Thury-Harcourt and then we'll be leaving town." He shrugged his shoulders and asked, "Why don't you think of a reasonable price and then double it. I'd be very happy with that and maybe your husband will be as well."

Nicole was puzzled by this generous offer and was not certain whether Edward was serious until he said, "We'll go downstairs again and sort any other items we would like whilst you think about it. I really would like to purchase these two pieces so please let me have them." He looked at the canvas once more, "And just let me know what you decide."

He did not want her to have any second thoughts about selling them without Julian's approval, so he decided not to give her the option, "You need not bother to wrap the canvas. I'll carry it down stairs for you and then I'll get Philip to fetch the car and we can just pop it the boot, but it would help if you've got a piece of card to put with the drawing, so as to keep it safe until I can get it framed?"

As soon as they had descended the stairs Philip handed the photograph back to Edward who asked, "Are you going to buy anything, Philip?"

"Well I like the poppy field painting. It's so like I remember it."

"I guess you must have a better memory than me." He laughed, "But then I suppose the only thing I could see that evening was Juliette."

Philip went to look again at the gipsy paintings that had so intrigued him and pointed to No. 2. "But I love this painting as well. I'm fascinated by the spirit of it, and the pleasure it gives me merely looking at it."

"Why don't you buy it then?"

Philip went to the frame and looked at the price tag. He was very tempted but he had not brought enough currency with him to pay its 4,350 francs price tag as well as the landscape.

Edward must have realised his friend's dilemma because he punched him on the back saying, "If you like it, Philip, you must have it. And you must let me buy both of them for you as a gift."

He would not listen to Philip's protestations against the offer and insisted, "After all, I've got all the money I won at the casino burning a hole in my pocket." He smiled and added, "Actually that gives me an idea how I can use the money I won to Juliette's satisfaction," and with that he took his notebook from out of his pocket and started to make a note of the price of a number of the paintings and of Nicole's sculptures."

By the time Nicole came downstairs with a large envelope containing the sketch, Edward had decided on the piece of Nicole's sculpture he wanted to take with him. It was a piece about ten inches high cast in bronze of a young girl about two or three years old. She was dressed as a vagabond, complete with grubby peaked cap with her long hair flowing from under it; baggy patched trousers, a ragged waistcoat that was far too large for her frail body, being worn over a torn and tattered shirt hanging loose at the wrists and frayed trousers which were patched in several different materials. From a distance the effigy created a comic image but as you studied the piece closely, the sorrow and drama of the child's tragic predicament was clear in the pretty but cheerless face, creating a heart-rending vista of the little girl's sadness.

Edward had liked the piece when he first saw it, but now that he examined it more closely, he realised that Nicole had used her own daughter as the model; a fact that made the melancholic look on her face even more poignant for him.

Nicole placed the envelope on the desk next to the painting that Edward had carried downstairs for her. She turned to Edward and said, "I'm sure my husband wouldn't want you to pay too much for these pieces so give me a minute and I'll try and come up with a fair price for you."

"Thank you, but don't forget what I said. Actually there are a couple of pieces Philip likes." He walked to the paintings and pointed to them, "These are the ones. Can you add these to the bill, please?"

The delight at selling two more paintings was clear on her face, "And is that everything?"

But instead of answering he picked up the sculpture and was surprised at its weight. It was far heavier than he had imagined. "I'm fascinated by this little girl, am I right in thinking it's the same girl as the one in the painting?"

"Yes, it's my daughter Amélie. She was sobbing her heart out one day when she couldn't go out into the garden to play and I sketched her sad face whilst my husband tried unsuccessfully to console her. And that became the motivation behind the sculpture."

Edward placed the sculpture on the table in front of her, "It's so wonderful, I must take it as well."

"I don't want to put you off buying it but you do realise it's not an exclusive piece, don't you?"

She picked the sculpture up and looked at the side of the base, "If you look here against my signature you can see that this is number 1 of 10. So there are another nine of the same model. It is too expensive to only have one model cast." She looked at Edward, "Do you still want it?"

Edward smiled and nodded his head, "Yes, of course," as he took the envelope containing all 36000 francs he'd exchanged at the casino from his winning chips and original stake from his inside pocket. He took the money out of the envelope and placed it on the table next to the chosen pieces, "Actually there is another piece I'd like your husband to sell me."

He pushed the money across to her, "I believe you'll find more than enough money there to pay for the items we are taking with us, and with what is left, I would like to give your husband a commission."

She shook her head yet again, "Please don't be offended but I have to disappoint you again. Julian doesn't take commissions. He doesn't like to have his work dictated by others, so I can't accept money for a commission." She saw the disappointment on his face and asked, "But just out of interest, what was it you had in mind?"

He picked up the envelope containing the sketch, "Well I was hoping he might consider painting a smaller version of this lady; a smaller version of the painting upstairs."

She looked at him with wistful eyes, "I'm sorry, it's was obvious you were taken by it, but I cannot accept the money for a commission." She looked at the pile of money on the table, "And as I've said, I cannot sell you the original either. Are you sure I cannot interest you in something else?"

Edward wiped his hand across his mouth and stroked his chin, "Much as I would like that particular painting, I do understand why Julian would not sell it, and I hope he never does." He laughed nervously as he added, "But if ever he does decide to sell it, perhaps he will give me first option to buy?"

He smiled at her but felt certain his comment had fallen on deaf ears. "It's such a wonderful painting and I would so have liked a copy of it, but if he doesn't take specific commissions, then I'll have to remain disappointed."

She almost ignored his comment and immediately asked, "So shall I make out the bill for these five items then?"

Edward was not yet willing to give in. He wanted to make sure, one way or another that Julian and his wife had all the money he had won. He knew a straight gift was totally out of the question without giving some reason for the generosity. If he admitted to being Julian's father then the rejection of the money would probably be more violent.

He decided to try another approach, "I do understand why your husband won't accept a specific commission and I respect that, but I am impressed with everything he has here. So can I suggest that you take the extra money and that he creates any piece of work he chooses for me? Any subject, in any medium he wishes. That way, it isn't really a commission is it? It's just paying in advance for his next project."

"This is terribly confusing for me. I have no idea what he will say."

Philip stepped in, "Please do as my friend requests. He has his own reasons for asking."

"I've never met anything like this before. I really don't understand it."

She looked at the money and without counting it knew it was probably almost double the amount for the pieces already purchased. They could certainly do with the money.

After a few moments of thought she said, "You will have to leave me your name and address and I'll get Julian to write to you when he has completed it. I just hope he will be happy with the arrangement."

"Please try and convince him. And don't worry about getting in touch. I shall be back here some time next year and I'll collect the item then." He laughed as he suggested, "Until then perhaps you can display it here with a 'sold' ticket on it."

She was even more confused by this but had decided against placing any further obstacles in the way of this most unusual sale. She picked up the money and started counting it, "I'll give you a receipt for these five items and I'll give you a separate receipt for the rest of the money. What name shall I put on them?"

Edward was thrown by the question and did not want to give away his identity as he was afraid of Julian's reaction when he found out it was his absent father who had been so generous with the commission. He was sure Julian would react violently if he knew and refuse to have anything to do with it, so he merely gave her his Christian names instead, "Edward Thomas." She then asked him for his home address. He could not think what to do about this and did not answer her, but when she asked a second time he gave her his correct address.

She gave him the receipts and he put them in his wallet and whilst she was packing the sculpture, Philip went and fetched the car. Nicole and Edward were standing together as they studied and discussed some of the other works together when Philip returned. They were both laughing and Philip sensed a newly found familiarity between them, which made him feel almost like an intruder as he walked towards them.

Nicole thanked them both for their purchases and said, "I hope you will get a lot of pleasure from them. And thank you for the generous commission. I'm sure Julian will try to give you something that you will enjoy."

"I'm sure he will. And please tell him for me that he is very talented and so are you. You should be very proud of all your work."

Nicole followed them out of the shop. She shook Philip's hand as she thanked him for the purchases again, but when she held out her hand to shake Edward's hand, he took a step closer to her, "Do you think your husband would mind if gave his very talented artist wife a kiss on the cheek, Madame?"

She smiled, "Non monsieur," and with that she leaned forward and gave him a kiss on his cheek instead.

"Merci beaucoup, Nicole." He squeezed her hand slightly before releasing it, "Et au revoir. It has been a pleasure to meet you."

"And you too, Monsieur." She noticed the bunch of flowers on the back seat as Philip put their purchases in the boot and without thinking asked, "Who is the lucky lady?"

Philip looked at Edward wondering how he would react to the question, but Edward just smiled at Nicole and replied, "A very special lady who I haven't visited in a very long time."

"Never mind, she will forgive you when you give her those. They are very beautiful."

Edward's face dropped, "I don't think she can ever forgive me for what I have done, or rather haven't done since I last saw her," and with that he got into the car before she asked any more awkward questions.

Both Nicole and Julian had the answers to all their questions however, when they went past the cemetery later that evening and saw the same bunch of flowers placed lovingly on Julian's mother's grave.

After they had visited the grave, Edward asked Philip if he would mind if they made their way home on the next day rather than wait until the following Tuesday as they had original planned. Philip could see that seeing his son and spending all that time with his son's wife had taken its toll on him. The visit to the graveside had been even more harrowing for Edward, and as he had placed the flowers, it was as if all the years of trying to avoid the pain of her death; not visiting the grave; and having no direct contact with their son, overpowered him. He had fallen to his knees and cried inconsolably. Philip moved to his side and tried to comfort his friend, "Are you sure you're all right? You don't look at all well."

But Edward would have none of it, and answered him angrily, "I'm fine. I just want to be on my own for a bit, so do you mind waiting for me in the car?"

It was at least half an hour before Edward was able to control himself sufficiently to return to the car during which time he poured out his heart to Juliette. He asked her forgiveness for abandoning their son and for not coming to see her as he knew he should have done, but doing so did not bring him any contentment. He tried to explain how traumatised he'd been at her dreadful death, but soon felt that it all sounded like an excuse for his unpardonable behaviour. It was only when he started to talk to her about his own illness and the realisation that his own death would bring an end to all his pain that he began to feel any peace of mind. He was no longer afraid that he could die at any time, and for a short time, even welcomed the thought that he could somehow be reunited with Juliette.

By the time he rejoined Philip he was quite calm and, even though he had no real belief in the afterlife, he knew exactly what further favour he needed to ask of Philip.

CHAPTER TWENTY-EIGHT

DECEMBER 1978

Samantha rang for the ambulance at three o'clock in the morning. She had been awoken by a noise and when she got out of bed to investigate she found Edward lying on the floor in his bedroom gasping for air. He was unable to speak and could not move his left arm or leg. The ambulance man thought it was a stroke or heart attack and immediately rushed him to hospital.

It was touch and go for the first few hours, but when Philip visited him late that afternoon, his treatment was beginning to have effect and he was trying to speak with barely understandable grunts and groans through a very twisted mouth and face. It took Samantha and Philip quite some time before they fully comprehended his requests; the most important of which was that he wanted to see Louise.

"I'll phone her this evening after her classes and let her know. Trouble is she doesn't always go straight back to her digs after lectures."

Edward became disturbed at Samantha's response and after a time it became obvious to Philip that he was trying to say he did not want Louise to be told of his condition over the telephone. He looked at his watch and said, "Look don't worry I'll go to Edinburgh and let Louise know what's happened and I'll bring her straight back. With a bit of luck she'll be here to see you first thing tomorrow morning."

"You can't drive all the way to Edinburgh, and then drive straight back through the night without a break. I'm sure Edward would rather wait a bit longer to make sure you arrive back here safely than fall asleep at the wheel and not get back at all."

Edward clearly understood what Samantha had said, and shakily pointed to Philip before placing his right hand to the side of his head to indicate that he needed to rest when he got to Edinburgh before driving back.

Philip leaned forward and took Edward's hand, "OK I'll go home first to collect a few things and I'll find somewhere in Edinburgh to sleep tonight." He released Edward's hand saying, "I'll pick Louise up first thing in the morning and we'll see you tomorrow afternoon."

As Philip went to kiss his friend on the forehead Edward whispered to him. Philip just about managed to understand his warped words, "You will keep your promise about phoning Madeleine and scattering my ashes, won't you? Please don't forget."

Philip nodded his head and whispered back, "I promise," and then decided to add, "But you're going to get better so there's no rush for now," to which Edward replied, "I think not," before closing his eyes as if ready for sleep.

Philip left his side and kissed Samantha on the cheek saying, "I'll go now to get Louise and yes, I will drive carefully and safely," before making his way out of the ward.

All the way home, Philip couldn't get Edward's last words to him, and his need to see Louise so urgently, out of his head. It was totally out of character for Edward to disturb Louise's studies in normal circumstances particularly when she would be coming home for the Christmas break in a week in any case. So there was obviously more to the request. And why would he feel it necessary to remind him of the other promises? The only possible reason was if Edward did not expect to get better and was preparing everyone for his death.

As he opened the door of his house, he had almost convinced himself that he had seen his friend alive for the last time. He was not one for prayers, but could not stop himself from silently pleading, *'Oh God, please get him through this. And at least keep him safe 'til I return with Louise.'*

He packed a few things in his overnight bag and after phoning his secretary to let her know he wouldn't be at work, he looked up Madeleine's phone number in France and started to ring it.

He put the phone down at the first ring and immediately picked it up again. He stood there with the receiver in his hand trying to decide whether he should speak to Madeleine now or wait until later. Try as he might, he could not get the thought out of his head that if he left it until later he might be telling her that Edward was already dead.

At Juliette's graveside earlier in the year Edward had asked Philip to telephone Madeleine and let her know of his death when it happened, but surely it would be kinder to prepare her and let her know he was seriously ill? *'She would want to know wouldn't she?'* he thought, but then recalled that Edward had also told him when in France that he did not want Madeleine, and particularly Julian and his family, to know he was ill. *'Perhaps I should leave it,'* but hesitated every time he went to put the phone down. Eventually he made up his mind that it was only right that Edward's son should know his father was dying whatever their relationship had been or even what Julian's feelings on the matter were. He rang the number again and this time he waited until it was answered.

It turned out to be a much longer telephone conversation than he had anticipated. Surprisingly, Madeleine seemed to not only have much warmer feelings towards Edward than he'd expected but also knew more about him than he had imagined. She knew of his operation a few years earlier but she did not know how serious the prognosis had become. When the conversation got round to Julian she became tense and was certainly more circumspect in what she said. Eventually however, she relaxed more and started to ask about Edward and Philip's visit to France, "I do wish Edward had stayed and spoken to Julian." There was some semblance of anger in her voice as she added, "He should have contacted Julian a long time ago and now you phone to tell me that it's probably too late."

"I'm sorry Madeleine but I don't understand it either. I can only think he's always been afraid that Julian wouldn't want anything to do with him and he didn't know how to deal with that."

"Maybe you're right, but he should have stayed and spoken to Julian in September." Neither of them spoke for a few moments and then Madeleine said, "It would have been far better to do that than just writing to me to tell me about how I had done such a good job of bringing him up and how proud he was of Julian's artwork." She then went on to say how angry Julian had been about the so called commission and how he had wanted to send back all the money including the payment for the pieces purchased.

"You know it took Nicole and me several days to calm him down and it was only when I showed Julian the letter Edward had sent to me as soon as you got back to England that he started to calm down."

"Why? What did the letter say?"

"Well it was a rather long letter saying all the things he should have been saying to Julian and not me. It told about all his feelings for Juliette, but perhaps more importantly, he spoke of all his regrets about abandoning Julian. There was too much in there to go into now, but if ever you are over here, I'll let you see it."

They spoke for another ten minutes, but at the end of the conversation Philip did not know whether Madeleine was going to say anything to Julian or not. He put the phone down and wondered whether he had done right to make the call.

He woke early the next morning and did not wait for any breakfast before setting out to see Louise. He hadn't contacted her the previous evening, deciding it would be better to break the news that her father was in hospital after she'd had a good night's sleep instead.

He looked at his watch as he arrived at the house Louise shared with three other girl students, *'Five past seven, she's probably not awake yet. I'll leave it a bit,'* but he only waited a couple of minutes before getting out of the car and ringing the bell. No-one came to answer. He rang a further three times before a girl he had never seen before opened the door. Her hair was soaking wet and she was holding a dressing gown tightly around her with one hand whilst drying her face on a towel with the other. She had obviously just got out of the bath and the water was still glistening on her bare legs. She merely looked at Philip without saying anything.

Hello, I'm Philip Matthews. I'm Louise's uncle. Do you think I could speak to her?"

The girl did not answer but continued rubbing her face as she closed the door and left Philip standing outside. Five minutes later he was just about to ring the bell again, when the door opened and Louise stood there.

She was also in her dressing gown but by the state of her hair and general demeanour it was clear she had been asleep until a few minutes earlier. She looked bleary eyed, but that quickly changed as she saw who her visitor was, "Uncle Philip, what arc you doing here? What's happened?" The panic in her voice grew as she asked each question, "Is it Mom or Dad? What's happened to them?"

Philip had been concentrating on how to break the news to Louise for most of the journey up, but he forgot all his planned lines and said, "Your father isn't very well, but otherwise everything's fine. Can I come in and I'll explain everything?"

"Sorry, yes of course." She opened the door wider and when he stepped into the hallway, she gave him a kiss before saying, "Shall we go into the kitchen and you can tell me all about it there?"

By the time Philip had explained that her father was in hospital and why he had come to fetch her, Louise was sobbing on his shoulder. She made no attempt to move her head as he gently stroked her hair. Eventually however she wiped her eyes on the sleeve of her dressing gown and got up, "Do you mind making yourself a cup of tea whilst I go and get ready then?" She pointed to one of the cupboards and managed a smile as she added, "That one's mine. You might find a bit of bread in there if you fancy some toast." She pointed to the fridge, "I think there might be some butter in there and if you're lucky you might find some jam or something in the cupboard."

Philip had tea and toast ready for Louise when she came back downstairs. She looked so different now that she was dressed, had combed her hair and put make-up on. She grabbed a piece of the toast saying, "I must give mother a call and find out how Dad is. I don't suppose you've got some 10p's I could use for the phone have you?" He gave her all the loose change he had as she took a swig of tea out of her mug.

Philip was beginning to wonder whether Edward had taken a turn for the worse as the telephone call seemed to take such a long time before she returned. "How is your father then? What did your mother say?"

Louise looked a little bemused, "Oh, I haven't spoken to her yet. The line was engaged, so I'll try again in a minute."

Philip shook his head and smiled, "And it took all that time to find out the line was engaged?"

She gave him a look that made Philip feel he was being too nosey, but she answered anyway, "No, of course not! I've been chatting to a friend." She pulled a bit of a face, "We were supposed to be going to supper with his grandmother tonight. He's really disappointed I can't make it."

She looked concerned as she asked, "Do you think his grandmother will understand?" She did not wait for Philip's answer adding, "I do hope she will," before dashing back into the hall to call her mother again.

She came back saying, "Mum says the hospital said that Dad had a comfortable night and that his condition was the same as yesterday." She frowned as she mumbled, "Typical hospital 'non-speak'. They never give you any real information."

The girl who had first answered the door came into the kitchen and Philip had to sit and wait whilst Louise explained everything to her and make arrangements with her to let the University know of the reason for her own absence, after which, she grabbed another piece of toast and covered it with the remains of the jam. "I won't be long," she said to Philip, as she took a bite of toast, "I'll just go and sort out a few things to take with me," and dashed out of the room, taking another mouthful of the toast as she did so.

Philip was anxiously looking at his watch wondering what on earth she was doing all this time, when she came down the stairs carrying two bags. She dropped them in front of Philip, saying, "Can you put these in the car." He picked them up and she immediately turned and went back the way she had come, "I must get some of my books. Won't be long," but by the time she came lumbering down the stairs carrying three further bags stuffed with books and other student paraphernalia, he was beginning to think they would never get away.

He insisted on carrying all three bags but was soon regretting he hadn't accepted her offer to carry one of them. He was thankful when they reached the car and was able to drop the heavy burden into the boot with the other bags. Louise got into the passenger seat and was fastening her seat belt as he got into the car, but she suddenly pointed back to the house and shouted, "Oh there's the postman." She jumped out of the car, "I'll just see if there's anything for me."

He shook his head and laughed, muttering to himself as he watched her dashing back to the house, "Will we ever get away? I don't remember everything being as hectic as this when I was a student."

Eventually she came back carrying a couple of items of post and, after putting them in the glove compartment, fastened her seat belt and turned to Philip. He couldn't believe it when she said, "Right, I'm ready if you are."

They had been travelling for almost an hour before Philip plucked up the courage to ask, "So who is the friend you were supposed to see tonight then?"

She answered almost dismissively, "Just Robert."

But Philip wanted to know more about this Robert. Mere friends don't usually want a girl to meet their grandmother unless there is more to it than simple friendship. "And who is Robert then?"

She laughed and looked across at her uncle, "I suppose if I don't tell you everything you're going to pester me all the way home, aren't you?"

He quickly looked at her and laughed back, before concentrating on the road again, "I guess so. It's not all a secret though, is it?"

"No of course not. His name is Robert Andrew James Cameron." She paused for a moment, "Well actually, it's Dr Robert Cameron."

Philip was expecting it to be another student, but a 'Doctor' Cameron was obviously older than Louise. He suddenly felt a paternal concern and wondered whether this 'Doctor' would treat his niece properly, "So he's a Doctor is he? Does that mean he's one of your tutors?"

"No, but his mother is." She sat back quietly for a few moments before continuing, "Look I was going to mention it to Mom and Dad over Christmas, so if I tell you all about him, you won't say anything to them before I've had a chance to tell them will you?"

"Not if you don't want me to." He took another quick glance at her, "But now you have aroused my curiosity, so you must tell me everything, or I will be pestering you all the way home."

"He's twenty-five. He qualified as a doctor last year and is now working at the Royal Infirmary. I met him there in September when he came to pick up his mother at the end of the afternoon. She's the professor of obstetrics and we were watching her do a Caesarean section at the hospital one day. All the girls fancied him and I couldn't believe it when he starting chatting to me whilst he waited for his mother to change out of her theatre clothes. And we've been seeing each other since."

"And that's it, is it?"

She laughed, "Yes. And that's it."

But Philip wanted to know more about this boyfriend. Louise had always had plenty of boys paying her attention, but the way she spoke of this one suggested more than the usual way she spoke of such friends. "So he wants to introduce you to his grandmother does he? I guess that means it's getting a bit more serious than just seeing each other."

She smiled and merely replied, "Perhaps."

Nothing more was said by either of them on the subject, but after Philip had stopped at a garage to fill up with petrol, he got back in the car and, as soon as they were back on the road, he asked, "And what does Robert's father do? Is he a doctor at well?"

Louise did not answer immediately and Philip was about to change the subject when she suddenly exclaimed, "Actually he doesn't have a father."

"Oh, I'm sorry. Does that mean he's dead?"

"No, it means he doesn't have a father."

Philip was somewhat shocked at the way she'd blurted this statement out so forcefully and decided he should not query the matter further and they both reverted back to saying nothing.

It was Louise who eventually broke the silence, "I suppose I might as well tell you the full story. Robert wasn't ashamed to tell me about his father, so I guess I shouldn't be either." She touched his arm as she said, "But you'll let me tell Mom and Dad when the time's right won't you?"

Philip was concerned about what was to come and all sorts of tragic situations flashed through his mind. "I'm all ears, and of course I won't say anything to anyone if you don't want me to."

Louise sat back and seemed to relax as she related how Robert's mother, Rachel Cameron, had been a brilliant student when she was studying medicine at Edinburgh after the war, and when she had qualified, a consultant at the hospital had invited her to work with him in his private practice.

Philip feared that Louise was going to say that this consultant was Robert's father but he soon realised his mistake as Louise continued.

"Rachel had only been working for him a couple of months when he died quite suddenly, and his wife asked Rachel to help keep the practice going. It was at the funeral that Rachel first met their son." Louise let out a sarcastic laugh, "Apparently he was very charming and good looking. He'd studied medicine before the war, but didn't complete his studies and became a career soldier instead." She let out another snigger. "But when he came home for the funeral he told his mother he'd resigned his commission and was going back to University to complete his medical studies. His mother was over the moon and was even more pleased when she realised Rachel had fallen for him. She thought that at last her wayward son would settle down, marry Rachel, and between them they could continue the practice."

Louise hesitated and shook her head, "And that's when Robert's mother became pregnant and all the plans were quickly made for the wedding."

Philip thought he knew what was coming next and said, "So did they get married or did something else happen?"

She responded with, "Or something else," but did not enlarge on this immediately and the silence pervaded the car again. Eventually however she decided to tell the full story, "I suppose I might as well tell you all there is to tell."

"Look, you don't have to tell me anything you don't want to. On the other hand, I think you know me well enough by now to know that I'm not a gossip. So I leave it to you."

She touched his arm again, saying, "Well I suppose it's an interesting way to pass the time." Nevertheless she was quiet for a few minutes as if trying to decide how to recount the tale.

"I suppose this is where I should tell you about the money his father left in his will. Robert hasn't told me how much and I don't think he knows. Anyway, unbeknown to Robert's grandmother, he'd apparently been pestering the solicitor to speed things up and let him have the money before the wedding. He said he wanted it to buy a home for him and his new wife, so they wouldn't have to live with his mother. The solicitor did his bit and handed over the money to him a few days before the wedding. And then as soon as the cheque was cleared he vanished. Nobody knew where he'd gone. He didn't leave a note or say anything to Rachel or his mother. Nothing!"

"So did they ever find out where he was?"

"Oh, yes, he'd gone to South Africa with the daughter of his Colonel."

Philip didn't know whether he should act shocked at this point and say something appalling about the man, but he couldn't think of anything apt to say, other than, "And how long had that been going on?"

"Well Robert's grandmother eventually got in touch with his regiment to see if he had actually resigned his commission as he'd said, and she was told that he'd been cashiered a few weeks before his father's death. Not because of the affair with the Colonel's daughter, but for some sort of dishonesty. They wouldn't say what he had stolen or done."

She pointed to a sign showing that there was a petrol station with toilets and food a mile ahead, "Would you like to stop for a drink or anything?"

"No I'm fine at the moment, but we'll stop if you want to." She said not, and he responded by saying, "Let's go on for a bit longer. We'll stop at the next place and you can take a spell at the driving if you want to." He looked across at her, "In the meantime, I want to hear what happened after that."

"Well, as you can imagine Rachel was distraught. She was unmarried; she was pregnant and she had no income if she couldn't work, but Robert's grandmother was brilliant. She insisted that Rachel move in with her, saying the house was far too big for one person anyway. She also insisted that Rachel should continue seeing patients in the surgery, but the number of private patients had already trickled to virtually nothing after the husband's death and as soon as the word got out that the young female doctor was pregnant and unmarried it dried up almost completely."

She thought for a moment before continuing, "And this just made matters far worse for poor Rachel. She said she was letting everyone down, but Grandma just closed the surgery and the business saying they'd sort something out after the baby was born. She supported Rachel and Robert, but when he was nearly two years old, Rachel said she wanted to pay her own way and continue her career. So that's what she did, whilst Grandma looked after Robert."

"And she's now your professor?"

"Yes and a brilliant doctor."

"And what about Robert? Is he a brilliant doctor as well?"

She laughed out loud, "He's the best."

Edward seemed to pick up during the next couple of days and when Philip visited him on the Sunday afternoon he was sitting up in his bed with most of the tubes and other trappings removed from his body.

Samantha and Louise were sitting at his bedside. Philip walked up to Edward and took his hand, "How do you feel today, Edward?"

Edward replied still in a fractured voice, "Fine thanks."

Philip looked across at Louise, "And how do you think he is Louise?"

"Much better than when I saw him on Thursday. In fact I'm thinking of catching the overnight train back to college. I really need to sort out a few things before the holiday. I'll be back for Christmas at the end of the week anyway and by the way he looks today I'm sure he'll be back home by then." She stood up and took her father's hand, "You'll be all right now won't you?"

Edward merely smiled and said, "Sure, you get back and I'll see you next week."

She moved away from the chair, "Sit here and talk to Dad, Uncle Philip. I could do with stretching my legs a bit."

Philip moved round the bed and sat down next to Samantha. He always wanted to touch her hand whenever he was this close to her, but they had both learned to control their feelings for each other, even when no-one else was about. Louise stood at the bottom of the bed, picked up the chart that was hanging there and started to study it.

Edward smiled at her and asked, "Anything on there that they're not telling us?"

Louise smiled back, "Nothing that I can see. Everything is virtually back to normal." The smile turned to laughter as she added, "Well if anything can be normal for a man with a heart as knackered as yours is."

Edward laughed back at her, "And that's your professional opinion, is it doctor?"

"I guess so," she replied, but even though she still had more years of study ahead of her, she knew that the long term prognosis was not good, but like most doctors did not want to upset the patient unnecessarily. She stood studying the chart before replacing it, "Keep going on like this and I'll definitely being seeing you at home for Christmas, no problem."

He had just said, "That's good," when the colour totally drained from his face as he stared at the people speaking to the nurse at the desk. She was pointing to Edward's bed and soon the man, the two women, one of them heavily pregnant, and the child walked towards them.

Madeleine was the first to speak, "The nurse said she couldn't allow all of us around the bed, but she relented when I told her we had come all the way from France to see you."

Edward was dumbfounded and couldn't speak as he tried to take in the fact that his son, his son's wife and their child were standing in front of him. The tears flowed in his eyes, and soon both Madeleine and Philip were also wiping the moisture from their faces. Philip stood up, kissed Madeleine and shook hands with Julian and Nicole, "It's good to see you again Nicole." He took hold of Julian's hand and shook it again, speaking directly at him so he could lip read his words if necessary, "And it's so good to meet you at last, Julian."

Julian pointed to his ear, and said in a rather guttural and rasping voice, "I can hear OK, when I've got this thing in." He laughed and added, "But don't all speak at once, that's when I can't follow what's said."

Philip introduced everyone and when Samantha was shaking Julian's hand, she said, "Your English is very good. Where did you learn to speak it?"

"From Grandmother. She's English and spoke it a lot of the time, so I grew up understanding both French and English."

Edward still had not spoken when Madeleine went up to him, kissed him on the cheek and asked, "And how are you, Edward?"

He picked up a tissue and wiped his eyes, "I think they must have given me something to knock me out and I'm dreaming this."

She kissed him again, "You're not dreaming anything."

"But I don't understand?"

"Nothing to understand, except that you've got Nicole to thank for this."

She leaned forward and spoke directly into his ear, "Just enjoy it and for God's sake, speak to your son. It's about time you did."

He looked across at his son, the panic welling up inside him as he tried unsuccessfully to think of the right words to say. Nicole took her husband's arm and pushed him towards his father, "Say hello to your father, Julian."

And so the spell that had traumatised Edward for all of Julian's lifetime was broken. The two of them, tentatively at first, touched hands and spoke.

By the end of visiting time they had talked at length and got to know each other for the first time ever. Edward also learned how his visit to the studio, and particularly the commission, had caused so much trouble between Julian and his wife. But he also learned how eventually Nicole had talked sense into her husband, by making him think seriously about what his reaction would have been if she had died when giving birth to Amélie.

He eventually saw her point and when Madeleine told them how ill his father was, had reluctantly agreed to come and see him before it was too late. By the end of visiting Edward was loathe to let his son go, and only did so when he agreed to come back for evening visiting.

Ten minutes later however, Julian was back at the nurse's desk asking to have a quick word with his father again. He was carrying a large square parcel wrapped in brown paper and tied with string. He placed it on the bottom of the bed and unfastened the string. He pulled the paper off the painting and showed it to his father, "I thought you would prefer to have this now rather than wait until this evening."

Edward was overwhelmed. It was a head and shoulders portrait of Juliette. The smile on her face was perfect and Edward could sense the same love in the eyes looking out from the canvas at him that he had experienced so often when she was alive. He beckoned Julian towards him and gave him a hug. As they held each other, he muttered, "Thank you" over and over again to his son.

When Sam, Louise, and Julian came to visit him that evening, Edward was lying in his bed with his eyes transfixed on the portrait leaning against the bottom of the bed. He smiled as each of them gave him a kiss and lay back on the pillow. Samantha held one of his hands and Julian held the other. Louise sat next to Julian gently stroking her father's arm as he closed his eyes, happy and content for the first time since Juliette's death. He had three of the people he loved most in the world with him, but his real contentment came from the fact that his beloved Juliette was smiling at him from the bottom of his bed.

He fell into a coma and died before the end of visiting time.

Julian and his family left the next morning, saying they had a booking on the ferry that day and would be unable to stay for the funeral. He promised Samantha that they would all visit again sometime the following year after the baby was born.

It was Nicole who had to explain the real reason they could not stay, "I'm due in three weeks, and when I suggested we should come, Julian wanted to leave it until after the baby was born." She gave Julian a peck on the cheek, "He is so protective of me, bless him, but I'm so glad now that I convinced him we should come straight away. But we do need to get back, I have a hospital appointment on Wednesday and Julian is insistent that I don't miss any of those." She took Samantha to one side, "I think he is worried that the same thing might happen to me as happened to his mother."

"I understand perfectly. You must get back. I am so pleased that Edward and Julian were able to be together at the end. I'm sure Edward died a happy man and that's more important than your being at the funeral."

At the funeral on the following Friday, the church was packed with local businessmen and both local and national politicians, many of whom Samantha did not know and others whose names she couldn't remember.

Joanna Hurst was sitting at the back of the church but Samantha did not notice her. Louise had telephoned to tell Joanna of the funeral arrangements without telling her mother and at first Joanna said she wouldn't come as she didn't want to upset Samantha, but Louise said she had obviously been an important part of her father's life and virtually insisted she should be there.

Joanna was not amongst the crowd who turned up for drinks and refreshments back at the house however, having decided that to do so would be too much of an intrusion.

For the next two hours Samantha made the necessary small talk and listened, with ever lessening grace, to all the condolences and good wishes from people who meant absolutely nothing to her.

Eventually only a few family and friends were left and she slumped herself on to the settee, closed her eyes and spoke to Louise who had flopped down next to her, "Thank God that's all over. I hope that's the last time I have to make pleasantries with all your Dad's old political pals. I think I've done my bit over the years, but I didn't expect as many as that today. How did you get on with them, Darling?"

"Some of them were OK, but I don't think I could have taken much more of it either."

For the first time that day they both smiled. Louise reached forward and gave her mother a hug, "It's going to be a bit odd at Christmas without Dad. Will you be all right when I go back to Edinburgh?"

Samantha hugged her daughter, "I was on my own all the time your Dad was in London and even when he was home, he was often at meetings and all the other stuff he had to do, so I guess I'll manage."

"It's been better the last couple of years though with him here, hasn't it?"

Samantha pulled back, touched Louise's cheek with her hand, looked into her eyes and smiled, "Yes but you weren't here, so I guess I now have to manage without either of you." She stroked her cheek, "But don't worry, I'll be fine."

Philip came up to them carrying two glasses of whisky and gave one to each, "Here drink this, you both looked whacked."

Louise took the drink and held on to Philip's hand, "You'll look after Mom when I go back to University won't you Uncle Philip?"

Philip wanted to say that that was all he had wanted to do since before Louise had been born, but had become accustomed to saying uncompromising things instead on such occasions as this.

"Your mother knows she can call on me anytime she wants." He kept his eyes on Louise, knowing that to look at Samantha could easily give more away than it should, "And when are your going back to Edinburgh?"

"I ought to go back for a few things before Christmas, but with Christmas day only a week away, it just isn't worth it so I'll have to manage and go back in the New Year."

He looked at Samantha and then back at Louise, "Actually there are a few things that Edward asked me to do for him; things I need to talk to the two of you about. Not now though, probably best when others aren't around. So will you both be here in the morning if I come to chat to you then?"

Louise responded with, "Sounds intriguing. Do we have to wait until tomorrow?"

They both turned and looked at Samantha, who said, "Why don't you come back this evening? Say about seven. We can all have a bite to eat and sort it out then."

Philip was ringing the doorbell at precisely seven o'clock and Louise answered it. She had changed out of her funeral black and was dressed in skin tight jeans and a white sweater, which together showed off every curve of her body. She gave him a kiss as she took his overcoat from him. "Mom's in the kitchen. She said she won't be a minute and that I'm to get you a drink, so what would you like?"

"I'm fine thanks. I have to drive home later so I better keep off the alcohol." She looked questioning at him. "OK, I'll have some lemonade if you've got it."

She laughed, "We've got loads of it. Mom got it in for the booze up today, but everyone was drinking the beer and spirits, so how much would you like, a couple of pints?"

He laughed back, "Just a small glass will be fine, thanks."

She went to fetch the drink but he called her back, "By the way, I've just found these in my glove compartment." He took two envelopes from his inside jacket pocket and handed them to her, "I'm sorry but they've been there since you took them from the postman last week."

She took them from him, looked at them, and threw them on the coffee table, "They're nothing important, I'll open them later."

When Louise came back with the drinks, Samantha was with her. She was no longer wearing her black either, but was wearing a discreet sleeveless dark blue woollen dress which would not have offended any of the puritans who believed that widows should not wear anything but mourning for a goodly time after their husband's demise. She was still wearing the row of pearls with matching earrings she had worn earlier in the day and as she walked towards Philip he became acutely aware of her perfume; the same perfume she had worn the very first time he'd met her.

He wanted to embrace her but felt awkward and not sure what to do. After all it was the day of her husband's funeral. It was as if she recognised his dilemma and made the decision easy for him when she merely took his hand, squeezed it, and said, "Hi. Supper will be another twenty minutes or so, so why don't you tell us what Edward asked of you?

Louise and I have been dying to know ever since you left this afternoon."

They all sat down on separate seats. Philip took a sip of his lemonade before speaking, "It was on the last day we were in France together. We'd spent time choosing the paintings at Julian's studio and then we visited Juliette's grave. After that Edward said he wanted to come straight back home, and as soon as I started driving, he said he wanted me to do a few things for him when he died."

Samantha shook her head slightly, "What did he want you to do that he couldn't talk to me about?"

Philip shrugged his shoulders, "Well I did ask him to speak to you about it but he said it would be better coming from me when he was gone."

She continued shaking her head and spoke as if she had not really heard what Philip had said, "But there again, he always seemed to avoid talking to me about what was going on in his head, so I suppose I shouldn't be surprised he spoke to you, should I?"

"I don't know about that Samantha, but the first thing he asked was that I should take care of you and Louise. I told him I'd be there for both of you anyway and that there was no need to ask such a thing." He looked at each of them in turn, "I'd hope that you both know that if there's anything either of you need, you only have to ask."

Louise reached across and touched his arm, "Of course we know, but what was the rest?"

"Well this is where it gets a bit awkward for me. He asked that I should phone Madeleine as soon as he died. Well that's where I was a bit naughty. I phoned Madeleine before I went to Edinburgh to pick up Louise and told her how ill he was. I know that's not what he wanted me to do, but in the event I think it turned out for the best."

"I'm certain you did the right thing, Philip. I'm sure he was delighted to see Julian and his family and they certainly wouldn't have come if you hadn't phoned Madeleine."

Louise nodded her head in agreement as Philip continued, "Apparently, he sent Madeleine a letter for Julian as soon as he got home from our trip to France but told her that he didn't want Julian to have it until after his death, but when I told her how ill Edward was, she told Julian and gave him the letter straight away. At first he wasn't interested, but it was Nicole who talked to him after she had read the letter. And I guess we have her to thank for the fact that Julian came to see his father." He was silent for a few moments and then said, "Even so, it wasn't what Edward had asked me to do. He only wanted me to phone her after his death."

"I don't see why you should feel awkward about phoning Madeleine.

Dad should have done more about Julian ages ago. It was years before I even knew I had a brother, and I could never understand it, or why it was never spoken of. It was only when I spoke to Madeleine last week that I found out the full story. I suppose the one good thing now is that perhaps, in the end, he died with some sort of peace on that matter."

Samantha interrupted, "Perhaps we should get Julian and Nicole over here and all talk about it." She looked at Philip, "And was there anything else he wanted you to do?"

"Yes, but I don't know how you are going to feel about the other two things." They both sat expectantly waiting for him to continue. "He asked that his ashes should be spread on Juliette's grave."

Neither women spoke as they looked questionably at each other. "I guess he never said anything about that to you either, did he?"

Samantha pursed her lips and shook her head and there was silence until Louise spoke, "If that's what he wanted Mom, then that's what you should do. What does it really matter where his ashes go?"

Philip decided to take the initiative, "I thought we could all travel to France on the Saturday after Christmas, visit the grave on the Sunday, see the New Year in over there and come back on New Year's Day." He did not know if Samantha would recognise the significance of spreading the ashes on New Year's Eve, but decided not to say anything.

Louise looked at her mother, "You and Uncle Philip can go if you want to, but I've made arrangements with Robbie to spend New Year with him in Edinburgh."

"I didn't know you'd arranged that."

"Well you do now," was Louise's response.

Samantha decided to avoid any problems with her daughter and let the matter drop. "Perhaps I can think about it over the next couple of days and let you know Philip? And what was the other thing he wanted?"

He had been dreading bringing this matter up. He had argued with Edward when he asked him and only reluctantly agreed when Edward had said that he could not destroy the things himself. He looked sheepishly at Samantha, "Edward has kept all the letters he had from Juliette before they were married and they're in his desk in his study."

Samantha stared at him as she wondered what was coming next, "So?"

"So, there are also all the letters Madeleine has sent to him over the years telling him how Julian was getting on. There are photos of Juliette, as well as childhood pictures of Julian and all that sort of thing as well. He didn't want you to just find them when you were clearing out his things and asked that I should deal with them."

Samantha stood up and said icily, “Fine. You do what you have to do. I’d better go and sort out supper. It should be ready by now.”

When she had closed the door, Louise smiled, “I don’t envy you having to put that one right with Mom. He’s always cut her out of anything to do with Juliette and Julian and he’s still doing it. I know he’s my father but he could be a pig sometimes.”

Philip smiled back without comment as Louise picked up the envelopes from the coffee table and opened the larger of the two. She took the Christmas card out, read who it was from and stood it on the table in front of her. She put her finger into the flap of the other envelope, ripped it open and took out a small blue card that fit easily into the palm of her hand. She looked inside it and put it on the coffee table next to the card. She opened the letter that was also in the envelope and read it.

“Anything interesting,” asked Philip.

“Oh no. I gave blood for the first time a couple of weeks ago and this is just my blood donor card. She went to put the letter back in the envelope, but quickly looked at its contents again. The colour drained from her face as she snatched up the blue card and read what was inside it again. Her hand went to her mouth as she stared at the document. Suddenly she let out a scream.

Samantha came running back into the room, “What on earth’s the matter?”

“Why have you never told me that I’m adopted?” She handed the letter to her mother.

“What are you talking about? Of course you’re not adopted.” She looked at the letter and laughed, “So you’ve become a blood donor. What’s that got to do with anything?”

Each time Louise spoke her voice got louder and more perturbed, “But it say’s my blood type is O negative.”

“So what’s that got to do with anything?”

“Dad’s blood group was AB. I read that on his chart at the hospital.”

“But darling, you’ve probably got your blood group from me. I’m probably ‘O’ as well.”

“That doesn’t make any difference. Dad still can’t be my Dad. So am I adopted or not?”

Samantha was beginning to dread where this was leading, but still could not admit the truth to herself, “Of course you aren’t adopted. You must be mistaken about something.”

Louise stood rigid, “Mother, I’m a medical student, remember? Now just tell me what this is all about?”

Samantha look intently at Philip, who had remained silent throughout the whole of the clash between the two women, willing him to get her out of this mess. He stared back open mouthed; the reality of the situation now patently obvious to both of them.

Louise glanced from one of them and then the other several times unsure of what was going on between them, but gradually the truth behind the expressions of horror and pleading on each of their faces dawned on her.

She let out another scream as she pointed her finger at Philip, "Oh, my God." She put her hand to her mouth for a moment as the certainty of her thoughts sank in. "It's you isn't it? You're my father. I know you're O negative, my Dad told me often enough about how you saved his life by giving him your blood and how you knew it would be OK to do that no matter what group he was."

She slumped back into her seat and sobbed uncontrollably. Through her tears she kept muttering, "How could you? How could you?"

By now, Samantha was also crying. She wanted to comfort her daughter, but had no idea what to say or do. She knelt on the floor next to Louise's seat and went to put her arms around her.

Louise pushed her mother's arms away and stood up; her words hardly distinguishable through the sobbing, "How long has this been going on?" She let out a shriek which added to the pain being felt by Samantha and Philip, "Did my Dad know?" She stared at them with piercing eyes that displayed the hatred she felt for them at that moment, "Sorry I mean did your husband know you were having it off with his best friend?" The words husband and best friend were both spoken with venom in her voice.

Philip got up and moved toward her. He, like Samantha, was still struggling to come to terms with the shock of the last few minutes, "Louise, sweetheart we didn't know, we genuinely thought Edward was your father."

She gazed intently at him as she wiped her eyes on the sleeve of her sweater, leaving a great streak of soggy mascara on the white material; the remaining mascara now covering most of her cheeks in an erratic patchwork of squishy and ravaged make-up. "I don't want to know what you thought and I definitely don't want to know any of the sordid details." She glared at each of them in turn, "I hate you both," and looked at her mother, "I thought the problems between Dad and you were because of his affair with Joanna, but now you must have been having an affair long before Dad met her."

Samantha could not believe what Louise had just said, "How do you know about Joanna Hurst?"

Louise screamed at her mother, "Because I'm not daft, that's why." And then she screeched even louder wishing to hurt her mother even more, "Did you know she was at the church today?"

When Samantha shook her head in disbelief, Louise took the opportunity to push the knife in further, "Well she was, and I'd invited her, so there."

Philip wanted to comfort both women and stop all the hurt from happening but chose to move closer to Louise; he so wanted to stop her pain and stop her hurting Samantha, but she clenched her fists and pummelled his chest, muttering, "I hate you. I hate you," continuously as she did so.

Philip stood statuesque willingly taking the punishment. Eventually the anger and rage within her took its toll. Her mind was still in turmoil, but the emotional strain and struggle of dealing with her father's death and funeral, followed immediately by this devastating revelation that her father was not her father, finally drained every bit of the fighting spirit from her. She could no longer cope with the situation; her whole body started to shake; her outraged squeals became the heartbroken and inconsolable sobs of a very young lost child who no longer knew who she was or where she belonged.

She allowed Philip to put his arms around her. Her head rested on his shoulder as the throb of her heart pulsated through her body and made every muscle and fibre judder and tremble in concert with it. Her mother came and enclosed her arms around both of them. All three were shaking; their synchronistic sobs being the only sound to break the otherwise stillness and silence.

Louise's response to this brief moment of love and empathy from her mother and her real father soon passed however. Her tormented mind returned and she once more wrestled with the shocking disclosure that continued to overwhelm her.

She pulled away from both of them, "I'm going to phone Robbie and make arrangements to spend Christmas with him and his family." She turned and as she made her way to the door, spoke once more with bitterness and acrimony, "And I'll leave you two lovers to sort out your own consciences, but don't you dare tell anyone else about this mess. The man we buried today is my father and always will be."

Philip and Samantha stood together, neither speaking nor moving. They each mentally grappled to come to terms with the precise consequence of their one night of love making; a consequence that had lain unknown and dormant for over twenty years. Eventually Philip mouthed the words, "I love you," and went to put his arms around Samantha. She moved away, a look of shock and fear on her face.

"I'm sorry, Philip. I can't deal with any of this, right now." She moved further away from him and dropped into the armchair. With her head in her hands she muttered, "I've often considered leaving Edward for you, but I can't lose Louise, not for you or anyone. I have to somehow get her back and I don't think that will happen with you around."

Eventually she looked up at him, "I can't deal with my feelings for you as well, so please go home. I'll phone you if there is anything we need, but I think it'd be best if you didn't telephone or get in touch with us."

Samantha had not meant her words to sound as cruel as they seemed to Philip. She had never spoken to him in such a barbed manner before and her words had cut through him like a knife. He struggled to comprehend the true meaning of her words as he drove home. The significance of Louise's comments about blood groups had hit him well before Louise had worked it out, and for a very brief moment he had been overjoyed with the knowledge that Louise was actually the child he had always wanted with Samantha. But now things had changed dramatically. Half an hour ago, Louise and Samantha were both happy to have him as part of their lives, but that had all gone now and he wondered if either of them would ever let him back into their lives again.

CHAPTER TWENTY- NINE

CHRISTMAS 1978 TO JULY 1981

Samantha sat disconsolate as she waited for her daughter to finish speaking on the telephone. She felt bad at the way things had been left with Philip, but knew she had to try and make amends with Louise before making any contact with him. But how could she put this thing right with Louise?

She heard Louise finish the call with, "So you'll meet me at the station tomorrow then?" before giving a final, "I love you too," and storming up the stairs to her bedroom, banging the door behind her.

Samantha knew she had to do something to try and sort out this mess with her daughter, even though she had no idea what or how. She followed Louise up the stairs and knocked on her bedroom door. There was no reply so she entered the room saying, "I need to talk to you sweetheart."

Louise did not even acknowledge her mother as she entered her room. Her case was already on the bed and she was pulling things out of drawers and throwing them haphazardly into it. Samantha sat on the bed and tried to take Louise's hand but she pulled away and went to the next drawer without saying a word.

She started by saying, "Sweetheart, we honestly didn't know. This is all as much of a surprise to Philip and me as it is to you." Louise looked at her through piercing eyes and shook her head disbelievingly and continued her packing.

But Samantha couldn't let Louise leave without at least trying to explain things to her, even if it meant admitting to things she'd never spoken of to anyone else. So, for the next hour she was entirely honest about her relationship with Philip; how he was already married when they first met and how she had already married Edward by the time their feelings for each other had been openly expressed. "But even then we both resisted doing anything about it. The one and only time we spent together wasn't planned and it's never been repeated again."

She wanted to compare this to Edward's affairs and how he had almost financially ruined them with his gambling, but knew it would only inflame the situation so avoided doing so. She also avoided telling her that Philip had always thought himself infertile. She finished by saying, "Honestly sweetheart, neither of us ever thought for one moment that Edward was not your father, and the fact that he isn't is as great a shock to Philip and me as it is to you."

Louise however, completely ignored her mother and acted as though she wasn't even in the room. The only time she did speak was when Samantha stood up to leave and said. "Please try to understand and forgive us, we really didn't know you weren't your Dad's child."

The anger in Louise was again aroused, "But my Dad isn't my Dad is he? My Dad is the man you had a one-night stand with, so what does that make me?"

Samantha responded with, "A girl who is dearly loved no matter whose child you really are."

Louise turned her back on her mother and the sobs returned as another thought crossed her mind. "I was so pleased to meet my brother for the first time a week ago and now you've taken even that away from me. And now if you don't mind I want to go to bed."

Samantha knew that she had said all that she could say about the matter without inflaming her daughter more, so she left by saying only, "I'll give you a lift to the station tomorrow if that's what you want."

After Louise had left, Samantha thought about contacting Philip but stupidly did not do so. He, for his part, had taken to heart what Samantha's final words to him had been and patiently waited the call that never came. As a result Samantha spent a melancholic Christmas with her parents and Philip had endured a cheerless Christmas Day with John and his family. None of their relatives understood why they were so moody and miserable, and, as Louise had demanded, neither discussed the facts of her true parentage with anyone, not even between themselves.

Initially, Louise had not coped any better than her mother. She had travelled back to Scotland by train on the day after Edward's funeral and had had a very perturbed journey as she turned over the events of the previous evening through her mind. She just could not accept that Philip was her father and by the time Robert met her at the station in Edinburgh, she was in a very distressed state, but the only thing she would say to him was, "I've had an argument with my mother," and when he pushed her for details, she asked him to, "Please leave it. I don't want to talk about it."

He was sensible enough to do so, but it didn't help Louise's situation when he told her he was on duty at the hospital that night, "Mother is out as well. She's going to be at a Christmas shindig at the University, so I've made arrangements for you to stay with my grandmother."

Louise not only felt rejected again but totally alone as he dropped her off at his grandmother's house. His farewell kiss and, "I'll come and see you in the morning," did not help one iota.

Grandmother was nothing like Louise had expected. She had imagined she'd be like her own Grandma Prior; a round faced, fussy, down-to-earth and unpretentious housewife, but she was nothing of the sort. She was dressed in superbly cut designer clothes that accentuated her perfectly preserved slim body. Her expertly applied makeup was exactly right for her; not too heavy but just enough to hide any tiny blemishes she may have wished to hide. Louise thought she was possibly in her eighties, but she did not look anything like that age.

Although the house was in the old part of Edinburgh and was probably at least a hundred years old, the inside did not show any of the ravages of time. The tall rooms with their superb sculptured ceilings and covings were perfectly maintained. Some of the walls were decorated in expensive wallpaper, whilst others were painted in rich solid colour which heightened the sense of luxury. The original paintings on the walls; the choice of carpets and the magnificent furniture all added to the perfect 'Country and Homes' feeling of this beautiful home, which seemed the perfect and natural surroundings for this particular lady.

She pointed out the various rooms before showing Louise where the bathroom was and then leading her to the bedroom, "This was Robert's bedroom when he was little and he and his mother lived here, but it has been redecorated since then."

Everything about the room was perfectly designed down to the last detail. The antique four poster bed with its heavy brocade curtains, which matched those at the window, stood on a heavy plain wool carpet. Two easy chairs; an oak dressing table and large oak wardrobe were the only other pieces of furniture in the room, but the other ancillary furnishings complemented and completed the splendour of the whole.

Louise had always considered her own home to be special and well furnished but this was something else, "This is a lovely room. Did you have an interior designer to help you choose the things in here?"

She smiled and shook her head, "I like to do these things myself," and then continued with, "Make yourself comfortable and just treat the house as your own." She walked to the door, but stopped with her hand on the door handle, "I expect you are hungry after your journey, so come down as soon as you're ready and we can have a bite to eat together."

When Louise went downstairs she was unsure which room to go into until a voice called, "I'm in here Louise. I thought we'd eat in the kitchen, it's so much warmer and friendlier than the dining room."

Louise walked towards the voice and entered the large country style kitchen, with its large Aga cooker; its marble working surface; its dark oak cupboards and pots and pans and other cooking implements hanging from the heavy oak beams. In the middle of the room was a plain wooden table on which had been set two place settings with crystal wine glasses. In the middle of the table a large candle in a broad glass vase had been lit, giving a warm glow across the room. "Sit yourself down Louise and pour us each a glass of wine whilst I finish dishing out this food."

Louise did as she was bid and, although she was no expert when it came to wine, when she took a sip of the dark red liquid, she knew it was not regular supermarket plonk.

In no time at all Louise relaxed and felt totally at ease with Grandma. She was not at all pretentious or patronizing, but was a very warm and pleasantly open person, who was genuinely interested in Louise without being nosey or inquisitive.

When they had finished the meal Louise stood up and said, "I'll clear these things away and wash up for you."

Grandmother winked and gave a mischievous smile, "No let's leave it all where it is, we can clear it away in the morning," and then she added, "Why don't we make some coffee and take it into my snug? We can finish nattering in there. It's much more comfortable than here."

The 'snug' was in fact a large orangery attached to the back of the house and filled with exotic plants. The place was kept warmer than even the kitchen by several large radiators around the low brick wall under the large glass windows. They each sank into one of the cane chairs in the centre of the room and Louise poured the coffee.

Louise could not believe how quickly she had become totally at ease with this dear lady. So much so in fact, that as they sat drinking the coffee, all the events of twenty-four hours earlier just came tumbling out and she revealed everything that had been said and happened the previous evening. Louise felt so comfortable talking to her that she knew instinctively that nothing being said would ever be repeated, and certainly never be gossiped about by this wonderfully gentle and warm-hearted woman.

The old lady listened sympathetically and compassionately without saying anything and gradually Louise's anger and pain subsided, as she exposed more and more of the thoughts that had been torturing her mind since the previous evening. Eventually, all her torment exhausted, her counsellor and confidant soon convinced Louise that it was who she was, and not who her parents were, that created her identity.

She then surprised Louise by talking at length about her own painful upbringing; about the loss of her brother in the First World War and of how she had married a man she did not truly love. She also talked about her son and showed some regret that she had not stopped her husband from being such a task master and disciplinarian to him.

She looked sad as she spoke, and Louise wondered how much personal guilt she felt when her son had deserted Robert's mother so cruelly.

Louise was now the counsellor and somehow she intuitively knew that the things being said had never been spoken about to anyone before. She was even more certain of this as she continued with, "I should have followed my heart when I had the chance." Louise looked questioningly at her without saying a word. She smiled at Louise, "I fell madly in love with a wonderful man once. He was in my brother's regiment and he was the love of my life." She touched her chest several times, "He's still in here with me now."

Louise was fascinated by the disclosure, "What happened? Did he die in the War?"

"No he survived."

"So why didn't you marry him?"

"Things are different now, and you probably won't understand, but he was not an officer and because of stupid social conventions, nothing actually happened between us. I never told him about my feelings and I never knew what he felt for me, if anything."

The two women were silent for quite a time as they each reflected on all the things they had disclosed to the other. Eventually, the old lady said to Louise. "I guess this Philip and your mother probably found themselves in a similar situation. Living by other people's standards can be a terrible burden."

She handed her cup to Louise and as Louise poured her another coffee, she said, "I did what other people expected of me for most of my life and it was only when my son left Rachel in that mess, that I decided to do what seemed right to me, and to hell with what anyone else thought." She laughed, "It did help that my husband was no longer around though."

She took Louise's hand, "If your mother and this Philip have loved each other as much as your mother suggests, then things will not have been easy for them." She lifted her hand to Louise's cheek, "Don't hate them for loving each other. I can tell you from my own experience that the pain of not being with the one they loved will at times have been unbearable for both of them."

When Louise got into bed later that night she no longer felt troubled by the previous evening's arguments at home and was soon sleeping peacefully and contentedly. She woke early the next morning and washed up all the supper things from the night before. She was making coffee when she was joined by Robert's Grandmother. Soon breakfast had been made and the two women were once more talking easily and relentlessly to each other.

"Tell me a bit about your family Louise. Robert hasn't told me anything about you."

When Louise called her Mrs McPherson for the second time, she stopped her and said, "Please call me Evie. That's what all my friends call me."

It was only after Louise started talking about Philip's family that Evie appallingly realised that the love of her life was in fact Louise's grandfather; a fact she chose not to tell Louise.

Philip tormented himself all over Christmas about the way Louise had reacted so violently to the knowledge he was her father and how Samantha had told him to get out of the house. He tried to make sense of all the questions going through his head but most of all he couldn't work out why he and Samantha had so easily accepted that Louise was Edward's child.

Why had he believed Teresa so readily about his inability to father a child? He had even missed her obvious confession on her deathbed that she had deceived him and that it was she who was unable to conceive because of the abortion. Why had he been so ready to see Louise's red hair as a sure sign that she was Edward's child? His own mother had been a redhead before it had turned white after his sister's death. Edward inherited his red hair from his father but Philip's mother was born Grace Richards and was Edward's father's sister. He was so annoyed at himself for ignoring the obvious and spoke aloud to no-one, "Damn it, most of the Richards' family had red hair, including my mother before Kathy died." He was furious at himself when he suddenly remembered that his sister, Kathy had also been a redhead, "Why the hell didn't I remember that years ago? I'm bloody half a Richards myself so why wouldn't I father a red haired child?"

But most of Philip's torment was about Louise herself. He had always loved her as his own child even though he had always thought she wasn't. She was Samantha's child and that was all that mattered to him. He would have done anything for that child and now, because he had accepted things so readily, he had done tremendous harm to the two most important people in his life. Louise was the innocent party in all of this mess, and now she was the one most hurt by things. Why couldn't it just be himself? He knew that if he and Sam were the only ones involved they would probably both have happily come to terms with it in no time at all.

The question he couldn't answer and couldn't stop thinking about was, 'How can we ever put things right with Louise?' but he didn't discuss the question with Samantha, and even more stupidly, didn't even consider the possibility of asking Louise.

After Christmas, Philip went to France on his own, and spent several days with Julian and Nicole, who both wanted to take part in the scattering of the ashes on the 31st December, making it a much more moving event than Philip had anticipated.

He returned to work as soon as he got home and Samantha returned to work a week later. After a while, some sort of a normal working relationship was restored, but both were still unsure how to deal with the realisation that Louise was Philip's child and not Edward's. It seemed to each of them that to even talk about the matter would bring dishonour and shame on Edward's memory. But worse still, neither of them made any move to discuss the matter with the other and neither made any move to overtly rekindle the electric intimacy that had existed for so many years between them. They had been able to talk openly and honestly to each other on all matters no matter how private or personal, but now things had reverted back to how they were before Philip first declared his true feelings to Samantha; both waiting for the other to say something.

Philip did not want to add to the distress he imagined Samantha was going through about Louise and so the things that should have been discussed remained unsaid.

He had never wanted his friend to die, but had nevertheless often considered a life with Samantha if Edward had died before himself. The events on the evening of his funeral had shattered all those thoughts and he knew that he could not, should not, even attempt to contemplate such thoughts again. And even though, every day she was around, Philip hungered to take her in his arms he did nothing about it. He was constantly afraid that to even attempt to do so would upset Samantha even more, and because he never said a single word to her about his feelings, he never found out that Samantha was desperately willing him to do exactly that.

Instead they both tried to push the shock and concern caused by the dramatic events of that evening behind them and immerse themselves in the every day business of work. Nevertheless the effort did not adequately deal with the problem for either of them and, in no time at all, Philip had decided that he had absolutely no wish to continue going to work every day and was openly talking to the rest of the family about selling the business. By the end of the year the decision to sell was made. John's furniture business was segregated from the rest and, along with the original factory premises, had been transferred exclusively and totally to John, his wife and his children.

On Samantha's advice the family agreed to retain the freehold of all the shop premises and buildings they owned, and not dispose of them to the purchaser of the business. After months and months of negotiations, a large retailer was found to purchase all of the retail businesses as one lot and take a lease on all the freehold premises. Philip, his mother, John, Lucy and Louise now had the sort of money that Philip's father Frank could only dream about when he had made plans to start the business in 1919.

Although Louise never actually admitted it, even to herself; the words of Robert's grandmother had rang true and had helped her enormously to put the matter behind her and she totally accepted the situation. Unfortunately however, she never told her mother or Philip that she had, even though she had made a sort of peace with them. This together with their own feelings of guilt at what they had inadvertently put their beloved Louise through, meant that even by the time Louise had completed her degree course two and a half years later, the uneasy tensions between Samantha and Philip had still not been properly dealt with by either of them.

When Samantha went to Edinburgh to attend Louise's graduation ceremony and celebrate her first class honours degree, Evie insisted that she stay with her. Although Samantha realised why Louise had fallen for Robert the first time she met him she had still not met his mother or grandmother and was quite nervous about meeting them. Louise often talked about Evie and Rachel and the extent to which she praised both women and extolled how wonderful they both were, sometimes made Samantha feel they had a better relationship with her daughter than she had and now felt some resentment towards each of them.

But by the end of that first evening alone together, Evie had managed to achieve the same magic on Samantha that she had performed on Louise.

Samantha was completely relaxed in the armchair, drink in her hand, and felt totally comfortable talking about anything and everything with Evie. She understood perfectly why Louise was so taken with her as she talked at length about Louise and how proud she was of her and her achievements. "It's a pity her father is no longer alive to see her graduate. He always tried to be there for her and would have been so proud to be at her graduation tomorrow."

Evie listened as Samantha spoke of Edward and their life together in glowing colours. She felt so sorry for her. Why did she feel it necessary to avoid the truth and persist in such a charade? She saw images of herself from years earlier when she had also tried to always do the right thing for others rather than what felt right for herself. She wanted to scream at Samantha and tell her to stop living her life on other people's terms but live it for herself. Even so, she had no intention of bringing up the fact that she knew that Philip was Louise's father, but nevertheless somehow steered the conversation round to him and was not surprised at the warmth in Samantha's voice whenever she mentioned his name or anything about him.

"I understand he sold the family business earlier this year. So what is he going to do with himself now?"

"I haven't spoken to him about it so I don't know if he has any plans or not."

"And what are you doing yourself now that you are no longer working with him?"

Samantha hesitated slightly before saying, "I haven't any plans either."

Evie laughed, "Louise says the two of you get on well together, so why don't you sort out what you're going to do and do it together?"

Samantha did not answer, but in bed that night she could not think of anything but Philip and how much she still loved him, and how much she wanted to be with him.

After the graduation ceremony, when all the guests and graduates were mingling outside the hall chatting and taking photographs, Robert fell to his knees in front of Louise and asked her to marry him.

A great cheer went up from all around them when she said, "Yes," and, when the nearest graduate threw his mortarboard into the air it was quickly followed by every other fellow student doing the same.

Louise planned to return home a couple weeks after her graduation, visiting family and friends before returning to Scotland to extend her medical training at the Royal Infirmary of Edinburgh. Samantha wanted to arrange a party whilst she was at home to celebrate both her daughter's degree success and her engagement and had already started to make enquiries at various hotels before she even mentioned it to Louise. Louise was against the idea and refused outright to such a grand event. Eventually however she reluctantly agreed to a small gathering at home where Robert, his mother and grandmother could meet the rest of her family.

And so, three weeks later, a small army of helpers descended on Samantha's house to prepare for the event. The back lawn was mown, a large awning erected, under which the trestle tables were covered with white table cloths awaiting the arrival of the caterers to fill them with food and drinks. Other small tables with garden chairs were placed in groups around the lawn and finally the banners with, 'Well done Dr. Richards' and 'Congratulations to Robert and Louise' were stretched between trees at the bottom of the garden.

Robert and Rachel, who had arrived by car the previous day, were staying with Philip's mother, whilst Evie, who had arrived by train several days earlier, was staying with Lucy. Although the two women had occasionally spoken on the telephone they had not seen each other in almost forty years and it wasn't long before they were talking about what had happened in their lives, each conveniently missing out the hurtful personal details of their disastrous relationships with men. Instead Lucy concentrated on her part in helping Frank and Tom build up a very successful business.

For her part Evie talked about her life since her husband had died and how for the first time ever she had become content and happy with her life. It was not long however, before Lucy was talking about Robert and Louise and saying what a lovely couple they made. But Evie was interested in other things. She wanted to see Samantha and Philip together and, as part of her plan, suddenly asked, "And what's this Philip like? Louise mentioned his name several times but she always changes the subject if I start asking questions about him"

Lucy smiled a knowing smile, "Well you know he's Frank's son and was my boss when he came into the business after the war." Evie nodded as Lucy continued speaking, "But I suppose you really want to know about his personal life?"

Evie grinned, "Yes please."

"His wife died quite a few years back and they didn't have any children."

"And has he got anyone else in his life now?"

Lucy merely answered, "Not as far as I know," but that was not the answer Evie had hoped for so she decided to be more direct and try and steer Lucy's answers around to the question she really wanted answered, "And what about him and Samantha?" She stared intently at Lucy, "Now they would make a lovely couple, don't you think?"

"Perhaps," was all Lucy would commit herself to saying.

Lucy had always been quite open about things when talking to Evie, and Evie was intrigued as to why Lucy was being somewhat evasive on this particular matter and pushed her further, "Well I reckon they'd be good together and what's more I think he'd make a good new father for Louise. Don't you think so?"

Lucy laughed uneasily as she danced around the subject, not wanting to offend Evie by refusing to answer but not wishing to say anything she may later regret, "I've never thought about it."

Evie continued to stare directly at Lucy, "I don't believe you."

"Well maybe I have, and yes I think they would make a lovely couple."

"And do you think he would be good for Louise as well? It's nice for a girl to have a father figure to look up to, don't you think?"

"Maybe that should have happened a long time ago when she was born," was all Lucy would say before raising her voice as she demanded, "And now can we talk about something else?" without making any further comment about Samantha's relationship with Philip.

Evie decided to drop the subject, but nevertheless wondered how long ago Lucy had known that Philip and Samantha's relationship was more than a working relationship; and more importantly, when she had realised the thing that no-one else had realised; that Louise was not Edward's child.

Samantha had invited far more people to the party than just the immediate family and friends and so, when Louise got back from picking up her Grandma and Grandpa she was greeted by a cheer from over fifty guests. They were everywhere; in the lounge, in the kitchen, in the conservatory, but most were in the back garden enjoying the wonderfully warm sunny weather.

Samantha was somewhat startled but was nevertheless overjoyed when Louise followed her into the kitchen and threw her arms around her neck declaring, "And this is just a few friends is it?" She continued to hug her mother as she whispered in her ear, "And in case you haven't already worked it out, I stopped being angry about that other business ages ago, so can we get back to how things were before?"

Samantha kissed her daughter and merely replied, "Yes please," before saying, "We do both love you, you know."

Louise pulled away, a big grin on her face, "I've always known that." She took her mother's hand and led her into the garden, "Let's go and make small talk with everyone."

Robert joined Louise and before long they were surrounded by people congratulating them and making a fuss of them. No sooner had one group of well-wishers moved away, than someone else had taken their place.

Philip watched as they slowly made their way around the garden, talking at length to everyone as they did so. He was waiting patiently, desperately trying to think of what would be the right thing to say when Louise reached him. He had sent a letter to her congratulating her on her degree success and had sent an engagement card to her as soon as he heard about it, but had not actually seen or spoken to her since she had popped home for a few days over the previous Christmas holiday. On that occasion they had acted in the same polite and courteous manner to each other as had become the norm over the last couple of years. He wondered if the same spontaneous warmth that had always previously existed between them would ever return. A couple of times, Samantha looked across at him and smiled. He desperately wanted to go to her and Louise and throw his arms around the two of them but held back as usual.

He had seen little of Louise since she went to University and as he stood watching them, he wondered how often he would be able to see her after she was married. Would this be how things would be in future? Would the only chance he ever had to see or know his daughter be on such rare occasions as this? He tried to put the thoughts behind him and for now just enjoy seeing her. She was no longer the young hesitant girl who had nervously gone away to University, but was now a very beautiful and maturc woman, with the man she was so obviously in love with at her side.

Suddenly Louise looked across towards him and grinned when she saw him looking at her. She had not grinned at him in that way in a long time. She quickly made her excuses to the couple she was talking to and pulled both her mother and Robert across to where Philip stood. She was beaming as she reached him.

She gave him a, "Hi, Philip," as she reached him. He wondered when she had decided to drop the 'Uncle' bit and was even more taken aback when she threw her arms around him and kissed him on the cheek. He kissed her back on her cheek before taking Robert's hand firmly and saying, "Congratulations to both of you. I really am pleased about your engagement." He quickly kissed Louise on the cheek again, "And as for you, Doctor Louise Richards. Well what can I say? I am really pleased..." He hesitated slightly before adding, "And I am really proud of you and your achievement."

The ice now broken they chatted away as if the last two and half years had never happened.

Evie sat at the table a few feet away, smiling to herself. She felt almost smug as she contemplated how hard she had worked over the last few months, subtly bringing Philip into the conversation whenever she was alone with Louise. She had privately become impatient at the knowledge that neither Philip; Samantha; nor Louise seemed prepared to talk about the things they should have discussed together a long time ago. She had been so troubled by the way it was affecting all their lives that just before she left Edinburgh, she sent for Louise, and in total frustration had brought up the subject again, "Secrets! Why can't people just deal with things as they are? Don't you think it's about time you made your peace with your mother and Philip?" And after she had apologised for her outbreak, she had virtually insisted that Louise should do exactly what she had just done and see what happened after that.

She sat admiring her handy work, until the spell was broken when a woman about the same age as Louise arrived and straightway made her way to Louise. Sally-Anne and Louise screamed and acted the role of the schoolgirls they once were, as they hugged and jumped up and down with exaggerated joy at seeing each other. Louise released her hold on Sally-Anne as she saw Sally-Anne's husband Steve carrying their two year old daughter and dragging their four year old son alongside him.

"Louise stepped forward and took the child from Steve and speaking to the child said, "And what is your name then?"

Steve beamed and answered for his daughter, "This little princess is Jessica." He then picked up the boy and with a great beam on his face said, "And this little tinker is Dominic."

Sally-Anne took Jessica off Louise and went and put her arm around her husband before kissing him on the cheek. She leaned forward and almost in whisper said to Louise, "And they said it wouldn't last five minutes, but having Dominic and then marrying Steve was the best thing I ever did." She took hold of Robert's hand and shook it, "I hope you'll both be as happy as Steve and me are," before adding, "I'll see you in a bit then Louise. If you've got time whilst you're home, why not pop round and we'll have a good old natter?"

Philip stood uneasily at Louise's side but had finally moved away leaving the girls to it. He hoped that Samantha would move with him but she did not do so, deciding instead to stay with her daughter.

"Come and talk to us Philip."

Philip looked across to where the voice had come from and then walked to where Lucy was sitting with two women he'd never met before. He leaned forward and gave Lucy a kiss, "You look well, Lucy. I hope retirement is going to suit me as well as it has you."

Lucy just smiled as Evie leaned forward to shake Philip's hand. She shook her head as she did so, "You don't remember me do you?"

"The face is familiar, but I'm so sorry, I can't place you."

She laughed, "Long time no see. We are both a lot older than the last time we met."

Philip was desperately trying to place her, "Well, seeing you with Lucy,

I'd assumed you were Robert's grandmother but I'm having difficulty placing where I've seen you before."

She was about to say something, when he stopped her, "I remember now, it was at my father's funeral. We spoke together at the old George hotel." He looked at her with some uncertainty, "But you're Robert's grandmother, aren't you?"

She laughed again, "Yes, I'm Robert's grandmother." She took the other younger woman's hand, "And this is Rachel; Robert's mother."

Philip took Rachel's hand and shook it, "I'm so pleased to meet you at last and put a face to the name. I've only met your son two or three times, but he seems a very fine young man. I'm sure he and Louise are going to be very happy together."

He looked back at Evie, "I can't believe you are Robert's grandmother. Louise has mentioned you several times but she's never said that I might know you."

She smiled again, "That's because I've never mentioned it." She patted the empty chair next to her, "Now sit down and tell me everything you've done since we last met."

He sat down and as Evie gradually interrogated him he started to realise that this lady knew more about him than he could have imagined.

Rachel sat spellbound as she watched Evie gradually work her magic on Philip in the same way she did with everyone else. She was fascinated how, in no time at all, Philip was sitting back, completely relaxed and talking quite freely and easily to Evie. Rachel had so often wished she had the same charm and power to make her patients feel as calm and at ease, but no matter how often she'd witnessed these events, she'd never quite managed to work out what the real trick was. She had come to the conclusion a long time ago that it must be something about the woman herself, and not what she said or what she did, and had stopped trying to find the technique. Instead she just kept quiet and enjoyed the enchantment being played out in front of her.

Lucy however, had never been a witness to the process before and knew little of what was really happening. She suddenly interrupted and said to Philip, "What are you doing with all your spare time these days, Philip? Have you seen much of Samantha since you retired?"

Evie glared at Lucy and kicked her leg under the table. Her charm offensive wasn't yet at the stage when such a direct question should be asked. The situation was made even worse when Louise arrived at the table with Robert saying, "You don't mind if we take Rachel and Evie to meet some of our other friends, do you Philip?"

Evie was reluctant to go with Louise, knowing it might be difficult to capture Philip again that day. But she was determined to make sure that things were sorted before she went back to Edinburgh and touched him on the shoulder as she stood up, "I'd like to continue our chat later, Philip."

He patted her hand saying, "I look forward to it."

Philip did not want to get into a conversation with Lucy, and so suggested they move to join his mother and Aunt Alice at the nearby table. No sooner had they sat down than the caterers announced food was ready and invited people to, "Come and help yourselves."

Later, Philip had been dispatched back to the food table to fetch his mother and Lucy a helping of the strawberries and cream, when he felt a tap on his shoulder, "I'd like to have that chat with you now Philip." Evie pointed in the direction of the conservatory, "Why don't you come and join me in there when you've finished eating?"

Evie was on her own when Philip arrived next to her. She stood up and took his hand, "I want to ask you about a photograph I saw in the lounge when Louise was introducing me to everyone earlier." She led him into the room and picked up the double photo frame, "You know what this is, don't you?"

"Yes; it's Joe's medal and citation." Philip took the frame from Evie and suddenly realised the significance to her, "Of course, it was your brother that Joe saved wasn't it?"

"But what's it doing here?"

"Well Joe was Louise's great uncle."

"I don't understand. I thought this Joe was just an army friend of your father's, not a relative." Evie closed her eyes as she realised that Philip meant that this Joe was the uncle of either Samantha or her husband and not his own uncle. She managed to avoid disclosing that she knew Philip was Louise's father by quickly saying, "So is he Samantha's uncle or her late husband's?"

"He was Edward's mother's brother." He laughed as he continued, "Edward's father was my mother's brother. So I suppose I am related to Joe, but only through about three lines of marriage. He isn't a blood relative."

Evie was relieved that Philip had made light of her 'faux pas' and chose to try and move on to a different matter, "But you do know who really saved my brother's life don't you?"

"Of course, Joe did."

Evie could not believe that the real truth about this matter was yet another family secret, "Didn't your father ever talk about it?"

"Well nothing more than the citation says."

Evie decided that she owed it to her brother to tell Philip the truth even if no one else would ever know it. She touched Philip on the arm and looked round as if checking that no-one else was watching, "No Philip, it was your father who saved Mark's life and from what Mark told me, if the Germans hadn't shot Joe as he was getting back into their own trenches, he would have saved Joe's life as well."

Philip shook his head in disbelief, "But that can't be, why would they give Joe the Military Medal if he hadn't been the one to save your brother's life?"

"Because your father convinced my brother that it was the right thing to do." She then told Philip the full story of how, during a charge on the enemy lines, her brother, Joe and Philip's father had managed to get within twenty or thirty yards of the German lines, when they fell into a large hole. She took the photo frame from Philip, "This citation correctly describes the event but the name is wrong. It was your father who pulled Mark all the way back to their own lines after nightfall. Oh, sure, Joe was there but he was only crawling back with them. He took no direct part in saving Mark's life."

She put the frame back on the table, "Joe was killed when he stood up slightly to get back into his own trench. When your father gave his report of what happened, he said Joe was the one who'd dragged Mark back."

She shook her head, "Your father got to Mark as soon as he came round in hospital, and told my still groggy brother what he'd said about the incident and Mark agreed to tell the same story. I guess it was because Mark was an officer that they gave Joe the medal, but really it should have been Frank's."

Evie held on to Philip's arm and they started walking back to the garden, but she stopped as they reached the hall and prevented them going further, "I'm sorry about that. All I wanted to know was why the medal and photograph were here. I hope I haven't put my foot in it but I assumed you would know the true story. I should have known better though. I should have known your father wouldn't have told the true story to anyone and spoiled things for Joe's family." She squeezed his arm, "And although I don't know you very well, I doubt you will either."

He turned and faced her and shook his head, "Probably not!" before adding, "From what you've said you obviously knew my father better than I thought."

She stood with a grin on her face, "Not as well as I would have liked to."

Philip gave her a questioning glance and Evie tried to explain the comment by recalling the times that she and her brother had spent with Frank during the war. Mostly the reminiscences were amusing and accompanied with smiles and occasional laughter, but when he asked her what his father was like at that time, her voice gradually softened and she was obviously finding it difficult to say out loud the things she was thinking. So much so that she stopped speaking mid sentence and just looked at Philip with a smile on her face. She touched Philip's cheek and gently stroked it with her hand, "You are so like your father. He was a good man and meant a lot to me."

Philip wanted to ask more, but they just stood looking at each other, neither saying a word. It was at that moment that Philip realised that this woman had almost certainly loved his father and probably still did. He felt he could almost read her mind behind those normally sparkling eyes that had suddenly become so sad. Had she loved his father in the same way that he loved Samantha? As soon as he had this thought, she gently stroked his cheek again as if to acknowledge that his thoughts were correct. She stared at him intently as she continued touching his cheek. Philip knew from the heart rending look on her face that although she was seeing the Frank she loved, in him, the pain behind the eyes meant that she had never had the strength to tell his father how she felt.

Suddenly, the moment was gone, and she started recalling the time she had first met Philip in the Arboretum and how she had pushed the obnoxious boatman into the lake. Soon they were both laughing until tears were running in their eyes.

Evie grabbed hold of Philip's arm again, "Come on young man, I think we've ignored everyone else long enough don't you."

She stopped again for a moment and held so tightly on to his arm that it almost hurt, "Louise's mother is a wonderful woman, don't you think?" and without waiting for an answer said, "I'm sure there must a man somewhere who would be just right for her. She's been a widow long enough and she's definitely not the sort of woman to spend the rest of her life on her own." She laughed and pulled on his arm yet again, "And come to think of it, you've been on your own long enough as well."

He looked at her, unsure how to reply, but she just continued smiling as she said, "Take some advice from an old lady who knows about these things. Stop worrying about what your head tells you and just do what your heart says instead."

She did not give Philip any time to answer or comment, but started to pull him towards the garden, "And now you can take me to talk to your mother. Your father spoke of her often but I've only met her for the first time this afternoon when Louise made me do the rounds of all her family."

"Of course, I'm sure mother would love to learn more about you and your brother."

Philip took Evie to join Grace, Lucy and Alice at their table and before long the four women were chatting excitedly between each other about Frank. Philip and his mother listened as each of the other women told their story of how Frank had helped them at various times in their lives. As they spoke it dawned on Philip that each of these four women, all now in their eighties, had all loved his father. He looked at his mother and saw the amused smile on her face: a smile that suggested to Philip she was probably thinking the same thing. The only difference was that, no matter how much or little her husband had loved these three other women; she was the one he had married and given his love to.

Philip left the women to their discussion and went to collect the small book he had seen on the hall table when talking to Evie, before sitting in the conservatory from where he could see Samantha and Louise talking enthusiastically to Rachel and Robert. He imagined that they were probably making wedding plans and sighed as he watched them. He felt sad and alone. As Louise's father he ought to be there with them. Why couldn't things have been different?

He looked at the book. He had recognised it immediately as the copy of the Rubáiyát he had given to Samantha on the day Louise was born and from the state of it, it had been well used since then. Had Samantha deliberately left it on the hall table for him to find?

He opened it at the page where the bookmark rested; the same page he had placed it all those years ago. Had Samantha deliberately put the bookmark there for the same reason he had? He started thinking about what Evie had said to him as he looked up at Samantha again. They smiled at each other as their eyes met and he silently repeated the words of the verse several times in his head without looking at the page and wondered if the words still meant as much to Samantha as they did to him

Perhaps it was about time he sorted out this sorry scheme of things? He had never been a gambler, but he knew at that moment that he had to risk everything in an attempt to settle the matter with Louise and Samantha once and for all.

CHAPTER THIRTY

JUNE 1982

Louise couldn't believe her wedding day was finally here. Waiting for it to arrive had seemed like an eternity, but today was the day. She had set her alarm for seven-thirty, but she jumped out bed well before that and looked through her bedroom window. The sun was already shining and there wasn't a cloud in the sky. The weather forecasters had predicted it would be warm and bright and she was thankful it appeared that they were correct.

As she sat wondering if she should get back into bed until the alarm went off she looked at her engagement ring and grinned to herself at the thought that later today she would be wearing a wedding ring on that same finger.

She stared at the dress hanging on the back of the door. She had originally wanted to buy a dress but her mother had said she would like to make it for her adding, "If it's a disaster we can always go and buy one, but my mother made mine and I'd really like to have a go at making yours."

Louise had reluctantly agreed but now she could hardly believe how beautiful the very special dress was. The light cream brocade material augmented with its pattern of raised roses in a very slightly deeper shade was perfect. How lucky they had been to find this material and then when they found the heavy lace for the over jacket in the same shade, she couldn't believe it. The grin on her face broadened even more as she admired the unique finished article and she muttered aloud, "Thanks Mum, you were right to insist on making it."

She couldn't sit waiting to start the day any longer so she put on her dressing gown and went down to the kitchen to make coffee. Her mother was already in there; a pot of steaming coffee ready and waiting, "Couldn't you sleep either sweetheart?"

"It took me a while to get off, but actually I slept quite well."

They sat drinking the coffee and Samantha produced one of her infamous lists. Everything they needed to do that morning was listed, from going to the hairdressers to checking that the smallest bridesmaids, Julian's three year old daughter Cécilia and her elder sister Amélie, went to the toilet before setting off to the church. Louise laughed and produced her own list from the pocket of her dressing gown. She placed it on the table next to her mother's with a, "Snap."

Samantha picked it up and checked the list against her own, "My word! You! Making a list?" She looked at Louise and teased her daughter with, "Today must be important for you to even think about making a list."

"Well I guess I'm getting more like you every day."

Both women were soon giggling together like teenagers; a thing that couldn't possibly have happened eighteen months previously. Samantha stopped giggling when Louise's alarm suddenly went off upstairs, "I suppose that means it's time to go to item number one on the list." She took hold of Louise's hand, "But first I want you to know that I'm really pleased the way things have worked out for you. Robert is a wonderful man and it's obvious you're meant for each other. Be happy sweetheart, you deserve it."

"Thanks Mum, I'm sure I will be." She let go of her mother's hand and got up, "We best get a move on, according to your list we both have to leave here for the hairdressers in half an hour.

At five minutes to twelve precisely, the car carrying the bride arrived at the church. Samantha was waiting in the vestibule with the bridesmaids and once the photographer had taken his arrival photographs, she checked the bridesmaids for the last time before making sure that Louise's headpiece was properly fixed and the train at the back of her dress was spread on the floor behind her. She turned to the bridesmaids with her final instruction, "Now stay just far enough behind Louise. We don't want you stepping on her train do we?" before walking up the aisle to take her seat at front of the church.

The vicar gave the organist the wink and everyone stood up as the first chords of the wedding march rang through the church. The whole congregation turned to watch the bridal group slowly making its way up the aisle to the beat of the music.

Philip looked at his daughter and smiled. He wondered what his own father would feel to know that his granddaughter was not only considered as good as the Harper family, but was actually about to marry the grandson of Evelyn Harper.

He quickly glanced at Evie, resplendent as always, but on this occasion she had clearly decided not to outdo the groom's mother. He glimpsed at his own mother and then back at Evie, and inwardly chuckled; pleased that Evie and his father had never been more than friends. He shuddered for a second at the thought that this day would never have happened if they had been lovers.

He smiled to himself at the broad smile on Louise's face as she saw her husband to be waiting for her. Robert beamed back at her with an even broader grin. Philip knew from the way they looked at each other that this was a marriage based on total love that would last.

Both of them continued grinning at each other through the whole of the first hymn and it was only when the vicar began the, "We are gathered here today to witness the wedding of….." that the grins turned to mere smiles, as they wished to honour the seriousness of the commitments they were each about to make.

When the vicar got to the point of asking, "Who givest this woman to this man?" Philip proudly took a single step forward and placed Louise's hand into the hand of the man waiting to be her husband.

They both gave him a quick smile as he moved to sit next to the woman he had married at the Registry office two weeks earlier.

Philip and Samantha had insisted that they did not want their wedding to overshadow Louise's in any way, and so Louise and Robert, acting as witnesses, were the only other people present. Philip took Samantha's hand into his and squeezed it as the bride and groom were repeating their wedding vows. At that moment he considered himself to be the luckiest man alive. Everything was finally remoulded nearer his heart's desire!